I0779196

THE HIDDEN KINGDOM

KINGDOM OF THE WHITE SEA BOOK THREE

SARAH M. CRADIT

Cover Design by Regina Wamba of ReginaWamba.com
"Five Sacred Vows" Art by Offbeat Worlds
Portrait Art by Lauren Richelieu
Map by The Illustrated Author Design Services
Editing by Emily A. Lawrence of Lawrence Editing

Publisher Contact:
sarah@sarahmcradit.com
www.sarahmcradit.com

Complete character guides by location can be found at the end of the book. These are spoiler-free and include only information that is true at the start of the book.

You can find a complete list of content warnings on my website: sarahmcradit.com

HOWLING SEA
WHITE SEA
N
S
W
E
MIDNIGHT CREST
ICEBOLT MOUNTAIN
MIDWINTER REST
WITCHWOOD CROSS
WHITECAP
NORTHERLAND RANGE
FOREST OF LYCANA
WULFSHEAD HAVEN
9
TORRIN'S PASS
WESTPORT
EASTPORT
DUNWOODE
1
6
DARKWOOD RUN
SALTHILL
WULF'S NECK
7
MAYKE
SALEEN
ASGILL
2
DRUMAIN
BYTHESEA
TERMONGLEN
RUSHWOOD
WHISPERING WOOD
12
VALLEYBROOKE
EVERLEIGH PIKE
STREAMSTOWNE
WILDWOOD FALLS
EVERHART THICKET
PARTH
RESPLENDENT RELIQUARY
5
THE SEPULCHRE IN THE SKIES
10
BRIARHAVEN
THE SEVEN SISTERS
GAP O' EVER
GREENFEN
RIVER RUSH
WINDWATCH GROVE
FIONN'S PASS
PINE BLUFF
WHITEWOOD
OLDCASTLE
OAK HILL
3
EAST DERRY
IRON HILL
BLACKPOOL
STONE MAWR
NEWCARROW
4
SANDYMOUNT
GREENCASTLE
GOLDTHORPE
SANDYCOVE
LEECASTER BAY
11
HORNSEA
PORT WORTHING
CAMP ATONEMENT
GREYSTONE ABBEY
WHITECLIFFE
8
CAMP RESTITUTION
1.) NORTHERLANDS
2.) HINTERLANDS
3.) WESTERLANDS
4.) SOUTHERLANDS
5.) EASTERLANDS
6.) ISLE OF BELCARROW
7.) DUNCARROW
8.) WASTELANDS
9.) WULFSGATE
10.) LONGWOOD RUSH
11.) WARWICKTOWN
12.) WHITECHURCH
KINGDOM OF THE WHITE SEA

For Laura Trujillo and Pam Beckford, who helped me get this one over the finish line

PROLOGUE

Kian trapped the lament deep in his chest. He turned from the funeral pyre, leaving the devastating sight behind him. Dozens of Medvedev, mostly Drumain, but some Saleen, followed behind in dazed concert.

It had taken weeks—and many caravans—to bring all the Saleen home, and only hours to see their bodies spent to flame and ash.

The largest share of the work had been taking the Saleen through the veil. The Easterlands men brought them to the borders of the Hinterlands. Kian couldn't permit them to come any further, despite their solemn eyes and remorseful intentions. He explained this as best as he could, thanking them with authentic gratitude as they delivered the last of the bodies, taking especial care with their tending of Ohsmha, the beloved Chieftainess of Clahnn Saleen. The great sorrow following these men in their steps pierced Kian's heart. There were some crimes big enough to swallow everyone around them. For the men of the Easterlands, nothing would ever be as it was.

It was Kael who believed all men were bad. Kian saw there was yet light. Even in those who would take it for themselves.

Eithne laid a hand between his sore shoulders. She let it fall away as quickly as it had landed.

This work was done, but there was more ahead.

For a Keeper, the work beckoned eternal.

KIAN BROKE FAST ALONE THAT EVENING. HE PREFERRED IT THIS WAY; whispering his gratitude to the soil and the creatures who walked it, as the last sigh of orange light fell like a careful veil behind the trees, fleetingly restoring the branches to life in ethereal wonder. Kael had never understood Kian's solitude, but Kael wasn't a Keeper. Kael didn't comprehend that a Keeper was, by nature, alone.

He couldn't shrug away his worries about leaving Kael to tend to their mother. Kael loved their mother, but that didn't shield her from his questions. His incessant challenges of her authority, her wisdom, her truths. Kian knew where it would lead, but it was not his role to come between present and future.

There'd been no choice but to leave his home and come here. Only a Keeper could choose and train new Keepers. The few Saleen remaining in their lands huddled in the shadows, saddled with a fear they'd never known before.

Despite the inconceivable efforts of the Meduwyn, Mortain, who had lured the Saleen from the safety of their lands, some had resisted this magic. They'd huddled high in trees as their brethren were led away, lulled into a submission that wouldn't find release until their spirits had transcended to the Halls of Light.

These few left were the Saleen who had seen the terrible events in their visions. But their magic didn't allow for intervention; for warning. They could only hide away, quietly sobbing into their arms for the horrors they could foresee but not prevent.

These were Saleen lands, not Drumain. On that, Yseult had been firm. Kian would train a Keeper and return. One Saleen or one thousand, it was all the same. For it was magic, not the Medvedev, that kept the veils.

That was the true betrayal of the Saleen. That the man, Lord

Quinlanden, had gained the trust of Ohsmha, only to use this gift to destroy her and her people.

It wouldn't happen again. Not here. Not in Drumain lands. Not in Mayke or Asgill lands. Not again, ever. The Light was dying. The veils had begun to thin. Soon, it would take no more than determination to pass through them. If one could pass the veils into their lands, it stood to reason they could, one day, enter the veil to The Hidden Kingdom. If this were to happen...

No. It could not. It could not, and so it would not, as his mother often said.

Not all the Meduwyn who'd been banished to Ilynglass bore such evil in their hearts. Those who sought to counter the malignant efforts might yet succeed. Yseult had been right about the boy, Drystan. Kian sensed in his heart that Lisbet was pulled toward the purpose awaiting her and her father, Dain. Kian would never see her again. This wasn't a traditional premonition, but a feeling that burned deep within, resembling fear. Beyond that, acceptance that a thing couldn't become a fear if it didn't have life and legs to carry fear upon.

He consoled himself in knowing he would see her bravery come to life one day, if she ignored her innate willfulness and rose to her purpose. If she could be satisfied in being merely the catalyst that sent Dain and Jamesan to their own fates.

"You do not always need to be so alone. The Saleen are your kin, even if we were not so familial before the great tragedy."

Kian set his meal aside. Eithne spoke as a Medvedev, but Kian now heard all words in the parlance of man, filling in the absent words himself. He'd become attached to their world, though it had never belonged to the Medvedev. He would take this with him, if nothing else.

"A Keeper is always alone."

"I would know this if you would begin our training. When, Kian?"

"When you are ready."

Eithne lowered herself and sat across from him. She wore her blue hair plaited in elaborate tangles around her head. It was very unlike how the Drumain women dressed their hair. He hadn't decided yet if he was fond of it, or her. "I am ready."

"You are not." Kian regarded her more closely. She was young and as yet unmatched. If Yseult were here, she might encourage the union. As the eldest son of the Chieftainess, it was Kian's responsibility to bring the daughter who would inherit the role from his mother.

She'd reminded him of this before he'd left. *You know your purpose. There is none greater but, should you find a mate during this time, I would not turn away such a gift. Would it be so terrible if our clahnns were united once more? The Saleen may bear the burden of the Light, but that charge belongs to us all.*

"Why is for you to say, and not me? Can you see into my heart?" Eithne's wide eyes wore a wounded look.

"I can, if I choose. But that is not how I know."

"How, then?"

Kian tossed the last of his berries to a deer grazing nearby. He stood, dusting the grass off. "When you no longer seek this answer, then you will be ready."

Kian entered the temple. The steps crumbled away, but that was the way of things. They didn't have stone or marble in their world, as men did in theirs. All things fell away. All things could be rebuilt.

Dusk settled a purple haze over the world behind him. Ahead, there was only light.

The same Light that was dying.

The Great Light of the Worlds.

Except, it wasn't the Light itself. No matter how far he reached, how desperate his hand, he couldn't touch it.

Only protect it.

He couldn't pass through to The Hidden Kingdom. This was not part of his charge.

There was one who could.

If they did not—if they could not—then the Light would die, and with it, all the worlds.

Kian pressed his hands to the warmth that kept the world and sent silent entreaties to his ancestors. He didn't know if they received them, but he couldn't believe that, after millennia of service, those still welcome beyond this veil would not have some love for those who kept them safe.

THEY WILL NOT BE
AS YOU REMEMBER
THEM

I
MANY WORLDS

Jesse's balance wobbled as a precarious battle waged between his eyes and his mind. There was only this sense—this absolute certainty—that though only seconds had passed, the world he'd left behind had advanced into the future without him.

World. The word no longer meant what it once had. Lysanor and Isdemus hadn't outright stated they'd left the White Kingdom for another, but there were things that could be understood before explanation was dealt. Jesse *knew* he was no longer in his world, and if there was now this other world, of strangely soft sand and sharp red peaks, there might then be other worlds.

The very thought was dizzying.

Jesse willed his lids closed. Again, the sense he was falling, not down, but away. Away from himself. Away from time. The troubled gazes of the two sorcerers burned through his eyelids. Let them be troubled. Their feelings couldn't be half of his own.

Stand, Jesse.

You do not descend from men who cannot, Jamesan Strong.

Lysanor had said this. Moments before. Weeks before. Either. Both. He was a man of two worlds now, split by opposing realities.

Why are you doing this to me? Why?

After everything you saw, you would ask us that?

Yes, he'd seen it, through the eyes of his father, and then his own eyes, tracing his heritage through the Rhiagains, and...

I'm a trader. I'm the son of Hamish Strong and Yanna de Medvedev. I'm known for my skill, for my loyalty, for my—

You've known your whole life you were not like your brother, or your father. Look at me!

Leave me alone!

Lysanor and Isdemus implied he'd known these things all along. That simply wasn't true. Jesse *had* always wondered about the effort required of him to fit neatly into his father's world; at how this contrasted with Ryan's relative ease with everything. A leather tome in a library otherwise devoid of books, his father called him once, and the Jesse of then had laughed at the silly analogies his father employed to explain a world whose clarity often eluded him. The Jesse of now...

Who are you?

I'm a trader's son.

Who are you?

He was the son of Yanna of the Medvedev. Yes, he'd known this. Perhaps, not *all* his life, but enough to accept this truth about himself, enough to—

Go on.

Ahh, did he have to? He could've gone the rest of this life happy in his ignorance.

Go on, Jamesan. It will not be less true if you fail to claim it, but your life will be half-lived if you choose that path.

Half-lived. His life was already this, for he'd been one man for almost twenty-five years, and was now meeting the other man he was supposed to be. He wasn't a Strong of Sandycove. He was the son of Dain Rhiagain, the grandson of a great sorcerer of Ilynglass. Sorcerer. A word he'd only known in passing was now a word that sought to define him, to give him meaning when he'd never believed himself to be lacking one, to put him in a box chosen by others bearing this name.

"Are you quite all right?" Lysanor's voice broke the reverie.

Jesse swallowed a deep breath. Nodded. The rich, heady scent passing on the wind, belonging to this world and not the one he knew, was yet another attack on his steadiness.

"See?" She aimed a pointed look at Isdemus with a harried head shake. "It's as I told you. He's ready. He's fine."

"Fine and ready are *not* tantamount, Lysanor. Will you look at him? He can hardly stand. He's practically green in the face," Isdemus rejoined.

"He's standing perfectly erect, and if anything, he's actually quite *pale—*"

"I'm fine," Jesse insisted. Blood flowed to his limbs more freely now. He awakened from head to toe, at last—regretfully—free of the vision of his mother, of his past. "Or, I will be."

Lysanor and Isdemus nodded in tandem as they inspected him, seemingly coming to different conclusions. They were an unusual pair. They possessed none of the mystique he'd expect from creatures belonging to another place and time. It was only in their eyes that their age and wisdom betrayed them.

"I've done what ye asked. Now I need something," Jesse said. He planted his feet in the silken sand.

"I suppose you can ask," Lysanor said.

"You're going to tell me where we are. And donnae lie to me. If you want me to believe anything else ye say, you cannae play me false."

Lysanor exhaled. She glanced at Isdemus. "I'm rather chagrined to say Isdemus and I have never given it name."

"That's a touch misleading, Lysanor, as you're implying this is *our* world, and not simply *a* world, in which we've occupied only a small corner," Isdemus countered. "It clearly has a name, given to it by those who belong here, which is to say, not us."

"But it *is* another world," Jesse pushed. "We're no longer in the White Kingdom."

"No, we are not," Isdemus said.

Jesse resisted a fresh wave of disorientation. "Aye. I see."

"I rather think you do not," Lysanor said tenderly. "But you begin to."

"And here... in this world... time..."

"Time finds its own way in every world," Isdemus said. "It passes as it chooses."

"And does it choose to pass slower or faster here than in the White Kingdom?"

Lysanor cut Isdemus off. His mouth closed. "In the time you've been here, I'd guess close to a month in the White Kingdom has passed."

Jesse stumbled back. Sand kicked up as his feet pedaled in reverse. "No." But it *felt* right. How he'd naively hoped they'd disprove this feeling, not confirm it. It was far worse than he imagined. "Esmerelda..."

"Still? Still?" Lysanor sighed in exasperation. "After all we've shown you, your concern belongs to a *girl*?"

Isdemus snaked a hand out, landing it on her arm. "Consider, perhaps, that when I said he wasn't ready, it was *you* and your impatience to which I was referring."

Lysanor scoffed.

Jesse's heart skipped so hard his eyes pulsed. A month. A month in here. A month since Esmerelda was taken. "You brought me in here and kept me from finding her? She could be *anywhere* by now. She could be—"

"I can find her," Isdemus said, stepping toward Jesse. Both arms were out. He seemed to search for a way to console Jesse, but fell short of knowing precisely how. "I can find her for you."

"Isdemus!"

"Sister," Isdemus cautioned. He narrowed the space separating him from Jesse. "We have, after all, asked much of you. We took you from a mission that meant a great deal to you, one you did not get to complete, because of us, did you? We owe you something in return."

"We do not have time for this!"

Isdemus ignored her. His focus belonged entirely to Jesse. "You must know we're preparing to ask a great deal of you."

"Aye, so I expected. All this trouble ye spent getting me here," Jesse answered him, but his mind played havoc with his fears, as myriad possibilities wove together into the new tapestry forming his adjusted reality. Had Lord Warwick discovered Esmerelda's deception? Was it a band of brigands? The king?

"*Isdemus.*"

Isdemus stepped closer. "We will. And if you do not or cannot do as we ask, then this world, all worlds, will cease to be. Your father. Your brother. Esmerelda. Everyone you've ever known, loved, or even hated. Everyone you could know, or never would. Gone."

Jesse snapped his head up. "What do you—"

"We will ask the impossible of you, for there is no other way. Our love of you won't keep us from asking it. Would it also be true to say, Jamesan, that there's nothing we can ask of you that you'll hear until you've seen the girl is safe? With your own eyes?"

Jesse, breathless, mind torn in two, nodded.

"You're a fool to pander to this whim of man. What does it *matter*, Isdemus? What does one life matter, when we speak of many? When we speak of all?" Lysanor's face burned bright with her anger.

"Ah, but sister, is that not the riddle lying beneath the worth of all life? Can there be a value on all, if there is not value on one? Does what we do matter, if his care for this girl does not?"

Lysanor snapped her mouth closed. She glared at them both.

Isdemus again looked at Jesse. "I can find her. In my mind's eye. And then you will go to her, so that you can know her fate, for better or for else. For though we have waited a long time for you, Jamesan, we cannot ask what we prepare to ask of you without recognizing your own needs. But you must swear an unbreakable oath."

"Anything." Jesse stepped forward, heart racing. "Anything. Just find her."

"No, Jamesan, not anything. What we ask of you is *everything*."

Jesse swallowed. Hot tears tickled the backs of his eyes. "Aye. I dinnae care the cost. I'll do whatever ye ask of me. Once I know that Esmerelda and her bairn are safe, I'll do whatever it is you say you've been waiting for from me. Just take me back to my world and show me where to find her. Please."

GRETCHEN'S BREATH HITCHED AS SHE WARILY RECHECKED HER rations. She swiped one hand along her moistened brow as she regarded the contents with rising dismay. The oppressive heat assaulted her senses with relentless persistence. The air's inexplicable density blurred her resolve. This wasn't the heat of her world. Even in her visits to the Southerlands, she'd not known this cloying stickiness that clung to her flesh, gripping the surface like a sentry tasked with keeping away anything resembling relief.

She'd told herself she brought enough, but *enough* was an intangible idea based on nothing more than what she knew. What she *knew* did little service to her here, in a world she didn't even have a name for.

In her hopeful imagination—and she must admit it now, when she had only a week remaining to her of the dried meats—she'd seen Pieter sitting just beyond the veil, waiting for her. In this vision, they'd turned together and returned home without words or fuss, for she'd taught all her children the necessities for survival in an unjust world, a role often reserved for the fathers. *If you're lost, you stay where you are. Go no farther than you must to find cover, not unless you're under immediate threat. Never wander, for I will always come for you, and a safe place to await help is the precious difference between life and death.*

When Pieter hadn't been waiting for her on the other side, it didn't dampen her spirits. He had, after all, been in flight from imminent danger, which wasn't the same as being lost. Ransom had been all but certain that the foe who had assailed Princess Assyria and Lady Blackwood was coming for them next. Pieter had taken this fear with him through the veil. Only a fool would assume their enemy couldn't do the same, and Gretchen had raised capable children.

When she'd initially stepped through the veil, Gretchen thought she was surrounded by sand. A turn to look behind her, where the veil *should* be if it were an actual door and not some strange form of magic, revealed a forest of sorts. She'd added the *of sorts* in her head, for though there were trees, they were not the tall towering green kings and queens that decorated the Northerlands, nor even their leafier cousins to the south. They sat low enough that it seemed a very tall person could touch the tops, their orange fingerlike branches spreading together to form a canopy. The copse in the middle of the desert was both a promise and a warning.

She saw no other choice but to go in.

Gretchen applied what she knew of her own world to bring some sense into this one. Trees required water to thrive, so she reasoned that, within the macabre dance of colors, she might find that source, and that source might provide for more than the trees.

It was all there was, anyway. Every other direction she looked was only the yawning beckon of desert, as far as her vision could stretch. She could walk hours or months. It was all the same when she didn't know these lands. The forest was the only reprieve.

A promise. A warning.

Pieter was a smart boy. He would've done the same.

So in Gretchen had trekked.

SHE CHECKED THE CLAY HONEY JAR, ALSO WOEFULLY LOW. HOW SHE wished to dip her finger and avail herself of a taste. It was the very last of the blackbee honey Earwyn had brought back from her visit home to Longwood Rush. They'd hoarded the spun gold as a delicacy, for celebrations and festival days, but Gretchen had brought it on this journey for another reason entirely.

Her father taught her the trick, taking her along on his hunting expeditions that could last a fortnight or more. Her mother took to her bed in horror on the eve of these trips, declaring, to no joy, that they were no place for a young girl, who had more important things to learn, like being a mistress of a household. That Chasten had sons for such things. But Gretchen *wanted* to be there, and was always grateful when her father paid no mind to his wife's weary objections.

There are things one must always take when leaving the world behind.

Food and weapons, Papa?

Does one really need reminding to bring such essentials?

No, Papa.

No, Gretchen. What I try to show you and your brothers is what you might not *think about bringing. Do you suppose I've ever been lost?*

Guardians, no!

Well, I have. But I've always found my way home. For I rediscovered the way I had marked for myself. You'll want honey. Sap if the bees aren't producing. And the extra bits of cloth your mother tosses aside for the handmaiden who collects her refuse. Best to use the bright colors that have spent the longest time in the dyes.

She hadn't understood until he showed her. As they moved beyond their known world, Chasten Quinlanden slowed to remove a discarded cloth strip from his pack. He dipped the end of one in the honey and used it to tack the bright fabric against the bark of a tree. Just when it felt they'd lost their bearings, he'd tack another. A trail to lead them home.

"Pieter," she whispered, leaning back against the bark of the last tree she'd tacked. There was only enough for a few more. This was the story of all the things protecting her life in this strange world. She'd refilled her waterskin at a stream several days back, gambling on her foreign body accepting the precious liquid, but it was almost empty, and she hadn't come across another stream to refill it. She had just enough food to return, if she rationed herself down to nearly nothing, but not if she continued on. "My cub."

Sweat crept into her eyes, obscuring her vision. The pearapple tree ahead split into two, three, four, five more. Gretchen laughed. The water hadn't killed her, so why not this? She could try it.

Gretchen heaved herself forward and approached the tree. It looked identical to the one guarding the veil in her world, the one everyone called a pearapple tree. Gretchen chose the brightest orb she could find. With a light twist and tug, it fell, and she opened both palms to receive it.

It didn't *look* dangerous. Its skin was smooth and inviting. But it wasn't always the thorns and barbs one must guard themselves from.

Gretchen had two paths. One behind, where she could return to the world she knew, without her son. Or ahead, where Pieter awaited, knowing, deep in his heart, that his mother would come for him.

If there was ever a time she wished Ash would return to offer his sage wisdom, it was now.

She sank her teeth into it with a satisfying popping sound. Juice streamed down her chin, falling in fat drops on her leather armor. The sweetness of the fruit sent a wave of surprise straight to her head. It tasted nothing like pearapple, with its subtle flavors that made it a favorite among bakers. This would be better enjoyed as a dessert course. She made her own name for it. *Honeycrisp.*

Gretchen gathered as many as she could carry in her satchel. As she fiddled with the clasp, a sound stopped her. She held her breath, waiting. There it was again. A crunch of action on the forest floor. She listened for the assurance it was only some animal. Like all forests, this one had its fair share of creatures. Most avoided her, but she'd seen a few regarding her from a distance.

More crunches, this time in chorus, folding in around her in an arc of sound. Gretchen's hand fell to her sword, the other reaching beneath her jerkin for a dagger. She stopped short of drawing it.

The next sound she knew well. The creaky responsiveness of a bowstring.

"Stop!" Gretchen cried out. "I am no beast!"

The bowstring eased. Was hers a language they understood? Did they pause from curiosity or surprise?

"Name yourself!" a male voice cried out. She strained to follow it, but he was well hidden, and she didn't know this forest.

"I am Lady Gretchen Dereham of Wulfsgate! I come in search of my son who came before me. I'm no threat to you, and have taken only what I require for my survival."

The man stepped closer. Still, she couldn't see him. Her eyes darted through the forest, but still, nothing. "Wulfsgate. No place here bears this name."

"She's one of them," another said, this voice coming from behind. She resisted the urge to spin toward him, afraid the sudden movement would draw their attack.

"Are you?" The first man again. "One of them?"

"I don't know what you're asking me," Gretchen called back. "I have only come to find my son."

"She mentioned a boy, Brahim." Female this time. Gretchen nearly sobbed in relief. A woman would understand.

"My son?" Gretchen cried out. "Pieter! Have you seen him?"

"There are no children here," the man who wasn't Brahim said.

"Do you bear arms?" Brahim asked.

Gretchen thought of the dagger she'd left tucked into her jerkin. She was glad now of her restraint. "I have the sword I brought with me."

"Lay it down."

"If I don't?"

The other man laughed. "Our arrows are aimed right between your eyes. The questions belong to us."

"Please," Gretchen pleaded. "I need to find my son. His name is Pieter. He is fourteen, but tall for his age, has reddish hair, and—"

"Lay down your sword," the other man insisted. "Or die arguing about it."

She had no choice. They could kill her where she stood, or she could hope her acquiescence bought her the goodwill required to continue on.

Gretchen slowly knelt. She laid her sword against the root of a tree and stood, arms lifted above her head. "It's down."

She gasped as someone bolted through the nearby brush and flew by her, taking her sword quicker than she could make out any discerning features.

"Very well, Gretchen Dereham of Wulfsgate. You will come with us."

2
OBLIGATIONS

Lisbet sat atop the dusty crypt of her grandfather, legs dangling against cobwebs older than she was. Drystan's tomb was just across from Hadden's, though the darkness hid all but the door, which was shut, but not yet sealed. She could open it; anyone could. They'd put him in Holden's tomb, for by now it was broadly assumed that Holden had either been discarded crudely in a ditch, or hastily interred in an unmarked grave, a final gift from an enemy vanquished only hours too late. There was much debate over whether a man should have a tomb with no body, and as yet, remained unresolved. So in Drystan went to the crypt of the heir, and no one but Lisbet and Ash knew he didn't have a drop of Dereham blood in him.

Well, her mother knew, but no one expected to hear from Gretchen Dereham anytime soon, did they?

The stonemasons would come to seal the crypt today. It was said their seals lasted a hundred years before they required tending, though none alive today would be around to see it done. Uncle Alric tried to show her the meticulous record keeping maintained by her ancestors, thinking it would soothe her nerves, but it only put them upon a finer edge. Talking about the dead made them more dead, not less. The loss of Drystan might never fully settle, and she liked it that way. Half-expecting him to walk through the door again kept her hope from dying with him.

On the return to Wulfsgate, Ash regaled Lisbet with story after story about his life with her mother, from their playfulness as children, to their illicit trysts in the Dereham crypts, of which he spared her all the salacious details when repeating. Gretchen came alive for Lisbet in new ways, some welcome, some not. The more he talked, the less inhibited were his words. Lisbet had never been with a man, and had no interest in it, but she could think of better places to do it than atop the cold stones of the dead.

Still, Drystan had been conceived here. It seemed fitting it was where he now came for his eternal rest.

Even from the depths of underground, the celebrations in the courtyard and beyond, in the main streets and quarters of Wulfsgate, carried down to her. The Great Sacrifice of Drystan was a refrain spoken in every conversation worth having, from the shops to the smithhouses to the pubs. Songs had been written and were sung in private and public alike, new verses created with every fresh crowd gathered. Hadden's Bane was ended, they said, thanks to the courage and resolve of Holden's brave sons. The prodigal son had returned and the sacrifice of the spare had at last sent the dark clouds running for the mountains. The veil had lifted. The snow, at last, would melt, and that mythical season of midsummer would return to their Reach, after centuries of denying them, to warm the earth.

Did no one care about the truth? That Drystan had died because men had failed where he felt he must succeed? That Christian was loath to be home, loath to take up the mantle he'd never wanted? That *both* Gretchen and Holden were lost to the world, perhaps forever?

Harried steps sounded to her right. She turned in time to see Eavan. Her troubled face was lit by the last embers of a dying sconce. She clutched her belly in the other hand. She'd gone to some trouble to hide it, but there was no fabric capable anymore.

"What? What is it?" Lisbet asked. "Is it the baby?"

Eavan shook her head. "It's Christian... and Ash. Christian just threw a fist at Ash, and Ash returned it, twice as hard. Someone needs to step in before they kill one another."

Lisbet winced. "He told him, then."

"Lisbet!"

"All right! All right. I'm coming."

"LADY ESMERELDA? IT CANNAE BE."

Esmerelda braced herself. She knew this voice. This man. Both things were from another world, one she'd fled without looking back.

She wouldn't be able to hide from this. It had to happen, and now it was. She had no choice but to ready herself for this moment and all the ones that would come after.

She slowly spun around to face him. Lowered her hood. "Steward Rutland."

Rutland's mouth parted. A gasp escaped. "Nay. It cannae be. 'Tis a trick of the eyes. The dead donnae return."

"Your eyes haven't failed you," she said softly. He was the first of her old life to bear witness to her truth, but he wouldn't be the last. From here, these encounters would only get harder, though she hoped each would strengthen her for the next. "Nor am I returned from the dead."

Rutland closed the door and turned back to her. "Aye, I can see that with my own eyes, Esmerelda. Where have you *been* all these months? And why did ye lie about it, let him believe... your father... do ye know the torment ye left the man? Believing his only daughter lost to the sea?"

Esmerelda nodded. "I had no other choice. He left me with none."

"No other choice? How can that be?"

"He was ready to sell me to a king!"

"Nay. He wouldnae have done it, in the end. You know that."

"Even you do not sound convinced."

He had no defense of this, so he tried another tactic. "You're the only daughter of a great lord, girl. He gave you everything."

"No. Not everything, Steward."

His gaze fell to her belly. He tried to speak, but words failed him.

Ravenna squeezed her hand from behind, reminding Esmerelda of her strength.

"Who did this to you, Esmerelda? What ratsbane—"

"The bairn is Ryan Strong's, and let me reassure you nothing passed between us that I didn't want. My father didn't see it this way, and so my choices were to stay, and become property of a cruel boy king, or leave, and take a path that might lead me to the only happiness I've ever known."

"That's why he sent the boy to the Wastelands, then? Aye?"

She nodded.

"Son of a crow." He rubbed his hand over his beard. "Why come back at all, then?"

"I never intended to return, Steward, but I understand Ryan is unwell, so I saw no choice. I've come in hopes my presence may be the balm he needs to make a recovery." She gestured around. "It seems I've arrived too late to find him here, though. Is it true that he's already awakened? And departed Whitecliffe?"

"Aye, he's awake." Rutland paced the room, still running his hands over the rough stubble painting the lower half of his face. Fresh gray appeared at his temples. She didn't remember them being there before. How many other things had changed in her time away? "He's awake, lass, but..." His eyes again traveled to the swell under her cloak. "I ken he willnae be as ye remember him."

"I know he's been through a great ordeal. I'm prepared to be there for him in any way I can."

"Does your father know? Does he know you're back?"

Esmerelda shook her head.

"Feck-all," Rutland muttered.

Esmerelda reached a hand forward and touched his arm. "He doesn't have to know you saw me."

"You'd have me lie to me lord, would ye? My best mate?"

"No, that wasn't what I meant, I was only—"

"I ken I'll take you to your lad, Lady Esmerelda. Though it's as I've said, he isnae the same and may never be again, they say," Rutland said. "I'll even give ye a day to sort the matters between the two of you. And then I've no choice but to tell him. I cannae keep such a secret from any man, least of all my lord and dearest mate. I donnae envy myself *that* task."

"Of course, Steward. You offer more than I would ask."

"Aye. You mad, mad girl." He exhaled into a whistle. "I ken you've returned just in time for the boy to make right by ye, though. That bairn is coming along any day now?"

Esmerelda nodded. "I suspect so."

"Business for your mother," he muttered. A softer look passed across his face. He touched her shoulder. "Are ye well, otherwise, Esme? Do you need the ministrations of the stewardess, before we get on our way?"

"I'm well enough." She hesitated before asking the next question. "Has... has Jesse Strong returned home?"

Rutland's face twisted in surprised. "Jesse?" His head and shoulders twitched in a light shrug. "Last I saw of him, he was in a right hurry to leave Greystone Abbey. But that was weeks ago."

"Did he say where he was going?"

"All I know, wherever he was aimed, he felt it more important than the business of a realm at war. Hamish would know better than I would."

"I see."

"Right. Put that hood back up for now, or you'll have all the Southerlands flapping their jaws before we even make it to the road." He reached for the door. "Ryan's gone home to Sandycove. When we returned from the Easterlands, he'd already left. I havenae spoken with him myself, understand, I only know what others have told me."

Esmerelda brightened. She beamed back at Ravenna, who met

her gaze with hopeful eyes. "He's home? Well, if he's well enough for all that!"

"He's awake, aye, and his body is healed, but they say it's his mind, lass."

Esmerelda ignored him. "I've ridden this Reach to every corner with my father. I know the way."

"I dinnae care if ye could do it in your sleep with your limbs tied, I'll not let you out of my sight. Your father expects me in Warwicktown end of the week, as it is. A head start on the trip cannae hurt." He nodded at her belly. "You in a condition to ride that far? Will I end up in the fish house when my wife finds I've allowed it?"

"I didn't get here on foot, Steward Rutland."

Rutland grunted. He looked past her and seemed to notice Ravenna for the first time. "Who's she?"

Esmerelda smiled to herself. "A dear friend."

Lisbet found the men in the Great Hall. Ash half-hung from the hearth by a bloody fist, winded to the point of panting. Christian dropped over the far edge of the table, nursing a split lip with a deep scowl.

"What's all this?" she demanded. She stepped into the path between them before they could go at each other again. "Have you forgotten how to be men?"

"Where did you find this brigand, Lisbet?" Christian asked. He pushed his sleeve down, revealing a large red stain. "And don't tell me again that he's your friend. No friend would claim the things he does. No *friend* would deign to bring such filthy falsehoods to their lips, nor even to think them."

"I claim nothing but my own truth," Ash spat. "Which is not yours, nor any man's, to take from me. Not anymore."

"You're not helping," Lisbet muttered. She lifted a hand to stay him as she stepped closer to her brother. His rage was lit by the hearth's flames flickering across the stone. "Christian, I understand this is hard. I know what you're feeling right now."

"Safe to say you do *not*, Lisbet."

"I do know, because I once felt as you do. This anger and confusion. These... ideas that go against what we know of our own mother. It took me time to come around to them."

"They are not ideas, they're desecration. They're lies!" Christian looked past her. "Though, to what end, for what aim, I cannot even fathom!"

"They aren't lies, Christian."

Christian laughed. He wiped more blood from his mouth. "You're a child, Lis. A child who this creature took advantage of, after letting *our brother* be *murdered*, and doing *nothing*!"

"He was my *son*!" Ash boomed from behind them.

"You dare come here and say this! To us!"

"You can level your rage at me all you wish, Lord Dereham, but I'll not hide away from this any longer."

"You dare! You dare... with my father *gone*. You waited for my mother, the only one who could put these lies to bed, where they belong, to be conveniently away—"

"Enough!" Lisbet screamed, throwing her hands to her sides. She turned to her brother, panting. "Do you truly believe I would allow a strange man into our home, our lives, if I didn't have good reason?"

"You're so young, you're—"

"No," she countered. "Don't say it to me. Don't call me a child again after all I've endured these past months. But you don't want to know these things, do you? Whenever poor Eavan comes near you, you act as if she's anything *but* swollen with the child of one of the men who assaulted her... men who would've killed her, killed all of us, if not for Ash. And me, your own sister? You can't even look me in the eye. You've hardly looked in my direction at all since my return."

Christian's mouth curled into a sneer. He diverted his gaze.

"See? When was the last time you knew me? You were a child yourself, when you put our world behind you and ran away to the Sepulchre. You left us, and I can't blame you for it, though it hurt.

But you can't return and be the claimant of all knowledge where our family is concerned, not when you'd forsaken us and pretended to be someone else. You say you miss Drystan, but you hardly knew him, either! He became who you should have, when you left him no choice. And in the end..." Lisbet's voice caught. "In the end, the very end, he was every bit the man Father wanted him to be. Every bit the man you were supposed to be."

"Stop. Lisbet. That's enough."

"Is it? Have I said the words that will turn your eyes to me, to who I am, what I've been through? To the *woman* standing before you, who never intended to be such, but has become so? If you can't do that, then you aren't *ready* for the truth Ash and I bring to this house."

Christian's hand shook as he pointed at Ash. "You cannot look *me* in the eye and tell me this man isn't responsible for our brother's death."

"I will do just that, if you'd look at me."

Christian dropped his gaze to his feet. He drew a shuddering, inward sigh. "They're expecting me in the courtyard."

"Go, then. Let them see their new lord. Let them see what their hope has bought them."

"You think you're clever, mocking me, Lisbet. You've been through an ordeal? Well, so have I. And now the entire future of this family rests of my ability to pretend that none of that matters."

Lisbet said nothing. He glanced at her once more without meeting her gaze and then stormed out.

When his heavy footfalls died to echoes, she spun toward Ash. "Fighting with him? You thought this was wise? That it would win him to your cause?"

"I didn't intend it."

"I told you to let me tell him!"

Ash dropped his hands away from the hearth, sighing. "I wasn't going to say a word to him, Lisbet. I've been avoiding him since our arrival, but his eyes follow me everywhere. His unasked questions lingered, waiting, and it was only a matter of time before he cornered me. When he did, I found the truth came easier than lies, for once."

"He'll never believe you now."

"He was never going to," Ash replied. "And I don't need him to."

Lisbet looked toward the fire. Of all her family, it was her mother she'd been so desperate to see again. Now she might never. If Gretchen's letters were to be believed, and she hadn't gone entirely mad, she'd left intending to cross the same veil Uncle Alric claimed to have gone through years and years ago. The search parties had failed to turn up anything. All that remained was the horse carrying her belongings and the letters.

"It doesn't matter what Christian thinks. We won't be staying, anyway," she said.

"Is that right?"

"That's right."

"Where would you have us go?"

"We did what we came to do, bring Drystan home. Now there's something else out there, waiting for us."

Ash stepped to her and laid both hands on her shoulders. "Do you know what that is yet?"

"You remember what I told you? That there was another child out there? A child of yours?"

"You think we should find them?"

Lisbet leaned into him. "I don't know. Kian said the answers will come to me. I have to trust in that."

Ash kissed the top of her head. "And I have trust in you, little one."

ESMERELDA'S SIDES AND BACK WERE ON FIRE. SHE'D LIED TO STEWARD Rutland. Though she had come to Whitecliffe by horse, riding was harder now, getting harder every day. If her mother knew she was so far along and taking such chances, there'd be no end to the lectures.

How she both dreaded facing her and ached at the promise of her warm comfort.

But she was *so close* now. At the end of a journey she'd often struggled to see herself completing, despite the brave front she put on for Jesse and her protestations about the power of love. She only needed to get herself to Ryan. Then, they could send for her mother and the midwife, and she'd bring this bairn into the world just in time to know their father, and it would all have been worth it.

The past weeks had been harder on her than all the ones before. She and Assana had rowed so hard in that tiny vessel, maneuvering against an impossible current for their very lives, certain Oldwin's men had caught them in their sights and would catch or kill them before they could make it to shore.

But Ravenna had saved them. In her heart, Esmerelda had hoped Ravenna made it far away from the creature that had tried so hard to break her, but she'd stayed, awaiting her opportunity to keep her vow to Esmerelda.

Esmerelda had looked back only once, and what she saw would haunt her nightmares forever.

Dozens of men, flailing in horror, their bodies consumed by flames. Ravenna's new bright orange avian form raining more fire down upon them as she dipped and rose in the precise movements of a trained assassin. Like the fire dragons of lore.

They never talked about it. Not before Assana left them at Briarhaven, nor after, when their new but already unshakeable bond should have allowed for such raw reflection. Ravenna said very little at all on their journey to Whitecliffe, most of her measured words reserved for inquiries into Esmerelda's health. Esmerelda didn't ask the questions desperately burning in her belly. In this way, she was looking after Ravenna's well-being, too.

One night, as Ravenna kept watch, she informed Esmerelda that Drystan had died. She'd known the precise moment it happened, for the magic he'd carried with him had returned to Ravenna, where it would stay. The shock of her smooth confession, how it rolled off her tongue without the ebb and flow of emotion trapping its progress, left Esmerelda with a terribly hollow feeling. Ravenna was mourning. She could see it behind the priestess' cool eyes, no matter the trouble she took to hide it. But she wasn't ready to share it, not even with the one she'd not so long ago called *the sister I chose.*

Was it their bond that kept Ravenna at her side? Or was it fear of facing a past that would never stay that way forever?

Esmerelda approached this suggestion only once.

I understand if you need to leave, Ravenna. It'll be no betrayal of me. You have done more than enough for me.

How could I leave you, knowing what awaits? The shock of seeing your father again, of your realm knowing your truth. And to deliver a child in the middle of it all? You mustn't be alone for that.

I won't be alone. I'll have Ryan.

I'll be here until your child is born, whether you like it or not.

Ravenna, that isn't—

I know what you meant. Selfless love is the purest form of love, Esmerelda, and I know your heart. It's selfless love I return to you by refusing your offer. Please don't suggest it again.

"Almost there," Esmerelda said to Ravenna, who'd been silent for hours.

Ravenna nodded. Her face disappeared behind her hood, but Esmerelda didn't miss her gloved hand reaching up to wipe her eyes.

STEWARD RUTLAND WENT ALONE INTO THE MANOR HOUSE. Esmerelda challenged this choice, but his wisdom stayed her from following. *Everyone in there believes you dead. Let it be me to soften the blow that might knock a lass down.*

"What do you think he's saying to them?" she asked Ravenna.

"It wouldn't surprise me at all if a bribe exchanged hands."

"I shouldn't have put him in this place. I regret it."

"Not as much as he does," Ravenna said. A light laugh was the first sign of ease she'd shown in days. Esmerelda laughed with her.

"What if Ryan won't see me?"

"Don't be foolish. He went to the Wastelands for love of you. He's been through it, that's all."

"You heard what Steward Rutland said. About him not being as I'd remember him."

"That could mean many things, Esme. But your task is to stay strong, and remember why you're here." Ravenna's violet eyes traveled downward. "What binds the two of you."

"I fear it's not me who needs to hear these words." Esmerelda raised her hand against the glare of the setting sun. "I'm worried that Jesse hasn't returned."

"I'm worried too."

"You can't sense him?"

"No. Not for weeks."

Esmerelda chewed at her bottom lip. She feared giving more power to her fears by speaking them.

Hardly a tick of the sun passed before Rutland's return. "Steward Strong has already ridden for Warwicktown. It's only the stewardess, her staff, and Ryan."

"Thank you, Steward Rutland. For everything."

He laughed. "Donnae thank me as if this is where I leave ye. I'll be taking a guest apartment for the eve, and tomorrow you and I ride for Warwicktown. Together."

Esmerelda swallowed. Nodded.

"He's in his father's study. He's waiting for you."

She breathed out, closing her eyes as the briny air passed over her flesh. Memories of those nights in the barn swelled against her heart. Of a before that promised an eternity of after.

Rutland touched her arm. "Leave your hope here, lass. He doesnae remember things as you do. He may never. It does no good wishing for what was."

Esmerelda straightened. She looked up, meeting his gaze. "He will remember when he sees his child growing. A child created not by chance, but by love."

"Aye, but when he doesnae, your father and I will be sure he does right by ye, just the same."

. . .

ESMERELDA ENTERED THE MANOR HOME ALONE. SHE PASSED THROUGH a door familiar to her, though the sense she was in a foreign land, unwelcome, overpowered the happy memories. Stewardess Strong stood at the entrance to the dining room, arms crossed. She said nothing to Esmerelda, offering instead a curt nod through a strained look. Esmerelda was certain if Rutland hadn't been there, Andrija Strong would already have the news of Esmerelda's return spread half across the Reach.

Esmerelda turned toward the study. It was a large room for the size of the manor. Books that neither Hamish nor Ryan would ever read—books, which had a value nearing gold, a luxury of the wealthy—lined the shelves built into the sturdy walls. These books were Jesse's. He'd told her this, one of the many nights they'd lain awake searching for common ground. Esmerelda wished now that she'd told him how she always snuck one of the old tomes in her gowns when she'd visit Sandycove. Her father had no such flights of fancy in his own keep. What books he possessed had practical use, nothing more.

But not even wealth had been enough to elevate Hamish Strong's son above those of men like Law or Rutland in her father's eyes.

Ryan was just inside, bowed over and wringing his hands on the settee. She lingered in the doorway, awaiting his invitation to enter, but he didn't look up. The fear curled off him in sharp waves.

"Ryan?"

His head shot up like an animal caught in the sights of a hunter's bow. He stood, then sat, then stood again. "Lady Esmerelda."

She tried to smile. "You haven't called me that since we were children."

"I cannae recall ever addressing you any other way."

She turned and closed the door behind her, her heart pulsing so hard against her flesh she wondered if it was possible for her heart to break clean through.

"They tell me I'm in love with ye," he said. He was again seated.

He'd wedged himself into the center of the settee, leaving no chance for her to share it with him.

Esmerelda lowered herself to the chair across from him. She pressed her hands into the rough fabric to steady the trembles coming on. "They tell me you've forgotten that love."

"Aye, if it ever was."

She peeled back her traveling cloak, revealing the swell of her belly more fully. "It was. It more than was."

Ryan's mouth twitched as he regarded the sight in barely disguised horror. "Is that..."

"I haven't suddenly taken to wearing pillows in my gowns."

"A bairn? And you're saying it's ours?"

"You really don't remember?"

"You and I? I cannae put my head around it. I ken the Guardians aren't that funny, creating such a pair. It must have been the brandywine, or a festival night, or—"

"It wasn't the wine." Desperation crept into the back of her throat. Esmerelda steadied her voice. "It wasn't once. And it wasn't an accident."

Ryan pressed his lips together in a tight smile. He shrugged, sighing.

"We both gave up our lives for this, Ryan," Esmerelda pressed. She leaned forward, but the swell of her belly held her back. "You were sent to the Wastelands for it. I let my whole family believe that I'd *died*. I gave up *everything* to wait for you."

Ryan's eyes glassed over with tears. "I donnae wish to hurt ye, Esmerelda."

"Then *don't*." She was crying now, too.

"To tell you I love ye, it would be a lie."

"When you look at me, what do you feel?"

"I..." Ryan lowered his eyes. "'Tis nothing you'd want to know. Nothing that wouldnae cause ye harm."

Esmerelda dropped to the floor. On her knees, she approached him. She gazed up, her teary eyes imploring him. "Look into my eyes and tell me you don't love me. Tell me you have no memories of all those months, of loving me by the moonlight, all those tender words. I'd never heard such pretty words." She pulled his hand and rested it against her belly. "Feel that love here, and then tell me it means *nothing* to you!"

Ryan's lower lip quaked. He met her gaze. "I truly donnae remember any of what ye say."

She laced her fingers through his as they rested against her dress. "And this? Does not even my touch stir your recollection?"

He shook his head.

Esmerelda felt the breath leave her body. A hardening encased her heart to prevent it from shattering. Ryan once said the Guardians were without humor, but what, then, was this? They'd watched as Ryan and Esmerelda chased their love against the odds, allowed them both to steer toward chaos to protect it, only to lead them here?

She peeled herself away from him and forced herself to stand. "You may not remember, but I'll never forget. Soon the entire kingdom will bear witness and see what you cannot, for this bairn will not wait much longer to show itself."

"Ye need not worry. I ken what my obligations are."

Hot tears fell down her cheeks. "Your obligations."

"Aye." The miserable look he wore broke her heart more than any words he'd spoken. "I know what I must do, for your honor and mine."

"For *honor*."

"Aye. What else is there?"

Esmerelda wiped away her tears. She re-buttoned her cloak. "Aye. What else, indeed."

3
ABSENCE

Brandyn backed up several steps to better appreciate the handiwork of the goldsmith. He'd never seen one man's head encased in gold before, let alone two, so he had nothing to compare the eager smith's work to. The man came highly recommended from Uncle Khallum. As far as Brandyn could tell, it was a fair job. A good one, at that. He'd even taken the trouble to work around Mortain's final shock, and Mads' pleading horror, which Brandyn hadn't known he'd enjoy so much until he saw the completed work.

"My lord? Is the work to your liking?"

"Do I like it? That hardly seems a strong enough word. Fantastic work, Childress."

"Thank you, sir." Childress bowed lower than he needed to.

"See my Master of Purse for your coin and tell him I said you're to be paid double. I'll put in a good word with my uncle as well. Should he ever have need of... well, these services."

The man's eyes lit up. He thanked him as he backed away, affecting several haphazard bows that were as unnecessary as the first. Brandyn wasn't used to this yet, but he smiled.

He turned to Storm, still grinning, this time with pure joy. "So? What do you think?"

"As far as molten gold heads go, they're quite striking," she answered. "Where will you put them?"

"Next to my mother's sword, The Betrayer, I was thinking. Oh, please don't let me forget to send a raven to my uncle thanking him for the gold. I'd also like to invite him to see the result for himself."

"Brandyn, you don't thank a man for what is owed. The gold was payment for the fruit and grain. He should be thanking you, for keeping his men from starving to death."

"I'd still like him to come see it."

"All right."

"What? Say it, then."

"Nothing."

Brandyn leveled a glare at her. "I know you. Nothing has changed between us that I can't see through you. "

"Everything has changed," Storm said with a light laugh. She waved her hands. "Look around you. Longwood is ours again, but more truly, it's *yours*. You're the Lord of the Westerlands, Brandyn. I should start getting used to addressing you by your proper title, before someone accuses me of being an impertinent, unfit for service."

"Lord, *for now*," he reminded her. He turned away from the heads, aiming his gaze into the courtyard and the gardens. He'd always preferred this place. It was like stepping from one world into another, the lush flora shielding those on both sides of the vibrant veil. One could forget there was still a kingdom, still troubles requiring solving. "My mother will return soon, and then she'll ship me back to the Sepulchre, where I belong. It's only a matter of time."

"Many will thank the Guardians when she returns," Storm answered. "For your family can't handle more change, in addition to all your losses."

Brandyn set his jaw and walked faster, cursing the way he still limped. He might always wear the scars from his torture at the hands of Mortain, the healers had said, but then what good were healers if not to erase the pains? "Mother really believes Ember isn't dead. Without a body, she won't accept it. Arturo tells me Ember never gave up on her, and she'll do no different. There's no turning her mind around on it."

"And you?"

Brandyn stopped in front of a series of vines decorated in deep pink berries. He plucked one and handed it to Storm before dropping a handful into his own palm. "If anyone could cheat death, it's Emberley."

"And?"

"You're annoying sometimes, you know that?"

"Tell me. If I'm to lead your council, it does neither of us good when you keep things from me."

"It's nothing you don't already know."

Storm crossed her arms, dropping the berry back into the dirt. "Remind me, then."

"It's only that I still believe Mother intends to make Emberley the heir. She's always regretted naming me. She's proud to have the Westerlands led by women. If Ember is dead, she's stuck with me."

"Or Gabi."

"She wouldn't choose Gabi. She'll have her wed to a Richland or a Tyndall."

Storm lifted her shoulders. "All right. So? Lady Asherley is young still. She has another forty years in her, is my guess. You'll be an old man yourself before this becomes more than a needless worry."

Mouth full of sweet cinderberry, he pressed, "Now tell me what *you're* holding back."

Storm inhaled hard through her nose. "I can understand why you'd want your uncle to visit. You've developed quite a bond with Lord Warwick, which will, of course, serve you, and this realm. Too long have our differences divided us."

"But?"

"He won't approve of your council."

Brandyn laughed. "It is *my* council!"

"When you say this you sound like a child. Which is precisely what he will claim," Storm countered. "For your council *is* mostly children. Me, Kaslan James—"

"Kaslan is twenty-two. Practically old enough to be a grandfather."

"Jonah Tyndall and Asher Richland."

"So? There's also Arturo Blackfen and Grand Minister Tyndall. Both seasoned, respected men of the realm."

"You have Blackfen spending most of his time delivering messages to and from Wulfsgate, and Tyndall is Grand Minister of the Westerlands. They're away more than they're here. And that's to say nothing of the men supplanted by your choices. Your mother's men, who have long served her and this Reach. Men who will want a role in the chaos ahead."

"Men like your father, you mean."

Storm sighed. "My father is dead. But there are others like him, who once had a seat at the greatest table in the Westerlands, and have now been put to pasture, like sickly cattle. Putting their sons in their place is a slight, not a consolation."

"You think I chose poorly, then?"

"Your uncle will think so."

"Then it is a good thing he's not Lord of the Westerlands." Brandyn stole another handful of berries and stuffed his mouth. He flashed a pink grin at Storm. "Race you back!"

ALASYR MET THE GOAT'S EYES, AND FOR ONE FLEETING MOMENT, IT seemed they'd come to an understanding.

It ended just as quickly, the creature's eyes drawn to some new distraction.

These scruffy animals lining the mountainside weren't the majestic midnight goats that had so captured his boyish curiosity. They possessed none of their rare beauty or unanswered mystery. Their coat, unlike the shimmery silvers of the immortal beats in the Courtyard of Regents, was matted by the day's sleet, a lifetime of filth and struggle crusted between fur and flesh.

Still, it lived and breathed. It was real. Ravenwoods were taught to revere all that drew breath. He had still, in the near eighteen years of his life, never tasted the flesh of any creature. After all that unfolded at The Rookery, this reverence for life seemed more ironic than scrupulous, but the teachings still resonated. All their teachings did, though he'd now begun unraveling the world he'd been created in, separating tenet from trickery.

He had a powerful urge to reach for the goat, to assure him of his intentions. He resisted the lie. Was it bred into him, this instinct to beguile another before drawing them into his full deception?

He would speak the truth now. That Emberley was weaker with each passing day. That the sustenance of meager berries and root plants that dared grow this high in the Northerland Range barely kept her these days. That the risk was too great for him to fly to the gardens at Midnight Crest for more diverse foods. She *needed* this meat. It might make her sick, after the paltry diet he'd been able to provide these long weeks, but then she'd again grow stronger. She might even find her mettle again, and with it, her wings, so they could leave this cursed place of cold and death.

Alasyr possessed no weapon capable of felling the beast. Emberley was the one who was good with a bow, but she'd flown here with only her strange courage and the tenacity that had turned flesh to feather.

Varinya had taken this from her. Seconds was all that had been needed for the lightning to arc and flow from the fingertips of the High Priestess of Midnight Crest, shattering the newly found wings of Emberley Blackwood. Late at night, when Emberley tossed by his side, as she struggled through fitful rest, he tried to imagine her final moments. Had she perished immediately, or had she suffered? Had it been the sundering of her wings mid-flight to steal her life, or the impact when she spiraled into the unforgiving terrain of Icebolt Mountain?

He wanted to ask. He was afraid of the answers. If there was any kindness in this world, Emberley would remember only the moment of her resurrection at Alasyr's shaking hands.

Alasyr, too, had his mother's power to take life. He hadn't *known* he possessed it until after he'd found refuge with Emberley in this cave, just as he hadn't known he could restore life until he'd reversed the dying of the midnight goat.

He'd practiced bouncing lighting against the walls, against the branches of trees fighting for purchase on the steep slopes beyond. On everything but the living.

I'm sorry. He dared not say it aloud and spook the pitiful beast, but he said it to himself, to his humanity, to his old life. To who he was, and who he may still come to be.

Alasyr closed his eyes and let the bright light pass from his fingers into the goat.

ASHERLEY BLEW ON THE DARK RED WAX, WAITING FOR IT TO FORM into a more exact seal before handing the vellum over to Rider Blackfen.

"Just one this time, Lady Blackwood?"

"Were you expecting more?"

Arturo shifted before her, but didn't drop his eyes. The Rush Riders had a boldness about them she'd always been attracted to. They practiced appropriate reverence, but didn't seem particularly intimidated by those in greater power. This one, Blackfen, often seemed to hide some particular amusement in her presence. The suggestion in his impertinent grin bordered on sensual.

Perhaps another time, when she was less distracted.

"Lady Gabi was hoping for a word from her mother."

"Lady Gabi had a letter from me on your last visit. And she will see her mother soon enough," Asherley replied. "She's no longer a child requiring a bounce upon my knee. She's the sister to the current Lord of the Westerlands, and she'll do well to act like it."

"Have you had any signs of Lady Emberley?"

Across the room, Marsh sighed and closed his eyes. She should send the boy back with Blackfen. She'd told herself it was time. The Tyndalls had been without their son and heir long enough. But she'd come to appreciate his presence. Where the others trod around her determination to find Emberley with delicate patience, Marsh threw himself into the action, refusing to sit idly by while others searched for her.

Like Asherley, Marsh believed Emberley was out there.

Besides, he was also old enough to decide for himself, and he'd decided to stay.

"None more promising than the last," she said with a terse smile. "But every day we find nothing, we are closer to finding something."

"As you say, my lady." He turned to Marsh. "Have you completed the letters to your mother and father?"

Marsh stood and passed them to the Rush Rider. "They expected my return by now. You'll... will you..."

Blackfen nodded and tucked them inside his vest. "I'll ensure they understand that your continued presence in Wulfsgate is one of devoted service to the House of Blackwood."

"Thank you."

"And Brandyn? He appreciates your counsel?" Asherley asked.

"When I'm there to give it." There was more Arturo didn't say, but Asherley didn't press him. Unless the Westerlands were falling into the sea, she preferred not to know. It would only make her business here that much harder.

"Hm. Perhaps your time is better spent at his side, not divided between us. Find another to send in your place next time, another Rider. I wouldn't want the ideas of his friends to find greater voice than those of his seasoned elders."

Blackfen said no more. He bowed and then left as quickly as he'd come.

"I always wanted to be a Rush Rider," Marsh mused, more to himself.

"Oh, yes? Then you know they begin their training when they're hardly out of their swaddling. You'd be an old man by their standards, Tyndall."

"I know everything about them," he answered, for a moment still possessed of the raw innocence of a boy. He *was* still a boy, just as

Emberley was still a girl. Yet neither of them were children any longer. The past months had seen to that.

Would this be the man who would settle her Emberley? Sometimes Asherley believed the young man aiding her on her long days and nights in Wulfsgate would make a fine match for her daughter. His name was strong. She'd never lack in affection or devotion. No matter what Blackfen might tell the Tyndalls, it wasn't service but love keeping Marsh in the Northerlands.

Yet, it took more than a decent man and the purity of his love to tend to the spark that lived within young women like Emberley.

"When the next Rider visits, ask him about it. That is, if you can trap him long enough. They're a restless crew," Asherley said. She'd only just replaced the cork in the jar of ink when another familiar face appeared in the door.

"Sister," Asherley said. She didn't feign a smile for Earwyn, who understood her anguish and required no façade from her. How grateful she was for this. How exhausted she was from the mask she put on for everyone else.

Marsh glanced at them both before excusing himself.

"He's a good lad," Earwyn said. She leaned against the desk on the other side of the room, her long white hair dangling down, tickling her fingers. "Hopelessly devoted to Emberley, and to you."

"He is."

"You know who he reminds me of?"

Asherley waited for her answer.

"Byrne."

Asherley scoffed. She started to rebut, but Earwyn was right on the mark, as usual. Marsh and Byrne *were* similar creatures. Devoted and kind, lacking the fire that lived within women like Asherley and Emberley, but nonetheless unafraid of it. "The third search party has returned?"

Earwyn slowly nodded. She looked down at her slippered feet, crossed at the ankles. "Same as the first two. Not so much as a scrap of cloth. It's as if Lady Gretchen disappeared from this world altogether."

"You sound like your husband."

"Do I? And what if I believe him, about what he says happened? About the veil?"

Asherley gave a light twitch of her right shoulder. "Then I say, you're a good wife, Earwyn. For every man deserves someone who believes in their strange whims."

"I don't believe what happened to him is a whim, Asherley. I believe it happened, just as he says it did."

"Then why can he not return? Why has the search party not also *fallen* through this veil?"

Earwyn still looked down. "Alric thinks the veil is shown to those in great need. It opened for him when he was moments from becoming a bear's meal. It may have opened for Pieter when Argentyn Ravenwood killed Princess Assyria, and the boys ran for their lives."

Asherley's response froze on her lips. She again saw Assyria Rhiagain disappear into the void. She felt the lightning arc from her fingertips, a magic new to her and altogether ancient, tearing down two Ravenwoods with such little effort it only added to the dream-like sensation coating everything that had happened to her since escaping Duncarrow.

And Emberley. So proud of her flying. How quickly that pride was snapped in two by the vengeance of a weak woman.

"Ash?"

She again composed herself. "No signs you say?"

"None of Gretchen, but there's evidence of an avalanche."

"This is their third trip over the pass. Is it new or did they fail to notice it the first two times?"

"I fear the latter, which has cost us precious time. We sent a different group of men this time, and they bore witness with different eyes. The tree where Alric went through was branch-deep in snow. It would've buried anyone there when it hit. And yet, when they dug out the snow, she wasn't there."

"We don't know she was even there at all."

"It's where we found her satchel, Ash."

"Means nothing, does it, without Gretchen herself?"

"Her letters were quite clear on her intentions. And though I adore Nyssa and Torrin, and will do as she has asked of me with gladness, I cannot believe she would surrender them to my care if she wasn't serious about what she meant to do. And... and fearful that this intention might render her unable to return."

Asherley tapped the quill against the desk. Like many others, she had no patience for the strangeness of Alric Dereham, but this was her sister, who was quite possessed of her sanity. She couldn't so easily dismiss her without creating a rift between them. "Any word of Maeryn?"

At this, Earwyn chuckled, a dark, pained sound. "She always was exceptionally slippery, even as a girl. She could be down the hall and we might not know it."

"It can't be true, what they're saying about her. She would never turn traitor."

"Can it not? Has that not always been the way of Maeryn, folding herself neatly against any wall that would take her?"

"Aiden, yes, she would betray him. But her own children?"

Earwyn shrugged. Her brows rose. "Then let us hope the truth is discovered soon, for they've already decided her guilt."

Asherley pressed the fate of her misbegotten sister down into the corner of her mind, for now. "Blackfen tells me Brandyn does well enough in my absence."

"Blackfen is a man of honor. All the Riders are. Did you read his whispers?"

"He's too cunning for that. He might not even realize his mind is so guarded." Asherley exhaled. "He won't have to suffer my absence much longer. I'll find Emberley, and then I can return Brandyn to his studies, where he belongs."

Earwyn smiled tightly. "Of course, Ash."

EMBERLEY DIDN'T AT FIRST COMPREHEND WHAT SHE WAS SEEING. So often now when she woke it was like emerging from a dream; the mercilessness of reality, an unwelcome lover. She slept as much as her body would allow, for it was her only defense against this.

But this wasn't that. This resembled a dream, but the shock of the icy morning wind assured her it wasn't. It was Alasyr, bloodied and bent over the corpse of some unfortunate animal. He struck at it with the sharp edge of a stone, over and over, his grunts quickly descending into something closer to sobs.

"Alasyr," she whispered. She was afraid of the strange echo in this cavern; how it made her voice sound. She'd come to prefer speaking low. "What are you *doing*?"

"Trying... to... feed... you..." he managed between gritted teeth.

"You've been feeding me."

"A lot of good that's done."

Ember pulled herself up, drawing closer to the fire. It was their only source of warmth. That and the meager clothes they'd had when they started. "I'm alive, aren't I?"

"For now."

"Well, if I die, you can just bring me back to life again, right?"

Alasyr didn't appreciate her attempt at humor.

The view beyond the cave was a mess of flurries and wind. Another storm, then. Nothing made her miss home like the weather in this treacherous world.

Emberley gathered the mental strength to leave the fire and join him. She knelt beside him. "You're only creating a massacre. Come, let me show you."

Alasyr hid his tears as he passed the stone to her.

"Here, you start under the breastbone, and then slide downward. We'll have to remove the entrails, for they can carry disease, but it'll allow us better access to the meat."

Alasyr nodded. His hands hovered above the mess, searching for purpose. She wrapped her bloodied hands in his and pushed them down into the carcass. "Feel here? Behind the ribs? That will cook up nicely for us. Might even taste good."

"It's just for you. I can't eat it."

Ember felt her sadness creep into her smile. "You should try."

He lifted his shoulders.

"Is that how it's going to be, then? You, looking at me with those heavy eyes, all the while starving yourself?"

"It is until you realize you can still fly just fine." No sooner than the words were out, regret passed across his face. "Forgive me. I know why you won't fly."

Ember tried not to appear too stricken by his declaration made in frustration. He'd been good about not reminding her of her failings. He had the uncanny ability to help her forget them.

"There must be another way down this mountain." She shook the goat. "Do you not think he's been to the bottom? And others like him?"

"I think he lived here. Like I did. Like we do now."

Ember dropped her eyes. "I don't want to live here."

Alasyr laced a bloody hand in one of hers. "I know, Emberley. We'll find our way."

"Me, you mean. I'll find my way. For nothing stops you from flying away and leaving me here."

"I wouldn't just leave you here," he insisted. "But I'm worried. Our resources have run too thin, and I can't return to Midnight Crest. I can't fly far from you at all, for fear I won't find this cave again, or that someone else might stop me before I can."

"When you look into my eyes, you no longer see the girl you told to fly, do you?"

"I still see her." Alasyr's throat ebbed as he swallowed. "But I've never recognized the bravery that lives in you. I've never possessed anything like it. It's because of this that I've failed to help you find it again."

"It was bravery that bid you to leave your home, to come find me." She sighed. "Though I fear I have also ruined your life, in ruining mine. I never meant for that to happen."

"No," he said quickly. "You opened my eyes. To things I should've seen, should have *known*, but instead chose the path all Ravenwoods choose. You've given me a gift you'll never understand. One I can never repay."

These words left a strange feeling in Ember. She returned to the work of dressing the scrawny goat, and when she extracted what meat she could, the two of them dragged the carcass out of the cave, and with a shared breath, hoisted it off the cliff, where it disappeared into the storm.

"Now we just put it over the fire?" Alasyr asked.

"You still have some of those sticks? The ones you collected and dried out for kindling?"

He nodded.

"Come. I'll teach you."

4

MALFENZA

The strange forest that had seemed to Gretchen so out of place in the endless desert no longer seemed that way once she reached the other side. When they emerged from the dense brush and trees, she found herself staring into a proper kingdom.

The desert remained a fixture in the background, but the sense of endless desolation was superseded by a barrage of tan and orange structures packed so tightly she couldn't make out the roads connecting them. The dense living circled high into a hill, winding until the keep at the top... no, this was no keep like any she'd seen. It was a castle of myth, its domes and spires beaming the most dazzling and brilliant colors and shapes as the midday sun dusted sparkles along the tops.

Gretchen had held her question so tight they nearly choked her. "Is that where you're taking me?"

Brahim pointed to the town. Nodded.

"To kill me?" she half-joked.

No one laughed.

"We're taking you to our home," Brahim answered. "I'm told yours looks very different."

"You're told?"

Brahim didn't answer.

"Do you have a name for it?" Gretchen asked, trying another question. She no longer felt like their prisoner, which emboldened her words, but she hadn't forgotten that though they'd sheathed their own weapons, they'd not returned hers.

"Malfenza," his wife Maura answered. "There aren't many of us left now, though one day, right?"

"One day," Brahim agreed. The corner of his mouth twitched. "We still have our dreams."

"The size of this city. I cannot even fathom something like this where I come from," Gretchen mused. "It must be three times the size of Wulfsgate."

Brahim frowned at the foreign word. "Ah, you mean our province."

"Province," Gretchen repeated. "It's all so familiar, yet not at all."

"We wouldn't know anything about it." Curran, Brahim's brother. She needed no magic to discern his animosity toward her; his barbs stuck to the ends of every word she dared speak. She wondered what had birthed such anger in the younger man, who had far more years ahead of him than behind.

"Have you been through the veil?"

"That's your word," Brahim answered. He angled them down a path. "To us it's a door. A door that should be closed forever."

"We do our part to keep those like you out," Maura added.

"Why?"

Maura averted her eyes.

"Why do you think, Intrusa?" Curran volleyed.

"I don't know that word," Gretchen said, though she'd gathered the general meaning.

"Pay no mind to Curran," Maura muttered.

"You won't tell me what it means?"

"He's saying you don't belong here," Brahim told her. "It's a word we use for... for the others."

"How many others have there been?" Gretchen tried to recollect how many had been lost in Torrin's Pass, but her disorientation blurred her memories. When no one answered her, she tried another question. "Malfenza is your... your province. What do you call your kingdom?"

He turned to Maura. "Ah. We know this one, too."

"It's what the others call their world."

"Your world, is what I'm asking," Gretchen amended.

"Tenestela," he said after a pause. He seemed loathe to release the word, and it occurred to her that her questions could lead her into more danger. She'd never heard this word. Brahim and his brood had seen enough visitors from the kingdom to be wary of them, to have a *word* for them. So where were they? Had they been allowed to return? Did no residents of Tenestela ever escape into the White Kingdom?

"Next you'll ask us what it means, as they all do. We don't know," Maura said.

"We know what it means," Brahim gently corrected. "But the language is not our own."

"The endless earth," Maura said, sighing. "There's little sense in it. Our world isn't so big. The Old Ones who named us are long gone."

"You speak too much," Curran accused. "Both of you."

"They're only words," Brahim said.

"You know better than any what words can bring."

"I mean no harm with my questions," Gretchen said quickly. The path shifted to the packed dirt of a proper road. "You say you've never passed through the veil, but you can imagine how strange it must be to find yourself in a world that isn't your own."

"We've heard this before, too," Maura said with a light cluck of her tongue. "Are you hungry, then? You must be, if you dared eating from the forest."

Gretchen paled. "Is the fruit poisonous?"

Maura laughed. "Not the kind that'll kill you. But mind your bowels later."

"Oh."

Curran grunted a laugh behind her.

Brahim stopped near a wagon left to the side of the road. A mule was tethered to a nearby post. He reached for Gretchen's pack. She tightened her grip by instinct, but relented at the weariness in his eyes, at her resistance.

"The way is steep. You'll appreciate a lighter burden," he muttered as he secured the wood handles to the harness on the mule.

"Thank you." Gretchen didn't know how to feel. She was grateful for their aid, but wary of how easily it was offered. She hadn't survived her turbulent formative years by trusting any but herself, but also hadn't found joy until she'd relented and let others in. This was the war she'd fought with herself for nearly forty years. A game of survival that ended only with death. "We're going to the top of that?"

"We live in the palace."

Palace. This word she knew, for her own father used it to describe their world in the trees of Arboriana. It was an old word, one that had fallen out of use elsewhere in the kingdom.

Already she'd become used to the way the dirt responded to her boots; the sharp, earthy aroma that permanently lingered in the air no longer burned her chest and nostrils. This wasn't a world of fantasy, but one parallel to hers; a continuation.

"Are you lords? Or... are you kings?"

"We take no such names for ourselves. The reinar are long gone. We are the ones who remained, and so the palace is ours."

"Where did they go?"

Brahim returned to his thoughts.

They continued on, passing through two elaborate arches as they entered what Brahim had called their province. A word was carved over the first gate. Malfenza, she guessed. It was written in an ornate script she couldn't read. Once through the entrance, Gretchen braced herself for the bustle of the packed town she'd spied from the hill, but in place of this energy was the startling absence of it. To her right and left, stalls lay abandoned. A harsh wind ripped past her, filling her face with dust. A snapping sound drew her attention to a standard flying high off the side of a tall building, but the flag had seen better days. Only half of it remained.

"Where is everyone?" Gretchen mused. She looked around, searching for eyes peering out from windows. For children playing in alleyways.

"Departed," Maura said without elaborating.

"All of them? There's none let?"

"Some. A couple dozen at last count, but most keep to themselves, as we do."

"A couple dozen? That's all?"

"Hm."

"Is all of... all of Tenestela like this?"

Maura paused and turned to Gretchen with a sigh of impatience. "Not yet. But it will be, if your kind cannot resist the temptation of coming to a world that doesn't belong to them."

"The light is passing, Maura. We won't make it before dark if we can't keep our pace."

Maura shot her one last knowing look, long enough to make Gretchen's blood cool, before moving on ahead to walk by her husband.

"If it's welcome you're after, you should've stayed in your own world," Curran said as he came up beside her. "There's nothing for you here, Intrusa."

By the time they reached the crest of the winding main road of Malfenza, Gretchen's legs threatened to collapse beneath her. Brahim, Maura, and Curran seemed oblivious to her exhaustion, all three still just as spry as when the journey began.

She took a moment to look back on the path they'd taken. The last slice of sun disappeared across the horizon, but there was still enough light to see the endlessness of Malfenza's tightly coiled sprawl. Squinting, she even made out the forest, now so far in the distance it seemed impossible they'd come all this way before sundown.

Gretchen let herself sink to an iron bench in the courtyard. She felt Curran's scrutinizing eyes on her, but she didn't care. She had nothing left except what she'd reserved for Pieter.

Vibrant orange fruits decorated the trees littering the courtyard. She'd seen some like them in the Southerlands. It seemed impossible that they could be the same. Everything here had been close enough, but not quite. *Almost*, she thought, as she took in all the unfamiliar sights and smells.

A young woman met Brahim and began carrying the contents of the wagon into the palace. Gretchen had to shield her eyes to follow the girl's path, as the dazzling white of the domes and spires, combined with the setting sun, blinded her.

She didn't dare hope Pieter might be waiting inside. Every time she'd said his name, asked after him, their lack of response was intentional. She didn't know how to interpret their strange silence.

Nor could she deny her curiosity. What a world this was already, and she'd only seen a glimpse. Alric would be beside himself when she at last sat before him and told her tale; if the Guardians were on her side, all her children would again be with her to hear this story. They'd laugh and muse over the strangeness, in the safety that everything was as it should be once more.

"Gretchen, you coming?" Maura's voice broke her reverie.

By the time Gretchen looked up, Maura was already climbing the long steps. Gretchen looked for Brahim and Curran, but they must have slipped inside when she was lost to her thoughts.

Gretchen followed. She froze as her feet connected with the first step, which was neither stone nor wood, nor even the rare marble of the Seven Sisters, but something more dense and lovely. She hurried as fast as her tired legs would carry her, and when she stepped between the massive alabaster pillars welcoming her into the palace, she couldn't resist kneeling to press her palms to the strange floor, cool to the touch. The colors were startling swirls of cream and light blue, but it was the texture, more solid than rock, more brilliant than any stone she'd known in her own world.

The young woman who'd helped Brahim cast a small shadow as she stood before her. "Are you unwell?"

Gretchen winced as she found the strength to again stand. She would hurt twice as much in the morning if she had the good fortune to make it that long. "Fine. Thank you."

"I'm Jassmyn, the attendant here at Malcazara."

"The palace."

Jassmyn nodded. "I can see to your needs, whatever they are."

The way Jassmyn said *whatever* left Gretchen with a strange feeling. "I appreciate your kindness. Where did Brahim and the others go?"

"It's sundown. Brahim and Maura have gone to temple."

Gretchen was too exhausted to ask for further explanation. "And Curran?"

Her expression darkened. "Retired for the evening. He won't emerge again until the sun rises." Jassmyn turned and pointed to a broad, winding staircase. "Can I show you to your room?"

Gretchen nodded. She strained to keep up with the younger woman, who climbed the steep stairs with ease. "You said you're the attendant?"

"Yes."

"Are you kin to Brahim and Maura?"

"No."

Gretchen pushed through her fatigue and quickened her pace. "How did you come to be their attendant?"

Jassmyn kept her eyes ahead, but Gretchen still caught a flash of wariness. "I was among those who stayed."

"Stayed?"

"Here," Jassmyn said, pointing with her arm at the hall awaiting them. It was long... so long the other end disappeared into a blur of white. "You won't mind the dust, I hope. We go many years between visitors."

"I'm not afraid of dust," Gretchen responded, but Jassmyn was already ten steps ahead. She practically sprinted to the door, throwing it open and disappearing within.

"Here you are. There are extra garments if yours need washing. You may come down once the last light has turned to darkness, for temple will end and the evening meal will be served." Jassmyn ran her eyes over Gretchen. "Yes, extra garments. I'll have warm water brought to fill your wash basin so you can clean yourself as well."

Gretchen tried to smile. "Is it that bad, then?"

Jassmyn's mouth twitched. "We cannot control the dust, but we don't have to drown in it," she said. "You'll find your bag on the chair. I've taken care to remove the offensive fruit you had inside, but have touched nothing else. Have you any further needs?"

"Not that I'm aware of, no."

"Wait for darkness, then return to the base of the steps. If you continue back straight from the entrance, you'll come to another courtyard. You cannot miss it, for there's only way if you follow what I've said. This is where the evening meal will be served."

"Thank you, Jassmyn. I will be mindful of the time."

Jassmyn assessed her one last time, backed out of the room, and closed the door.

GRETCHEN WAITED UNTIL THE LAST LIGHT DISAPPEARED OUTSIDE THE circular window in the center of her room before slipping downstairs.

While she bathed, Jassmyn had slipped in and unceremoniously removed her filthy clothes and grime-covered boots. Although the clothing awaiting her was cleaner—nay, nicer, silks and gold cloth were as rare as they were impractical in the cold north of her kingdom—she couldn't squash the sensation that every step farther into their world was a more secure prison.

The ease in which they'd taken her into their home, given her board and provisions, didn't calm her fears, as it might have someone like Holden. She couldn't help waiting for the invisible sword to slice from the shadows the moment she relaxed too much.

She decided she'd let them speak and then again ask about Pieter.

The courtyard was easy to find, as Jassmyn said. Trees with bowing branches and patterned bark provided cover as she stepped inside. Unfamiliar but sweet scents, like fruit and bread, carried across the cool evening breeze. The strange stone was warm beneath her feet, like the wind on their trip from the forest to Malfenza.

"Gretchen." Brahim waved from ahead. "Join us."

She made her way through the veil of exotic flora. It reminded her of what her kin had tried to create in their kingdom of trees.

The table was large enough for a king's feast and seemed to be spun from gold itself, though that was impossible. There couldn't be enough gold in this world to waste on something men and women spilled their food upon.

Gretchen slipped over the bench across from Brahim and Maura who, despite the great length of the table, sat side by side. Maura offered her a practiced smile, one that, Gretchen guessed, Brahim had coerced from her before Gretchen's arrival.

Her bowl steamed with a dark, thick broth smelling of spice and smoke. She inhaled the scent and closed her eyes for a moment.

"Others have found this meal fitting to their constitution," Brahim said. He was more at ease now, in a flowing white tunic and loose pants. His long hair was undone, falling over his shoulders in waves. "Not unlike the food of your world, I understand."

"It smells wonderful," Gretchen said. She lifted her spoon, and they both nodded. As the first hint of flavor touched her tongue, she resisted the urge to moan. She could eat twelve bowls of this. "It *is* wonderful." She noticed their empty bowls. "Have I come too late?"

"We finished before you arrived. We expected you would want words from us."

Gretchen moved to set her spoon aside, but Maura shook her head. "You eat."

"All right, then." Gretchen's heart sped in her chest. She forced herself to take another bite.

"You aren't the first to come to us. Each time, I say to the one who has stepped through, how can we ensure you'll be the last?" Brahim started. "They say, can we bring more, can you come to us? Some cannot handle the dismay of the door not reopening for their return and go mad with grief. Others stay in gladness, for they find this world more amenable than the one they left. But none can ever answer our question."

"Nor can I, I'm afraid," Gretchen said. "Until I passed through in search of my son, I didn't fully believe it was real."

"So there are those who know of your... veil, then?"

"There are whispers... but those who make the claim are dismissed as mad. My husband's brother is one such man. He claimed to have fallen through, but only just. He saw the desert, a tree like the one in our world, and then he returned."

"Better that your kind think he's mad than attempt to follow his example," Maura said.

"I don't think it's so easy to just step through," Gretchen said, shaking her head. "Or more would have done it."

"Yet some do."

"I'm aware of no others."

"Do you doubt what we say?" Maura countered.

Brahim tensed at her side. "Is it so unreasonable, belleza, when we haven't found a way to send them back to their world?"

"It's not that I doubt you," Gretchen said. "But I can't help you understand it any better. There are still moments I think this must all be the remnants of a dream. It goes against everything I've believed in my life." Gretchen raised her spoon. "Despite how real this feels going down, despite what I can see with my own eyes, this still defies reason."

"Now that I don't believe," Maura said with a surprising grin. "I've watched you watching. Things aren't so different for you as you would've expected."

"It may be more fair to say I had no expectations, as until I actually stepped through, I still didn't believe I could."

"Well, you're here now, and it's too late to send you back, so we must find another way to deal with this," Maura said as she sighed.

Gretchen froze. She looked down at her empty bowl. No telltale signs of a bellyache, but it could be slow-acting poison. She wouldn't know until it was too late.

Maura turned to her husband. "We protect her. We home her. We feed her. Yet the distrust in her eyes doesn't wane."

"Perhaps if you told me why I'm here. Why you helped me at all, when you had no reason to. When you had more reason *not* to, given your strong feelings about others like me," Gretchen countered. She pushed her bowl aside. "I wouldn't have come here at all, if I didn't believe my son, my Pieter, had come through here first. You couldn't possibly know this, but I have already lost two of my children to the fickleness of fate, and to lose Pieter would be more than my heart could bear. It already is. Forgive me if I find it hard to trust, Maura, Brahim, for I've grown so used to the world taking that I cannot fathom why it would now give anything."

The couple exchanged a look. Brahim surprised her by reaching forward and clasping one of her hands in his. "We won't harm you, unless you harm us. We've harmed none who have come through the veil, as you call it, even though it's our mission to keep more from coming."

Maura joined him, linking her hands around their knot. "I, too, am a mother, Gretchen. I know the pain of which you speak. All too well."

"Have you lost a child?"

"There are no children in Malfenza. There will not be children in Malfenza again, not until the day where we can be certain no more of your kind will ever come here."

"I don't understand."

"Your people have brought a disease that claims the lives of our little ones," Brahim said. "Malfenza was once... it was once what it should be. And then your kind came, and the children fell, one by one. It took us far too long to understand why."

"We sent them all away, every last child," Maura said. "The few women remaining in Malfenza know better than to bring a child these days. But, if one does, then she kisses them, and sends them away, before her love can take root. They are sent to be with others until they are old enough that the disease can no longer take them."

"Disease," Gretchen whispered. "I know of none that kills only children, and so swiftly."

"Your world is not ours, and ours is not yours," Brahim said simply. "Some who have come here have perished from things that would do no more than set us back for an afternoon."

"Where do you send them? The children?"

"Cadsella. A province, like this one, except they haven't had the fever of the outsiders sweep through. You asked us before, why we stayed," Maura said. "If we don't keep your kind from traveling farther into our world, then Cadsella will no longer be safe. Our children will no longer be safe. And there will truly no longer be any hope for us."

"Where are the others? The ones you say have come through?"

"One or two are still in Malfenza. The others... they've either succumbed to disease, or moved closer to the sea. But never Cadsella. They come there, they're killed onsite, no second chances. For our children won't let them."

"I..." Gretchen released both of her hands, breathless. "I have no words adequate."

"Your Pieter," Maura said. "He came through, just as you did, and he, too, found the forest, seeking aid. When we came upon him, he was scared, calling for you, for his father."

Gretchen was stunned. Her hope surged. "You've seen Pieter! Where is he, then? Did you send him to Cadsella with the other children?"

"How could we, if he might have carried that disease with him?" Maura again looked at Brahim, who nodded. "Gretchen, he's here, but we couldn't tell you so without first preparing you, for he will not be as you remember him."

"Not be as I remember him? Has he been hurt?"

"He's as well as he can be. He even stopped crying out for you in his sleep. But that was years ago."

"Years? What are you saying?"

Maura choked a soft cry into her palm. Brahim took over. "Pieter didn't come to our world mere weeks before you joined us. Years have passed since we found him, alone and afraid. He is a man now, old enough to have his own family. And he has..." Brahim bowed his head.

"Let him tell her, Brahim. That's Pieter's tale to share."

Gretchen shook her head. "No. That's impossible. That's not my Pieter. It must be some other boy."

"Through the years, we returned with Pieter to the door. Many times we tried to find it again, to send him back to those who loved him. But it would never appear for him. It has never appeared for us, which is why we've never been to your world." Brahim sighed. "I'm afraid, Gretchen, that there is no return. Not for Pieter. Not for you."

"We'll help you settle into a life here, as we helped Pieter," Maura insisted. Her smile faded to worry. "Brahim, she's gone pale." She scrambled to her feet.

"I'm fine, I'm fine," Gretchen insisted as she stumbled away, the warm stones no longer welcome, the pretty scents now foreign, cloying.

Gretchen fell against a tree just as the nourishing meal turned to bile at the back of her throat.

5

IF NOT LAND AND LOVE

Darrick considered the strange table centering the room in Lord Warwick's Hall of Warring. Though no one spoke of it directly, the teakwood monstrosity consumed the thoughts of all gathered, evident in the way the other men never let their comfort lull them off their guard, lest they lose a limb or more to the unforgiving and intentional serrated edges. They sat back in their chairs, some even fully erect, but not a one leaned forward.

This was analogous with the man himself. In their short acquaintance, Darrick knew Khallum as passionate and loyal. He demanded the equivalent in others, sustained by the belief that neither of these commitments could be earned absent of regular doses of fear. He made all acutely aware of the fate awaiting those who fell short.

"Right, men, as ye know, we're here to discuss the matter of Oldwin."

Khallum's men alternately grunted, cheered, or—carefully—pounded their fists upon the sharp, briny table. This was theater; the expected response. The fire behind their eyes was not yet lit.

"Do ye not mean *King* Oldwin?" Garrick quipped.

Khallum addressed this with an involuntary twitch of his eye. "The Knights of Duncarrow now guard the isle. Their ships have been anchored beyond every port in the kingdom large enough to bear a vessel to sea, for near a fortnight. I ken they'd make landing if they wanted a war, so it's time we understood what they do want."

"What else could they want?" Rutland asked. "Their presence in our harbors incites only one thing."

"Yet no goading from us lures the rats to port, aye?" Hamish countered.

"They mean to keep us in. Keep us from sailing for Duncarrow and ending this," Law said. "There's not enough of them to win a war."

"The Knights, no. The Rhiagain Guard is far larger," Darrick rejoined. "They'd already outgrown the Isle of Belcarrow when my father was king. I doubt Oldwin even knows their numbers. Assyria would, but... but she's gone now. Do we know, have they been deployed to the kingdom?"

"We've word from young Lord Quinlanden that Oldwin has the Rhiagain Guard scouring the forests of the Hinterlands. Cian's men brought a couple of the guards to Duncarrow, to the prison, to see what they could learn. Seems Oldwin has them searching for something."

"The Hinterlands? Lick of sense that makes," Rutland said.

"How would ye know?" Garrick challenged.

"Mortain wanted something from the Saleen, badly enough to slaughter them. Oldwin and Mortain are cut from the same cloth. With their lands empty, Oldwin and his men only need to find a way in," Darrick said. "Not knowing what he's after may be our greatest weakness."

"There's still more of us than them," Garrick grunted. "If we all take up the sword."

"All of us? If you mean the kingdom, they've long abandoned us," Allarick Nye said.

"You're ready for war, Garrick, and we donnae even know what they want," Hamish countered. "What we're fighting for."

"Aye, are we not fighting for the realm, then?"

"We aren't fighting for anything if they won't engage us."

"Perhaps we've nay sent enough men to entice them!"

"We'll have no shortage of men, now that the whole of the kingdom knows Prince Darrick is back. They'll nay stomach a wily magician in his place!"

"Aye, they're just waiting for someone to rise up and lead this!"

The men argued in pockets of charged cross-talk. Darrick returned to his own thoughts, where the truth niggled at him, there, but beyond his reach.

When Darrick was a boy, his father had no interested in the Medvedev. His own curiosity about the kingdom led him to approach Khain with questions the king wasted none of his time in answering. *If you've a care for trees, boy, you have a whole kingdom full of them.*

"Aye, aye," Khallum boomed, restoring order. "We've a few things to consider, but let us nay forget that *we* have the rightful king here, at *our* table." He nodded at Darrick. "The sorcerer is no Rhiagain. He's a blight upon this kingdom. Have ye seen even one lord or lady of this realm bend the knee in deference to their new sovereign? Nay, and ye willnae. He has no power here unless we allow him to take it."

"We could have a hundred rightful kings at this table," Law said, the only calm voice at the table. "And they'd do us no good at all, if we can't get to Duncarrow to restore them."

"Who says the king has to be in Duncarrow? Aye, high time he sits in the Southerlands, donnae ye think?" Garrick said. "The least the Rhiagains can do for us after all they've taken."

"The other Reaches might have something to say about that," Law said with measured patience. "Duncarrow has long been a symbol of power to this realm. It would take more than our words on vellum to undo this. It's time we invite the other lords to this table."

"Which lords? The *boys*, you mean, running the Westerlands, Easterlands, and Northerlands?" Khallum countered.

"You were a boy when you rose to the title," Law reminded him, unruffled.

"Aye, with bigger balls than the three of them combined."

Law applied admirable restraint in not rolling his eyes.

"Lady Yesenia will talk sense into young Cian," Rutland added, with a brief flush in his cheeks. Khallum remembered something he hadn't thought about in years; how his sister used to slip out in the night to meet Rutland, in what they both thought was secrecy, when the entire Reach knew. Khoulter was negotiating their betrothal when Yesenia was sold to Corin Quinlanden. Rutland licked his wounds and found another wife, but Khallum saw now his flame for her had never quite died.

"Tuck yer cock back in, Erran. She's a Quinlanden now," Garrick quipped.

"Yesenia is a Warwick," Khallum gruffed. "And aye, she'll straighten the boy out, like she did Byrne and me, I've no doubt. But in time to do anything about our present trouble with the sorcerer claiming our crown?"

"Oldwin has no interest in being king," Darrick said, voice low. The raucousness died down. All eyes turned his way. "The world of men is beneath him. To assume he possesses the same concerns and motivations as us would be to underestimate him in a very fundamental way. Declaring himself king is but a means to an end. To defeat him, we must discover what end he's after, for if he succeeds in whatever machination drives him, the business of kings and queens will no longer matter."

"Do you have a suggestion, Your Grace?" Law asked.

Darrick pushed his chair back and stood. "Not yet. But you'll forgive me if my mind is elsewhere at present. My wife and son have arrived this morning with Scholar Edevane. They're waiting in the gatehouse, and after five long years, not even an immortal tyrant can keep me away. The business of this kingdom remains my priority, but the business of my family calls to me now."

. . .

"HE THINKS HIS COCK MORE IMPORTANT THAN THE KINGDOM, DOES he?" Garrick growled when most of the other men had left.

"Mind your tongue, lest I take it," Khallum warned. "The prince has waited years for this, and we'll nay stand in his way. A man whole is worth more to this cause than one severed from his purpose."

Garrick grunted.

"What, then, do we fight for, Garrick, if not land and love?"

"Lord Warwick." Rutland, from behind him. "A moment?"

"Aye, what is it, then?"

"Alone. Sir."

"Go on with ye," Khallum said, waving his hand at Garrick. "What are ye jawing at? Waiting for one of us to turn into a fully trussed boar to whet the hunger in your eyes?"

Garrick shuffled out with a defiant swagger in his step. Khallum wanted to knock it right out of him. Unlike Hamish, who still agonized over his unwitting role in the slaughter of the Saleen, Garrick carried himself a victor. Khallum would need to put a stop to this, before it grew legs and ran ahead of them all.

"Make it quick," Khallum said, turning to Rutland. "Ransom is expecting me in the armory."

"How is he?"

"Not as he was. I haven't lost hope." He glanced into the open air beyond the balustrade of the room. He'd never tire of seeing his men again working; their strength returned to them. How their smiles had returned when Gwyn went to visit them with her baskets of bread and fruit. They'd never voiced their gratitude, but he saw it in their eyes, and it was one less thing to keep his nights long. "But I have other sons."

"I have something I need to tell you. Something I donnae quite know how to say."

Khallum snapped his attention back to his friend. "Aye? Was there another collapse in the mine?"

Rutland shook his head. He wouldn't meet his eyes. Khallum's impatience became fear.

"Say it, then. Donnae leave it hanging for the air to take."

"Someone has returned to the Southerlands. Someone you believed lost to you."

Khallum snorted. "That all? It cannae be anyone so important. I have everyone I need here."

"It's Lady Esmerelda, my lord."

The stone floor beneath Khallum's feet shifted. A light, airy feeling swam up behind his eyes, right as his knees buckled. Erran rushed to steady him, but Khallum flailed his arms in defiance. "Aye... aye, so they've found her then. Her body is at last returned to us."

"No. She's not dead, Khallum. She's alive as you or me."

"I *know* you cannae think this is something to jest about!"

"I would never," Rutland said with a pitiful look. "I regret not knowing the right words, my lord, for a situation such as this. I've nay found myself in one like it before. But what I say to you is the truth, and though I know 'tis a great shock, it's also a great blessing. Your sweet lass is alive, and she's here, waiting to see ye. Waiting to see her father."

He reached for the shit-stained ledge, his breaths pushing hard against his chest. "What you say isnae possible, Rutland. *Isnae possible.*"

"As I would've said, before I saw her with my own eyes."

"One doesnae return from the sea after *months*!"

"Lady Esmerelda wasnae ever in the sea, my lord."

"How? How hasn't she been in the sea?"

Rutland looked away. "That story isnae mine to tell. You should hear it from the lady herself."

"She's *here*, you say?"

"Aye. In the gatehouse."

"The gatehouse of the keep? *My* keep? Does Gwyn know?"

"I donnae ken so." Rutland shifted uncomfortably. "Ryan Strong is with her."

"Ryan Strong? He wasted no time."

"I cannae say more."

"What *can* ye say?" Khallum demanded, panting. Dark spots danced before his eyes, pulling the room away from him. "What *can* one of my most trusted advisors and mates *tell* me about the return of my dead daughter!"

"Only that my lord should prepare himself. For though she's alive, and acquitted of injury, she'll not be as you remember her."

"MAMA!" STEFAN GASPED. ANABELLA HEARD IT, TOO. THE RESPONSIVE creak of the double doors yawning open in the great hall beyond. The ring of fresh steps. The pause as he considered his next move.

All at once, she lost the nerve she'd gathered for this moment. She was now painfully aware of every thread out of place on her dress in desperate need of mending, or the dry spot against her jaw that she couldn't cover with the powder Lady Gwyn had lent her. Her hair, which had been set in flowing curls, had fallen flat. Time and circumstance had aged her, and she was no longer the woman Darrick Rhiagain once called *Isa*, his beautiful, but an old hag with little more than disappointment to offer a prince.

Anabella swallowed these lies. She recognized them for what they were. The moment was here, and if Darrick's love for her lived in such shallow spaces, then it wasn't love at all.

She'd survived worse, but she hoped to live for better.

"Wait here, Stefan."

"Why, Mama?"

"As we talked about. Just give Mama a moment alone with your father, and then I promise, I'll bring him in to you straightaway."

"Will he know me?"

A sob trapped in her throat. "Oh, darling. He'll know you. He would know you in a sea of a thousand faces."

"Wait here? You'll come get me?"

Anabella nodded and kissed him on both cheeks. "I promise you, it won't be long. This day is as much for you as it is for me, sweet boy."

Anabella turned toward the door. Steps sounded on the stone

beyond the doors, and glimpses of him passed through the narrow space between the door and the wall. Darrick.

Anabella exhaled and reached for the door.

Esmerelda sat at the other end of the room from Ryan. The half-barren space was the nearest to resembling a proper study, with one shelf of old ledgers and dozens upon dozens of rolled maps protruding haphazardly from wicker baskets. An old musk, of sweet smoke and long-spilled liquor, hung heavy over the dim light coming through cloudy windows. The dusty floor had seen better days, and perhaps never met the ministrations of a mistress at all. She'd never been in here before. It was a room for men, for warring and plotting. For all those things unfit for a lady.

Her heart had been shattered in a room like this one. Now it would be split another way, as she prepared to see her lies play out across her father's face.

For all her anger toward him, toward his curation of her life without a thought to her happiness, Esmerelda never wanted to hurt him. Most of her memories of her father were filled with love; a kind of love he could never give her brothers as he doggedly prepared them for the hardness of a life of duty. She'd always been his darling. His emerald of the sea. And no matter the bitterness lurking dark in her heart over this role he'd chosen for her, being his princess had been her foremost joy in life until Ryan came along.

She wondered, sometimes, if it was for this that Khallum couldn't forgive Ryan. Not for reaching beyond his station, but for reaching for a prize another man wasn't yet ready to surrender.

All for nothing. She chanced a look at Ryan, but he was still working hard at avoiding her. He traced his fingers along a dusty game table, pretending to be properly mesmerized by the results.

Soon, she'd need to examine what remained of her heart after the devastation of her reunion with Ryan in Sandycove. Of how greatly everything had changed since she last kissed him in the stables, before they both left to embrace the sacrifices required for the life awaiting them. She'd never known such fear as she had speaking their final words to each other by the moonlight, but to be so afraid was the most powerful emotion she'd ever known. She, a lady of the realm, a beautiful and precious pawn of powerful men, was doing what few before her had ever dared. The pull of comfort was potent even then, but she'd resisted it, laughing through her tears as they kissed and embraced and spoke of what it would be like, one day, when they were no longer chained by the world that had created them.

She'd never understand the cruelty of a mind that would keep such happiness away from him. It was a harsh reminder that all things were fleeting. Her sadness couldn't last forever, no matter how sharp the dagger felt buried so deep in her heart.

Esmerelda heard her father before she saw him. His guttural howls, sounding out letters that seemed to form her name, matched by the desperate pleas of Rutland. Esmerelda closed her eyes. She pressed both hands to her belly and said a silent prayer to the same Guardians who had forsaken her.

"I ken he means to murder me," Ryan said. He was on his feet, eyes scanning the room. Looking for a way to defend himself, perhaps. She saw he wasn't wearing his sword, which was strange.

"Not you," she said, turning away from him, rising to face the door that would soon no longer separate her from her deception. Had this always been the end? Her dreams, only that?

Esmerelda opened her mouth wide and sucked in a pocket of air. She trapped it there, enjoying the soft dizziness that eased her nerves.

The doors flew open. Khallum Warwick tramped through them, arms wide, eyes wild.

"*You*," he charged, chest heaving. The word lasted seconds, lingering in the air between them.

Esmerelda's discomfort nearly elicited a laugh, but she feared he might strike her if she didn't quell it. "Me."

"Your letter." For all his bluster upon entering, he was now rooted in place. His flushed face grew deeper red. Unaware of his disheveled hair, his shirt half-open. "You told me ye went to the sea. Ye *told me* you'd spent your own promise!"

Esmerelda desperately wanted to avert her eyes, but she dared not. "I almost did. I considered it."

"Almost? Is that what stands before me now?"

"I knew if you believed there was any hope of finding me, you'd search every corner of the kingdom."

"To protect my dearest and only daughter? Aye, ye can bet on it, and do ye even know how fortunate ye are, girl, to have a father who cares? Or were ye only thinking of yourself?"

"You were going to just hand me over to the king! Sell me, in marriage, to a man known for his cruelty!"

Khallum snorted. "Let us not pretend this isnae about a boy, aye?"

"And what if it is partly about a boy? You would've never let me wed him!"

"You lying whore. You filthy, traitorous whore."

"Lord Warwick!" Ryan jumped to his feet. "She's your *daughter.*"

"And you're a dead man, according to the word of law, so to kill ye again wouldnae be a crime," Khallum said without looking at him. His cool eyes burned holes in Esmerelda, one at a time. Her tears mercifully blinded her.

"I can only say I'm sorry for hurting you and Mother." She surrounded her child in the protection of her palms, and it was then that her father at last saw what his rage had kept him from seeing. "I know now how foolish I was. That love... that even real love can be ephemeral, taken as fast as it's given."

Khallum pointed to Ryan without looking up from her belly. "*He* did this to you?"

"We did this together."

"And why is he not at your side, then, girl? Why does he hover like a criminal awaiting the law to come take him to justice?"

"He... says he doesn't remember."

Khallum laughed. He ran his hands over the dark stubble on his chin. "Aye, 'tis what Hamish told me as well. I've seen better excuses from men who wouldnae lie in the bed they've made. All fun till it's not, aye, Ryan?"

Ryan tried to speak, but Khallum silenced him with a scathing look.

"Nay, you've nothing else to say that I care to hear. Not if you cannae even recall taking my daughter away from me."

"It's not his fault, Father."

"Not his fault?" Khallum's mouth hung, incredulous, as his eyes traveled between the two of them. "Aye, I may not know much, but there's only one way a bairn is made."

"Not his fault he doesn't remember," Esmerelda said, lower.

"I could've... ahh, if you'd just come to me, girl."

This time she couldn't withhold her laughter. "Come to you? You're not serious. And what could you have done, Father, other than shame me and call me a whore, and then send me off to Duncarrow just the same?"

He employed great effort to stay calm. "I shouldnae have said that. I was wrong for it. But 'tis a woman who does as she's told, and a whore who cannae..." Khallum exhaled slowly. "Your mother is better at this."

"It does no good, dwelling on what was."

"Some wisdom there, aye? And where were ye, all these long months, if not in the sea?"

Esmerelda didn't want to drag Jesse's name through this if she didn't have to. Nor would she share Yanna de Medvedev's secret. "All over the kingdom." She almost told him about her time in Duncarrow, but something stayed her.

"And I'm to believe it's this louse in the back ye returned for?"

Esmerelda drew a shaky breath. "When I heard he'd returned and wasn't himself, yes. I thought seeing me might help bring him... bring him back to us."

"Oh, girl. This is why, Esmerelda. 'Tis why it's the job of a man to provide for a woman. Why a father chooses his daughter's husband, knowing what she needs better than she ever could. Do ye now understand? Has it taken all this for you to see?"

"No," she answered, meeting his eyes. She summoned the salt and sand within her; that he'd given her. "I willnae *ever* understand how this world came to see women as no more than pawns of men. I willnae accept it. I *meant* to give myself to the sea. That wasn't all fable. It was Ryan who showed me another way, who saved me and gave me cause to believe there could be more."

Khallum's mouth trembled. "That *boy* who pretends not to know ye? That one, ye mean?"

"He once loved me," she said, head high. "And I still love him. Guardians help me, but I do. And if ye love me, Father, as ye claim to, then you'll catch me before I fall, for my heart has nay *ever* been so heavy."

A scream formed at the back of Esmerelda's throat. It pressed at every inch of her flesh, not content to escape her mouth alone. She buckled forward, face buried in her hands, crying her pain into her palms. Darkness flooded her eyes as she turned, in her agony, toward the chair, but it was the strong arms of her father encircling her from behind that caught her, and she surrendered, not knowing if he meant to comfort her or crush her; not caring in her bleak desperation.

"Forgive me," he cried, his breath hot at her ear as he held her so tight she gave up trying to stand. "Esmerelda, forgive me."

"Isa."

His words floated between them. Anabella had words, too, many of them, years' worth of them, but as her mouth parted to give them life, it was only a soft groan that escaped.

Darrick stepped closer. She sensed his own fears, his own inadequacies, and they weren't so different from his inexplicable reticence with her all those years ago in the Wintergarden, when he led their unlikely courtship with an even more unlikely insecurity, unable to imagine she, a commoner, could love him, a prince.

He was changed. She witnessed the hardships of his time in prison, in his heavier gait, in the trenches lining the corners of eyes more befitting of a man twice his age. But he was still Darrick. Still *her* Darrick.

The unseen weights tethering her fell away and Anabella flew forward, pressing herself into his chest like she'd done in all the hope-filled fantasies that ushered her through the long, early days in Duncarrow. His arms tightened around her with such intensity that it forced a gasp from her chest, and she laughed, inhaling the scent of him, headier but still one her heart recognized.

"Anabella. I'm struggling to believe this is real."

"*You* are? I'm still not certain this isn't a dream," she managed, through her laughter and tears. She peeled away so she could look at him once more. "My husband. Can it be that we can actually be this now, married, to each other?"

Darrick wound both her hands in his and brought them to his mouth. "We have always been married. Memories of those days and nights kept me alive, when nothing else did. It was always you, until I..." He swallowed. "I forgot that old life. I had no choice, for in my heart I feared the worst for you, despite Assyria's promises."

"And now?"

Tears cut paths down his cheeks, falling between them. "Now is all that matters to me. Now is what we have, what cannot again be taken. You're here! You're standing before me, and somehow just as beautiful as you were standing in the cherry blossoms of the Wintergarden. No, more. How can that be possible?"

"You have always known the right words," Anabella whispered. Their lips hadn't yet touched. Once they did, she feared her ability to stop, and there was something even more important now than mending her heart, waiting only a room away.

Darrick decided the matter when he stole her breath with a kiss. She melted into it, and the years fell away.

With a happy sigh, she peeled back. "There'll be time for us still. Right now, there's a very excited little boy on the other side of that door who's been waiting a very long time to meet you."

. . .

KHALLUM HAD NEVER GIVEN SUCH ATTENTION TO HIS EMOTIONS. HE'D been raised by a lord to become a lord, and a lord didn't temper his response to those less than. As the father of lords, he'd shown no less restraint in their rearing, preparing them to command respect, not return it.

But this was his daughter. His glimmering emerald of the sea, the light in his darkened heart. Khallum had been free to love Esmerelda in a way he couldn't love his sons, and when she'd left, she'd taken that, taken every last soft piece of him until there was only the hardness left.

Women were prone to whim. He believed this. He *knew* this. And yet, how many women had he known who subverted this sacrosanct conviction? His own wife deferred to him, not out of requirement, but love. The same woman who had raised his beautiful Esmerelda, sitting before him not in contrition, but in the resolve unique to men.

He once thought if only he could have her back, he'd let her have what her heart most wished for. That he would've defied The Pretender and given her leave to marry the man of her choosing.

Now that she was here, he found this to be less simple. She had a bairn coming any day, and the father, the very one who'd caused all this, was now someone neither Esmerelda nor Khallum recognized.

"No," Esmerelda was saying. "I won't force Ryan to marry someone he doesn't love."

Khallum scoffed. "Love? For what, I ken, does love have to do with marriage?"

"Stop it, Father. You know you love Mother."

"Aye, I do *now*, but it wasnae love that forced our union, as ye well know." Khallum leveled a hard look on Ryan, who sat near Esmerelda but seemed as if he'd never relax until there were miles between them. "I dinnae care how ye feel, boy. You lay with a woman, she's yours to see after."

"I said I would, aye? I said I'd marry her," Ryan said. He didn't look at either of them. "I know my obligations."

Esmerelda laughed. "There you are again, with that word. Obligation! I don't want to be any man's *obligation*, Ryan." She looked at Khallum as if to say, *can ye believe this one?* "I'd not be the first woman to care for a bairn on her own. And it isn't as if marrying a woman means a man will have any hand in the rearing."

"That isnae the point, and you know it." Again, Khallum had to pull back on the anger broiling at the center of his chest. It wasn't for her, anyway. "A lady cannae bring a bairn unwed. You are Lady Esmerelda Warwick, Our Emerald of the Southerlands, and that willnae be your fate."

"*Your* fate, you mean? For is that not all you care about, what they'll say about you?"

Khallum inhaled through his nose. *Steady.* "Aye, my reputation is like gold to me. But you are worth more."

"I could take a husband later in life. Many women do."

"Widows, lass. Widows do. Unless ye want me to have this one dealt with, to earn ye this title properly?"

"Tempting," she murmured.

Ryan squirmed in his seat, crafting more distance between him and Esmerelda. "Your father's right, Lady Esmerelda. You cannae be unmarried with a bairn, and if... if the child *is* mine—"

"*If* the child is yours?" Esmerelda turned on him with fire in her eyes. "You'll watch your tongue with me, Ryan Strong, for there has *never* been another! 'Tis only for you I surrendered my innocence!"

"Apologies," he muttered, eyes on his lap. "That isnae what I meant. 'Tis only that, since the child is mine, it should be me, and not another, to take on—"

"So help me, if you call me and my child a *burden.*"

"Easy. Both of ye," Khallum said. "Esmerelda, you're pale. Let's find you some rest before word gets out. Your mother and brothers will give ye quite a fuss, and you'll need your wits."

"I'm..." Esmerelda's eyes widened in horror. "I..." She gripped her belly. Ryan gasped as the cushion they shared spread dark with liquid.

"The bairn," Ryan whispered. "This is what happened to me ma, when..."

"Go!" Khallum cried. "Go fetch Lady Warwick. She'll know what to do!"

"Aye... aye," Ryan said in a panic. "Aye, I'll go."

Khallum knelt before his daughter. He took her sweaty hands in his and bade her to breathe.

"Is this really happening?" she cried.

"Aye. Aye, I ken it is."

"I'm not ready," she managed through her harried breaths. "I'm not ready for this. I thought I had more time."

"A Warwick is always ready," he urged, brushing her matted hair away from her eyes. "And I willnae leave your side."

Sweat poured from her brow as she regarded him in shock. "A man? In a birthing chamber?"

"And?"

Esmerelda started to laugh. Then her eyes swam back in her head, and she lost consciousness.

6

A PROMISE SPENT

Christian stood at the head of the great roaring fire at the center of the courtyard, stone-faced and sick to his heart. The Grand Minister recited the dead-given rites with the proper solemnity, pausing at all the right moments to underscore the tragedy of Drystan's life lost at the peak of his youth. Those gathered to pay final homage nodded in time, repeating back the most sacred of the verses, as if they hadn't danced around this same fire the night before. Declaring their troubles over; Hadden's Bane ended.

Later, when the moon was at its highest point, Christian would join with what remained of his family, and they'd journey down into the crypts to offer their final words to Drystan, before the Guardians ushered him on to his final journey.

Christian reached for Aylen's hand, but she was several paces away, holding fast to Nyssa and Torrin. Nyssa's little face disappeared in the silver folds of Aylen's flowing robe, while Torrin tried to be strong, staring bravely forth with his hand clutched tight in Aylen's. The whites in his knuckles gave away his agony.

He should be grateful for Aylen's natural way with them. They'd lost almost everything, too swiftly to make proper sense of it. Christian should offer his own comfort, but an icy numbness had spread over his heart and mind. One not even his wife and siblings could thaw.

Bitterness crept into his gloved hands. *He* needed Aylen's touch. *He* was drowning in his grief, in his regret, which was becoming as infinite as his ire. He'd lost not only a brother, but a way out of this tangled mess.

Lisbet stepped to his side. He felt her eyes on him as she turned her head toward him. He pretended not to notice. Her presence drove him near to madness. All his relief at seeing her home and safe had been replaced by suspicion. Bringing that man here. Loading them all up with lies that made no sense; that only made the unfathomable loss of Drystan worse.

"The ice lives within us. We live within the ice. In the valley, as in the mountains, we persist in dualities. Ice. Flesh. Blood. Snow. Bones. Crags." This was a different Grand Minister. Not the one he recalled from boyhood. He didn't know his name.

"We beseech you, Guardian of the Unpromised Future, who has weighed the life of Drystan Dereham and demanded its promise ended, to protect him in his travels from your kin, Guardian of Trial and Tribulation. For though Drystan's life wasn't long for this kingdom, his sacrifice has earned him the reward of eternal, peaceful rest. His braveness against this kingdom's greatest foe will be recalled in memory, word, deed, and song, for all of time to come. We beseech you to see him as we do. As we always will, until time ends."

Lisbet sniffed. She dropped her face in the arm of her gown. She seemed so out of place in the garment, but Earwyn had gently insisted, spending the morning helping her find one she could bear wearing for a few hours. It was what Gretchen would've done, but Gretchen wasn't here, so Earwyn had taken her place; another who had done what Christian could not.

That man, that brigand called Ash, sobbed alone, leaned up against a tree. Christian directed glares at him throughout the ceremony, though the man was oblivious. The only visible signs of enmity between them now were the respective bruises from their shared blows, and the occasional worried glance from Lisbet that they might seek to repeat the exchange.

If you truly doubt his motives, then why is he still here? Aylen asked him as she'd reached for his face, intent on healing him. He'd shaken her off.

No, don't. I want others to know the monster he is.

He wears a similar story on his own face, you know.

Am I the monster, then? Is that it?

She'd backed away from him, wearing a stricken look. *You're not yourself. You haven't been since your father left. Would you like to know what I think? No, well, here it is, anyway, for I'm your wife, and I can only hold my tongue for so long. I think you know this man comes to us with his truth, and your inability to accept this, to break bread with him and share your words, and the kindness I know you possess, both keeps him here and will eventually drive him away, leaving you with only your regret.*

The crowd began to move. The sea of furs dispersed into smaller circles, where they would undoubtedly speak of Drystan in the solemn reverence afforded all dead; faults erased from existence, invented strengths repeated as new truths. How bold and brave Drystan always was! A true hero, from the moment of his miraculous birth! A lord of the realm in blood and deed! Christian wanted to scream, to slice through their deceptions and remind them that neither of Holden Dereham's eldest sons ever possessed the mind or heart for any of this. That Drystan's sacrifice was needless! Where were greater men? The ones clamoring for war? The ones who failed the children of the realm, who then did what they could not?

"You'd do well to take a breath," Alric said from behind him. "Anger with nowhere to go hardens and becomes part of us."

"I don't know what you're talking about," Christian muttered. He pulled the furs from his hood closer to his face.

"Holden was my brother. And you are his son, through and through."

"Was. You say that, as if we know his fate, but we don't."

"We might never," Alric replied. "And that's something you must learn to live with."

"Learn to live with." Christian laughed. He rolled his tongue into the side of his mouth. "How has that become the foundation of my very existence?"

"I know it isn't necessary for me to ask you if the alternative would have been preferable. That he leave Lady Aylen to die at the hands of those men."

"Everyone speaks of this choice as if it was the only one. The only way," Christian hissed. He dropped his voice. "A more cunning man could have saved them both."

"A man more cunning might have caused both their deaths."

He caught sight of Aylen once more. She bowed with the weight of an exhausted Nyssa hanging in her arms. Torrin was tight at her side, looking up at Earwyn, who was no doubt saying something kind and comforting, and exactly what they all needed.

"She's good with them," Alric said, following his gaze.

"Aren't all women?"

"No," Alric said with a laugh. "A woman knows it's her duty to bring a child, but to love a child comes from another place. A woman who would embrace another woman's children as her own is rare indeed."

"I know who my wife is."

"And where she is. Over there. Where you should be, at her side, as she has shown herself to be at yours."

Christian started to retort, but Alric was already hobbling back toward his wife.

MARSH LEANED AGAINST A TREE IN THE WINTERGARDEN. *THEIR* TREE, as he'd come to think of it. He and Emberley had their pick of thousands, and they'd chosen this one, even long after the Ravenwood boy began his illicit stalking, putting his vile stamp on happy memories.

Alasyr knew what had happened to Ember. He *had to* know, because it had happened in his kingdom, with his people.

Problem was, Marsh hadn't actually seen the raven warlock since before Emberley had flown away.

Flown away.

No matter how many times he said these words, they felt no more real. But she had, she'd turned into a raven and flown, Torrin said, and though he was a child and could be mistaken, there was a devastation to his words that left no room for doubt. Lady Blackwood confirmed this herself when she returned to Wulfsgate, though she still hadn't spoken of what happened to her at Midnight Crest. Or to Emberley, after she'd found her wings.

Thinking of Emberley struggling through this alone kept him awake at nights, separated from the much needed rest after long days searching for her. He never should've left her. If he'd listened to his gut, she'd still be here with him.

Memories of her happy giggles, the soft light hitting her freckled cheeks as he leaned over her, peppering her with kisses... he inhaled them. They lived within him, promises of a future he could still feel. She *was* out there. No one that full of life could die before it had been lived.

Alasyr no longer had cause to dip down and train his beady eyes on them, but Marsh still watched for any sign of his dark wings in the sky. He had his bow ready if Alasyr wouldn't come willingly.

"Hunting in the Wintergarden? Be glad Lord Holden isn't here. He'd have you in the stocks," Eavan said. She stepped delicately through the high snowbanks, sidling in next to him. He didn't really know her, but it hurt his heart at how everyone in Wulfsgate averted their eyes whenever she entered a room. By now they all knew how she'd come to be like this. That should have been cause to hold her close and rush to her aid, but instead she was now marked by this terrible thing beyond her control, made worse by her father's status as a traitor. Everyone whispered of how she'd never find a husband now, or have a future as a proper lady of the realm, but no one spoke of how they might help her find either of these things.

Marsh turned and met her eyes. "My arrows are reserved for one bird in particular."

"The Ravenwood," she said, a hint of humor playing in her voice. "Would you really shoot him?"

"Do I not look serious to you?"

Eavan's face dissolved into a laugh. "You in fact look very serious to me."

Marsh turned his eyes back to the sky. "I'd rather not shoot him. But I will, if he won't land on his own."

"You think he knows about Emberley, is that it?"

"I know he knows."

"How do you know?"

"I just know."

"I see." He felt her eye roll from the corner of his gaze.

"No one sees. That's the problem." Marsh nodded to her belly. "How long do you have?"

"I look ready to burst, don't I?"

He shrugged. "I really wouldn't know. I haven't been around many women in their delicate condition."

"Delicate condition." Eavan snorted. "That's one way to describe what's happened to me, I suppose. Months yet, but too late to find a husband who might not know any better."

"If he has eyes, anyway."

Eavan turned to him, offended, but then they both laughed. "It really does seem as if there might be seven of them in here."

"Is there, do you think?"

"Guardians, I hope not!"

"When they're old enough, you'd have free labor."

"Do you think four is too young to turn them on to the loom?"

"Too late, if anything."

Eavan nodded, smiling. "Will he come down? Your raven?"

Marsh inhaled and released a hard breath. "Well, I hope so,

Eavan. It'll be a lot easier for me than having to find a way to come to him."

THE FIRST SWALLOWS OF THE GOAT MEAT HAD SENT EMBER straight to the cliff's edge, bowled over in retching agony. Alasyr could only watch, helpless, as she expelled what was supposed to be her relief. But true to Ember, she'd wiped her mouth, forcing a half-hearted smile as she said, "Just need to get used to eating meat again, is all."

She'd tried again the next night, this time mixing it with some of the bitter berries they'd come to think of as decadent. This time, she forced it all down, lips curling as she fought against the rising bile. "Right. Better."

A fresh storm swept more snow inside the mouth of the cave. It would never warm enough to melt. Much more, and it would become ice, especially if there were snowbolts. Alasyr used his hands to brush it to the sides before the challenge became insurmountable. Before long, she'd joined him to help.

"Emberley. I can manage."

"Four hands are quicker than two."

"You need your energy."

Ember spun on him. "We've been eating the same food, both of us, for weeks. If you can do this, I can do this."

"This isn't so different from the food I ate at Midnight Crest. I'm not skin and bones now. You are."

"Not that you'd notice, in all that leather and feathers."

"Is that envy? Want me to put in a word with our seamstress?" Alasyr hadn't noticed himself slip from concern to teasing. He enjoyed her defiant attempt to hide the growing smile.

"Only if I had a mind for town theater," she muttered, flashing her mischievous eyes at him once more before returning to the task of the snow.

They finished as the last of the light faded. Alasyr added more logs and a few sticks to their fire to give it life through the night. He glanced over at Emberley, expecting to hear her tiny snores any moment, but she was huddled against the cave wall, watching him.

"I didn't mean to let the fire wane. There'll be more warmth soon," Alasyr said.

"I'm as warm as I ever am in here," Ember said. "Though we could both be warmer if we bundled together."

Her suggestion ignited something unwelcome in him. Despite the intimacy of their arrangement, they'd hardly touched at all since that first night, since... well, a kiss was all it had been, but it was the only kiss he'd ever known, and he wished he could stop thinking about it.

Her words brought it all back. The way her arms flew about his neck after he returned her to life, devouring him in her desperate confusion. He'd kissed her first, but her recoil left him afraid he'd offended her, until she surprised him by kissing him. How long they'd held one another like that, he couldn't remember, for the immediacy the moment required caused him to surrender all sense of time. When he'd awakened the next day, she'd moved to the other side of the cave.

Since then, nothing like that had happened. Some nights, the hard nights, she laid her head against his thigh, and he'd touch her hair, the way Ravenna had once liked, until her stubbornness surrendered to rest, but that was as far as it went.

That was fine. He didn't want that... that other. He assured himself of this so often that he even believed it now.

"Alasyr? Was I speaking Medvedev or something?"

"What? No... no, you're right. We should've thought of it sooner."

"We both thought of it sooner. I was just the only one brave enough to say it," Ember countered.

Alasyr flushed. He hoped she couldn't see it in the dark, but her own pale cheeks, lit by the rising flames, were clear as anything as he walked toward her.

Ember patted the cold ground beside her. "Here."

Alasyr pressed his back to the wall and slid down. No sooner than he'd settled did she lay her head against his arm, narrowing the polite gap he'd left.

"You can put your arm around me."

Alasyr swallowed. "Oh, can I? I have your permission, then?"

"I just said you did."

Alasyr pretended to be annoyed as he lifted his arm and settled it around her. She moved in even closer.

"That's better."

"As long as you're comfortable," he said. When he sounded like himself, and not some lost bunny, he could almost forget how the smell of her soft skin, even after weeks of punishment from the elements, made his heart do a flip.

"You're not?" she teased.

"I didn't say that," he said. "You want to sleep like this, then? Is that it?"

"I want you to tell me about Ravenna."

Alasyr stiffened. "Ravenna? What about her?"

"You two were close."

"Was that a question?"

"You say her name sometimes. When you sleep."

Alasyr balked. "I do not."

"Please don't be as you used to be, pretending not to like me. Challenging me at every word," Ember pleaded. "I won't ask you to be vulnerable, only to be who you really are, with me."

This stark earnestness of Ember had always been what both pulled and repelled him. No one at Midnight Crest was so open with their intentions. He wasn't tuned to respond in kind, and so he responded in defense, and she'd seen through that, too.

Alasyr closed his eyes and leaned his head against the hard cave wall. If he met her eyes, he'd be tempted to slip into the man she was asking him not to be. "You're close to your own sisters and brother, are you not?"

Ember nodded against his chest.

"Your mother and father, they encouraged this? Your playing together, your joy?"

"They did."

"The very idea of that is foreign to me. Ravenwoods aren't taught closeness; we're discouraged from it. Our loyalty is first to our kin, then to the bonds chosen for us, then only lastly to ourselves, if there's anything left." Alasyr chuckled. "I remember when Ravenna first started visiting Wulfsgate for her training. She'd come home, struggling to make sense of their ways. She told me of the games the little ones played. The twins. I forget their names now, but she'd remember."

"Nyssa and Torrin."

"And the gathering at mealtime. The large table full of food, the laughter and stories. Ravenna and I both mused over this, how these things the men and women of Wulfsgate did went against all we were taught of the men of the kingdom. That they were warlike, evil running through their blood, born and bred into them. But these weren't her experiences at all. It was the iciness of our own world that felt cold and joyless."

"You don't share meals at Midnight Crest?"

"Most take theirs in solitude, or with their mate and their young children. There are times, celebrations, where we all come together. The High Priestess will invite those to her table she decides are worthy. But there was no laughter or playfulness there. If we spoke at all, it was meaningless pleasantries."

"Is that why Ravenna left?"

Alasyr pressed his lips together and grunted. "Ravenna *left* for a man."

Ember shifted at his side. She looked up at him. "Your anger about this feels like a recitation now. Like you don't really believe it anymore."

Alasyr turned his head away from her. To look into Emberley's eyes was to be lost in them, or be challenged by them. He could withstand neither. "I'll never know why she left. She never told me... maybe because when she shared with me her experiences in Wulfsgate, I insisted she was being lulled into their web, just as Mother said could happen."

"You can't blame yourself for that, Alasyr. We're all meant to heed our mothers and fathers as children. We don't begin to think for ourselves until later."

"I was the older one. How did she see it first?"

"Not everything has an answer. Can't it be enough that her leaving led to your own eyes being opened?"

"No. It's not enough."

Ember nodded against him. Her arm snaked over his belly, winding around him. "Then let me express my appreciation of who you've become. For the Alasyr who watched his sister leave would've left me dead on this mountain and never given it another thought."

Her words pushed a lump into his throat. This hard truth left him without defense, but she wouldn't have accepted one from him, anyway. She had never accepted anything less than his clearest self.

Alasyr dropped his head on hers and pulled her closer.

He'd hardly finished four sips of the liquor, and already his vision was blurred. It tasted like what fire might if liquefied, blistering his mouth and throat long after it had passed to his belly. He'd found this one not in the kitchens, where the watered down spirits served at meals were kept, but in his father's private cabinet.

Christian kicked his feet up onto the small desk in Holden's apartment. His defiance in the act was dulled only by the realization there was no one there to scold him. No one who *would*. For he was the Lord of the Northerlands now. He could do as he pleased, oblivious to the judgment of others. If anyone ever shared their real thoughts with him again, it would be a minor miracle.

He dropped his boots on the wood, enjoying the dirt falling out and onto the desk. How the ever fastidious Holden would rail if he saw it! He'd order the desk scrubbed and sanded before using it again. He'd remind Christian of this misdeed every so often, for years to come, a permanent refrain in their strained relationship.

"Do you know what foul things those boots have seen?" Christian muttered through his drunken laughter, affecting his best impression of his father. "Even the horses take better care."

His laughter bounced along the empty walls. It came back to him, dying there. He took another swig from the cloudy bottle. "Agghhhhh!" he groaned, dropping forward at the burn. His feet hit the ground with a loud thud.

The sound of the door catching on the lock turned his attention there. Another push, then two, then three. A soft sigh. Aylen. Her steps disappeared down the hall.

Christian's eyes filled with tears. He gazed longingly at the door. Aylen. He was ruining that, too. Ruining the only thing he cared about. Straddling the precipice of happiness and sorrow only made both harder to attain.

His mother's letter lay crumpled on the desk. He grabbed the nearest candle and tilted it toward the vellum. Wax fell upon the wood of the desk, hardening. His hand shook, and more wax dotted the desk. The flame grew closer to the paper. The edge curled slightly inward, blackening.

Christian set the candle back in place. He pushed away from the desk with enough force to send his father's ledgers to the floor. He paced the room, one eye on the vellum, his inebriation drawing the dimly lit room into a haze of his regrets.

Read it. You already loathe her. Loathe me. You seek power in your loathing, so go on, Son, claim what is rightfully yours.

Christian turned at the sound of his father's voice. He winced as the room spun away from him. He closed his eyes, but heard it again.

What stops you? Your fear she's right? That I was right, and this is where you belong, have always belonged? That we've always known what's best for you?

"Stop it!" he cried.

Go on, then. Prove me wrong.

"Christian?"

"I said stop it!" Christian screamed, breathless.

There was a pause, and then the words came again. "Christian, it's Alric. I need a moment of your time. The Southerlands have sent word."

Christian's eyes darted around the room. He rushed to the fallen books, quickly tidying them. He shoved his mother's letter in a drawer. Hurriedly, he ran his hands over his disheveled hair and then, blinking several times in a futile attempt to clear the drunkenness, unlatched the door.

Alric's expression was of immediate concern. "Are you all right?"

"The Southerlands. What do they want?"

Alric watched him closely as he responded. "They want to force action on the naval blockades."

"And invite war?"

"We're already at war. The recent absence of battles and blood doesn't exonerate us from reality."

Christian waved his hand. "They have a king in their pocket. They worked so hard to get him, and now they're afraid to use him?"

"Until Prince Darrick commands the Knights of Duncarrow himself, he'll never be the king. Half the kingdom believes he's a pretender as it is. They think Warwick is making his own play for the throne."

"And why doesn't he, then? Command them?"

"The sorcerer is wily," Alric replied. "He's taken the Rhiagain claim for himself, and no doubt used his magic to persuade circumstances to his liking. Lord Warwick believes if we can disrupt the blockade and get the prince to Duncarrow, it will be enough to show the kingdom their true king has returned."

"Too many hold Duncarrow in too high an esteem."

"I won't disagree. But it's been our isle of kings for hundreds of years. The one who commands those rocks and the men who serve them is the one we call king."

Christian snorted. "I take it they want our men again? We already gave them men. We *were* those men. Remember?"

"This is a new campaign."

"Led by the Southerlands? Then they should use their own."

"Any men we provide would be focused on Eastport. Every Reach focused on their own."

"Eastport is peaceful."

Alric's concern deepened in his brows. "There are fifty ships docked just beyond our port, preventing all sea trade and travel, Christian. That isn't peaceful."

Christian braced himself against the door as a wave of dizziness hit him. "Inciting them is even less peaceful, would you not say?"

"Oldwin's actions affect us all. This entire kingdom. He holds the crown hostage."

"The crown has never bothered us here in the north."

"Are you drunk?"

Christian laughed. "If I am?"

Alric sighed. "Cian Quinlanden and Brandyn Blackwood will most certainly heed the call of their ally. Do you want the Northerlands to be the only one who does not rise to meet the greatest need this kingdom has seen?"

Christian shrugged.

"Your father would send men to Eastport. Even he, in his reticence, wouldn't deny our need to come together now. He'd see the wisdom in ending this stalemate. And he'd appreciate that Lord Warwick is the only lord of this realm even bothering to *try* and end this madness."

"My father, you say."

"Yes, Christian. Your father. Holden Dereham. A man who you may not respect, but many did, and still do."

"Oh yeah? Curse him," Christian spat and slammed the door.

Ash looked up to see Gretchen descending the last of the mossy steps leading into the crypt. Her red plaited hair refracted the light from her torch, her heavy eyes conveying the weight of everything she carried in her heart.

It was only a trick of the light. It was Lisbet's voice; her face, her crimson hair, bound in the same braids Gretchen had always employed to keep her wild locks in place. He hadn't told Lisbet the whole truth when she'd asked why he initially kept his distance from her. That looking at her was like peering into an obscure past, as terrifying as it was inviting. It pulled him through time, and he was again Gretchen's greatest secret, sneaking around in darkness in order to love her.

"I came down to be with Drystan and then lost myself to old memories."

Lisbet settled the torch into the sconce. "I know you'd hoped to see her again."

"Would you believe me if I denied it?" Ash's laugh bounced off the stone. "Your mother created a truth she could live with. My return would only take that from her. I had to come, for Drystan. But I was afraid to come, for her."

Lisbet leaned against a tomb. Hadden's. "Maybe she already knew the truth."

"Your mother was always strong, even in her weakness," Ash answered. His smile faded away. "I know that look. It was Gretchen's, when she was puzzling over something."

"I think I'm done with the puzzling," Lisbet said. She leaned forward, her gaze traveling to her feet. "It's time for the doing."

"Tell me."

"We've had word from Uncle Khallum. They mean to disrupt the blockade, drawing and isolating their attentions to several ports across the kingdom. They've named key ports in each Reach. For us, it's Eastport. He believes that the only way to move forward and put Darrick Rhiagain on the throne is to incite them."

"And in doing so, thin the fleet guarding Duncarrow, I assume. Making way for Lord Warwick to sail to the isle with the prince."

"I assume."

"I'm sure your brother will do what's asked of him."

"He should, anyway," Lisbet went on, musing over her words as she said them. "But that's the business of a lord." She swung her foot, tapping it against the stone tomb. "It's our business that concerns me."

Ash tilted his head. "You can't mean for us to join the front lines? You and me?"

Lisbet shrugged.

"Lisbet, I'll do what you ask. This you know. But I can help us both better if I understand."

She kept her eyes down. "It's what Kian said, about placing my trust in my instincts. What I understand... ah, well, what I understand is next to nothing. It's less than nothing, it's... of no use to me." She looked up. "But what I *feel* is that we're meant to be in the Southerlands."

"The Southerlands?"

"When the scout from Warwicktown delivered the message, it was as if a great fire kindled within me, and the only way to quench it was to say, yes, all right, I understand. I'll go. *We'll* go. And I think this is what Kian was talking about."

Ash nodded. He wouldn't fail her as he had Drystan. Any doubts he possessed would stay his. She would never know of them.

Though it wasn't doubt at all he was feeling now, but fear.

"Then we go," Ash said. "We go as soon as you say it's time."

"It's time," Lisbet said. She hopped off the tomb, dusting herself. "I'd hoped to have some words with Christian, but he isn't ready to speak to me, or to you, or to anyone. It may be years before he is, and we don't have years. I feel that strongly. Do you?"

Ash hesitated only a moment. "Christian's battle is one he wages with himself. He must address that before anything else will matter to him at all."

"When this is all finished, we'll return here. Together. Mother will be back, maybe even Father, and we can repair the cracks that have taken over Wulfsgate."

Ash tried to smile, for her. He didn't think he'd ever return to Wulfsgate. A brief but potent feeling hit him that Lisbet wouldn't, either.

He caught his breath. "Let us get one good night of rest, then. I see the fire in your eyes, but I'm not so young as you anymore."

Lisbet yawned. "I'm tired, too. I thought being home would soothe me, but all I feel is agitated. Unsettled."

Ash, too, had feelings. Feelings that seemed to be, as Lisbet called them, awakenings, though he had less clarity, even, than she did. He would keep them to himself, for now.

"Your home isn't as you remember it," Ash answered. "Perhaps one day it can be so again."

Lisbet wore a skeptical look. "Yeah. Perhaps."

"Tomorrow, then?"

Lisbet gave him a brief, awkward hug before skittering back up the stairs.

ALASYR PEELED AWAY WHAT WAS LEFT OF THE LEATHER KEEPING HIM warm. He draped the vest of feathers over Emberley, careful not to wake her. The prickled flesh on his bare arms stood erect. Even a Ravenwood couldn't withstand cold without cover for that long.

He had a sudden urge to kiss her. He wanted to kiss her. He could deny it forever, and it would still be untrue. He wouldn't do it unless it was what she wanted.

He didn't know how long he'd be gone; how hard it would be to find what he was after. He'd made certain the extra meat was buried under a snow pile, staying cold enough not to go to rot. Emberley had showed him this. She'd showed him so much.

Mostly now, she was showing him how slowly a stubborn person could die.

"I'll come back," he promised. If he didn't shift soon, he'd freeze to death. "I'll come back, with help, and we'll get you off this mountain."

7

THE BUSINESS OF THE RENTS

Gabrianna Blackwood sat in the corner of the Great Hall, alternately harnessing her growing horror as she observed Brandyn holding his first Citizen's Day, and employing all her willpower to keep these thoughts from appearing on her face for all to see.

This last, she thought, was proof she was the daughter of the most cunning woman in the land, and not simply plucked from the nest of a cave troll. In her defense, the cave troll jest had been a running joke her entire childhood, as she more closely resembled her Warwick father in both face and demeanor. More so than the other girls, who'd either inherited Asherley Blackwood's beauty—Hollyn, or her great wit and cunning—Emberley.

How excited Brandyn had been to sit before his people and hear their grievances. Their mother had loathed this sacred tradition, telling them that any happiness granted to one would lead to the misfortune of another. There was no pleasing everyone, but there were always enemies to be made.

Gabi, half-hidden by the dense velvet curtain pulled to the side for the day, watched as Brandyn said yes to nearly everything asked of him. They needed a loan, they got one, even though he'd not had a single look into the treasury since returning to Longwood Rush. They wished for their trade rights restored, he returned them. Never mind that they'd been taken in the first place for illegal freebooting.

By her count, he was on the seventy-fifth citizen. His council, made up of mostly his friends, hid yawns in their arms. Kaslan James and Jonah Tyndall exchanged less than subtle looks over their lord's head, and Rhydian Tyndall seemed on the verge of collapse. Asher Richland cleared his throat enough that Brandyn asked him if he needed some tea with honey. The sun itself had little left to give the day, but Brandyn's energy seemed without limits.

Gabi wasn't there as a member of his council. He'd never even asked her, though she was the only other Blackwood from the direct family still in Longwood Rush. Still, he couldn't ask her to leave, either. She was a Lady of the Rush, who outranked everyone but him. And she was a year older. If she'd been born a male, it would be her holding court before the people of their Reach.

Brandyn at last cast a surprised glance toward the sky dome, where the first whispers of dusk showed.

"I believe our day is coming to an end. We'll hear one final grievance," he said. His council did little to hide their palpable relief, but the excitement from the remaining citizens drowned out their dramatic sighs.

There'd been over a hundred who'd come to see their lord that day. They hadn't expected him to get through so many, and now there were only a few left. They vied for their chance to steal this coveted spot, but it was Asher who impatiently reached into the waning crowd and drew the final citizen.

The man dropped to his knees so hard, Gabi winced.

"Elliott Cantwell, Lord Blackwood. I've traveled to you from Newcarrow, in hopes you might spare us some relief."

Kaslan James curled his lip at the mention of Newcarrow. Gabi stifled a laugh. No man still living in the remnants of Greystone Abbey had any love for the upstart town that had taken their place on the trade route. The men of Newcarrow were more than traitors, in their eyes; they were lightweights, incapable of weathering diffi-cult times, too delicate for the real world.

"Newcarrow. You've come a long way. You can stand," Brandyn answered. "If you're a man of Newcarrow, then you are under the protection of Steward Stanhope."

"Yes, my lord, but it is the matter of Steward Stanhope which I had hoped to bring to you."

"What matter of Steward Stanhope?"

"You see, for many of us in Newcarrow, we rely on our license to use the port. Our entire livelihoods are tied to our trade. Many of us are from Greystone, which has fallen out of favor for any man desiring a future. We gave up our homes, nay our lives, to aid Steward Stanhope in his quest to establish a more fruitful city, one more habitable for our families than the one we'd left."

Kaslan shifted in his seat, deepening his glare. If eyes could murder, Elliott Cantwell would be a pile of dust.

"Abandoned Greystone, you mean. Leaving it to rot," Brandyn corrected him.

Cantwell's eyes widened at what seemed the first sign things weren't going well. He stuttered his next words before finding his pace again. "My lord, our rents have increased each year since. And not the standard raises, the kind one can expect when a steward works to make a place welcoming, worthy of life and work. Rents not only on our lands but also our trade licenses. Many of us have been pushed to choose between our homes and our places at the port, but that's no choice at all. If this continues, we'll be forced to return to Greystone."

Brandyn sensed Kaslan was ready to blow, so he lowered a hand gently to his side. "Greystone is only what you see now because of men like you who abandoned it."

Cantwell's lower lip dropped, lowered. "Sir—"

"If more men were to return, it might again be a place of pros-perity." Brandyn sighed. He leaned sideways, slumping in the high chair. "And what reason has Steward Stanhope given for raising of these rents and fees?"

"To accommodate growth, my lord. But—"

"Have you not benefited from this growth these past years?"

The man shook his head wildly. "We don't know where the money goes! Our docks are in terrible need of repair. There's rot in the storehouses, so we can no longer move product, except in small quantities. The rats have become as citizens themselves, so numerous that the bakers have moved their business off the wharf."

"My lord," Tyndall whispered. Gabi leaned in, straining to hear. "If I may, Lady Blackwood never placed herself in the business of the rents, for good reason. It's a steward's right to govern his land as he sees fit, so long as the taxes are paid to the Rush on time."

"But should there not be a place for accountability in this Reach, Grand Minister?"

"I can explain this to you better when this is done. I advise you to send him on his way and let us put an end to this long day."

Brandyn set his jaw. He stayed this way for several excruciating moments. "Cantwell, you have said 'we' more than once. Do you speak on behalf of yourself, or have you come representing others in Newcarrow?"

Cantwell straightened. "I come representing forty of us who have signed a petition, requesting either a lowering of rents, or an inventory of repairs and other benefits that will put this increase to use for all of us."

"Forty, you say?"

"Yes, sir."

"This is an adage as old as time," Tyndall muttered. "No man is happy when his expenses rise."

"Risen, yes, but to what end?" Brandyn shot back.

"We cannot know, for the man capable of this answer isn't here. We should send for Steward Stanhope, to let him present his side and provide such records as necessary."

"But that will take weeks. These men are having to choose between their homes and their trades, Tyndall. You heard him."

Tyndall screwed his mouth into a frown. "So he says to you. But he had the means to travel from the farthest end of the Reach, did he not? That isn't the privilege of a poor man."

Brandyn shook his head. "We're all tired. You're right, it's time to end this." Louder, for all to hear, he said, "I am overriding the increase of rents for this year, and all years henceforth, until such time that Steward Stanhope can present evidence of the benefits to all. A steward's job isn't to horde their wealth, but to use it for the betterment of their people." He stood. A flurry of cloth echoed as all moved to kneel or bow. "And I would like this proclamation sent not only to Newcarrow, but to all the Great Cities of the Westerlands. An increase in rents must *never* be issued without the good of their people front of mind. Of our people. Storm, please have this message prepared and sent in the morning. All rents are suspended until the stewards can come to me to plead their cases. That is all."

Brandyn lifted the hem of his robe and disappeared into the hall behind his chair.

The powerful, competing waves of anger, disbelief, and stunned joy nearly bowled Gabi over.

She didn't have the mind for politics, but she understood emotion quite well, as an empath, in a way others were incapable. Brandyn might have left with a sense of pride in what he'd done for Cantwell and the other men of the realm, but he'd made a grave error, of a magnitude none of them could yet understand.

He'd never listen to her, but that didn't mean she wouldn't try.

"That won't go over well at all," Kaslan said as Gabi fled past, after her brother. "Not well at all."

She paused and turned to him. "Yes, well, you're on his council, are you not? Then counsel him!"

She raised her own skirts and dashed off in pursuit of Brandyn.

Brandyn felt them all trailing behind him like a chorus of conscience. Ready with their opinions, their censure, their carefully chosen words meant to instruct, but not estrange. *This isn't what Lady Blackwood would have done.* Well, she wasn't here! Not here, and

Brandyn was, and if his mother had something to say about his choices, she could return and make them herself.

"Brandyn! Wait!" Gabrianna. His sweet sister, who wanted a role in this game of children playing adults, but was even less equipped to the task than him.

"I wonder if you would all be following me so closely if you knew I was headed to the privy," he said. He winced through the throbbing pain in his leg that never quite left him.

"I've seen you in your undergarments. Do you think I have a care?"

Brandyn came to a stop. "If you have an opinion about today, it can wait until after we've supped, for we've already gone well past mealtime."

"Yes, and whose decision was that?"

"Gabi." He sighed. "I'm exhausted."

"Why can you not see I can be of use to you? That I can read what you cannot?" Gabi pointed toward the other end of the hall, where they'd emerged moments before. "Mother always said empaths offer the most valuable service to a lord or a king, for we can read intentions... we can sense when our own have caused trouble for us."

"Those men were happy when they left my chamber. They'll return home, their voices heard. A feeling that will soon be shared by all the Westerlands. I suppose you'll tell me now that this was misguided? Evil?"

"Even they were not expecting it, for good reason," Gabi countered. "They know a lord doesn't take from the plates of his stewards, and that's what you've done, Brandyn, do you not see?"

"Why do you think you know more than me? More than my council?"

"Your council is as fearful of what comes next as anyone. They know that the suspension of rents will lead to *more* starvation, for do you really think the stewards will take from themselves? No, they'll expel these men from their lands and take what's left. Your council knows this, for they've been raised by the Great Families. Whether they'll tell you is another matter."

Brandyn laughed. "They're my council, Gabi. That's their whole purpose."

"If you respond to them as you do me, then their purpose matters not."

"Are you done?"

"Lord Blackwood!" Harried steps sounded down the corridor. They both turned just as Arturo Blackfen pushed through the stalled group of Brandyn's council. His crimson cape flew behind him as he made purposeful strides in their direction.

"He's on a mission," Gabi muttered.

"Rider Blackfen. I wasn't expecting your return so soon," Brandyn said. Something was wrong. He felt himself paling. He hoped the others couldn't see it. "My mother... has she..."

"Your mother is fine," Blackfen replied. "I'm afraid her efforts continue on the matter of Lady Emberley, and so she sends her regrets through letter." With an apologetic look at Gabi, he added, "Only a note for Lord Blackwood this time."

Gabi dropped her eyes in disappointment.

"What is it, then?"

"Some of my Riders made contact with a scout headed your way. By morning, maybe sooner, a request will come from Lord Warwick in the Southerlands, calling for action."

"I thought we agreed war is in no one's interests."

"You've seen the blockades along your coastline."

"Doing nothing beyond obstructing the view."

"And your trade."

"We need nothing that cannot be sent overland."

"Your uncle doesn't believe it's for nothing. He thinks it's an intentional distraction, and I'm inclined to agree."

"A distraction?" Gabi repeated. "From what?"

"From what indeed," Blackfen answered, but he was looking at Brandyn.

"Isn't engaging the distraction falling right into that trap?" Brandyn asked.

"The sorcerer wants something. Not the crown," Blackfen said. "He draws our eyes away from him, away from whatever he has his sights on. The Knights of Duncarrow are his protection. Lord Warwick believes if we can focus the ships at the key ports by drawing them into battle, they'll have no choice but to come to the aid of their brethren, leaving Oldwin vulnerable. The returned prince can be restored, and we can end this."

"This sounds a bit like throwing a rock into a beehive and hoping for honey."

"That's exactly what it is, but if one wants honey, one must take the risk."

"Why not them waste their time on their ships, doing nothing? These past weeks have been quiet. Our people are just starting to feel safe again."

Blackfen lowered his voice, dropping his stance so his eyes met Brandyn's. "As long as Oldwin the sorcerer sits upon the throne at Duncarrow, not a single person in this kingdom can call themselves safe."

Brandyn waved a hand. "I'm tired. Can we discuss at the council meeting tomorrow?"

Arturo forced a smile, but his eyes betrayed his frustration. "Yes, my lord."

8

OLDCASTLE

"No chance. It's nearly springtide."

"You heard what Master Dilliswhane said."

"Dilliswhane is old, and there's never been snow in springtide."

"Says who?"

"I heard your mother say it to our stable hand, last time she was over."

"Wasnae my mother, then. She prefers the blacksmiths."

The boys laughed, continuing their playful banter all the way down the long hall of the library. Balfour Dereham didn't look up until their voices disappeared, followed by the satisfying thud of the double doors announcing their exodus.

He exhaled and fell back against the velvet cushion of his chair. Why did they even bother coming here? It was a place of study, not for Firth Garrick and Rolph Edevane to huddle in the corner and whisper about the girls they'd taken behind the Wayfarer's Inn in the village. There were dozens of places in the castle for this, but only one where Balfour could find some peace from his thoughts.

He slipped the book from under the stack. Hiding things was second nature, and he hadn't even given it conscious thought when

104

he stuck *The Great Mystery of the Veils* under the pile of the more expected fare, such as *Duncarrow: Lineages* and *The Most Unusual Beast Life of the Northerland Range.*

Both his Ancestral Studies and Faunal Species classes bored him to tears. But he was an excellent student, one of Emeraldcastle's finest, and if anyone knew his long hours in the library were merely a disingenuous ploy to access the secret back room, reserved for masters and their aides, they gave no indication.

Balfour pushed away from the desk, checking the hallway once more. There was only the library warden, asleep at his post. Satisfied he had the privacy required, he slipped back into his chair and opened the tome.

"*A brief word from the long-suffering scribe,*" he muttered, running his fingers over the paper that was thinner than vellum, twice as delicate. At the sign of a smudge, he lifted them again, instead leaning in closer. "*About the unusual phenomenon in the White Kingdom most will argue is mere myth. This scribe speaks, of course, of the veils, or those places where the walls between worlds are thin, and can usher one from our world to another. A number of such veils are said to exist across this kingdom. The precise locations can neither be agreed upon, nor, this scribe wishes to point out, believed to be real at all. Furthermore, this scribe feels more than compelled to call out that this is a work of fiction, and having said so, wishes for no further threats upon his family and their continued well-being.*" Balfour laughed. He flipped forward to find the name of the scribe, but there was nothing.

Balfour nearly leapt from his seat as the library warden snuck up behind him. The wily old turd was slow, but he was sly. He'd never even heard him coming.

"I dinnae know this one." Warden Liddle sniffed over his shoulder. "Doesnae even smell right. Ye got that from the room in the back. Didn't ye?"

Balfour quickly closed the book. "Yes, Warden. I'm doing research for Master Frost."

"Maassstterrrr Frossssst." The warden drew the words out so

long Balfour nearly fell asleep between them. "I ken he didnae tell me he had one of his pubes doing research for him."

Balfour squeezed a fist under the table. "In the future, if you would prefer, I can ask him to do so."

Liddle whistled between his teeth. "I cannae believe a master of Emeraldcastle would commit such an oversight."

"Perhaps Master Frost didn't know he was to inform you of the research done on his behalf."

The old man whipped his hand around Balfour so quickly he didn't notice until the bony fingers were running along the gold lettering. "Veils? Eh? *Well*, now. This shouldnae be in this library at all, or any proper library. A blasphemous stack of paper, this one. How it got here without me noticing, I cannae say, but I'm none pleased. None pleased at all."

Balfour slid the book away. "If there's trouble around this book, it's Master Frost you should speak with."

"Master Frost knows better, and I'll nay have ye maligning his name."

"Master Frost will be none too pleased himself once he learns you've not taken him at his honor."

Liddle grinned. He leaned in again. "For now, just the same, I'll be taking *this*."

Balfour's heart sailed into the back of his throat. He'd never been so close to anything that might offer answers, and it couldn't end like this.

It wouldn't end like this.

He cast his eyes toward the hall and then, with a subtle but swift blink, sent out his command.

Liddle gasped as the sound of dozens of books crashing to the stone floors pulled his attention away. "Ah, feck all, and feck her," he muttered and dashed off. Before he made it around the first row of shelves, he peered back. "Donnae ye be going anywhere with that book, lad. 'Tis requiring of proper disposal, lest we're caught with it."

Balfour nodded, and when the warden was gone, blinked his eyes again and sent even more books careening to the library floor.

"Feck all and feck her and feck the whole village," he muttered with a laugh, gathering the tome under his jacket as he rushed away to the gratifying sound of Warden Liddle sifting through all the best curses a salt and sand upbringing offered.

BALFOUR THREW THE BOOK ON THE BED ACROSS FROM HIS, INTO THE teeming pile of random junk he'd been stacking there. It once belonged to the other boy boarding with him, Sam Forrest, but one day Balfour had come home and all of Sam's stuff was gone. He didn't bother asking the chamber warden what had happened, because he already knew. He'd never had a chambermate last longer than a year. *You should work on being less strange, Dereham.* Either they came to the deduction on their own, or someone finally told them that Balfour was the son of Alric Dereham. Yes, *that* Dereham. The crazy one.

But Balfour's father wasn't crazy. It was his burden to prove it.

He went to latch the shutters on his narrow window, pausing only briefly to observe the joyful melee just beyond. By the Guardians, it *was* snowing, just as Master Dilliswhane said it would. Undoubtedly the boys would take the armor scraps the good-natured armorsmith left outside for just such occasion and trudge up the hill, catching great speed on their way back down. Soon enough, the girls from Crimsoncastle would join them, and there'd be another kind of fun.

Balfour latched the shutters. He'd never been up the hill with the other boys.

The latest letter from his mother sat unread in the top drawer of his small desk. The rumors had reached him before she could. He already knew about Aunt Gretchen and what was said about her disappearance. But unlike his father, Gretchen hadn't returned. Nor Pieter.

For years, Balfour had done his best to be *less strange* around those he felt could help him. Masters, usually, some apprentices. Most—even the kind ones—laughed away his talk of veils, reducing the idea to myth. This astounded Balfour. If he couldn't find the truth in a place of learning, then where could he?

His time at Emeraldcastle was nearing an end. He'd soon be a man in the eyes of the kingdom and would have no choice but to leave this place—the only place he might find what he was after—forever.

He'd almost given up when Master Frost found *him*.

I understand you've been asking around about the veils.

Master Frost taught alchemy, but Balfour had never taken his course. He didn't even know the older man. *Yes, Master, it's for... for an assignment.*

It is certainly not for any assignment here at Emeraldcastle, and we both know it. It is quite normal to possess a natural curiosity for those things beyond explanation or reason. But it would be unnatural to expect most to understand this. You must wield your curiosity with a feather, not a mallet.

The subject of the veils didn't come up at all again between them for several months. Until one evening, Master Frost pulled him aside and told him about a book he'd purchased from a trader at a pub in Oldcastle. He didn't dare keep it in the instruction hall, and the library warden was too fastidious with his inventorying for it to go unnoticed for long.

I've placed it in the secret room. Warden Liddle is not authorized to be in there without a master present, and most don't care for the old man very much.

You snuck a book into Emeraldcastle, and you're telling me?

And who else would care about the contents but the boy still struggling to make sense of them?

Balfour's worries crept in then. Was it a trap? Being caught in the secret room of the library was grounds for expulsion.

I'm leaving my key to the room with you, Pupil Dereham.

Balfour had eased some at this. *Have you read it, Master?*

No, and my instincts tell me there will be time for only one of us to do so before the book is confiscated.

Why me? Why not keep it for yourself?

Dear Balfour. You're the only one between us who has lost something to the veils. My interest in them is purely academic. Yours is personal.

Balfour promised to tell him everything he learned, and that was the last they spoke of it.

He blew out all the candles but one, then stoked the coals in the fire, adding a few more logs for the long night ahead.

Satisfied, he climbed beneath his heavy blanket and began to read.

9
LIFE AND LIMB

"She's a right beauty, this lass," Hamish said. He hid a snuffle against his arm. Esmerelda held her daughter out, but he shook his head, wearing a look of terror. "Ahh, no. She's jus' so little. A big'un like me might break her."

"Felicitations on your first grandchild, Hamish," Gwyn said. She filled her tone with as much diplomacy as she could muster, loosening the clench in her jaw that seemed now permanently set there. The sight of any Strong man was enough to elicit the darkest corners of her protectiveness. Though she knew it wasn't Hamish's fault his youngest son was a louse. He'd raised his other son well enough.

"Aye, 'tis a most joyous day, Lady Warwick. For us both." Hamish stretched his chubby hand, holding it right over little Gemmasyn's face. Her little face contorted. She was too newly born to assume it was joy, but she wasn't crying, either. "And to name her such? You've given this man a gift I cannae express, Lady Esmerelda."

Exhaustion decorated Esmerelda's smile. Her labor hadn't been easy, and Gwyn had never beseeched the Guardians as much as she had in the hours before her granddaughter was born. She wouldn't lose her only daughter after only just getting her back. Not after...

Gwyn cleared her mind.

"Ryan told me about your own little Gemmasyn. He and Jesse loved her so," Esmerelda said. She settled Gemma into a more comfortable position. "I couldn't think of a better name for the next generation of Strong women."

"Aye, 'tis a loss I still feel, day after day."

"We'd, of course, hoped she might name her for one of our own mothers, but Esmerelda is young and full of vigor. This won't be her last child," Gwyn asserted.

Hamish nodded. He puffed out a breath between pursed lips. "I ken ye both think poorly of my Ryan, and I cannae blame ye for it. But I'll nay let the boy abandon his duties. Ye must know, Lady Esmerelda, I'll nay let ye go on unsafe in this world, you and the bairn."

"She wouldnae ever be unsafe," Khallum gruffed, appearing behind Gwyn in the door. "She's a Warwick."

"Aye. Aye. I ken ye understand my meaning jus' the same, my lord."

"Ryan should consider himself free of all such duties," Esmerelda said. Some life returned to her cheeks at the declaration. "I won't go through the rest of my days feeling as if I have taken his."

"You were always a thoughtful girl," Gwyn said. "But thoughtfulness has no business in the early days of marriage, dear. He'll come to appreciate the gift he's been given, in the most beautiful and sought after daughter of the Southerlands. You found each other once, you can do so again."

"You've seen how he looks at me." Esmerelda's mouth twitched. "How he loathes me."

"Nay," Hamish said, drawing out the word. "Nay, my lady, he doesnae loathe ye. He never has. Only he's used to young women more... more..."

"More salt and sand? I'm not hard enough for him, is that it?"

"Too hard, maybe," Khallum muttered with a brow raise, a smile playing at the edge of his mouth. "The bairn has come. There'll be a wedding soon enough, but we've more pressing matters now. Hamish, can I steal you from your granddaughter?"

"Aye. Aye, 'course," Hamish said. He let his hand fall gently upon the baby's cheek, brushing it ever so lightly. "Lady Esmerelda, you'll tell me if there's anything I can do for ye, you and the bairn? Anything at all?"

Esmerelda nodded. "Of course. Thank you, Steward."

When the men had gone, Esmerelda handed Gemma to the wet nurse and pulled herself higher on the bed. "I meant what I said, Mother. I won't marry him."

Gwyn settled herself into a spot at the end of the bed. "Oh, I know you mean it. You've always been one to mean things. You're very like your father in that way, though don't tell him I said so."

"I know you'll always be angry with me for leaving as I did."

"Angry?" Gwyn rolled the word around in her mind. Was she angry? She'd still not put her head around the meaning of it all. Not just Esmerelda's deception, but everything since; all the rest. A time-line of failures. "No, dear. I'm not angry with anyone but myself. Had I been someone you could come to, confide in, you might not have felt such desperation."

"There are things one can confide to their mother about," Esmerelda said. "And those they cannot. You would've held me, soothed me, and still conspired against my desires. For as a mother, your duty is to see your daughter off to a worthy marriage. Even if you could've kept me from the king, you would've paired me off to a Law, or even a Rutland, and I would've never forgiven you or Father for taking this from me."

"In the end, it was still taken." Gwyn massaged her daughter's swollen ankle. "Whether you'll believe this or not, I *am* sorry for your heartbreak, Esmerelda. This world can be very unfair, and I'd hoped you had many years ahead yet before you wore this mantle yourself."

"My heart will mend," Esmerelda said. "But not if I'm forced to face him, day after day. Not if I'm to become the object of his greatest resentment."

Gwyn smiled. "Oh, my dear. He's confused now, but he won't be when he again holds you in his arms. There are some things more powerful than what a man has in his mind to be true."

"Next you'll remind me how it was for you and Father. How cold he was until he warmed to you."

Gwyn laughed. "I intended to, but I see you've cleverly seen through my intentions, so I suppose I'll keep my wisdom to myself. You know most unions are not born of love. They are born of expediency. Of practicality. You're more fortunate than you know, for you will be wed to the keeper of your heart. One day, he will remember this, and he'll come to you with welcome arms, and not ones spread of duty alone."

"I'm tired," Esmerelda said. Her head fell to the side. "I can't seem to get enough rest to recover."

Gwyn pulled the blanket up and tucked it around her. "Bringing a bairn is no small chore, Esmerelda. There's a reason it is the business of women. No man could endure it. Your energy will come to you again. For now, sleep."

Esmerelda smiled through bleary eyes. "Thank you, Mother. For everything."

"Of course, dear."

"Oh, I forgot to ask the steward. Has anyone heard from Jesse?"

"Jesse?" Only at her daughter's question did Gwyn note his absence. He should be here, at his brother's side. "Why, no? Not that I'm aware. Would you like me to ask?"

Esmerelda shook her head against the pillow and closed her eyes. "No. If he's meant to come, he will."

"Our munitions at Port Worthing have been destroyed," Khallum said, once the few men he still trusted had joined him in the Hall of Warring. He was sick right to his stomach that his mental inventory of his men and their capability for betrayal left him with only his closest mates. "Burned, under the cover of darkness," he added before the question could come. "Law, we'll be requiring a full accounting of the events of the night."

Law gave a weary nod.

"An accident? Some fool drawing his pipe too close?" Rutland asked.

"No accident," Khallum said. "It was a betrayal."

The other three men exchanged looks. Rutland, Strong, and Law. Had it come to this, that these were the only ones he could trust? That when he rolled over names in his head, men he'd known all his life, like Garrick, he just couldn't be certain.

"Who knew we were storing it there?" Rutland asked.

"Only my men," Khallum said.

"And Law's," Rutland countered.

"The men guarding the storehouse never saw the contents, nor had they any access," Law replied. "Far as they knew, we'd rented out the storage to a local silversmith who'd had some trouble with brigands running away with his goods when the shop closed for the night." He bowed his head. "Besides, they paid with their lives last night."

Khallum hadn't the patience to grieve for dead guards. "Then only us. Thorpe, Nye, Garrick, Leecaster, Barne, Clayton, and Bradford. Prince Darrick, of course. Twelve total."

"Not Clayton. He's been looking after his son. The accident."

"Ah. I'd forgotten. Eleven, then."

"Eleven."

Hamish ran both hands over his face in disbelief. "Yer men, my lord, they'd never. Not even tha' codswallop Garrick. Law says it wasnae his guards, aye, but what about the men who moved the munitions?"

"Leecaster and Bradford did it themselves, by moonlight. There were no others. There were no others for precisely this reason," Khallum answered. "We have a ratsbane among us, men. And if we donnae draw him out soon, t'will not only be the munitions destroyed."

"Could someone have followed them?" Rutland looked away

when he asked the question. Khallum could read his old friend as well now as ever. He was already sorting the cause; already preparing the judgment.

"Leecaster and Bradford knew better. They knew the risks. If they cannae spot a tail, we've other problems."

"Then why are they not here?" Law asked. He waved his hands. "Why are they not here, answering these questions?"

"Because I donnae know!" Khallum boomed. He dropped both hands on the table, narrowly missing the sharp edges when his palms connected. "I can guess, aye, but I cannae know, and what I want is the wisdom of those closest to me, not more questions!"

"All right, Khallum. We're here. We're here, and we'll sort out this mess, the four of us," Law said peaceably. "But I need to know what has you so convinced this is treason from the inside, and not some other force at work. Oldwin is a creature known for his tricks. Why would he need one of our men to do what he could do himself?"

"Well, I donnae know anything, Samuel, and that's the problem, isn't it? If I cannae rule out my own men, then how can we carry out any plans at all?"

Law nodded. "Very well." He turned to the others. "We'll not waste a minute."

"Aye. Aye, thank you." Khallum inhaled the briny air, and for once, it steadied him. "And, eh, tell yer wives there'll be a wedding soon."

"In the middle of war?" Rutland countered. "You donnae ken it's better to wait?"

"No man enters a war knowing how it will end. I'll see matters at home settled before I find out."

"She's sleeping, then? Gemma?"

Esmerelda nodded, pressing a finger to her lips. "She just went down. You can return later if you want to see her. She seems more sociable after she's been fed."

Ryan didn't dare step beyond the doorway. "I've seen her. Not today. Before, I mean."

Esmerelda pulled her robe tighter. She struggled to tie it, and he nearly reached to do it for her, but he neither wanted to be this close to her nor expected she'd want it, either. Most of his life since waking had been guessing the intentions of others, and at times, his own. His feelings didn't match his memories, nor what he knew of himself, but there seemed no doubt from any but him that he'd lain with and even loved Esmerelda, and the child sleeping in the cradle was a result.

"Yes, Ryan. I knew what you meant. If your father sent you, let's you and I agree right now that it's not necessary. I'll even tell him you came."

"My father didnae send me."

"Are you lost, then?"

"Come on, Esmerelda. If we're to be married, we cannae always be at each other's necks."

Esmerelda laughed. She pulled herself up by the post of her bed. "We're not getting married, Ryan. No matter what our fathers might say. Now, try not to look so relieved. Might need to practice your heartbreak, before you get it right for the others."

He wasn't relieved. He lived constantly on the edge of... something. A feeling. A revelation. An agony ready to reach forth and take him away to a place of despair. His father had said, *aye, but she's a beauty. More than I couldhae fetched ye.* Esmerelda *was* a beauty, but that same beauty was a bane when it belonged to a spoiled princess.

But that, too, was different. *She* was different. Colder, more assured than he remembered her. There was still that hint of entitlement, but it was layered in with the hardness of all she'd evidently endured since... since...

"I donnae know what ye want from me," he said at last. "I willnae... willnae *lie* to ye, but I can do right by ye. By our daughter."

Esmerelda's anger softened. "You may think you're doing right by me, but I'll die before I allow a man's pity to sit in the place where love should be. You don't remember me? Us? Then move on, as I am."

"They'll never let us do that."

She laughed. "Telling me what I can and cannot do hasn't worked out so well for my mother and father, has it?"

Ryan took a single step forward. "They're only doing what they believe is right. You're a mother yourself now, with a bairn, and that bairn needs a father."

"Aye, Ryan. A father is what she needs. But what she'll get if I marry you is fulfillment of an obligation."

"I donnae want this any more than you do!"

"Then stop... *this*." She gestured her hands between the two of them. "Stop making things harder than they need to be."

"Why are you so feckin' impossible?" he screamed, realizing his error immediately as Gemma's sharp cries sounded from the corner of the room.

Esmerelda closed her eyes, inhaling through her frustration. "Please, just leave." She buried her face in her hands. When he didn't move, she looked up, her eyes brimming with tears. "*Go*, Ryan."

He did as she asked, and he left.

As he made his way back to the gatehouse, another face he should know better than he did appeared, waving.

Darrick.

Darrick Fecking Rhiagain. Back from the dead. His supposed best mate in a prison he couldn't remember.

"Visit with your daughter?" Darrick asked. He waved at his own son, who knelt by the pigpen. His little hands vied for pig flesh, but the pigs had all backed themselves to the other side of the muck. "Anabella and I both send our felicitations. And to think, you didn't even know she was with child when you were sent away. Your Guardians have a strange way, don't they?"

"Attempted to visit, anyway," Ryan answered. He almost added *sir*, but Darrick had already scolded him more than once. A prince scolding him for not being familiar enough. It was more than he could fathom.

"Esmerelda's heart is wounded, and her body is recovering. Time will heal both."

"It's my memory keeping her broken," Ryan said. "Three healers now have come, and all three have said I may never get that time back. I cannae love her, but she willnae let me do right by her, either. There's no winning with her."

"It may take longer than you want it to, but you'll find your answers."

"She says she willnae marry me. That she doesnae want my pity. I think she'd run away again, before she allowed it."

Darrick laughed. "I see what brought the two of you together. She shares your stubbornness."

"I cannae see the connection at all." Ryan sighed. "I want to do my duty by her and Gemma, but I willnae force her to take the vows. She's already suffering, and adding to it feels cruel."

"Perhaps if you stop speaking about it as a duty, that might help?" Darrick smiled at Anabella, who'd come out to join Stefan with the pigs. Ryan remembered what Darrick had said to him, just a few nights past.

What kept me alive in those early days was remembering what I once had with Anabella. What kept you alive was knowing what you still have with Esmerelda.

Now, their experiences were flipped around. Upside down.

"I'm lost for what to do."

Darrick dropped his hand on Ryan's shoulder. "Even in her anger, she must know she has to marry soon. If it's not you, Lord Warwick will find another. But what if she marries another, and all your memories return to you? All the love, the love that made little Gemma?"

"What if they don't, and we loathe each other for all time?"

"Well," Darrick said with a light chuckle. "Then I suppose your marriage will be no different from most." He dropped his hand, and his smile faded with it. "You're a good man, Ryan. Maybe it's not the man you remember yourself to be, but I'd guess there's no one who knows you better than Esmerelda, Jesse, and me. We all have more love for you than we know what to do with." He looked past him with a distant expression. "I've been summoned to see your betrothed's father, so please excuse me."

"Everything all right?"

"I don't think so."

RAVENNA STEPPED CLOSER TO THE WATER. THE SEAFOAM LAPPED AT her bare feet, eliciting a surprised laugh. How had she gone her whole life never knowing how saltwater felt rolling over her flesh? How many more delightful discoveries lay ahead?

Her joy was short-lived. Anytime something happy passed through her mind, and threatened to stay for long, the hard, jagged memories of her darkest moments returned. Raining fire and death upon the brigands who'd assaulted her friends. The exact stinging moment she felt Drystan's life force snap. The day she ceased to be Ravenna Ravenwood and became someone else—*something* else— entirely. This new horror, born upon the dais of Duncarrow.

Except... it wasn't all horror. She'd never felt this freedom in her dark raven form, but as a phoenix, her troubles fell off into the wind as she aimed herself higher. By the time she spread her wings to glide upon the tempestuous sea air, her terrestrial concerns belonged to another world and time.

Oldwin, and the Rhiagains present at her transformation, no doubt still puzzled over the mess she'd left behind. At least one Rhiagain dead, maybe more. She'd never know. She didn't care this time, like she had the last. Any who'd participated in her agony deserved death, and she'd spare no time mourning them.

This was new, too. This apathy.

A lot of things were new, and she was only just beginning to discover these changes. But it seemed no accident that she'd first stolen fire from the brigands to bring it down upon them, and now could breathe her own fire through her sleek, curved beak, making her own chaos.

Ravenna only flew at night, while the rest of Warwicktown slept.

Esmerelda held her secret tight. She didn't mind her new nocturnal life. She'd never been more free than when she was alone with herself.

It was exhilarating to fly here, in this world so unknown to her. She'd been surprised when her wings worked so well, after the stories of Rhosyn's clipped wings, when she went to the Westerlands. But then, she'd only heard the stories of Rhosyn from other Ravenwoods.

One day, when she was certain Esmerelda was safe in body and heart, she'd fly high and never return. She'd decide her destination later. Her instinct would guide her. She couldn't help wondering what was stronger. The pull to draw more fractured truth from Oldwin? Or her surprising indifference to it, and him?

Was he hoping she would? Return? Or had he delivered this information, knowing it might drive her to madness? Would he then be surprised that it wasn't her "father" she was called to seek out, but her former home, Midnight Crest?

She pressed a hand to her belly. Her breath stopped as she waited for any sign there might be life in there.

There was nothing.

She knew there wasn't actually nothing. It wouldn't be long before she became all too aware of whatever Oldwin's magic had done to her.

Ravenna checked once more to be sure she was still alone before taking to flight. She soared high above the keep, settling into a small nook on the highest tower. Below, Lord Warwick's men patrolled, waiting, but not one knew what they were waiting for.

Ravenna knew who she was waiting for, though there were yet days ahead before he arrived. She'd at last sensed him again. That was, if her new magic could be trusted.

Magic or no, Jesse *would* come. Of that, she was certain.

IO
MAGIC OF NEED

Over the years, Oldwin had contemplated how he might summon the Magic of Need.

How did it decide a need from a want?

Oldwin *needed* Correen's rotting, bloated body to lose the unspeakable stench that now hit him with every foul wind—but his magic held no power to speed the untenable process of decomposition.

He *needed* the kingdom distracted by his threat of war in their seas, and by his missives that the Rhiagain line was ended—but the pull of the tales of Darrick and Dain stirred a hope that had been thought long dead.

He *needed* the Rhiagain Guard to find the door, the only door worth finding—but reports returned daily of pockets of massacre at the hands of the Medvedev, and a counter-magic that left them so disoriented they lost all progress made in their charting of the Hinterlands.

He *needed* the Knights of Duncarrow to finish their own business in the Wastelands—but they'd delivered only a pile of bodies.

He *needed* to possess the Great Light of the Worlds—but it

seemed as if the magic was working entirely against the purpose, thwarting him at every attempt.

There was the Magic of Want, but it was too self-defeating. Sorcerers lost limbs, and even life, as the cost. It was volatile and unpredictable. A last resort, when all else failed.

"Your Grace."

Oldwin braced himself at the high pitch of young Gilford Rhiagain. Oh, to just kill them all and relish the solitude. But even traveling the kingdom under illusion posed significant risk to him. For now, he needed these fools.

"You must have news, to disturb me like this."

"Fifty more are dead in the Hinterlands. Their commander sends word requesting an audience with you, sir."

Oldwin turned. "With me? Why would I grant that?"

"I believe... I believe he will beseech you to reconsider sending more men to their deaths."

Oldwin laughed. "He can aim his beseeching elsewhere. I care not if ten thousand die. Their service is to me, not themselves, or their very mortal fears. Is that all?"

Gilford dropped his eyes to the side. "The Southerlands know they've been betrayed, but they do not know by whom."

"I wouldn't expect them to possess the wit for that discovery. Are we done?"

Gilford reached inside a sack that Oldwin only just noticed. He pulled out a filthy shirt, balled in his fist. "Lord Warwick sends a gift."

"How has Lord Warwick managed to send anything, with the knights guarding the seas?"

"They sent a scout in a smaller vessel, who was invariably killed for his efforts, but they retrieved the gift."

"Am I expected to believe they sent a man to his death for a shirt?"

Gilford reached again into the sack. This time he pulled out a roll of vellum. With a shaking hand, he passed it to Oldwin, who ripped it away with a scathing look.

We've grown far too accustomed to the inhabitants of Duncarrow reaching beyond their means. This comes to an end. The whole kingdom knows the limits of your power. Consider this a gift. A shirt off the back of the rightful king, Darrick Rhiagain. One of your magic will know this for what it is. A promise.

"Burn it."

"The letter, sir? Or the shirt?"

"Both!" Oldwin boomed. Gilford stumbled back several paces. "Go!"

Gilford couldn't scramble out fast enough. Unlike Eoghan, who'd lamented the fear his own blood had of him, Oldwin had no patience for fealty of any color. Not this, nor the confident smoothness of some of the others, who seemed to have decided he had a problem with weakness and showing strength might save them.

Neither their strength nor their weakness kept them alive. The expediency of their presence wouldn't last forever. It couldn't last much longer at all, for Oldwin was now certain that the tickles he felt, that unthinkable loss of potency that reminded one that a longer life wasn't the same as immortality, was the start of his final days. Days that would either end in obscurity, or continue on, forever, in infamy.

He hadn't come this far for anything but the latter.

If he had to sacrifice every soldier in the Rhiagain Guard and the Knights of Duncarrow to find the doors, he'd do it.

For if they couldn't find the doors, he'd have to risk everything to do it himself.

"THAT'S ENOUGH, DARLING." ADYNORA SNAPPED HER FINGERS. Another Ravenwood, one of lower birth, came forward and removed the bowl in front of Ryandyr, to the young girl's obvious dismay.

"But I'm still hungry!"

"A feeling you'll grow used to. A feeling you must grow used to, for you'll stay hungry the rest of your life."

"Mother says I'm small for my age. That I need to grow."

Adynora lowered a steely gaze on her granddaughter. "You'll grow taller with age. But you'll not grow wider while I draw breath. I didn't return from my retirement just to watch you become a plump little embarrassment." She leaned in. "And don't think I missed the sacred rule you just broke. Tell me what it was."

Ryandyr curled her small mouth in a pout. "Don't stuff my face like a sow."

"You know very well that isn't the one I mean."

Ryandyr diverted her eyes. She crossed her arms, thought better of it, and placed them again neatly in her lap. "Don't speak of my mother."

"And why?"

Ryandyr sniffed. "Because she's... she's a traitor."

"A traitor. Who died the death of one, and was banished henceforth from the line of succession, as Ravenna was."

"Yes, Grandmother."

"Yes, High Priestess," Adynora corrected. She willed the hardness in her face to fade to something softer. "I know this is difficult for you. Despite that your mother and father committed treason against us, they were still your mother and father. Ravenna is still your sister. Do not think I've forgotten those things."

Ryandyr kept her eyes lowered.

"But it is my responsibility, as High Priestess of Midnight Crest, to prepare you for the same role. For your own ascension will be here before you know it. I will not have that day arrive without your readiness."

Ryandyr nodded to her lap.

"Ryandyr. Look at me."

Warily, Ryandyr raised her head. Even in her restrained grief, she was a lovely girl. One of the few Ravenwoods to possess silver hair, considered a rare gift given to only the most worthy among them.

But then, Rhosyn was said to have had silver hair, and she was the last Ravenwood Adynora would ever want Ryandyr to take after.

At thirteen, she was still a girl, but it would be a woman Adynora presented to the Ravenwood men in less than two years' time at the next Langenacht. It would be a woman *worthy* of the role, so that Adynora, at last, may rest.

There was no gain in paying homage to the rage she'd harbored when she'd discovered that her Varinya, the sparkle in her heart, had given herself to a *man*, years after the magic chose her brother Argentyn. To disgrace herself so. The very idea that Holden Dereham's bloodline could taint her own was maddening. She hadn't been certain until Ravenna was born.

Spirited Ravenna. Adynora had loved her, despite all of it. But it wasn't until Ravenna had aged, coming closer to her own time as High Priestess, that Adynora at last found the means to rid the Ravenwoods of the taint that had started with Varinya's betrayal.

"When we are alone, you and I, you can speak to me as your grandmother," Adynora said. She'd let the girl hang on the potential of her words. As with everything, this, too, was a test. Ryandyr wasn't ready now, but she would be.

Ryandyr nodded.

"That is also when you may make known your grief, but only if it may help you in overcoming it. Do you understand?"

The girl again nodded.

"For no one else here must ever see you shed a single tear over any of them. Not one. A High Priestess isn't without heart, but she *is* expected to possess the strength to conquer it, to do whatever is necessary to lead from here." Adynora pointed to her head. "Not from here." This time to her heart. "At some point in your tenure as High Priestess you may be required to make decisions that will seem impossible to most. But they won't be impossible for you. *You* will do what is needed to protect our legacy, for you will have learned that nothing, *nothing,* is more important, and this hardening of your heart will be what gives you the power to believe it."

· · ·

Oldwin turned at the ripple of the water in the stone basin coming to life. The sound startled him. Sent a chill to his bones, a sensation he hadn't experienced in many years.

Only two had ever come to him in such a way, in this world. One of them was dead.

Oldwin approached the basin. Adynora Ravenwood's face appeared in the water, swimming into focus.

"I wondered if you'd still be on the other end," she purred. Her raven hair fell in deep waves; she was a High Priestess twice retired but still possessed a youthfulness that would draw any suitor. Oldwin was past such base needs, but she reminded him, as Ravenna had, that he was still capable of desire.

"It is me who calls on you," Oldwin answered, surprised at the soft lift in his voice, as if he intended to court her. "Our arrangement is ended."

"So Ravenna is gone, then? It's done?"

Oldwin stiffened at the mention of Ravenna. Of his normally impeccable judgment. Of his undoubted failure. "No. But she will not return to Midnight Crest."

Adynora's lovely face hardened. "What do you mean, no? How can the answer be no and our arrangement be ended?"

"I was to ensure she never returns to Midnight Crest. She will not."

"That wasn't the agreement."

"It's what I can offer you."

"I had Assyria Rhiagain killed for you!" she exclaimed. Then, seeming to realize how loud she'd said it, again dropped her voice low. "I had a princess of the realm murdered, for *you*."

"A realm and crown you have no time or interest in. Such a sacrifice you made!"

"Tell me why you're so confident," Adynora challenged. "That she will not return."

"Or what? You'll raise Assyria from the dead?"

"I wouldn't be the first Ravenwood to do it."

Oldwin pursed his lips.

"I upheld my end, Oldwin. Tell me."

Oldwin sighed into the cold room. "Ravenna will not return to Midnight Crest because she will be as foreign to it as it is to her."

"How so?"

Oldwin contemplated whether to release or hold this information. All information had the potential for power. As he considered this, he saw that telling her *was* a form of power, to sow great discord, and he wouldn't even have to go north to Midnight Crest to do it. When would this opportunity present itself again, with the end so near?

"Ravenna," he said slowly, enjoying the impatient look she wore, "has come into the powers of her father, and these powers have changed her. Changed her in a way that will render her unrecognizable to all who once knew and loved her. Including herself."

Adynora laughed. "Holden Dereham has no powers. Even his son can do no more than scry obscure futures with an accuracy I'd certainly not wager my fortune upon."

"Holden Dereham," Oldwin said, coming upon his first real enjoyment since discovering Eoghan Rhiagain dead at Esmerelda Warwick's hand, "is *not* Ravenna's father, and it's rather disappointing that someone of your power needs to be told this at all. No, I rather say it's appalling, Adynora, for you have, for years, lived mired in your revenge over a half-truth."

Adynora's mouth tightened in a thin line as she glared at him through the water. "Argentyn is not Ravenna's father. That was clear to me from the time she was an infant. I may have agreed to conspire with you, for mutual aim, but that doesn't mean I trust a thing you say. I know all too well of your loathing of me, of us. It runs many lifetimes."

Oldwin grinned. "Which is why it brings me such great joy to tell you that Ravenna's real father is Mortain of Ilynglass. He has his own reasons, for wanting to strike against your ilk, more than he ever told me. Told us he could destroy your entire world with a single act."

"You lie. Lies are all you know."

"He created the illusion that deceived both you and your daughter, an illusion you both fell for utterly. Now that Ravenna has reached the maturity of her magic, she has taken the form of her father. She is no longer a raven, but a *phoenix*. So this, Adynora Ravenwood, is why I can be so confident that she will not return to you."

Oldwin laughed as he waved his hand over the water, clearing their connection.

Perhaps he'd misunderstood the Magic of Need all along.

For, until he'd seen the look of horror painted across Adynora Ravenwood's face, he hadn't known just how much he needed that.

TO PROTECT AND DESTROY

II

TOO CLOSE TO HOME

It was well past the dead of night, trailing into the first hint of morning, when Ravenna spotted the lone rider passing through the gates. He hung heavy upon his horse, astride by sheer will alone, the promise of relief just around the bend.

He dropped to his feet as he entered the town proper, leading his horse the rest of the way. It would be much quicker for Ravenna to fly down to him, landing at his side, but she wasn't ready for the inevitable questions he'd have at her change in plumage.

She glided down from the parapet, conscious of keeping to the shadows. When she touched ground, she went the rest of the way on foot.

Jesse's tired, drawn face first froze in cautious anticipation, then slowly thawed as recognition passed across his weary eyes.

He quickened his pace, giving a gentle tug on the exhausted beast. Ravenna had only just opened her mouth to welcome him when he had her against him in a hard embrace.

"Ravenna," he whispered against her hair, his breath hot at her ear. "Thank the Guardians you're safe. I'd hoped I might find you here, too."

Ravenna put enough distance in their hug to look at him. Whatever had happened to Jesse in the intervening distance had aged him. He wasn't the same. She wasn't the same. She wondered if he could see this change in her, as she could in him. "Did you? I thought I'd overstayed my welcome."

Jesse kissed the corner of her mouth. He lingered a moment, indulging himself in a quick study of her, before dropping his arms. "These past... weeks, I suppose, I cannae say how long... have given me a needed perspective on many things."

"Will you tell me about them?"

"No," he blurted. With a drowsy exhale, he added, "Not tonight. Tonight, I need a rest so powerful that I can forget it all. Any chance of sneaking in without drawing Lord Warwick's eye?"

Ravenna grinned. "They have me in one of the guest cottages, near the gatehouse. They think me so inconsequential that I don't even have guards like the others do."

"Inconsequential? They donnae know who ye are, then?"

"Whatever they think they know would be wrong. So if there's a place more private, I'm not aware of it."

Jesse's flush painted his cheeks, even in the dark of night. "I accept your offer, if that's what it is."

Ravenna touched his cheek with her palm. "No magic. Just me."

Jesse's eyes closed. "And Esmerelda... she's..."

"In the keep. Resting."

"They kept their word to me, then. She's here, and she's safe." He exhaled, releasing a breath that sounded years in the building. "She's safe."

"Who? Who kept their word?"

Jesse dodged the question. They turned down a path that took them away from the keep. "I can only imagine how Lord Warwick reacted when he saw her, alive." He winced.

"Oh, whatever you're imagining, it was worse. He's calmed since. He knows he must be calm, or he'll drive her away again. Besides, his attentions are on matters in the kingdom now. Much has happened since we saw you last. Or do you already know?"

Jesse shook his head. "I cannae even say for sure how much time has passed since I left Greystone, set after the two of you." He glanced up at the moon with a frown. "You dinnae suppose I might get in to see her tonight?"

"Not if your aim was to avoid Lord Warwick. And Esmerelda needs her rest. Her daughter was born the day we arrived in Warwicktown."

Jesse's jaw fell into a beaming smile. "The bairn has come? And a little lass, then?" He mused on this. "I cannae wait to meet her."

Ravenna nodded. "I know you're eager for it. And Esmerelda will be so happy to see you. She's been asking about you."

His throat ebbed as he swallowed. "Has she?"

"And your father. Your brother, too. He's also here."

Jesse came to a halt in the middle of the path. "Ryan's here? In Warwicktown?"

"He is, and awake. Recovered in body, though in mind, he's still troubled. You'll want to prepare yourself for this."

"Aye..." Jesse said these words into the wind. "I've seen it. But I didnae see he was here."

"Seen it?"

Jesse pointed to his head, but didn't elaborate. "Where's he staying?"

"In the gatehouse, I believe."

"Not the keep, with family?"

"He fears Lord Warwick might have him killed in his sleep. I don't know that I blame him. I wouldn't rule it out."

"I see."

"They've all been so worried, and will be so relieved you're back. But not tonight."

Jesse offered a sleepy grin from the side of his mouth. "Not tonight."

"This one's too close to home for you, Khallum. If this one isnae a message..." Rutland shook his head. "We have no choice but to sort it. No choice."

"Aye, Erran, ye think I donnae know that?" Khallum paced the Hall of Warring, one eye to the Golden Coast, and the thin haze of dark smoke that had traveled downwind from Goldthorpe. Even the mine workers, lungs hardened by years of inhaling the black dust, coughed into their arms as they milled about.

The keep at Goldthorpe, and some of Steward Nye's relations, had perished overnight in a terrible fire. "I've sent Hamish to take a look with his own eyes. Not that I donnae trust Nye, but..."

"We donnae know who we can trust anymore," Rutland said. He whistled through his teeth. "If we cannae trust our own men."

"Aye, that's the heart of it, isn't it? Coming right down to it, the list of men I'd trust with my life is dwindling each day."

"Surely Nye wouldnae have razed his own keep, with his family inside?" Rutland countered. "One of his lasses is among the dead. His wife willnae last the day."

Khallum leaned over the open window overlooking the sea. "If I had answers, we wouldnae need speculation, would we?"

"Where's Law?"

"He rode north with Hamish. He's gone to sit with Nye, proffer some comfort in this nightmare. Poor man." Khallum shook his head. "Aye, if he had any hand in it, then I just donnae know anymore, Rutland. I just donnae know. But I trust Hamish to sort out the ruins, and Law to sort out the man, if ye ken."

"Aye, I ken."

Khallum spun around. "Can I speak to ye as a man, not a lord? As a mate?"

Rutland dropped his head in a solemn nod. "I'll always be whatever you need me to be, Khallum. You know that."

Khallum pressed his palms into the shit-stained ledge. It had a permanent sliminess to it, but he dug in, held fast. Had he not always done this? Held fast? Was this not the way of all Warwicks?

And where had it gotten them?

"I was wrong, Erran. About the blockades."

Rutland scoffed with a *pfft* sound. "It may not have worked out, but you were the only one with a plan. The only one who ever comes with a plan. Did ye see anything from the other Reaches at all? No, nor did I. Nor do we ever. It's always you, Khallum. Always a Warwick. Every time."

"Khallum's Folly, they're calling it. Can ye believe the nerve of these spineless cowards?" Khallum waved a hand. "Nay, I know, I ken your meaning, but that's not... does it not bother you, the way the Knights of Duncarrow, the way they all just *stood* there, on the decks of their ships, and watched as our men sent the bombardments up into their hull? How they did nothing? The lot of 'em, burning alive?"

"That's what the men said. We didnae see it with our own eyes."

"They had no lie in them. These were the accounts of the men in Port Worthing *and* Bythesea."

"It's strange, I'll admit, but they didnae leave, either. They held their place at sea."

"But do ye not see? 'Tis what I feared all along. That Oldwin doesnae want *war* from us. He wants us caged, like animals. If Prince Darrick is right, then he doesnae want the crown, either, so what does he want?" Khallum threw his arms out. "What does he want?"

"To break us," Rutland said. "To bring you to where you are now, confused and lost."

"Aye, but *why?*"

Rutland approached him carefully. He dropped both hands on Khallum's shoulders. "Brother, does it matter why, if this is where it's put you? If this is the state you're in? You cannae trust anyone anymore. You've run mad with speculation. If that's what Oldwin wanted, it's what he's gotten. It's what his actions have bought him."

Khallum set his mouth tight, huffing hard breaths through his nose. "Aye. Fine. But then what are we doing to do, Erran? What are we going to *do* about it?"

"What I wouldn't give to have the right answer for you now," Rutland said, his eyes heavy.

"So do I just let my Reach burn to the ground? What if next time it's Mariel, or Agnes and Esther, in their beds when a fire starts? Would ye still say 'tis my passion getting the best of me?"

Rutland dropped his eyes. "Perhaps Darrick is right, and the answer lies in the Hinterlands. Whatever it is the creature wants so badly there."

"And how are we to discover this with thousands of Rhiagain Guard patrolling the forests?"

"I donnae know, Khallum. But if the way to stop Oldwin from Duncarrow is closed, then it's time we decide on another way." He let his hands fall back to his sides. "The prince has had enough time to reunite with his family, wouldnae ye say?"

Khallum looked at him.

"He's had more to say about Oldwin than anyone. He's the only man we know who's met the sorcerer, has any firsthand knowledge of him. It's time. It's time we bring him back in and allow him to do what we pulled him from prison to do. Lead this kingdom out of the chaos his father and brother led it into. The kingdom waits for us to make this move and wonders why we donnae."

"Wonders why? Do they not realize a tyrant has Duncarrow hostage?"

"You've done enough, but it willnae be Khallum Warwick who unites this kingdom. Donnae bristle at me. You know I say these words with fealty and love. You rescued Darrick Rhiagain for a reason. Time to use him. All the way, not the way we're doing now. Despite the risks. Maybe even because of them."

Khallum nodded. He searched for words, but nodded through his lack of them.

"We'll sort it. One way or another," Rutland assured him. "I'll go find the prince." He moved toward the door, then abruptly stopped. "There's word Jesse Strong is here. That he arrived in the night."

"In the night? Where'd he sleep then, under the Guardians in the sky?"

"In one of the cottages, with Lady Esmerelda's... friend."

"Aye, I see." Khallum raised a brow. "Just in time for the wedding,

I suppose. Where is he now, Strong? We know how he likes to run off."

"I ken he's gone to see his brother. Or Esmerelda."

"Esmerelda?"

"It's been said it was Jesse she was with, all these months. That he secreted her away, at his brother's behest."

Khallum scoffed. "You paying heed to fishwife gossip now? We both know Jesse was in Greystone, aiding Steward James."

"Was Ryan himself overheard saying it."

"And you're just now telling me?"

"We've had bigger matters to mind. Jesse's here now," Rutland said. "Why not ask him yourself?"

The ride to Warwicktown had felt long. Longer than it needed to be, for certain, for if he'd had any sense of direction from where he'd re-entered the kingdom, he might've been able to orient himself quicker.

He'd not wasted a moment of this time on his way back. He'd stopped fighting the truths Isdemus had shown him, and when he did, when he at last let go of his dogged urge to cling to what was comfortable and known, this magic that first awakened in him in Greystone Abbey began to take greater form. He could see things now. Things that were not in front of his eyes, but were no less real. For one, he'd seen the man Ryan had become.

He saw other things, too. Things about himself. All his life, he'd craved simplicity, when he'd been born for anything but. There was no use in denial, or wasting time wishing for what he'd had. When he'd concluded his business here, Isdemus would expect Jesse to uphold his end of the agreement, and if he thought his life was complicated now, he could only imagine where the sorcerer's demands would lead him.

Not all things were so complicated. Family. Loyalty. The bonds linking both together.

Ryan's feverish pacing made Jesse dizzy. The joy of their reunion had been short-lived. He could hardly recall his worries, with how swiftly anger had replaced them.

"Would you stop that?" Jesse said from the other side of the room.

"Stop what?"

"Moving. Can ye not sit still for even a moment?"

"Ye sound like Father."

"And you sound nothing like yourself."

"Oh, aye?" Ryan laughed, but didn't slow his frenzied strides. "I suppose you think you're the first to say this to me in recent days?"

"I'm not just anyone, Ryan. I'm your brother. Your oldest and truest mate. Do ye think I would've given up everything to take her halfway across the kingdom for the fun of it?"

"I never said it didn't happen. But I cannae lie about remembering it, either. Nor does it help, everyone telling me how I should feel, how I once felt. I'm not that man now!"

"Not to you, maybe, but to Esmerelda? She only sees that man."

"Jesse." Ryan stopped moving and stepped closer. "You know me, better than any. How, *how* could I have fallen in love with someone like Esmerelda Warwick? Did someone spell me? Help me understand how it happened, for I cannae ask anyone else around here without drawing their fist."

"Oh, aye, well, I asked myself the same, many times," Jesse replied. "It defied all reason, but ye loved her, and there wasnae a thing I could do about it. You loved her enough to go to the Wastelands for her, enough to ask me to take her away for ye."

"Darrick... that is, the prince... he told me. I guess I told him about her, in the prison."

"Aye, well, ye did. Ye asked me to take her to our mother's people."

Ryan balked. "To the Hinterlands? You took her there?"

"I tried," Jesse said with a light shrug. "They made to attack us. We escaped before they could."

"Did they not know who ye were?"

"Who knows? It doesnae even matter now, for the secret you

both were so desperate to keep is no longer one. You both got what ye wanted in the end."

Ryan snorted. "No. This isnae what I wanted. Not ever."

"Yes, it fecking was," Jesse said, charging toward his brother. The rage flickered in his cheeks. After everything. After *everything* Esmerelda had been through, that *he* had been through. "It *was* what ye wanted, and t'was what I gave up my life protecting. What I advised you against, for *months*, and ye had not a whit of care for my words. You were a man lost, and for what? For this? So you could disappear to a place in your mind where even the mention of her name curls your lip in disgust? The woman ye once loved, and now has delivered your firstborn? Perhaps you're right, in the end. You're nay the man I once knew you to be."

"Jesse—"

"Do you know how many nights I held her while she cried, sleepless in her worry for you, assuring her you would make it through and be waiting? That all she'd endured would be worth it in the end?"

"I already said I'd marry her! I've nay run from my obligations, no matter how I might feel. You're supposed to be on *my* side! Why are you having a go at me still?"

Jesse's hand trembled as he pointed it at his brother. "Because Esmerelda deserves more than your pity."

"Oh, aye? Then why don't *you* marry her?"

Jesse dropped his hand. "In case no one else has told you this, it's more than your memory that's left you."

JESSE FROZE WHEN KHALLUM CALLED HIS NAME. HE OFFERED A strained smile. "Lord Warwick, sir."

"Jamesan Strong, as I live and breathe."

"I've only just arrived. I wanted to see my brother first, and then I'd planned to come to pay my respects to you as well. Sir."

"You were with Ryan, aye? Then ye know he's even more of a louse than before he got my Esmerelda in a bad way."

Jesse dropped his eyes. "I was on my way to see her next."

"Oh, aye?" Khallum squinted as the mid-morning breeze dusted sand into his eyes. "There a particular reason you might want to see her?"

"I'd like to offer my felicitations on the arrival of her daughter. My first niece." Jesse fumbled through a nervous nod. "And, of course, to you, sir, for the birth of your first grandchild."

"Hmph," Khallum said. "Ye seem appropriately joyous of the news, but not particularly *surprised*. Why is that?"

Jesse pointed behind him, at nothing specific. "Both Ravenna and Ryan told me the happy news."

"Happy," Khallum repeated. "Happy for whom? Esmerelda? Not your louse of a brother."

"Aye, I know. I ken the situation."

"The situation?" Khallum narrowed the space between them. "The situation? The situation. Aye. Yes, the situation."

Jesse's hands flexed in agitation at his side.

"I've heard that you may know more about this *situation* than even I do."

"Sir?"

"I'll ask ye as man, but if you lie to me as a boy, you'll never set foot in Warwicktown again."

Jesse hesitated. Nodded.

"Is it true, that Esmerelda was with *you*, all this time? All this time, when we believed her lost to the sea?"

Jesse pressed his lips tight. He inhaled through his nose and blinked a moment longer than he should have. "Yes, my lord. She was with me."

Khallum saw the spots behind his eyes before he was aware of the boiling rage surging up from his toes. "And..." Khallum closed his eyes. He rolled his tongue along the roof of his mouth. "When we spoke in Greystone, ye didnae think that might've been the time to tell me?"

"I'd sworn a vow. To my brother. An unbreakable one."

Khallum leaned in, mere inches separating their faces. "And what of the unbreakable vow a steward swears to their lord?" he boomed. Nearby merchants pretended not to listen as they reluctantly went on with their business.

"I made my choice, and it's one I must stand by, as a man of honor. All I can do is apologize to you, my lord."

"Apologize. Aye. Aye. And was she with you in Greystone Abbey, then? Was my daughter, whom I believed to be dead by her *own hand*, there, with you, perhaps just in another room? Right under my nose?"

Jesse's lips twitched. "She was... she was there. But not at the tavern. We made use of Dungarde Keep."

Khallum's mouth and eyes flew open in tandem. "So now you're telling me one of my oldest mates was in on it, is that it? That Steward James conspired to keep my daughter from me?"

Jesse shifted in the sandy dirt. "Lord Warwick, I did all I could to keep Esmerelda safe. I would've given my own life to see it done. I'm only here long enough to see this with my own eyes, and then I'll be on my way once more."

"On your way? Do ye always have somewhere more important to be, or is it only when you've been forced to face me?"

Jesse at last dropped his eyes. "I gave my word that if I could see that Esmerelda was safe and cared for once more, I'd return and give my aid."

"To whom?"

"I cannae say. I'm sorry."

Khallum raised his finger to rail on him some more, but his mind at last caught up to his ears. "You're telling me you returned only for Esmerelda? To see if she was safe?"

Jesse nodded. "I'll not trouble you much longer."

Khallum narrowed his eyes. "If she was with you, then why did she return without you?"

"Her stubbornness, I suppose. She felt she'd become a burden to me." Jesse sighed. "It wasnae true, and I assured her as much. But when you told me, that is, when I learned of Ryan's fate, I couldnae keep it from her. I said I'd bring her home, but she slipped away before I could do so."

"When? When did she slip away?"

"A few nights after ye told me, I ken?"

Khallum gaped at him. "But that was almost two months ago. It doesnae take months to travel from Greystone to Warwicktown, does it?"

Jesse's expression shifted to concern. "Are ye telling me she hasn't been here all this time?"

"She only just arrived a few days before you, lad!"

Jesse paled. He took a step back, eyes cast to the sky in thought. "You're certain of this? That she wasnae... I dinnae, hiding somewhere here?"

"You dare question what I know, Jesse Strong?"

Jesse shifted his gaze toward the keep. He ran his hands over his face. "I need to see her."

"So the two of you can compare your betrayals before I can ask her? I ken not."

"Lord Warwick." The tension between them was immediately severed at Darrick's arrival. "Am I interrupting?" He caught sight of Jesse, and a wide smile brightened his face. "Jesse. What a pleasure. Steward Strong will be so happy you're home. You've been to see Ryan, then?"

Jesse seemed caught between this moment and another. "Your Grace. I've just come from seeing him."

Darrick laid a hand on his arm. "It was Ryan who taught me that miracles are not fable. He'll come around to the man you remember. The man we both remember."

Jesse nodded. "Aye. I hope so."

"Don't let Hamish wait too long to see you." Darrick turned to Khallum. "You sent for me?"

"I did, Your Grace." Khallum sent a hard glare at Jesse. The business of Esmerelda would have to wait. The business of the kingdom could not. "Jamesan. You'll nay be leaving Warwicktown until I decide we're finished. In case 'tis unclear what I mean, that's an order. From your lord."

Jesse nodded through relief he didn't hide. "Lord Warwick."

When Jesse was gone, Darrick asked, "The sharpest sword wouldn't have cut through whatever lay between the two of you."

"Doesnae matter," Khallum muttered. "I need to bring ye up on matters. It's time."

"Time?"

Khallum blew a choked breath between his lips. "For me to step aside. For you to take your place in leading us through this."

"IT GIVES MY HEART JOY TO SEE YOU OUT OF YOUR BED NOW. AND that gown," Ravenna said, circling Esmerelda with a growing smile. "I can see now the lady you were raised to be."

"Oh, nonsense," Esmerelda retorted, blushing. "Though it's nice to feel well enough to be amongst the living once more. Even if it is hard to resist hiding away from the world with Gemma. When I look at her, I can almost forget... the rest."

Ravenna squeezed her arm. "She's beautiful. She already looks so much like you. She has your eyes."

"And her father's mouth." Esmerelda frowned. "How I always loved Ryan's mouth. The curve of it when he smiled... that mischief..."

"Jesse has the same mouth."

Esmerelda turned away, pretending to tidy an arrangement of irises. "Does he?"

"I came to tell you something."

"Everything all right?"

"Esme, please, look at me."

Esmerelda turned. She was so lovely in the royal blue gown, the flush rising to her pale cheeks. Ravenna saw Esmerelda's whole life ahead of her, suddenly. Saw everything, for all its beauty and joy, all its heartache and sadness. A vision that was as imprecise as it was certain, for though Ravenna rarely experienced these looks into the lives of others, when she did, they weren't the unreliable prophecies of man.

Ravenna shelved these thoughts. "We swore there'd be no lies between us, and I've been keeping a great secret from you. Don't be cross with me, Esme. I had to be certain you'd make it through those dark days before I added to your troubles. Nothing was more important than seeing you and Gemma survive that."

Esmerelda's practiced smile fell away. "Go on, then."

"When I went to see Oldwin, that night. You remember?"

"Ravenna, there's nothing about our time in Duncarrow I'll ever forget. Ever."

"He told me that the Langenacht would be only a charade. That he'd blessed his..." Ravenna paused for strength. Saying these words aloud gave them flesh and bone. "His seed. That no matter how many Rhiagain men came to take their place with me, the child born of the Langenacht would be his. And that, knowing this, I must still go forward and go through with the ceremony just the same."

Esmerelda gasped. "*No.*"

Ravenna moved through the rest of her words in a haste, before her courage failed her. "During the ceremony, Oldwin told me something that's been chipping away at me ever since. He told me that *he* was my true father. He told me how it had come to pass. So now I must come to face what is before me. That I'm carrying the child of my greatest enemy, and that this same enemy claims he's my father."

"Ravenna," Esmerelda whispered. "Oh, Ravenna."

"Take the pity from your eyes. I can't bear it."

Esmerelda pressed both hands to her mouth. She shook her head. "It's not... is it true? Can it be true?"

"You've seen me fly in my new form, even if you're kind enough not to ask me about it. We both know I didn't get that from the Ravenwoods."

"But he's a liar! A deceiver! Could there not be another explanation? Maybe he's spelled you!"

"I trust nothing that comes from that creature's mouth, but there must be some truth in there, somewhere. I *feel* there's some truth in there, though I won't find it here."

Esmerelda's mouth parted. "You're leaving."

Ravenna nodded. "Not yet, but soon." She approached Esmerelda, taking her hands. "I wanted to wait for you to be well again. To be strong. And there was something else I was waiting for. The other thing I've come to tell you."

Esmerelda's eyes prickled with tears. "Will it break my heart?"

Ravenna leaned in and kissed the corner of her mouth. "I believe it'll mend it. Jesse has returned. He's here, and he's waiting, quite impatiently, to see you."

"Just us?" Darrick gazed around the empty Hall of Warring. Without the rumbles and energy of all the great Southerland men, the room seemed somehow less imposing. The table, only that. The great open window, boasting bird excrement older than he was, let in a glare from the morning sun that cast the filth of the place into crude display.

"Aye. Just us," Khallum repeated. He stood on the opposite end of the room, under the row of swords from his forebears. Darrick remembered the Warwicks melted down only small pieces of their father's steel to make their own, so that every sword wielded by the present lord was from all the men before. "Rutland has brought you up on the events at Goldthorpe overnight then?"

"This one was close to home for the Southerlands."

"Those were Rutland's words."

"You didn't bring me to ask who's behind it, surely."

"I may not yet know the hand who wields these atrocities against our own men, but aye, you and I know who issued the command," Khallum said. He crossed his arms. "What I donnae know, what I cannae ken, no matter how I spin my mind around it, is why he comes for *us*. I can increase my guard, which I've done. I can send men at his men, which I've done. I can wait, which I've done. None of these things make my men and their families safe again."

"Is it my counsel you're after?"

"I have all the counsel I need already," Khallum replied. "Your governance is what I'm after, Your Grace."

"I see."

"All these long years, the Warwicks have been the only strength in defiance of the crown. It's been my burden, as it was the burden of my father, and his, to stand against what others refuse to. Is that why Oldwin sets his sights on us? I donnae know. But 'tis my own failings that have laid bare a truth I find myself hardened against confessing, even as you stand before me ready to hear it."

Darrick listened to the man speak of his failings, keenly aware of his own. He'd first stepped back, allowing the Westerlands to lead their own war. When it was over, he'd launched himself forward, declaring himself king in all but name, riding a momentum that required more than simply his desire, though he hadn't known it at the time. And then, nothing. What had he done, but sit idly in the shadows, contemplating the words and strifes of Khallum and his men, daydreaming of a wife and child that were now his? Even Wyat had asked, before he'd left to return to his responsibilities at the Reliquary, what he was waiting for.

What was his purpose, if not to do as Khallum was now asking him to do?

"Khallum," Darrick said, stepping forth. "The failings are my own, in waiting for this moment, rather than seizing upon it, as is my duty. For lazing about with Anabella and Stefan, while the Southerlands burn. While *my kingdom* burns."

"I wouldnae have said it quite as such," Khallum muttered. "It's been the great honor of all Warwicks to stand where others have refused. But I fear, as my men now do, that it isn't the Southerlands Oldwin is after, though I've no doubt he'll raze it to the ground before this is ended if we donnae stop him. What he's after is bigger than us, in a way that leaves me trembling straight to my boots."

Darrick folded his hands over his mouth, thinking. He'd done nothing but these past days. Lying awake next to Anabella, long after she'd fallen asleep. In the long, lazy mornings. All the while returning to one thing. "The Hinterlands. The Hinterlands are the key. I don't understand why. Not yet."

"Does he mean to enslave more of them? The Medvedev?"

Darrick shook his head. "I don't think the enslaving of the Medvedev was ever about control."

"Then what?"

"Entry."

"How do ye ken?"

"Mortain knew enslaving the Medvedev, violating the most sacred of all our laws, would draw outrage and ire from the kingdom, and it did. Of course it did. But where did it lead? Not to a victory for the Easterlands, or even Mortain. It ended in the Saleen's total slaughter."

"Leaving their lands undefended," Khallum said, coming around to Darrick's understanding. "Leaving whatever is there, undefended."

"I know this doesn't help us, not with the Rhiagain Guard crawling about the forests by the thousands. But what if..." Darrick paused, searching for the right words. "What if..."

"We need an ally, on the inside. Medvedev," Khallum interjected.

"Do we have any?"

Khallum snorted. "We've never been welcome in those forests. After the Saleen died at our hands, I'm nay holding my breath for an invitation, either."

"That wasn't your doing. They know that."

"Changes nothing."

"Do you know yet? Or suspect?"

"What?"

Darrick waved his hand. "Who from your men is working with Oldwin on these attacks."

Khallum bristled. "I still donnae know if it *is* one of my men."

"But you suspect this."

"I'm nay ruling anything out. Would be a fool who did."

Darrick paced, working out his thoughts. "We don't believe what he wants is in the Southerlands, and yet he attacks you, and not the others. Why?" Before Khallum could answer, Darrick went on. "You don't stand between Duncarrow and the Hinterlands. The Easterlands does. The answer is here, somewhere, Khallum. It's *here*."

"Which is it, then? Is what he wants in The Hinterlands? Or the Southerlands?"

Darrick's mouth parted as the pieces of understanding came together, not quite connecting, but coming closer. "What if it's both?"

RAVENNA WATCHED THE REUNION OF JESSE AND ESMERELDA FROM A distance. The gentle, awkward dance as they decided whether they should embrace or not, and how much; Esmerelda eventually burying her tears against Jesse's chest, as he waged a battle with himself, and what, precisely, to do with his arms.

Ravenna's night with Jesse had been pleasant. A man and a woman meeting on equal terms, with no expectations when the morning arrived. She'd commissioned no magic to bring him to her bed, nor to keep him there through the night. He'd fallen into her arms willingly, and she his. Only when it was over and behind her did she recognize it as the one and only time in her short life that she'd had as much to give as to receive.

She also understood it would be the last time she shared a bed with Jesse Strong. His heart was pulled elsewhere, even if he was unaware of it.

But so was hers.

Hers had been pulled elsewhere for years, and now, inexplicably, it was called to the one place she'd sworn to herself she'd never return.

Home.

Oldwin had found a way into her nightmares. She didn't know how he'd done it, nor did she have the means to defend herself against these nocturnal violations. She supposed it had to do with the child growing within her, linking her with Oldwin for time undefined. Each time, he employed new and more horrible ways to threaten her. Last night, while Jesse lay sleeping at her side, Oldwin reminded her she'd never be welcomed back at Midnight Crest; that she was his now, but it didn't have to be a punishment. Together, they could find the answer to eternal life and bring forth a child born knowing it would live forever.

An answer he claimed to already possess.

Ravenna didn't know what any of it meant. She only knew the truths she needed would never come from Oldwin.

From the one who seemed all too insistent that she never again go home.

Ravenna didn't expect her mother to be any more forthcoming than Oldwin, but Ravenna knew Varinya's tells and tics, in a way she could never, and didn't want to, know Oldwin's. If her words didn't reveal the truth, then her eyes would.

Then Ravenna would know.

She would know, and then she'd have to decide what to do about it.

"WHERE HAVE YOU *BEEN*?" ESMERELDA RAN THE EDGE OF HER PALM down the hard spurs of his fresh beard. "Where have you been, that would keep you from being acquainted with a sharpened blade?"

Jesse reached for her hand to pull it away, but changed his mind. He flushed safely behind the evidence of his self-neglect. "I went looking for you."

"But that was many weeks ago," she said. Her obsidian hair fell in unspoiled waves over the shoulders of the blue velvet gown, painting the perfect picture of who she was born to be. She'd changed in their time away, but he could see her again for the lady she was, the life she'd intentionally left behind. Still, there was an uneasiness in the act; as if she was playing a role.

"Aye, it was," he answered. "But I understand that you've only just returned yourself."

Esmerelda laughed. It was a practiced sound, the kind he imagined worked on the sort of men who had once vied for the opportunity to court her. "Ravenna and I were waylaid. Foolish women, you know, thinking they could fend for themselves."

Jesse pulled her hand away from his face, twining it through his as it fell to their sides. He didn't immediately release it, not until she looked down, bringing attention to the strange connection. "You know that willnae work on me, Esme. Others, maybe, but not me."

The amusement faded, replaced by a hard smile. Hard, but real this time. "One day, but not... I haven't the heart to tell you now. Have you seen Ryan, then?"

Jesse nodded. "It's more than his memory. He's not himself at all." He sighed. "I'm so very sorry. I was always afraid he might not return, but I never considered he might return a different man."

"It's not your fault," Esmerelda said. "It's not anyone's. Except my own, I suppose, for believing in something that was never meant to be mine."

"He may not be who you remember, but it wasn't a whim that you gave up your whole life for. If anyone knows this, it's me."

"No? Perhaps you're right. It changes nothing." The sea breeze caught her dress, and she steadied herself against the rocks. The tide would come soon. When it did, they'd be trapped here, if they didn't leave soon. A fairer reality, perhaps, than the one awaiting them both. "And I swear to the Guardians, Jesse, if you *dare* attempt to reassure me he'll come around, that he'll—"

Jesse laughed. Esmerelda's face froze in indignation. This was a look he knew well. She'd gifted it to him often in their early days together on the road. "Aye, I ken I value my life too much, for that, Princess."

Esmerelda aped slapping him, then joined him, laughing along. The sound was near musical to him, like a happy memory. She was here, home with her people, and she was safe. He'd upheld his vow to Ryan, and to her. He could move on with his life now, once he'd fulfilled one final promise.

"I'm afraid I willnae by staying long," he said with reluctance. "I came home... I came to see you. And the bairn. A girl, they say?"

Esmerelda's face fell. "You're leaving?"

"I'll stay a few days, but then I have business, away."

"Business? What business could you have when you've only just returned to the Southerlands, after months away?"

"I'll tell you one day, if I can."

"If you *can*?" Esmerelda was incredulous. "What trouble did you find on the way home to us, Jesse Strong?"

Jesse tried to smile. "Only if you tell me your secrets."

"You're too clever, by far," she charged. "I'd ask you to stay for the wedding, but there won't be one."

"Esme, you cannot be unwed and a mother."

"When have you known me to be concerned with the rules the men in my life have set on my behalf?"

Jesse shook his head. "You'll get no more lectures from me. I only want your health and happiness."

She nodded. "I know. And though my heart is broken, I find it hard to dwell on this for too long, not when I look into my Gemma's eyes and see what my life is now, and will be forever after."

Jesse stopped breathing. "You named her Gemma."

"My mother wanted me to call her Mylannie, and of course my father said she deserved a proper Warwick name, but..." Esmerelda looked up at him, head tilted to the side. "I remembered how you and Ryan both spoke of your younger sister. How you'd both loved her so much. I wanted a name that showed her how loved she was, and I couldn't think of a better one."

Jesse's voice choked. "Aye. We loved her, but it wasnae enough. The Guardians still took her."

Esmerelda reached up and pushed a rogue tear away with her thumb. "The Guardians are fickle bastards. Would you like to meet her then? My Gemma?"

"I'd like that very much."

12

FAILURE TO SERVE

Rhydian's heart still lived at the back of his throat, thrumming so hard his eyes threatened to pulse into oblivion. Beside him, Arturo was already recovered, eyes cast in the direction of his thoughts. Rhydian often wondered if the man was possessed of an internal lever he could flip from one Arturo to another. He lay on his back, wearing nothing but the sweat still glistening from their reunion to remind him of the past hours. His mind, though, had long since traveled somewhere else.

Arturo sensed the examination. With a quick smile, he rolled over and planted a kiss in the hollow of Rhydian's neck. "I promised to stop doing that, didn't I?"

"Doing what? I hadn't noticed," Rhydian said drily.

"I would like to be more present with you," Arturo replied, settling his head against his hands, folded above his head on the plush pillow. "I do try, you know. Sometimes I even believe it'll work."

"I know you do." Rhydian slid his hand over Arturo's torso, enjoying the slip as it passed over the evidence of the passion that still lived between them, after all these years. Since they were boys, even before their mothers and fathers were plotting their marriages to the eligible young ladies of the Reach. Arturo chose a life with the Rush Riders early, and although he never said aloud that he'd done so to escape the inevitability of a traditional family, Rhydian understood. He understood well enough to find his own avoidance by joining the clergy. Moving up the ranks to Grand Minister was never the plan, but it afforded him the privilege of autonomy in movement, and more stolen hours with the only one he wished to give them to. Their respective professional travels provided them with the cover required, and the freedom from questions. "But since you cannot, you know what I think you should do."

Arturo shook with a light laugh. "You've always found comfort in words. Why do you think you've been such a darling of the Reliquary, Rhy?"

"You do too, even if you're loath to confess it."

"Ah, there we are. Confession. I knew you were on the job."

Rhydian nestled himself under Arturo's arm as they both laughed together. How he loved Arturo's laugh, which slipped through so seldom the further he aged away from the boy who used to sneak with him down to the falls to steal kisses and more. "I wouldn't dare. Not with you. I'd need an entire year of cleansing when you finished your unburdening."

"A year? You insult me. I'd expect at least three."

As their laughter faded, and the solemnity settled over them once more, Rhydian angled his head up to look at the only man he'd ever loved. "I would do anything for you. Sometimes I wish you'd let me. Other times, I know your refusal of this is your only means of protecting me."

Arturo grunted, but it faded to a sigh. Contentment slipped into the sound as he transferred it to a kiss atop Rhydian's head. "You might get the chance. You'll be seeing more of me now."

"You're staying?"

"Lady Blackwood believes my presence is more valuable here, guiding her son."

Rhydian propped himself on an elbow. "Turo, she's not wrong, but I don't think she has any inkling of how bad things have gotten here. Or even if you do, with how seldom you've been here."

"I might not be here to witness it, but I've heard more than enough on my travels. Jasmine Wakesell was only the first to declare her intention to withhold taxes, but Fairchild Bristol is preparing for the same, and once he does, the rest will follow, one by one. Brandyn's council may soon be forced to choose between lord and family."

"I'm disappointed Stewardess Wakesell didn't use Storm to reach Brandyn."

"Storm didn't return to hear the dead-given rites read for her father. For now, that door is closed."

"Everyone deals with loss in their own way," Rhydian said with a sad shake of his head. "The plain truth is, Brandyn listens to no one. Not me. Not Kaslan, or Asher. Not even Storm. He's decided that a true leader must take on the burden of decisions alone, and the council exists as a matter of ritual, no more. News of the unrest in the Reach will soon find its way to Lady Blackwood, no matter how we might try to shield her."

Arturo's face hardened. "She's changed. Perhaps it's what she's been through, what she's lost. It isn't for me to say. But I don't believe Asherley wants to hear about her Reach falling apart, no matter the truth in it."

"Turo, you know that isn't true. No one has given more for this Reach and our people, and right now she looks to us to take the mantle so she can protect what she still has left."

Arturo scoffed. He turned his head to the side, away. It was in these small ways, these little reminders, that Rhydian saw the distance that would always exist between them. Formed not by the absence of love, but the impossibility of it.

Then he surprised him. "I know you're right," Arturo said, turning back to him with a tight smile. "What I most fear is failing to serve her by failing to understand her needs."

"You could never fail to serve, Arturo Blackfen. It's simply not within you."

"And yet, I left her in Wulfsgate with the reassurance all was well."

"So, return. Tell her the way of things. Let her decide what to do."

Arturo sighed. "She was clear. I'm to stay and help guide Brandyn."

"Instructions she gave without understanding how bad things have become here. Surely you've heard what Lord Warwick deals with in the Southerlands? His own men turning against each other, against him?"

"We're not the Southerlands," Arturo said, with some force to his words. "She'd take my longbow for making that comparison."

Rhydian pulled himself up higher. "Thinking we're immune to this could be what brings this very thing to our doorstep. Brandyn is a good boy, a loyal, intelligent child, but he's drowning in his inexperience, and any attempts to save him, by us, draw him farther out to sea. This is a boy who took the head from his enemy and now forgets an even greater one still lurks in the shadows, waiting for his turn. Who may yet get it, if our Reach is divided by Brandyn's well-meaning but terrible decisions. Tell me, what's the very worst thing that could happen if you're candid with her on what's happened since her son took over?"

Arturo lifted his shoulders. "I don't know. She turns her anger at us for letting it get this far."

"She's wiser than that."

"You have an answer for everything, don't you?"

"Tell her, Turo. You have given over your life in service to this Reach, so go to her and *serve*. If she stays in Wulfsgate, then you've done your duty, and you'll rest easier knowing so."

Arturo twisted his mouth. "You want me to leave, and I've only just arrived."

Rhydian reached under the blanket. "I wish you could never leave. But that is not the way."

Arturo winced at Rhydian's ministrations. He ran his teeth over his bottom lip, moaning. "No, it's not the way."

"So it's settled then, and you'll go? You'll tell her?"

Arturo tipped his head back in pleasure. "Yes. Yes. Yes!"

"YOU WANT TO READ IT SO BAD? READ IT." BRANDYN THREW THE letter from his uncle on the table. When Storm reluctantly extended her hand, one eye on him, he tore it back and crumpled it in his fist. "Better yet, burn it."

"Are you going to tell us what it says?" Storm's voice climbed higher as he stepped closer to the roaring hearth and the high flames meant for just this moment. Her question echoed off the stone walls.

"You wanna know? I'll tell you," Gabi said with an impertinent little *humph* at the end. She flounced down on the bench across from Storm. "Though, you probably know already, for it's no different than any of us have been saying, only our uncle has his own especial way of expressing his displeasure."

"This is a meeting of the council," Brandyn gruffed. "You're not council, Gabi."

"Go on, tell us," Kaslan urged Gabi. Brandyn caught a flash of his mischievous grin from the corner of his eye as he bounced in his seat in anticipation.

"Brandyn will share if he chooses to," Arturo said, his strong voice the decisive end to the cross-squabbles. "We have more urgent business to discuss than family quarrels."

"So it *is* a quarrel," Asher mused.

Brandyn spun on them all. "I shouldn't have said a word. Gabrianna, go."

Gabi defiantly folded her hands over the table. Brandyn waited for the others to join in chiding her, but they did nothing.

"Fishwives, all of you," he muttered. He wished he'd never said a thing. When he first read the dressing down from his uncle Khallum, it was anger rushing through his head and limbs. Now he was simply embarrassed. He dropped the letter in the fire, ignoring the gasps of disappointment, relieved to see the harsh words blacken and burn. "If you must know, he was displeased with our choice not to attack the blockade at Newcarrow. He claims it's a breach of our alliance. If he were here, I'd remind him that an alliance isn't me sitting back and taking orders from another Reach!"

"Does he know why?" Asher asked.

"What do you mean, why?"

"Does he know," Asher replied. "That you've drawn the ire of all your stewards, who now refuse to raise a hand in your name?"

"Is there something else you'd like to say to me, Richland?"

"Come now," Arturo said, playing the role of long-suffering father. "You speak like boys, but the business of men is before us." He shot a look to the Grand Minister, but Tyndall had his eyes fixed on the fire, wearing a half-dazed look. "Lord Blackwood, we must discuss the matters of the rents."

"What is there to discuss, Rider Blackfen? I was perfectly clear. They may again collect rents when they have presented to me how those funds are used."

"It's not for the Lord of the Reach to decide how the landholders spend the funds they collect," Arturo countered. "It has never been. These lands are theirs. The tenants making lives upon those lands are theirs to serve or not. This is a free Reach, where a man can move anywhere he likes, without applying for dispensation, not like the Easterlands."

"It wasn't a free man who spoke to me from Newcarrow, but one beholden by a system that fails him no matter how he turns."

Arturo gripped the bench with both hands. "If there are no rents, Lord Blackwood, then those men suffer infinitely more than they were before. The rents fund the resources these tenants require for basic survival. If the steward chooses to dip from his coffers and build another barn at his keep, or add to his litter, it is no business of ours, so long as the men on his lands don't starve. But you must see that these men *will* now starve, for a steward will use what little is left in his coffers to feed his own first."

Brandyn raised a hand. "You weren't here, Blackfen. You didn't hear the man."

"It's a story as old as time is, Brandyn! I don't need to hear this particular man's complaints, for I have heard it before, as my father has heard it, as his father has heard it. No man is ever satisfied with what they have, whether he has one gold coin in his hand, or a thousand."

"My lord," Brandyn replied through gritted teeth. "Is the only appropriate way of addressing your lord."

"Brandyn," Gabi hissed. "What's gotten into you? You aren't yourself!"

"I told you to leave!"

Arturo leapt from his seat with unnatural speed. "Lady Gabrianna, if you'll excuse me."

"Not you, Blackfen," Brandyn shot back, sighing. When Arturo made no move to retake his seat, he groaned. "I said *not you*. Where do you think you're going?"

Kaslan and Asher exchanged wide-eyed looks. Tyndall finally stopped making love to the fire with his eyes.

"Taking the advice of an old friend, my lord," Arturo answered. "Before you inadvertently undo everything the Blackwoods who came before you have worked so many generations to build. Before, despite your true heart, you see it all burned to root and ash."

"Sit *down*, Arturo."

Arturo's icy eyes pierced him. "No."

The rider's cape snapped against the air as he turned and left.

Brandyn turned to the others, waiting for them to have something to say about it, but they were too stunned to speak. Were they wondering how he could allow such disrespect from his own council? Or did they agree with Rider Blackfen, fearful of the consequences of speaking the same words?

Sudden, hot tears burned the back of Brandyn's eyes. The matters of the Reach seemed so simple to him as a boy. There was good, and there was bad. There was right, and there was wrong. He'd done what seemed right, and now everyone was angry with him. None of the stewards backed him, a predictable outcome to everyone *but* Brandyn. Kaslan and

Asher both hinted that their fathers were demanding they return to their homes. Tyndall and Blackfen plotted from their bed, a bed Brandyn was well aware they shared. But did he care? No, for that wasn't his business. Protecting this Reach was.

They all stared at him. Waiting.

Uncle Khallum's letter crackled behind him as it burned. *I hope you're paying mind to what's happening in the Southerlands, nephew. For it's coming your way next. After my men rose to your aid in the Wester-lands, I thought we understood one another. I see now that you're as I suspected all along. A boy, barely out of his swaddling, unripe for the task at hand.*

Brandyn swallowed an unsteady breath. It trembled in his chest. "Go on, then. We're done today."

A**SHERLEY** **MOVED** **TO** **THE** **CENTER** **OF** **THE** **CLEARING**. D**OZENS** **OF** glowing eyes peered at her from the shadows of the tree, creeping in from the protection of the dark forest center. She'd entered here an intruder. She intended to leave this place as one of them.

She closed her eyes, and the world disappeared. The thrum of her heartbeat was the only sound she allowed in, and she latched tight to this, riding the rise and fall of her breath's rhythm. *In. Black-wood. Out. Ravenwood.*

In her mind, her arms pulled inward and bowed, becoming wings. Her flesh, tickling over muscle and bone, sprouted feathers. Her great height disappeared in an instant as her long, lean legs pinched inward, shrinking, becoming talons. She opened her mouth to speak the raven's words.

But it was her own voice, through the same ruby lips she'd known her whole life, breath rasping from the same lungs.

"Damn it all," she hissed. Her friends in the forest returned to their own business. She didn't think she imagined their disappoint-ment as they each turned away from her failure.

Daily she tried to find the wings she'd discovered at Midnight

Crest. Not once with success. With no one, not even her beloved Earwyn, could she share this.

Asherley turned her eyes toward Midnight Crest. The clouds had dropped low that morning for a late season storm, but she would always now know exactly where it was. She could be standing in Warwicktown wearing a blindfold and she'd know where to look. Her life had ended there. It seemed only right that she could return whenever she wished.

She'd taken lives there, as well. The two most powerful beings in all of Midnight Crest, and she'd dispatched them with no more than a surge of terrible grief and anger. They were not her first, but they were the first she'd taken down with magic alone.

Where the guilt and confusion should live was only further pain. An almost hollow numbness that kept her from feeling *anything*, if she couldn't feel what she needed: relief, understanding, closure. All this magic she now had, and none of it brought her closer to finding her daughter.

The kingdom was spinning out of control. The others thought she didn't know, but Asherley Blackwood had never missed much. She wasn't oblivious to the messages passed around Wulfsgate, complicated by an absentee lord who she could help, could guide. She could rip Christian Dereham so far from his melancholy he wouldn't recognize it when next it came knocking.

But as with the matter of the wings, Asherley was learning she had limitations.

"Even if you could fly, Lady Blackwood, I don't think you'd find her at Midnight Crest."

Asherley wasn't startled at Marsh's intrusion. She'd half-expected it. When he wasn't helping organize the search party, he was fixed on the skies, awaiting the Ravenwood boy to magically swoop in with answers.

Though comfort was elusive these days, she found what little remained for her in his presence.

"She's not at Midnight Crest, Marsh."

"Will you ever tell me what happened there?"

"No," Asherley said. Her eyes fell away from where the towering spires should be had the clouds not taken them. She turned toward him. "I'd never want you to think of Emberley and see her as I did, in those final moments."

Marsh swallowed. "Would you tell me, if you really believed she was dead? If all we're doing now was chasing a false hope?"

Asherley slipped the hood from her cloak back over her head. "What do you think we're doing?"

"I think we're going to bring her home. Not the way Lisbet brought her brother home. But properly."

Asherley nodded. "Then we will. I'm beginning to think you're right, Marsh. About the flying."

"Yeah?"

She again cast her eyes toward the invisible peaks of Icebolt Mountain. "And I don't believe for even a moment that's the only way up there."

13
RESTITUTION

Captain General Edmund Gilgowan wiped away the last of the day's sweat. It provided little relief; his sleeve was soaked from both sides. Armor would kill a man in this heat, leather too, so he and his men wore cloth. It wouldn't even be enough to protect themselves against the sand mites if they raised arms. But his men weren't here, at Camp Restitution, for battle.

The map, too, was soaked, and the ink was a mess of dark blots, but he checked it anyway. He'd memorized it by now, but Gilgowan was a man of structure and routine. His evaluation of the day's end was unsurprising. They'd covered less today than the day before. Yesterday, he'd made the same observation. He'd been making it for a while now, though he'd lost track of the days, same way it seemed they repeated their steps with each new one.

This wasn't what he'd given his life training for. Not what he'd forsaken the call of a traditional family to do. He could still have a family, like all Knights of Duncarrow, but with a wife plucked from the crown's pleasure, at his side only long enough to bear him a son before moving to the next knight. Some of these women, he heard, would carry ten or more children by ten different men, before being sent to retirement, which often included a life in the kitchens of some noble.

He'd of course known this when he came to Belcarrow as a boy, but back then there'd been honor in serving a king of Duncarrow.

That was part of what had been eating at him these long, joyless days in the heat. These orders hadn't come from the king. That was clear enough. Still, they bore the crown seal. They always had, though he'd always known better. Something was amiss in Duncarrow, but Captain General or no, he wasn't in the position to question the politics of the Rhiagains.

"Captain?"

Gilgowan tensed in anticipation of the predictable question. "Yes, Lieutenant?"

"We'll reach the end of our rations tomorrow. Has there been word yet on a new shipment? The men are…" Lieutenant Worley hesitated to say the words, for the same reason Gilgowan tensed to hear them. "They'll soon starve."

"Yes," Gilgowan agreed, though what to say next eluded him. All these months, he'd upheld the deception. That they were here under secret but honorable orders, and that all they were asked to do—the death pits, the stolen rations—would result in a reward unlike any they'd ever known in their days of service. More soldiers would come once the camps were clear of prisoners, and they no longer had to practice such discretion. They'd be treated to great feasts.

But the prisoners had been gone a while now. They'd burned the last of them a fortnight ago, smoke and ash billowing their sins, and the last of the evidence, into the night sky. Still, no replenished ranks. No feasts. At this point, he'd give his right arm for even a full bowl of gruel.

"What do we do, sir?"

"What we came to do, Worley."

"We've hardly covered half the map, sir. How are we to finish without food for the men?"

The way Worley looked at him, the raw anticipation burning in his eyes that emboldened him just enough to speak his mind, left

Gilgowan hollow. Worley hung his hope on the thin supposition that Gilgowan had a stash for such a day as this. If not that, then answers. Something. Something that only the man at the top of the chain could have, in the eyes of the men lower.

But Gilgowan had no secret stash. He had no magic at his disposal to employ and turn their situation from dire to bountiful. He had no answers. Least of all, why this supposed veil was so important. Important enough to murder thousands of men, who might be criminals of some sort, but hadn't been sentenced to death by any court or law.

"The king knows this as well," Gilgowan replied. He squinted as the last of the disappearing sun blinded him, its light bouncing over the red and orange peaks. "He'll not let us starve."

Worley was clearly anxious about his next words, but spoke them anyway. They were all past the point of restraint for the sake of order. Whatever his lieutenant said next, Gilgowan wouldn't hold it against him.

"He ordered us to kill those men. What if more men come, and their orders are to do the same to us?"

"Hmm," Gilgowan replied. He'd considered this late at night, belly empty. It left him unsettled. "Don't forget so easily who we are, Lieutenant Worley. We are the Seventeenth Artifact of the Knights of Duncarrow. The Knights are the highest servants of the crown. We are not the same as the men we disposed of."

Worley nodded, looking entirely unconvinced. "As you say, sir."

"It's not enough."

"Your Grace." Gilford, who possessed only enough bravery to conjure a pause in place of the words he would never say.

"You think I'll dispatch of you with a flick of my finger if you say what you want," Oldwin prompted. "That my especial demands of fealty do not come with the clarity you so desperately wish to provide."

"Um."

Oldwin spun around. The smile he wore was genuine for once. He *was* amused, and he certainly hadn't felt this in a while! Was this to do with the other terrible business, then? Was a taste for humor part of these last days? "Go on, then. I say it's not enough, and *you* say..." Oldwin rolled his hand in the air like a parent encouraging their child through a basic instruction.

"That... that it is my wish to serve you, Your Grace, in all things, in any things, in—"

"Say what you mean, or I will do exactly what you expect me to. I'll pull the precise details of your greatest fear from your mind and employ them in exacting precision," Oldwin said through an over-stretched grin that deepened the boy's terror.

"If there's something, or someone, in the Southerlands that you wish for us to secure, or to have dispatched, then we will do so." Gilford looked terribly relieved once the words were out.

"And? These are the orders I've given. Continue to give. This is how it works. I give the orders. You see them done. Is there confusion on your orders?"

Gilford wanted to sigh. He trapped it in his chest, with the rest of his fear and inadequacy. Oldwin wished he'd do it already. He'd begun to understand what annoyed Eoghan so much about this part of the job. "No confusion on the orders, sir, only a... a desire to understand them. To understand what the, well, objective is, if you will."

"The objective."

"Yes, sir."

"You want to know what the objective is. You want to know to what end I am taunting Lord Warwick, stealing from him, burning his lands. You fail to see the *objective* in this."

Gilford shook his head wildly. "I don't wish for you to think of this as a failure, sir, but rather, a desire to serve you better. To understand what you're after in the Southerlands, so that I may help you achieve it."

The young man bounced back several paces when Oldwin

laughed. "You wish for me to explain to you the point of torture, then?"

Gilford's eyes widened. "Torture?"

"Is this so obscure a concept for you?"

"No, well, yes, I mean, that is, it hadn't occurred to me that this might be your intentions, Your Grace."

Oldwin shook a finger at him. "Because you didn't ask. Your fear of me blinds you. Represses you. From more than you'll ever realize, and it isn't for me to teach you this, nor do I possess the time or desire to spend another moment on it."

"Sir." Gilford nodded. "I understand now. You simply wish to torment Lord Warwick, until such time as..."

"Torture, Gilford," Oldwin corrected. "Until such time as I grow weary of it."

Gilford was too caught in his relief to have survived another encounter that he had no sense left to detect the lie. Oldwin would continue to torture Lord Warwick, but it wasn't something he did for his own amusement.

He would torture Lord Warwick until he had what he needed. Eventually, these 'distractions,' would break the man.

"Is that all? Or will I next have to explain to you the art of detecting when a conversation has reached its natural conclusion?"

"There is one other thing. The Wastelands, Your Grace. The camps are clear."

"Good!" Oldwin clapped his hands and laughed. "That only took several months more than it should have."

"In this same letter, Captain General Gilgowan writes that his men have exhausted their provisions. That the next phase of his assignment is incomplete and they will need more provisions, and quickly, if they're to complete it."

"Why are you bringing this to me? This is your business, not mine."

Gilford's fears returned in a flash. He shifted from one foot to the other, clearly weighing whether his next words would be his last. Oldwin almost regretted the quick deaths he'd issued to so many after Eoghan died. Now everyone expected one. "We cannot get to them, Your Grace. To deliver any."

Oldwin scoffed, loading another sharp barb for the ginger-haired imbecile. But he supposed Gilford had a fair point. The crown no longer enjoyed passage through the Southerlands, and the Wastelands had no ports to send the provisions by sea. "Have you come to me seeking answers, or is it possible that, for once, you might provide one?"

"I do have a suggestion, sir."

"Go on, then." When Gilford again stumbled, Oldwin closed his eyes in impatience and pulled it from the boy's head. "Why, you are much more devious than you let on, aren't you? Let them starve? Gilford!"

Gilford flushed.

"And when they do starve? What then? What of the task I've set them upon?"

Gilford didn't seem to know how to answer this, either.

Oldwin dismissed him. Gilford's idea was useless, but Oldwin had no better idea himself. If he couldn't get resources into the Wastelands, he couldn't get more men, either.

He was reminded that anything he'd ever needed done well must be done himself.

When the boy was gone, Oldwin dropped the smile. Even something as simple, as mundane as pulling a thought from another's head had become shaky and imprecise. He'd pulled the word, but not the thought. Oh, he could piece it together just fine *now*, but what would happen when he couldn't?

How swiftly could the last several thousand years come to an end? All his searching? His sacrifices? To come so far and simply... fade away.

Oldwin had traveled through many doors to get here. Only one would lead to The Great Light of the Worlds.

He now knew where it was, but not how to enter. Not how to breach the impenetrable doors that stood before it.

It was said there was a door that would take him through the ones where he wasn't allowed. It was said he could step through this door and exit to the precise place he needed to be—no competing magic to stop him. No one in this kingdom understood that the Medvedev didn't simply hide behind their magical doors; they stepped into other realms, other kingdoms, when they disappeared through trees no one but they could find. Within one of these kingdoms was the door to everything.

Not if he couldn't get there.

But the Wastelands... for many years, the Warwicks had protected this land, passing down tales they didn't understand, shouldering a responsibility they were forced to surrender when the Wastelands was taken from them. Not even the one they called Fynne the Good gave the land back, when he set everything else to rights.

Because Oldwin wouldn't let Fynne give the land back.

Because Oldwin knew the door that could slip him beyond the magical trees of the Hinterlands and into the kingdoms he couldn't otherwise enter was said to be there.

Lysanor was the one who told him, and was now the one conspiring to keep him out.

She could spin her deceptions with the reincarnation of Dain. With whatever other designs she and the weak-minded Isdemus planned to distract him. The business of kings and queens was so inconsequential now, had always been, except to those who understood what lay at the center of all the worlds, what could give life.

Life eternal.

ADYNORA STROKED THE SILVERY CHIN OF HER MOST FAVORITE midnight goat. She'd singled this one out when she was still a girl, and the goat, in turn, recognized the importance of this choosing, always making his way to her when she stepped upon the ice of the Courtyard of Regents. She was his, and he was hers, in a world where nothing was anyone's.

Oldwin's lies still burned in her mind, threatening to take root.

She'd known, long before searching for solace and answers in the space between the worlds, that the great Meduwyn sorcerers were not to be trusted. This was a truth as sacred and simple as needing air to breathe, or the light of the sun for precious food and flora to grow. The ancestral visions running through the eldest daughters might have long left them—if they'd ever been real at all—but they hadn't abandoned all the stories of where they'd come from. Ilynglass. It was their home, once, but they'd fled long before the Meduwyn found their way to the shores of Duncarrow. Fled for their very lives. For, though it was said that the Meduwyn couldn't kill Ravenwoods, and they couldn't kill the Meduwyn, there were always imaginative ways around any problem. They would call down storms and wash them out, or ignite the fires that burned them in their beds. The hatred burning beneath the surface of the history between them had boiled to the point of no return, driving the Ravenwoods out of their home, seeking new lives in a world that seemed untouched by the foul magic of the sorcerers.

They'd traded one danger for another. The men inhabiting the White Kingdom were uninspired and closed of mind. These were men who had named their very kingdom after the color of the foam that passed on the waves of the seas. Unimaginative men were dangerous men.

The Ravenwoods found themselves in exile until they were at last taken in by King Torrin of the Northerlands.

A plague had swept Torrin's lands, one he was powerless to slow or stop. The Ravenwoods offered healing in exchange for protection. The Northerlands again thrived, and the Ravenwoods had their peaceful, if isolated, kingdom in the mountains to keep them safe from harm. The agreement had always been one-sided. It took next to nothing for the men to offer protection, but the Ravenwoods were eternally bound to provide aid to the men, whenever asked. They sent their daughters, and sometimes sons, to the Great Cities, to what the Ravenwoods called training, but was more of a gentle bribe. A reminder to each generation of what the prior generations had sworn to do. While the alliance with men had warmed and cooled over the centuries, no real danger had ever reached Midnight Crest.

Not until Adynora's weak-willed daughter had given her heart, and then her body, to one of these same men.

All these years, Adynora had carefully observed Ravenna for any sign she might be Argentyn's. Spotting Argentyn in her was no simple matter, for Argentyn and Varinya had been siblings, and so when one said Ravenna had her mother's nose or mouth, they could also say she had her father's, for there were more similarities than differences between them.

Ravenna was not Argentyn's, though, and this was a fact Adynora had convinced herself of by the time she discovered a means to drive her away from Midnight Crest.

But... she'd struggled to see Holden in her granddaughter, either. There *was* something else there. Something in Ravenna's blood that impeded her progress with magic. That kept Varinya and Argentyn on their toes, in fear.

Oldwin was a great liar, with every reason to drive further enmity into the small, careful world the Ravenwoods had curated in the kingdom over the past centuries.

And yet.

"Grandmother," Ryandyr said, her small, timid voice almost a disappointment when compared with the great fire that had burned in Ravenna. Ravenna would have made a fine High Priestess, but the same qualities that made this so were the very ones that Adynora must keep from their order. "High Priestess," she corrected in a rush.

"Yes, Ryandyr?"

"We haven't yet spoken of what I'm to do when I fly down to Wulfsgate on the morrow to begin my training."

"Tomorrow?"

"Yes, according to the sacred calendar, my training is to begin tomorrow if my magic is to be fully formed before my Langenacht when I turn fifteen. Ryessa has been preparing me for this day, though she has not herself been to Wulfsgate and so suggested that I should ask you, as you completed your own training there when you were preparing for your own ascension."

"She's right. I did," Adynora mused. Ah, and she hadn't been immune to the Dereham charm, either. Hadden had followed her everywhere, and she'd allowed it, enjoying his fixation. But not once did she indulge it. She understood she was purchasing the continued safety of her people, not betraying them. She wasn't weak of heart, like Varinya, or Ravenna. Was Ryandyr?

"What can you tell me that will aid me in making you proud?"

Adynora pushed back from the table. Her attendants rushed to her side to ensure her path was clear.

"Nothing. For you won't be going."

"Not going?" Ryandyr looked as if she'd been struck. "How will I complete my training?"

"Training with men has long since reached its expiry of usefulness. I'll be training you myself."

"Have we fallen out with men?"

"You could look at it that way," Adynora smoothly replied. "Or you could choose to see that training with those who are so far beneath us only holds us back from our potential, rather than helping us to realize it."

"But who will protect us?" Ryandyr wore her panic in her eyes.

Adynora laughed. "We've always protected ourselves. It's time we stop pretending otherwise."

MARSH HAD BEEN CHASING THE CURSED RAVEN FOR DAYS IN A GAME OF barn cat and mouse. The raven would emerge, then disappear, leaving Marsh to wonder if he'd seen him at all, or mistaken him for some other bird. Then at last he'd appear again, a day later, continuing the game. Marsh would take aim, his vision throbbing in and out of focus with his escalating pulse. Each time, something stayed his hand.

The raven would repeat the game, drawing Marsh farther from the keep, only to disappear entirely until the next day.

This time, though. This time, Marsh had him.

At first, it seemed as if Alasyr would bolt and take back to the skies, beyond the reach of Marsh's arrows. Instead, he swooped and dived, swirling through tree branches, deeper into the Wintergarden.

He wants *me to follow him.*

Marsh didn't return the arrow to its quiver just yet, though. He clutched it tight in his fist, dropping his bow to his side as he trudged through snow to his knees, cursing himself for not shooting Alasyr when he had him in his sights.

He wove around the trees and benches, slipping farther away from the comforts of a place known for its beauty, deeper into a forest he was less familiar with and had always been slightly afraid of. These weren't the colorful, inviting woods of the Westerlands, but a darker, more forbidden place, where one could lose themselves if they were not absolutely certain of the way.

He paused near a tree with a thick bark, propping his gloved hand against it while he bowled over to spit out the bile that had filled the back of his throat. He heaved hard breaths into the warmth of his vest, having learned that to invite the icy northern air in was asking for death. When he'd caught enough rest to continue, he wiped his mouth on his arm and straightened his posture, preparing for another hard sprint.

When he looked up, Alasyr Ravenwood stood only ten feet away. Wearing the patterned shirt of a Northerland man, cheeks only lightly flushed, as if having a bit of fun.

Marsh reunited his hands, getting ready to load the arrow into the bow. Alasyr shook his head.

"If you kill me, Emberley will starve," Alasyr said, his soft, deep voice muffled by the endless snow. "We may not ever be friends, you and I, but we both want the same thing."

Marsh's chest heaved in exhaustion, heart racing. "You're a liar."

"If I was a liar, you wouldn't have followed me. You wouldn't have been out here waiting for me."

"I wasn't."

"Now who's the liar, Marsh?"

"If you knew," Marsh said, stepping closer. His chest burned. His legs threatened to turn to liquid. "If you knew I was out here, then you're no better than I thought you were. That you would let me suffer. Let Ember's mother suffer." He tried to flex his numb fingers, but when he did, the bow and arrow fell from his hands, disappearing into the snow. He was afraid to go for them. Afraid Alasyr would again be gone if he looked away for even a moment. "She's alive?" His voice cracked. "Let's say I believe you. Where is she?"

Alasyr nodded. "She's been with me, in a cave high on Icebolt Mountain. But she's unwell. I have no way to bring her down the mountain on my own."

"Unwell? What does that mean?" Marsh narrowed his eyes. "What have you done to her?"

"I *saved* her." Alasyr tried to laugh, but the sound was bitter. "I saved her life, but there's no magic for what troubles her now."

Marsh pushed his tongue to the roof of his mouth to quell the rise of emotion. "What troubles her now, then?"

"She's afraid to fly. If she can't fly, then she'll..." Alasyr turned his head to the side. "She'll never leave that cave alive."

"Why are you here?"

"I need your help."

"If you needed my help, why did you waste several days taunting me?"

"I hadn't decided if you were the right person to give it."

"How..." Marsh struggled for words.

"As it turns out, it isn't quite so easy to slip into a man's kitchen and steal food without being chased away, or hunted down. I managed to get my hands on his foul shirt, but..." Alasyr sighed. "It pains me to be standing here. With you." He rolled his hand. "Conspiring."

"And now you want my help? Now that your days of thievery are behind you, and you've decided no one else is capable?"

"Now *Emberley* needs your help," Alasyr clarified. "I suspect you're uniquely qualified to offer it, even if you are a man."

Marsh laughed, pointing toward the sky. "I still have trouble believing Emberley flew, and now you think *I* can? A Tyndall from Wildwood Falls, without a drop of magic in my blood?"

"Who said anything about flying, Wildwood?"

Marsh shook his head. "Now I know you're playing games."

Alasyr took a step closer. "There must be other ways up that mountain. Ways only men know about."

"You'd know better than any man."

"I know of no other way, so if men don't, then we're agreeing we cannot save Emberley. Yes?"

"If there were ways up that mountain, we would've found her by now."

"If we don't find one, then her blood will be on both our hands."

"Why should I believe you? Why should I believe anything you say?" Marsh dropped the quiver from his shoulders and moved closer to Alasyr. "Why should I believe you know anything at all about Ember?"

Alasyr reached into his pants. He pulled out a patch of fabric and stretched his hand toward Marsh.

Marsh took another couple of steps and leaned in to grab it, backing up again once he had it in hand. He watched Alasyr through distrustful eyes, dropping them only reluctantly toward the swatch of bright red. His suspicion faded to the powerful sensation of being kicked in the gut.

"Mother's blood," Marsh whispered. He pulled the small bit of fabric to his face, inhaling. "Where is she?" When he said the words again, they came out as a scream. "WHERE IS SHE?"

"I told you where she is. And now I need your help."

Marsh laughed through fresh tears. "You haven't told me anything!"

Alasyr folded his hands before him. "What would you like to know? What can I say that will convince you quickly enough, so that she doesn't die waiting for you to come around?"

Marsh stuffed the fabric into his own jacket. "Tell me what Lady Blackwood will not."

"What has she said?"

Marsh laughed. "I don't think so. You first."

Alasyr drew a steadying breath. He stood straighter, as if powered by the words. "Emberley found her wings, and she flew to Midnight Crest to save her mother, who'd been taken there by my father. But... my mother couldn't abide the idea of half-bloods at the Rookery, and had no interest in diplomacy. She intended to kill Lady Blackwood, to throw her from the balustrades, but the arrival of Emberley interrupted this plan. And instead... instead..." Alasyr squeezed his eyes shut, wincing. He exhaled the next words. "My mother struck Emberley from the skies, ripping her wings apart. I watched her fall into the abyss of night and storm."

Marsh stumbled backward, reaching once more for the tree. The sickness started in his belly, but he willed it down. "No. She couldn't have survived that."

"She didn't," Alasyr said after a hard pause. "When I found her, she'd already been gone a while, I... I meant only to take her somewhere safe, somewhere the buzzards couldn't..." Alasyr again had to take a break. "I don't owe you, a man, an explanation of my magic. I don't owe you anything, but I'm telling you, for *her*. For her. Do you understand?"

"What did you do?" Marsh said the words slowly. "Alasyr. What did you do?"

"I brought her back," Alasyr said. When at last the confession was done, the boy smiled. "I brought her back, and until I felt her warm breath, saw her chest rise and fall, I didn't think I was capable of it."

"Emberley died?" Marsh pressed his hand to his mouth, this time to stop the sickness from spilling forth. "She died, and you brought her back?"

Alasyr nodded.

You have no choice. You've been waiting for this. There is nothing else. There won't be anything else but this.

"And then?" Marsh pressed.

"We've been in the cave ever since. I bring in what berries and leaves I know we can safely eat, but she's declining without proper food. I know she needs more. I offered her goat meat, but she's not taking well to it. As I told you, I've tried foraging, and even stealing, but none of it is enough. I'm out of ideas. Out of options."

"Why didn't... why didn't you come to me sooner? Or since you loathe me so much, anyone else here? All these weeks! All these weeks, and we could've found a way to her?"

Alasyr dropped his eyes. "I was afraid of what would happen if I took to the skies. I left my home in exile. What if they caught me, kept me from returning to her? She'd die if that happened."

"You're here now."

Alasyr again stepped forward. "I'm weary of explaining it to you. Accept my reasons, or do not. I don't care."

"You must have a plan, then? Some idea, to come here, to me?"

"I can carry some food back to the cave. Not much, but my talons can support the weight of a small satchel, if I take regular rest. Some bread. Perhaps some wine, and some better meat."

"And the two of you live in the cave for all of time?"

"No, Wildwood," Alasyr said. "The food is to give us time to figure out a way to get her down from there."

Marsh bristled at the nickname and Alasyr's derisive delivery of it, but bit back his retort. "Why did you save her?"

A look more suited to Alasyr appeared; that smirk he recognized from the raven's days of stalking them in the Wintergarden. "I don't know."

"I don't believe you," Marsh said, now feeling something else, something that made him sicker deeper in his belly. "But if I have to load you up with meals for Emberley for the rest of my life, to know she's safe, then I'll do it."

"You won't have to. We'll find a way."

"You heard what I said, if there was—"

"You're not *asking* the right people. Did you know there once was an alliance between the Ravenwoods and the men of both Midwinter Rest and Witchwood Cross? The Derehams protect us from the rest of the kingdom, but do little against their own men. The Frosts and Wynters were once our trusted friends, too."

"So?"

Alasyr's laugh cut straight through Marsh's confidence. "I don't suppose you might know one."

"Aylen," Marsh whispered.

"Ask her," Alasyr commanded. "For I can't guarantee my safety in these skies, and this means I can't guarantee Ember's on the mountain."

Marsh nodded. He was dizzy with all the ways this conversation had taken them. "Stay here. I'll come back with food."

"I have to be able to carry it in flight."

"Yeah. I got that," Marsh said, kneeling in the snow to recover his bow and quiver. "I'll be back before dark."

"Tell no one."

"Emberley's *mother* is in the keep, she—"

"No one. For you don't know what Lady Blackwood is capable of either, do you? I came across the body of my father, broken against the mountainside. I know she did it. And in my heart, I know she did the same to my mother. We can't be certain of *anyone* anymore, can we? You and I?"

Marsh turned and ran without responding.

14

INTRUSA

Gretchen cast her gaze to the canopy of stars while she waited for Brahim and Maura to return with the man they claimed was her son. She didn't dare let her eyes drop in searching desperation, scrutinizing every movement of the trees as the warm evening breeze passed through, wondering if it was them; him. She refused to squint through the dimly lit garden, illuminated by the night sky. All these things, these little, terrible moments, would break what was left of her, and she needed all that was left for what awaited.

He's away, is all they would tell her, when she demanded they prove their claim that Pieter was here and had grown into a man in the time he'd been missing.

Then tonight, after they broke their fast, they confessed he'd returned.

Then where is he? Why is not here, with us?

He asked for some time to himself before seeing you.

Before seeing me? His mother? How can that be?

You've searched for him for weeks. But Pieter has awaited your arrival for years.

She felt Curran's hawkish gaze long before he announced his

presence. "You've come a long way, Intrusa, for what you want. But fate has other ideas for us when we refuse to heed the path given. Even in your world, that truth cannot be so foreign."

Gretchen wanted to swat him away like a cloying insect. Away. Gone. From her, from this moment, awaiting her just ahead, if she could stamp out the nerves making her hands shake and her eyes well up with tears. "Brahim and Maura have already prepared me. In a kinder way than you."

Curran paced in an arc behind her. "In their kindness, have they told you where Pieter has been? Why he couldn't come to you the night you arrived?"

"Away. He's been away."

"I wonder," he mused, "who the kindness is for? For you? For him, so that he does not feel compelled to share with you his heartbreak?"

Gretchen turned before she could stop herself. "What heartbreak? You enjoy tricking me, but I won't fall for it."

"It's no trick."

"Then his mother is here, and can soothe any wounds he might have."

"He went into the desert for his seven days of mourning. Do you do that in your 'kingdom,' as you call it? Or do you move on from the dead toward the living, knowing they, too, will die? Will leave you?"

Indulging him was a loathsome idea. But Brahim and Maura kept things from her, offering truths in small morsels, never filling her up. Curran was a foul, sad creature, but even if wielding truth as a weapon, she would take it.

"You obviously want me to know, or you wouldn't be here, taunting me with it. So tell me."

Curran stepped closer. Close enough that his hot breath tickled her nose as he leaned in, his stance strong and defiant. "And what would you do with the truth, Intrusa? Would you hide from it, as the others do, or challenge it, head-on?"

"I—"

Gretchen didn't get to finish. She and Curran both turned toward the steps in the courtyard.

"Gretchen." Maura's soft voice pierced the air. "He's here."

Pieter Dereham stood before his mother for the first time in almost a decade. Though he was much changed, she looked exactly as he remembered her when he last saw her, howling after him in Termonglen, when he was dragged away in chains.

"Cub," she whispered, and he was both relieved that he'd be spared hours of examination from his own mother, questioning his identity, and also annoyed, that she was here, that it had taken so *long*. Maura and Brahim had prepared him for this even before she'd arrived. Time passed differently here. No one knew why.

But Pieter was weighted by his exhaustion, by a soul-deep grief. And now, he'd have to explain that, too, to his mother.

"You found me," Pieter said. What else was there to say? He could share all the many things he'd practiced saying in the first days, after Brahim and Maura found him eating that terrible fruit that had turned his bowels liquid. He hadn't believed back then, about time. Not for a while. Not for years. Even then, there'd been no solace in their claim, nothing to validate it. Until he saw his ageless mother standing before him after a decade of waiting, he hadn't realized there was a part of him that still doubted.

"How? How can this be?" She reached for his face, a look of bewilderment beset by tears. "You look so much like your father when I met him."

Relieved when she dropped her hand without touching him, Pieter tried to smile. "You always said that."

"But now you're the age he was when I was told he would be my husband."

"He's not with you?" Pieter already knew the answer. Holden Dereham's lack of imagination had kept him from many things in his life. Of course it would keep him now from his son.

"I left when he was at war," she said, nearly breathless. She couldn't stop staring.

"At war?"

"Doesn't matter now. Doesn't matter *here*," Gretchen said. "Can I hold you?"

Pieter's eyes stung with tears he willed back. "You never would've asked me when I was a boy."

"This is like a dream to me. And although I wish, in a way, that it was, that I could awaken and find you in your bed at Wulfsgate, covered in piles of furs, as you always liked, I equally fear waking and finding you still lost to me. I've never feared the unknown, but seeing you now, I've never been more afraid of anything than that we've become strangers to each other."

Pieter lifted his shoulders, lowering them into a sigh. "I'm still me, Mother. But I've already had a life here. I had…" He looked past her, at his surrogate mother and father. He'd even called Brahim this, though with Maura it was guilt that stayed him from giving her the same familiarity. "I had a wife. And a son."

Gretchen's mouth dropped. "You what?"

"I just returned from the desert, where I buried them, side by side. Far from the city, where their bodies might spread the disease that killed them."

"Pieter," she whispered. "No, my cub."

"This world isn't ours, Mother. It's not meant for you or me, but here we are, and I must live with knowing that it's possible that it was *me* who killed them both. I'll never know with any certainty, but it will haunt me just the same."

"You've been here… ten years, as you say. It couldn't have been you."

Pieter laughed and pointed in the general direction of the veil. He'd once called it this, too. A veil. But to call it that didn't denote its potent danger. Instead, it drew men of the White Kingdom in with their curiosity and their disease, only to ruin this world. "Rehana was a child when I came. She was a child, as I was a child, and this is not a disease that kills quickly, but rather, sets down roots and waits. It waits for happiness, for joy. For new life. And when it sees it can take so much more than it initially thought, then it strikes."

"Diseases don't work that way, cub."

"This one does."

"All the more reason we must leave here, Pieter. You said it yourself. This isn't our world. We aren't meant to be here." Gretchen dropped her voice low, shaking her head back and forth. "They may want us to stay, for their own reasons. I don't know what those reasons are. Perhaps you do, as long as you've been here. But we cannot stay here a moment longer than is necessary."

"Don't speak of my friends as if they're your enemies. Without them, I would've died out there, eating food that wasn't meant for men, crying myself into oblivion while I wondered if anyone would ever come for me. If my *mother* had forsaken me."

Gretchen dropped her eyes. "I did come for you. I came for you as soon as I knew the searches we sent into the pass were in vain."

A sudden thought struck Pieter. "Ransom. That morning. Did he survive? Did he make it to Wulfsgate?"

Gretchen nodded. "It's how we knew that you'd disappeared near the pearapple tree. Alric couldn't stop himself from theorizing, he never can, but this time he was right."

"He was *always* right, but it was simpler for you all to think him insane. And Lady Blackwood?"

"I didn't learn her fate before I left to come looking for you. Emberley was still searching for her when I came after you."

"Drystan and Lisbet?"

Gretchen shook her head.

"Maybe they found their own door."

"Pieter, we have to leave here. We can catch up on all we've missed when we're home, and safe. Don't you want to see Nyssa and Torrin? Your father? Christian is home now, too, and Aylen is with him. You remember Aylen Wynter? She's your sister now. Christian wed her at the Sepulchre, and he'll be the lord one day, when your father's time is done."

"You're describing a world that isn't mine, Mother."

"Of course it's yours! Even if you have spent ten years here—"

"Even if I have?" A hard flush rose to Pieter's cheeks. "Look at me!"

"Even if you have," Gretchen continued, and now this was the mother he remembered, all fire on top of hardened ice. "You spent more than that in the White Kingdom. *That* is your home, Pieter. I don't know why these veils exist that allow us to leave our worlds for others, but I know you're right. Maura and Brahim are right. They should be closed, and travel between them forever forbidden. They cannot even have their children with them, because of us! You buried your own wife and child, because of us."

"My wife's name was Rehana. And my son was Drystan. Your grandson, Mother. Don't speak of him as some obscure thought. He was real. As real as you and me."

Gretchen's anger settled into something calmer, but harder. "You wouldn't have named him so if you were not still tethered to our world."

"I named him so because there are some things that shouldn't be forgotten. If we'd had a daughter, she would've been Lisbet. You let them go, but not everyone did."

"That's not fair. In letting them go, I helped save them."

Pieter laughed. "You'd never struggled to control Father before, so why was that different?"

"It's never been that simple with your father. You might have seen that, as you aged, had that happened at home and not here. The whole kingdom was watching. To deny King Eoghan would've been to bring war to our doorstep."

"From what you said, war came anyway."

Gretchen looked down at her hands. "I don't want to argue with you, Pieter."

Pieter softened. He reached forth and ran his palms over his mother's arms. "I don't either."

"Do you live here? In the Malcazara?"

"No," Pieter answered. "Brahim gave me my own home when I joined with Rehana. He'll give you one, too."

"That won't be necessary. We'll be leaving soon."

Pieter drew from the last of his patience. "This is my home now. The sooner you accept that it's also yours, the sooner you'll find something resembling happiness here."

15

THE GOLDEN CASTLE

Cian pressed his body to the railing at the perch atop Arboriana and leaned over the edge, surveying the land that had become his even before word of his father's death had reached them. It was always supposed to be his, but he'd thought he still had many years ahead of him before he had to think about what that might be like. Aidan Quinlanden had always been in robust health. Something about the man made it seem like he might even live forever. He'd once joked that Cian would himself be old and near the end of his own promise before he'd have to concern himself with the matters of the Easterlands.

Below him, the world moved on as if the last few months had never happened. Workers worked. Civilians went about their business, gathering, gossiping, exchanging gold for wares. Their lives hadn't been upended, only inconvenienced. They weren't the ones who now must face the seditious reputation that had fallen upon the leadership of the Easterlands.

A surge of bile formed in the back of Cian's throat. He willed it down. His father wouldn't hurl his lunch from the perch. His father wouldn't be so afraid.

My father was a traitor.

He was fortunate to have his aunt and uncle here to guide him. Corin treated Cian as his own son, and Yesenia always had precisely the advice he struggled to find on his own, in his woeful inexperience. He needed them now more than ever, when the rest of the kingdom judged all by the actions of one.

But even surrounded by loving aid, he'd never felt so alone. Breandan and Dorrin were away at Oldcastle, and hadn't even applied for a temporary leave to return home. Eavan hadn't even said goodbye before she turned her back on Whitechurch. And Assana... Oldwin had shared no word of her in his declarations to the kingdom. She had to be dead. Or a prisoner. She must be one of these things if she hadn't come home to him yet.

"There's not enough strength in the world for what you must do," Yesenia said from the lounger behind him. "You'll feel better when it's done, though."

"How?" Cian turned to face her. "How will I feel better? How could I?"

"You'll know you've done what you must, as the Lord of the Easterlands. As a man of strong moral character, who has chosen right from wrong, even at the expense of his own heart." Yesenia tried to smile. "She has always loved her children, no matter how your father sought to break her down. She loves you still, of that I have no doubt."

"Then how could she do this? To me? To us?" He heard the boyish desperation in his voice and wished he could take it back.

"You'll ask her that, as you must, but be prepared for an answer as unsatisfying as it is false. If she lies to you, I suspect that, too, will come from a place of love."

"We're talking about treason, Aunt Yesenia. Allying with the same man who led a war against the Westerlands, conspired to kill Uncle Byrne, and led the Saleen to their deaths. What does that have to do with love?"

"No man, or woman, is so simple," Yesenia said. "I'll not defend your mother's actions. I only want you to find peace in what you must do, in reconciling the same woman who sang you to sleep, was also the one who betrayed your Reach."

Cian's mouth twitched with anger. "There's no reconciling that."

"You may find that easier to live with." Yesenia nodded. She pushed herself forward, standing. "Are you ready?"

"No," Cian said, but reached for the rungs on the ladder and climbed down.

ASSANA PULLED THE HOOD OF HER TRAVEL CLOAK DOWN OVER HER face as new patrons shuffled into The Golden Castle. Two brought the snow with them, stomping forward onto the wood like ill-behaved cattle. The third snuck in behind, huddled low. Unlike the other two, he paused at the door, kicking the white chunks from his boots to the side before entering.

She nursed the ale in the mug between her palms, coolly regarding all three new arrivals to the tavern. The two men settled into a booth at the opposite end. They were so consumed by their chatter—far too raucous at this hour—to even glance her way. The other, who Assana could now see was younger, probably a pupil of one of the universities, tucked himself into a small table, far from the hanging lanterns providing the only illumination. Outside, the strange late season storm took most of the light from the sky.

There were only three types who came to taverns at this hour. Travelers. Drunkards seeking reprieve from judgment. Or those, like her, who didn't want to be seen.

The two men at the other end were already on their second tankard by the time she'd decided they were most certainly drunkards. Night workers, probably, ending their shift here instead of slipping in next to their wives.

The other, though. The young man. The barkeep returned to his table with only a hunk of bread. No ale. No wine. Some men carried their own, in their skins, but she saw no furtive reaches inside his vest. Whatever was in the book he had spread before him was the sole focus of his attention.

Maybe him, she thought. It would not be just *any* pupil of one of the five universities. She knew that now, though she couldn't have known that when she started. The others had been all too eager to take, with nothing to give. She was no longer willing to give if they had nothing for her to take.

If he was still here when she finished her ale, she'd decide then.

"MOTHER."

Maeryn Quinlanden looked up from the bench in the corner of the cell. Her once radiant hair hung tangled in filth. This was a choice. He'd sent combs and basins of water for her to tidy herself. He wasn't surprised to see them abandoned in a heap, unused, with all the other things he'd sent her.

Yesenia hung back, far enough to give him his privacy, close enough that he felt the steadying effect of her presence.

"Cian." Maeryn brushed some mats off her face, squinting. "I've been in here weeks, and yet this is the first I've seen you."

Cian pointed at the discarded offerings. "I sent you things."

"They're just things. They're not my son."

Cian turned back to look at Yesenia. She offered a gentle, encouraging nod.

"Ahh." Maeryn looked past him. "You brought that trollop."

"Don't speak that way about Aunt Yesenia," Cian warned. "She's been good to me. Helped me, when you..." He swallowed, setting his lips in a tight line. "Left."

"Did you know that I once loved Corin Quinlanden?" Maeryn's hard look faded to something whimsical and altogether inappropriate for the moment. "She stole him."

Yesenia chortled from behind.

"The king chose your marriages," Cian pointed out. "I didn't come to talk about the past. I came to tell you that the council has ruled, and you'll be tried for treason for your actions against the Easterlands and the kingdom."

Maeryn leaned her head back and cackled. She looked nothing

like his mother, then. Not in her many, many forms he'd come to know, as she learned to adapt to her husband's cruel world.

"There's nothing funny about this, Mother."

"You aren't brave enough to tell me you've decided, so you hide behind the decision of your council. That's something your father would've done."

"Father is dead. And the punishment for treason... is..."

"I know what the punishment is, Cian. But do you? Do you fully understand what will happen next? Can you handle the sight of me swinging from one of the same trees you once climbed as a boy? Are you ready for that?"

"Maeryn," Yesenia warned. "Cian is here as your son, and it may be the last time you can meet him on these terms. Don't squander it."

"And how very convenient for you, Lady Yesenia," Maeryn said in a drowsy, singsong voice. "Treason." She was looking at Cian again. "Isn't it funny how that word means something different, depending on where you're sitting?"

"You conspired with Mads Waters, Mother."

"I also informed Khallum Warwick of the unpleasant business with the Saleen, so he could spread word of your father's treachery to the kingdom, but I suppose that doesn't matter a whit to you now, does it?"

"You conspired with our enemy! You pretended to be allies of Aunt Yesenia and Uncle Corin, and then told Mads everything they said! And then… then, you disappeared!"

"Mads was always a malleable man. Built to bend to the strongest voice. Ah, and I thought if I could get deeper into his ear, into his..." She closed her mouth, thinking. "That I, too, could bend him."

"But you didn't, did you? For you're here, in a prison his ancestors helped build. And for what? What did you think he might do for you, once you bent him? Once you betrayed the rest of us?"

"I assumed he would win this war. He and the sorcerer," she said.

"And that when they did, my children would be safe, for his love of their mother."

"Love? Mads shares responsibility for the annihilation of all the Saleen."

"Will you put him in the tree next to mine, then?"

"He's dead," Cian said. "Brandyn Blackwood killed him."

Maeryn again laughed. "Little Brandyn? Asherley's baby boy? Good for him. A true vengeance exacted, in payment for his father. Byrne was a good man. He didn't deserve what Aiden did to him."

"Father is dead, too. Has anyone told you?"

"Your father was dead the moment he sailed for Duncarrow. He just didn't know it yet."

Cian reached for the bars, wrapping his hands around the dense metal. "Do you not have anything to say for yourself? Anything at all?"

"What would you have me say, Cian?"

"Anything! Anything that might stay what is coming for you! Anything that might explain how you could abandon me!"

"Do you remember when you found me in the stables that night? When I told you that your time was coming, and you must be ready for it?"

Cian nodded. Tears welled in his eyes.

"It's here," Maeryn said. She drew her knees up into her arms and turned to the side, closing herself off.

"Mother?" Cian cried.

Yesenia moved behind him, laying her hands on his shoulders. "Come, Cian. You have what you need. She will not give you more."

When Assana left Esmerelda and Ravenna just north of Briarhaven, she'd told them she was returning home to Whitechurch to help salvage what remained of the Quinlanden name. That witch, Ravenna, knew she was lying, but said nothing. They had that in common, Assana thought. They had so many lies between them that the truth was the elusive thing.

If Esmerelda knew Assana had no intentions of ever returning to Whitechurch, she was either too spent from their thrilling flight from Duncarrow, or too focused on her own reckoning ahead to say so. They said their farewells with cordial hugs, no mention made of the emotional wreckage between them. Assana didn't suppose she'd ever see her cousin again, and that was fine. She wished Esmerelda well, but anyone or anything that reminded her of Duncarrow would fit better in her past.

Even that was almost laughable. Wasn't her time in Duncarrow, particularly that last part, why she was in Oldcastle to begin with?

Assana sipped the ale slowly, hood low, eyes on the boy.

She never asked herself why she'd done it. Why she'd allied with Oldwin. She needed to justify nothing that contributed to her survival. When she was past her bitterness at being forced to take Eavan's place, her thoughts more clear, she accepted that Eavan wouldn't have survived a place like Duncarrow. She didn't have the survivor's instinct Assana possessed, the convincing adaptability that had allowed Assana to smoothly handle the volatile Eoghan, while also keeping herself just useful enough for Oldwin.

It almost hurt at the end, watching Eoghan's conscience take shape. She didn't know Esmerelda would kill him, but she'd known he'd be dead soon, and that her less-than-gentle push for him to free Esmerelda would lead him there. Not because Oldwin had told her, but some things didn't need to be said.

You want to be free, Oldwin had said.

What do you mean, free?

Gone of this place. Done. Home. Wherever you wish to go.

This question feels like walking into a trap.

I'm not Eoghan. If you want to be free, I will make you free. But you must do one thing for me.

What thing?

Convince Eoghan to free Esmerelda Warwick.

She'd laughed. She couldn't help it. *Free Esmerelda? Was it not you who went to such trouble to get her here?*

Explanations are not part of this arrangement. A simple yes or no.

And if I say yes?

You and Esmerelda may both go free.

How do I know I can trust you?

He'd laughed. *You cannot trust me, girl. But Duncarrow will be the last place you'll want to be soon.*

Assana had done her part. Warily. Suspiciously. But what other option did she have? Eoghan was outmatched. She was expendable. She hadn't believed Oldwin, but his offer was the closest she'd come to a way out, so she'd taken it.

Assana glanced up at the sound of wood scraping wood. The boy leaned back in his chair, wearing a troubled look. His exhale was long, measured.

He briefly glanced her way. Assana gasped inwardly, dropping her eyes. She knew him. But from where?

If he shared this recognition, it wasn't enough to draw him away from his table and the book. He returned to his studies and she, her thoughts.

Oldwin had given her no indication of his plans, but she'd learned quick enough when she returned to the cell to find Eoghan dead, at Esmerelda's hand. Of all the outcomes she'd pondered in her imagination, somehow she'd never seen this one.

She knew it, then. It was more of a feeling, but her instincts had earned her survival, and she wouldn't ignore them. Oldwin meant to kill her. He'd used her, and he had no reason to keep her alive now. Esmerelda, too. Poor Esmerelda. She'd done what she needed to do, but she'd be forever haunted by it.

And how long had Oldwin known Esmerelda would do it? Had he planned this even before Assana sprang him from his prison? Had it been his influence invading her thoughts, helping her to see his use and sell it to her husband?

These questions kept her up, night after night. They ate at her, taunting her, first as they hid among the dry food of Duncarrow, waiting for death, and then later, once they'd escaped it.

She was certain Oldwin had known they were in the food cellar. Known and was waiting for them to die a slow, cruel death.

I'll go home. See how I can help Cian rebuild our reputation in the kingdom. She'd almost believed the words. They sounded reasonable. Right. Had she been released under some other condition, they might have even been true.

There was no home to return to as long as Oldwin lived. It was said no man could stop him. That there was no magic in this kingdom more powerful than a sorcerer's.

But all things in the world had limits. Even Oldwin.

Here, in Oldcastle, where the *Book of All Things* was written, rewritten, and shared with the kingdom... here, she would find the answer. For like all great things, there were those parts meant for all, and those meant for only some.

Eight pupils she'd taken to bed. Eight pupils who'd bragged about a level of access they didn't have, to impress her. Nothing about any of them was very impressive, but she understood now to avoid the loud ones. Anyone with anything of real use wouldn't be shouting about it from the rafters.

The boy looked up again, and this time, their eyes locked. Her instinct was to push her gaze down again, back into the last few drops of ale, but the recognition was more powerful now. It had been years, many years, but those eyes. When had she last seen them?

Balfour. Aunt Earwyn's son.

They'd sent him away. For a proper education, they said, but everyone knew it was because Balfour's father was crazy, and Balfour, even as a boy, was showing signs of the same.

What had her brothers, Dorrin and Breandan, said about him? *He's weird. None of the boys like him.*

He quickly closed the book and slipped it inside his vest. She read the panic in his eyes, not born of recognition, but fear. Was he afraid she'd take the book?

Assana had just decided to go over to him, when he flew from his chair, toppling it, racing out into the snowy morning.

16

THE WARWICK BURDEN

"I didn't expect you'd still be here."

Jesse pushed his sword back into its sheath. He flushed and quickly pivoted so she wouldn't catch his embarrassment at getting caught practicing his swordcraft. She had seen it, though, as she'd seen all the other little things men and women tried so hard to hide in their daily lives. She'd had nothing to do here *but* observe and wait. The waiting was agonizing, a slow death, but now she knew her way.

"Still here?" he repeated, still facing away. He fussed with his sword belt.

"In Warwicktown," Ravenna said. "You made it clear to us all you wouldn't be staying. That you had some other undisclosed business that took precedence."

"Aye. I am leaving. Soon. I was actually coming to see you," he said as he turned. "There's something on my mind. I've been running through it, over and over."

"Sounds dangerous. You're not one who likes to spend time with their own thoughts."

Jesse frowned. "Which is why I may need your counsel, before I settle on a decision." He slowly tilted his head. "You already know, don't you?"

"No," Ravenna said, navigating careful steps through the moldy piles of hay. This was the private armory of the Warwicks, so she'd expected something more bold, assuming, but it was no more than an overstated barn. Then again, she'd heard one of the men, Rutland, whispering about moving their arms again. There'd been another attack, on another town Ravenna had never heard of. It seemed as if the Reach was on the verge of all-out war. "I haven't read your thoughts, if that's what you mean. But I can guess, because I think you're coming around to an idea that's been building longer than you know."

Jesse tried to laugh. "Have ye? A guess?"

Ravenna nodded. "Say the words anyway. Hearing them will give them legs, make them real. Help you decide if you truly mean it."

"If I mean it?" Jesse scoffed. Then he did laugh. "Aye. Do I mean it? I think so. I ken the situation for what it is."

"You sound like Ryan, going on and on about duty."

He sighed. "That's exactly how I donnae want to sound."

"Tell me, then. Go on."

"You're the one who came here looking for me. Everything all right?"

"Everything's fine."

When she offered no more, Jesse nodded. He lowered himself to a thick bale of hay and sat, gesturing for her to do the same. He seemed as nervous as a boy when first realizing the girls he'd been playing with weren't just friends anymore.

"It's about Esmerelda."

Ravenna grinned. "*That* I already know."

"Aye, and how would I know that's true? You could say that about anything I say next."

"I *could* pull it out of your head..."

Jesse shook his head. "It's true, what they say about you witches. Evil."

"You're still going to tell me, though," she said.

"You're enough to keep a man busy the rest of his life," he teased.

"Aye?" she asked, mocking his accent. "I ken I'll nay know, for it isnae *my* heart you're pining for."

"Terrible," he retorted. "I never liked that word. Pining."

"Ryan might yet recover."

"Esmerelda says you've tried to heal him."

Ravenna dropped her eyes. "My magic is different here, but I've never been able to mend a mind, even at Midnight Crest. If I could, my entire life would've been very different."

"He might recover," Jesse said, nodding. "But Gemma is here now, and Esmerelda, stubborn as she is, would raise the bairn herself. And 'tis not that I donnae think she's capable. I do. I think Esmerelda Warwick is capable of anything she's determined to do."

"But you can see a future she cannot," Ravenna said, helping him along. "One where the shame this brings upon her family eventually breaks her heart, and then her."

"I cannae see the future, exactly. It's more like I can see what is, even when it's not in front of me. It's how I knew Ryan was in a bad way. I donnae know why I couldn't see her, though. It's like I have a blind spot with her." Jesse hesitated, his mind catching up. "You've seen her future?"

Ravenna didn't answer. She'd not seen enough to help him, but had seen too much to be fair to him. She'd also picked up on his brief allusion to some new magic.

"All right, then. Here it is. I mean to ask Esmerelda to be my wife," he blurted, looking first surprised by the words and then relieved. "To be a father to the bairn that shares my blood, and to make right what has become wrong."

Ravenna reached forward and clapped him on the knee. "There you are. Do you feel better now?"

He winced. "It's a terrible idea, isn't it?"

Ravenna shook her head. "I think it's the best idea you've had since I've known you."

"I cannae decide how to take that."

"You'll want to work on your delivery, though. Esmerelda will send you and your intentions packing if she detects even a hint of pity in your asking."

Jesse nodded. "It's not pity. It's not duty, either, exactly. It's..."

"I know what it is and I think, if you really wanted to, you'd know, too. I've seen the way you two look at each other. How you are with each other. *What* you are to each other. It might ease your conscience, to think of how you feel as brotherly, but there are no greater lies than the ones we tell ourselves, Jesse."

"We..." Jesse trailed off. "I ken I donnae know much anymore. I came here to see that she was safe, that's all. Upon the Guardians, that was *all*. But I didnae expect to find everything so changed. With Ryan. Esmerelda. With me."

"Something happened to you, didn't it?" Ravenna pressed. "Those weeks you were gone?"

Jesse gazed down at his hands, clasped in his lap. "I came looking for the two of you as soon as I'd found you gone. I rode hard, as hard as I've ever ridden, but by the time I came across your horses and belongings, I was too late. But I wasnae alone." He looked up. "I want to tell you. I do. If I donnae say the words to *someone*, I might burst from the weight of them. But I cannae do it if I think you'll doubt me. You know I'd never lie to you, and that has to be enough."

Ravenna was suddenly nervous. "I'll believe you. I promise."

But when Jesse finished telling his tale, of the great sorcerers of Ilynglass, of Dain, and Yanna and the vow that would soon draw Jesse away from Warwicktown, Ravenna was struck dumb with how small her mind felt as she tried to understand any of it.

"I don't... I *believe* you, I just don't..."

"I know, I know," Jesse said. "I'm still coming around. My whole life has been a lie. I donnae quite know how I'm supposed to feel about that. How I'm supposed to *be*, around my father, my people. I'm not even a man of the Southerlands, not by blood."

"You're whoever you say you are. And it's only a lie if the truth matters."

Jesse regarded her with a strange look. "Does the truth not matter to you, then?"

How I wish it didn't. "Are they..." she whispered, breathless. "Isdemus and..."

"Lysanor."

"Lysanor. Are they like Oldwin? And Mortain?"

Jesse nodded. "Except Lysanor and Isdemus want to save this world, and Oldwin and Mortain want to destroy it."

"So they told you."

"Nay, Ravenna, they *showed* me. Visions of my past, before I was born, who I was meant to be. They *told* me next to nothing, because they knew I had to see it for myself to believe it."

"The sorcerers are liars! Great deceivers!" Ravenna jumped to her feet. "And it is for them you'll forsake everything to follow? That you'll leave Esmerelda behind, just when you've decided to stand at her side?"

"I'm not forsaking anything. I'll do as they ask and then return."

"There won't be a return! Whatever it is they want from you, it'll be the last thing you ever do!" she screamed. "Don't you see?"

Jesse stood and reached for her. "What's really troubling you, Ravenna?"

Ravenna spun away from him, dizzy to the point of exhaustion. "Esmerelda hasn't told you. Has she?"

"Told me what?"

"What happened to the two of us after we left Greystone Abbey."

Jesse released her and took a step back. "No. She hasn't."

Ravenna clutched her belly. She focused on the smooth inhalations and exhalations keeping her standing, to again find her calm. Was she really going to tell him this story? Every terrible, sordid detail? It wasn't only her tale to tell, but Esmerelda's, too. Would Esmerelda want him to know? Would she be relieved that someone else said the words, so that she didn't have to?

Yes, she decided.

She nodded toward the hay pile. "You'll want to sit back down for this."

. . .

ODRAHN WARWICK, THE ONCE FIERCE WARRIOR OF THE SOUTHERN Reach, trembled as Khallum held the wine to his wrinkled lips. Instead of thanking him when he was satiated, Odrahn swatted him away, clinging to one last vestige of pride, with his final hours lingering.

Khallum had neglected his great-uncle. When he'd returned to Warwicktown, bedraggled and nearly spent, Khallum put the man in a cottage and the matter behind him. If he had a gold piece for every time Gwyn—sometimes gently, sometimes not so—reminded him of his duty to his only remaining elder, he could build a ship capable of sailing away from this kingdom and find another. Where his duties didn't outweigh his hours in the day, and his failures didn't cost men lives and home.

Odrahn was the last of the old ones in his father's line, and the only one who hadn't succumbed to some mysterious illness or accident after the Epoch of the Accordant took from the kingdom almost all of those belonging to the older generations. Khallum hadn't given this exclusion nearly enough thought; how Odrahn had escaped what few others did. Now that the old man was dying, Khallum wished he could ask, but he was here to see the man off to his final journey, not burden it with his own needs.

"I didn't think ye would ever come, boy." Odrahn's voice, though gravelly from age and disease, was still as bold and strong as always. Even now, Khallum feared him. He always had. "Took me staring down my promise to stir ye, did it?"

"I should've come sooner, Uncle. Forgive me."

"Aye? Forgive ye? That's what men do on their deathbeds, they say. Go forth into the unknown, unburdened." Odrahn laughed. "Feck what they say. There is no they, boy. Only us." He rolled his face toward Khallum. "Soon, only you."

"War is coming to our sands. I'm doing all I can to keep it away, but it may not be enough. Our enemy isnae like us. Even when I can guess his moves, I cannae stop them."

"Your father failed you," Odrahn said. "Didn't he?"

"Pardon?"

"Your father. He taught you nothing. He left you with half a story, and none of the right parts."

"The crown failed my father," Khallum countered. "Failed him, then murdered him."

"Aye, he failed ye. For ye'd not be speaking of the trivialities of war if ye knew anything at all about the Warwick Burden."

"I'm living the Warwick Burden day into night, Uncle. The sorcerer, he's burning our lands, killing our men, our *children*—"

"Will ye shut yer mouth and listen? Or do ye suppose there's naught else for ye to learn, so seasoned ye are?"

Khallum dropped back in his chair. This wasn't what he'd come to do, but he had no choice now but to stay and listen to the angry ramblings of the old man.

A shock of lightning lit the room. He forced himself into discomfort by saying nothing.

"The Warwick Burden isnae about pissing on each other's pyres. Have ye really never asked yourself why? Why the crown cares so much about the business of a Warwick, when they couldnae give a plum about the Derehams, the Quinlandens, the Blackwoods?"

Khallum waited to see if his uncle's question was meant for answer, before responding. "We know why. Our minerals. They've always wanted them. There's none like them anywhere else in the kingdom, not even in the hard soil of the southern Westerlands."

"What *value* is a mineral in a kingdom this small? What does wealth buy us, but a surplus of coin? Food? Trade? Aye, but there was a time, not so long ago, when we looked after our own. We ate our own food. We cut our own timber. We donnae need the bounties from the half-wits in the Easterlands or Westerlands. We donnae need anything we cannae make ourselves."

"The Southerlands cannae grow the greens needed to sustain our men. They nearly starved to death when the trade routes were closed."

"Half-truths. Who told you the Southerlands cannae make our own greens? Ye think this whole reach is but salt and sand, do ye?"

"No one had to tell me what I already know."

Odrahn waved a bony hand. "Nonsense. Someone told ye. For if ye just *knew* it, Khallum, then you'd know it's a lie. When all you children were rounded up and sold off like livestock, that wasnae all that changed for us. Alliances donnae start and end with a marriage. They thrive on mutual advantage. Aye, ye have minerals, and others desire them, but what did they have to give us in return? Nothing. Nothing we didnae already have, and so our farmers in the north lost their lands and livelihoods when the crown needed us to need others. Many of them ended up here, in the mines. And so that's how we've come to require the Easterlands and Westerlands to feed our men."

Khallum was aghast. "Father wouldnae have taken food from his men's tables."

"Khoulter Warwick was a boy when he became Lord of the Southerlands, just as you were. His father died fighting this crown. He had no one to guide him, so he learned to fear the crown, even as he railed against them. Once Khain had what he needed, he had Khoulter and all the others killed."

"Where were you, then?" Khallum groaned inwardly at how easily he'd been baited. He'd come to perform a duty, and instead was ready to fight an old man. "When all this was happening? How were you so fortunate as to escape that fate?"

"I was away, shouldering the weight of the Warwick Burden."

Khallum was proud of himself for not releasing the exhausted sigh building in his chest. He looked beyond his great-uncle, past the glass of the fogged window to the storm beyond. If it kept up like this, it would wash out the miners for a day or so. Maybe longer.

"Ye have somewhere to be, Khallum?"

He had many places to be. Many fires to put out, even more to anticipate and prevent. But he forced a smile and said, "You seem to want to tell me about the Warwick Burden. Aye, go on then."

"Donnae think me blind to what's in your eyes. My own may have lost their color and life, but I can hear. Your father did fail ye, though we failed him, too. I'd ask ye if ye knew why the Rhiagains wanted the Wastelands bad enough to take it from us, but you'd only say minerals again. Wouldn't ye?"

"Aye, I suppose so."

"You already know you're wrong, for I've told ye so. Long before the Rhiagains had the idea of turning the place into a prison to keep us out, some of us found ways of slipping in past their guards and gates, continuing what our fathers taught us, and theirs taught them. Mind, some were caught. Some were killed. But some things are bigger than life and death, ye ken?"

Khallum nodded. Another bolt of lightning ripped through the sky. Some screams sounded seconds later. He supposed that meant it had touched down. Another matter to eat at him, for him to neglect in favor of another.

"The old maps are long gone, but when I was a bairn and sneaking my way in, I had the fortune of being shown the way by those who no longer needed maps. I would've shown my own son, had the Guardians given me one. Khoulter knew, and he kept promising he'd take you and Byrne on a run. He swore he would. And then you were married off, and my nephew died."

"Maps? Maps of what? There's nothing there in those barren lands. Nothing but—"

"Minerals? Aye, I ken there's still plenty of those, too. Better ones than ye mine here in this forsaken town too close to the sea. But 'tis not the true gem of the Wastelands, and never has been. 'Tis not why the Rhiagains risked an all-out war and rebellion to take it from us. Was only the reason they gave to keep the true one buried."

Khallum's mind wandered. He left his eyes on the old man, but his thoughts ran elsewhere. They'd emptied the armory in the night, moving it to the ruins of an old monastery, but they couldn't keep it guarded without drawing eyes. They'd move more again tomorrow, if their attentions weren't drawn to yet another attack, and they were due. They were overdue, by Khallum's count, and each one had been more personal than the last. He half expected to wake one morning and it be Gwyn, or the boys, taken. Darrick's idea that the sorcerer wanted not only something in the Hinterlands, but also in the Southerlands, never left him. Nor did the fact that it had to be one of his own men, conspiring with the demon. Was it Garrick? Barne Holton? Both of them, wily enough, but disloyalty? *Treason?* Were they really capable of it?

"...veils. It's always been the veils."

It was as if being slapped back to the present. "Veils?"

"Aye, donnae play the fool with me. Ye know the veils I speak of. They're all over this kingdom, and where they all lead, who can say? I donnae even quite know where the ones in the Wastelands go, only that it was our task, our burden, to see that none ever entered them before they could be destroyed. Really, it was one in particular."

"Veils. In the Wastelands."

"Are ye daft? Or have I been speaking the old language?"

"Did ye say that the Rhiagains took the Wastelands... for veils? For something that's nay even real?"

"Nay real! I know you're a Warwick, but are ye truly so lacking in imagination that ye cannae grasp anything your own eyes haven't seen?"

The old man was losing it. This often happened in the end, reality and fantasy blending into one, to ease one off on their final journey. "Aye, well, I'll eh... be sure to get someone on that."

Odrahn's bony hand snaked out and grasped Khallum's. "Donnae condescend to me, Khallum Warwick. I may've never been a lord, but I've given my life, all of it, every tick, every second, every day, every year, to service of this Reach. Down to the last. Ye come here, crying about a sorcerer burning your lands when ye donnae even know *why*. Not what he takes, but what he *wants*. Ye believe in his magic, while disbelieving in the magic I've spent my life guarding, but *'tis the same*! The same magic created him that created the veils, and 'tis the same magic needed to end it. That foul being has no use for munitions or minerals or murder. He could create it all with but a wave of his hand and wipe it all away with the other. What he wants is what we've protected, kept him from, all these years. What he, even after locking us out, keeping us from our task, still cannae find, because 'tis not something that one stumbles upon. Ye know." Odrahn tapped his free fist against his chest. "Or ye donnae know. He may yet possess the magic to find it, and there's none there, none of us, anymore, to stop him. To save what he would take and destroy. Destroy. Tha's always been the answer, boy, to destroy the veil, but you'll need his blood, or another sorcerer's, to do it. They opened the veils, it was said, only they can close them. No longer 'tis about protecting. Destroy the veil and only then will ye have the upper hand ye crave, the answers to save this land. And you've now wasted what's left of my energy trying to convince ye of what our blood has been *born* for, for centuries. Centuries! And I still have nay told ye how to find it without the map, how to get in there, to—"

Odrahn's face suddenly froze. His hand went stiff on Khallum's, his rheumy eyes fluttering with fresh tears. A desperate croak sounded from the back of his throat.

"Uncle?" Khallum reached for the wine, but before he could bring it back, Odrahn Warwick had spent his promise.

"Ah, feck-all," he whispered.

"Lord Warwick?"

Khallum looked up, still absorbing the strange confession and the utterly shocking swiftness of the sudden loss. He was present in neither moment. Not his uncle's death, nor the awkward lingering of the page arrived to deliver a message.

"Steward Strong and his son have asked to see you in the Hall of Warring." The page said the words to Khallum, but his eyes were fixed on the dead old man.

"Which son?" Khallum asked absently. His gaze returned to the motionless stare of his dead uncle. Only moments before, he'd been fully alive with the power of his confession. It had taken everything he had left, which hadn't been enough for all he still had left to say.

"The older one, sir. Jesse."

Khallum released himself from his uncle's grip. He laid Odrahn's hand on his chest, folding the other one over it. With a silent thought to the Guardian of the Unpromised Future, he stood, dazed, and nodded to the page.

RAVENNA RAN STRAIGHT INTO A MAN.

"Easy," he said, dusting himself off. He had a pleasing smile, the kind that seemed made for others. They'd never been introduced, but she knew who he was.

"Sorry," she mumbled, but when she returned to her path, he stepped in front of her.

"You're a Ravenwood," he said, now with a different smile, this one not meant for her, but for himself.

Ravenna looked past the prince, to the other end of the hall where Lord Warwick had just disappeared. She was too late to tell Jesse what she'd heard. Her heart felt lodged in the back of her throat.

"I'm Darrick."

Ravenna affected a half-hearted curtsey, eyes still on the closed door ahead. "Your Grace."

He laughed. "We both know a Ravenwood does not bow to a Rhiagain."

This elicited a small, distracted smile from her. "You're the one who said I was a Ravenwood."

"You were listening in on Lord Warwick."

Ravenna's attention snapped back to the prince. "What did you say?"

"You heard Odrahn Warwick's deathbed confession," Darrick said. "Is that not what Lord Warwick went in to witness? This is a tradition of the men of this kingdom. Rhiagains don't trouble themselves with last hour regrets."

"I don't know what you're talking about," Ravenna answered, flustered. "I was looking for Jesse."

"You could tell me what's troubling you," Darrick said with a light shrug. "I understand some find comfort in that."

"You do not?"

"My wife is teaching me. I spent most of my life knowing that my words would neither be understood nor welcome to the people around me. I've always found the most comfort in my own counsel."

"You and I aren't so different, then."

Darrick grinned. "Even if we are sworn enemies."

"You're mistaken. There are no Ravenwoods in the Southerlands. Your Grace."

"As you say." He wasn't fooled.

Ravenna regarded the man, sizing him up. He was younger than she realized, around Jesse's age, perhaps a year or so more, and looked nothing like the gnarled monster his brother had become. He was welcome to the eyes, but haunted, in a way she found both inviting and repellant. He was capable of great love, but also great harm. She couldn't see his future to determine which would be his legacy. "What do you know about the veils in this kingdom?"

Darrick didn't seem as surprised by the question as he should. "I've never stepped through one. Or seen one. But as Rhiagains, we've been exposed to the kind of magic that leaves little doubt as to their possibility. Have you? Seen one?"

Ravenna shook her head.

"There's one closer to where your people are, in the pass, they say."

"Not my people." The door at the end of the hall was still closed. "But where do they go?"

"Other worlds."

Ravenna laughed.

"The Rhiagains and Ravenwoods both came from another world. Why do you find this so difficult to believe?"

"And Oldwin. What might be his interest in a veil?"

Darrick's playful, easy façade fell away. "Oldwin? Why is his name on your mind?"

"He and I are, unfortunately, acquainted."

"Ravenna," Darrick said, stepping closer. "You cannot trust a sorcerer. Especially not that one. My father had him locked away for good cause, and my brother was a fool for releasing him."

"What would he want with a veil?"

"Why are you asking this?"

Ravenna leaned in. "Lord Warwick will want to dismiss what he heard as the ramblings of an old, dying man, but you can't let him do that. *You* cannot let him."

Darrick dropped his voice. "What did Odrahn say to Khallum?"

"And whatever plan Lord Warwick and his men, and *you*, come up with to stop Oldwin, Jesse is to have *nothing* to do with any of it."

"Jesse?" Darrick's voice trailed after her as she fled the way she'd come.

"I KEN WE'RE BOTH VERY SORRY TO HEAR OF THE LOSS OF OLD Odrahn," Hamish said, whistling through his teeth. He rapped his knuckles on the wood. "The last of the old ones." He raised a small glass of dark amber liquid.

Khallum raised his own, emptying the contents in one large gulp.

Jesse joined in the toast, but set his glass aside, untouched. His stomach was a mess. His nerves a mis-tied knot.

"I ken you're here because your boy must've finally confessed to you what he's been at all these months," Khallum said. He didn't sit. He leaned against the window overlooking the sea. The tide was in, and the current was rough. There'd be flooding from this storm, to add to their mounting troubles. Jesse imagined himself in action, helping move sand in front of doors, shoring up the irrigation in the mines. He missed *doing*. He missed his trade. A life that was no longer his, no matter what Khallum Warwick said today.

Hamish glanced nervously at Jesse. "I ken so, my lord. He's sorry for what he did, too. He'd do it all differently, if time could be turned."

Jesse closed his eyes and sighed. "Father. I'm not sorry for helping Esmerelda."

Hamish shifted at his side. "Let's stay to it as we discussed, aye?"

Jesse looked up. "I'm deeply regretful of the hurt it caused, but

I'm not sorry for aiding her. If I'd turned her down, she would've found another, someone less devoted to protecting her and her child. I donnae know what would've happened to Esmerelda if she wasn't in my protection, but I know she's home, safe, after being in mine."

Khallum grunted. When he spoke, he was looking at Hamish. "This is what you pulled me away for? The Reach is burning. My great-uncle just spent his promise." He pointed his hand out the window. "Now we can add *flooding* to our list."

"My lord—"

Jesse wrung his hands together. He knew the words. He only had to say them. "I've come with an answer to Esmerelda's dilemma."

"Her dilemma," Khallum repeated. "If ye mean her boar-headed refusal to do what's right for herself and the bairn, then you must also be a worker of miracles."

Jesse looked at his father. No matter what Jesse had learned, Hamish Strong was his dad. He'd raised him as his own. Jesse had never lacked for anything.

Hamish, red-faced, nodded. "Esmerelda willnae wed Ryan. She's retreated, wounded, and I cannae see her changing her mind."

"What does this have to do with you, then?" Khallum volleyed, this time to Jesse. "Why is it you, and not your brother, coming to me about my Esmerelda?"

"Esmerelda is as a sister to me. I've come to see her as my own kin, and Gemma, her bairn, shares my blood. I believe that, if I ask her to be my wife instead, she'll find the offer an agreeable alternative."

Khallum's corner-of-the-mouth grin chilled Jesse's blood. "*You* want to wed my Esmerelda."

"My lord, there's sense in the boy's offer. I ken he's right, Gemmasyn is one of us, and Lady Esmerelda, her heart is bruised, aye, and she'll nay see reason. But she trusts my Jamesan, and he, my eldest and heir, will sit in my chair one day, and there isnae shame in weddin' a firstborn son of a Strong."

Khallum ignored him. His eyes bored holes into Jesse. "Why?"

"Why, sir?"

"Aye, why you? Why are you offering this?"

"I made a vow to protect her."

"Spare me the horseshit. Your vow ended when she returned to my protection."

Jesse looked down at his hands. "I care for her."

"You care for her? What does that mean?"

"As I said, she's like kin to me. As a sister."

Khallum snorted, laughing. "Most men donnae wish to fuck their sisters, Jesse."

Jesse shook his head to clear it. This wasn't how it was supposed to go. Khallum would accept nothing less than his truth. "Esmerelda and I became close, those months away. Not like you're suggesting, but there's a bond there, a friendship. My father always said that a successful union isnae about what happens in the marriage bed, but everywhere else. I believe Esmerelda could see me as that kind of husband, who looks out for her, who sees her as equal in all things."

"Only a fool sees women as their equal," Khallum replied, but the sting had faded from his words. His eyes moved to the side, thinking. "Was this your idea, Hamish?"

"No, no, sir. But I ken I couldnae have come wit' a better one."

"You think I should give my daughter to your son?"

Hamish looked down at his hands. "I ken we're where we are. Esmerelda has a bairn, and that bairn needs a father. My Ryan wouldnae ever turn his back on duty, and though Esmerelda should've taken that offer, for it was a right good one, she didnae, and short of tying her down, my lord, what else is there? Jesse cares for her, as he's said, and it may be she cares for him. It may be that we can put an end to this matter before Esmerelda's reputation is ruined."

Khallum looked at Jesse. "The Guardians must favor you. It's only because matters of greater urgency draw my attention that we haven't had the words that we're long due for having, you and I."

Jesse nodded.

"But that time has also given me leave to see that, however the means, my daughter is alive, and she's home. I willnae thank ye for it, but I'll suffer you to live another day."

Jesse swallowed. "My lord."

"You're happy on the sea, are ye not?"

"I am."

"A Strong man belongs on the sea. It's in his blood. You gave that up, for her."

"For Ryan, but aye, also for her. He intended to finish his business in the Wastelands, come find us, and then I'd return to my trade and leave them to their happiness."

"What if to fulfill your vow meant giving it up for years? A lifetime?"

"I would've done whatever it took to keep her safe. I would've done right by Esmerelda, to the very end."

"The very end," Khallum repeated. "Right. Well, Jamesan. If Esmerelda accepts your offer, you have my blessing. If she fails to see the wisdom in it, I ken she'll have to satisfy herself with loathing me for the rest of her days, for she'll be wed by week's end, either way."

Jesse exhaled in heavy relief. "Thank you, Lord Warwick."

"You still have to convince that stubborn girl," Khallum replied. "Now, go. Not you, Hamish. We'll send for Rutland and Law. We've more pressing matters at hand."

"And the prince?"

"Aye," Khallum said after a measured pause. "This is his game to play now, isn't it?"

"Stefan, go on."

"I don't wanna go, Mama. Everything is wet."

"Not outside, little one." Anabella rested her hands on her hips with a deep sigh. "Just out in the hall, for a few, please? For Mama?"

"Isa, it's fine," Darrick insisted, but the look she shot him prevented further objections.

"Stefan, Mama rarely asks you to do anything for her. I'm asking you now to please go take your ball that Wyat gave you when he left, and go play in the hall. Just for a little while."

Stefan hung his head. "Fine."

Anabella reached down and scooped him into her arms, peppering his face with kisses. Despite himself, he giggled. "I love you, and to prove it, tonight I'll show you the abandoned ship you've been asking about. Lord Warwick says we can walk right up to it when the tide is right."

Stefan's eyes lit up. "Really?"

"Yes, really. But now, go play."

"Yes, Mama."

"Isa, that wasn't necessary. I'm fine," Darrick insisted when Stefan had left.

"You're not fine. I think I know my own husband, don't I?"

"You look at me as if you believe I'm keeping secrets."

"And? Are you?"

"To keep something from you, I'd first need to understand it." Darrick sank down in the tall chair near the hearth. "I don't want to overreact to something that may not require it."

"Tell me, and perhaps I'll have counsel. I may be a woman, but I'm no fool."

Darrick looked up at her with a soft smile. "You're wiser than me, on most things."

Anabella clucked her tongue. She sat at the edge of the bed. "Tell me, Darrick."

He lifted his hands in a half-shrug. "I had a very peculiar encounter with Esmerelda's friend outside the Hall of Warring. Ravenna. You remember me telling you I thought she might be a Ravenwood?"

"And I told you, Ravenwoods don't come this far south."

"That's what she said. But I'd stake my crown on it. She's a Ravenwood. She has her reasons for not wanting others to know this, so I'll keep that to myself."

"If you're right, she'd be in danger here. Keeping her secret is the right thing."

Darrick nodded. "I found her outside Odrahn's room, listening."

"Listening? Why?"

"I don't know, but it's been troubling me ever since."

"What did she say to you?"

"It's not so much what she said," Darrick said. He leaned his head back against the soft leather and looked at his wife. "It's what she asked me. She wanted to know what I knew about the veils."

"The veils? What could you know about something that's not real?"

Darrick tilted his head to the side. "A woman born and bred of the Northerlands, and you don't believe?"

Anabella was aghast. "Why would I? The only men who have ever claimed to have any knowledge of them are madmen."

"Like Alric Dereham."

"Alric is a good man, but he's never been right."

"And if I told you I believed?"

Anabella laughed. She couldn't decide if he was serious. If he wasn't, the troubled look he wore under his odd smile made no sense. "Are you saying you've seen one?"

"Of course not," Darrick said. "But you know I don't need to see something to believe in it. In the ordinary or the magical. It's all the same."

Anabella scoffed. "All right. What else did Ravenna want to know about the veils?"

"Just that. If I knew anything. If I knew where they went."

"What did you tell her?"

"Other worlds, I said. She didn't believe me. Then she asked me what Oldwin's interest in the veils might be."

"Oldwin?" Anabella gasped. "What would a Ravenwood want to know about him?"

Darrick held out his arms. Anabella moved to him and fell into his lap. Their reunion had surpassed her most vivid dreams from those long nights in Duncarrow. He'd rarely let her out of his sight, always looking for ways to be touching, to be connected. He'd neglected the realm for her, and she knew this, but had selfishly allowed it, saying nothing, drinking up every moment with the only man she'd ever loved. When she saw his guilt over the neglect grow into a near tangible form, she'd forced herself to pull back, to not appear to need from him what she would desperately require for the rest of their lives together. It was her love for him, a feeling bigger than herself, that made her hide these fears from him, so that he could do what he was born to do.

"I don't know, Isa. But I think... it may have to do with something my father once told me. It made little sense to me then. It's only starting to now."

Anabella buried her face against his neck and listened.

"He said..." Darrick hesitated as he moved through his thoughts. "He called the Warwicks defenders. He said we'd taken the Wastelands from them, but they wouldn't stop coming for it. He said they'd caught some Warwicks inside the gates and had them executed."

"That's terrible."

"Defenders," Darrick said again. "Everyone knows we stole the Wastelands because we wanted what was inside. But you wouldn't call someone a defender when speaking of a gold that now belongs to you, and not them, would you? Or minerals on a land that now belonged to you? Would you?"

"I don't suppose so, no."

"So what if it's not that?" Darrick didn't seem to want an answer, but as he asked the questions, he grew more animated, more resolute. "What if it was never about that at all? That the Warwicks possessed... *defended*... something much more valuable?"

"But the Rhiagains have the Wastelands now. They've had it for generations."

"Maybe we haven't found what we're after yet."

"What does Lord Warwick say?"

"I haven't spoken with him about this yet."

"Because he'd know, wouldn't he? If his family was, as your father said, defenders?"

"I'm not so sure," Darrick answered. "For it would better explain

Oldwin's targeting of the Southern Reach. Khallum hasn't even mentioned it."

"I don't see how that fits. Oldwin assaults the Southerlands, and the prize is in the Wastelands, which the Southerlands no longer has control over."

"Perhaps he means to back Khallum into a corner, force him to reveal what he knows."

"That doesn't feel quite right, Darrick."

"No. Nor to me, Isa. This all starts and ends with the sorcerers, somehow. I know it does. I just cannot put my finger on the source. And through it all, an old rumor keeps nagging at me."

"What rumor?"

"That my elder brother, Dain, wasn't my father's son at all, but a bastard of one of the sorcerers." He shook his head. "It can't be true, of course. Both my father's wives were terrified of him."

Anabella felt herself pale. She slowly pulled herself up to look at him.

"What is it?"

"I should've told you this sooner. But I wasn't ready to speak about those days. You've asked me to, but I couldn't."

He dropped his hands to her waist. "Tell me what?"

"Your brother, Eoghan, he... he visited me frequently, in the sky dungeon."

"No." Darrick's cheeks edged with red.

She shook her head. "Not like that."

"Isa," Darrick whispered.

"I don't think he had anyone he could talk to. No one he trusted, could confide in. Who was I, except a woman at his utter mercy, who could never tell a soul anything he shared with me? You know, of course, that Dain was taken away to be killed by your father's Lord Chancellor."

Darrick nodded. He held her tighter. She sensed his fear through his touch.

"Before the Lord Chancellor died, he confessed he couldn't bring himself to kill a small, defenseless child, and so instead had Dain given to a childless couple, to be raised in complete obliviousness of his true identity. Even Oldwin didn't know, and Oldwin was the one who convinced Khain to have his son killed. When Eoghan found out, he went into the kingdom, in disguise, to search for Dain."

Darrick released her. "Did he find him?"

"No," Anabella said. "But knowing he was out there, the fear of it, ate away at Eoghan, making his black heart blacker. If Dain was *not* the son of Khain Rhiagain, but the son of one of the sorcerers, then..."

Darrick gently nudged her from his lap and reached for his sword belt, buckling it. "This conversation hasn't happened between us by accident. There's a reason that rumor won't leave me. There's a reason Eoghan told you what he did." He took her face in his hands and gave her a long, hard kiss. "We might yet best Oldwin after all."

"I don't understand," Anabella called after him when he rushed to the door. "How does this answer anything?"

"Dain is out there. Oldwin went to great trouble to have him killed and failed. The veils. The keepers. It's all related, Isa! I don't yet know how, but it has to be."

"Where are you going?"

"To find Lord Warwick."

17
THE LIGHT

Kian wrapped his fingers around the edges of the great glimmering pool. Eithne's eager eyes bored holes in his back. If he lingered on his dread much longer, she would read it.

It wasn't the sensation of drowning that scared him anymore. He'd long ago surrendered such base fears, under the careful guidance of his mother's instruction. But unlike his own visions, the ones from the Light were volatile and unruly. This pool was but a glimpse of what the Light could do, but its power was a greater magic than he or any other Medvedev possessed.

He would see what had been, in order to understand what would be. He would see what he needed, which conflict with his capabilities. He would see those things he could control, and those he had no power to stop.

"Kian?" he heard Eithne say just as he plunged his face into the cool water.

Lisbet huddled in silence near the fire while Ash slipped the sharpened stick through the last of the rabbit meat. When he was occupied with other things, she liked to study his face, to see where she might witness herself in it. Lately, she'd also taken to wondering how she might resemble her Rhiagain lineage. Red hair was a known Rhiagain trait, but Gretchen was also a redhead. Drystan, Lisbet, and Pieter had all inherited the red hair, but only two were Rhiagains. So where had hers come from? These were the types of things that made her wish she'd been sent to Oldcastle for higher learning, rather than sitting through what had been provided by the old men and women in Wulfsgate.

These thoughts brought her no closer to telling Ash who he was. She had to. There was no one else who could. But any time she tried to say the words, they failed her.

"It may be dark, but I can see you staring at me," he said. "Drystan used to do that when he was summoning the courage to ask me something."

"I was thinking about my father," Lisbet said. It was only a half-lie. She *had* been thinking of Holden, before she turned her examination on Ash.

"Which one?" Ash said with a light smile. He settled the meat into the holder he'd fashioned and sat back against the log. Travel had been easier this time, when they could take the Compass Roads and stop at inns and taverns when the path allowed. Starcaller certainly appreciated the fairer path, sounding her approving snuffs every so often.

They were south of the Reliquary now, closing in on River-chapel. Ash had said Warwicktown wasn't far off, though he admitted this was a guess. He'd never been.

"I was wondering if Holden will ever come home, or if they've killed him, as Christian thinks."

"I don't know, Lisbet. But it's dangerous to hope for something too much. I hope Holden comes home. Gretchen will need him, when she returns."

"If," Lisbet corrected. "If she returns."

"She will."

"You still don't believe she went through the veil?"

"The veils aren't real."

"What if they are? My uncle, Alric, he's a good man. Holding so fast to his story has cost him respect, kinship, reputation. There's no reason for him to keep saying it, unless it's true."

"A man can believe something with his whole heart and still be wrong."

"Hm." Lisbet wrapped her arms tighter around her legs. "I believe him."

Ash poked at the fire with a stick, his face blank. "All men deserve someone who believes in them."

"Ash," she said, leaning forward. "I believe in you. I wouldn't be here with you right now if I didn't."

Ash relaxed some. "Don't mind me, Lisbet. I've been lost to some darker thoughts these long days. Happens to us all from time to time."

"What kind of dark thoughts?"

"Nothing you don't know. This awakening magic, the way it's changing. Now I can see things in my dreams, and I know... I know they're not dreams."

Lisbet nodded. "I have those, too."

"Do you?"

"Two nights ago, I dreamed I was standing on the rocks at Duncarrow, and the keep was in a pile of rubble and ash," she said. A chill passed through her as the memory settled over her. "And though I've never been to Duncarrow, I know in my bones that if I were to go there, it would look just as it did in my dreams. Except it wouldn't be in rubble and ash. Not yet."

Ash dropped his stick in the dirt. "I had the same dream."

"No."

He nodded. "I did. But last night. And then I dreamed of the red rocks and peaks of the Wastelands. Another place I've never been, but I knew it like—"

"My own heart," Lisbet finished. She exhaled slowly. "I had that one, too. What does it mean?"

"If I knew where this strange magic has come from, then I might be closer to answering that."

Lisbet reached forward and turned the rabbit. She hoped he couldn't see the guilt in her eyes. "Maybe Lord Warwick will have some answers."

EITHNE PASSED KIAN A BOWL OF WARM STEW. WARM NOW, NOT HOT, because he'd been in the glimmering pool for hours, far longer than he'd intended. He smiled and lifted the bowl in thanks, though introducing food only threatened to turn his belly.

In the corner, Aian feasted upon some small creature he'd hunted in the forest. Eithne's own familiar, an otter named Leithna, swam in the river nearby. Kian had moved their camp closer to the water, so she wouldn't feel the pain of separation.

"What did you see?" she asked, judiciously waiting for him to have several bites down before speaking.

She was enthusiastic, but young. The Medvedev didn't measure age in years, but experience and understanding. Eithne was chosen because there wasn't anyone else. Of the handful of Saleen remaining in these lands, she was the one most suited to the task. The Keeper of the Light for the Saleen must be Saleen, just as Yseult was the Keeper of the Light for the Drumain. These rules were not his own.

Although the temple that protected The Hidden Kingdom was on Saleen ground, all four clahnns had doors that brought them here, and any of them could be here as quickly as it took to pass through a veil. The Keepers of Mayke, Asgill, and Drumain kept the veils that opened here. This was the first lesson he'd taught Eithne, but he found this only confused her, and so it was time to begin at the start.

"I've told you how three of the four came to us. In our lands," Kian told her. "You remember?"

"Drystan and Lisbet," Eithne answered quickly, a dutiful disciple. "And their father, Dain."

"The fourth came, too. We turned him away."

"Why would you do that?"

"He had not yet had his own awakening," Kian explained. "We are meant to do what we do in the way it is meant to happen. I see this is confusing for you, as it once was for me. It means that though Jamesan was always going to return to us, to his mother's people, he could not do so until he had witnessed the history of his father."

"Dain, you mean?"

"Dain is a branch connecting other branches. Without Dain, there would be no Jamesan, no Lisbet or Drystan. But without Isdemus, the Meduwyn, there would be no Dain. Even Dain did not have the power to create Jamesan, without Yanna."

"Did the Light create these connections?"

Kian shook his head. "The Light does not drive the actions of men, sorcerer, or Medvedev, Eithne. The Light is absent of all three, and the source of all three. The center of what is, what will, and what won't. You must never forget, it was the sorcerers responsible for the Great Sundering, tearing apart the world and time itself with their treachery. It is because of them the Light is now vulnerable." He watched the confusion rise in her face. She tried to fight it, fearing disappointing him, but he read it clearly. "I say you must never forget, but you are not a Keeper, and so you do not yet even know. The ones who did are gone."

Eithne dropped her head low.

Kian reached forward. With a finger, he lifted her chin. "You are here to learn. Not to feel shame."

Eithne nodded.

"I have already told you the Great Light of the Worlds gives life to all things. That it is our duty as Medvedev to protect it from all who seek to take from it, to offer harm."

"Yes."

"You have asked me *how* we do this. Simply, we are the ones who hold our histories. We protect the truths that other Medvedev will never know. You might even say, we keep the truth *from* them."

"Why would you do that?"

"To prevent the past becoming the future." Kian went on. "Once, the worlds were connected. All the many worlds now separated by veils were one, and time was one. But the Light was always separate. The Light belonged to its own world, which has many names, but we call now The Hidden Kingdom.

"The Meduwyn and Medvedev were both protectors of the Light. We were few, then, but immortal. Our magic, though different, was complementary. It is not so simple as this, but some among us have described the magic of the Meduwyn as the Magic of Dark, and ours as the Magic of Light. That the Meduwyn practice Magic of Want, while the Medvedev practice Magic of Need. It's enough to say that all things must have balance, and in The Hidden Kingdom, this balance was struck and kept by our differences. The Light was the giver of our immortality and our seemingly limitless magic. It asked for nothing in return, only that we never take more than what was given. This was our way for many thousands of years."

Eithne's mouth slowly parted in wonder as she listened, rapt.

"Some of the Meduwyn decided their gifts were not enough. They wanted more. One of them, Enivera, The One Who Betrayed Us, went to the temple and reached for what was not hers to take. The power of this betrayal sundered the world of men, dividing it into many worlds. It sundered time itself, throwing us into chaos as we were spread across the worlds, expelling Meduwyn and Medvedev alike. But it was the opposing magic, from Enivera and those who had followed her, that created the veils that passed between, like pressing their hand in a door before it can fully close.

"The Meduwyn found themselves in a world they later called Ilynglass, which had been their word for The Hidden Kingdom. And we came here, to what the men call the White Kingdom. But the Light was not done with us, Eithne. The Light knew the hearts of the Medvedev, knew that the betrayal came not from us. But the Light was wounded. It could never again be so vulnerable."

"But we are not in the White Kingdom," Eithne said. "Not once we pass through our own veils."

"No, but that was not always so. In those early days, we

wandered the forest of the Hinterlands. Men were few then, but they were enough to overtake us. We were slaughtered, enslaved, and worse. Our immorality had been stripped away when we were exorcised from The Hidden Kingdom, our magic dulled. We had never been so defenseless. Just when it seemed as if hope was lost, the Light returned to us our magic, allowing us to create our own veils within the Hinterlands that protected us from the men hunting us. Veils created by our magic, not the foul sorcery of the Meduwyn. These veils took us to a world entirely of our own, where we were again offered safety, in return for a second chance. For though the Meduwyn had been struck out, they were unwavering in their determination to find a way back, to at last take the Light for their own, united in this task. If they succeeded, an endless darkness would fall upon everything the Light had once fed and protected."

"No one has ever told me this," Eithne said when he had finished. "We don't speak of where we come from, only where we are."

Kian nodded. "Only the Keepers pass these stories. Only the Keepers know these stories."

"Why? Why only the Keepers? This history belongs to all."

Kian chose his words with care. "We keep our truths to the few chosen to protect them."

"But the Medvedev are peaceful! We're not the ones who betrayed the Light!"

"The Meduwyn committed the betrayal, but they are not so different from us. We are not so different from them. Can you be certain everyone you have ever known would be as committed as you are now?" *Kael*, Kian thought, then banished it.

"I do not know how to answer that," Eithne said. She lowered her eyes.

"That *is* your answer. That you do not know. And so we guard our history, as we guard the Light."

"But..." Eithne's eyes traveled with her thoughts. "The Meduwyn. They know where we are. It was one of them that killed my people."

Kian nodded. "They know the way to The Hidden Kingdom is here."

"But they cannot enter our veils?"

"Not the ones created with Medvedev magic. But there is one, created when all the veils were formed by the Meduwyn betrayal. As it was not our magic that crafted it, our magic cannot destroy it, either. It's in the Southerlands, in what the men call the Wastelands."

"Where does it go?"

"Here, Eithne. It leads the traveler here, to our world."

Eithne's eyes widened. "But there are no Keepers there."

Kian pushed the now cool remnants of his bowl side. "Long ago, we forged an alliance with men in the south. We blessed their lands with valuable minerals, and in return, they became Defenders of the Veil. For hundreds of years, the Warwicks fulfilled their end of the vow, but when the Rhiagains were brought to these shores by the ambitions of four Meduwyn, it was only time that separated them from learning what the Warwicks protected. They took the land from the Warwicks. They have searched for the veil ever since."

"Why haven't they found it yet?"

"Through the years, some resilient Warwicks attempted to sneak in and continue their duty, but they were found and killed. And so the passing of the sacred mantle of Defender was no more, and we have been awaiting the arrival of the Meduwyn ever since." Kian looked past her, watching the sun disappear beyond the horizon. He would need to return to the temple soon. "Not all Meduwyn mean to take the Light for themselves. There are some who have seen the wickedness of their ways and sought to mend it. Dain and his children come from these Meduwyn, and they will either be our salvation or our undoing."

"Can it be mended?"

"It can."

"But?"

"But that does not mean it will." He reached for his cloak and refastened it. "I had hoped the water would show me, but it did not."

"It showed you something. You won't tell me, will you?"

"I would not be a very good teacher if I kept things from you, would I?" Kian smiled sadly. "What I saw, Eithne, was that though the Meduwyn Oldwin does not yet know of Dain's children, he will. Soon, Oldwin's eyes will be opened, will be turned to us, on the back of a betrayal from within our own ranks. Where he was once blind, he will see. When he does, there will be nothing left to stop him."

Eithne crossed her arms and returned the smile, though hers was brighter, full of hope. "*We* will stop him, Kian."

18

A PROPHECY OF THREE

Asherley stormed down the endless hall of Wulfsgate Keep, hands pressed into fists at her side. At the other end, Joran Rosewood looked as if he might fall over dead, and that to do so might be preferable to whatever awaited him. He'd always been afraid of her, and sometimes she liked this, because sometimes that was exactly the power she wanted over him.

"You were said to be a dead man, Joran Rosewood!" she screamed. Her words didn't carry the weight she'd been aiming for, the depth of her rage trapped by the thick tapestries lining the walls on either side. "Unless you now claim to add haunting me to your many gifts, Enchanter?"

Joran bowed his head, bracing for impact. She drew closer, the sleeves of her dress catching the wind as they made tiny snapping sounds. His head was so lowered his chin touched his chest.

Breathless, she came to a stop uncomfortably close to him. She wanted him to feel the heat rising off her flesh. To absorb it. "You owe me so much more than your silence."

Joran at last looked up. His lids hung heavy over his eyes, weighted by an exhaustion that colored in the rest of him. Another time, it might have softened her. "Lady Blackwood. I have always given you everything I have to give, and even when you left for Duncarrow, my service did not end. I followed your son across the kingdom when he brought me into his own trust and counsel. When I knew my usefulness to him was spent, I followed my visions hoping they, too, might serve you."

"If you feel your debt to me and my kin is fulfilled, then tell me, why did you come? For if it is only for me to look upon your sullen face and find myself filled with immutable rage, then I would've preferred to think of you dead, and more fondly besides."

Joran gave her a strange look. "My vow to you is for a lifetime, unless you release me from it. Forgive me, Lady Blackwood, but I believe you have misunderstood me."

"I've misunderstood you abandoning Brandyn in his darkest hour? Or have I misunderstood your months of absence since?"

"It was to Wulfsgate I was aimed when I left Brandyn near Whitechurch. Or, I should say, when he was taken from us, by the sorcerer, Mortain," Joran explained. In the months since she'd last seen him, in Termonglen, his hair was now much whiter, and there was less of it. The lines on his face telling his story were nearly conjoined, becoming one long narrative, nearly spent. Perhaps he really was dying now. "It was not an Enchanter Lord Warwick needed to recover Brandyn. That was a job for the warriors of our company. And then I was overcome with a vision so unlike any I have ever had before. It was so powerful I changed my course from Wulfsgate, where I had the strongest sense I might find *you*, to return to the Sepulchre, because I feared I was dying, and my last wishes have always been to be sent into the fires at Briarhaven, as you well know."

"Joran, get to the point."

"Head Magus Tymagen assured me I was *not* dying, but that I was having a Life Vision."

Asherley shook her head. "Am I supposed to know what that means?"

"Most seers have but one in a lifetime, which is why they are so named. Which is why when a seer experiences one, they don't have the understanding, on their own, to properly identify it. The Head Magus worked with me, for weeks, as I lay in a fever, speaking nonsense. He sat at my bedside and wrote down everything I said. When it was over, we went over all he'd written, and he gave me leave to come to you right away. What I've seen are things you must know about, Lady Blackwood. I would wager my life that they will come to pass, exactly as I've seen them. But the Head Magus was clear. There are those things I am permitted to tell you, and things I am not. Yet I believe the things I *can* tell you will guide you down the right path, just the same."

Asherley's blood cooled. She didn't like this side of Joran. He'd always hedged with her. He never wanted to commit to anything, waffling through generalities to avoid anything overly specific that she might hold him to later.

"Is it Emberley?"

Joran nodded. In his eyes, she saw there was more.

"And Brandyn?"

"Yes, Brandyn as well."

"Is there more?"

"What I saw was a Prophecy of Three." Joran gestured toward the Great Hall. "And for all three things, Lady Blackwood, I believe you will want to be sitting down."

MARSH STARED IN HELPLESS DISBELIEF AT THE MASSIVE ROWS OF BOOKS lining the walls of the library at Wulfsgate Keep. The Blackwoods had one like it, but the endlessness of words had never felt so crushing as they did now, when he was against time itself to find the right ones.

He ran his fingers along the spines as if the answers could be divined by touch alone. Some were old, crumbling at his intrusion. He recoiled, searching for hardier ones. He pulled one at random from the shelf and flipped it open, quickly closing it again with a frown. He had no use for the migratory pattern of seabirds in the Southerlands.

He pulled down another. This one was a record of the snowfall for the past two hundred years. The next he opened was a book of songs believed to induce the proliferation of crops in springtide. On and on he went, flipping through enough pages to determine each book's uselessness before moving on to more disappointment.

He dropped the last book on the large table that swallowed up the full center of the room. He leaned into the hard wood, determined not to let his frustration get the best of him. From the corner of his eye, he spotted a tall barrel with long scrolls protruding.

"Maps," he whispered, and rushed over. He pulled one out, nearly stumbling back with surprise at the heft of the thing. He unrolled it just enough to see it wouldn't be of use, then reached for another. The third one he pulled out gave his heart a quick slip. *The Northern Kingdom*, it said at the top, followed by a marking of time that predated the Rhiagains' arrival to the realm.

If there *had* been roads up Icebolt...

"I saw you with the Ravenwood boy."

"Guardians, you nearly stopped my heart!" Marsh exclaimed. He clutched his chest, bouncing back several steps. "What are you doing here?"

Eavan moved into the center of the room. She ran her fingers over one of the discarded books. "I saw you with him. And I heard some of what you two were saying. I heard about Ember."

Marsh's breath caught high in his throat. "You don't know what you heard."

"Given the look on your face, I'd say I confirmed it."

"Eavan—"

"I didn't come here to hold this over you. Or to insist you tell Lady Blackwood, or even ask why you haven't. You must have your reasons."

Marsh held the map behind him. It was a silly thing to do. It was nearly as tall as he was. "Then why did you come?"

"To help you." Eavan stepped closer. "I know you don't *want* my help, but to help *someone* would be an immense relief to me, when I feel as if I'm not even in service to myself. I have no one here now that Lisbet is gone. Besides... it will take two of us less time to go through all these things, will it not?"

Marsh shook his head. "I don't want to involve anyone else in this mess. I don't even know if the bastard is telling me true or playing games. We could be long down the rabbit run before we ever heard him laughing from his cursed perch in the sky."

"You don't think he's playing games," Eavan replied. "Or you wouldn't be in here."

"I *know* he's playing games," Marsh said, shaking his head. "He doesn't know how to be any different. But I also know he's seen Emberley. And if there's even a chance she's still alive, I'll spend the next fifty years tearing this library apart, page by page, to find the way to get to her."

Eavan laughed. "That's very dramatic, but I don't think it'll take you fifty years. This room is only so big. What are you looking for?" She nodded at the map. "In there?"

Marsh inhaled through his nose. He held the breath, watching Eavan, knowing he should send her away, but relieved to have *someone* to share this with. "Alasyr said there used to be an alliance between the Ravenwoods and the Frosts and Wynters. That they once guarded Midnight Crest as the Derehams do, which maybe means there were ways up the mountain from Witchwood Cross and Midwinter Rest. Or else, why would the alliance be necessary at all?"

"Have you asked Lady Aylen?"

He shook his head. "I wanted to. I was going to. But she has enough on her mind right now. And if I ask her, then she might say something to Lady Blackwood."

"You don't want Lady Blackwood to know?"

"It's complicated, Eavan."

"Complicated and I are well acquainted. So what else, then?"

"I already studied the great map on the wall over there. There's nothing. But there might have been, once." He held up the large rolled vellum. "This map pre-dates the Rhiagains. It might have something."

"Well, what are you waiting for?" Eavan unbuttoned her cuffs and rolled her sleeves. "Let's take a look."

EARWYN ALLOWED SOME DISTANCE BETWEEN HERSELF AND HER husband. Alric had awkwardly propped himself against the east balustrade. He always stood this way, leveraging whatever was closest as relief for the leg that had never healed.

She'd first spotted him there from the ground. By the time she made her way to him, he was still in the same position.

Being wed to Alric Dereham was a continuous exercise in patience and understanding, but neither of those things was a hardship. Many said that Earwyn Blackwood had fared the worst of all the young ones married off at the Epoch of the Accordant, but that had been one of many lessons life forced her to learn; to drown out the perpetual noise of what others said. Alric had never raised a hand against her, nor spoken a word of unkindness. He loved her reliably and never questioned her choices. When she'd sent Balfour away to Oldcastle—which she'd done not to spare her son from his father but from the ridicule surrounding him—Alric had simply said that it was high time a Dereham attend university.

He'd always been good to her, and in return, she did her best to be good to him.

"Alric," she said softly into the chilled wind passing across the top of the keep. "You used to talk to me."

Alric stretched a hand behind him. She took it. "I've never been a man accused of the right words, my dear. But they've never been so neutered as they are here and now."

"What's happened? Is it Christian?"

"That's part of it."

"Give him time. He's suffered so many losses, and now he's being asked to do the last thing he ever wanted. It may be years before he can look past his own youth and desires to see this time as anything but unfair."

"For a moment, when we were at the encampment, after Holden

was taken, I saw a glimpse of the man who could lead his people. Losing Holden was a great shock to me. There was enmity between us, of course, but we were brothers, and that was never forgotten. Though he didn't need me, he always made a place for me. Rinn did that, you know. Rinn had a way of bringing everyone around him with him, making them feel part of whatever and wherever he was. They liked to say Holden was a poor replacement, but Holden had that way about him, too."

"I know you miss him."

"I miss them both," Alric agreed. "But I'm grateful Holden isn't here to see Drystan returned to the Guardians, Gretchen gone through the veil, Lisbet again disappeared with a man claiming to be her real father, and Christian sulking around like a petulant child. Did you hear him yesterday? Deep in his cups, practically boasting that Lord Warwick's plan to disrupt the blockades fell afoul. Celebrating Khallum's folly, as if it isn't ours as well. As if the failure to stop an enemy could ever be cause for celebration."

Earwyn joined him at the stone wall. "Christian *will* come around. He will. He has Aylen, and she's already become so beloved of the people of Wulfsgate that I daresay they don't even notice that their lord is so absent. She's taken my place with the twins, and she leads a household like a woman well experienced. One day, he'll see it and will know what he has, and that it's greater than what he's given up."

Alric shook his head. "It's more than that, Earwyn."

Earwyn pressed her hands into the cold stone. Gretchen would've chided her for not wearing gloves, but Gretchen wasn't here. She might never be here again. "You haven't been the same since Pieter and Gretchen went through the veil."

She'd chosen these words intentionally. There was nothing supposed about what had happened. They'd gone through, and that was that, because she believed her husband. She would always believe him. The brief but grateful look Alric flashed her from the side told her she'd chosen her words well. "I always accepted that I wasn't meant to stay there. I thought it was an anomaly of magic, protecting me long enough for me to be free of the bear, but no more. Because I didn't belong there, you see? It was a gift, but with limitations. But if Gretchen and Pieter were allowed to stay, that means I was wrong, wasn't I?"

"Maybe they don't know how to return. Or cannot."

"Yes? Maybe. But why, then, was it not like that with me? Sometimes I take myself back to that moment, and my memory tells me I didn't choose to return, but was spat out, like a wulf expelling a bite of rabbit meat that had gone foul. So, why?"

Earwyn slipped a hand over his. "I wish these answers hadn't always eluded you so."

Alric turned to her. He reached forward and cupped her cheek in his gloved hand. "Your gentle handling of me all these years has never gone unnoticed, my darling. I only wish I could give you more in return."

"Nonsense," Earwyn said. She tried to smile, but a fresh sadness has taken hold. "You have given me more than enough."

"That's a lie," Alric replied. He returned to his view of the snow-covered town. "But a kind one. Is your sister staying much longer?"

Earwyn laughed. "Is that your way of suggesting she's overstayed her welcome?"

"Me? No. No. Welcome isn't mine to extend or rescind. My wonder comes from concern, actually. As one who has been consumed for most of his life by an obsession, I wouldn't want that for anyone else."

"You mean her belief that Emberley lives?"

"You say that as if you think I don't share her belief. It would be hypocritical of me, wouldn't it? A man who has only wished for others to understand mine, failing to understand hers?" He turned to her again. "Earwyn, the point of obsession, of the madness born from it, has nothing at all to do with whether you're right, and everything to do with whether you'll ever get the chance to prove it."

. . .

Asherley held out her hands. "We're sitting."

Joran ran his palms over his upper arms, affecting an overly dramatic shiver. "Is this as warm as it gets? Indoors?"

"There's a fire in a hearth larger than some homes, Joran. Shall I have blankets fetched for you?"

Joran dropped his arms, properly contrite, and leaned forward. "It's time for you to return home, Lady Blackwood."

Asherley laughed. "Is this what passes as prophecy these days at the Sepulchre? Or did Lord Dereham hire you to find a less direct way of asking me to leave?"

Joran didn't return her humor. "The first thing you must know is that Arturo Blackfen will soon arrive."

"I've ordered him to stay and counsel Brandyn. Anything he needs to tell me he will send by raven, or another Rider."

"He will come, and soon," Joran countered, "for in his counsel of Brandyn he has unearthed concerns strong enough to ride here, against your orders, and warn you."

Asherley's eyes narrowed. "Like what?"

"When he comes," Joran answered, dodging the question, "you will return to Longwood Rush without delay."

She laughed. "Why would I do that?"

"When you return, you will find the politics of your Reach in shocking disarray. It will drive you to anger, but it is with love that you must deal with Brandyn, for in that you will discover the answer that will save your Reach, and your son. I cannot tell you what this answer is. On that, the vision and the Head Magus were clear. But when it comes to you, you will know it is right, and when you know it is right, you must follow it."

Asherley slapped her hands down against the wood. "Joran, what are you even talking about right now?"

"The second thing you must know," Joran continued, as if she wasn't on the verge of losing her mind and patience, "is that you must abandon your search of Emberley. Before you take my head off, hear me out, my lady. Emberley *is* alive. She is safe, for now, and it will be the task of others, not you, to help decide her fate."

Asherley stopped breathing. The only sound hanging between them was the hard thrum of her heart and the sharp crackles of the fire behind her. "She's alive. You've seen her."

Joran nodded. "In my vision, yes."

"What do you mean, the task of others to help decide her fate? What fate? If she's alive, we will bring her home!"

"I cannot provide more clarity for you. I wish I could." Joran's eyes were sad. "But you must know that if you do not heed my counsel, Lady Emberley will not reach forward and take the destiny afforded her. She will be tethered to you, and her responsibility to you, and though it would be with love that you allowed this, it will require a greater love for you to stand back and let others aid her."

"What others? All you've done so far is speak nonsense to me."

"The last thing you must know is that once you have saved your Reach from the infighting rotting it from within, you will again have to leave it."

Asherley flopped back in her chair with a sigh. "And go *where*, exactly?"

"To seek out one of the sorcerers for a cure for what ails you. It will take your life if you are not healed."

Her blood cooled. She was suddenly aware of every ache, every ailment, every imperfection across the surface of her flesh. "I have what Hollyn had. Is that what you mean?"

Joran nodded. He lowered his eyes to his hands. "You do have it. I've seen it. Only those who hail from Ilynglass know the cure. But if you return to Duncarrow, Oldwin will take you as a trophy."

"But there is nowhere else."

"There are other sorcerers."

"And where am I to find these other sorcerers?"

"I do not know yet," Joran answered. "That part is still unclear to me."

"Unclear!" Asherley exclaimed. "You come here, telling me I'm *dying*, that my son is destroying my Reach, that I must forsake my beloved daughter, and that's supposed to be enough that I follow everything you say, just as you say it?"

"Lady Blackwood, we have known each other for many years. Through good times and hard, you have trusted me. That trust took you to Duncarrow, blindly, but with confidence that you were aimed true. That trust sent your children into the world and spared three of them. That trust must still mean something to you. I will serve you until the day my promise is at last spent, and in that service I will never lie to you. I *have* never lied to you. The visions I've had of you were so powerful that, still in service to you, my lady, I traveled back to a place I swore I'd never return, after how I was treated. Three separate seers independently confirmed all I saw. If I cannot tell you everything, it is only because some things have the power to alter history, and a seer must always seek first to protect, second to counsel."

"You ask a lot of me, Joran," Asherley said, finally, after taking a moment to let his words settle over her. She did trust him. He was an old fool, who never liked to commit to anything, but he was her fool. "More than you realize."

"I realize more than perhaps you know," Joran said, turning her words around. "But if you need one final push, then here it is. In these next moments, Arturo Blackfen, the greatest Rush Rider the Westerlands has ever known and the most loyal man in your service, will come striding down that hall with the very message I've just told you he'll be carrying."

"That's quite a bit more precision than your visions typically offer," Asherley said, near teasing, but her humor died away as footsteps sounded in the distance. Joran watched her. She looked back at him. She was almost afraid to turn toward the sound, to confirm what would be so much simpler, so much more satisfying, to deny.

Joran gently nodded once.

She glanced toward the hall and saw Rider Blackfen making his way toward them.

"You came back."

"You sound astonished."

Ember pushed the stick down into the last of the fire. She looked tired, but as always, had gone to great pains to keep this from him, angling her face in such a way that he could only guess how deep her exhaustion ran. "You seemed to believe you'd be at risk, leaving here. I'm only thinking of your own worries on the matter."

"It is a risk," Alasyr said. He watched her mess with the fire. Her hand shook almost imperceptibly. She watched him watching and stopped.

Alasyr stepped deeper into the cave and set the satchel down by the fire. "When was the last time you had bread, eh? And boar?"

Ember shook her head with a delighted laugh as she tore through the provisions. "And cheese? Where did you find such delicacies?"

"I can get more, when we run out."

"A slice of pearapple pie? Alasyr! This is a right feast!"

Alasyr flushed. He leaned into the stone of the cave, enjoying the return of a more animated Emberley. He hoped none of it made her sick again.

Marsh. He has to find a way.

"It's all I could carry," he said, shrugging. "I'll return for more."

Ember looked up from her bounty with a wide grin. "But where, Alasyr? Where did you get all this? Did you steal it?"

"Ah," he started, shuffling in place. "No, I didn't steal it."

"Well, I know you don't eat like this at Midnight Crest."

"No," he agreed. Even in the ice cold, he was sweating. Why was he hesitating?

Because Marsh loves Ember. And you...

Ember's smile died. "What is it? What aren't you telling me?"

"Marsh," he choked out. "Marsh gave it to me."

Ember pushed the bag aside. Her face went pale, paler than usual. "Marsh? He's here?"

"In Wulfsgate."

"Why is he in Wulfsgate?"

Alasyr dropped his eyes. "He's searching for you."

Ember pulled both hands to her mouth as she choked out a gasp.

"He stayed, with your mother. Your mother made it back to Wulfsgate safely, Emberley. I didn't see her with my own eyes. I had to lure Marsh into the forest, away from the keep and others."

"My *mother* is in Wulfsgate, too?"

Alasyr nodded. "They haven't given up on you." Alasyr felt a sudden urge to cry. He wouldn't. A Ravenwood reserved their tears. They didn't waste them on past dwelling.

Still. He couldn't help but compare the resilient commitment of Ember's loved ones to the cold detachment displayed by his own parents when Ravenna left.

Ember turned her head away. Her expression disappeared into the darkness. "You didn't see my mother, but you... you did see Marsh? You spoke with him? Is that right?"

"Yes."

"How was he? How did he look?"

"I thought he might shoot me out of the sky, so I wasn't concerned with how he *looked*." Alasyr closed his mouth tight, resetting his words. "He looked exhausted. I don't think he's slept much."

"You told him, right? That I'm alive?"

"I don't think he believed me at first. By the end, he did." Alasyr nodded at the food. "He gave me that, and then I asked for further aid that he seemed less confident in his ability to provide."

"Which was?"

"There may have once been a path up this mountain, guarded by men. I asked him to find it."

"He doesn't know these lands, Alasyr. Better men have died in the passes and foothills."

"I don't think Marsh is concerned with the business of better men. He seems blissfully unaware of his own limitations."

"If he does find it?"

"Then I'll ask him to take the path himself."

Ember leveled a shocked look. "Alone?"

"I'll be with him, flying back and forth between the two of you. If he makes it all the way here, to you, then I'll follow you both back down the same path until I know you're safe."

Ember held her hands over the fire. She didn't look at him. This avoidance was intentional. "Let's say it works. Your plan. Then what?"

"I don't understand."

"Come over here, Alasyr."

"Why?"

"Just come."

Alasyr ignored his racing heart and troubled mind and went to her. They were never quiet for long, and he'd learned to let them settle into the background, rather than consume him from temple to toe. But they were still there, always. With her, they were always at their loudest.

She reached a hand up to him to pull him down. He lowered to a crouch, but she tugged him harder, and he fell beside her. "I'm asking what will become of *you*?"

Alasyr cast his eyes toward the fire. "I'll find my way. Ravenna did."

"What if I said your way is my way?"

"*What?*" The word came out harsher than he intended.

"What if I said, when we find ourselves free of his cave, I don't want that to be the last we see of each other."

Alasyr twisted his fingers together. "I'd say that... you're only being emotional. There's no world for the both of us."

"Yet here we are. The both of us."

"You know what I mean, Emberley."

Emberley reached a hand forward. She pressed a finger to his chin, turning him toward her. "You once loathed me. Now you give up your life to keep me safe. And still, you cannot see a future that has me as anything but your adversary."

"No, I don't see you that way, I—"

Ember silenced him with a soft kiss. Inexplicable warmth coursed through him. He was incapable of movement and yet also weightless, connected and disconnected, present but away. When she deepened the kiss, slipping her tongue between his lips, Alasyr forgot every objection, every caution. He was hers, lost to her, his fears belonging to another Alasyr, not the one here, with her.

The small sound made when she at last pulled away—the bit of spittle still settled atop his lips, not his, not hers, but theirs—pushed his heart into his mouth, where the taste of her still lived. When he looked at her then, in the *after*, he swelled with something bigger and brighter and warmer than anything he'd ever known in his cold kingdom.

Ember smiled, a light laugh trapped at the back of her throat. "Tell me again, Alasyr Ravenwood, about this world that does not exist."

"Marsh loves you. He'll come for you, and take you back to the life you left behind."

"I know he does. And I love him, something I couldn't see when I was so blinded by my own needs," she said. "But love isn't that simple, is it?" Ember reached for his hands and wound them in her own. "Is it?"

Alasyr looked down at their pile of twined fingers. His breaths were imprecise. He feared words wouldn't be what came out if he tried to speak.

"Twice now you've risked your life for mine. Will you really find it so easy to leave me, when the time comes?"

Alasyr tightened his fingers, squeezing their knot tighter. "I only did what was right. What my conscience would tolerate. When Marsh finally makes his way here to you, I'll again do what's right. For you."

Ember leaned her head into his shoulder. "And you say you've never known love."

19

EVER THE GAP

Assana slipped into the pub every morning at the same time, and predictably, Balfour always shuffled in moments later. He had his table. She had hers. He'd become more guarded with his book since that first day, pulling the sides of his cloak over the top to form a tent. It made her laugh. Did he think she could see that tiny print from all the way across the pub? Did he think she cared? She'd heard about the books the boys snuck from the dark corners of their parents' libraries; the ones that would make even the most ribald man flush from head to toe.

That laughter faded when she considered that whatever he was reading was serious enough to go to ridiculous lengths to keep it from her. If it was a filthy read, as she'd guessed, he'd want the privacy of his own room for that. Instead, he was after a different kind of discretion. Coming into the pub at odd hours. Settling in the shadows of the light, far from any other patrons, or even the barkeep.

One day, he didn't come. He'd apparently decided her continued presence was a problem. So Assana slipped back into the frosty morning, cloak wrapped tight against the unusual mid-season snow, and trudged through the small village of thatched roofs and dormered windows in search of his next chosen spot. There had to be a next spot. Otherwise he'd be doing his reading in his room, or at the university. He needed this, and she needed him.

Assana entered a tavern called Ever the Gap. Like the one she'd just departed, it was empty at this dismal hour, and she almost turned to leave when she saw a cloak draped over a table in a dark corner. The barkeep twisted a dirty rag inside a clean mug, staring at her.

"Did a pupil come in here?" she asked.

The man nodded toward the table with the cloak. "Aye. Taking a right piss in the back, or so he said. Been gone too long for that."

"I'd like to buy him an ale."

The barkeep flipped the dirty mug right side up, slamming it on the bar. He grabbed a nearby pitcher and filled it, then slid it across the uneven dark wood. She barely caught it before it fell to the floor.

"Thanks," she muttered and dropped the proper coin on the bar.

"None for ye, lass?" he called after her.

Not unless I want to be out back with Balfour nursing watery bowels. "No." She dropped another coin. "The drink was on you, should he ask. I wasn't here."

He grunted and slipped the coin into his pocket.

Assana took the chair across from the one wearing Balfour's cloak. She waited for the barkeep's attentions to be drawn back to his shoddy cleaning and then slipped the sachet out of her own pocket.

Assana learned this trick from her mother. Maeryn had very little usefulness to pass on to her daughters, but the Blackwood women were all purveyors of poison, and Maeryn proudly taught both Eavan and Assana everything she'd remembered from her girlhood in the Westerlands. Aunt Asherley had an entire garden at Longwood Rush devoted to her passion in this, though their skills weren't limited to nefariousness.

Assana's eyes always glassed over at all the rest. Poison was her only interest.

This concoction of elderflower and rosewood was said to put a man at ease.

With the barkeep focused on his ineffective tidying, Assana tilted the sachet upside down over the mug of ale and tapped out the contents. She stirred the ale with her finger. Leaned in to smell. Faint, but only if one was looking for it.

This next part she dreaded more than the idea of going to bed with Balfour Dereham. Standing outside in the cold. Waiting for minutes, for hours. She wouldn't know until he at last stumbled out. When she'd have to quickly determine how far the concoction had taken matters, so she'd know just how much she'd have to do to bring him the rest of the way.

He was alone, but that didn't mean he was lonely. It didn't mean he'd fall into her arms and then take her where she needed to go.

She was drawn to his need for secrecy; the very idea he had something important enough to protect. That he had the mettle to first seek and then protect anything.

He was the one, if she could get him there.

Assana exited the pub and leaned against the side of the building, waiting.

THEY'D TAKEN TO EATING THE DRY BRUSH.

Gilgowan hadn't been certain it was edible until the first man grabbed a handful, his fear of death having been chipped away by his now daily addressing of it. They'd, all of them, watched in nervous anticipation as the brave soldier first chewed, albeit uncomfortably, and then swallowed, wincing. Moments passed. An hour. He hadn't died, nor had his bowels turned—least not any worse than they had already—so the rest went at it. It was a right feast when compared to starvation.

For Gilgowan, the sad celebration was short-lived. It wasn't enough to sustain his men. Not enough for the energy required and spent. If only he *knew* when relief would come, he could relax and laugh with his men.

But he didn't know. No word had come in place of food. He'd finally considered the possibility that the crown had abandoned them. Was it for their failures? Was the object of their work no longer important? He didn't know. He had no way *to* know. Gilgowan, a man built to both take and give orders, had only ever needed the *what*, not the *why*, but the beckoning call of death had a way of making things important that hadn't been before.

They could leave and find relief beyond the Wastelands, but then they'd be tried for treason and executed. He could send another scout to Duncarrow, but the last hadn't returned. He couldn't blame him for not returning to this, though he suspected his scout had been killed. It was this fear that kept him from sending another. Gilgowan might never know if he was sending men to their respite or their death.

It was the not knowing, he told himself, that kept him from speaking up when the first of his men suggested that some of the dead were still fresh. Fresh enough to eat.

It was the not knowing that stayed his hand when a group of them dragged a corpse to Camp Restitution and discussed the proper way to dress it, evaluating what meat was still fit for consumption and what was too rotted to do more than make a man ill.

It was the not knowing that kept his mind from grasping fully what it was to put human flesh into his mouth, chew, and swallow, so that he could live another day.

It was the not knowing.

The not knowing.

The not knowing.

"It was a rat's ass!" Balfour cried, nearly doubled laughing as he stumbled out of the pub, repeating the punchline to the barkeep's jest. It wasn't even funny. He didn't know why he couldn't stop laughing, but it was a nicer feeling than the ones he was most accustomed to on the average day.

He was still so snared in his amusement he didn't see the girl step out in front of him. He knocked her back a few steps when he ran straight into her. He mumbled a hollow apology, until he saw who it was. It was *her*. The one from The Golden Castle who'd suddenly started keeping his hours, watching him as if she knew something properly scandalous.

Balfour was in possession of but one scandal, though he doubted very much this one had any interest in *that*.

"You," he charged.

"Me," she said with a light, quick lift of her shoulders, and a curated smile. She was familiar, but he supposed she looked like all the girls in the universities who pretended to give him the time of day, only to turn the interaction into a quick joke for their mates.

He pressed his hand to his cloak, relieved when he still felt the response of the hard lines of the book. Something about this one made him worried it might not be.

"You aren't a pupil in the universities."

"Do they allow girls now?"

"They always have, if their kin has the gold for it. Crimsoncastle, mainly."

"Crimsoncastle? Is that a jest about women and their moon flows?"

"Don't know and don't care."

"Hmm," she said, in an offhand way one might comment on the weather.

"I'm late for instruction," he lied. He tried to step around her, but she matched the landing of his boots in perfect response. "What do you want, anyway? Following me around?"

"Is there somewhere private we might go? To talk?"

Balfour snickered. "You and I have nothing to talk about."

"How do you know?" The girl tilted her head, flashing her wide eyes at him. She was quite lovely, and she knew this, which made her less lovely. That wasn't all that made her less lovely, though. There was something dark in her. Behind that smile and bright eyes was something dangerous, and for the first time in her presence, she intrigued him.

"I just know," he replied, but now he was taking her in, all of her. The cloak disguised her figure and dress, but if she removed it he expected there to be some fine fabric, like velvet, hugging her slim waist, denoting her as highborn. Only a highborn had the fortune to possess the brash confidence of this one. Her teeth were white and straight, proof of a fair diet. She had no telltale bulge around the middle from an abundance of bread and grain.

Balfour tossed aside his caution, and, with a flick of his hand, opened her cloak. Rich red silk, tailored just for her pleasing figure. It was almost too easy.

The girl laughed. "Am I supposed to be impressed by your magic? I've seen better."

"Have you?" Balfour stretched his arm out with a snap, and the blacksmith's sign across the road came crashing down into the snow.

The girl shrugged. Yawned.

Balfour wanted to knock her from her feet, but there were enough men milling about that he'd be taken down in an instant. And then he wouldn't get to experience the conclusion of his strange, enticing encounter.

Balfour rolled his tongue into the corner of his mouth and with a forced look of boredom stretched his arm out once more and this time sent the wood of the same shop splintering and flying into the air. A crowd gathered, pointing and then gasping as the blacksmith's shop first fell apart and then caved inward.

The girl pressed her mouth into a line and nodded approvingly. "All right. That's proper."

The blacksmith came running out of his shop just before it collapsed entirely. He screamed, arms flailing, searching in furious misery for the culprit.

The girl buried her laughter in her arm. Balfour eyed her with still-growing interest. She was a devious one. He'd just destroyed a man's livelihood, and she could hardly contain herself.

Balfour found himself laughing too. He took her by the arm and guided her away from the wreckage before they drew eyes to their heartless amusement.

"Not my finest moment," he muttered, more to himself. He glanced over his shoulder, but no one was following. All gathered shared in the sudden and inexplicable misery of the very confused blacksmith.

"I'll send an anonymous donation," the girl said, waving her hand.

"Will you?"

She shrugged. "Probably not."

He would, then. He had enough gold from his mother's unwelcome packages to rebuild the shop twice over.

"Who *are* you?"

Balfour gasped when the girl snaked her arm out and cupped her hand between his legs. "Do you want my name, or do you want me?"

"I don't have a roommate," he managed through clenched teeth. Her hand squeezed tighter. He'd lain with a woman, once. Not a girl. An ale wench in a pub he could no longer patronize because of the folly.

"No?" she asked. "How are the walls?"

"The walls?"

The girl stretched upon her toes and whispered the words against his ear. "I'm not the least bit quiet."

20

THE STRANGE MATTER OF TIME

Gretchen helped Maura pin the washing. She used small scraps of thin metal that she curved into place using her fingers, shaping the dresses and trousers and quilts to the line. It reminded her of the way her mother used to do it, a lifetime ago in Whitechurch, at Arboriana. Though they had servants, the Lady of the Easterlands often threw herself willingly into the minor household tasks. She used to say to Gretchen that it was her way of reminding the staff that she was always there, watching to ensure they didn't slack in their duties. But Gretchen remembered the easy calm that fell into her mother's eyes as she took fastidious care in every twitch of her fingers. Mariana Quinlanden had once been a Skylark, and though Skylarks were among the ranks of the Great Families, there was a hierarchy, and the Skylarks were not Oakenwells or Edevanes. Many whispered that Chasten had chosen too low for a bride, and it was her comfort with the chores they often cited as proof of their claim.

But Gretchen, too, liked the predictability of tending the household. As she aided Maura, this world, this reality, began to have an air of normalcy. She could almost forget that her little Pieter was now a man old enough to have lost a wife and son, and to be hardened by the cruelty of both. That the rest of her children were lost to her, unless she could find an answer that Brahim and Maura had not.

They were in Pieter's residence. Brahim had gifted it to him when he'd taken a wife, but he'd not lived there long enough to tend to most of the repairs needed to make the place livable. Like most homes in Malfenza, it was in a state of disarray, the remnants of choices made in a rush; of families who couldn't take everything when they fled the city for a safer one.

Yet the natural light spilling in through the reddish walls, the vines climbing around the sills of the open windows, seemed more a welcome than a goodbye.

Curran helped Pieter reinforce a wall that had crumbled away near the bottom. To see how patiently he showed Pieter how to pack the mud in place was like looking at a different man than the one who glared at her through persistently narrowed eyes, whispering, hissing, *Intrusa*.

But it was Pieter, not Curran, she couldn't take her eyes from. When she'd last seen him, his scrawny arms had barely been capable of pulling his bowstring. This Pieter had filled out. The cut of his now developed muscles reshaping the shirt as he flexed to press the heavy mixture into the wall.

"Pieter can feel your eyes on him," Maura remarked. She ran her hands down a dress to smooth it out.

"If you hadn't seen your son in months, only to discover he's become a man, you would do the same."

"The strange matter of time between our worlds haunts him, too. In his life, he has been without his mother for years. He'd made peace with this absence." Maura reached into the basket for another shirt. "But you also come at a difficult time, with the loss of Rehana and Drystan so fresh. Loss has shaped Pieter's entire life. Though, it can be easier that way, for some."

"Easier?" Gretchen repeated. "He may look like a man, but only hardly. It's taking all my will not to scoop him into my arms like I did when he was a boy, which for me was only yesterday."

Maura nodded toward where Curran and Pieter worked. "Yet that isn't the comfort he wants or needs, Gretchen. A man needs to keep busy. Curran knows that as well as anyone. You may see his quickness to cruelty, but what he does now, for Pieter, is more like what a father would do for a son."

"I would thank him, but he'd only curse me for the effort," Gretchen murmured, snapping a blanket between her hands to straighten it.

Maura stopped her work. "Curran also lost his wife. She was carrying their first child."

Gretchen felt the blood rush away from her face. "How did she die?"

"Same way the children died. The disease attacks the young and infirm, but they didn't know Needrah was unwell until she was already gone. Sometimes the disease lies in wait, as it did in Rehana and Drystan. Other times, it moves swiftly, without mercy." Maura looked at the two men. "A bitterness took over his heart. He would help Pieter from becoming the same way, if he can."

Gretchen closed her eyes and leaned into the table, sighing. "This is why he loathes me."

"He loathes all outsiders who would bring more heartache to our world," Maura answered. "But he never felt that way toward Pieter. Maybe because Curran was no older than Pieter is now when he lost Needrah. He saw Pieter was only a boy, lost, afraid, and took to him immediately. They've been quite close ever since." She paused. "I said Curran was like a father to Pieter, but it's more like an older brother. Pieter rarely spoke of his life in your world. Was he close to his older brothers?"

Gretchen never took her eyes off Pieter. Seeming to sense this, he turned, flashing her a brief, uncomfortable smile, and then went back to his work with Curran. "His eldest brother left home when Pieter was very young. He was close to Drystan, though. Only a couple of years separated them."

"The one he named his son for."

"But then Drystan's attentions were drawn elsewhere, and there may as well have been a decade between them."

"The sorceress," Maura said. "Yes?"

"He told you about that?"

"In the early days, his story came out of him like a whirl of dust on a hard wind. After that, he said nothing at all. It was only when he named his son Drystan that I even remembered the name, what it had meant to him."

Gretchen watched as Curran rested a tender hand upon Pieter's back, as he led him through the rest of his instruction. Curran was someone else with Pieter, and Pieter was someone else altogether. She was the foreign entity here, the piece that didn't quite fit. No matter the kindness she'd been offered, or how this strange, beautiful world appealed to her, she couldn't envision a future where she fell so easily into a life as her son had.

She kept these thoughts to herself. They wouldn't be welcome.

"Maura," Gretchen said. "There's something I have been meaning to ask you."

"You want to know about the veil. Why some can return and others cannot," Maura said. She emptied the last cloth from the basket and pinned it. "You haven't accepted there will be no return for you."

"How did you know?"

"It's the question I'd be asking if I were you."

"You say I haven't accepted it, but how could I, when I lived with a man who came into your world and returned to mine? When I know it *is* possible?"

"If you believe it's possible, why have you not tried?"

Gretchen balked. "I would never leave here without Pieter. I cannot risk going through and then being unable to return here."

"You want to know why other men have returned when you and Pieter cannot?" Maura propped the basket under her arm and met Gretchen's gaze with cool eyes. "You ate the fruit, Gretchen. Once you'd eaten the fruit, you became a part of this world."

"That sounds absurd. What does fruit have to do with anything?"

"The fruit is only a symbol," Maura answered. "Once you have taken from Tenestela, you become permanent. A man can step through and return right away, and that is for the best. It's why we watch the forest. To drive men away before they make a choice they cannot take back. But we were remiss with your arrival. Pieter had lost his family, and we were distracted. Our failure to send you back quickly enough made you one of us. At least, this seems to be the only truth we've found that has any sense."

"I ate the fruit because the alternative was a slow death," Gretchen retorted. Her thoughts returned to those long days, the sight of her dwindling rations threatening what remained of her thin hope. "I didn't have enough rations to return through the veil again and journey home."

"Would you rather be dead, Gretchen, or here, with your son?"

"Of course I'd rather be with my son."

"Then learn to embrace the gift for what it is. For you can see it as a gift, or as a curse, but it changes nothing. This is your home. This is your life. There is nothing else." Maura nodded at Curran. "You might find yourself more at ease if you had a man to warm your bed. That's a truth that must be consistent across all worlds, no?"

Gretchen gaped at her. "Curran?"

"Do you see any other men here?" Maura waved a free hand. "You make do with what you're given. Happiness follows acceptance."

Gretchen watched Maura walk into the other room to retrieve more clothing from the washing basin. Could it be true about the fruit? There had to be some explanation that reasoned how Alric could return, and Pieter could not. Why Alric hardly seemed aged at all when he returned from his ordeal, and Pieter had aged a decade in what she knew as weeks.

One thing Maura had said stood out above all the rest. *If you believe it's possible, why have you not tried?*

Maura was right. She would always believe it was possible until she tried. But she couldn't risk stepping through and being unable to return to the world, leaving Pieter behind. Somehow, she'd have to convince him to come with her.

She turned toward the sensation of a violent heat. Curran, again, boring holes in her with a gaze so intense she had to turn away.

He might be the only other man in this city, but he was the last man in this world, or any other, that she would ever take to her bed.

21
WHAT LOYALTY LOOKS LIKE

Asherley requested a private meeting with Lord Dereham to offer her formal farewell and gratitude for the extended hospitality. Christian sent his wife in his place.

Aylen made all the right excuses for her husband. She was convincing enough, and someone who hadn't borne witness to Christian Dereham's dereliction of duty would have believed every word. Asherley had advice for this young woman who had married a man in the throes of a crisis, but Aylen's love for the man would blind her to any wisdom not gleaned on her own.

"Do you need anything at all? For your journey?" Aylen asked. She was a lovely woman. The silver hair of the Sepulchre had branded her, but she seemed to fit easily into both worlds, both native and exotic. The Northerlanders adored her. She'd fallen naturally into the role of lady, and not only because she'd been born and bred for the possibility of this moment.

Asherley gestured toward the courtyard. "I have the Rush Riders to accompany me. And a very old, cranky mage."

Aylen chuckled. "Don't let him hear you call him that. He's a very proud Enchanter."

"Prideful is right," Asherley quipped. "I have one bit of unfinished business. I haven't been able to find Marsh. I need to speak with him before I depart."

"Marsh," Aylen mused, drawing her eyes away in thought. "He's been spending an awful lot of time in the library these days. With Eavan."

"With Eavan, you say?"

"Poor girl. I think she's been looking for a way to be useful. Marsh is a kind boy and has been making a place for her in his studies."

"Marsh Tyndall fancies himself a scholar now, does he?" Asherley muttered. "Would you mind having someone inform Rider Blackfen that I'll be a few more minutes?"

Aylen nodded. "I'll tell him myself, Lady Blackwood."

On a whim, Asherley reached forward and clasped the younger woman's hands in her own. "Lady Dereham. Don't let his shadows blunt the warmth of your sun. You can love his darker parts without sacrificing your light."

Aylen's fractured smile and twinkle in her eyes expressed the objections she couldn't quite voice. She squeezed Asherley's hands once and then released them, turning to go.

Asherley continued toward the library. It was the first time she'd been alone all day. Her morning and afternoon had been a flurry of goodbyes, of last-minute considerations, of Blackfen and Joran going over the maps with her, as if she had anything of use to offer the conversation of overland journeys.

She shouldn't be leaving. Her place was here, waiting for Emberley. The deep stubbornness, that had as many times been her savior as the architect of her sorrow, pushed back against Joran's visions. She'd always done this with him, pushing, then pulling, then pushing more until he was desperate to please her. He liked to remind her that visions didn't serve any but the vision itself, and that he wasn't in the business of telling her what she wanted to hear. And of course, she would smartly retort that she *knew* that, for when had he *ever* told her what she wanted to hear?

This time was different. Not for the troubled confidence

brewing behind Joran's eyes. Not because he'd traveled to the Sepulchre for guidance, after he'd sworn never to return while still a man living. Not even because he was right about the precise moment Rider Blackfen would arrive, and the exact words he would use to persuade her.

Would these things have been enough? Perhaps. Perhaps not. But it was her own instinct, the Ravenwood magic that pricked her heart with promise every moment she was near the source. *This is not the place for you. You must go. You must go before the option to return is stolen from you.*

Asherley pulled open the double doors to the library.

Marsh and Eavan were leaned over the table in the center of the room, whispering over an enormous map.

"Tyndall," Asherley said, loud enough to make him jump. His eyes darted to the map in a panic, exchanging a similarly frantic look with Eavan.

"Lady Blackwood." He nodded. "My apologies. I didn't hear the door open."

"Quite right," she said, moving into the room. "This map has laid claim to the entirety of your attention." Asherley ran her fingers along the edges. It was very old, the tiny precise lines belonging to a time long before theirs. "What an interesting thing to be so taken by."

Do not divert the boy from his task. You heard what Joran said. He is Emberley's last hope.

Marsh looked ready to crumple to the floor on the spot, even eager for it. Eavan smiled sweetly. "Aunt Asherley, this is really only me being silly. You see, the armorer's son, Angus. Argus?"

Marsh nodded. His throat ebbed. "Uh, yeah. Argus."

"Argus," Eavan continued. "He *insisted* that Salthill didn't exist a hundred years ago. And *I said* that Salthill had been around since the Reach was a kingdom, which is to say, it's at the very least, many hundreds of years old. And seeing as I have five gold coins riding on being right, of course I couldn't let it go."

Marsh listened in surprise, and then shrugged as if to say, *it's true*.

What terrible liars. She'd trained her own so much better than this. Asherley pointed to the lower corner of the map. "It's right here. Where it's always been."

"So it is!" Eavan exclaimed, laughing. Marsh nervously laughed with her.

"I'm leaving Wulfsgate. Today," Asherley said. If she stayed here any longer, she wouldn't be able to stop herself from tearing apart the thin layers of their deception. Joran was clear she wasn't to do this. "Returning to the Westerlands."

Marsh stepped out from behind the table. "Lady Blackwood?"

"Don't look so panicked, Tyndall. Your place is here, searching for Emberley. I'm trusting you and you alone with leading this most important task, for I know that you'll not fail me, or her."

He bowed, dropping his shoulders lower this time. "I won't leave until I find her. If I ever step foot on the soil of my homeland again, it will be with Emberley at my side, and only then."

"I look forward to that day. And Marsh..."

"Yes, Lady Blackwood?"

"I meant it. There is *no one* else I would trust to this task. No man, nor woman. No lord, or soldier, or king, or lady. For there is no one who loves Emberley as much as I do, or so I believed until I witnessed your commitment."

Marsh lowered his eyes.

"I won't ask what it is the two of you are getting up to in here. It isn't for me to know. That much is clear." Asherley let her eyes fall on Eavan. "You won't change your mind about returning to Whitechurch, will you? Your brother continues to ask about you."

Eavan shook her head. The playacting from earlier had melted from her practiced expression. "That ceased to be my home when my mother and father sold me like a slave. And now they've become traitors, not only to me, but the entire realm. If I could shed myself of the Quinlanden name and be free of all of it, I would."

Asherley sighed. "I received word today that your mother will be tried for treason. The council has already decided her guilt, so the trial will be a mere formality, I expect."

Eavan's lip trembled. It was the only sign the news had shaken her. "She should be. Poor Cian. He deserves better. We all did."

Asherley hadn't let herself dwell on the imminence of her sister's execution. It seemed like a truth belonging to another world, not theirs. Nor could she intervene on her behalf. If what was said was true, then Maeryn had betrayed her blood, her Reach, her kingdom, and herself, then she'd forgotten who she was, and that was a crime beyond any power Asherley possessed.

"You could come with me to the Rush," Asherley said. "I'd make you a fine marriage in the Westerlands. No one would dare question where your child came from. You would be as my own daughter, no less. You would never want for a thing, Eavan."

Eavan glanced at Marsh before returning her attention to Asherley. "I appreciate that, Aunt Asherley. But I find myself unexpectedly invested in Marsh's passion. I believe I can still be of aid to him, here, and would like the opportunity to continue, for as long as I can."

Marsh flushed a dark red. Asherley didn't detect any attraction between the two of them, but Eavan Quinlanden was still one of the most beautiful young ladies in the entire kingdom. A man could find himself with worse partners to spend their days with.

"Marsh?" Asherley prodded.

"I could use her aid, if she's willing to still give it," he fumbled. "When Emberley is safe, I'll escort both of them to Longwood Rush."

"Good," Asherley said. She held her arms out to Eavan. The girl nearly ran into them. She held her niece, absorbing the sharp pangs of the girl's desperation for love and affection. Asherley vowed to do right by Eavan and the other children who had been left to wade through the murky waters of their seditious parents.

Asherley looked over the top of Eavan's blond curls at Marsh. "This all comes down to you now, Tyndall."

Marsh nodded. "I won't rest until she's safe."

. . .

"She knows," Eavan whispered. She was the first to speak, and the words didn't come right away. They were both frozen in place until they heard Lady Blackwood's steps disappear down the hall, leaving them with only the rhythm of their pounding hearts.

"You don't have to whisper anymore," Marsh said. "And yeah. She knows."

Eavan spun on him. "She didn't stop you. She *encouraged* you, Marsh. She wants you to go up that mountain."

"That's sure how it sounded."

"Even if it kills you."

Marsh scoffed. "It won't kill me."

"We've only *just* found evidence of a pass. The world looks much different when you're in it than it does on a map."

"Yes, thank you, Eavan, I'm aware."

"Don't get cross with me." Eavan folded her arms. "I'm helping, remember?"

"That was a good offer Lady Blackwood made you," Marsh said. He still had both eyes on the door. His thoughts spun webs around the encounter, which should have left him empowered, and instead he felt as if he'd been left out of something very important.

"To go with her? She *has* to offer. Who else will take me in?"

Marsh turned around and looked at her with a gentle smile. "I didn't sense duty, or pity, in her words. You should consider them."

"I probably will. But it's as I told her. I have something more important to do here."

Marsh dropped his hands on the table, holding himself aloft. "You can't come with me up the pass."

"Because I'm a girl?"

"Because you're with child," Marsh said with a nod to her belly. "Because as you pointed out, I don't know what I'll find, or what dangers lie ahead."

Eavan rolled her eyes. "We don't even know if the path still exists, do we?"

"I've spent my life in forests, finding paths I'm not meant to. Even in the Westerlands, where anything that can grow grows aplenty, you can still find evidence of places long abandoned. Doesn't take much to put them back into use."

Eavan's gaze was so intense, so lingering, he was suddenly and acutely aware of things he normally never gave passing thought to, like how strange flesh felt on bone. And then she said, "Do you know your eyes are different colors?"

Marsh sagged into his laughter. "Yeah. I'm aware."

"I've never seen such a thing! One is green, and the other is... violet. I thought violet eyes were reserved for witches and derelicts. Mother's blood." Eavan squinted, as if that would help to better evaluate the phenomenon. "Does Ember love this about you?"

The blood rose quickly to his face. "I've never asked what she thought about it."

Eavan nodded appraisingly. "Oh, yes. She must. I'm going to say with certainty that she loves this about you the most."

"I suppose I'll have to ask her when I see her, won't I?" Marsh glanced out the window, to the setting sun beyond. Alasyr would come only at night now, but he'd not come the night before, or the one before that. The food Marsh had sent him with would be dwindled to scraps, if not already gone. Tonight must be the night. "You'll think of a fair excuse for why I'm absent at supper?"

"You don't want me to go with you?"

Marsh shook his head. "I don't want to scare him off. He's anxious enough with me. He doesn't know you."

"Does he look like Ravenna?"

"What?"

Eavan sighed with a dreamy look. "Nothing. Only he might be more eager to speak with me if he knew I spent weeks with his sister on the run."

"I don't know, Eavan, but I think that might make him less inclined to be in your presence."

"Why's that?"

Marsh shrugged. He rolled the map and tucked it under his arm.

He felt small compared to the massive scroll, which was already a weight he was ready to be well rid of. "Just a feeling. Ravenna's leaving changed him. All he wanted was for her to come home. Now, I'm not so sure that's what he wants at all."

"Why wouldn't he want her to come home?"

Marsh looked toward the north. "Maybe he finally understands why she left."

MARSH DROPPED THE SACK OF FOOD ON A TREE STUMP. BEFORE Alasyr could even gather his bearings, Marsh was asking him to hold the other end of a grotesquely long, rolled hunk of vellum. Alasyr started to ask what he was playing at, but Marsh cut him off, urging him to follow his lead.

Alasyr grunted and held the edges of one end while Marsh backed away. "We have nothing to set it on, but I didn't bring it to entertain you. Only to show you this one thing." Marsh used his elbow to pin down the side he'd been holding and then, using some mild contortions, pointed at the top right corner of the map.

Alasyr shrugged. "What am I looking at, Wildwood?"

"You don't see it? Just north of Midwinter Rest, behind the Frozen Vale?"

"Your corner of the map might as well be in the Southerlands for as well as I can see it from over here."

Marsh groaned. "Fine. I don't need you to see it. On the map, anyway."

"See what already?"

"A *path*, Alasyr. Remember, you were the one who told me about the alliances your family once had with the Frosts and Wynters?"

"I told you to talk to them. Don't you have one living with you in the keep?" Alasyr waved a hand.

"If Aylen knew about a path, she would've mentioned it long ago, when all our searches came back empty. She wouldn't have let us endlessly search if she had the answer."

Alasyr was so surprised, he released his side of the map. With a hard whistle it went rolling back toward Marsh, nearly knocking him back. "You really found it."

"It took some doing. It's not on the new maps. I don't know if they've let it return to its wild state, or they just don't want others to know. But it existed, once. I know that, now." Marsh turned to grab the map again, but then decided against the effort. "It goes almost all the way to The Rookery and then stops. Why would it stop?"

Alasyr shook his head. "You can't reach The Rookery on foot. You think it really stops that close?"

Marsh bobbed his head from side to side. "As far as I can tell. The scale of the mountain is difficult to comprehend in a map."

"And from the air," Alasyr muttered. "I'll try to fly around tomorrow, in the early hours. I'll see if I can find any signs of the path coming near to the cave where we've been staying. If I can get you close, I suppose I'll have to guide you the rest of the way and hope you don't go careening to your death."

"How... how's Emberley? You told her, about me?"

Alasyr nodded. Fresh snow dotted his eyelashes. He swatted it away. "Yeah. I told her."

"What did she say?"

Alasyr's heart caved at the sign of Marsh's, so clearly worn in the hopeful look in his eyes. He shouldn't feel this way, but he did. "You need to go there in the morning. To where the path begins. I'll meet you there."

"The morning? You make it sound like a quick trip into town. It will take me *days*. A week, longer. I have to cross Torrin's Pass to get there. That is, if I don't find myself lost. I'm not from here, and much more skilled men than me have gone missing in these lands."

"You have others like this? This map? Something that won't knock you over every few steps?"

"I don't need it. That is, it's in the Frozen Vale, which can only be accessed from Steward Frost's lands, and he... well... they say he's a bit of a shut-in."

"What, like he doesn't like people?"

"I don't know, he… I don't guess he'll be too eager to help us, is all."

Marsh's vulnerability was touching. Alasyr almost enjoyed it. Emberley was attracted to strength, not hesitation, or weakness.

"All right. All right. I'll leave in the morning. But now that you know there's a path, what's stopping you from taking her down herself, before I get there?"

Because, you weak, silly boy, for me she has only empty reassurances, but for you, she will reach so much deeper. "She's been unwell. We might need to carry her."

"But if she's sick, why would you want me to come alone? Why shouldn't I go back to the keep right now and demand a search party join me, with proper resources, proper Northerlanders who know these lands and how to navigate them? Who will know what to do if we run into problems?"

"I thought you were a smart boy, Wildwood. Ember says you are," Alasyr said, clucking his tongue. "If a company of men are spotted on the pass, it will draw the eyes of Midnight Crest. You want to save Ember? Then you'll help me by not letting those who killed her the first time do it a second."

JORAN RODE AHEAD. HE CLAIMED HE NEEDED SPACE FOR HIS thoughts, but Asherley sensed the truth in Wulfsgate and she sensed it now as they traveled south on the Compass Road, headed for home.

He was afraid of her.

He'd never say so. Asherley could threaten him with great suffering and he'd still never explicitly confess what had him rattled. Perhaps the old wizard could sense in her what she could now sense in herself; that her time in Midnight Crest had changed her in a deep, irreparable way. Her losses alone had made her someone else, but this was different. This was a change to her blood, her flesh, her heart, and bone. She had flown! Only once, and never again, but Asherley Blackwood had shifted that same blood, flesh, heart, and bone into the form of a raven, and had flown from the kingdom in the sky to the one on the ground.

Only Emberley would ever understand. And now she was being led away from her daughter, toward a problem that belonged to another lifetime, where Asherley was only a sly, highborn mistress of poisons with a sharp tongue and a long memory.

"Your son was angry at me for leaving. I directly disobeyed an order to come to you," Arturo said from her side. He spoke low, his deep voice cresting just above the hum of the wind. "I felt it only right to be the one to tell you this and accept what consequences may come from this act of defiance."

Such a mild confession it was, compared to the ones she might share if prompted. But it weighed heavily on his heart. "Not all orders are meant to be blindly followed, Blackfen. That's not what loyalty looks like."

"What does it look like for you, Lady Blackwood?"

"Knowing my heart, even when I do not. Even when I will not." Asherley realized she was talking about Byrne. Only now could she wholly appreciate what he'd meant to her and what his absence had taken from her.

"I don't yet know Brandyn's heart. Is that my failure, then?"

"Brandyn is too young to know his own heart. He wasn't ready for the mantle of leadership, and *that* is *my* failure."

"Not a failure, my lady. To allow it to continue, that would be..." Arturo trailed off.

"You can say it. It would be my failure. That's what you were going to say, was it not?"

"I was, but I should not have been so bold with you."

Asherley drew in a hard drink of cool air. She'd never felt so unfalteringly alive as she had in the sky kingdom of Midnight Crest, and yet so less a part of anything. She couldn't forget the world she'd come from. Not for the curiosity burning deep in her heart, nor the immortal love she bore for Emberley. She must reconnect with who she was, in flesh, and heart, and bone, and blood.

"What if I would like you to be bold with me, Blackfen?"

"My lady?"

"You enjoy the company of Grand Minister Tyndall. But do women ever find themselves in your bed?"

Arturo pointedly kept his face forward. "I... yes, from time to time. Travel can be a lonely business. I look for ways to make it less so."

"I understand loneliness. I'd like to be well rid of my own, even if for a night. Do you have aid to offer me in that regard? Now, I ask you not as the ruling lady of your Reach, but as a woman who hasn't lain with a man, a real man, since her husband, and that was another lifetime besides."

If Arturo had heard the rumors of her deeds with Eoghan, he was too good of a man to say so. "A real man, you say?"

"Are you not a real man, Arturo Blackfen? I hear there's something a Rush Rider and their horse have in common."

"Not always true."

"And for you?"

"Well. For me, it is."

Asherley was lightheaded with the soft rush of flirtation. She almost tried again to read his whispers, but it was more fun this way. How many years since she'd felt this? This exciting, delectable dance of man and woman, drawing closer to the one language they both spoke, always. "You'll show me tonight, then?"

Arturo grinned from the corner of his mouth. "With pleasure, my lady."

22

THE TRUTH OF MY HEART

"She likes you," Esmerelda said with a knowing nod. "See the way she reaches for your fingers?"

Jesse's smile widened in pure delight as he dangled his pinky just close enough for Gemmasyn to grab it. "I ken a baby doesnae know the difference between friend and foe."

"I ken she knows her own blood. And I haven't seen her this way with anyone else yet," Esmerelda replied. "Does she look like your Gemmasyn? I know she's still too little to tell, it's a silly question."

Jesse wiggled the knot of pinky and baby fingers as the infant giggled, squirming in her simple joy. "I donnae remember what she was like as a bairn. My mother stayed to the nursery in those days. I think she knew Gemma needed something more, even then. She didnae come out until Gemma was already walking."

"My mother nursed me," Esmerelda said. "But not my brothers. Father wouldn't let her. He said it would make them weak, too 'tied to the teat.'"

"And yet, you're the only one who ran from it," Jesse teased. Esmerelda pretended to be shocked and then laughed with him. His laugh always soothed her, in the same way achieving a challenging goal was immensely gratifying. She knew it was more real than the brooding he wore like a shield.

When the moment faded, Jesse's face hardened. "You said she knows her own blood. There's something I need to tell you, Esme, not because I have to, but because I want you to know."

"All right."

"But first, I need to know... would you have ever told *me* what happened to you in Duncarrow?"

Esmerelda wasn't expecting the question. "I... yes, eventually."

"Will it be a problem for you if I say I already know?"

Esmerelda paled. "Ravenna told you."

"She thought you'd want me to know. Is that true?"

She looked down at her hands, fanned out. Her mouth opened, but she didn't speak right away. "You're the only other one in this kingdom that I ever want knowing about it." She looked up. "The only one I ever want knowing any of my secrets, because you're the only one I trust with them."

"Aye," Jesse said. "And to that, I have one of my own that I want you to know, and all I can hope is that it doesnae change matters between us."

Esmerelda accepted Gemmasyn into her arms when Jesse passed her back. "You can tell me anything, you know that. I'd never tell another."

"It isn't who ye might tell. It's what ye might think of me."

"Your salt and strong is stronger just now. You *are* nervous," she said with a light laugh. Her smile shifted to a more solemn one. "As for changing things between us, Jesse, we're well beyond that now, you and I. The hard stuff has only brought us closer, hasn't it?"

Jesse pushed to his feet and moved to the other side of the nursery, putting distance between them for reasons he didn't understand. He leaned against the windowsill, watching the relentless rain that had been falling for days now. Solid ground had caved to muddy slush. Not even the keep had escaped flooding. "You met Oldwin in Duncarrow. I met two others like him."

"Sorcerers!" Esmerelda was breathless. "That's what you mean?"

Jesse nodded.

She took a moment to drink in the information. "It couldn't be Mortain," she said. "He was in Whitechurch, and he died there, at Drystan's hand. You're saying there are others?"

"There are others. Others who aren't like Oldwin or Mortain. But they come from the same place. They began their journey with the same aims. Somewhere along the way, they chose a different path. I donnae know why. They had no cause to explain themselves to me."

"How in the Guardians did you meet two sorcerers? That doesn't just *happen*, does it? Until I saw Oldwin with my own eyes, I didn't even believe they existed, and now you're saying you just happened upon two more?"

"I didnae just happen upon them," Jesse explained. "They were *looking* for me. And they found me at the worst time. They kept me from coming for you. I had no defense against their magic. I'm sorry, Esme, for failing you when it mattered most."

"Nonsense," Esmerelda countered. "The Guardians always have their own ideas. Nothing to be done about that. And you're here now, right? You came back. You came back to me, long after you needed to."

"Did you really do it?" Jesse dropped his voice low. "Did you really kill the king?"

Esmerelda laughed. The sound was shrill and unnatural. The darkness in her eyes betrayed her. "You sound as if we're speaking of a game we'd play as bairns. Kill the king! He was going to force me into marriage, and I'd already let myself die once to keep out of his hands. I'll never let any man take my power from me again. Never. But I didn't kill him for myself, Jesse. I did it for Gemma. They were going to throw her into the sea when she was born. I had no choice."

"I wish I could've done it for you."

Esmerelda looked away. She bounced Gemmasyn against her chest. "I don't. Now that I know how thin the thread between life and death is, I'll never fear another man again."

"You've changed," Jesse said.

"Is that a problem for you?"

"Not at all," he answered, half-smiling. "Though I've changed, too. The sorcerers saw to that."

"I've noticed the changes in you. I won't lie to you. I *have* felt slighted since you returned, keeping your secrets to yourself. Though I've been no better, have I?"

"We're righting that wrong now, aren't we?" Jesse leaned back against the window and met her eyes. "You said Gemma recognizes our shared blood. She and I do share blood, through my mother. But Hamish isnae my father, Esme. He and I aren't bound by blood, only honor and love, and he knows this, has known this all my life, even if he doesnae know who my real father is."

"But..." Esmerelda stopped bouncing Gemma. "Ryan looks just like Steward Strong."

"Ryan is his son. I'm not."

"I have so many questions," she said, breathless. "I don't know where I should start with them."

"I have them, too, but I'll tell you what I know. My mother, Yanna, was already far along with me when she met Hamish. She'd been expelled from her homeland by her sister, for having relations with a man. Hamish knew she was in a bad way, and he didnae hesitate to sweep her away, and when the time came, to raise me as his own. He didnae know then, and he doesnae know now, the name of the man who got her in her that way." Jesse hesitated. She might believe him. He feared she would not. But he couldn't ask what he'd come to ask with any lies between them. "Do you recall the story of how Dain Rhiagain died?"

Esmerelda nodded. "Of course. Everyone knows the story."

Jesse told her, then, about the prophecy and the betrayal. Of the sorcerer, Isdemus, slipping into the queen's bed. Of the Lord Chancellor's failure to carry out the terrible deed, leaving Dain to be raised by the Sylvaines. "They never knew where their son had come from. They were desperate for a child and never questioned it. And Dain, who grew from boyhood into maturity as Drystan Sylvaine, never knew, either. He might not know now. He may have known nothing at all when he spent those nights with my mother in the Hinterlands."

"But that would mean..." Esmerelda had stopped moving altogether. "That would mean..."

"That I am part sorcerer, part Medvedev, and part Rhiagain."

"No! How can that be? We would've known, wouldn't we? You haven't even come into your magic as a Medvedev, but now you add sorcerer to your blood, and there's been not a sign? Not a one?"

"Not until Greystone."

"What do you mean?"

"That's when the strangeness began. Things I knew I couldnae do began to happen around me, and, even knowing it's magic, I still donnae know a thing about it. But it's there, and I feel more and more of it every day. I can see things I have no business seeing. I can feel things I couldnae before. And though I wish I could put it back where it came from, Esmerelda, that isnae the way this world works, is it? We get what we're given. We do with it what we can."

"Why... why would they tell you this? Why come for you?" Esmerelda settled Gemmasyn into her bassinet and began pacing the room. "Why?"

Jesse went to her. He stood before her to ease her agitation. "They need something from me. Something they've waited my whole life for."

"They want to use you," she whispered, looking up into his eyes. "And you... you intend to let them."

Jesse rested his hands on the outer edges of her shoulders. He patted the soft satin of her dress, then let his touch fall away. "I traded my promise for your location. I had to be certain you were safe."

"Jesse!"

"Esme, it's fine." He tried to smile. He wanted to; it felt right. But as he saw her heart break in the soft flush of her cheeks, in the panic ringing her eyes, he wondered now if any of this was right at all. "It's all right."

"That's why you're leaving?"

"I'll return as soon as I can."

"If they let you return. If they let you do anything that doesn't serve them." Esmerelda exhaled, sinking down into the chaise. "You say these sorcerers are different. But I've seen evil with my own eyes. They're the same, but somehow they're good, and kind, and benevolent? How can you know?"

Jesse looked down at her. "I have no answer for it. I've felt now, for some time, that something wasnae right about me. This awakening of magic, it may've begun in Greystone, but there's always been something there, Esme. Something that kept me from ever feeling as connected to this world as I wanted to be. I thought it was because of who my mother was, but I've never come into her magic at all, have I? None of it made a bit of sense, until they showed me who I was."

Esmerelda seemed to hold back tears. "And now it all makes sense, does it?"

Jesse knelt down before her. "Will you come with me?"

GWYN PRESSED HERSELF FLAT AGAINST THE STONE WALL. HER BREATHS came fast and hard. Her chest caved in, and then arced outward, as she struggled to control her panic. She'd never known such pain. Not when she believed Esmerelda to be lost to the Guardians, nor even when Ransom was taken away in chains. For these things, as terrible as they were, as unbearable as they were, had been beyond her power to control. She'd not made peace with these losses, but she had accepted them as part of the chaos of life, and the unknown path that awaited them all. Any of their promises could be spent at any moment. There was simply no defense against it, and the only path to survival in this world was to embrace what you were given and ask for no more.

But this... this was a choice. A choice she'd been offered, and then made. Not once, but continuously, and as she watched

Esmerelda step tentatively into the sand, hand in Jesse's, Gwyn knew she'd make the choice a thousand times over.

"Mother?"

Gwyn willed her eyes open, blinking through the darkness spreading across her vision. She inhaled once more and then, turning, slowly released the breath, turning it into a smile. "Ransom, darling. Everything all right?"

"It's you who looks like you've seen a ghost."

"Me?" Gwyn laughed. She hoped he didn't hear it the way she did. "Oh, no. Just watching your sister. She might at last have her chance at happiness, if she's willing to take it."

"What does that mean?"

"I've been sworn to secrecy by your father. You'll know soon enough."

Ransom looked at her like she was mad. "I'm on my way to the Hall of Warring. Father has finally decided it's time."

Gwyn choked back the tears. They weren't for Ransom. For once they were for herself. "I agree with your father. It's time."

"I hear he's found a wife for me. Do you know anything about that?"

Gwyn did not. "Where have you heard that?"

Ransom shrugged. "You know how whispers are."

"Well, I suppose it's time for that, too, isn't it? You're a man in the ways that matter."

"Has there been word from Wulfsgate about Pieter?" Ransom looked like a boy again when he asked this.

"I'm afraid not. Neither Pieter nor Gretchen have returned."

"Are you sure you're all right, Mother?"

"Perfectly so. Only lost to my thoughts."

"Women," he said with a sly grin and sauntered down the hall, toward the future that had always been his. She would've done all this for him, too, but fate had brought him home on other terms.

Gwyn pretended to laugh. But when he was gone, she doubled over, dropping to her knees.

When would it end?

When would it be enough?
When?

"YOU BROUGHT ME ALL THE WAY TO THE COVE TO TALK?" ESMERELDA lifted her dress as the tide moved in. The warm water splashed over her ankles, sending streams of sand between her toes. How she'd marveled over this sensation as a girl. She'd loved the sea, the sand. Played as hard as her brothers, and twice as long.

Jesse hung behind, close enough that she felt the heat of his breath on the back of her neck. It was a small thing, but a reminder that she was alive, here. After giving up a life for love that didn't endure, she would never again take it for granted.

"This is the best place in all the Southerlands to be at sunset. I donnae care what they say about Whitecliffe. It's here, in the hidden shadow of the rocks and sea and sand," Esmerelda mused. She kicked at the wet sand, enjoying the satisfying *sploosh* as she first dug her toes into it and then pulled them out.

"Your Southerland speech still comes and goes, I see."

"With my moods."

"You have your share of them."

Esmerelda turned to laugh, but the look on his face stilled her. "What is it?"

"I don't quite know how to ask what I mean to ask ye."

"Ask me?"

"So, I'm gonna just do it, and hope if ye turn me down, then you'll do it without taking offense to the question."

"You're worrying me."

"I've come to ask ye to be my wife."

Esmerelda cawed out a sharp laugh. "Are ye being clever?"

"Esmerelda, I mean it." Jesse stepped closer. He looked down at her hands and she thought he'd take them in his, but he instead shoved them into his trousers. "I'm asking ye to marry me."

"You want *me* to be your wife?"

He nodded.

Esmerelda took several steps back. Her laughter died. "You ask me this, why? From pity? From duty?"

"I'm not Ryan." Jesse shook his head. He winced as he waged an internal battle. "I'd give anything to see him returned to himself, and to you and Gemma, but that isnae the world we live in, is it? One where we can turn gold into wishes?"

"You're not Ryan," she agreed. Her heart sputtered against the back of her chest. It caught in her throat. "So why are you here, offering what he once did? Because you feel sorry for me? Because you feel... what? What do you feel as you ask me this?" Esmerelda trapped a scream in her throat as the first of her tears made their way to the surface. "I can bear this pity from anyone else, Jesse, but not you!"

"I swear to you, that isnae why I'm here."

"Then tell me why!"

Jesse stepped forward. His head was bowed low, too low to see his eyes. His mouth parted as he took her hands in his. "Do ye trust me?"

"You ask me this now..." she said. "I don't know what to think. I don't know what this is. Why you're here, doing the only thing that could ruin things between us."

"I promise you. I promise you, Esme. I wouldnae ever do that to you. Never would I do anything to cause ye pain, not intentionally."

Esmerelda's eyes fell to their joined hands. It was a touch that had once felt familial and now... now she didn't know what she was feeling, only that her heart was rising and falling all at once, creating a confused mess of unanswered questions and lingering but unspoken words. "There are thousands of women in this Reach you could choose to warm your bed and keep your heart. You could have your pick of them. If not pity, then you'll tell me why you're asking for it to be *me*."

Jesse's breath hitched. "I *should* have been wed by now. I have my own life, places I look forward to returning to after I've done a proper run. They say I return to a place empty and cold, but that isnae how it's ever been for me. I've always had all I need. All I thought I'd ever need. Aye, my father and Andrija introduced some lasses to me, and they were fair enough. Some even made me laugh, and a couple even warmed my bed for a while, as ye say. But the thought of coming home to any of them, day after day? *That* left me empty and cold. Ryan, he had a new lass every fortnight, and it exhausted me to watch him. He would've done his duty and settled down with one, but it wouldnae have stopped him from carrying on. And I never... never would have believed him capable of what he made with you, had I not seen it with my own eyes. I didnae understand it myself at all. Which is why I cannae understand how what he felt for ye could be swept aside, lost memory or no."

Tears streamed down Esmerelda's cheeks. She tightened her hands in his, afraid to say even a word that might break his confession.

"If I thought he might come back to ye—"

"I'm not his anymore. I'm not *anyone's* anymore."

"I see that. I see who you've become. I was there for it. I suppose what I mean to say, Esme, is that he loved ye for who ye were, and I..."

Esmerelda angled her head up, imploring him. She held the gaze, drawing him to a place that was safe to speak. "Is it so hard to tell me how you feel?"

Jesse swallowed. "Aye, but not for the reason you think."

"If you want me to believe this offer is anything other than pity for a woman you care for as a sister, then you have to speak true to me, Jesse. For both of us."

Tears tickled the front of his eyes. She wanted to reach forth and wipe them away, but she would need to break their touch, and though she didn't fully understand what was happening, there was nowhere else she wanted to be more.

"I couldnae understand the attraction between you two," Jesse went on. "I still... I still donnae, not really. But now, it's 'cause I *see* you, and I *know* you. I know ye like my own kin, and you're not made for sneaking about, or illicit nights. You aren't some man's beautiful prize. Not a husband's. Not a father's. You're my equal, and I couldnae ever see it another way. For though I'd once loved ye as a sister, after all we've endured, together..." Jesse closed his eyes briefly before reopening them, looking straight into hers. "It's not nearly so simple now."

Esmerelda's hopeful heart dropped. He was as afraid of the words as she was. Pride buoyed her head high. "And what if to me you're still just a brother?"

Jesse squeezed her hands. A few quick beats that said more than anything he'd spoken. "Would it be so terrible to be wed to a man who's already kin to ye? Who'd care for your daughter as his own? Who's already sworn to give his life to see you safe and happy?"

"There are worse things," she whispered.

"There are worse things," Jesse agreed.

"Never in a thousand years would I have ever seen us standing here, you asking me this. Ravenna would say she saw it all along. She accused me of having untoward thoughts about you."

"She said something like that to me, too."

"What you said before, about Ryan, and all the other lasses. I remember it that way, too. It was part of the excitement of loving Ryan Strong, I suppose. Knowing how it all might end. No matter how he loved me, I knew better than to think I was so different from any of the others. Months, it might have taken. Years, if we were fortunate. But eventually I wouldn't have been enough for him anymore. As a woman, we accept this is our lot. That we must be satisfied with the life we're given, while our husbands will spend their best years searching for their own joy anywhere but home."

"He would've done his best by you."

"But would it have been enough? I'll never know."

"*You* are enough," Jesse whispered. "For any man who knows what he has, you're enough."

"Who is this changeling standing before me, and what have you done with Jesse Strong?"

Jesse twisted the corner of his mouth into a smile. "I've been wondering myself."

Esmerelda sniffled as she laughed. "What will my father say when he discovers I've traded one Strong man for the other?"

"Lord Warwick already knows my intentions," Jesse said, flushing. "I asked his permission, or I'd not be standing here before ye now."

"You went to my father first?"

"It was the right thing, Esme. I'll nay have any more midnight flights in your future. You deserve better."

Esmerelda sighed. Her breath shuddered with the last of the trapped emotions leaving her. The moment had passed, and she was as relieved as she was sad about it. "I suppose there's *some* sense in doing things proper. Not that I'm the best person to speak on the merits of *that*."

Jesse laughed. "Aye, proper can be good sometimes."

"He's pushing for a quick wedding. He's eager to be rid of the problem of his unwed daughter. We'll have it here in Warwicktown, if we can find a place that hasn't been taken by the flooding."

"Is that a yes, then?"

"I'm already plotting the food and drink we'll serve, so what do you think?"

She thought he would kiss her then. She could almost feel the urgent press of his soft lips, that gentle arch of his mouth forming a defense against the world as it connected with her own.

But he didn't.

Jesse only watched her as he held fast to her hands.

"Everything I am is yours now," he said. "Yours and Gemma's."

KHALLUM STARED IN HELPLESS DEFEAT AT THE TOMES LINING THE jagged table in the Hall of Warring. Rutland, Hamish, and Darrick each regarded the new arrivals with the same befuddled scrutiny. He'd known the books would be long and full of detail, but hadn't considered they might be massive enough to make suitable weapons when ordering them from Oldcastle. The one from the Northerlands was so enormous it had to be carried in by two men.

"Where's Law?" Hamish asked. "He should share in this suffering."

"On his way from Goldthorpe," Rutland answered. "He wouldnae want us to wait."

"Right," Darrick said. He clapped his hands together. "Anabella has given us our first proper direction, and Wyat has sent us the books we requested. Let's not waste a moment." The other murmured unenthusiastic agreement. "We have more reason to believe Dain was sent into the kingdom to be raised in anonymity than we do that he died as a boy. Eoghan wouldn't have gone to such trouble to find our brother otherwise." He pointed to the four books. "He's in here somewhere. In some lineage, in some town, there'll be a young boy, adopted by a childless couple, around four decades ago."

Khallum nodded as he listened. It was a solid plan. It was their *only* plan. He struggled in silence with his great uncle's words, his revelation of some obscure past that elevated the Warwicks to heroes of the realm. As he'd watched Odrahn Warwick's body turn from flesh to flame, and finally, to ash, before sending his remains to the sea, Khallum wished he'd not waited until the man was dying to palaver with him. All the questions he had would never be answered. Odrahn had been the last of them.

Even if there was a veil—and an ancestry of Warwick Defenders —what use was knowing any of it without knowing all of it?

Darrick believed. He'd heard the word before: Defender. He'd watched his father and grandfather do nothing with the minerals mined from the land that had been stolen, supposedly, for its riches. He was certain this confession from Odrahn, and Anabella's remembrances of Eoghan's obsession with Dain, had been revealed in tandem for a reason. He seemed unwilling to consider any other explanation.

Oldwin wants this veil, Khallum. He needs this veil. He's desperate to find it, enough that he was killing everyone in the camps to make way for the discovery. We have to find it first.

But even if they found Dain, they wouldn't know what to do with him—or the veil.

"Well? Get started then!" Khallum barked when the men hesitated in shared contemplation. He detected their annoyance and the source. This was a task for lesser men. But lesser men were conspiring with their enemy. Lesser men were responsible for what happened in Goldthorpe to Steward Nye's family.

When they did no more than flip the leather covers over, with all the daintiness of women, Khallum dropped into his own seat and pulled the closest tome to him with overstated flourish. *The Book of the Westerlands' Ancestry.* Hamish was next, sliding the Northerlands records closer. Rutland settled on the Easterlands, and Darrick took the Southerlands. When Ransom arrived, he slid in next to Hamish and jumped right into the task.

It would be a long night. It might lead to nothing at all.

They were nigh an hour into their reading when Ryan Strong burst through the door. His flushed face and panicked eyes drove all men to their feet.

"Lord Warwick. Your Grace." He rushed the formalities. "You need to come quickly."

Khallum pushed to his feet. "Is it Esmerelda?"

Ryan shook his head. He dropped it to gather breath before looking up again. "A horse just arrived in town. There was a man... a man lying over its back. Murdered." Ryan pressed one hand to his neck, breathing in. "It's Steward Law, my lord. They've killed him."

All the air inside Khallum rushed outward. He reached for his chair, but it wasn't enough. Both palms fell into the jagged edge of the table, and he let the cut do its worst, pressing his immediate grief into the pain. The scream lodged in his throat transferred downward, radiating out through his toes.

Rutland had fallen back into his chair. He buried his face in his hands.

Hamish was the first to break through the pained silence when he released a deep, guttural wail into the air. The sound ricocheted between the men as they each felt the knife enter their chests. It had always been the four of them. From boyhood. Everything since.

Ryan, rattled, dropped his eyes between them, searching for direction.

It was Darrick who had the words they needed. "Find Lady Warwick and all her children. They're not to leave the keep. Ransom, you go with Ryan to help gather your kin. Oldwin has now taken everything but Lord Warwick's own blood, and you can be assured that'll be next, if we let him. Rutland. Hamish. I'd advise you to bring your own families here to Warwicktown, bring all the guards here and fortify the city. Stone and wood can be replaced, flesh and blood cannot."

"We'll go together," Rutland said to Hamish. "Whitecliffe, and then return through Sandycove. Aye?"

"Aye," Hamish said. He blew his nose on his sleeve. "Aye."

"Lady Warwick already knows. She was the first to get the news," Ryan said. "She has all but Esmerelda in the keep now. She's sent some men to bring her back."

"Where's my daughter?" Khallum boomed. "Find her!"

"I'll find her, sir," Ryan said, but Hamish stopped him.

"She's with Jesse. Doing what we agreed, my lord. He took her to the cove, I ken."

"With Jesse?" Ryan repeated. "Why would she be with Jesse?"

"Donnae ask why, boy, just go!"

"Lady Esmerelda!"

Jesse released Esmerelda's hand. They stopped in the sand as Ryan ran toward them, wearing a look that chilled Jesse's heart.

"What's happened?" Jesse asked, but Ryan looked past him.

Ryan reached for Esmerelda's arm. She ripped it back before he could take hold. He seemed surprised; even wounded. "Your father needs you in the keep. Now."

Esmerelda wrapped her arms over her chest. "Why?"

Ryan briefly glanced at Jesse. With it, a flash of anger.

"He believes your life is in danger. He wants all of ye under his watch."

Esmerelda's nostrils flared as she squared herself. "You'll tell me why, or I'll go nowhere with you."

"It's best ye donnae know, my lady."

"Just say it, Ryan," Jesse pushed. "She's not a child."

Ryan screwed his mouth into a scowl. Jesse could see it hid something else. "It's Steward Law. He's been..." Ryan lowered his voice. "Murdered."

Esmerelda gasped. "No! By whom?"

"Same monster who's been burning the Southerlands, stone by stone, I ken," Ryan said. "The creature is done warning us. Next time, it'll be a Warwick." He looked at Esmerelda. "That enough cause for ye to pay mind to yer father, for once?"

"My father... this will crush him. Law was as a brother to him."

"Come on, Esme, let's go," Jesse urged. He placed a hand behind her back. The first whispers of shock stung the backs of his eyes, under his skin, the weight of the loss of Samuel Law settling in. Law had mentored him; been a true friend to the Strongs. He stretched his jaw, widening his eyes, pushing it all back and down. There'd be a time for grieving once she was safe.

"*I'll* take her to Lady Warwick," Ryan insisted. "You're wanted in the Hall of Warring."

Esmerelda threw Jesse a helpless look over her shoulder as Ryan practically dragged her up the sand.

"I'll come find you!" he yelled after her.

Ryan was right. Law was the final warning. And though everything ahead for him was shrouded in the unclear promise of darkness, he knew, in the way he knew many things now that were not available to him before, that the task ahead of him was connected to all of this.

With every breath, Jesse was pulled away from the life he wanted, and closer to the one Isdemus and Lysanor had created him for.

23
MOTHER

Kael found his peace in the arrival of sunset. The first promise of amber, giving way to the red and ochres of the world beyond theirs, before settling once more into the hazy dark of night. It was a reliable reminder that he was bound to the same world as men. The same hours. The same lifespan. The same fate.

It shouldn't be this way.

Once, long ago, it wasn't.

He shouldn't know this. He wasn't a Keeper, like Kian, or Fasten, the young Medvedev Yseult chose to take Kian's place while he was tending to the business of the Saleen. Fasten didn't have the blood of Yseult running through her. She was lithe and fast of body, but lacked in wit and curiosity. *The role of the Keeper is to be incurious,* Yseult said when Kael confronted her about passing him over. *It should have been me, Mother.* There was no apology in her tired eyes when she answered, *it was never going to be you.*

Kael was well acquainted with anger, but not this white hot rage burning him from the inside out. He had more questions. Demands to make. Answers owed him. But when Yseult de Medvedev was finished speaking, she was finished.

She was weak, and not just from the business of the Saleen dying, but yes, that, too, for her suffering had been a *choice*. The Saleen's plight was not their own. Had Yseult been as foolish as Ohsmha, led from her lands by a mere man, she would've deserved the same fate. The utter absence of aid or even word from the Mayke and Asgill clahnns all but sealed this truth.

Yseult was weak for being incurious. Kael wasn't alone in this thinking. Many of the Drumain, once they learned more about the Keepers and the Light and all the things kept from them, would feel this way, and they'd support him. Once they understood the things he did, they would follow him.

Kael liked how this made him feel. To be chosen. Wanted. The one. All this time he'd been reaching too low, seeking his mother's attention, when he could have had so much more.

The sunset ended. Night arrived.

Kael started down a path long overgrown. Brambled bushes of berries bearing thorns greeted him, tearing small threats into his flesh. He rather liked the feeling. To bleed, knowing that to do enough of that would lead to an end he couldn't prevent. The death of man. It spurred him forward, reminding him. There were two Kaels sometimes, like now, when he could be both satisfied in the way of things and also utterly embittered. That first, Kael only fought for comfort. He would have to die. Kael had already started the ritual of the slow death of the one who wouldn't do what was needed.

He'd known about the Light before Kian departed. It was fortunate it happened before Yseult commanded he go heal Yanna's boy in the Southerlands, a task so far beneath him that it drew his exclusion from the cabal of Keepers into a finer, darker relief. He'd done what she asked—in his way. For his reasons, which had been shaped by what he learned watching the training of Fasten.

Kael licked fresh blood from his lips. It tasted of mortality. He relished the coppery tinge as it rolled down the back of his tongue.

The deeper he went down the path, the more dense brush

assaulted him. He drew the blade from his boot to fend some off, but it had as much usefulness as engaging a pail to drain the sea.

This was the path he must take. The only one that would lead him where he needed to go.

He peeled back his hood. And why not? His face was one of their own. Not that any here would know his true face. None except Esmerelda, but she was tucked safely away in her father's protection now. Needless, for though Oldwin's word to others was ever in doubt, his word to himself was not. He'd paid for his needs with Esmerelda's safety. He still had needs to purchase.

That he must purchase them at all was maddening. A hundred years ago... even *ten* years ago, Oldwin of Ilynglass wouldn't have needed a single other soul to meet his aims.

There was less truth in this than he liked. The magic of the doors had always been elusive. Nearly a thousand years it had taken to find the one to bring him here, to the White Kingdom. He'd only been at the task of uncovering the one in the Southerlands for just over a century.

He didn't have a thousand more years to search. He might not have ten. He might not have one.

Oldwin was dying. His magic waning was at first subtle, and now so rapid in its deterioration that he wasn't certain the tricks he'd employed to cross the sea to get to the sands of Warwicktown would get him back to Duncarrow.

Oldwin moved through Warwicktown with the measured pace of a shopkeeper. No one questioned him or looked twice to confirm recognition. They were in the chaos of grief, and this chaos was a selfish kind. Every man for themselves was the theme of the evening, as buildings were boarded and swords sharpened. What would they think if they knew the architect of their fear was passing by them in the night, enjoying the spoils of his handiwork?

He wasn't *really* enjoying them, though. The business of dying distracted him.

He ducked inside the stables and waited. It wouldn't be long. Their minds were linked now; or, more truly, he had access to theirs. Forever, if he liked, but forever meant something different to him than it did to men. It still could—would—once he found the way to the Light.

Oldwin tapped his hand into an impatient song against the hay as he waited.

KAEL FLEW BACK, GASPING. YSEULT'S EYES FLASHED OPEN, BUT SHE didn't jerk forward, as she should have. She didn't call for aid.

He gaped down at his hands. Had he... had he? Had he put them at his own mother's throat with intention?

He had.

But this shock, this regret, wasn't what it should have been. It wasn't an indictment of the horrors living within him, but at his failure to fully embrace them.

"I know why you're here," she said. Still, she didn't move. Didn't sit. She merely rolled her head to the side, eyes blinking slowly. "I've been waiting for you."

"As man. You speak such. You would. You would. Become."

"And what are men, Kael, but creations of the Light, just as we are. A Light you think you understand, but how could you?"

"I do. Understand."

Yseult's smile wasn't warm. "You heard what I allowed you to hear. You think I did not know you were there, as I delivered my training to Fasten? That I did not choose my words for you? That I did not know they would, one day, lead you here?"

Simmering rage peppered dark red blotches into his cheeks. He knew it was there. He hated her for bringing him to this. "Your fault."

Yseult laughed. "I suppose it is my fault, isn't it? I delivered you into this world. I created you. I could have drowned your life in the river, but a mother's love makes her foolish and blind. You have seen your future. I have seen it, too. But the one behind your eyes is clouded by your desires. Remember that, when I am gone, and you have no one to help you understand."

Yseult closed her eyes and lay back. "Go on, Kael. We all have infinite paths available to us in this life, but you have already chosen yours. There is one last door you must close before you can step forward. You already know what you came to do. You knew before you took the way closed to you."

Kael's hands trembled as if alive for the first time. He didn't want her permission. Her kindness. Her understanding. It was wrong, all of it!

"Why?" he asked.

"Oh, but there are so many ways to answer this, and the door is closing."

"Why?" he demanded.

"Soon, it will be too late. Your fear won't serve you. It stifles you."

"WHY?" Kael cried, sobbing without tears.

"You will never be a Keeper," Yseult hissed. "It is for creatures like you that the Keepers exist. You are an abomination, and I will fight to my last breath to stop you if you leave this place without finishing what you started."

Kael launched himself forward. He flung himself over her, pinning both sides of her neck with the hard curve between his forefinger and thumb. He grunted into the tightening, a sound that escalated into a scream as he came to realize how difficult this actually was. How long it took to steal the life away, even from one who lay in perfect acceptance of the crime.

Yseult's eyes slowly widened. Red spindles crept into the whites, and at last her irises flexed, released, and then she was gone.

Kael tried to climb off her, but he tripped and fell to the ground, to his knees.

"Mother," he panted.

. . .

LIGHT STEPS SOUNDED IN THE MUD BEYOND THE DOORS. THEY stopped. The hesitation annoyed him. Had he not given them the one thing they wished for in all the world? What he asked in return was nothing by comparison.

Khallum Warwick wouldn't see it this way, but Samuel Law had been a gift. A gift in the form of replacement.

The doors opened. Moonlight spilled in. The hooded figure entered slowly, but was quick to shut them in, away from prying eyes.

"You look different."

Oldwin laughed. "You'll never see me the same way twice. Nor will you ever look upon me as I am."

"I don't care what you look like. I don't care about your trickeries, or deceptions. This has to end."

"I say when it ends." Oldwin rose. "Or it ends as it should have begun."

"You've taken enough. Find someone else. It cannot be me!"

Oldwin stepped closer. He lifted his finger, and, with his nail, tilted her head back. "I say when it ends, Lady Warwick. Was that not clear, when I delivered your daughter in place of a second death? When I spared her life and sent her home to you? Unless there is a price greater than her life?"

"You promised," Gwyn whimpered. Tears of weakness streamed down her red cheeks.

"I promised nothing that I have not given you."

"I don't understand. I don't understand what you want from us! Why have you chosen my husband, my Reach, to torture? What do you *want* from us?"

"Your husband has something I need. He has kept it from me. So I will take, and I will take, and I will take, until he is ready to offer it to me."

"What? What does he have?" Gwyn sobbed. "Whatever it is, he'll give it to you! He wants this to stop. We all want this to stop."

"He knows what it is," Oldwin answered.

"I'll tell him, then! I'll tell him he has something—"

"That wouldn't be very wise of you, Lady Warwick. Not unless you want your husband to know it was you who delivered the Southerlands to me, not once, nor even twice, but over and over and over."

Gwyn held her head proudly. Her lower lip curved inward. "If he knew this was why Esmerelda was home, he would understand."

"Even you don't sound convinced of your words."

"Then tell me what to do!"

Oldwin grinned. "With pleasure."

DEATH HAS
OFFERED ME LIFE

24

THE FIVE SACRED VOWS

Ryan followed Esmerelda. She went into the room she and the other women had spent the better part of the morning getting ready in. The ceremony was set to begin soon, once the sun hit the center of the sky. She'd probably forgotten something, or else she'd already be up the hill where hundreds of Southerlanders were crowded into the large tents, waiting for the two brides to appear.

Why was he doing this? Continuously seeking her out? What must lay dormant within him to even want to do this? This was his constant battle. The war he waged with who he was, and who he was expected to be. Only one of these men was familiar to him, but the other was the only one familiar to those who knew him.

He'd employed healers and doctors alike. Even that sorcerer still lingering, the one they all pretended wasn't a Ravenwood. In a moment of desperation, he'd once run his head into a stone wall to jar loose whatever was stuck, but all that had earned him was a week of dizzy spells and one monster of a headache.

Ryan forced himself to see Esmerelda through different eyes than the stubborn ones insisting on an outdated truth. This was as much physical as a mental thing, squinting when she was in his sights, blurring his vision; he pretended the words she said were charming, even funny. He recited in his mind his love for her, over and over, on the chance he might wake one day and be capable of attaching feeling to word. She'd always been pretty, but that didn't make her special. Still, he told himself that she was the most beautiful in the realm, a prize unlike any other. Over and over and over.

He'd tried all these things in the hope he might eventually unravel himself, so that he could again be a man of honor. A man who fulfilled his commitments. A man who could look upon his own daughter and remember what must have happened in order for her to exist. Who others could meet in halls without dropping their eyes in disdain.

But that wasn't possible, was it? That wasn't possible because the man he was now had never loved her, had never seen her beyond the spoiled highborn who would've never given him more than a passing glance.

Still, Ryan followed her, not exactly knowing why, willing one foot before the other.

Esmerelda closed the door behind her. His hand caught it before it latched, and she turned back in surprise, her eyes first widening in disbelief, and then narrowing into deep, angry slits.

"What are you doing?" she demanded. "The room for the men is at the other end of the hall, as you well know."

"No, I... I wasnae looking for the men. I came to see you. To see how you are."

"You came to see how I am?" Esmerelda said. "I'm fine. I'm getting married today, and I've never been better."

"If you say so."

"If I say so?" Esmerelda said the words slowly, underscoring them with a rage that had developed in the handful of moments since he'd blocked the door. "I'm already nervous enough without you coming in here, looking like you need reassurances. If you've something to say to me, it can wait. Or, perhaps you could instead just never say it at all. That might be better."

Ryan moved farther into the room, deepening his terrible judgment. She didn't want him here. He didn't want to be here.

She looked beautiful. He didn't even need to take himself through his recitations to convince himself this time. One of the women had wound her silken raven hair around branches and petals of some white flower he didn't know the name of. He could fashion a hundred different knots, but the designs women employed to make themselves beautiful were a mystery to him. And her dress, a long white gown made of silk and lace, dropping down through her bosom into a sharp cut, left his stomach full of butterflies when he let his gaze linger overlong. Someone had painted some rouge into her cheeks, atop her eyes and mouth, and she was like a dream.

Ryan realized she'd done this for Jesse. Was that why he was here, he wondered. For Jesse?

"Esmerelda, I know you're doing this because ye have no choice. 'Tis my fault. My failure has brought you to this day, and I ken I want ye to know how sorry I am. And that I'll do whatever ye need for me to make this right."

The look Esmerelda gave him wasn't the stubborn-eyed petulance of the willful child who'd turned her nose at him as a girl. It was the cold regard of a woman.

"Today is my choice. Not yours. This isn't some unfortunate situation I find myself in for a lack of options. I chose this."

"Aye, but," Ryan said, "it's nay a choice you would've made, if not for me."

Esmerelda dropped her hands to the white lace hugging her hips. "And what would you know about me, about my choices? Nothing, right? For was that not the problem, that you don't know me at all? You cannot see me for the person I've become, so do you linger upon this matter, still, now, when I've freed you of your obligation? Don't you understand, Ryan? You're free!" She made an ushering gesture with her hands, like he was a bird being pushed from the nest.

"I'm sorry." Ryan chanced a closer step. "I wish I could turn time around and become the person you want me to be, or, if it helped ye more, to take it all back, so that you're no longer hurting."

Esmerelda's brief hesitation made her subsequent laugh cut even deeper. "You think I'm heartsick for you?"

"I ken that's how ye looked when we reunited in Sandycove, aye."

"That's really how you see me now? That you've made such an impact on my life that I couldn't *ever* possibly recover and find happiness elsewhere?"

Ryan hadn't expected this. He hadn't seen this cruelty in her; this unkindness. And yet, as soon as these thoughts formed, he understood how unfair they were. He deserved these words from her, and she deserved her happiness.

But with Jesse?

"I only want to be sure you've chosen the right man, Esmerelda."

She again laughed at him. "That you believe you have any place in this matter at all is quite astounding."

"Equally befuddling to me, and yet I couldnae keep myself away."

"What could possibly be your intention in coming here to me now, on the day of my wedding? Is it your fear that you know the truth lives in you, still, and one day you'll wake and have to face it? You know you don't love me. So tell me why!"

Ryan thought about this. He toiled over his confusion ever since he'd learned of Jesse's offer to Esmerelda. And though it should be Jesse he was asking, all he could find for his brother was icy silence. Was she right? Had he stored their truth in some dark place that would elude him until he was well past the point of making things right again? Was he afraid that Jesse would wed her, and only then he'd remember?

"I donnae know," he said.

"You donnae know?" she repeated. "You donnae *know*?"

"No, I donnae know why I'm here. I donnae know why I keep finding myself back in front of you, trying to save ye, trying to save..." he let his words trail off.

"I don't need you to save me," Esmerelda said. "I don't need you to love me. There's only one future for us now. As kin." She reached down and plucked a woven floral bracelet off the table, slipping it over her wrist. "I won't be late for my own wedding." Esmerelda pushed past him, but he grabbed her by the arm.

"Why Jesse?"

Esmerelda regarded him with a disgusted look.

"Why Jesse? Why him? Why not Nathenial Law, as your father wanted, or a Nye, or a Thorpe, or any other man in this Reach?"

"My father learned the hard way not to make my choices for me."

"But why *Jesse*, Esmerelda? Why him?"

Esmerelda wrenched her arm free. "Why not Jesse? It's because of him that I made it through those long months away, waiting for you. It's because of Jesse that Gemmasyn is safe. It's because of Jesse that I can now see through the haze of my regret and find hope. So why *not* Jesse, Ryan, when he's the only man who's ever been there at all the times I have needed him?"

The force of her words gave him pause. "But do you love him?"

"Do you care?"

"Aye, for he's my brother, and he deserves happiness, too."

"That's not what I asked."

"Aye, well, fine, I do care. I donnae know why. I think I've convinced myself I feel this way more than anything else, but here I am, and I do care, Esmerelda, or I'd not be standing here before ye."

Esmerelda's mossy eyes flashed with something that lighted within him a new sensation, a glimpse of an old life he couldn't remember. She wasn't a girl, nor a woman, but something in between, infinitely more interesting.

"Aye, I love him," she said. "I don't understand how it even happened, or how I could feel as I do now, after loving you as I did. What I feel for him isn't that. What's between us took time, and patience, and pain, and fear and... and though I may not know what it is to steal kisses from him by moonlight, or sneak about for the excitement of it all, I know I've never felt safer than when Jesse is at my side. What I feel when I'm near him are the most inexplicable, indescribable feelings. And I know that if I don't step out of this room and become his wife, I'll regret that for the rest of my days, however long they find me."

Beyond the keep, the bustle and hum of the guests milling about grew into loud refrain. They were all here for this, to watch Esmerelda and Jesse wed, and to see Ransom, the heir, take his own bride, Lilja Nye. There hadn't been the excitement of a wedding in Warwicktown for so long. This was the way forward for the Reach, the way they could heal from the losses and turn their swords up at whatever new ones awaited, because *today* was about joy. They would see this day through, no matter what, and the battle on the other side of it would stay there until tomorrow.

Or so they said. Ryan thought they were all fools.

"I guess there isnae more that needs saying, then," Ryan said.

"Except for this," Esmerelda said. "You *will* find it within yourself to be happy for Jesse. He's given up so much for you. You won't take this, too."

Esmerelda pulled at the iron handle and slipped away.

HAMISH CUT CIRCLES AROUND THE ROOM, WEAVING AN UNEVEN PATH, lost in a search for thoughts that he could tap into words. This had always been the way of Jesse's father. And Hamish *was* his father, would always be his father. He was proud to call himself the son of Steward Strong.

"Ye ready, then?"

"Aye," Jesse answered. "Ready as a man can be."

"Esmerelda is a lovely lass," Hamish said. "I couldnae do any better for ye, Jamesan."

"Thank you, Father. I know you've been waiting for this day a long time."

"Aye, longer than I would've liked." Hamish laughed. "But I ken you're where you're supposed to be, and just when ye needed to be."

"Time has a way of strengthening some things and weakening others, I ken."

"I suppose 'tis true, isn't it? I'm happy for you. You deserve to know a man's joy in rearin' a family of his own. Yer own bairns, running around, wit' your eyes and hair and other bits that remind ye life goes on even after you're gone. Aye, 'tis true I used to wish this would happen sooner for ye, but I see now the Guardians had somethin' else in mind for ye. Fortune smiled upon me, gifting me a wife I *liked*, ye ken, one I *chose*. 'Tis not duty standing awaiting ye today, Son, but happiness."

Jesse smiled toward the door. Somewhere down the hall, Esmerelda would be tying up her own loose knots, enjoying her last official moments as a free lass. "I am happy," he said. "More important to me is her happiness. That she can see me as more than a choice she felt she must make when she had none better."

"Nay. Nay. I donnae believe that, and I donnae ken ye do, either."

Jesse nodded. He tugged at the crisp linen, newly stitched just for the day. It made his skin itch. He couldn't wait to be free of it. "If I didnae lack the proper words for it, is all."

"I ken ye come by that from me," Hamish said with a light scoff. His expression shifted. "I donnae wish to make ye late for yer own day, Son, but I've sat upon a truth for some years, one I've long since owed ye."

Jesse braced himself on the back of a nearby chair. He knew what was coming, but he couldn't tell his father without revealing why. "All right."

"When I met yer ma, she wasnae in a good place, Jesse." Hamish trailed off, his face reddened with an anger that was both fresh and also very old. "Some louse had taken advantage of yer ma, and she was carrying a child from tha' crime, ye ken. I knew she was wit' child when I took her wit' me, but I grabbed Yanna by the hand, and by the Guardians, I asked her to return to the Southerlands and do me the honor. I didnae even know her. I knew nothin' about her! I didnae know who'd done it to her, 'course, but nor did I know what foods she liked on her table, or whether she fancied wine or tea, ye ken? I knew *nothin'!* I only knew she belonged with me. So I took her home with me, and I made her my wife. And when her bairn was born, I made him my son. It wasnae even a choice, really. It was as if I'd been born to do what I did, and t'was not a day, not a single one, I ever looked back with regret."

Hamish whistled through his teeth as the confession ended. He closed his eyes, bracing.

Jesse slowly nodded. "I've always known there was something that set me apart from the other Strong men. I learned so much from you, but I was never really meant for the sea like you, and like Ryan. I came to love it, but that isnae the same." Jesse couldn't tell his father he already knew, but he could give him the reassurances he deserved. "It doesnae matter to me whose blood sired me. It willnae *ever* matter to me. What does is that my true and only father is standing before me now. The only father I'll ever have, the only one I'll ever call by that name. He's the only man I want at my side on the day of my wedding. The man who gave me my skill, my sense of honor. The man who gave me everything that was his to give. I have never wanted for anything." Jesse pushed the chair away and stepped closer to his father. "I mean that, Father. Anything."

"Ye say..." Hamish cleared his throat. He tapped his fist against it. "Ye say you donnae, it doesnae bother ye to know there's another man out there—"

"No," Jesse insisted. "Because that man isnae my father. He's only a man. He wasnae there to patiently teach me, to toughen me. To ease me, when it was proper. He isnae standing before me now, on my wedding day, as I prepare to make my own family."

Hamish ran his meaty fist over his nose, sniffling away the snot. "Yer a good boy, Jesse. Ye ken, always been a good boy. I used to think that was yer mother in ye, or even the ratsbane that got her with child, for it couldnae be me."

"Everything I am," Jesse said, "is because of you. Please never think otherwise. For I will not."

Hamish went to clap his son on the shoulder, but Jesse fell into his arms. The two men clutched each other in silence.

"Well," Hamish said. "I ken we should go meet yer bride on the hill, aye?"

Jesse wiped at his eyes with his thumb. "Aye. I ken we should."

· · ·

Esmerelda trembled from her neck to her toes. She told herself it was the harsh wind whipping across the hillside, sending the chills rippling down her back, but the wind was warm, and these anxieties came from within.

Her father had drawn this day together almost overnight. He'd waited only long enough for the Great Families to arrive, urging them all to make haste, as they all knew, too well, that they must have this day in order to welcome the inevitable next.

She didn't quite understand his insistence to put this behind him before addressing the business of Oldwin. But she didn't have to understand it to see nothing could sway him. He'd always been this way, and it was because of this she'd known he'd never understand or accept her love for Ryan; why she'd made the choice she did, launching them forward into the future they now stood upon.

There would be a second union made, between Ransom and Allarick Nye's second daughter, Lilja. A Nye marrying a Warwick would've caused a scandal in any other time, but there was no one else left in the upper hierarchy of the Great Families. They'd waited too long to choose a bride for Ransom. Steward Law's daughters were all married. Steward Rutland's only daughter of marriageable age wasn't of marriageable mind. And what wasn't said, but was certainly felt, was Khallum Warwick's sense of duty to a man who had lost so much for the crime of being a man loyal to the Warwicks.

Esmerelda's mother had pulled her aside that morning to ask if she knew how the day would go. She confessed she didn't. She hadn't been to a wedding since she was a girl, and she recalled nothing except the scalding heat and the ripe scent of cabbage boiling in the noonday sun.

It will be over very fast, Esmerelda. You'll say your vows, and then it'll be done, and you may enjoy the food and drink and the dance your father has prepared for you. There's nothing to it. Truly.

What if it happens so fast that I don't remember it?

You will. Perhaps not tonight. But the words will never leave you. Not if you've chosen to speak them. And you, my darling, are one of the most fortunate of women who has chosen for herself.

She *had* chosen. She'd chosen the same man who'd once looked upon her with derision, calling her *princess* in a way that left her heart wounded.

But was that not also why she'd accepted his offer? It was easy to love someone who had always loved you. But to earn that love—to fight for it, even when you didn't know you were fighting for anything at all—was infinitely more powerful. To meet somewhere in the in-between of each other, and from there, begin, at last, to understand.

In his vulnerability she found her own strength, and together, without realizing it at all, they'd both become who they were meant to be.

Now, she would face this life with him, together. But though she was confident in her choice, envisioning them moving through the ministration of their daily, ordinary lives was as yet beyond her grasp.

The chorus of voices settled down. Esmerelda saw the minister before her, lowering his hands to indicate the need for silence. At her side, Jesse fiddled with the clasps on his vest. He ran his tongue over his lips, widened and closed his eyes. She wanted to take his hand, but the minister hadn't said she should, and she was so afraid of doing wrong.

She was grateful to be doing this before Ransom. If she had to watch his ceremony first, she might lose her nerve.

"You are all here to bear witness to the Five Sacred Promises that begin all blessed unions of the Southerlands. These promises are binding. They are for life and cannot be undone." The minister lowered his eyes to Esmerelda and Jesse. "I will soon ask you both to confirm your commitment. Once these words are said, they are said forever."

Esmerelda's mouth was a dry riverbed. She wanted to look at

Jesse, to join in some shared look that might ease her, but she was rooted in place.

"Salt and sand," the minister went on. "So begins all sacred happenings. So ends all promises. In the salt of the sea, we are most free, like a bird of upon the wind, or a fish in the deep. But the sand is there to ground us, to remind us of our tethers, our bonds of duty and fealty and love. This is the lot of a man or woman of the Southern Reach, to be both free and bound, both of the sea and of the land that connects it. There can be no greater manifestation of these truths than the joining of two who have chosen to temper their salt and cultivate their sand, together."

The minister exhaled a long, intentional breath and looked at Jesse. "Jamesan Strong, son of Hamish, son of Yanna, do you enter this joining, heart open, mind willing?"

Jesse at first spoke the words in a whisper. He swallowed and tried again. His voice shook. "Aye, Minister, I come before you, heart open, mind willing."

The minister turned to Esmerelda. "And you, Esmerelda Warwick, daughter of Khallum, daughter of Gwyn, do you enter this joining, heart open, mind willing?"

Esmerelda feared nothing would come out when she opened her mouth, but her words were strong and crisp. "Yes, Minister, I come before you, heart open, mind willing."

"Then I will ask you both to repeat the Five Sacred Promises. Turn to one another. Jamesan, fold her hands in yours, now, as you will for all the rest of your days."

When Jesse pivoted toward her, Esmerelda's breath hitched at the sight of his red, swollen eyes. But it was his smile, full of nerves but also heart, that brought tears to her own eyes.

"I have reached into the sand, and the sand has offered me strength. This I offer you, until my promise is spent."

Jesse and Esmerelda repeated the words, horribly out of accord. Jesse bit his lip to keep from laughing, and she squeezed his hand to maintain her own composure.

"I have faced the wind, and the wind has offered me breath. This I offer you, until my promise is spent."

This time they did better. Jesse had a smile behind his eyes; there was mischief there. He was always so serious, but she loved him most when he was not. To her, his solemnity was a wall; his playfulness, the door through.

"I have mined the gold from our cliffs, and the gold has offered me prosperity. This I offer you, until my promise is spent."

Esmerelda took a deep breath.

"I have submerged myself in the salt of the sea, and the salt has offered me courage. This I offer you, until my promise is spent."

One more, Jesse mouthed, and Esmerelda understood he was trying to ease her, and she smiled back, as if to say, *donnae ye worry about me.*

"I have faced the deaths of those who came before me, and death has offered me life," the minister finished. "This I offer you, until my promise is spent."

"... until my promise is spent," they both finished. Jesse tightened their hand grip.

The minister reached for some rope lying on a nearby stand. He set his book aside and tied a Whitecliffe knot around their hands. It was a strong knot, Esmerelda knew. The kind they couldn't easily untie themselves.

"It is these vows that bind you. Let this rope rest eternally upon your hearth, as a constant reminder of what you have both surrendered, and also gained, in this union," the minister said. "Jamesan, Esmerelda, you are now one, and naught but death can sunder this bond."

Behind them was an eruption of cheers.

Was this the end?

The minister leaned in toward Jesse and whispered, "You may kiss her now, lad."

Jesse's throat ebbed. He rolled his bottom lip inward and then, closing his eyes, leaned in and pressed his mouth softly to hers. Esmerelda gasped at the connection; that their first brush with intimacy should happen here, now, in front of everyone. She buried this sensation for another, slipping her tongue into his mouth to deepen the kiss, enjoying, just a little, the rise of the excitement rolling from the crowd at her emboldened move.

Her father stepped forward, and, brandishing his ancestral steel, Sandspire, cut through the center of the knot. He handed the rope to Jesse.

"Donnae ever lose sight of this, Jamesan. Not for a single moment."

The entire evening had been a welcome blur. A soft mix of laughter and light; of the rich aromas of a lingering feast mingled with the now wilting floral designs woven all around the tent, the tables, the wood holding it all in place.

Khallum had set up several tents for the occasion. It was farther from the keep than he was comfortable with, but the muddy ground at sea level was no fit place for a wedding. They'd moved to higher ground, in the hills, where the sea wind whipped hard enough to make the women clutch their dresses and hair, and left the men to wonder about the structural sturdiness.

He'd never seen so much silk and velvet. Gwyn had never cared for the finer things. He supposed a Northerland woman, in her hardness and practicality, wasn't so different from the ones bred from salt and sand. It had been Hamish to suggest; that it would be the richness of it all that would hold the evening fast in everyone's memories, long after it had all faded, and the fears returned.

The bar wenches earned their wage refilling the drinks of the men and women alike. There wasn't anyone in attendance who didn't partake. Khallum himself had two mugs, one in each hand, and when he'd drain one, he'd hold it out to be refilled while quaffing down the other. One wench gave up circling the room and camped near him.

Rutland stood with him in the corner. Neither had the heart for dancing, but they both tapped their feet in time to the lively music.

Nye had chosen the musician, and the man thumped and swished across the tent, three separate instruments on his arms. He switched between each one with inexplicable ease, and Khallum couldn't help but think this man might be better utilized in a soldier's life, with such dexterity.

Neither man reflected their thoughts aloud, and though they were caught up in day's joy, they preferred enjoying it from the corner. They smiled as their wives were passed through the other men, as the children animatedly danced and laughed and sang along to the strange songs of the musician.

Darrick and Anabella swept across the room. Darrick was a right dancer, a skill he'd unlikely picked up from either Duncarrow or the Wastelands, and Khallum made a note in his mind to ask him about that later, though he wouldn't. He wouldn't even remember wondering about this tomorrow. It wouldn't matter then.

Hamish had Mariel, Rutland's wife, in his arms as he cut strange patterns through the crowds into what seemed to be his own poor attempt at dancing. Rutland laughed and drew another sip from his ale, ignoring her wide-eyed pleas for rescue. Hamish's boorish wife, Andrija, had Allarick Nye coerced into some kind of jig, and as father of a bride that would become the next Lady of the Souther-lands one day, he had no choice but to smile and comply.

Rutland raised a glass. He waited for Khallum to do the same.

"Even Samuel would've approved of these festivities," Rutland ventured. "The old gold catcher."

Khallum chuckled into his ale as he sipped in honor of their old friend. The loss felt so fresh that he wondered if it would ever dull.

"Ye remember that day, when we were boys? When he gathered the shopkeepers round, and took them to task for not accounting for theft in their reports to the Reach?"

"Oh, aye, and though he had no authority for it, told them he'd see it that their taxes were raised for the deception."

"Even as a boy," Rutland said with a whimsical head shake. "Even as a boy."

"Even with the ladies!" Khallum cried. "When he met the stewardess, his first words were a censure on how she shouldnae be wearing such rich fabrics when men were starving in the Reach."

"If she'd slapped him right then, wouldnae have been a soul to say he didnae deserve it."

"Aye. Aye. Makes ye wonder how he lured her into his bed."

"Wasnae with gold."

Both men laughed. Law should be here, too, to appreciate these jests. He had better humors in his middle age. He could appreciate the ribbing.

They had always been four, and now they were three. And what they didn't dare say, or even think, was that tomorrow there could be two, or even one.

But tonight wasn't about that. The dark thoughts could wait another night.

Khallum spotted Gwyn dancing with Ransom. If the boy was displeased with Khallum's choice of wife for him, it couldn't be found in the magnificent smile that had been plastered across his face all day and evening. Lilja Nye might not be a Rutland or a Law, but she made up for it in an especially pleasing face, and other parts.

"You did well, by Nye. You could have thrown him a pile of gold, but now he'll be the father-in-law of a proper lady."

"Aye, well, Samuel had no unwed daughters left, did he? And Nye has suffered for this Reach. There must be some reward."

"Law's son, Nathenial, still needs a wife. We'll need to see to that."

"Ye think I didnae try to sway Esmerelda up to the very last about it?"

"Did ye?" Rutland drained his ale. "Of course ye did."

"Aye, and the stubborn girl had nothing for it. It's what I'd planned for her, before the damn girl ran off. Before the king made his demands of her."

"She did run off for a reason."

"Ye on her side, then?"

Rutland laughed. "If anyone's earned the right to her own happiness, I ken it's Lady Esmerelda. Look at her. She's nay danced with another man. Her eyes are for Jesse alone."

Khallum turned to look at his daughter. It was as Rutland had said. Jesse flushed with purpose at her side. He was keenly aware of her surroundings, ever on alert for anything that might cause her harm, even here, when there were a hundred armed men at the ready. He cared for her. It was clear when he'd come, heart in hand, to ask to wed her, and it was clearer now. Khallum just couldn't fathom how it had happened. "I didnae have the heart to push any harder," he muttered. "But I ken she'll dance with her father."

Khallum set both mugs down on a nearby table and made his way to Esmerelda, pressing through the throngs of bodies dancing and laughing. The potent scent of sweat and ale filled his nostrils. It was like battle, in a way.

He passed Stewardess Rutland struggling through her dance with Hamish, before smacking right into Ryan Strong, whose face was colored a deep purple from his night at the drink. He stumbled past without apology.

Esmerelda's happy, flushed face lit up when Khallum appeared. "Thank you, Father. For today. For everything."

"Today was for us all," Khallum muttered. "I ken you may have saved a dance for your father, then?" He nodded at Jesse. "Your husband will allow it?"

Jesse returned the nod, though Khallum could see the light panic in his eyes. Khallum understood this fear. He was pleased Esmerelda was in the hands of someone whose regard for her safety matched his. It was her face he saw in his nightmares, as she was taken from him once more. The Guardians having returned to finish what they couldn't before.

"Is this how you imagined your wedding day?" he asked. Her hand, so small in his, reminded him she was still so young, only a girl. But she wasn't that anymore, either.

"I never imagined it at all," Esmerelda said. She moved with grace and ease, and he realized she was the one guiding them both through the movements.

"Isnae that what all little girls dream of?"

"I never thought of this day as one that would bring me happiness," Esmerelda said. "Until now."

"And are you happy, my emerald?"

"I am," Esmerelda said, reflecting on the words as she said them. "I am happy."

"I ken you're both eager to get on with it. But, for now, you'll remain in Warwicktown. You cannae go to Sandycove, not until matters are resolved."

Esmerelda moved them into the center of the floor. "I know, Father."

"Esmerelda, I mean it. You willnae be pleased with me, but you'll be under constant guard, you and Gemma. I willnae have it any other way."

Esmerelda smiled indulgently. "I *know*, Father. It's all right. I understand your fears, even more so now that I'm a mother."

"A mother," Khallum said gruffly. "Hmm. My little gem. You grew too fast, you know?"

Esmerelda nodded.

"Will ye be starting on the rest of your brood, then?"

Esmerelda's face darkened a deeper red; not a color of joy, but confusion and embarrassment. "We haven't talked about it. I suppose I don't know."

"Ye donnae know?"

"Jesse loves Gemmasyn and will be a good father."

"A man needs a son, Esmerelda. You're the only one who can give it to him now."

Though the love between his daughter and her new husband was clear, it was familial, almost too much so. Jesse's guilt over his feelings for Esmerelda should have been washed away with their vows, but it now seemed heightened. As if he was afraid of his feelings for her.

"So long as you're happy," Khallum said. "That's all I can ask for."

Esmerelda laughed. "Really?"

Khallum cleared his throat. "Seeing ye like this, I ken it'll make it all worth it if I donnae survive the coming days. I ken now that you're not like the other women. You cannae be told what to do, or pushed into a line you donnae belong in. So aye, I am happy for you. Your happiness brings me joy."

Esmerelda reached her hand up to rest it on his stubbled face. "How deep in your cups *are* you, Father?"

Khallum chortled. "Deep enough, I ken I willnae remember it tomorrow."

"I'll remember," Esmerelda said. "I might even be decent enough not to remind you."

Jesse stood across the room. He hadn't chosen a dance partner.

"You oughta rescue that boy, Esme. He doesnae know what to do with himself."

Esmerelda pivoted their dance so she could see. "No? Nor do I, I suppose."

"Go on, ye, back to your husband." He released her with a gentle nudge.

"Husband," she said. She repeated the word again. "It'll take some getting used to."

"The night is ending for the lot of us. It's only beginning for you."

RAVENNA WAITED UNTIL SHE SAW JESSE DISAPPEAR FOR DRINKS. HE hadn't left her side all evening. She'd grown impatient waiting for a moment alone with Esmerelda.

Then he was replaced by Lord Warwick. She waited for him, too, to take his leave.

She hurried through the crowds, aware of the eyes falling on her in the beautiful crimson dress Gwyn had prepared for her. Gwyn seemed like such a lovely woman. Possessed of the unconditional love of a mother, something entirely foreign to Ravenna, Gwyn had pulled Ravenna aside and said, *you need something beautiful to wear. You're a part of this day, too.* Ravenna felt like crying as the weight of this unnecessary kindness threatened to crush her.

"So this is how normal people throw a wedding?" Ravenna

quipped. "No grand orgy? No brothers and uncles eyeing you with unslakeable lust?"

Esmerelda turned toward the sound of her voice. She didn't seem to know whether to laugh or cry at the strange jest. "Aye, well, in the Southerlands we donnae think much of sharing," she played back. "Least not with our own kin."

"I can see the appeal," Ravenna said. She twisted her mouth into a grin, and this prompted the laugh from Esmerelda she'd been after.

"Did you enjoy it?"

"It's *your* wedding day, Esme."

"I don't know what this day was like for others, because I was... I was right in the middle of it all. But it seemed like a lovely day, did it not?"

"It was a very lovely day," Ravenna agreed. She searched for Jesse. He was still near the serving stand, now occupied in conversation with Lady Warwick. "The very best. You look so happy, and beautiful, and I must say, I've never seen Jesse so radiant. Did we even know that was possible?"

"Is he? It's all been very overwhelming. I hope my memories don't settle into the same haze the day has been."

"You'll look back on this day, seventeen children later, with nothing but joy."

Esmerelda gasped. "I'll cut your tongue out for that."

Ravenna shrugged with a wink. "You're the only one I'd ever fear capable of seeing it through." She didn't have long. "Look, Esmerelda. This is right. You and Jesse. Don't ever pay mind to your doubts, for they serve no one, least of all you."

Esmerelda's smile faded some. She dropped her eyes. "I'm sorry I've not been there for you more since we came to Warwicktown. You must feel so out of place here."

"Nonsense," Ravenna insisted. "You're a mother now, and Gemma needs you. Now you're a wife. Whether you see it or not, Jesse needs you, too."

"Now that the wedding is behind us..." Esmerelda sighed. "That means nothing, does it? Not when war looms over us."

"I came to tell you I'm leaving. I don't want any prolonged good-byes. I'm going tonight. Now, in fact."

"Already?" Esmerelda paled. "Where will you go?"

"Midnight Crest," Ravenna answered. "There's something I've left unfinished. I would stay here forever, with you and Jesse, if I could, but that's not my path. Now that I know you're safe, and Jesse is safe, I can leave in something at least slightly resembling peace."

"What if I'm not ready to say goodbye?" Esmerelda's eyes welled with tears.

Ravenna reached forward and wiped them away. "No tears, Esme. This isn't the last for us."

"I hope you really mean that, Ravenna, for in my heart I feel as if I've both gained and lost a sister before I knew what to do with her."

"I wouldn't deceive you. Not about this." Ravenna looked past her and saw that Jesse was making his way back. "There's one last thing. Jesse will be leaving soon. I know he's told you about this deal he made with the sorcerers."

"I don't trust it, Ravenna, not at all."

"As you shouldn't. I fear if he travels alone to them, he won't return."

"Well," Esmerelda said, a look of mischief spreading through her eyes, "Jesse can say about it whatever he pleases, but he was never going alone. My mother can care for Gemma until we return, but there's no one but me, now, to look after Jesse."

"Good," Ravenna said. A heavy burden was lifted from her heart. "If there's anyone who can stop him from agreeing to something foolish, it's you."

She'd said no goodbyes, and Jesse was close now. Ravenna leaned in and quickly kissed Esmerelda on the cheek. Before withdrawing, she whispered, "Sisters. Always." And then, before she could change her mind and stay forever, with the people who now seemed more family to her than her own blood kin, Ravenna darted past the crowds and pressed into the night.

She felt Esmerelda's eyes on her and glanced back only briefly, to see her sister, dress hitched, mouth parted.

It was for her that Ravenna took to flight when she did. She burst into a spray of orange light and twirled in tight circles, showing Esmerelda, in a display of love and trust, her true self.

Esmerelda raised a hand to wave. Ravenna spun for her once more before soaring high into the sky, into the evening night, and away.

"You look so beautiful tonight, Isa." Darrick gazed into his wife's glassy eyes. It was the first night he'd seen her at ease, and it might be the last for a while. But tonight... tonight she was his, and she was happy.

"All Gwyn's doing," Anabella answered with a light, girlish giggle. Even that was new—or not new, but from another time, one where he'd fallen in love with her under the brilliant white blossoms of the winter-blooming cherry tree. "It's been far too long since I've known my way around a ladies' chambers and dressing room. I don't recall how to do any of this anymore."

"It's not the rouge," Darrick said, "or the dress. Those are just ornaments. It's the look in your eyes. I know you've been through so much. More than you should have ever had to endure."

"We've both been through so much. Too much. But..." Anabella linked their fingers tighter as they danced. "I know that's all behind us. No matter what waits for us tomorrow, we've already been through the very worst we can endure. The Guardians would never dare take more from us."

"I—" Darrick was cut short. He watched Ryan stumble through the crowd in a drunken haze before crashing into Khallum. Khallum was too surprised to do more than gape at him, and before he could say a word, Ryan rolled away, ambling out of the tent and into the night.

"What do you suppose has gotten into him?" Anabella asked.

"I'm not quite sure, but..." Darrick frowned in the direction Ryan had gone.

"You should go to him. He seems very alone these days. He could use a friend. Don't worry about me."

"You wouldn't mind?"

"No, no, no. Stefan appears to need rescue himself, all those little girls fawning over him. It's quite more than he knows what to do with."

With a distracted laugh, Darrick planted a kiss at the corner of her mouth, his eyes still fixed on his friend. He pushed through the celebration and eventually landed on the cool, soft ground of the marshy hills still inundated by the weeklong rains.

Ryan struggled up the hill, bested by the tall grass that whipped at him. He headed higher, missing steps due to the uneven ground, his bottle of swill held high to avoid spilling. Not so drunk he couldn't prioritize, then.

"Ryan?" Darrick called out. "What are you doing?"

"Aye, and what does it look like?" Ryan slurred. He wiggled the bottle in his hands and continued climbing. He added a song to his trek, which he sang loudly and badly. Darrick didn't recognize the words. He suspected Ryan was making them up as he went.

"Upsetting yourself and your family," Darrick answered. It was a tougher love than he'd planned to give. Ryan's kin had danced around his slow regression, failing to aid him through it, and this was where it had brought him. "Burying your sorrows in a bottle that's near empty?"

"There are other bottles!"

Darrick caught up to him quickly. He grabbed him by the arm, turning him with a light jerk. Ryan's head flopped around in a strange spin before falling into a nod. He was on the verge of tears. "What's going on with you?"

"You might be our king soon, but you are nay our king now."

"What does that mean?"

"I donnae answer to ye!"

"I'm asking as your friend. You can talk to me."

Ryan cackled, a high, desperate sound. "When has there ever been any use in talking to anyone about anything?" He took another hungry sip from the bottle, nearly empty.

"If that were true, you wouldn't need that bottle. It doesn't hear your words, it pushes them down deeper within you, where they go to rot."

"Ye must be new to the Southerlands." Ryan belched. He seemed befuddled by the sound. "'Tis what we do. Salt and sand and... swill. Aye, that's it?"

"That's not true," Darrick insisted. "Lord Warwick isn't like that."

"Ye see him tonight, lad? He's had alllll the cups."

"He's celebrating. That's not at all what you're doing, is it?"

Ryan shrugged. He looked down the hill, toward the town and the sea. The act made him woozy. Darrick reached out to steady him. "There's never harm in speaking our pain. You taught me that, you know. You might feel better if you tried it yourself."

"Why would I feel better?" Ryan rolled his head back. "Does everyone else here feel better? Having a wedding on the eve of war, pretending like there's naught wrong? Like Samuel Law wasnae *murdered* on the back of his own beast. Like Steward Nye didnae lose his wife and bairn, and the very stones over their heads. Like one of us willnae be next!"

Darrick wanted to reach for the bottle, but it didn't seem wise. Ryan had stopped looking toward the hill ahead and was here, now, speaking. That was enough. "What else do we fight for, Ryan, if not what we would live for? Lord Warwick planned this day to remind us of all we have. Not to forget. Not to put it behind us, or ignore what's coming. No one is more aware of what tomorrow might bring than Khallum Warwick. But tonight? Tonight there will be joy."

Ryan's laugh was dark, pained. "Yeah? I donnae know what that feels like anymore. Joy."

Darrick risked stepping closer. He positioned himself on slightly higher ground to keep Ryan from bolting up the hill. "We were once friends. Good friends. We went through it, the two of us.

Things no other man here could ever understand. I've left you alone, because I know you don't remember, and I don't want to make things worse for you. But I've missed you, missed our friendship. I've had friends, yes, but most were loyalists, people who chose me for who I was. You didn't have to befriend me in that cruel place. That wasn't part of your charge. I wouldn't be standing here, desperate to help you find your way back, if you hadn't once done the same for me."

Ryan drained the bottle. He regarded it with a look of deep disappointment and then sent it sailing into the tall grass. It disappeared before it landed. "There is no way back from this... this... emptiness." His eyes rolled back, but this time he fought it. "Esmerelda had the right idea, telling them all she went into the sea."

"You've lost your memories, Ryan, but not your life! Move on. Put it in your past. You might never get them back, and you have to find a way to accept that. Life is rarely so neat and fair. Who else could know that like a man who gave up five years of his life in prison? Five years of my son's life, time with my wife, that I will never ever get back. We don't always get what we want."

Ryan pointed toward the tents. "Jesse got what he wanted, I ken."

Darrick shook his head. "That's not fair. Jesse gave up everything to do right by you. You told me about this, even if you don't remember. How he tried so hard to convince you to let her go, but when you couldn't do it, he gave up his life, and his own freedom if Lord Warwick were to discover his deeds, to take her to your mother."

"I may not remember it like ye said, but I didnae ask him to marry her!"

"Jesse would never have married her if he wasn't sure the door to you was closed. He's a man of honor. More than most of us are. Even in your anger, you know this is true."

Ryan's nostrils flared. He grunted.

"And, today?" Darrick went on. "Today, he deserved a brother to stand at his side in happiness for him. Instead, you're running around in your cups, embarrassing yourself and him. If you have no memories of any of it, why are you worked up about it?"

Ryan licked his lips. He wiped the spittle away with the back of his hand. "Aye, and what if I am remembering?"

Darrick froze. Even in the warm breeze rolling off the hills, his blood chilled. "Are you? Are you remembering?"

Ryan stumbled back a couple of steps. "What does it matter now?"

Darrick reached for him, but Ryan tore away and stumbled off into the grass, disappearing into the night.

Gwyn had called it the bridal suite, but it was the old chambers of Esmerelda's grandparents. The set of rooms had been abandoned since their untimely deaths, and Khallum, who had the right to this apartment, had never taken it for his own. It remained empty and unused, not even opened for guests, until this night.

Jesse had never been inside. It was bigger than anything they had in Sandycove. It was bigger than it had any need to be. But it had been lovingly prepared for the night ahead. The hearth roared with a seasoned fire to keep them warm through the rainy night. Candlelight dotted the otherwise dim room. Two pitchers of wine, filled to the brim, sat upon the table, next to a basket of fruit.

The vows had been spoken; the celebrations ended. Everything here was a reminder of their next duty, as husband and wife.

If Esmerelda was considering these same things, she didn't show it. She stood on the other side of the room, warming her hands near the hearth. Her ornate dress, crafted just for this day, had come apart. The lace had frayed from her dancing, and the precious, delicate silks were torn in several spots. Her hair, having fallen out of the woven floral design made by the women who loved her, now tumbled in gentle waves around her face. It had grown since she'd sliced it off with his sword in desperation, and the ends curled just below the soft rounded edges of her pale, bare shoulders, tickling the top of her breasts.

Jesse swallowed a hard lump. He'd never looked at Esmerelda this way before. He shouldn't be doing this to himself; this guilt and fear of being alone with her was nonsensical. He'd asked for this. He'd been certain it was right for them both. He was still certain, and yet didn't know if this was where they really belonged, right now, together.

Esmerelda turned, and now he could see in her eyes that she was contemplating the strangeness of it all, same as he was. They were friends. Perhaps the best of friends. They were brother and sister, and now, in addition to these things, they were also man and wife.

"This room is lovely," Esmerelda said, an attempt at conversation that Jesse had already failed at. "I don't know how I've lived my entire life here and never seen it."

"We could house an entire family in here." Jesse tried to laugh, to make a jest of it. The effort was instead trapped in his chest. Esmerelda attempted to smile, but all he could see was the ebb of her throat, throbbing with her racing heart.

"Can you?" Esmerelda half-turned. She pointed behind her, to the stays on her dress. "It's a bit of a task, compared to the dresses I usually wear. I'd ask one of my ladies to aid me, but they're not here. I can't... well, I cannot get out of it myself."

Jesse knew nothing about getting a woman out of a dress like this. All the women he'd been with had been ready for him, and as he thought of this, this comparison to other women he'd lain with when Esmerelda stood before him, waiting, he suddenly felt ill.

His hands hovered, unsure, until she guided him through how to untie the crisscrossed ribbons that had held her together. He pulled, one by one, gradually loosening the dress, amazed by the generous give. Amazed that she'd been capable of even breathing these long hours.

The dress had loosened enough to fall from her shoulders. Jesse stopped before it could fall all the way off.

"Thank you," she said, arms crossed over the fabric to keep it in place. She glanced toward the bureau, where her nightgown had been chosen for her, probably by her mother.

"I'll let you..." Jesse stopped. He turned from her to give her time, waiting for the sound of fabric rustling in the exchange of one garment for another.

But the sound didn't come. In its place was the light rise and fall of her breaths. "I don't want it to be like this, Jesse. You nervous, fearful. Me, not knowing what to say, or do."

"I..." Jesse didn't know how to answer her.

"What I mean to say is, I expect nothing from you. If we never... if we never... it won't be a failure of you, or our marriage."

Jesse should turn. He should reassure her there's nothing wrong with them, with wanting to be here, together. That it wasn't that he'd never considered this, because he had. He *had* thought of her this way, in his dreams, more times than he should have; her serene smile, her wide, trusting eyes. Imagined her soft arms looping around his neck as he lifted her.

But he could never say this, could he? He could never tell her that, at some indeterminable place in their time together, he'd stopped seeing her as a sister, because, to Esmerelda, that same shift had not occurred.

"Aye. Right." These were the only words Jesse could manage. Then he heard it. The rustle of fabric. The exchange of one gown for another.

When she was done, Jesse turned. Esmerelda wore a slip of fabric so transparent he could make out the smooth arcs of her breasts, meeting at the press of nipple against cloth. The sheer muslin clung to her hips, creating a perfect outline of her.

Jesse realized he hadn't breathed in some time.

He peeled away his jacket and vest, then angled away from her as he unbuckled his trousers, careful to pull his shirt down to cover himself. Offending her was the very last thing he wanted.

He normally slept in the nude, but if he did that, she'd think he'd done it intentionally, his desires raging against her gentle rejection.

Jesse peeled back the blankets and nodded for her to get into bed. She climbed in, watching him, and when she was settled, he joined her. It wasn't the first time he'd slept at her side, but it was the first time he'd not had his honor lying between them. It was the first time he'd felt terrified at the notion that he wouldn't make it through the long night without saying or doing something untoward.

"What I said before," Esmerelda ventured, her voice low, rhythmic. "About seeing you as my brother."

"There are no other words needed. I respect how you feel."

"But what I mean to say," Esmerelda went on, "is that you *aren't* my brother anymore, are you? I wouldn't have married a man I saw that way. For the same reason I couldn't marry Ryan, when I knew there was nothing left between us. Do you understand?" She climbed into his arms, as if she'd always fit there. The piece he'd not known was missing.

Jesse wrapped his arm around her and his hand fell against her waist, his fingers splaying against what felt like bare flesh beneath the thin material that had been left there for just this purpose, to incite passion. Esmerelda slid one leg over his thigh, dropping it between both his legs. Her heat radiated against his flesh. It was a welcome heat. The kind, he now understood, was an invitation.

He dropped his head to the side to look at her. The look she gave in return launched a battle within him, where he was torn between knowing he could pivot just so and enter her, be inside her, within her, *one* with her, and knowing he could do no such thing.

Esmerelda seemed to wait for this, and when it didn't come, she rested her head on his shoulder in resignation. Her lips brushed the side of his neck, lingering here.

Jesse dusted a kiss against her forehead. He didn't trust himself to be so reticent against the wet heat she had pressed into the side of his thigh, so he forced his thoughts elsewhere.

He held her like this, neither of them moving, hardly breathing. His heart, a mess of speed and movement and fear and longing, knew there would be no sleep for him this night.

25

MIDWINTER REST

Adynora and Ryandyr departed the Courtyard of Regents in perfect unison. Ryandyr passed smoothly down the corridor, shoulders back as her grandmother had taught her, every movement the result of Adynora's careful curation.

She'd tended to the girl's instruction since the early morning hours. Ryandyr was exhausted. Adynora wasn't concerned about her exhaustion. Her ascension to High Priestess would come with at least fifteen years of this weariness—or more, in Adynora's case. But she must be prepared, in a way that neither Varinya nor Ravenna had ever been, and there was no one else to do it but the dowager High Priestess who had failed first one, and then the other.

Adynora watched the girl as her hand fell upon her pinched waist. She was just about the right size now for the gown she'd wear at her Langenacht. It wouldn't have been so had Adynora not taken her diet under careful watch. Ryandyr whined that she was starving, but Adynora assured her she would starve a little less when it was all over.

It will be fine, Adynora had said, so much even she was tired of hearing it. It had to be fine. All she'd done, everything over the years, every choice and misstep, to this point, it was all so that *it, they, all of it,* would at last, be fine, recovered from the shock her grandmother Rhosyn's defection had settled upon their careful world.

She marched across the stones, away from where her granddaughter had turned off. Her attention was pulled down another corridor, toward the Hall of Hours. It was one of two gathering spots at The Rookery, used officially for the Feast of the Langenacht, where all but the future High Priestess availed themselves of the finest meal they'd ever have until the next ceremony. Unofficially, it had become the meeting place of the men, and even some women, to gather and share stories. It was said the stories they told were relics of their past, but Adynora didn't know this from experience. Only the unimportant ones reduced themselves to such pastimes.

She had no interest in these stories, at least not outwardly. How could she, when it was the women, the chosen women in their line, who were said to be possessed of these truths as part of their many gifts? It was the women who carried this burden; who knew from where they'd come, details the men could never possess for they were not special.

This lie held their entire world together.

Adynora had never liked this tradition, this gathering behind the backs of the High Priestess. But her mother had cautioned her that there were small deceptions they must accept, for those who were not special still possessed the need to feel part of something. She must allow it, her mother said, for if she didn't, they would become restless and seek more sinister betrayals.

Now, though, Adynora wasn't simply annoyed but threatened. This was no innocent exchange of stories, not anymore. Not since Ravenna and Alasyr had left; since Varinya and Argentyn had been murdered upon these very stones, by an outsider. It was now a place where they could speak those things that couldn't be spoken in front of her, and if they couldn't speak in front of her, then their words were dangerous.

Rillyn, her husband—and once, her brother—exited the Hall of

Hours with one of the little ones, Nevyn. It was too bad about the boy's age, Adynora thought, for with Alasyr defected, Ryandyr had no other brothers to win her hand at the Langenacht. Adynora had no qualms over the limitation of youth as a precursor to eligibility, but at eight, he couldn't do what the greenlight fires would require of him. Ryandyr must be satisfied with an uncle, or a cousin.

"Taking your grandson to your secret meetings now, are you?"

"Adynora," Rillyn acknowledged, frosty. "Our meetings have never been secret, or you wouldn't know about them."

"This is what you would teach him? What you would poison his mind with?"

"Nevyn will never be High Priest, so what concern is it of yours what he learns?"

"If he was even a year or two older... but alas..." Adynora smiled coldly at her grandson, who seemed afraid of her.

"Do you not have more important matters, like the indoctrination of poor Ryandyr?"

"Ryandyr's *instruction* has concluded for the day."

"Then perhaps you could spare some of your precious time for Ashara and Nyana. They've lost both their parents, a brother, and a sister, in only a few short months. You can imagine the confusion they must feel."

"Ryessa has done a fine job taking them under her wings," Adynora countered. "Perhaps if *Ryessa* had been my eldest, we wouldn't even be having this conversation. We both know Varinya took after you. Your precociousness that can only lead to dark troubles."

Rillyn ignored the slight. "They see you with Ryandyr. Day in, day out. It would take so little to give some of that time to them."

"Yes, well, Ryandyr is important now, and they are not," Adynora replied. "As you well know."

Rillyn ran his thumb over the beard he'd grown when he was no longer called to the duty of High Priest. She hated it on him. He looked more like a man than a Ravenwood. Now that they'd resumed the mantle in the absence of Varinya and Argentyn, she should demand he remove it. "And you wonder, Adynora, why we feel compelled to meet separate of our leaders. There are other ways to be important."

Adynora bristled. She knew he could read this upon her face, and this made her even angrier. It was for this reason that she said this next thing, deciding it as the words flowed. "You should know that I've moved up the Langenacht. It's time for us to have a new High Priestess."

"You *what?*"

"The other Ravenwoods are restless."

"The other Ravenwoods have no care! Adynora—"

"She's ready, and it's time."

Rillyn was stunned. She expected this; counted on it. Enjoyed it. "She's thirteen."

"So? In two years she will be the same person."

"There's a reason we wait! And even at fifteen..." Rillyn took a sharp intake of breath. At his side, Nevyn's terrified eyes traveled between them both. "There has always been a reason we wait. Has she even had her... no, don't tell me. I don't want to know."

"Every generation, the mantle has passed, without fail," Adynora said.

"Not always. We both know, not always."

She turned to her grandson, ignoring Rillyn. "Do you not agree, Nevyn, that we should embrace tradition?"

Little Nevyn looked up at her, eyes wide with fear. He should be afraid of her. They all should. It was fear that would keep them in line.

"The weakness of men is why this decision will always fall to a woman," Adynora said, her grin now real, empowered. "Go on, then."

Rillyn pressed his hand to Nevyn's back to ease him forward. "Think about this before you make a decision that will bring upon us the very reverse of what you intend. You and I both know there are paths we cannot return from. You want to avoid ruin? This is how you invite it."

He left her without a proper goodbye.

RAVENNA SOARED HIGH ABOVE A TOWERING MOUNTAIN PASS. SNOW coated the very tops, but the rest were downward slopes of dark brown and red, denoting she was still somewhere in the southern half of the kingdom. She didn't know what the name of this pass was called, or the towns dipping into the foothills on either side. She had no sense of orientation, no familiarity of landscape that might come from someone who was born into this land. She wasn't made for this world. She was a witch, crafted in the icy mountains of the far north, carved into a life that had been crafted for her long before she was even born.

A life she'd left behind, but was once more drawn to.

Returning home didn't mean a return to the old Ravenna, though.

Her new wings came with more than a change in plumage. Her wings, stronger than they'd been even at Midnight Crest, were no longer exhausted in flight. She could go higher now, into the clouds, and face the wind, something she'd been afraid to do as a raven. But she wasn't a raven. She was a phoenix. A gift, if it was in fact that, from her real father.

Ravenna would return and approach her mother. She'd demand her version of the truth that Oldwin had dripped into her ears like steady poison. She wanted to know how a wise witch like Varinya wouldn't detect the deception. How she could have loved a man like Holden at all, and then cast Ravenna from her heart for the near identical crime of loving his son.

Even if her mother lied, the truth would live in her eyes, which Ravenna could now read more clearly following her many iterations of self.

But her return to her mother wasn't only to demand answers, but to warn her.

Esmerelda had worried about Ravenna in Warwicktown, picking up shrewdly on her craving for solitude. Ravenna didn't know how to listen to her own thoughts when surrounded by the noise of the busy world, and now that she was free of all the many things that had tried to harm her, now that they no longer lingered over her like a waiting promise, she wasn't afraid to listen. She was remembering things her mind had suppressed from her, to protect her.

She couldn't weave all the threads together into something coherent, but she understood that spinning this web, at the very center, was her grandmother, Adynora. Adynora had known about Drystan. She'd understood Ravenna's struggle, and even suggested that Ravenna should follow her heart, which was the very antithesis of all Ravenna had been raised to think, believe, and feel. She'd been sympathetic. Too sympathetic. Ravenna only understood now that this wasn't a kindness, but *why* was still a thread she needed to connect.

Something else had seeped into Ravenna's thoughts late at night. In leaving, she'd abandoned her sister to the same fate she'd fled.

So many before her had accepted their fate with blithe acceptance, but not Ravenna. Not Rhosyn. How many others had seen it for what it was; a tradition meant not to empower, but to enslave. How many had escaped after all, and gone on to live a full and beautiful life, like Rhosyn?

Ravenna caught a tailwind and rode it down the mountain pass, drawing closer to the green of beckoning land. She needed rest for the evening. She wasn't tired, but her thoughts were, and she couldn't stifle them when her wings were spread and the world was hers.

She didn't know what she'd do when she arrived at Midnight Crest. She knew only that whatever future awaited her—the joy and purpose Rhosyn once found, or the banishment and isolation Ravenna felt more keenly was her calling—this was the bridge she must cross to get there.

· · ·

By the time Marsh finally passed through the town gates of Midwinter Rest, he was all too aware that another day or two and he would've been crawling past the meager guard patrol. His rations had dwindled to scraps. The horse he'd borrowed—stolen, really, for he could tell no one of his plans, except Eavan—foamed at the snout. His first stop was the town stable, where she could get a meal, rest, and a good long brush. His heart couldn't take losing another horse to exhaustion.

He next used his coin to procure a warm bowl of stew and a tall ale from the tavern recommended by the stablemaster. It was one out of a whole row of them, an indication of what passed for fruitful commerce this far north.

When he'd finished his meal, he hitched a ride from a clothier who was delivering shipments into the foothills. He said the Frosts were just past the end of his route. Marsh tossed him more coin than the ride was worth and jumped into his cart.

The climb steepened the higher they went. Marsh huddled in the back, knees drawn to his chest, waiting in excruciating cold for the clothier to complete each delivery. When they'd climbed so high the snow was blinding, the clothier stopped his wagon and hopped out.

"End of the road, boy," he said.

"We're here? Where is it? I don't see it." Marsh shielded his eyes, straining to see through the white wall ahead.

"About fifty paces uphill. Cart won't make it any further."

"How does Steward Frost come and go, then?"

The clothier shrugged. "Steward Frost has not left his keep in many years." He eyed Marsh. "You've a way back down, then, when he turns you away?"

"He won't."

"Just the same." The clothier huddled under his furs and pointed down the path they'd come up. "The Blackmoors will offer aid. Last place we stopped before here. You'll remember it."

"Thank you," Marsh said, still looking into the abyss of blinding white. "About fifty paces, you say?"

"Give or take."

Marsh nodded. "All right, then. I'll take my leave with gratitude, sir."

The clothier tipped his fur hat. "Find me again at the first snow."

Marsh mumbled the proper response to that greeting, still hazy on what it even meant in a land that was always covered in snow.

A sudden pang of loneliness hit Marsh when the clothier disappeared into the storm. He didn't have his horse now. He couldn't see, and only knew he was pointed true when he felt himself climbing once more.

He was only a stone's throw from the gates when he saw them, iron curves peering through the snow. As he reached forward, Alasyr dropped from the sky in a flurry of dark feathers, unfolding before him with a self-satisfied grin.

"Nice of you to come," Marsh muttered as he pressed his whole body into the gates to move them.

"I said I would, didn't I?" Alasyr said lightly. "When you arrived."

"You could've come sooner. I've been practically starving for the past two days. I almost died in the pass. Not that you've any care about that."

"Of course I care," Alasyr answered, looking uncomfortably stricken. "At least until Emberley is safe, and then that will fade, as all things do." He laughed at the horror in Marsh's face. "I was scouting for the pass you found on your map, if you must know. Thought we might avoid this little dance with the steward. I saw what looked like a few hints of an overgrown trail, but I couldn't make out how to start. They must've covered it well. As for your food, how was I to know you're so inept at hunting, Wildwood?"

"I can hunt just fine, but there's nothing *to* hunt this side of the pass."

"Or you're possessed of the constitution of lady."

"We're off to a wonderful start, you and I," Marsh shot back with a scowl. "But we're here now, and I'd like to know how you expect me to get the steward to share his great secret with us?"

"Let me handle the steward," Alasyr said. "You're just a boy from... from... a place where the wealthy take their holidays, isn't that right?"

Marsh didn't answer. He was already regretting this alliance.

"And I'm a Ravenwood. We're worshipped in the Northerlands, or feared, or both. Either should serve us."

"With such high regard you hold yourself in, how could this go wrong?"

Alasyr reached forward and lifted the iron knocker, thumping it against the door. Marsh's whole body tensed in anticipation as he toiled over the right words for the servant who answered. But when the door opened, it was a young woman. She cast her eyes to the side. She was comely, with a kind face, her blond hair tied back in a loose braid. But it was her dress that caught his attention, for it was clear she was no servant at all, but a highborn.

"Miss?"

She still didn't look at him when she answered. "Two of you there are. Yes, two. Who are you, and what do you want?"

Marsh and Alasyr exchanged confused looks. "We're here for an audience with Steward Frost. Is he in?"

"Is he in?" she repeated with a wry smile. She tilted her head to the side, and, still looking sideways, yelled, "Father! It seems there are two guests here for you that you did not invite."

"She's blind," Marsh mouthed to Alasyr.

Steward Frost's heavy steps boomed in the hall behind her as he thundered toward them. He was a large man, whose appearance belied a man much older than he probably was. His beard had turned full white, like the snow all around his keep.

"Who are you and what do you want?" He repeated his daughter's words.

"My name is Marsh Tyndall, eldest son of Steward Tyndall of Wildwood Falls."

"Wildwood Falls is in the Westerlands, boy."

"Yes. It is. And this—"

Alasyr cut him off. "Alasyr Ravenwood. Though I don't believe further inspection into my lineage or familial home is necessary, is it?"

Steward Frost cradled his beard in one hand. "The Guardians are funny, aren't they? A Westerlander and a Ravenwood, standing at my door. Has my ale gone to rot, finally? There cannot be any sense in this worth explaining."

"I know how it looks, but we do have a reason to be here," Marsh said.

"Are you lost? Is that your reason?"

"We have questions we hope you can offer us an answer to. Do you have time for us, Steward Frost? I've come all the way from Wulfsgate to find you, and it was no easy voyage."

Steward Frost regarded him with a strange look. "You crossed the pass, then? The two of you?"

"Just me," Marsh said with a hard glare at Alasyr. "I did it alone. If nothing else speaks to my intentions, perhaps that will."

"Anyone who finds their way up here has no intentions I'm interested in."

"It's a long story," Marsh said with a sad smile. "But we'll share it with you, if you'll let us in. Even long enough for a warm drink and a few moments before a fire would be a kindness."

The steward grunted. He turned to his daughter. "Still some cider from Wulfsgate, ain't there?"

"Yes, Father."

"You'll fetch us some?"

"Yes, Father." The girl went to do as asked, cutting an intentional path down the hall.

"Has she always been blind?" Marsh asked.

"Half her life," said the steward. "The best fire is just off the kitchen. We're never prepared for guests anymore here at the top of the kingdom. I had to let most of my servants go, for work in town. Just me and Elena now, and the cook."

"Why?"

"The way of things sometimes. This isn't Wildwood Falls."
Alasyr grinned.

"Even locals don't make their way up here unless they have business, and I can't guess what business the two of you think you have here. But you've tickled a curiosity I didn't know I still had in me." He pointed to the small table. It wasn't the monstrosity in the Great Hall of Wulfsgate Keep, fit for a sumptuous feast. If he'd had such a table, it was gone now.

Marsh dropped in next to Alasyr, and the steward sat across from them.

Marsh looked at Alasyr with a nod. "Go on, then. You said you wanted to handle it."

Alasyr leaned in. "I know about the alliance that once existed between our people."

"Our people," Steward Frost repeated, and already Marsh could tell this was not going well.

"An alliance. I don't know." Alasyr shrugged. "But it involved a pass. A path. A road. Whatever you call it, but a *way* into the mountain that leads to Midnight Crest."

"And why do you think that, raven?" The steward's face was stoic, even.

Marsh inhaled.

"I don't think it, Steward, I know it."

"There's a map," Marsh cut in quickly. "An old map I found in the library at Wulfsgate. It shows the pass that used to exist behind you, in the foothills. Behind the Frozen Vale. But we, that is, Alasyr, hasn't been able to find it himself."

"You'll tell us where it is," Alasyr demanded.

"Alasyr," Marsh hissed. "Forgive him. He doesn't know how to hold a conversation in the company of gentlemen."

Steward Frost looked at Marsh as he asked, "Why would you need to know where this supposed pass is, then?"

"There's someone up there. She's stuck, and she needs us to rescue her."

Frost chuckled. "And how did *she* get up that mountain?"

"She flew," Alasyr said with a shrug. "And now she cannot fly back down."

"There's no sense in any of what you just said. You both know that, don't you? Only a Ravenwood could fly up there, and Ravenwoods don't need to come down. They don't want to come down. Isn't that the point? That they live in their little castle in the sky, with their magic and their feathers?"

Marsh wound his hand around Alasyr's thigh to warn him from whatever he planned to respond to that. "She's not a Ravenwood," Marsh answered. "She's a Blackwood. She found her wings, and then they were taken from her, and now she needs our help."

"A Blackwood, you say? Since when have Blackwoods had any magic in them worth talking about, let alone wings to fly?"

"We're not here to talk about the Blackwoods," Alasyr grumbled. "Do you or do you not know of a pass that can take us up this mountain to help her?"

Frost bristled. His dislike for Alasyr was as clear as Alasyr's disrespect. "Why would I help you?"

"Why wouldn't you?" Alasyr shot back. "We're talking about a young girl who will *die* in these mountains if she's not rescued, and you want to fixate on your jealousy of our castles and magic?"

Marsh held his hand up to Alasyr, silencing him. "If there's anything we can offer you in return, Steward Frost, we would be glad to do so. We're not here to anger you, or take from you. We're here because we both care about this girl, and we know of no other way to get to her. Alasyr can fly to her, but he lacks the strength to safely carry her down. I lack the wings. We need to take her by foot, and if there isn't a pass, then all hope really is lost to us, and I cannot accept that."

"Was the Ravenwoods, broke the alliance," Frost said. "You already know there's a pass. You wouldn't have come all the way here if you didn't know that. There *was* a pass. Years ago, the men of this Reach were driven by their curiosity. Our arrangement was no different from what the Derehams still enjoy; we protected the pass, the Ravenwoods gave us their magic in return. Healing, mainly. For hundreds of years, or so I've been told, until it was no longer desirable for the Ravenwoods to aid us. Then, they turned on us."

"Why?" Marsh asked. "Why would they turn on you?"

Frost didn't answer.

Alasyr radiated with annoyance. "How did your daughter become blind? You said half her life. An accident, then?"

The look Frost dropped on Alasyr was enough to cool Marsh's blood. "Fell as a girl. Hit her head. When she woke, she was fine, other than her sight. I took her down as far as Wulfsgate, but even they don't keep Healers around. And why would they, when they have ravens doing their bidding?"

"I can heal her. But you have to show us the pass."

Frost's disdain for Alasyr wasn't stronger than this enticement. "You would heal her? You would do that? Can do that?"

Alasyr shrugged as if it was nothing to him. "Of course I can. But what I ask in return isn't up for negotiation. I heal Elena. You show us the way, and tell us what we might expect on the trip."

"I've never been up the pass. I couldn't tell you what dangers await, only how to begin."

"Then you'll show us how to begin. Are we in agreement?"

"You will heal her first."

"Bring her."

Frost called for his daughter, who Marsh suspected hadn't returned with the cider because she was listening to their words. He turned back to them. "You must know this pass hasn't been traveled in over a hundred years. More. We don't tend it. No need now. I don't know what you'll find up there, as I said, but it can be nothing good."

"We know there are risks," Marsh said.

"Do you, though? I don't think you do. But you seem determined either way, and it can only be the Guardians that brought the two of you here, offering to heal my Elena, so I won't stop you. What's it to me?"

Elena returned without the ciders. Alasyr reached his hands toward her face. When she recoiled, her father assured her it was all right. She closed her eyes, and Alasyr pressed his hands over them. And then it was done. Elena Frost gasped when her eyes opened. She looked directly at her father, really seeing him, and then Alasyr, Marsh. Her mouth erupted into a sob.

"Can you see?" Frost stumbled from his seat toward her. "Can you see, daughter? Elena?"

Elena looked him in the eyes and nodded. She reached forward and, as if both afraid and elated, laid her palm against her father's scruffy face. Overwhelmed, she closed her eyes again. "I can," she said. "It's so—"

"Right," Alasyr said, impatient. "So that's done. Now show us the pass."

Frost sighed. He brought Elena's hand to his mouth with a light kiss, then let it fall away. "Wait here. I'll prepare the wagon."

"My horse is in town," Marsh said. "I'll need to go fetch her before we start."

"No, you won't," Frost answered. "Your horse won't survive these mountains. You go on foot."

Frost left, and his daughter, with one last tearful look at them both, followed.

"I don't like this," Marsh said. "I can't even take my horse. I'm out of food, I—"

"He'll restock your food. It's the least he can do, after the gift I've given him."

"It's not even the food. It's... this is bigger than us, Alasyr. We need people to aid us."

"You know that's not possible."

"Yeah." Marsh ran his hands down his face. "Yeah, I do know."

"Do you?"

"We'll do it your way. There's no other choice."

"You act like you'll be alone. I'll stay with you, for most of it, anyway."

"Comforting, seeing how well that's worked out so far."

"If something happens to you, Wildwood, I won't let you just *die* up there, all right? If that happens, I'll get help. All right? All right?"

Marsh didn't believe him. He knew Alasyr was lying. But what choice did he have? He'd already committed his life to saving Emberley, and this was how he could do it. This was the way to prove that he'd meant the words when he said them.

"All right, Alasyr. Fine."

26

TRUMPETS

"Did you hear that?"

Storm looked up from the chair where she'd been sharpening her knife. She did this a lot now, he noticed, drawing the blade over the whetstone with mindless precision. Any sharper, and that blade could slice through the kingdom itself. He was beginning to take it personally. She was bored. That was his fault, like everything else falling apart in the Westerlands.

"Hear what?" Storm asked. But a moment later, she stopped her ministrations and cocked her head. "Are those trumpets?"

"Sounds like trumpets," Brandyn said, mulling it over.

"But trumpets only come out for the lord and lady when they're returned to the Rush."

"Exactly, Storm. I'm here, so who decided the trumpets should be played?"

"And for whom," Storm muttered.

"Wouldn't surprise me if it was Blackfen who ordered them. All but fancies himself a lord now, the way he talked to me and then ran out like a traitor to go collect allies like sweetmeats. Perhaps he's come to stake his claim, make it official."

"Come on, Brandyn, that's not fair," Storm said. She gave him the same disappointed look she'd one day give her children, if she had them. "He's only trying to help you. You haven't made that easy for anyone."

"He *abandoned* me," Brandon pointed out as he hurried to the window. He saw the Rush Riders move into the courtyard in all their regalia, their long bows stretching from above their heads to nearly touching the ground as they rode in on their majestic horses. Four to a row they streamed in, peeling off to the right and left as they filled the open square. There seemed no end to them.

"How many Rush Riders do we *have* in this Reach?" he asked.

"I don't know. A fair amount, I suppose?"

"Well, I think they're all here," he said. "Come look."

Storm joined him at the window. "That's really something. Aren't they beautiful?"

"The horses or the riders?"

"It's almost as if they're not men at all, but something more. Doesn't it seem that way to you, too?"

"Hard for me to think about that right now when I'm watching this spectacle unfold and I don't even know why."

Storm laid a hand on his back. "Oh, come on, Brandyn, you're not yourself."

"You've been saying that, but I haven't asked for your opinion."

She turned toward him, her attention still half peeled to the march of the Rush Riders below. "There's an anger in you that doesn't want to leave. It seems to have taken residence. You shouldn't be so quick to allow it to get so comfortable."

"Oh yeah? You might have anger, too, if your father was murdered by your uncle—"

"My father *was* murdered. By *your* uncle."

"If your favorite sister was lost and probably dead in the mountains. If your other sister was taken from you by a king who's now dead and has left this realm in the hands of a monster. If you were *tortured* for hours by one of these monsters, and then instead of being allowed to recover from that, I was given a sword to take a man's head off!"

"You had a choice. You chose to take his head."

"No, Storm. I didn't. If I'd let him go, not one of the men who followed me there would've followed me home, and you *know* that. The choice was stolen from me, like everything else that matters. Like my very Reach, most likely, and all I can do is watch as Blackfen comes in and takes it from me."

"He doesn't want to take this Reach, he wants to protect it!"

"From me. Right?"

Storm sighed. "It doesn't have to be this way, Brandyn."

"Doesn't it?"

Storm started to say something else, some other piece of misguided wisdom he didn't ask for, but Brandyn silenced her with his shock.

"It's not Blackfen," he said.

"Then who?"

"My *mother*," he whispered. "She's here. She's home."

"She didn't say she was coming home, did she? I thought she was in Wulfsgate until Emberley was found."

"That's what she said in her last letter. But look."

Storm followed his gaze. "Well. That is most certainly Lady Blackwood."

"I haven't seen her in… in…" Brandyn felt like crying, but that's what a child would do. "It's been years. I could've seen her when I returned home to meet the girls in the Hidden Cave, but Emberley told me not to. She said… and then we left…" Brandyn twisted his face to avoid the tears.

"She's here now," Storm said, more gently than he was used to. "So let's go down and offer Lady Blackwood the proper greeting."

Brandyn nodded. He swallowed down the rest of his words. His mother was here. Emberley wasn't at her side, and there'd been no raven delivering news, good or bad. Was she here to tell him in person that Emberley was dead?

Or… or was she instead here to silence him, to punish him for his failure to run this Reach as she would have?

This was the one thing he could do for her, and he couldn't even do that.

Brandyn and Storm rushed down the stairs and into the courtyard to meet her. The last of the Rush Riders peeled away, revealing his mother in all her magnificence. Asherley Blackwood, the Great Lady of Longwood. As regal as she had ever been. He'd always seen her this way; as a great lady first and a mother second. She wore the brilliant emerald velvet of the Rush, laced with a deep crimson at the sleeves that matched the Rush Riders who answered to her alone.

All Brandyn wanted to do was throw himself in her arms and drink up the cool comfort only she could offer him. His mother was here, she was *here*, and he forgot, for the moment, his failures, his inadequacies, and rushed forward to do what he knew he should not.

But she raised her hand, stopping him. "We'll speak tonight, Brandyn."

Brandyn was mortified. He wanted nothing more than to disappear into the stones and melt away. His council had witnessed this public chastisement. Everyone had.

"Mother?" he asked. His voice cracked.

"In my chambers," she said, in the authoritative voice she used with her subjects, not her children. Never with them. "A private supper, you and I."

His mother and her retinue rode past him and continued on toward the stables, leaving him breathless and without words. As they passed, Brandyn locked eyes with Joran Rosewood, who'd vanished entirely at the most critical juncture in the war.

"You," he hissed, but the old Enchanter dropped his eyes, avoiding Brandyn.

Brandyn turned to Storm, but she could only shrug.

Asherley didn't sit. Each of the men alternately offered her some new place to rest, but she declined them, one by one. She'd been doing nothing *but* resting these past months. She wanted to stand. To pace. To do *something* that would lead to a result she could see and feel.

Before her stood Arturo Blackfen, Griffath and Rhydian Tyndall, and Easlan James. She'd summoned these four men specifically to the Halls of Longwood, choosing them carefully from among her most trusted men. She could count on these men to be honest and speak clearly, without fear.

That she could only be certain about these four was a stark reminder of how much everything had changed since she'd allowed herself to be carted off to Duncarrow.

She'd intentionally left Joran out of the meeting. She'd heard all she needed to from him, for now.

Asherley had seen none of this coming. Not her husband's murder, nor the war it had launched. Not Brandyn's call to lead, nor his failure of it. What good was a gift of sight when what it didn't show negated what it did?

The men, turn by turn, shared their concerns over the intervening weeks between the end of the war and now. They were so very careful when they spoke of Brandyn, cautious not to besmirch his name while remaining clear and true to their words about the troubles. This was also why she'd chosen them, for she couldn't be certain that other men's heads would be safe if they said anything about her son that didn't sit well with her.

She hadn't always been this emotional, but Asherley could say that *she hadn't always been* about so many things now. Both ends of her emotional pendulum swing were heightened with her losses, and all that had happened to her since she'd left Termonglen for Duncarrow.

Despite Blackfen having prepared her in Wulfsgate, their words were still ice to her bones. It was so much worse to hear the words in her own halls, on her own land.

"I taught him better than that," Asherley said, more to herself than the men.

"My lady, he's twelve," Steward James said, and Asherley started to correct him, to insist Brandyn was eleven, but, with a start, she realized he was right.

What else had changed all these months away?

"No one has endured more than you have, Lady Blackwood. You're back now, and that's what matters. It's what will matter to the other stewards." Griffath Tyndall, this time. He'd artfully avoided the subject of his son's return when she greeted him, though she saw the unasked questions in his eyes.

His brother, Grand Minister Tyndall, stepped forward. "If I may?"

Asherley nodded.

"I believe the boy is suffering, my lady. He has not adequately grieved the loss of his father, and he feels his shadow lingering here. Lady Gabi, as well, though she's not been tasked with running a Reach, either."

Asherley held out her hands. "I can't bring him back, Rhydian. I don't have that power." But wasn't part of the problem that she didn't *know* what power she had? She'd only just started to understand what she might be capable of when she was forced to leave.

"I know, my lady. Of course not. But what you didn't see was how he bonded with Lord Byrne's brother, Lord Warwick. They grew quite close in the war, and I believe it was good for them both. Brandyn needed that guidance, as all young men do. He's a smart boy, Lady Blackwood. He takes after you. But he benefitted more from the experience of his elders than I fear he's willing to acknowledge. He doesn't realize how this helped him win the war. Sometimes I think he believes he did it by himself."

Asherley turned her head away. "Let's move on from my son. I have to face him soon enough. But I thank you for your wisdom, Grand Minister."

Tyndall bowed.

"How difficult will it be to repair the damage?"

"The stewards are spitting mad," Easlan said, "but they know it isn't their lady behind this. If your return comes with the return of the way things were before, all will be well again. We've not come so far that we can't go back."

Asherley laughed. "That sounds too easy."

"As easy as it was for Brandyn to take."

"I do that," she said, "and they'll never respect him. You know that. He will one day be their lord, and their respect for him can never be in question."

"They know he's only a boy, my lady. No one could ever expect more from him."

"Yes, and if I'd died, he would still be a boy *and* their lord, wouldn't he?"

"You could call for a review of taxes," Blackfen said. "There's not been one in many years, and the stewards know this is overdue. They're expecting one."

"I haven't had a tax review because I haven't raised taxes. Something I would hope most men in this Reach would be very grateful for," Asherley said testily.

"You have not, but many of them have raised the taxes they levy upon their own people, my lady, offering no benefit in return for this. Brandyn perhaps chose the wrong path to address this, but he identified a problem that's been festering in this Reach, without doubt. This is a way you can help the people and keep the stewards from straying too far from the line. It's a small thing, but it will protect the spirit of Brandyn's command while not driving the stewards closer to revolt," Easlan said.

Asherley turned to the Tyndalls. "What say the two of you?"

Griffath nodded at Easlan. "He's right, my lady. Some have raised taxes against their citizens, and they shouldn't have without cause. They know this. You can right the wrong and still protect the people."

"I suppose this was what Brandyn was attempting in his misguided way," she said.

"He saw his people were suffering, and he acted as he believed was right."

Asherley let her eyes travel across all four men. "I will not tolerate a single word against Brandyn from anyone in this Reach. You understand?"

"Of course, my lady. That should not even need to be said," the Grand Minister said.

"No, but it *does* need to be said. Because there will be no coming back from that. Brandyn's reputation must be preserved. I trust the four of you to see to that."

"Of course."

The midday sun crested at the tops of the floor-to-ceiling windows, blinding her. A new but already familiar sensation followed, a deep pain that pulled the nausea from her belly and sent it straight to the back of her throat.

She covered her eyes and pointed to the curtains. "Someone draw them." When they hesitated, she yelled, from her pain, "Now!"

Blackfen rushed forward and worked at the long ropes, one at a time. The others joined him, and when their backs were turned, she leaned over the side of the table and retched upon the floor.

Asherley ran her ornate sleeve across her mouth and said, "And let them remain that way. I never want to see the sunlight in this room ever again."

THIS TIME ASHERLEY ALLOWED BRANDYN'S HUG. HE WAS LESS EAGER to the task than he'd been in the courtyard. She'd killed that in him, but she'd needed to, for his own sake. One day, he'd understand.

The embrace from her son should have been a sweet relief, a reminder that though she'd given up so much, she still had much left to her. Instead, it hurt her to do it. Her instincts screamed at her to put as much distance as she could between herself and everything precious remaining. She now understood how evanescent all of it was, how swiftly even this moment could be taken.

But she couldn't show any of this to Brandyn. He was her son, and right now he needed her to be more than his leader. He needed his mother.

Looking at him was like gazing upon a younger version of

Byrne. Brandyn had grown, and it was more than years that separated their last time together. The subtle signs that he'd aged out of his boyhood appeared in the lines on this face that had come too early; of the permanent scowl that settled more naturally over his face than the smile he gave her. He wasn't the same boy. He wasn't even a boy at all now, not really. Only in his immaturity of leadership had he shown signs of his youth, but that was her failing, not his.

"Emberley?" he asked. He'd broken the embrace. She'd waited for him to do it, knowing he'd be too hurt if she did.

Now that it was done, all she felt was relief.

Asherley shook her head. "She's out there. They'll find her."

"Why'd you leave, then? I thought you wanted to be the one to do it."

"We'll talk about that later."

"Have you been to see Gabi?"

"I have."

"You made *me* wait to see you."

"Gabrianna only needed my kisses and reassurances. That's not what you need, is it?"

Brandyn's hands turned to fists at his side. "I didn't know, for months, if you were dead or alive. If I would ever see you again. Until word came from Wulfsgate, I knew nothing at all!"

Asherley gestured for him to take a seat. The table in her chambers had been prepared for the two of them. She reveled in the rich scent of the lean meats that were more familiar to her than what she'd been given in the north. "I needed to understand what had happened here in my absence."

"Who better to tell you that than me?"

"I also needed time with my thoughts."

"You had time for that on the ride here, Mother."

"Time with my thoughts on you, Brandyn," she said, without dropping her eyes away. "You, and what I can do to help you."

"You could not leave me alone to run an entire Reach for months, and then to lead a war in our name!"

Asherley stood and held out her arms. "Come here, Brandyn."

"I don't want another hug. Not like this." He blinked hard. He fought tears. "I wanted my mother, but that's not how you're seeing me now, is it? You see one more thing you need to fix. I don't want that. I don't want you to look at me like that."

Asherley dropped her arms and returned to her seat. With some reluctance, he joined her at the table, but his wary, wounded look didn't dissolve. "You're my son. My *only* son. But you, and Emberley, and Gabrianna are not my only children. This entire Reach and the well-being of everyone who lives on its land falls to me to see after, as it will one day fall to you."

"That's what I was *trying* to do when the people came to me seeking my aid."

Asherley nodded. "You did right, taking that to heart. You should listen. That's what a lord does. It's wisdom that will show you how to act upon what you hear. That will come with experience."

"The stewards are taking money from their people and giving nothing in return."

"Not all of them," Asherley countered. "And yet you punished them all, for the crimes of one or two. Didn't you?"

Brandyn looked down.

"We need the stewards, as much as the stewards need their people. The stewards invest in the lands the people live upon, the same land they need to make lives, to prosper. The stewards, too, are your people. They're your partners. You could never do it all."

The tears he'd been holding back erupted. They streamed down his face. She resisted the urge to reach for his hand, for both their sakes. "I don't understand any of it. And you knew that when you left me here. You knew that and you did it, anyway."

"When I left," Asherley said evenly, "your father was alive. I knew he could handle things. He has before. I didn't learn until much later, until it was too late for me to do a thing about it, that we'd been betrayed. And then I was a prisoner once more. Powerless."

"Until you weren't."

Asherley leaned forward across the table. "I won't apologize to you for trying to save your sister. If you're waiting for one, you'll go your whole life in disappointment."

Brandyn sniffled.

"I left you with men I trusted, and you replaced most of them with boys who were too afraid to tell you that you were making things worse. You ignored those with experience and wisdom, and did as you pleased."

"You left me!" Brandyn cried.

"Brandyn. You are my baby, the sun in my sky. I know I failed you, but it will not happen twice. Our failures are lessons, and I needed time to reflect on what mine could be from this."

Brandyn leaned back in his chair. He pushed his plate of food aside. "What does that mean?"

"Women have led this Reach since Rhosyn's daughter. Some have questioned why I would break that, by choosing you. Our success leading the Westerlands has come with a sense of invulnerability, but it has also caused me to overlook the needs the men might possess. That *you* might need more than me, a woman, can give. There are things that even I cannot teach you."

Brandyn watched her in growing suspicion.

She took a sip from her wine. "I understand you've grown quite close to your uncle. Khallum."

He looked cornered by the question, eyes wide. He didn't answer.

"He's a good man. His methods are cruder than mine, and we don't always see matters the same, but I respect Khallum Warwick. Byrne respected him, and Khallum, most days, respected that Byrne wasn't just a reprise of his older brother, but his own man. And you're like this, both your father, and me. But it's your father's people who can teach you what I cannot."

"What are you saying?"

"You're leaving for the Southerlands at first light. I've already sent word ahead to your uncle. It will be good for you to learn how to be a man from someone who has survived the experience."

Brandyn pitched forward. "Do you even know what's going on in the Southerlands right now?"

"Yes," she said. "I know also that Khallum Warwick came to your aid when you needed him. And now Brandyn Blackwood will come to his aid when he needs you."

"Needs me? I'm just a child!"

"A child who, with the help from his allies, won a war before he was old enough to be called a man," she said coolly. "You'll repay that debt, and from that, you will learn a lesson more valuable than anything I could ever teach you, Brandyn."

"He doesn't want me there. He's angry with me, for not going along with what the entire kingdom now calls Khallum's Folly."

"You are not the entire kingdom. And I better not ever hear you speak of your uncle's devotion like that again." Asherley breathed out. "He loves you, Brandyn. Whatever anger he possesses will soon be replaced by an opportunity to help shape you into the man who will one day become his son's ally."

His lip curled inward. "What if I don't want to go?"

"You will. And this time, you'll go on your own. Storm's mother wants her home. It's time for you to let her go."

"Without Storm?" Tears streamed down his cheeks. "You'd really make me go without my protector? Why are you punishing me?"

Asherley quelled her own welling emotion. "Go on, eat your food. You know better than I do what passes for sustenance on your travels."

"Mother?"

She prepared to defend against his next rebuttal, but it was worry she saw in his eyes. She brought her hand to her face and gasped, recoiling. Her flesh was ice.

"I'm fine," she lied. "Eat."

27

THE ONLY PATH

Oldwin found an abandoned home to shelter in. Abandoned was perhaps not the most truthful means to describe the small cottage near the shore, as it hadn't been abandoned until he disposed of the old man and woman living there.

He should have sent a messenger to deal with Gwyn, instead of coming himself. Risky, but not as much as the situation he was in now. He'd known even as he left Duncarrow that a return was precarious, and now he was well and truly stranded here, his magic weakening at so rapid a pace that his thoughts could hardly keep up with the changes.

It wasn't only weakening. He was losing entire pieces. His visions had mostly left him. He could no longer render himself invisible, the magic he'd been employing to get to the Southerlands and back to Duncarrow without detection. A change in appearance wasn't enough, not when every ship in the sea was scrutinized, every man's purpose inspected.

Oldwin was tired. Tired, straight to his bones. He'd never known such fatigue—or any, really. He'd never understood when men lamented their exhaustion over ale, or to their long-suffering wives.

He'd never needed rest in all his years. He slept because the days were long at his age, and he didn't have a use for every hour anymore.

How *fast* it had all happened. He couldn't help but reflect on how the past thousands of years leading to this day had been fine, and then suddenly, with a snap of the fingers of fate, he wasn't at all fine. He was swiftly becoming less fine with every passing day and had been given no time to adjust to these changes. These *losses*.

He had a feeling he'd never see Duncarrow again. He possessed no sentimental ties for that rocky isle, but he was protected in Duncarrow. He couldn't see what the future would bring to his dwindling magic, and for the first time in his life, he now had to think about such base things as protection. He was vulnerable.

Oh, how he hated that word. Vulnerable. Oldwin of Ilynglass wasn't made to be vulnerable.

And yet...

A return to Duncarrow couldn't happen today, and tomorrow, he'd be worse. His magic was too unpredictable now.

His conversation with Gwyn plagued him. He didn't want to think about her, but he couldn't banish the surprise in her eyes when he'd said that Khallum had what he needed. Was she truly ignorant of the Warwick Defenders, a role they'd played for centuries? She was weak. Yes. So it was also possible that she was a fool, though she didn't strike him as a particular one. Did she really not know? And if she didn't know, what did that say about Khallum?

She'd not been as easy to convince as he'd expected. When he'd dangled Esmerelda in front of her, she'd hesitated. She'd demanded proof, and so Oldwin had sent a scrap of her daughter's traveling cloak, and that thin strip of fabric, which could have come from anywhere, was enough to light the hope in her simple heart.

Gwyn only continued aiding him out of fear that Oldwin would take back what he'd given her, but even that fear had its expiry of usefulness, for Esmerelda was now surrounded by a thousand men protecting her, and this gave Gwyn false comfort. A thousand men wouldn't be enough to keep Oldwin away if he was determined enough. She needed to understand this. The only power Gwyn Warwick possessed was the one Oldwin still gave her.

What he would do this night would remove all doubt of this. She'd confess to her husband her treachery, knowing she had no choice now but to involve him. Then Khallum would have a choice of his own to make. The door, or his children. And Oldwin would do it if he had to. He would kill every child of Khallum Warwick and every other man in the Southerlands. He'd crush every last life underfoot, even that mewling bastard infant of Esmerelda's. Especially that one.

But there hadn't been a Defender in the Wastelands for many years. Oldwin would know, for his men, under the guise of the king's business, had been the keepers of that land for over a century. Warwicks found their way in from time to time, and the guards dealt with it. But Khallum himself had never been, nor had his sons, his brother, his sister.

Had he given up the mantle? Did he even know about it? He had to know. Khallum Warwick wouldn't possibly care this much about the Wastelands, still, if he didn't know what was in there.

Oldwin rolled over on the hard bed. He'd stripped back the blankets, ripe with the old couple's dying stench. The straw mattress was enough. He didn't need the creature comforts of men. Only a place to refresh his energy. There wasn't much left now. What remained was enough to turn his attentions on one path, and one path only.

He could go to the Wastelands, where a door waited for him, unguarded. But if he didn't succeed where thousands before him had failed, he would die trying.

Or, he could travel to the Hinterlands, where the magic would prevent him from entering, but with what remained of his own power, his cunning, he might find another way.

But he couldn't do both.

He didn't have to decide tonight. Tonight, he would deliver a gift to the Southerlands of the likes that would cause songs to be written and sung, for years beyond.

Assana hadn't left Balfour's room for days. He'd stopped attending his courses. He had more important things to attend, he would say, falling over her, plunging himself inside and annihilating all except her illicit desire.

She could have pushed him sooner, but there was something about him that almost caused her to forget why she'd come. A small part of her saw herself never leaving this room, content to spend the rest of her days twisted in endless coitus with this strange boy.

He started calling her Assana days ago. She'd never given him her name. *I know who you are,* he'd said. *I knew it after that first day. I just didn't care.*

She'd been stunned. He had more cunning in him than she expected. *Did you?*

Is that a problem for you?

We're cousins. Doesn't that bother you?

You knew we were cousins when you were plotting to fuck me, while you were fucking me, and after you fucked me. Should I be bothered?

Balfour reluctantly unwound himself from her arms. It wasn't a temporary thing this time, but a call to the action Assana had come here for. He groaned to do it, and she resented that he was the one to break the fugue of this bliss. That she'd not found the where-withal to put her mission above her confusing desires.

He slipped on his worn and peeling boots. They weren't befitting the nephew of a lord, and Assana wondered why Earwyn hadn't sent her son any new ones. She realized it must be because he hadn't asked.

"What was it like, fucking the king?"

Assana was so taken aback by the question, all she could do was laugh. "Unpleasant. Why?"

"I've never met anyone who's fucked a king. Only curious." He finished with his boots and turned to her. "Did you see it happen? Did you see his murder?"

Assana was afraid he might read her mind. Could he do that? There was no way to know for sure. She pushed her memories of that day back. "No. I didn't."

"Oldwin let you go, after he'd murdered the king in his own keep? Just like that?"

"No, not exactly," she said carefully. "I hid from him until it was safe to escape."

"How did you escape? The word in the Easterlands is that you're either Oldwin's prisoner, or dead. There'd be a lot of people happy to see you."

"A boat. Why did you bring me here, Balfour?"

He shrugged.

"You must have some reason."

"I suppose I was curious why you'd go to such lengths to get my attention."

"I need something."

"Plainly. Bad enough to use me to get it. Most around here wouldn't have sunk low enough to come to me for anything. I suppose I had to know why."

"You weren't the first," Assana said. "But I do hope you'll be the last."

"Because you want to keep fucking me, or because you want to stop fucking me?"

Assana continued to be surprised at his artless way of speaking. "Because if I don't find this answer soon, it'll be too late."

"Well," he said, "tell me what it is, and if I can help you, I will. But if you lie to me..." Balfour tapped his head. "I'll know. Magic."

Assana laughed, nervous. "That's not how magic works, you silly boy. Most get one gift, if they're lucky."

"Most," he said with a wink. "But is that a guess you're willing to stake your entire claim upon?"

"First, tell me what's in your book. The one you hide from me."

Assana pointed to the deep pile of cloaks and clothing in the corner. She knew the book was at the bottom.

Balfour tensed. "No."

"Why not?"

"It has nothing to do with you."

"How can you know that, if I haven't told you why I'm here?"

"I just know."

Assana made as if she was going to the pile to get a reaction from him. She got one and stopped. She wasn't here to torture him. She needed his help. "Is it at least interesting? You know, of the sort that the stuffy scholars wouldn't want you to read about?"

Balfour cocked his head. "Interesting to me, anyway. Others don't care as I do. Now, tell me."

"How do I know you can help me?"

"You already believed I could. It's why you followed me, cornered me, and then fucked me. You saw a boy who knew the value of hiding something, and you thought, if I could go to such lengths to hide something, then perhaps I could find something."

"Then where would a boy like Balfour Dereham go to find something that another needed?" Assana employed her best coquetry, but they were beyond this part. He already knew he could have her. He'd had her dozens of times over the preceding days, and he'd have her again before this was over. There was no game here anymore.

He pulled his cloak over the top of him and checked the night sky outside the window. "Why don't I show you?"

"Where are we going?"

"The library will close soon. No one goes there at night if they don't have to."

"You mean I could've just walked into the library all along? I didn't need to fuck my way through all the colored castles?"

Balfour laughed. He liked her. She could see it. "Your plan offers infinitely more excitement than mine, but hopefully mine promises more satisfaction."

"What's your plan?"

"Put your clothes on, Assana. You'll need them. For now, anyway."

She lifted a brow. "For now?"

WARDEN LIDDLE WAS A STRANGE MAN. THE KIND THAT CAME TO A place like Oldcastle not to live but to die.

Balfour had given her one task. *I've already made all the books fly off the shelves. Often enough, he's going to realize it's me and report me to the Sepulchre, if I do it again. This one's all you.*

She had the old man well occupied by the downward hitch in her gown, revealing more bosom than her mother ever would have allowed. With Liddle's eyes buried in her chest, Balfour slipped past without notice.

"What's that you say, lass? A wulf?"

"Yes! Outside the library!" Assana panted out her pretend fear, aware of how her breasts heaved with every breath, pleased at his budding awareness of it.

"In these parts? I ken we donnae get wulves—"

"Well, there's one now, and you must go, you must do *something*."

"Well, I..."

"I was told you would know what to do, Warden. That I should come to you, because, as they said, Warden Liddle was the man capable of such a task."

"Who told you that, lass?"

"The other girls outside. They ran away in their terror. They're terrified! But before they ran for their lives, they said, go to the Warden. He's a Southerlands lad, salt and sand and he's never met a thing he was afraid of!"

Warden Liddle wore the conflicted look she'd been aiming for. Of course, this was all it would take. It was always all it would take.

"Well," he said, hitching his trousers, "I ken it cannae hurt to take a peek."

"Oh, thank you, sir! He was hanging around the trees. Stalking us, like prey." Assana pointed off into the vague distance. "He'll take one look at you and know he's made a terrible mistake, though."

"By the trees, you say? Well, I ken there's nay light out that way. May have to wait until morning."

"Oh, yes, he'll be hard to see, and you might need to wait for a while."

Liddle's doubts crept into his knitted brows and narrowed eyes. "I cannae just leave the library alone."

"Oh, it wouldn't be alone, sir. I'll watch it for you. It's the least I can do." Assana smiled.

"You donnae even know what to do. 'Tis no job for a lass."

"Do you get many people this late at night, Warden?"

"Aye, well, no, but..."

Assana guided him out, pressing herself against his back to remind him of the prize the wulf meant to take. "I simply won't feel safe returning to my room until I know he's been handled."

"What if I cannae find him?" Liddle called over his shoulder when she shoved him into the night.

"I have all the faith that you will, Warden!"

Assana closed and bolted the double doors and cast her eyes across the library in search of Balfour. She caught him waving her down from the back of what seemed an endless alley of books. She hadn't known there were even this many books in existence in the entire kingdom.

It wasn't the library, though, that Balfour was interested in. He stood at the doorway of a back room, and she made her way down to him, inhaling in wonder at all the many books.

"What is this place?" she asked when she'd reached him.

Balfour held up a key, dangling it. "The books no one wants us to read."

"You assume I'm after a book."

"I thought we were past the games, Assana. What else could you be after? You want information. Books are where information lives."

Assana slowly nodded. "All right, then."

"I give him half a tick before he loses his courage. You tell me what you need, it'll go quicker if both of us can search."

"Could it really be here?"

"You tell me. I've never met a rule I didn't enjoy breaking."

Assana turned to him. "The sorcerers. You know, the ones the Rhiagains brought with them. Like Oldwin. And Mortain, the one who helped my father commit atrocities."

"We're here about what you don't know, not what you do."

Assana groaned. "Is there anything here about them?"

He didn't seem nearly stunned enough at the target of her search. Instead, he looked excited.

"Well, I don't know, but there's only one way to find out."

28

OLDWIN'S GIFT

J esse was in the desert.

This wasn't the warm familiarity of the Southerland high-lands, where he'd spent so much of his youth. He *had* been here before, though. The answer came into focus as he recognized the jagged crags and fine, vivid sands.

He turned to look for Esmerelda, but she wasn't there. Of course she wouldn't be. She'd never be here. This wasn't a place for her. He wished it wasn't a place for himself, either.

Panic settled in. A hot rush of dizziness tingled behind his eyes, sending a spray of infinite dark dots into his vision. He stumbled, unsteady. Like before, he didn't know how he'd gotten here, or how to leave. He was stuck until someone or something released him.

Then he saw him. Isdemus.

"Jamesan," he said. His eyes wore a distant, sorrowful look. "Why do you linger?"

Jesse raised his arms to shield himself from a hard wind carrying a funnel of dust straight at him. It stung his eyes and coated his tongue.

When the assault ended, he spat out the remaining sand and

blinked his eyes. "How can you not know, when it was you who understood why I must go to her in the first place?"

"You bound yourself to her. You didn't disclose that intent when I told you where to find her." The words were an accusation, but were delivered on the soft stream of resignation.

"Because it wasnae my intent when I left you. I only went to make sure she was safe, to see my vow to her and my brother through to the end. But when I arrived..." *No, before that. Before that, because now I can see things I couldn't see before.* "Circumstances changed."

"You stay for her," Isdemus said. "But it is *for* her you must leave."

"I'm not clever enough for your riddles, Isdemus. You want me to go somewhere, but you won't tell me where. You taunt me about staying, but I've been waiting for *you*, to tell me where to go, and what to do. If you're expecting me to read your mind, or figure this out myself, you're going to be very disappointed."

"Something is happening right now, Jamesan. Right as we speak, in this very moment. A treachery so powerful it will change the course of this kingdom's redemption. Some will think there's no coming back. But those same people will think this because they do not know about you. What you can do. What you will do."

"What? What's happening?"

"You were never meant to stop it. That is not your destiny. But you can put halt to further loss and pain. Not from the warmth of your marriage bed, though. The noose draws tighter every moment you stay there. The safety of everyone you care about is transitory, a deception. For if you are there, you are not where you must be to put an end to this all. And it is only you who can do this."

"Stop what?" Jesse demanded. "Why will you not tell me?"

"I wouldn't ask this of you, my own blood, if there was another. If I believed your father was enough, I might have come to him, but would that have been a better idea? Any easier for me? You have a sister as well. I should have told you this. It seemed so unimportant against the weight of all the rest, but it's your right to know this. But whilst they have the blood of sorcerers in their veins, they are not

Medvedev, like you. They cannot pass through the veil that would take them to the end." Isdemus continued his rambling. Jesse wanted to ask about this sister, but already the desert was fading. His dream was ending.

"*Is* this a dream?" Jesse asked, though he didn't know who the question was for. "Like the others..."

"What else have you seen?"

"Colors." Jesse shook his head. "Emerald and violet and shades I donnae have the words in me to describe. And light... a bright light, so bright it eclipses everything around it."

"So then you already know where you must go?"

"That makes sense to you, does it?" Jesse asked, incredulous. "Colors and light and nonsense?"

"You've seen the end. You've seen your destiny."

"But where?"

"I cannot tell you where until you're ready to leave. This cannot live in your mind where it can be stolen by the same one who would take every life in this world to achieve his aims."

"I'll never be ready to leave." Jesse threw up his hands. "But I'll do it because I swore I would."

Isdemus nodded. "Then you'll leave tomorrow."

"I must see to the safety of Esmerelda and Gemma. Once that is done, then yes."

"Very well."

"Where, then?"

"When you last went to the Hinterlands, they denied you. Do you know why?"

"They didnae believe me, about who I was."

"You were not ready, but more importantly, you were not in the right land."

Jesse shrugged. "I went to my mother's land."

"Yet the one awaiting you, the one to whom you must go, is not in the Drumain lands, but the Saleen."

"You want me to go to the Saleen lands? The same Saleen slaughtered by the Quinlandens?"

"You'll wake now, Jesse."

Jesse started toward him. "Wait! I have more questions! Why would I go there? How will I even know where to go?"

"Esmerelda watches you. She worries for you."

"Isdemus!"

But he was already gone. The desert faded to the cool musk of their bedchamber.

Jesse shot forward in the bed, but Esmerelda caught him in her arms halfway through the motion. She wrapped him tight, pressing her face into the sweaty fabric of the shirt clung to his back.

"Every night now," she said. "These bad dreams."

"I'm sorry, Esme. I didnae mean to wake you."

"I'm *worried* about you, Jesse." Esmerelda rocked him in her embrace. "Don't keep me from this. Don't go somewhere I cannot go with you."

Jesse turned and gathered her in his arms this time, unwinding hers and folding them inward as he held her. "I have to find your father."

"Why, what's happened?"

He pressed his lips to her forehead and then slipped from the bed. "I donnae know. I donnae know anything of use at all, just that something will happen, or has happened. Something terrible."

"How do you know?"

He wouldn't lie to her. "Isdemus came to me."

Esmerelda's eyes narrowed. "What does he want now?"

Jesse looked back at her. "You know what he wants."

She exhaled, slowly closing her eyes. "So it's time then."

He nodded.

"Aye. Right. I'll pack our satchels. I've already spoken to my mother about Gemma. She can't go, of course. She's safer here, with the lot of the Warwick Guard looking after the keep. We'll return to find her spoiled rotten after a few weeks with my mother, but it can't be helped."

Jesse started toward her. "Esmerelda."

She recoiled gently. "Even now, you'd try to stop me? You, who knows me best?"

Jesse hung his head. "You know that isnae what I mean. You know."

"I go where you go," she said, landing each word with firm determination.

"I donnae know what we'll find when we get there. What if I cannae protect you?"

"*You* protect *me*?" Esmerelda threw her head back and laughed. "And jus' why do ye think I'm coming wit ye, Jamesan Strong? 'Tis *I* who will protect *you*."

Tears spilled over his eyelids. Esmerelda came to him, and, stretching on the tips of her toes, kissed both of them. "Jesse," she whispered.

"I'm afraid," he confessed in a whisper. Words he could only speak to her, and perhaps never again.

"Fears," she said softly, "are our comforts come to convince us they should triumph over bravery and honor. But it is bravery and honor that has won us our comforts, time and again. Now, you have been called. *We* have been called."

"But for what? I still donnae even know what they want from me!"

"Whatever it is, we'll do it together. As we do, in all things."

He twined his hands in hers. "I donnae deserve you."

"We all deserve exactly what we get. And I know it's true, for it was you who told me so."

The corner of Jesse's mouth twitched into the hint of a grin. "Did I? I thought you liked to let all my words flow right over ye, like air passing over the wind."

"You should be happy you've wed a woman still full of surprises." Esmerelda's smile faded so quickly it startled him. "Right, then. My father, you say. I suspect he's still in the Hall of Warring."

"At this hour?"

"I heard him speaking with Mother. There's been some new

revelation. Said not to expect him in bed tonight. He'd see her again when they broke fast."

Jesse released her hands and turned toward the door. "You'll go with me to find him, or you'll go to your mother, but you cannae stay here alone tonight."

"With you, of course," she said. "What will you tell him? How will you explain this... premonition you've had, without telling him who you are?"

"I'm not sure yet," Jesse said. "I'll think of something."

Drystan Sylvaine.

Son of Drystan and Raychelle, Steward and Stewardess of Rushwood, Easterlands.

They all spoke this name, Drystan, one by one, passing it between them, taking intentional turns with it, hoping, at some point, to discover an air of familiarity that might lead them down a more sure path.

It was Khallum's own son, Ransom, who'd proudly stood and declared he'd found Dain. *It's him. It has to be. All other orphans placed two decades ago have a history. But not him. Not Drystan. It says here that Stewardess Sylvaine couldnae have children, and the gift of an unknown boy was a miracle. Unknown boy. See, it says that right here. Boy of unknown origin. It has to be him, right?*

Khallum was proud of his son, whose presence in the Hall of Warring was long overdue. He'd been old enough for a while, but Khallum had never felt he was quite ready. None of his boys took after him. They were all Gwyn, through and through. He supposed that was his fault, for not giving them enough toughening as they grew from bairns. It had to be some reckoning from the Guardians that the only child who *was* like him was his daughter.

But this would all be Ransom's someday, tough enough or not.

The hour was late, and they were all tired. Or had been until Ransom's fortuitous discovery. The renewed vigor passing between the men would sustain them hours yet.

"So Dain Rhiagain was given to a Great Family," Rutland said. He ran his tongue over his lips. "All this time, he was hiding right in front of us."

"Ye s'pose Quinlanden knew about it?" Hamish asked.

"The ratsbane grasper would've used him long ago," Khallum countered. "Ye can bet on that."

Darrick paced near the open window, facing the sea. The night's wind had carried rain inside earlier, but the air was still now. Almost too still. "What do all of you know about the Sylvaines? Anyone know or trade with Steward Sylvaine? They must have acquaintances even beyond the Easterlands."

The men exchanged looks, alternately shaking their heads. "I ken the name Sylvaine, aye," Rutland said. "But not the man. We donnae trade with the Easterlands what we can get elsewhere."

"The book says he disappeared around twenty years past," Ransom said. "Beyond that, nay, nothing. No sightings. Nothing. However, it does say he left after the Epoch of the Accordant, and that—"

Khallum rubbed his beard with increasing angst. "Dead, then. That what you're saying?"

Ransom shook his head, still pointing proudly to his discovery. "I donnae ken so, Father, or at least, that isnae what it says here. The steward believed his lad left following a lass he loved. A Gretchen... Quinlanden." Ransom looked up. "Aunt Gretchen?"

Khallum's jaw dropped. He blubbered through a bout of speechlessness. "Read that again."

"Well, I ken, Father, it says right here. Aye, Gretchen. Gretchen Quinlanden, now Dereham."

"Gretchen," Khallum said. "And Dain Rhiagain. Is that what you're saying, lad?"

"Well, there's nay anything here to indicate he knew he was Dain, then or now. Was always just Drystan, to his father, his mother, the people of Rushwood."

"Aye, fine. He goes after Gretchen, and then what?" Khallum waved his hands, urging the boy on.

"There isnae anything else, Father. Just that about a decade ago, Steward Sylvaine transferred the stewardship to his brother's son. Drystan's name isnae mentioned anywhere else in their chapter. Aye, wait, there's this. I almost missed it. Maybe it's a fault in the transcription. But when Steward Sylvaine passed his heirdom to his nephew, it says he passed it from 'Ash to Barrie.' You suppose that was what they called him, then? Ash?"

Hamish wrinkled his lips. "Ash? What kinda name is tha'?"

"Lady Dereham will know," Darrick said. "We'll send a scout straightaway. I wouldn't trust this one to raven. If it's true, that he followed her, he would've given up everything to do it. That's no small thing. If anyone will know about this Drystan, or Ash, or whoever he is, it would be her."

Khallum hung his head, shaking it. "She's gone. She left in search of her boy and never returned."

"Dead, then?" Hamish asked.

Khallum shrugged.

"What about Lord Dereham?" Ransom said, then dropped his mouth into a sigh as he realized his error. "Christian?"

"The boy is a shame upon his house," Rutland said. "The stable hand would know more about the doings of the Derehams than their eldest son."

"Still. We have to ask," Darrick said. "Even something inconsequential could bear fruit. We'll send a scout north, and also to Rushwood, though I don't expect them to tell us much. A man doesn't give his title to another man's line if he doesn't believe the act is final."

"Hold," Khallum said. "Stop talking. That name... I ken it's been bothering me since Ransom said it. Drystan. That's the name of her son. The one who killed the sorcerer, Mortain. The one who died for it."

"And the man..." Rutland trailed off. "There was a man who came to take him back to Wulfsgate for the dead-given rites. Ye remember that? He was with one of the Dereham girls. The redhead."

"Lisbet," Khallum said. "Aye, I remember. Not well. We had our own business. I ken I remember them leaving with a wagon, aye? A wagon we helped pack. I thought he was a guard, or a footman of the Derehams."

"Was it him, then?" Hamish said, almost a whisper. "I ken there's something nay right about naming your son after yer old lover, unless..."

"Fishwife gossip," Khallum muttered. "Gretchen isnae here to defend her honor, and we'll nay besmirch it in her absence, either."

"What if it was him, though?"

"Pray it was, for that means he's still alive. Still out there."

"Ravens, then, at least to start," Darrick interjected. Khallum felt his need for action. His sense of having been neutered by the recent loss of Law. "At first light. Ravens, and then scouts. To Wulfsgate, and then to every town in the Easterlands. One to the new Lord Quinlanden as well, so he doesn't feel as if we're going around his authority. Rushwood was Drystan Sylvaine's home for two decades. Someone may know something. We'll just have to be a little guarded with our wording, in case the messages fall into the wrong hands."

"And just wait, then, for another attack?" Rutland countered. "Sit back and hope they find anything at all?"

"Is there a better way, Erran?" Khallum said. "The only other sorcerer we know of is the one we're trying to defeat. Dain may turn us away, aye, but he's all we have. He's the only thing we have. I donnae like it either. I donnae like sitting around, *waiting* for the creature to come at our people, with no defense! But we at last have a way forward. Unless one of you has one better, this is what we do. Until then, we keep our kin safe. We keep them so close we'll be ready to be well rid of them by the time this fight is ended."

The men traded nervous laughter. It was interrupted when the doors at the far end of the hall flew open. Jesse burst through them, with Esmerelda in tow. She cradled Gemma tight against her chest.

Khallum dropped both hands on the table. "What's gotten into ye, boy? It's the middle of the feckin' night!"

Jesse's flushed face gaped back in growing horror. "Something's happened, Lord Warwick."

"What? What's happened?"

"Everyone needs to gather to their wives and children now, make sure they're safe and accounted for."

Hamish rose. "Jamesan, what's the meaning of this?"

"Donnae just stare at me, go!" Jesse cried.

The men all shifted out of the room. Khallum watched them all, thinking, *this wouldn't have been enough. Even a month ago, they would've lit into him for daring to order them about.* Everything was different now. Nothing was safe. Taking anything for granted was flaunting a dare at the Guardians.

Khallum hung back. "Why'd you bring my daughter and grand-daughter to the Hall of Warring in the middle of the night?"

Jesse's hand dropped to his sword hilt. "They're safer with me."

"You will tell me where this came from, Jesse."

Jesse's eyes were glassy, heavy. "I felt it... I saw it."

"You know better than to think that's enough. You, coming in here, scaring the men like that. After all that's happened."

"Please, go to Lady Warwick and the boys. If I'm wrong, then the worst to come is that they're safe and you're ready to put your sword to me."

"Please, Father," Esmerelda pleaded. She bounced Gemma on her shoulder. "Please, just do as he asks."

Khallum's eyes shot between them. Landed on Jesse. He pointed a finger in his face. "You *will* explain this later."

Jesse nodded. "If I can, sir."

"No, not if you can. You've been acting afoul since ye returned, and I'm fed up to the gills with it. You're kin now, and ye owe me more than that."

Khallum pushed past him and stormed down the hall. He heard his daughter and her husband at his heels. Rutland was the first to appear in the corridor. With a sigh, he nodded to confirm his family was fine.

Hamish was next, confirming Andrija was fast asleep in her bed.

"And Ryan?" Jesse asked.

"Still in the gatehouse."

"Aye, we'll go there next."

They pushed farther down the corridor, rushing to the sounds of their breaths riding out their heartbeats. Ransom was at the door to the lord's chambers, but he'd waited for his father.

"Go on in then, boy!"

Khallum pushed past him and burst into the chambers. Though it was dark, he could see Gwyn's curved form under the heavy blanket. She shot forward in bed.

"What are you *doing*, Khallum?"

"Where are the boys?" he demanded.

"In their beds! Where else would they be?"

Gwyn asked these questions as she leapt from the bed, pulling her shawl around her shoulders. She followed them down the short hall leading to the bedchambers for the boys.

Khallum ripped back the covers on Garrick's bed. The boy slept soundly, knees pulled to his chest. Even the intrusion didn't stir him.

With a heavy sigh, he dropped the covers and headed toward the next room. Jesse was already ahead of him, and he turned, shaking his head. "He's not in his bed."

"Khallum, you'll tell me what this is about, or I'll scream!" Gwyn hissed behind him. "Why are you worried about the boys?"

"It's okay, Mother," Esmerelda said soothingly, but not at all convincingly.

Claybourne appeared in the doorway. He rubbed his eyes, squinting against the intrusion. "Father? Mother?"

"Where have you been?" Khallum asked, marching toward him. "Are you all right?"

Claybourne screwed his mouth into a frown. "I was in the privy. Willnae forget to ask your permission next time."

"Mind your mouth," Khallum warned him. To Jesse, he said, "The gatehouse."

Jesse turned to Esmerelda as he backed out of the room. "Stay with them? To gather them, to give them strength? There's at least a hundred guards just outside. Scream, and I'll come."

Esmerelda nodded. She pressed Gemma closer. "Of course."

Jesse nodded at Khallum, and together they moved back down the hall, turning toward the doors of the keep. The guards stumbled out of their sleep when Khallum cursed them.

Khallum pulled ahead, rushing through the mud, turning to a sprint. Jesse lifted his own pace when a curdling scream sounded.

"No," Jesse said. "No, not the bairn. Not Stefan."

But Stefan was the first face they saw. The boy flew from the gatehouse, howling. Ryan came out next, catching the boy around the waist. They were both covered in blood.

Ryan dropped to his knees, wrapping Stefan tighter. "It's Anabella," he managed.

Esmerelda held tight to the boy. Stefan was folded into her lap, his limbs wrapped together as if he could disappear and escape the terrible reality he'd witnessed. She whispered as she rocked him, easing him through the remains of the terrible night. All Jesse could hear was, *you poor sweet dear.*

She'd passed Gemma to the nurse, but nearly attacked her when the young woman tried to take the little one back to the nursery. *Did ye nay ken there's been a murder?* Esmerelda snapped as she returned to her ministrations of Anabella's son.

Jesse sat near his brother on the lounger. Ryan was the first to find her. He'd followed Stefan's confused cries, rushing from his own chamber into theirs to see Anabella's wide, lifeless eyes and Stefan climbing over her in desperation.

Ryan hunched forward. He held his bloody hands out and away. There hadn't been time to clean up. Jesse called for a guard to fetch a basin, but the guard didn't move. They had their orders, and they'd failed to stop the future king's wife from being murdered in her own bed. They wouldn't make this error again.

"Darrick..." Ryan at last spoke. His voice trembled. Jesse laid a hand on his back. "When he came in, when he saw her... the sound... it wasnae man, but animal, like a mother bear returning to her den to find her cubs have been taken down by hunters. I could live my whole life... if I never hear tha' sound again..."

"I'll get the water," Esmerelda said, but Jesse shook his head.

Rutland appeared in the doorway, drawing everyone's eyes. He'd come from the prince's chamber, bloody and bedraggled. Jesse felt there was some symbolism in all the men here covered in the blood of Anabella Rhiagain. Her blood was on all their hands, every one of them.

"Khallum is still in there with Darrick," Rutland stammered. He closed his eyes. His jaw twitched. "Took two of us to pry His Grace away from her. I've never... never heard such sounds in my life. I ken I'll die in peace if I never hear them again."

"Like an animal," Ryan said, looking up.

"Aye. Like that."

Ryan pointed a shaky, blood-crusted hand. "Is she still in there? Anabella?"

"Gwyn and Andrija are at the temple, tending her, preparing her."

"What does that mean?" Ryan pressed, his voice escalating in his increasing desperation. "Preparing her?"

"For the pyre. I dinnae what the women do. 'Tis their task. I'll happily leave it to them."

"You cannae burn her before he sees her again! He'll want to see her before she becomes ash and flame. All those years... it was for her that he lived."

"No one's gonna burn the prince's wife till the prince is ready."

"Mama?" Stefan poked his head up to see. "Does he mean Mama?"

Esmerelda passed a helpless look to Jesse over his head. "Perhaps not in front of the boy, Steward Rutland."

Rutland buried his ragged sigh in the back of his hand. "Apologies, my lady. I'm nay myself."

"None of us are."

"Where's Mama?" Stefan cried. "I want to see her!"

Esmerelda clicked her tongue gently and held him tighter. "It's all right, Stefan. Your father will come for you."

Rutland raised both brows, as if to suggest that wouldn't be happening anytime soon. He leaned into the doorframe, shifting his weight with a sigh.

Hamish pushed in behind him and dropped to his knees before Ryan. "How ye farin', son? Ye all right?"

Ryan barely had the energy to move his head back and forth.

Hamish blubbered a heavy exhale. "No man should have to see what ye did."

"Stay with him?" Jesse asked his father. "I want to fetch some water. For his hands." He passed his gaze to Esmerelda. "I'll be just a few steps away."

She nodded, pressing her face into Stefan's tousled hair.

Hamish swallowed hard, burying Ryan's hands in his own. "Aye, Jesse, go on."

Jesse backed out of the room and into the corridor. Candlelight from Darrick's chambers flickered through the small gap left by the cracked door, casting macabre shapes across the stones. He was frozen by the sight; by what had happened just beyond. Had Oldwin himself done this? Right under their noses. While they slept. While Lord Warwick and his men plotted.

Isdemus was right. The ripple from tonight would continue for many, many years to come.

The light disappeared when Khallum appeared at the doorway in response to Jesse's footfalls against the otherwise silent hall.

His eyes burned holes in Jesse. Then, shaking his head, he closed the door.

When he'd stood upon the sands staring into the same sea he thought he'd lost his daughter to, Khallum Warwick at last knew what a man meant when he spoke of helplessness. Helpless to ease Gwyn's grief, or explain to his sons how he'd let their only sister surrender to her dark thoughts. Helpless to recognize and embrace his own pain, which only came boiling forth when he saw her again, alive.

The helplessness he felt toward Darrick Rhiagain was something else entirely. It was raw and real and alive, terrible and tangible evidence of his inability to do for others that which he'd been put in this role to do: to protect.

"He'll face a reckoning unlike anything the foul creature has known before, Your Grace."

"Darrick," the grieving man corrected. "Don't call me that anymore, Khallum. You shouldn't have called me that before, and definitely not now."

"He's gone too far. Too far this time."

"And those are merely words, aren't they? What weapon can words bring to life? He'd already gone too far, with Nye's wife and daughter. Then with Law, our true friend. What are words against *any* of that?"

"We have our answer now," Khallum said, in the absence of comfort that would fall short of adequate. He said this knowing that while he couldn't ease the man's raw grief, he could perhaps provide hope in its stead. "We know what to do."

"No," Darrick cried. He watched him through bleary eyes, his red face lit by the candles the women had left burning. "You have your answer. I cannot stay here."

Khallum couldn't keep his eyes off the bed. The women had stripped the sheets and covers, making quick work of the mess, but the dark crimson stains would only fade, never leave. They'd burn this upon a pyre too, but not the same one they'd place Anabella Rhiagain upon.

Khallum's guilt pricked against the tiny openings of his skin, seeping out. Could Darrick see Khallum's relief, that it had been his wife and not Gwyn? Not his children, his first grandchild. The same relief would be his eventual pain. He knew this. "Where will you go, then?"

He'll change his mind. He has to. He's the king. This isn't about choice for him.

Darrick stared off to the other end of the room. "I should think about that, shouldn't I? I suppose the best place for Stefan is with his family. Steward Weatherford will want to know his grandchild, and perhaps he'll have a place for me as well. It would be more than I deserved."

"Not deserve his aid? Why would you say that?"

Anger crept into Darrick's voice. It settled into the way he pinched his nose as he curled his lip upward. "I had no right loving her. I knew that, even years ago. I was selfish to lead her along, and then I married her, a selfish act that cost her five years of imprisoned torment at the hands of my cruel brother, and saw my son brought into the world in the same horrible circumstances. And now, her life is done. For my love of her. My Isa." His anger transformed again into grief. His mouth hung slack as he cried, tearless.

"This isnae your fault, Your Gr—Darrick. To think of it like that is to suggest a man has no right living at all."

"Do you know why Oldwin killed her?"

"To hurt you, of course. And he will pay for it. On my life."

"I'm asking, Khallum," Darrick said slowly, "do *you* know why Oldwin took her, and not me? Not Stefan?"

Khallum hesitated. He'd failed the prince in his not knowing. He shook his head.

"Because a sorcerer cannot harm a Rhiagain. And Stefan has my blood, while Anabella did not."

"How do ye mean, cannae harm?"

"It goes way back into our distant past, when we all lived in the same land, in another kingdom. Some magic prevents it. Ravenwoods as well. The three of us cannot directly harm one another. And though Oldwin could've employed and easily bought hands to carry this crime out against my Anabella, I know it was his own that drove the dagger into her heart. He would have wanted to be the last to hear her voice, her breath. He would have wanted to take that, too, from me. So, yes, Lord Warwick, it is my fault. For bringing her close to me, knowing I was always safe from the creature's poison, but she could never be."

Khallum searched his mind for more hollow, ineffective sympathy, but Darrick wasn't done.

"But this is also... it's also how I know Oldwin lied about killing Eoghan. Someone else in Duncarrow turned against my brother. I don't know who. Maybe it doesn't even matter. I tell you this now because once I'm gone, any last bit of usefulness I might still possess goes with me."

Khallum leaned in. He had the urge to touch Darrick, but he held back. "Don't ye want vengeance?"

Darrick snickered. "And what has vengeance ever earned a man but more pain?"

"His crime must be answered, Darrick!"

"And it will be. But it's you who must answer it. Not only for Anabella, or Law, or the Nye family, but for the horrors yet to come. For it will be your family next, Khallum. He wanted me gone, and now I will be. I hate to give him what he wants, but I have nothing left to give to this cause. But you must know, it was never me he wanted. It's you. It's always been you. I don't know why, but you're running out of time to sort it out."

"The Rhiagains have always taken as they pleased from the Warwicks. Why does he need *me* to do more of the same?"

Darrick lifted his shoulders with a tired, sad smile. "You look to me for answers, but I've never had them. My leaving will free you to think as you must, without my influence."

"I would've failed without you."

"I'll take my gratitude with me for all you have done through whatever remains of my life. You freed me from prison and believed me to be a greater man than I am, enough that I believed it. Your faith in me was stronger than all the things that had worked so hard to bring me down." Darrick dropped a hand over Khallum's. The blood had dried now, but the pain was only beginning. "But I'm not the man who will deliver this kingdom from the treachery of Oldwin. Perhaps I never was." He stood. "I need my son now."

Khallum pointed toward the door. "You cannae stay in here with him."

Darrick's smile was faraway. "If not for him, I could stay in here forever. It was the last place my Isa drew breath, and the only place she and I ever knew freedom and happiness. But you're right, Stefan can't see this."

"You'll come to the keep. You should've been there all along. Gwyn will see a room prepared for the two of you."

Darrick turned back. "Thank you, Khallum. For everything. There'll be no need to send a scout to Wulfsgate, when you prepare your morning missives. I'll stop there myself, on the way to Anabella's father. It'll be my last act of service to a kingdom that never needed Rhiagains, and will do better once they are well rid of us."

Khallum rose. "I'll prepare a full guard to escort the two of you."

Darrick shook his head. "He's done with me. Save your protection for yourself and your kin, for you'll need all you have until this evil is defeated."

"THE SEA LIVES WITHIN US. WE LIVE WITHIN THE SEA. ON LAND, AS ON sea, we persist in dualities. Salt. Flesh. Blood. Foam. Stone. Bones."

The Grand Minister read the dead-given rites over Anabella Rhiagain. This wasn't like it had been when Eoghan sent the pube fresh out of the Reliquary to preside over Esmerelda's final voyage. Khallum was no longer a subject of the crown, loyal or otherwise. With Darrick moving on, Khallum would never serve another Rhiagain again.

When I find Dain, I could put him on the throne. Was his by right, until that was taken from him.

Aye, but I ken this is an opportunity for us. Time for a change.

The people donnae like change. They flourish under consistency.

What consistency have the Rhiagains given us but pain and theft and suffering? Aye?

Khallum ceased the internal battle, saving it for a time when there were fewer eyes upon him.

The flames roared high, and the beautiful young woman who

had loved the right man at the wrong time in history disappeared, becoming one with the pyre.

"Is this what mine was like, Father?" Esmerelda asked.

Khallum wasn't prepared for the sorrow that hit him in the chest at the question. "I dinnae dare say it was worse, Esmerelda, but it felt that way, then. We had no fire to make, for there was no body, to send to the flame." He turned to her. "I willnae ever tolerate seeing ye up there like that, my emerald. Do ye ken? Not ever. You ever think like ye did again, even a whisper of it—"

"I have Gemma now," she reassured him. "I could never leave her."

"And Jesse."

Something in her eyes wounded him. "And Jesse," she parroted.

"Have ye come to regret yer choice already?"

Esmerelda was quick with her rebuttal. "No, Father. Not at all."

"Then what is it?"

"Mother says all unions find their way. That I shouldn't look to the ways of others to find my own. Don't spend your worries on my happiness. We're finding our way. I wouldn't choose any different if the choice was offered to me again."

Khallum cleared his throat. "Are ye not... bedded, then, is that what you mean to say? Oh, aye, I should've known, when the boy came to me, talking about loving you like a sister—"

"Father!" she shot back in a loud, hissing whisper.

"Right, right, 'tis not my business."

"For once, anyway," she said. "They say Darrick Rhiagain is leaving us. Leaving our cause. Is that true?"

Khallum's eyes burned from the flames. He was desperate to close them, even for a moment, but blinked through the stinging discomfort. "He does what he must, as we all do."

"But he's the rightful king. He can't be content to leave it all to Oldwin, to just surrender!"

Khallum eyed her from the side. "You most of all should appreciate what it is to turn your back on what ye were born for, girl."

Esmerelda looked back toward the fire.

"And I dinnae have the heart to keep him. How can I ask him to fight for what he's already lost? A man has to think of his son."

"Do you still..." Esmerelda stared directly at the fire. He heard the hitch in her voice. "Do you still loathe me, for what I did?"

Khallum looped a rough arm around her waist. "I never loathed you. I couldnae *ever* loathe you. But if you ever wound me like that again..."

Esmerelda leaned into him. "I have all I need now, right here."

Khallum held his daughter as the fire roared high, billowing black curls into the noonday sky. Darrick stood alone, his arms crossed before him, wearing no expression that could later be torn apart and scrutinized by the few gathered. Whatever the man felt, he'd buried it deep.

Jesse returned to Esmerelda's side. He held Gemmasyn in her swaddling. This was no place for a bairn, Khallum thought, but little Gemma wasn't the only little one here, in a time where the only safe place for anyone was with everyone.

Khallum was struck by how easy Jesse was with the girl who was not his daughter. And he realized, as he considered this, that the circle that had begun before Jesse was born was now closed. For Jesse now did the same thing Hamish had once done for him, raising another man's child as his own. Never looking to the past that had made it so.

It wasn't a Strong man Khallum had wanted for his daughter, but he reckoned she could do no better, just the same.

Those gathered slowly filtered away as the fire waned. Darrick didn't seem bothered by the exodus or to even notice there were only a few mourners left. He stared blankly into the fire as it first dissipated and then turned to ash and ember.

When Esmerelda and Jesse peeled off, Khallum made his way over to the prince.

"We'll wait till morning," Darrick said, without looking at him. "I thought Stefan was old enough for this... but..."

"Where is he now, then?"

"With your wife. She and Esmerelda, and Andrija Strong, have been a blessing to me in these terrible hours. I cannot ever properly thank them."

"Anything you need for your voyage, you take. Anything mine is yours."

Still staring into the flames, Darrick said, "I should tell you now. I was never going to be king. I would've taken the crown only long enough to dissolve it all. To bring Duncarrow to the ground and return the rule of the kingdom to the men and women it belongs to."

"I donnae understand," Khallum said. "Did ye always intend this?"

"It's why my brother wanted me dead. Why I'll always believe my father knew and endorsed the act. I was born for this. To end it all." He at last turned to Khallum. "You don't need me, Khallum. You never did. The era of the Rhiagains is already over. It ended when someone spilled the last of Eoghan's blood upon the stones of Duncarrow. Should you find Dain, resist the urge to be a king-maker. You come from a line of men who were chosen to do great things, Khallum Warwick. Seize your destiny. You're a Defender, and now it is time for you to defend everything you love, until the very last breath leaves you."

29

THE BENCH

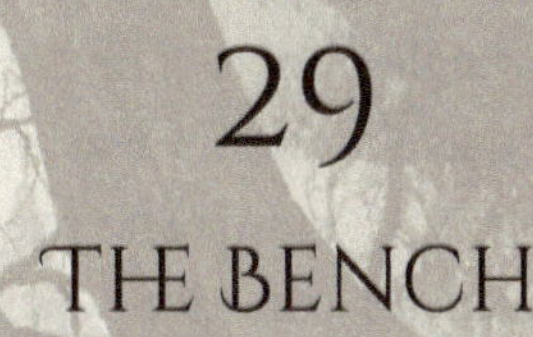

Ravenna began her descent, slipping through a gap in the dense clouds, and, lower still, angled herself in between the stone pillars. She wasn't used to her wider wingspan, and she nearly clipped the end of her left one as she underestimated the descent.

She landed on the side of The Rookery that gave her the least chance of being seen until she was ready. No one had business in this wing; it was the relic of a slowly receding bloodline, the death knell of a dynasty that didn't know it was nearing an end because no one among them possessed the objectivity of an outsider. There had once, she'd heard, been so many Ravenwoods, they had to put an order against procreation until another wing of the castle would be built; this wing. Instead, the Ravenwood women discovered they enjoyed not being brood mares, and the birth rate plummeted, never recovering.

She'd chosen her flight path with careful precision, coming up along the coastline, evading the eyes of Wulfsgate altogether. Not that they'd recognize her. How could they, now, as she was? It was her own guilt, and a grief still buried, awaiting address, that pushed her westward.

While she didn't expect to see anyone here, that didn't mean she should linger. Conscious of how brightly her new plumage burned against the darkness and ice of Midnight Crest, Ravenna landed swiftly, unfurling in a single move. The sensation of the damp stones responding to her heeled boots was startling, like haunting an old memory better left in the past. She pressed her palms to the walls. The responsiveness of the ice elicited a clipped gasp. Returning home ignited every last of her senses, sending the story of her life straight into her bones, like an unbreakable dagger.

This feeling wasn't welcome. *Repulsive* was the only word playing in her mind as the hard wind whipped through the corridor.

"Ravenna?"

In the moments it took to unravel the recollection, Ravenna froze, afraid to turn. She knew this voice. Her aunt. Ryessa. Ryessa had loved them all, in a way Varinya was forbidden from, until Ravenna had been plucked from the nursery and thrown into the harsh cruelty of her loveless training.

"It cannot be you. Can it?" Ryessa's steps sounded behind her, slow, cautious. "Varinya insisted you'd gone the way of our ancestors, but I never believed that. I think I would have felt if if you were truly gone."

Ravenna drew in a gulp of air and pivoted to face her. "Ryessa."

Ryessa gasped, stumbling back. "It *is* you. Gods."

"I won't be staying. I only came to speak to my mother."

"Your mother?" Ryessa's hands raised before her, but she made no move to touch Ravenna. She moved them around the way she might if hovering near fragile glass. "What happened to you? Where have you been?" She cast a worried look over her shoulder. "Has anyone else seen you?"

"You're afraid," Ravenna observed as she approached her. "Why?"

Ryessa all but shoved her farther down the corridor, to the very edge where the light didn't fall. "Have you truly not seen it then?" She tapped her head. "Is that not how it works, the histories? When does a history become a vision? I know it's forbidden to ask you this."

"That's not how it works," Ravenna mumbled. "I've seen nothing. You'll have to tell me."

Ryessa pulled at the dark curls dangling near her waist. "Oh, it shouldn't be me who tells you this."

"Tell me what?"

"If Adynora finds you..."

"Ryessa!" Ravenna grabbed her by the shoulders and shook. "Tell me!"

Ryessa's nostrils flared. Fear burned in her eyes. "Your mother and father are both dead, Ravenna, at the hands of..." She dropped her quavering voice even lower. "A Blackwood."

"What?" Ravenna released her, stepping back. "How would a Blackwood get close enough..." She didn't finish. Killed. Dead. If she didn't say it, then there was still time for it to be a lie.

"It's not safe for you here."

"Where's Alasyr?"

"Gone. He left after... it really isn't safe for you here. You cannot be seen."

"I'll speak with my grandmother, then."

Ryessa shook her head. "I really can't advise that. Come. Come with me."

"Where?"

"Somewhere you won't be spotted."

A dark fist encircled Ravenna's heart. There was so much more to this. She wondered if she would find enlightenment here, or if it would take her down an even darker spiral, one she couldn't climb out of. "If I go with you, you'll tell me everything?"

"Yes, but not here. Come."

Ryessa burst into flight and Ravenna followed.

Alasyr watched Marsh attempt his climb for hours, and now day had turned to night. The boy scrambled over fallen trees and untangled himself from gnarled branches, slower after each time he had to deal with a new obstacle. At this pace, Emberley might be waiting for years.

His wings ached. He almost longed for Marsh's struggle on foot, for it would break up the monotony of the endless circling, but that would invite conversation. He had no desire for this... to get to know the boy, to bond with him.

Marsh's grueling pace was further complicated by a fresh snow pelting the foothills. As he moved higher, that snow would become a squall, and there'd be no protection from that onslaught. The snowbolts would be a threat to them both. Alasyr was desperate to check on Ember, but he'd promised Marsh he'd stay close. Oh, he was resenting it now, but he wouldn't go back on what he'd said, for if something were to happen to him because of Alasyr's negligence, Emberley would never forgive him. Marsh could disappear into the sea when Ember was safe. For now, he needed him.

It wasn't only Emberley calling to him, though. But this other... he'd ignore it. For now. Forever, if his courage didn't fail him.

Marsh at last surrendered to his exhaustion and settled down for a break. Alasyr spent a burst of energy to fly ahead and scout the path. But like his trips before, he saw nothing but snow and brush. As Marsh had said when they started out, he could only see the path by looking down at his feet.

Marsh was resilient, he'd give him that. He'd pushed longer than he should have. His break would extend into the night. The grueling progress would come to an end, for now.

With reluctance, Alasyr swooped down and unfolded beside him. The boy made quick work of a fire.

"You're making camp here?"

Marsh pointed with a stick. "Snow is too thick. I can't even see my own feet now."

"There's no cover here."

"Have you seen any?"

Alasyr hovered close to the slowly growing flames. "I flew on ahead. The path will get harder from here. I can't even pick it up."

"Great."

"Try some enthusiasm, Wildwood. You'll need it."

"Will you stop calling me that?"

"Emberley is waiting for you. We're taking too long."

Marsh tossed the stick into the flame and fell back against the log. "I can hardly see. I'm frozen right to my bones. Hiking a mountain is hard enough without over a foot of snow to slow me. I'd like to see you do any better without those pretty wings."

"Will only get deeper the higher you climb."

"We're not made for this. Not you or I."

"Are you not enough for Emberley? Are you giving up?"

"That's not what I mean." Marsh looked down at his gloved hands. "You know damn well that's not what I mean."

"Then show me. And show her. Show us both you're enough."

Alasyr flew away.

"I DON'T UNDERSTAND," RAVENNA SAID, WHEN THEY WERE SAFE. Ryessa had brought her to the garden, where they grew most of their food. No one came here except the Ravenwoods who worked in the kitchens, and it was past meal hours. "The very idea of the Blackwoods is an affront to my father. Why would he bring Lady Blackwood *here*?"

"No one knows, Ravenna. There've been whispers, but no one can *confirm* anything. It's all been so strange, all of it, and the strangest of all was how Lady Blackwood could kill the two most powerful Ravenwoods in all of Midnight Crest."

"Power has nothing to do with title. You know that."

"Doesn't it? Is it not the magic that decides the most powerful and elevates them to lead us all?"

"You don't believe that."

Ryessa shook her head. "No. I suppose I don't."

"And how did she kill them?" Ravenna swallowed a hard lump.

"With magic. Some dark, foul magic that nobody had a chance to comprehend before she... well, before she sprouted wings and flew away."

"She flew. Lady Blackwood."

"Yes. She flew. Many saw it all happen. It started with the girl... Lady Blackwood's daughter. It all started with her."

"And my mother? She killed that girl?"

Ryessa dropped her eyes and nodded.

"How could she do that to another mother? Why... *why* would she do that?"

Ryessa picked at some cabbage that had fallen off the patch and lay rotting, forgotten. "Varinya has always been desperate to prove to our mother that she wasn't simply chosen by fate, but capable by deed, by talent. The Blackwoods were a threat to our way of life. They shouldn't exist."

"Yet they do."

"They should've stayed away..." Ryessa trailed off. "I believe your mother would've been haunted by her choice. She'll not get the chance now."

"But why? Why kill the girl?"

"You're really so distressed by the death of one of them?"

"All life is sacred," Ravenna whispered, stunned. "I can accept her anger at having them here, but to kill a child? There is no atonement in such an act."

"I don't have the answer you seek," Ryessa said with a sad smile. "She found out what your father had been doing, sequestering Lady Blackwood in the very halls you landed in. Her fury was uncontained, and she took it out on that little raven who had only just found her wings."

"And Alasyr went after her, you say? Why would he do that? Why would he care?"

"Oh, Ravenna. He hasn't been the same since you left. He has so much anger in him. Your father caught him lingering around Wulfsgate, searching for you. At least, that was his intent in the beginning, but then something else pulled his attentions."

Ravenna was stunned. "You're not suggesting Alasyr had feelings for the Blackwood girl?"

"I cannot do more than suggest, for neither Alasyr nor the girl are around to answer that."

"Do you know her name?"

"It was..." Ryessa turned her eyes up. "Emberley. Yes, I think that's right."

"I know her," Ravenna said. She tapped her hand on her thigh. "Or, I know that name. I met her brother, Brandyn, on my travels. He asked me about her. If I'd seen her, on my way south. I told him I hadn't."

"She came to Wulfsgate. That's where Alasyr met her, I suppose. But it wasn't your brother who told me any of this, Ravenna. It was your grandmother. She knew about their unlikely friendship, just as she knew about you and the Dereham boy. She knows everything. She always has, with her all-seeing eye."

Ravenna dropped into a low crouch. All these sharp truths tingled against her flesh. "She said that I should follow my heart. That it would be wrong not to."

"And where is your boy now? Drystan?"

"Dead," Ravenna said. "As I should be."

"I'm so sorry, Ravenna. Truly." Ryessa reached forward and grabbed her hands; an unusual show of intimacy. "She was the one who told your mother what Argentyn had done. I know Argentyn couldn't have brought that woman up the mountain by himself. So who aided him? Who aided him and then turned his own wife and sister against him?"

"You're not saying..."

"She knows everything. When I say that, you cannot understand. But she truly does, Ravenna. She always has. And knowing that, I can't help but wonder why she'd want you gone? Why she'd want my sister and brother gone? Alasyr, gone? She did not a thing to protect any of them, and if the whispers are true..."

"Say what you mean, Ryessa."

"She'll soon know you're here. And when she does, my darling, you must be so very cautious. Cautious with your life, yes, but also with every word she gives you because, without doubt, they will not be said with your best intentions at heart. Certainly, word will reach her of those wings of yours. The ones you think I didn't notice. The ones that did not come from a Ravenwood. She'll punish you for that, and everything else. She wished for you gone, and that wish was granted. But now you're back, and if there's one thing that Adynora Ravenwood does not deal well with, it's when her wishes fall short."

Emberley stood at the very edge of the cave, at the tips of her toes, staring down into the raw emptiness of the snowy void. She enjoyed how it was like looking into nothing at all. How she could see only the blinding white and occasional peak of light blue crags cracking through the gaps in the fog. She could well and truly disappear here, and no one would ever find her. She'd never know how far she'd fall, because death would come before understanding.

But it wasn't death that Emberley Blackwood had in mind today.

She *knew* better than to focus too hard on this. Had she not learned this lesson in the forest? Peace was the way, though in her darkest moments she knew she'd never know true peace again. And if peace would elude her now, in her greatest hour of need, what did that say about what she deserved?

Trust in yourself, her mother had said. Alasyr, too, had this message for her. Fly, he'd said. That's how you'll get to Midnight Crest, Emberley. You fly.

He'd been gone longer than he said he'd be. She tried so hard not to be angry at this. There was no cause for it. He was off helping Marsh, helping to save *her*, and yet her solitude, this sense of aloneness that eclipsed anything else that might have reached forward to protect her in a loving embrace, made her sick in her mind and her heart. She hated them both, almost as much as she hated herself. *Fly, you stupid girl. You stupid, incompetent girl.*

Emberley dangled one foot over the abyss, as if stepping out into the world below. She enjoyed the way the wind caught her boot, swaying her leg off balance. Not quite enough, though.

She closed her eyes. It wasn't Wulfsgate she saw when she imagined herself soaring down through the clouds on the skill of her fully formed wings. Not south at all, but up, up toward Midnight Crest, that same place she'd met her untimely end, where she'd seen final truth in her mother's horrified face, and Emberley had understood, in that terrible moment, that she was saving her mother's life at the expense of her own.

She had only enemies in Midnight Crest. Why she was called there now was as elusive as the wings that wouldn't appear between her shoulders to carry her to safety. They'd tried to kill her and succeeded, but their true failure had been in underestimating Alasyr.

If not for him, she wouldn't even be thinking these thoughts, breathing this air. *Daring* herself to fly once more.

Emberley had no answers, but she felt as if her heart might burst if she couldn't get there, and soon.

She pitched forward. That single moment. The weightlessness as her second heel left the ground, and she leaned into her intentions.

Then, with a gasping sob, Emberley stumbled back. She sucked at the air as she crawled backward into the cave, creating distance between herself and what she might do if she let her mind go to this place again.

When she hit stone, Emberley curled her knees inward and huddled against them, shaking.

Ravenna slowly made her way to the Courtyard of Regents. She'd pulled her hood tight, burying her face in the folds of fabric. It wasn't her desire to come into contact with anyone but her grandmother. At least not until she'd said what she wanted and heard what she needed.

It was against the rules for her to step foot upon the icy courtyard floor. She was no longer the intended High Priestess. Rather, she was now a defector, even a traitor in the eyes of some, or many, or perhaps all. She formed an inward smile as her boots made contact with the slick ground. The rules only applied to those who belonged here.

Yes, but those who do not are summarily executed. Only a fool would let down their guard here.

Ravenna stopped moving when she saw Ryandyr. Right in the center of the circular courtyard, facing away from her, but toward someone or something else. She was a wisp of the girl Ravenna remembered.

Ryandyr turned toward the intrusion of sound. The girl paled. And then, before Ravenna could say anything, her eyes rolled back in her head and she slumped into a soft pile of purple velvet against the white ice.

Ravenna began to rush forward when a shadow fell over her sister. Adynora. The older woman's shock at Ryandyr's quick decline was replaced by sharp fury. Without taking her eyes off Ravenna, Adynora called out for aid. Two Ravenwood guards rushed forward and then halted at the edge of the courtyard. They were afraid to go in. Adynora ordered them to stop being such fools and come take the girl to her chambers. "And find Ryessa to attend to her. She's had a scare."

When they'd scuttled away, with Ryandyr draped carefully between them, Adynora's careful smile faded. "I sincerely believed you were smarter than this, Ravenna. I cannot decide if I am pleased or disappointed to have been wrong."

"Nor did I expect my return here, Adynora."

"High Priestess," her grandmother corrected. "For now, anyway. Your mother and father are dead. Alasyr has defected, just as you did. You'll find our halls much changed. Perhaps for the better, we'll find, as time passes."

Ravenna's mouth twitched into a hard grin. "If you want to hurt me, you're too late. I already know."

"So you've come back to mourn them?"

Ravenna locked eyes with her grandmother. "No."

"Oh? Well. Perhaps you've come then to witness Ryandyr take her men by the light of the greenlight fires in a fortnight, to become

High priestess."

Ravenna's unsteady confidence dissolved. "You moved it up."

Adynora shrugged. Her jewels shimmered with the gesture.

"That was not your right. We have our ways."

"Your use of the word 'we' has long expired, Ravenna. You are not one of us anymore, if you ever were."

"But she's only thirteen!"

Adynora's heels echoed as she took a step closer. "*You* should have thought of that. But your own desires blinded you, didn't they? Just like your mother. Actions have consequences even beyond the ones you would foolishly bring upon yourself. It's a selfish person who cannot foresee that."

"You weren't always like this," Ravenna said coolly. "You were once kind."

"Your mother might have kept the Ravenwoods at ease another couple of years while she eased Ryandyr into the role you abandoned. She was well-liked, Varinya. Most didn't blame her at all for your leaving, and that would have bought her grace. But now... they will not tolerate a dowager High Priestess for any longer than it takes to ready the new one. The young one."

"The Ravenwoods don't care who is and who isn't High Priestess!" Ravenna boomed. "You cannot see that because you are so mired in your own self-importance, the same that was bred into all of us, even me. But I see it now. What is any of this to a Ravenwood? How does it change their life at all? What does a High Priestess do for any Ravenwood, other than herself?"

Her grandmother continued to ignore the questions. "Ryandyr will succeed where you have failed and bring a child from a union that will one day replace her."

"*She* is a child," Ravenna countered.

"And what does that matter to you? You had no care for Ryandyr's future when you abandoned her to it. When you left for your own selfish reasons."

Ravenna sensed the danger. In her heart, she knew her grandmother was behind all the terrible things that had surrounded her short life, and would find herself at the end of this once more if she didn't step carefully.

"I thought you wanted me to leave," Ravenna said, leading the conversation down the path she'd come here for.

"To shame our blood and ways! *I* wanted that?"

"You told me I should follow my heart."

Adynora laughed. "No, Ravenna. I reached *into* your heart and saw your weakness. It had no place here. I could have clipped your wings then and ended it all, but instead I took mercy upon you and allowed you to take another path. And for that, I should have your gratitude. Instead, you stand upon *my* courtyard, and accuse me."

"A path that led me straight into a sorcerer's hands."

Adynora's eyes widened; her mouth parted. At last she'd found the words her grandmother hadn't expected. "You met a sorcerer?"

"My father, he said. But before he told me this, he took me to his bed, bartering with my body, for the life of my friend and her child. Then..." Ravenna trailed off.

"Hmm," Adynora said. The revelation unsettled her, despite how she tried to hide it. "Well, I hear Mortain is dead now."

"Mortain?"

"Your father. Was this before or after he was killed? Or do you need more time to spin your lies?"

"Oldwin," Ravenna said. "I was speaking of Oldwin. What does Mortain have to do with any of this?"

"Oldwin?" Adynora paled.

Ravenna smiled. "Ah, have I discovered something Adynora Ravenwood does *not* know?"

"Oldwin *lied* to you. He's the king of liars. The emperor of untruths."

"And how would you know?"

Adynora looked away.

"One of you has been lying to me all along."

Her grandmother crossed her arms over her gown. "And why do I care if you know? It may as well be the worst kept secret in Midnight Crest. For years I thought the Lord of Wulfsgate was your father. It was bad enough, believing your blood was diluted with the fallibility of men, but it was even worse to learn it was tainted by our enemies."

"None of that was my fault."

"Those sorcerers drove us from our land and then followed us here to further taunt us, to push us into the very corner of a kingdom where we could never be free. There is no good in them, Ravenna, and you have that in you, too, so how does fault matter? Varinya didn't know she'd lain with Mortain, but only because she was too blind, in her vanity and weakness, to see his deception for what it was. She died in ignorance of this truth, and yes, she did have to die."

"You were their *mother*." Ravenna willed herself to stay calm.

"Do you know how difficult it is for a mother to realize her own children will bring down the very world they were sworn to protect? That your choice is between them and everyone else whose lives depend on yours? You will never know the pain of making that choice."

Ravenna was aghast. "Why would you tell me all this? Your confession is treason."

Adynora slipped a finger under Ravenna's chin. The edge of her pointed nail broke the skin, drawing blood. "Because you won't survive this return, Ravenna. You do know that, don't you? I gave you a chance to find happiness beyond our world, however fleeting and puerile, but you just had to come back. And now, once more, I must make an impossible but necessary choice. But as with your mother and father, it was never really a choice at all, was it? A High Priestess can only ever have one path."

Ravenna recoiled from her touch. "It was you," Ravenna said, "who first pushed me from the nest and then delivered me neatly into Oldwin's hands. You had no mind for my happiness. You devised a way to be rid of me, and it failed. You failed."

Adynora tapped her bloody fingernail against her cheek. "He must have a soft spot for you. He couldn't go through with it. I regret that I'll never know why he would lead you into believing he was your father, but it really doesn't matter in the end. Oldwin, Mortain, they're the same. Your mother decided your fate, Ravenna, and when you greet the ancestors, you can thank her for that ignorance."

"And Alasyr?" Ravenna's tears stung, but she forced them back. "Will he be there, too?"

"I expect he knows better than to return here. He's wiser than you, anyway."

Ravenna boldly stepped forward. Her eyes narrowed. "You cannot harm me."

Adynora held out her arms. Her jewels shimmered into song. "Ah, are you then to gift me with a display of your new sorcerer's charms?" She dropped her arms back to her sides. "You came home knowing your fate. If you cool your blood, I'll deliver you one final gift. A swift death. You can be at peace. Don't you want that? To end this suffering?"

"You. Cannot. Harm. Me," Ravenna repeated.

"Child—"

"Yes, *child*," Ravenna hissed. She gripped her belly. "*My* child will be the grandson of Mortain, son of Oldwin, the blood of sorcerers flowing through my veins and his twice over. You cannot harm me or my child, Adynora. You never could. No Ravenwood can. And now that I know it was you who brought this horror upon our house, I will make sure every Ravenwood knows as well. It will be theirs to decide what fate awaits you."

Ravenna couldn't resist the boiling rage that bade her to erupt into a sea of orange and red feathers. She twirled into the sky in delicious spirals, giving her grandmother the show she'd asked for.

Marsh had aches in places he didn't know existed. The cold had stopped bothering him at some point, but this wasn't the relief it might have been. He remembered something his mother said once, when Lyria complained about an unusual cold snap in springtide, in Wildwood Falls. The Falls were where the very wealthy spent their holidays, as Alasyr kept derisively pointing out, and the year-round warmth was part of the appeal. They weren't made for the cold, and when it reached their borders, they were all miserable.

But Clarissant had chided her daughter for disrespecting her own senses, which were, as she'd said, *given to us all by the Guardians, to keep us safe. It's when you stop feeling the cold that something is wrong. When that happens, you've already lost.*

More than something was wrong—he was afraid to put his hand to his mouth, for one, because he wasn't convinced it was still there at all—but Marsh couldn't linger overlong on these thoughts or he'd surrender to them. He disagreed with his mother. You weren't lost until you decided you were.

All around him, there was nothing. Nothing except the stark white of endless snow, on the ground, in the air, before him and behind him. He tripped on logs and brambles that he couldn't see until he was upon them. He now had so many cuts, scrapes, and bruises that he refused to examine until they were safe. Alasyr could heal him, of course. But he couldn't even see the raven anymore; didn't know whether he was still out there or had abandoned him. Marsh didn't trust him, but he was well past the point where trust had anything to do with keeping him moving forward. There was only one way to Emberley.

Time was no longer clear. He'd eaten a ration of dried meats Frost sent him with, but didn't know if that was hours ago, or days. He didn't know how long he'd been gone, or even if he was still going the right way. He'd lost the usefulness of all his senses in this sea of snow and ice and the beckoning unknown. Everything now lived in the moment, with him.

Marsh grunted as he stumbled into something. He navigated his leg up and tried to go over, as he had with all the ones before, but it seemed he'd stepped right into a wall. He pressed his hands against what felt like a block of ice. He ran his hands up, up, until his arms were stretched as far as they could go, but still he hadn't reached the top of this new obstruction. He dug his thick gloves into it and detected the texture. It was bark; a fallen tree, but much, much bigger than the trees in the foothills he'd been tripping over. Was he still even in the foothills?

He shuffled to the right, pulling his hands along the bark to guide him. He went slow, one foot, then the other, until he hit the mountain wall. He followed the sensation of the thick log until the tree curved up, disappearing into the mountains from where it had fallen. Where it veered upward, there should be a gap, he thought.

Marsh's knees and legs groaned as he dropped to a crouch in hopes he could push under, but the snow had drifted up into the tree, hardened to ice. He couldn't budge it.

There was no way around the stump on the safe side.

He closed his eyes and beseeched the Guardian of the Unpromised Future to look the other way on this day, and then moved this time to the left, toward an edge he couldn't see. One foot, stop. The other foot, stop. His senses screamed as he moved beyond the safe area, even slower now as he pressed one boot into the snow, waiting longer before pulling the next over. Marsh cried out when his foot stumbled at the edge. He heard and felt the snow break off and fall down into the chasm. He waited for the sound of it hitting bottom, but it never came.

He started to readjust himself back to the safety of the path when he felt the branches. His heart surged. He couldn't climb over this massive thing. He couldn't squeeze under, either. But if he was careful, he could use the branches to navigate himself to the other side. It seemed insane as he thought through it, but this was the only way forward.

No Marsh, he heard Emberley say. *We all have our limitations.*

Are you enough for Emberley? Alasyr goaded.

Marsh reached blindly for the first branch, and when his hand connected, he secured his fist around it and tugged. Sturdy enough. Holding tight, he carefully lifted his left leg and draped it over another branch just beneath it. He squeezed his thigh to test the pull of it, and it seemed capable of holding him. But as he slid more securely into place, his right leg left the ground. He looked back in a panic to spot where he'd been standing, but was unsurprised to see nothing.

He almost laughed. What would his mother think of him tangled in the branches of a tree, dangling high above the world?

With an unexpected burst of confidence, Marsh shifted his weight and reached his left arm toward another branch to advance his position. He silently cheered himself as he made real progress, his awkward navigation of arms and legs a perfect match for the maze of tangles as he eased toward the center of the massive tree.

Then he heard it. The snap, followed by the crack. All at once his left leg was a dead weight when the branch disappeared. He shifted, but the burden of his weight on the branch holding his right leg was too much. Marsh screamed. The sound disappeared into the snow, muted. His gloved hands clamped right upon the single branch he was now holding, but he felt the slipping come. He'd been so sure moments before. So certain he could do this.

Marsh squeezed his eyes closed and kicked at the other branches as he searched in desperation for something else to stop his fall. But the sudden, jerky movements caused the final branch he had purchase on to crack and then snap. Marsh opened his eyes just in time to see the branch no longer connected to the tree as he fell backward into the abyss.

RAVENNA CAME TO A GENTLE LANDING IN THE SMALL VALLEY NESTLED between two of the most northerly summits in the range. The copse of trees provided shelter from storms and a momentary peace from the tempest always brewing within The Rookery. The trees were old; older than the Ravenwoods and their arrival to the kingdom, she thought. It was their age that turned the small reprieve into a small but effective escape, blocking out the world beyond.

The bench was still there. She was surprised to see it, given the rudimentary construction. Alasyr had dragged some old logs from the edge of the tiny forest and propped them into something they could sit upon. And they did, sometimes for hours, often saying nothing, or speaking of inconsequential things. But it was also here that Ravenna confessed to her brother her fears about the Langenacht, and how she'd do just about anything to escape the fate awaiting her. He'd understood, he said, but then he, too, had cast his lot...

Ravenna exhaled, sagging down onto the bench. He *had* cast his lot, yes, but she'd been too furious to listen, to hear him when he tried to tell her he'd done it to protect her. But no matter his intentions, Alasyr couldn't protect her. She'd done that for herself, leaving this world behind, a choice she'd never regretted but had brought even more agony upon her.

They came here as children. But it was strange to think of herself that way, when she was, in many ways, still a child. She realized she'd probably turn sixteen soon, though she didn't know for certain, and was equally unsure it even mattered anymore. Varinya and Argentyn had them come here when they were learning their wings, in case their little raven bodies failed them, so they would have a safe place to land. They'd also come when they were children, they said. As brother and sister, before fate and duty made them husband and wife.

Ravenna and Alasyr never saw anyone else. It was their place; a reprieve from magic that was its own kind of magic.

Everything within her hurt. Her body, spirit. She'd turned her grief to power, because she'd needed it. But now that she was alone, the weight of all she'd suppressed passed into the thin air of the mountains, leaving her with the hollow understanding that all she'd once loved was no more. Drystan was dead. *Dead.* Not simply away, or out of mind until such time as she could address him, but *dead.* And he wouldn't be so if she'd simply discouraged a love that had always been more in her favor. He'd felt oppressed by the life awaiting him, but didn't all young men? He would've been a good leader. She'd known it then, and let him follow her across the kingdom, not for the unshakeable love of him, as he had of her, but because she was terrified of being alone.

Her mother and father were gone now, too. There'd be no

amends. No answers to the questions she now understood she needed to ask. No screaming fights, or desperate hugs. No chance for any of that.

Alasyr... he wasn't dead, at least, but he may as well be. He'd followed her lead, and now he could be anywhere. If he was wise, he'd stay away. Though it hadn't been for him she'd returned, in her heart she'd held to the hope she might see him once more. That she might say to him all the things she couldn't say when they were both prisoners of these dark, icy halls.

Ravenna would do as she'd promised her grandmother. She would tell them all. Tell them all and let those who remained decide what to do with the truth of Adynora's treachery. It had been one woman deciding things for so many, for so long. For the first time, they could decide for themselves.

But for now, Ravenna would steal these last moments where she was truly alone, buried in the silence of her grief and regret.

30

THE PASSING OF YSEULT

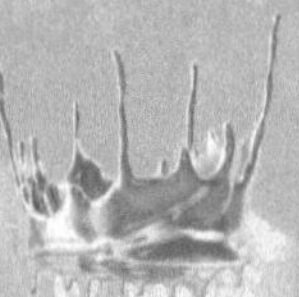

Kian awoke to the gentle but urgent hands of Eithne shaking him. He'd been riding the delicate path between sleep and wakefulness for hours. He'd not enjoyed a full night of rest since coming to the Saleen lands. It wasn't something he dwelled on.

Sorrow pulled him over the line into full consciousness. Oh, it was a strange, hollow feeling, deep and without end. His mother. That's why Eithne was here. His mother. The news had at last arrived here. Kian had known.

He'd known the moment her life force exited this world.

He wasn't here to linger in his pain. Time wasn't on his side.

Aian shrieked. Kian cooed, calming him.

"Kian." Eithne's urgent whisper deepened his pain. "Kian!"

"It's all right, Eithne. I know."

"You know?" She fell back into a crouch, settling against the backs of her feet.

Kian nodded. He pressed his hands to the sides and pushed forward. "I have known."

"You have known? How long?"

"I knew in the moment. I felt it."

Eithne brought her hands to her mouth in a muted gasp. "Why did you say nothing?"

"There is no need to speak when words add nothing." Kian jumped to his feet. "She is gone."

"But..." Eithne followed him when he rushed from the hut. "They say... they say..."

"She was murdered. Yes."

"You're not shocked?"

"No."

Eithne struggled to keep pace. "Why?"

Kian came to a halt. He squinted at the sunbeams breaking through the canopy of trees. The words weren't for her. He realized this before he said them. "Do you ever have the sense that there's something you've been waiting for your entire life? Something terrible, yet also unstoppable?"

"I... don't think so."

"No, Eithne. You haven't, then. You'd know precisely what I meant, if you had."

"You've been waiting your whole life for your mother's murder?"

"Not in the way you say it, no," Kian answered. He let the sunlight wash over him, bathing him anew. What he couldn't tell Eithne was that along with the sorrow was relief. An ease of conscience. He'd foreseen this day in his dreams, and now that it had come to pass, the waiting, the wondering, the guessing, it was all ended now. He could lay aside this fear and replace it with something more constructive.

Not anger. That was there, but he must not let it surface.

He turned to face her. "Kael will stand against the Light."

Eithne's eyes widened. "He—"

Kian squeezed a hand over one shoulder. "There are some among us who have never embraced the charge given us. Who look to a point in our past and cling to it, where they should disavow it. They have always been there. Kael will not be the first to attempt this."

Eithne's head shook in small, tight movements. "But why?"

Kian tried to smile. "Some see the world in colors or gray, and others good or bad. But the world is filled with color, with light, and with dark. Most live somewhere in between these places. Even you and I, who are dedicated to protecting the Light, we are not wholly good, are we? We have our share of dark thoughts, though we do what we can never to act upon them. Some live closer to the darkness... close enough for it to take them, and to take all of us with them."

"We have to stop him," Eithne said, horrified.

"We have to protect the Light," Kian gently corrected. "Until another can stop him."

It wasn't enough. It wasn't nearly enough.

It would have to do. He knew the words he needed. Persuasive, he could be. It was time he didn't have. And the eleven Drumain sitting before him in his mother's tent, waiting, wide-eyed and open-minded, would have to do.

For the others, his mother's people, would soon come for them. Their combined magic would fade, leaving them vulnerable.

"Kian," Kael said. His upper lip curled at the next word. "Murder."

Those gathered exchanged looks. Could it be true? Had Kian murdered Yseult? But he wasn't even here. Everyone knew it was Kael. Now Kael was saying it was Kian?

Let them think on that. To answer would be to remove the mystery. The very idea it wasn't possible would linger and then fade until there was only one answer.

It didn't have to be this way.

Was it not that very question that started his search from within for a better way?

It didn't have to be this way, and so Kael de Medvedev, newest High Chieftain of the Clahnn Drumain, would show them just how it could be.

31

THE LIGHT ENDER

There were only two books they'd stolen from the secret room of the library and snuck back to Balfour's room. Neither were directly about the sorcerers, but the subjects were promising enough, and it was all they could find in the time they had. *The Secret and Salacious Histories of the Rhiagains*, was the one Assana grabbed, because any title that sounded like the start of good fishwife gossip *had* to be promising. It seemed, at least, more interesting than the one Balfour had in his room already, *Duncarrow: Lineages.*

Balfour found one called *Ilynglass: And Other Secrets of the Kingdom*, and Assana's heart quickened at that word. She knew it. Oldwin himself had told it to her. *That one. Grab it.*

They'd had no more time. There were so many books to choose from, but Warden Liddle had given up on the matter of the wulf sooner than they'd expected. Assana had pressed both books to Balfour's chest and returned to the front with a light skip in her step. While Liddle's eyes were drawn to everything but the library, Balfour slipped out.

Now that Assana had answers before her, teasing her with their evasiveness, she found she couldn't as easily summon her desires.

Balfour tickled the back of her neck with his tongue; slipped his fingers under her dress. But her mind couldn't be swayed.

Assana stared at her book day and night, willing it to reveal its answers.

"What do you care about the sorcerers, anyway?" Balfour asked one night. He lay naked on his bed. It was an invitation that would go unanswered. "Enough to come all the way here?"

"They're evil."

He rolled his eyes. "We're all evil."

She glared at him. "You think you know evil? Take whatever you know, magnify it by the highest number you can count to. Even that wouldn't be enough."

"Do you know how dramatic you sound?"

"Have you lived in a castle with one of them? No? Then you cannot know." Assana turned back to the pages of the book on Ilynglass. She ran her fingers along the gibberish. The code was written by man. It could be deciphered by man.

"Anyone could've killed the king. Don't need great evil for that."

No, you don't, for it wasn't Oldwin at all but a brave girl who killed this king, and no one will ever know. "It's so much more than that."

"Then tell me."

Assana closed the book and set it roughly side. "You first. What's in your book? The one you hide? The one you get nervous about when I even speak of?"

Balfour dropped his arms to his sides. They crunched against the straw of his mattress. "I'm filled up with derision from everyone else. I can't take it from you, too."

"You hardly know me."

"I know you better than I've ever known anyone."

"That's sad."

"No sadder than you coming here to seduce me to avoid going home."

"Tell me, Balfour."

"No."

"Tell me."

"You'll think I'm a fool, like they all do."

Assana crawled over to his bed. She rested her hands and chin on the mattress. "I came here to find a way to stop the sorcerers, when everyone before me has failed. I'm the last person who'd think you're a fool. Whatever your interest, it can't be half as insane as mine."

Balfour turned to his side. His cock was half-hard, and she knew it wasn't for her, this excitement. He *wanted* to tell her. He'd wanted to tell her all along, or to tell someone, and he'd been sizing her up, to see if that someone could be her. "You know what they say about my father."

She nodded.

"What do you think about that?"

"I think people in this kingdom act as if their opinions of others were a trade that could bring them riches."

Balfour watched her closely. "But what do *you* think about what happened to him?"

"About the veil?"

"Yes."

Assana exhaled against her folded hands. "I don't know. I've never myself seen one. But I have seen an immortal creature manipulate a king and kingdom, so anything seems possible after that."

"What if I told you I believe him?"

"Then I'd say you were a good son."

"You wouldn't say I'm crazy, like him?"

Assana balked. "I don't think your father is crazy. I think any man in this kingdom who dares challenge the way of things as we want it to be is called many things. I don't know what happened to Lord Alric, but I know the Derehams are honorable men. There's no gain for him in lying about it. All his confession has done is bring darkness upon his house."

Balfour snorted. "Yeah. Darkness."

Assana nodded to the corner of the room. "That's what this is? The veils?"

"You say that as if it's as inconsequential as the history of herbs."

"I also said I believed you."

"You said."

"I *do*. Few in this kingdom have seen what I've seen," Assana said. She fell back on her heels. "And? Have you found anything?"

He shook his head. "It's all theory. I gave up halfway through from disappointment. The author makes as if he's an authority on the matter, but there's nothing in there that tells me where they are. How to... I wanted to..." He closed his mouth tight and swallowed.

"You wanted to what?"

"It's silly."

"Tell me anyway."

"I wanted to find a veil for myself and step through. So I could show others. So I could... prove my father wasn't lying. But if it was so easy, other men would've done it, wouldn't they?"

Assana reached forward and grabbed one of his hands. "So let's find one, Balfour. Let's show them."

He turned his head away to hide his glassy eyes. "You're taking the piss."

"I'm not." She tugged his hand. "I'm *not*."

He grunted.

"I'll tell you why I came. I want to learn about the sorcerers so I can destroy them. So they can never again hurt anyone in this kingdom. Man. Medvedev. Child. King. They don't belong here. They never did. My mother once said that a good man leaves a place better than he found it. A bad man takes until the place isn't recognizable by any who once loved it. The sorcerers are leeches. They take, and they take, and they give nothing, they return nothing. And though I don't know what they are after, I feel... I *know*, that they are preparing to take so much more than ever before. Maybe everything. Something terrible is coming, and it will come, unless someone can find the power to stop them."

He rolled back to face her. "You think they can be destroyed?"

"*Everything* can be destroyed, Balfour. And nothing is so elusive that we cannot find it with the right motivation. Together."

. . .

Enivera.

He hadn't thought of her in years. The echo the sound her name made as it bounced around his mind was both familiar and not, like a memory he'd stolen from someone else.

But Enivera? She'd belonged to Oldwin, and he to her.

He didn't count the years anymore. He thought of his life as before the Sundering and after. Before, when he was a child of the Great Light of the Worlds, and after, when he was a disciple of the same, determined to find his way back to what was now forbidden to him.

They'd all been there in the before. Mortain. Lysanor. Isdemus. Enivera. Many others. So many others, most of whose own lights had gone out in the years since the Sundering. There were a few still on Ilynglass when the four had departed, but he couldn't imagine they'd lived very much longer. It wasn't a life there. It was a punishment.

But not Enivera. Enivera hadn't come to Ilynglass. There was nothing left of her, only this hollow sound as her name traveled across the space of the few sentimental thoughts remaining. Only for her would he even allow them.

Oldwin plunged his fists into the ice of the riverbank. He'd not come so far, yet, that he couldn't change his mind and take the other path. But that would only be true for a little longer.

Enivera.

He'd now known Mortain and the others longer than he'd known her, as time stretched and bowed. They'd been allies—but not friends, never that—out of necessity. A shared vision that scared the others, who were still sore from being cast out by the Light. They reviled the name Enivera, called her the Light Ender, never pausing their melancholy to consider that only she'd possessed the bravery to try what they'd all secretly whispered about.

Mortain had understood. And Lysanor. And Isdemus. Until they no longer did. Even Mortain had lost his faith in the end. He would not have been bested by a mere boy if that wasn't true.

Oldwin's eyes fluttered closed as he channeled her.

He'd been standing right beside her when she reached her fists into the Light and demanded its power for herself. *You will not keep this from us any longer! It is not only yours!*

When the world was ripped asunder.

When she'd exploded into a million little balls of light.

He liked to think he'd absorbed some of her, her courage washing over him like a warm bath as the rest of her filtered into the air and sea. He thought this until he had no more time to think, for the world trembled, and from there, chaos.

A chaos that felt like a tumultuous slumber.

When he awakened, he was in Ilynglass. It hadn't been called that before he and the other Meduwyn landed upon the sands; they'd brought the name, along with their magic and their resentment. It was the name of the golden city of the Meduwyn in the Hidden Kingdom, and to declare this new land, cold and barren, this same thing was to ignite the rebellion that would one day see them returned. It was Lysanor who first named it that, and Oldwin thought, as the beautiful sorcerer stood upon the hillside of jagged rocks, that she, too, had absorbed Enivera and was now taking up her mantle.

What a fool to think so. There had only been one Enivera, and she lived only in his memories now.

They must be tired, Oldwin thought. How else could Lysanor and Isdemus have come so far, only to turn their coats and embrace the end? To be so ready to lay their own lives aside, a choice that could only be final?

Well.

He would never embrace the end.

It wrapped its tiny, black fingers around his ankles with a light tug, but Oldwin was still strong, even as he grew weaker. He was still Oldwin the Meduwyn, Lover of the Light Ender.

And with what little of his magic remained, he'd finally seen this hidden weapon that Lysanor and Isdemus had spent so much of their energy keeping from him.

Oldwin would meet this Jamesan Strong, descendent of Isdemus, child of the Medvedev. His way in. His end and his beginning.

Isdemus and Lysanor had created him to stop Oldwin, knowing full well if Oldwin ever discovered his existence, he would have his way in. His way through.

Using the boy, Oldwin would finish what Enivera began.

32
UNTIL THE VERY END

The slam of the door ricocheted across Gretchen's chest. It was a sound that meant something; that lingered, traveling beyond the gesture, running through and underneath and all around the intention behind it.

Gretchen pressed her palms into the wood of the table and drew a hard, inward breath. She held it far longer than was necessary. Her head spun in the delicious dizziness of a promise... to hold it until she surrendered to the sensation, or to stop, to *feel*.

Her lungs decided for her. She coughed out, sputtering, the dark dots dancing behind her eyes coming in and out of focus. The harsh light from the noonday sun burned her once more. Lit up the orange and yellow and red of the home in glaring exposure of all the cracks and dust they had yet to address.

"Gretchen?"

Her shoulders rolled forward in a cringe. She'd forgotten he was there at all. She hadn't intended for anyone else to hear her conversation with Pieter, but Curran never *left* these days. He was always there, working, helping, directing, judging. She shouldn't think of his quickness to aid with such derision, for he'd helped Pieter, but he'd started this cold snap between them the day they'd met and had never done a thing to thaw it. Over time, this had formed into the thick ice dividing them.

"It's nothing, I'm fine," she lied. Her breath may be recovered, but it wasn't nothing. Her heart wasn't fine. Nothing would ever be fine again. "Lost my breath for a moment, is all."

"I heard what Pieter said to you."

"Of course you did," Gretchen said without turning. She ground her palms into the wood, searching for stability. "You're always here. Always listening. Judging."

"That's not why I'm here."

"And why are you here?"

"To help him."

Gretchen laughed. "His mother is here now. You can lay your burdens aside."

Curran's steps sounded behind her, but stopped at a distance. "I can't blame you for asking him. I know what it is to need to see something for yourself, to believe it. Not everything can be given up to trust and faith."

Gretchen said nothing. This softness in his voice was new, and she didn't trust it. He wanted to lull her into vulnerability, where he could more easily crush her, punishing her for coming where she wasn't wanted. It was all he knew.

Maura's words came back to her, then. About what Curran had lost. But Gretchen had known loss her entire life and had never been so cruel.

But is that true? Holden's voice this time.

Come now, Sparrow. We both know better. Ash now.

"Pieter made it clear enough. He already believes. He's learned blind trust here. I didn't teach him that."

"You think Pieter believed this blindly? It wasn't you who was here, to collect him when he'd trekked off to the veil to try, in vain, to return to you. It wasn't you who tried to, each time, help him back through, only to watch him fail. To see his heart grow colder with every failed attempt."

Gretchen cast a hard look over her shoulder. "I suppose you'd like a reward for this selflessness."

Curran choked out a short laugh. "A reward, no. But an understanding from you would be nice. It isn't your fault that Pieter's life has passed by in here, but yours is no longer his only family. It took Pieter years to accept he couldn't return. Pushing your guilt upon him, forcing him to relive a pain he's only just gotten over, is unfair. It's more than unfair. It's hurting him, and he's afraid to tell you just how much."

Gretchen whirled around. She stepped to him. "I don't need anyone else telling me how my son is feeling!"

Curran didn't wince at her rush of emotion. His face was worn with sadness. "No. You only need to listen to what he himself tells you."

Gretchen couldn't say what did it. What word he'd used, or whether it was the resignation in his expression, but it killed what was left of the fight in her. Pieter's rush of anger when he'd left had pushed her to the precipice, and now all she wanted to do was fall over the edge. If the Guardians had any love left for her, she'd land somewhere familiar.

Why will you not accept this?

Because the kingdom is our home!

Was our home, Mother. It was our home. And now this is. Because there's no return.

Says Maura! Says Brahim!

Says your son! I can't go back there. I can't... I won't explain it to you. You're going through what I went through for years, and I don't want this for you. I do not want you to experience my despair... my... please. Trust me. If you cannot trust them, trust me. There is no return.

I'll trust it when I see it with my own eyes.

Oh, the hurt. The hurt that had broiled as the tears welled under his lower lids, spilling just as he turned to leave her. The slamming door. The font of regret.

Gretchen sank into an old, broken chair. "I came here to bring him home, and now everyone tells me there is no home. Only here, and whatever this is."

Curran dropped to a crouch before her. "Whatever this is? It's your home now, too."

"When I was..." Gretchen trailed off. Why was she telling him this? She didn't care. The words were more for her, anyway. "When I was still a girl, a king decided my fate. He pulled me from the only world I knew and forced me to travel to a land that was so unlike anything I had known and loved, that I thought I might drown in the sorrow of it all."

"But you didn't."

"No. Because once my children were born, I knew that wherever I was in the kingdom meant nothing. I could live on a ship in the sea as long as I had them. As long as I could look into their eyes, and listen to their voices, and tell them stories, and hear their own."

"All children become men and women someday. It then becomes their joy to do the same, with their own families."

"Not all do," Gretchen said. "And I'll never know, will I? I'll never know if Christian will break his silly promise to himself not to bring a child into his otherwise beautiful marriage. I'll never know if Drystan will find his way home, and his way in the world. I'll not ever see Lisbet ease her wild mind and embrace a path that might bring her the happiness she's been so afraid of. And the twins... ahh, they are still so little. I cannot even predict what they'll become! And I'll never know."

Curran pulled himself to his feet. He came to her and stood over her. "We have all lost, Gretchen. We all have a past that feels more inviting than the future. But we cannot go back. You could have a life here, with Pieter. Maura could be as a mother to you. Brahim is a good man and would lay his life aside for any of us in Malfenza."

Gretchen looked up at him. "And you?"

"I can help you get your new home fixed up." He lifted the hammer in his hand and attempted a smile.

Gretchen laughed. She couldn't help it. The look was so unnatural on him. He was almost handsome with this hint of joy. "I don't have a home here to fix up."

"Brahim has one picked out for you. He'll be angry that I told you first, but he plans to surprise you."

"You know what I meant."

"Home is a choice. It's a feeling." He pointed toward the cabinet he'd been repairing. "Light is fading. I should finish."

"You don't cancel Lord's Day, Christian. It's simply not done."

"Am I not the lord? Is it not my day, then, to cancel, or even be rid of altogether?"

Aylen planted herself in front of the door, blocking his escape. It was almost humorous. He seemed to be the last person she wanted to see these days, and here she was, trapping them together.

It wasn't humorous, though. He couldn't even remember the last time he'd laughed and meant it.

"Your people came from all over the Northerlands to see you. Some traveled weeks. Some brought all their possessions, for they had nowhere safe to store them. Not all of them possess the wealth to travel as you do, or leave their trades for weeks on end. Most cannot afford to do this more than the once a year granted them. And then you refuse to see them? How? How could you do that?"

Christian leaned into his father's desk. "We don't need a Lord's Day, just like we don't need a lord. The Reach would do better to govern itself. The coin they'd save in taxes alone would change their lives."

Aylen was aghast. She was often aghast these days. He was so used to it, he'd forgotten what joy looked like on her. "You may not need a lord, but they do." Aylen pointed. "I will go out there and, on your behalf, in *your name*, do what their lord should do. I will say the things I need to say, and grant the requests I should grant, and help the people you should be helping, and beseech the Guardians that I've not stepped wrong."

"I already told you, Aylen. It's cancelled."

"You may not care if you run this Reach into ruin, but that decision does not belong to one man!"

Christian couldn't help himself. "Actually. It does."

Her cheeks were a burning red. She flung her arms out. "Who are you? I don't even know you anymore. I haven't known you since you returned from war. Have you always been two different men and were just *that* good at hiding it from me?"

"I told you," he said, "that coming home was bad for me."

Aylen laughed. "Bad for you? Like it's a disease? Do you hear your words? You sound like a child. How you act now is a choice, Christian. You choose to behave like a child in the throes of a tantrum. Little Torrin wouldn't even act this way. He would know better. He would go out there, even in his inexperience, and do his very best."

"Then send him."

"Torrin *is* a child."

Christian shook his head with a scoff. He pressed his hands to the cloudy windowpane and looked out. The line was very long. They waited for him, still. So she hadn't lied. She *had* revived it. She really intended to go down there and speak with every last one of them.

"I didn't give you permission to hold this day on my behalf, Aylen. If you were not my wife..."

"You'd what? Hit me? Remind me of my place?"

"You know that's not what I meant."

"And what did you mean, then?" When he said nothing, she asked, "Oh, we're back to sulking, are we?"

He had to bite back the urge to take his fist to her face. Even the thought of doing it shocked him. It sent ice to his bones. Hit her? Could he hit her? His love? His Aylen?

"Is that..." The urge rose once more. He fought it harder than he should have had to. "Is that what you think I do when I'm in here?"

"I know very well you're not doing anything useful for this family, this Reach, or... this marriage."

"So you know nothing, is what you're saying."

Aylen's pause was filled with something he couldn't define, but it hit him hard. "Did you even know Lisbet is gone?"

"She's not gone."

"Left, with that man claiming to be her father. The one you took your fists to in anger. Do you even care?"

Christian's lip curled. "She's not gone. She would've consulted with me if she was planning something so foolish. And she only just returned home."

"And why would she tell you? A man who's supposed to be her brother but treated her like a stranger? She's gone, Christian. She left, with Ash. And I don't see her ever returning."

"I'm the seer, Aylen," he reminded her.

"Some things don't require magic. Why would she come back to you? To this? You say you didn't give her leave to go, but who needs authority, or leave, or permission, from a half-lord?"

Christian's eyes were bleary. He could hardly make her out anymore. He wanted her to understand, but all he could offer her was a million reasons not to. "I didn't want this. It was never my choice. I was *happy* at the Sepulchre. You'll never understand."

"Happy?" she repeated. "You were always haunted."

"That's not true."

"I've slept beside you for years, Christian. Long before our marriage allowed it. I was witness to your dreams. You can lie to yourself, but I'll never accept those lies because I know better."

He turned away and swatted his hand at the air. "You can think what you want. But I was happy, and I could have been happier with more years between me and this life. I could have been a good man."

"What's stopping you?"

"You could never understand."

"A good man wouldn't stake his goodness on whether his life of privilege made him happy or not! Nothing terrible happened to you here! You had a mother and father who loved you, imperfect though they, like all people, might be. More siblings than you knew what to do with. A safe home. A full belly. What could be so terrible about that?"

"You'll never understand," he said once more.

"I see we finally agree. If you miss it so much, then *go*. Go back to the Sepulchre, then. Go back begging, and pleading, and perhaps they'll even let you back in if you're as convincing at that as you are at failing your people here. I'll stay. I'll make sure Torrin comes up to be the man that you, for reasons I will never understand, reasons that no one will ever be able to adequately explain, refuse to be." Aylen reached for the door.

"You can't leave."

"Leave? I have over a hundred men awaiting me in the Great Hall, so that I can serve them, as their lady. As duty bids me. With luck, they'll be so enamored with my strange silver hair that they won't stop to ask themselves why their new lord couldn't be bothered to see them himself."

The door slammed. He'd hear the sound in his heart forever. It was more than a door closing. Something else had just ended. Something bigger and far more important to him.

Christian started to call after her, but a sob lodged in the back of his throat, choking his voice.

He bit into his sleeve and sounded a silent scream into the fabric.

YESENIA HUNG BACK AT THE BASE OF THE HILL. CIAN HAD WANTED them there, but he needed courage, not comfort.

This wasn't her first public execution. They were fond of them in the Southerlands. Khoulter Warwick had believed none of his children, not even his daughter, should be spared the spectacle.

Cian had taken his mother's words about the trees of his boyhood to heart, and had a scaffold erected instead. He stood, stoic, as the guards led her up the hill from the prison; as they pushed her up the stairs and sent her neck through the noose.

They waited for the Grand Minister to read the rites of the betrayer as a hard wind whipped over the top of the hill. Steward Oakenwell stood at the boy's side, but his presence was a formality. He was there to do what Cian was supposed to do, if Cian could not.

"Have you any last words, Maeryn Quinlanden?" Cian's small but confident voice carried even down the hill.

"You would deny me the name Mother, in the very end?"

"Have you any last words, *Mother*?"

"I should be there," Corin whispered. "I should be doing this. He's just a boy."

"Shh," Yesenia whispered. "And listen to the words of a man."

"No," Maeryn said.

Cian pulled back on the lever that released the rope. Maeryn dropped through the opening of the scaffold, her neck snapping. Corin winced, but Yesenia kept her eyes trained on her dying sister-in-law as she swung, twitching. It was the very least she could do for the boy whose childhood was now ended.

When at last Maeryn stopped moving, Cian turned away from her and walked back down the other side of the hill.

ALRIC SECURED THE STRAPS ON HIS OLD GIRL. HIS SWEET GIRL. THIS would be her last trip with him. He wished there was some way to repay her loyalty. To give her a life free of men, of burden, of service. He packed an extra satchel for her, full of food to leave behind when he could no longer be there to feed her. But the food would run out, and she wouldn't know how to find her own. She was a tamed beast, not a wild one. She'd return to the only home she'd ever known, and they'd find no work for her there. She'd never been built for the things she'd accomplished, his little miracle that he'd never named. He hoped they would do right by her. Give her the retirement she deserved. Aylen might. She had that in her heart, that softness for all things. It would be Aylen who saved the Northerlands, in the end.

"All ready then?" Earwyn had packed her own bag, but her horse stood four to five hands taller than his pony. It could carry more. But what mattered was what they could still carry on foot, when it was time to leave their beasts behind.

"You don't have to do this."

"I want to."

"Not even for me."

"There is no one else."

"We both know that's not true, Earwyn. What about Balfour? What about our boy?"

"Our son is haunted by his name. He doesn't return my letters. Hasn't for years. What Balfour wants is what you want, my dear. To be free. We can give him that."

"You sound so certain when you say it."

"Is this the life you wanted, Alric? To have been born the third son of a lord, held up for his name, and by those same people, ridiculed? Trapped, in a circle of love and loathing that you cannot escape?"

"But this isn't only about me."

"I, too, am a third child, so I know," Earwyn said. "My eldest sister has always been enough for the Blackwood name. She will always be enough for the whole of us, the light that only spreads far enough to allow us into the shadows. I've never been bitter about that. Because my place is with my husband, and my husband's place is wherever he can at last find the peace that has eluded him for so very long."

Alric's heart ached. "You've always been better to me than I deserved."

"That's simply not true." Earwyn cupped his face with her palm. "And it makes me sad to hear you say it."

"You told Aylen, then?"

Earwyn nodded.

"Did she try to talk you out of it?"

"No."

"Will she tell Christian?"

Earwyn shook her head. "She has her own struggles with Christian."

"Then that's all there is to it? We go?"

"We go."

"Over the pass."

"Over the pass."

On a whim born of the moment, Alric kissed his wife on the

mouth. He couldn't remember the last time he'd done it, though he'd thought about it every single day since the last. "I will keep asking you, until the very end, if you want to turn back. Until the very end, you can change your mind, and I'll never love you any less for it."

Earwyn's kiss in return was more demanding, longer. When she pulled away, the look she wore in her eyes made him melt right into his boots.

"And until the very end, Alric Dereham, I will be there with you, at your side. Where I belong."

33
DEFENDERS

"I trust the two of you more than any in this kingdom. With my own life. With the life created from me, and the lives they'll create, Guardians willing. I ken there can be no trust greater than this, and that we all know it already, but I'm saying it just the same. Aye?"

Rutland and Hamish nodded in kind.

"With Law gone to the Guardians, there's nay any others I'd have in this room to replace him. Ransom is still a bairn, in many ways. I donnae have the proper time to tend to him. The other men... aye, well, we cannae be sure about anything, can we?" Khallum passed his hand over the hair that was now a proper beard. It was no longer coarse. He'd let it go and was surprised that the sea air no longer burned his lungs so much, either; he was no longer so aware of his inadequacies. "I cannae be certain one of them isnae working with the enemy anymore."

"Son of a crow," Rutland whispered. "Do ye ken who it might be?"

"Would either of you be so willing to point the finger at men you've known your whole lives?"

Rutland bowed his head.

"Has word spread, then? To the other Reaches?" Hamish asked.

Khallum shook his head. "Only to our closest allies. Our rightful king's wife murdered in her own bed? Under my watch? By a killer I cannae stop? How can I put those words into the realm, into every corner and coast? And now... and now that the king has left us, left us no better than we were before, when Eoghan was raising his wee fists and throwing his cries into the kingdom."

"And Oldwin, why has he said naught?" Hamish asked. "He wanted unrest, aye? He'll get a right speck more, he spreads the word, so what's stopped him?"

It was a fair question. He might have answered different, even a fortnight ago. "Before he left, the prince told me something. Something I cannae quite shake from my thoughts, and I should've told ye all sooner, I know, but I needed time to think on it. Darrick doesnae think the message was for him at all, but me."

"This Defender nonsense again?" Hamish blubbered with an eye roll.

"Hamish," Rutland warned with a shake of his head. "Khallum, there's something I've not told ye, either. I should've, but I ken we've had more important matters on our minds until now." He cleared his throat. "'Tis about this. The Defenders."

Khallum nodded. "Aye, go on."

"Our fathers were mates. The best of. 'Tis why we are."

Hamish snorted.

"Why we all are," Rutland amended. "And mates, they talk. And fathers talk to sons. Did ye know, there are men who say t'was the Warwicks and the Derehams, were here before all others. Before the Reaches were Reaches. Before the Blackrooks became the Blackwoods, and the Quinlandens were naught more than upstarts. Was us. Not the Rhiagains. And aye, even before the Medvedev."

Hamish shook his head. "Aye, and who would know such a thing? We didnae even write our histories 'til the pretenders washed up on our shores."

"No one," Rutland conceded. "It's enough for me that men passed these tales down, that they saw the need in it. And at the side of the Warwicks, were the Rutlands. Rutland men have always been salt and sand."

"And Strongs."

"Aye, 'course," Rutland said with a light smirk only Khallum could see. "But my father, he knew about the Defenders, Khallum. Your father confessed it, that he was afraid, because he didnae know the way of his ancestors, as he felt he should. All the men who would were dead, save your uncle, and he was missing all those years. Until now."

"Until now," Khallum repeated. "I didnae call ye here to speak of Defenders."

"Aye, but I'm saying we should. What else did Darrick say?"

"He said..." Khallum waited for the thunder to pass, for the stones to cease trembling. "He said I was going about it all wrong, worrying about the Rhiagains and their crown."

"My son nearly *died* worrying about the Rhiagains," Hamish said.

"Law *did* die, worrying about 'em," Rutland replied without looking at him. "Nye's wife and girl died for it. But what if he was right, Khallum? And the Wastelands, the war between the two of you... what if it's all been not about gold or ore or whatever else they've found in those lands, but magic?"

Hamish laughed so hard it broke up into several disparate chokes.

"Did he crack wise, Hamish? I didnae hear a jest," Khallum warned.

Hamish's laughter faded into light coughs he buried in his fist. "Apologies, Khallum."

"Go on, Erran."

"That's all. I just wanted ye to know. Our fathers talked about this. What Odrahn said, 'tis no lie. The whole of it? I cannae say. But 'tis no lie. If there is a veil there, and 'tis the job of the Warwicks, the *Southerlands*, to keep it safe from those who would use it for ill, then it seems to me we know our task."

Khallum grunted. "Even if we could find it, what then?" He

shook his head. "We've got ourselves a kingless crown in Duncar-row, and that needs addressing. But the era of the Rhiagains has ended. So who do we crown?"

Rutland jumped to his feet. The sound of his boots smacking the stone echoed off the damp stones. "Forget the crown, Khallum! There willnae even be a *kingdom* if we cannae see past our own hands and feet to what really matters here!"

"Then what," Khallum began, through gritted teeth, "do ye suggest we do?"

"Find the veil," Rutland said. The crimson flourishes in his cheeks spread. His nostrils flared. "Find the veil and defend it until we have what we need to destroy it."

"MOTHER!" SHE CRIED, HER SCREAMS BREAKING INTO SHRIEKS OF desperation. "Mother!"

"Emberley! Where are you? I can't see you!"

"I can't see you either, Mama!"

"Keep calling for me! I'll find you! Don't stop saying my name. Don't stop until I have you!"

But every time Emberley called out, her voice was farther away. This continued until the only thing she could hear was the thrash of the storm.

"Emberley!" The sound was swallowed by the howling of the wind whipping through the center of the storm. The next time she screamed her daughter's name, there was nothing at all. She couldn't feel, hear, see, or sense anything but the utter nothingness.

Asherley bolted awake to fresh panic. She was pinned down. At first she thought someone was holding her back, but when the fog of her dream cleared, she realized each of her legs were tangled in between the legs of the two men. One to her left, the other to her right.

Ah, she thought. *That.*

She hadn't been asleep long. The moon was still high. She was still slick with the sweat of their coitus, which was among the most unusual things she'd ever done.

Asherley had never been with two men before. It seemed like something she would've tried many times over by now, but she'd been wedded since she was very young and had been true to that marriage. She didn't count what had happened with the boy king, and neither would Byrne.

She struggled to untangle herself, but Arturo's muscular thighs had hers in a death grip. With a defeated sigh, she turned toward Rhydian, but her breath caught when she discovered his eyes were wide open. He was staring at her.

"You're awake," she said. "It's the middle of the night."

"I never sleep much. You had a nightmare?"

She nodded. "About Emberley. I expect they'll keep coming to me until I've brought her safely home, where she belongs."

Rhydian watched her from the pillow. His dark eyes sparkled against the jag of moonlight spilling in through the tall windows lining the far wall. He was beautiful, like Arturo, as if they were cut from the same cloth of gold, but spun into very different garments.

"You were changed by what happened to you there." Rhydian could be speaking of war and he would still sound soothing. She didn't think this was his training. He was created for this.

"Everything about the past few months has changed me, Rhydian."

He ran his fingers over her belly, making a little game of it with a curious look. He always looked at her this way. As if she was a puzzle to solve. "I'd never lain with a woman until last night."

"And? Did you enjoy it?"

The quick little grin he flashed warmed her heart. "More than I expected to. You're exquisite, as you already know. Yet that's not what I find appealing about you. It's your mind that entices me, Lady Blackwood, if you'll forgive me for saying so."

Asherley closed her eyes and pressed her head into the back of the pillow. "We just fucked half the night, Rhydian. Call me Asherley, at least when we're sharing a bed. And never apologize for speaking truths to me. I happen to be proud of my mind. It's gotten me farther than most."

She caught his flush from the corner of her eye. "I enjoyed watching Arturo take you. His pleasure is my pleasure. And you watching me take him... that... that I also most unexpectedly enjoyed."

"The unexpected enjoyments are often the best ones."

He nodded.

Asherley wrapped her arms behind her head. "And that will not be the last time?"

"I should hope not."

"All right. Tell me then. What is it you find so enticing about my mind?"

"Well, you're not like other women, are you?"

Asherley laughed. "I should think more women are like me than not, Rhydian Tyndall. It's the men who seek to cut them into tiny little morsels that are more palatable to their delicate constitutions."

He chuckled. "Perhaps you're right. My brother's wife is colorful, like you."

"Clarissant? She's a proper witch. She came by her magic the honest way, just like Jasmine Wakesell. I've taught them both a thing or two, but I could learn more from them. But you'll find women like this not only in every corner of the Westerlands but also this entire realm."

"Clarissant thinks I don't know this about her, but I do. I know more than most would have me know, but I would never share another's secrets. I will die with the thousands that live in my heart."

"What secret of mine are you angling for, then?"

"I suppose it would be too forward of me to ask you about what happened to you at Midnight Crest?" Before she could answer, he sighed. "I sense that it's eaten away at you, and if I can help you, in some way..."

"There's nothing to say. I was a prisoner, first of Argentyn

Ravenwood, and then of his wife, Varinya. Varinya meant to kill me, and may very well have, had Emberley not arrived when she did. I watched that foul woman strike Ember down right before my eyes, and then I watched her fall from the sky. And, in my rage, I found the ability to strike them both down. Ah, and then I flew away."

Rhydian's mouth parted, speechless. "You... you flew away."

"How else did you think I came down off that mountain?"

"I... don't know."

"Yes, I flew. Just as Emberley had flown to me, to rescue me. But I couldn't find her. I flew for what seemed like hours, until my wings were so sore I almost fell from the sky. I knew then that I couldn't do this alone, and I found my way to Wulfsgate, and my sister. Unfortunately, once I landed, I wasn't able to fly again, or since."

"To hear you speak of it this way!"

"And how should I speak of it?"

"You have the power to fly. To *kill*. That doesn't interest you?"

"Well," Asherley said, as if she was discussing what they might have for their next meal, "I haven't had the time, really, to give it proper thought."

"You should find the time, Asherley. Make the time. These are no small things that have happened to you. They could have repercussions you cannot even imagine."

"I can imagine things most men could not, Rhydian."

Arturo shifted, and she took advantage of the opportunity to extricate her leg. It throbbed from the stifled blood flow. She flexed it under the covers. "Do you think Brandyn's travels have been fair? There should've been a good thaw south of us by now."

"You can talk to me—"

"I am talking to you," she snapped.

"Asherley—"

"I have no need for spiritual guidance, but if I do..." Asherley flipped herself over and rolled atop him. She knew of no better way to silence a man, at least not one that satisfied her own needs in the doing. She was happily surprised at the physical response this produced from him, and she rewarded this by taking it in her hand and rolling her fist over it in soft strokes. He might not be attracted to her in the same visceral way he desired Arturo, but she lighted *something* in him, and she would take whatever she could get.

Rhydian's eyes rolled back as she shifted to guide him inside. She arched her back and started riding him, and soon his hands were on her hips, encouraging her to go faster.

The swifter her stride, the quieter her thoughts.

Beside them, Arturo grunted. He stretched his arms and then turned toward them. He bit down on his lower lip. "Am I invited?"

Esmerelda waited patiently as the handmaid laid out the meal, dish by dish. It looked wonderful, but she wasn't hungry. Her appetite had left some time ago. She would need to eat, though, for Jesse, or he'd worry over her and she didn't want that. She'd given him enough reasons to worry over her, and now that they were married, she wanted less of them, not more.

When they were alone, she steeled herself and said, "So what is it you look so afraid to tell me?"

"Do I look afraid?" Jesse sliced into the boar on his plate. He started to take a bite when he saw her face.

"I know that look all too well."

He lowered the meat halfway. "I'd just hoped to wait till after we'd eaten."

Esmerelda flopped back in her chair.

Jessie's fork clanged on the plate, followed by a light, resigned sigh. "All right. I just came from speaking with your father."

"Why?"

"I told him I was leaving in the morning and that you're coming with me."

Esmerelda's jaw dropped. "You *what*?"

"I waited for you to tell him yourself. I knew you were anxious about it. We're leaving tomorrow, Esme. He had to know."

"We should have discussed this! It wasn't your right to tell him that!"

"I've tried to talk to you about it," Jesse said calmly. "Aye, I know you're afraid of what he'll think or say. But if you want to mend what's been broken with him, there can be no more lies. You cannae keep things like this from him. Not anymore, not after what happened. And you *are* mending things, Esme. Don't reopen that wound with your fear."

"That wasn't for you to decide!"

Jessie lowered his head.

"What, now you're angry with me, is that it?"

He inhaled a hard breath. She missed the days when he wasn't afraid to speak his mind to her. She wondered if that was gone forever, traded in when they said their vows that made some words forever impossible. "Your mother already knows, aye? You'd put her in that position, make her lie to him as well? And then what happens, when we return?" His head shook. "Ye think his pride would allow the slight a second time?"

"What I *think* is that he'll keep me from going with you at all, and *that* is why I didn't want him to know."

Jesse dropped his hands on the table. "It isnae his choice to make, Esmerelda! You're a wife now. And that is... that isnae even the reason. You're your own person. You're not his. You're not mine."

Esmerelda looked away. She hated that he was being so reasonable, when she was an emotional mess.

"I would've fought him to the end, but he didnae fight me at all."

She snapped her head back. "What did he say?"

"Well, he wasnae *pleased*, as ye can well imagine..."

"And?"

Jesse wore the look of a man waiting to take a punch. "He said it was my job now to protect you. That he couldnae stand in the way of a husband's duty."

Esmerelda's head fell back in laughter. "Your job?"

"Esme, all I could do was quietly agree. It's done. He'll say no more."

"So he knows about the sorcerers?"

Jesse paused, then shook his head.

Her eyes widened. "You didn't tell him."

"How could I? He'd never believe me, nor… aye, well, nor would he have let you go with me." Jesse smiled lightly at the attempt to lighten the tension.

"And what *did* you tell him, then?"

"That I had business, and you'd be coming along. That Lady Warwick would tend to our Gemma until we returned. That the road was no place for a bairn."

"Business? While the Reach burns?"

"Aye, none knows better than your father that to halt trade, even now, would be our death knell. We should've left sooner, but after the business with poor Anabella Rhiagain…"

Esmerelda bit down on her tongue. The anger burned just beneath, but it wasn't for Jesse. It wasn't for anyone. It had been building so long she didn't know who or what to thank for it.

She measured her words. "All right. And what reason did you give him for taking a woman along on a man's task, then?"

Jesse reached across the table and grasped her hand. "That as a man so newly wedded, I couldnae be parted from my wife, even for a day."

Esmerelda laughed before she could think better of it. "And he believed you?"

Jessie's face fell. He withdrew his hand, dropped it back in his lap. "I suppose I must've been convincing enough."

Her heart sank. She'd wounded him. He was the last person she ever wanted to hurt. "Jesse. I… please don't take my words to heart tonight. I've just not been myself since Anabella was killed. And this…" She waved her hands. "These elaborate meals, life just going back to the way it was, when nothing, *nothing* is as it was, and never will be. It's gotten to me, I suppose. Forgive me."

He nodded slowly. "No one's the same now. It's all right. Of course you're worried for Gemma."

"No, because I *know* he cannot harm Gemma. Her blood keeps

her safe. It's not that." Esmerelda sucked in her bottom lip. "I wake in the night, three, four, or five times. I watch you until I see the blanket move. And then when I see you're breathing, I feel like a fool because I *am* a fool. Only a fool would act in such a way, and then I know I'm exactly who my father thought I was all along."

Jesse pushed out of his chair. He went to her and pulled her up. "What ye just said, about Gemma's blood keeping Oldwin from harming her?"

Esme nodded.

"That means he cannae harm me, either. I've Medvedev blood running through me, just as Gemma does. It's why Oldwin went after Anabella, because if he couldnae kill Darrick, he knew just precisely how to hurt the man. Just as he must know how he can really hurt me."

"How?"

Jesse pressed his lips to the top of her forehead. He laid his head across her hair. "He could take you."

Esmeralda's heart thrummed so hard, her vision blurred. Every time she was close to him, close like she was now, she was simultaneously wrapped in her beautiful and complicated feelings and also standing back, watching, as if through the eyes of someone who could better understand what was happening inside her.

She was utterly incapable of being objective when it came to Jesse Strong, either before her marriage, or after.

She looked up at him. "That's why I'm going with you, so we can protect each other."

"You've killed more men than I have. I'll take whatever protection ye have to offer, lass."

Esmerelda lowered her eyes as she smiled.

"Do ye really still believe it was pity?"

"Pity?"

"You and me?"

"I never thought that, or I wouldn't have married you."

"You'd tell me if you thought that?"

"I..." Esmerelda shook her head. "I didn't think it then. I don't think it now."

"But our marriage, isnae like other marriages, is it?"

"Nothing about either of us is like other things, so why should our marriage be?"

"Are you happy, though? That's what I'm coming at, Esme. Are you happy with things, as they are? Or have ye regrets?"

Esmerelda pressed her face to his chest. It wasn't what her body, her heart, cried out for. That burning she'd had inside that never died, not since their wedding night where she'd thought, however briefly, he might need her as a man needs a woman.

But it was still the place she felt the safest, the most loved; more, even, than the hard squeeze of Ryan's muscled arms as he held her by the moonlight and made promises she'd believed.

"No, Jesse. I regret a good many things, but marrying you isn't one of them."

His relief passed through to her as he held her. "Tomorrow, then?"

Esmerelda threaded her arms around him and disappeared in the offered warmth. "Tomorrow."

Gwyn stood with her husband outside the keep as they waited. She held little Gemma tight to her breast to shield her from the coastal wind that kicked up, snapping the flags so tight it made her nearly jump out of her skin every time. There were others who could care for the bairn, but she wouldn't let her out of her sight, not until Esmerelda was safely returned. She hadn't been gone a day, but Gwyn had easily fallen into old patterns. A mother's role was never finished.

These days it was all she could do not to succumb to the strange, invasive thoughts, like the one floating through her mind now. Gemma ripped from her arms, carried across the wind and ulti-mately, into the sea. Penance for her crimes.

She could tell no one these terrible thoughts; to share even a little would be to allow the whole awful thing to come tumbling out.

And had it seemed like that was what Oldwin *wanted* her to do? Tell Khallum everything?

The sound of horses made her husband stand more erect. He brushed his hands over his leather armor and checked his sword.

And then Brandyn Blackwood appeared, rounding the bend in the road, wearing the telltale emerald of The Rush, followed by the crimson and silver of the Rush Riders who had accompanied him on his journey from the Westerlands.

As he came into full view, she was stunned to see him so grown. Byrne's boy was a baby when she last saw him. "Look at him. He's a boy, though he looks like a little man."

"You didnae see that boy take war to the Easterlands."

"Pfft. He's still a boy in his mother's eyes. I read Lady Blackwood's letter. She's worried for him. He's tried to do too much too soon. Byrne would've known what to do."

"Aye, and I wish she wouldnae have been so fecking impatient. Didnae even wait for my response. What'd it take him, five days to get here? What'd they do, ride and day and night? In some kind of rush, she is." He shook his head. "She'd nay be happy to learn she was sending her lad straight into danger. What am I to do with him?"

"She trusts you to guide him. You're Byrne's only brother."

"I donnae know what to do with him. Not now, in the middle of all... this."

"You'll find some use for him, won't you?"

"I ken I have to, aye?"

"Be easy on the boy, Khallum. He's lost so much." To herself, she thought, *we all have. And so much of it is my fault. How much longer can I live with knowing this?*

"Aye, and who hasn't?"

"He's only a child."

Khallum shook his head. He raised a hand in greeting as Brandyn and his retinue drew closer. "Nay, Gwyn. If he was here to be a child, it's to you I'd send him. He's here to be a lord, and I cannae think of a better, nor worse, time to do that than in the middle of a war for everything that matters."

Khallum leaned against the open window. The fresh morning sea air for once felt like a relief as it filled his lungs. He was changing. Everything was. "Shame ye didn't arrive a day earlier. Just missed Esmeralda. I ken she would've enjoyed seeing ye, after all these years."

Brandyn's expression froze. "Esmerelda… she came home?"

Khallum narrowed his eyes. "Donnae ye mean she returned to the living? Or did ye mean to say you're yet one more man who knew something I didnae?"

"I…" Brandyn stumbled. Sighed. "I saw her. In Greystone. When I arrived, she was there already. With…" He trailed off altogether. He'd spoken out of turn and was afraid now. His eyes were filled with the dread of where it might lead.

"Jesse Strong? Aye, I know. Now, she's made him a proper wife. Let the past live where it belongs, I say. The future is all we have now."

"She wed Jesse? But I thought—"

Khallum nodded to the table. "Sit."

Brandyn pulled out the chair that once belonged to Samuel Law. He couldn't have known this, nor what it meant now that it had lain vacant. It sent a strange feeling through Khallum. As if things were changing more, changing faster each day, and he could either accept this or die fighting it.

"This table!" Brandyn gasped. He recoiled his hands just in time to avoid slicing them clean through.

"Aye. Be mindful, lad."

"Your men *sit* here?"

"Well, where else would they sit?"

Brandyn's brows rose. He gave a light shudder and moved himself a couple of inches back. "I *tried* to speak sense into my mother, Uncle Khallum. I told her about the troubles here. She wouldn't see reason."

"Sounds like ye had your own share of troubles, in the Rush."

Brandyn cast his eyes away. "I won't make excuses for it. But she thinks that I... she thinks that I could... eh..."

"Learn something proper from a lord?"

"Yes."

Khallum nodded as he exhaled. "I ken that does fall to me now, with your father gone. First lesson, donnae set aside the men who know better than ye, aye?"

Brandyn looked down at his lap.

"Ye think I keep all these men around because I like to look at them?" Khallum gestured to the empty chairs. "What I donnae know, they know. What they donnae know, I know. Together, we lead this Reach. 'Tis not the work of one man alone. Ye ken?"

"I'm deeply sorry to be a burden. I don't want to add to your troubles, and if you'd prefer, I can make myself scarce."

"A burden?" Khallum laughed. "I've lost a good man, aye, perhaps my best, and now I've lost the prince. I'll take any hands I can get."

"You mean Prince Darrick? What happened to him?"

"Your mother didnae tell you?"

Brandyn shook his head.

"Anabella Rhiagain is dead. Prince Darrick has taken his son to find peace for them both, and I'll nay stand in his way."

"Anabella is dead? How?"

"Murdered by the ratsbane playing king in Duncarrow. The one causing all our troubles, terrorizing my Reach. He'll stretch his foul fingers into the kingdom next. Donnae rest thinking he'll stop with us."

"But who will be king when we win? All the other Rhiagains are dead!"

"The Rhiagains are no longer our concern."

"Why would they not be our concern? They're the cause of all our problems. Most certainly of yours!"

"Forget the crown!" Khallum groaned in annoyance, as if he, too, hadn't just asked these same questions; hadn't only recently believed who sat upon the throne was the only thing that mattered. "For too long, our vision for this kingdom has been as narrow as who wears the crown, but this kingdom was here long before the Rhiagains, and if the Warwicks have anything to say or do about it, it'll be here long after. You may wear your mother's name, boy, but you're a Warwick lad, to the bone. Was a Warwick who took the head from his enemy. Who led his men to an uncertain future and delivered upon his promises."

Brandyn eased a bit at the compliments. "I'll help however I can. But what can I do?"

"It's not what you can do that I need right now, but what you *know.*"

Brandyn twisted his mouth into a frown. "According to my mother, not much."

"What, eh, kinds of things did ye learn about in the Sepulchre?"

"The Sepulchre? You want to know about the Consortium?" Brandyn whistled through his teeth. "Well, they taught us some history of magic, I guess. Some of our coursework was from the universities, to keep our minds fresh, they said. But I wasn't there long enough for any of the good stuff."

Khallum pressed harder. "What did you learn about magic itself?"

"It's like I said, I wasn't there very long, Uncle. A year. What I mostly learned was that I still had much to learn." Brandyn laughed. "Magi Christian tried to teach me to be patient. It didn't work."

Khallum rolled his hands in the air. "What did they tell you about the *veils?*"

Brandyn's light smile died. "The veils? Like the one Mad Alric Dereham fell through?"

"Aye, like that."

"I don't think that's magic they wanted us knowing about. Maybe the Elder Magi would know, but they'd never... they would never talk to us about that. Should we send word and ask them?"

"No," Khallum snapped. "No, they like their secrets too much, and I'll nay beg any man for aid. What about the sorcerers? Or did they really teach ye nothing there?"

Brandyn shook his head. "Had I learned about them, I might have been better prepared to face one."

"You lived to tell the tale. Not all men have."

"Only because of Drystan Dereham. I owe a life debt I can never repay."

Khallum nodded. "He honors his kin with that death."

"Why do you ask about the sorcerers?"

"I find myself in need of one."

"What, why? Why would you ever need one of those terrible creatures?"

"Your magic, boy," Khallum said. "You're a seer, aye?"

"I am, but—"

"What have you seen for the Southerlands? For the Wastelands?"

Brandyn leaned forward, but nearly cut himself once more. "No, Uncle, it doesn't… it doesn't work like that. I have no control over what I see. I can't command my visions, or see what I want."

Khallum snorted. "And what good is it, then?"

Brandyn held his hands out. "I can't say it's been good at all, not for me. I was learning to interpret my visions when I left the Sepulchre, when Emberley needed me. I fear now I'll never be allowed to return and finish my training. If I can't learn to use my visions, they'll never be good for anything."

"Your mother never should've sent you there to begin with. You're a Warwick. You were meant for bigger things than silver hair and the robes of women."

Brandyn sighed.

"What if I asked you to see something?"

"I don't know—"

"Have you tried, to see what ye want?"

"I was afraid the things I wanted to see were the very things I shouldn't. Magic has a way of making you regret wanting more of it."

"Well, I donnae see it that way. And what I want *you* to see is the Wastelands."

"The Wastelands?"

"Think hard. I want you to find a veil. It's out there, somewhere, and we must protect it until we can destroy it."

"I don't understand. What veil? What are you talking about?"

"You're a Warwick, Brandyn. That makes you a Defender, too."

Brandyn kept shaking his head. "A Defender of what?"

"Settle in, boy."

34

YOU CAME BACK

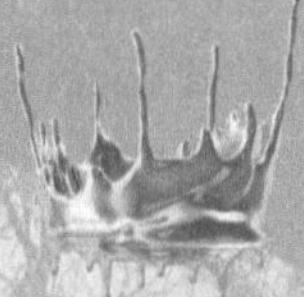

*M*arsh was falling away. His hands and feet no longer connected with anything to secure him to the tangible world. He could see, but no longer feel, the sweet relief of the branches still connected to the tree that had decided his fate. The ones that had betrayed him disappeared. The pull from safety was the last thing he remembered, that tug of urgency into the beckoning abyss.

Until something grabbed firm to his arm.

Was it a Guardian? Was it a bear? Was it—

Give me your hand, you fool! Quickly!

Alasyr.

He'd come.

He'd come back.

He had no sense of how long ago this happened. The mountain still dulled any proper use of his senses.

What he recalled of those harried moments were Alasyr's agitated words, a mismatch for the grave worry etching his face. Alasyr, tending to all his wounds from the treacherous journey, one by one, working hands over flesh, and when at last he'd finished, he, too, was spent, was as cold and worn as Marsh had been since he first set foot on the path.

They'd sat there like that, side by side. For how long, Marsh didn't know.

Now they climbed together. Alasyr took to the skies only long enough to scout ahead, but he always returned. He navigated the same obstacles, grunting at all the same difficulties that Marsh struggled against. But it was easier now. The two of them. The feeling that he wasn't alone buoyed his hope to new heights, and his spirits improved as they pushed together against snow-laden logs and helped untangle one another from the surprise briars that would catch them unawares if they got too confident in their movements.

Marsh never said to Alasyr the three words he wanted to say most.

You came back.

It wove between the tight smiles passed from one man to another when they overcame the small but important victories on their difficult path. It lived in the meager meals Marsh prepared and served to them, their eyes locking briefly as Marsh passed the cracked bowl.

The air was thinner now. He wouldn't have known this, how to identify it, until it hit him for the first time.

Alasyr patiently explained it when Marsh had to stop more often from the dizzy spells that stole over him.

You get used to it. We'll go slower, if that's what you need.

I need to get to Ember.

If you fall off this mountain again, I won't go after you a second time, Wildwood.

A silence fell between them as Alasyr underscored his point with a very serious look. Marsh couldn't help but laugh. Alasyr's stoic expression erupted. He joined in, and they sat like this at the edge of the world, the two of them laughing until they were almost warm again.

"How long have we been at this, do you think?" Marsh asked.

"Long enough."

"If you feel you should go on and check on Ember..."

"I made several trips with bags of food when we left Midwinter Rest. Remember?"

Marsh hadn't remembered this until Alasyr's reminder. As he thought about it, he barely remembered Steward Frost and his daughter. Most of the words they'd exchanged had slipped away, replaced by more practical thoughts, like how to survive.

"We're not far now," Alasyr said. He'd stopped moving. He pressed both hands to his lower back, which had to be screaming like Marsh's was. "I'm going to go look ahead again. You'll stay put until I return? Won't get yourself into any trouble?"

Marsh nodded. He didn't want to say it, but was relieved Alasyr didn't expect him to go on alone, even for the few extra steps it might take for him to return. Alasyr was his only safety up here... his only friend.

Alasyr pressed his lips into a tight line. He let his hand hover reluctantly over Marsh's shoulder before dropping it. He squeezed. "Right, then. Don't move."

Marsh nestled in under a small overhang of rock. There were a few of these spots on the path, where the snow hadn't blown all the way in. It wasn't much, it could hardly be called shelter, but it felt like relief just the same.

He wondered what his mother and father were doing right now. Lyria and Jonah.

The ravens had been mercifully light on the details of what had happened to the Tyndalls during the War for the Westerlands, but Marsh knew they'd suffered. He had faith in Lady Blackwood to make right any wrongs, but Marsh felt the pressure to return and take his place at his father's side, as his heir, and until he did, the House of Tyndall would remain incomplete.

This future seemed more and more elusive the higher he climbed. Really, his doubt of it started somewhere on the road with Emberley. He didn't know when he decided he'd go wherever she led.

But he struggled to see Emberley returning with him and becoming his wife, Stewardess Tyndall, or even one day, Lady Blackwood. These were the futures that lived in his deepest desires and dreams, but he could no longer grasp their potential as anything *but* dreams.

Did she even want him?

Alasyr dropped down, startling him from his reverie. "We're there. An hour by foot, at most."

Tears filled Marsh's eyes. He willed them back, but in defiance, they spilled anyway.

Alasyr reached down, his gloved hand open. Marsh sniffled and took it, rising once more as Alasyr pulled him forward.

Alasyr nodded.

Mash nodded back. Dusted the snow off.

Together, they made the final push.

EMBERLEY TURNED THE RABBIT OVER THE FIRE. IT WAS DONE. IT'D been done, but she didn't think her belly could handle another night of the same meat, so she kept turning it, hoping at some point she'd gather the resolve to survive another night.

When she thought about what she might prefer to this, trying to imagine herself sitting at her mother's long and bountiful table at Longwood Rush, she could conjure nothing. She had no desire for food of any kind, and she wondered if that meant she was dying.

Again.

The world, perhaps, righting the wrong Alasyr had undone when he revived her on this mountain.

Whatever the answer, she was stuck here.

And whose fault is that?

Mine. Mine alone. I shouldn't have come here if I couldn't find it within me to make the return.

And what would you have done if Varinya Ravenwood hadn't struck you down? Huh? Marched up to her and asked her nicely to release your mother?

I hadn't thought that far.

Right. You hadn't thought that far.

I just needed to get to her.

You sound like a child.

I am a child.

No, you were never a child.

Emberley's father used to say that most men indulged in talking to themselves from time to time, but it was when you started responding that you had a problem.

Losing her mind seemed the least of her problems.

And what *would* she do if she could again face Varinya Ravenwood?

I'll know when I'm standing before her.

The sound of snow falling off the mountain beyond the cave entrance brought her senses to life. This happened sometimes, when the small but hearty beasts strayed too far from the safety of their known world.

She'd watched one claw at nothing and fall away. Since then, she saw this in her nightmares. Sometimes, she was the beast.

More snow falling. Ember reached for a nearby rock, closed her fist around it.

But it was only Alasyr.

"Oh, thank the Guardians—"

And Marsh.

Marsh stumbled inside. He fell to his knees when he saw her.

Marsh. It was Marsh. He was here. When Alasyr said he'd gone to get him, it hadn't been some strange fever dream she'd conjured up in her desperate desires. Ah, it really was him, it was *Marsh*, that foolish boy, that silly boy, that beautiful, perfect boy—

Emberley cried out and ambled toward him, half-running, half-crawling. She knocked them both back as she threw her arms around him, and they rolled along the cave floor like this, both laughing, both crying.

"Oh, it's you. It's you, Ember. It's you," he kept whispering, his urgent warm breath soothing against her cold ear.

She pulled them so they were seated. She laid her legs on either side of him, and he yanked her forward, kissing her before she could do it first. How could she have ever, ever thought she didn't love him? That he wasn't enough for her strange and fiery heart? That what she felt wasn't this perfect, eternal bliss, of knowing you were with the exact person you were meant for, made for.

Marsh tangled his fingers in her hair and deepened the kiss. He gasped in her mouth, a desperate but wonderful sound that made them both laugh, and then she hugged him so tight she couldn't feel her arms anymore.

She looked up to see Alasyr standing off to the side, waiting. She stretched her hand out to him, and he regarded it as if he didn't realize what she was offering. But then Marsh, too, reached for him.

Alasyr's throat ebbed. His eyes were shot with red. He looked so unsure as he reached for their hands, but when they tugged him down, he, too, laughed, laughed until she silenced this with her own kisses. She felt Marsh's mouth at the edge of hers, and as she angled herself to receive both their affections, Alasyr's and Marsh's lips connected. She waited for the recoil, the disgust, but it didn't come. Alasyr pressed his palm to the back of Marsh's head, and the two men lost themselves to their own moment.

The three huddled together, arms twined around each other's shoulders, hands linked from behind. Both Alasyr and Marsh were so cold from their travels, but it was only warmth she felt from them.

A sense of peace stole over her.

Alasyr laid his hand on her cheek and kissed her. There was no hesitation now; nor jealousy from Marsh, who only watched and waited.

"I have something I need to do before we go," Alasyr said. "Before we leave this mountain behind."

"What is it?" Ember asked.

"I need to return to Midnight Crest." He shook his head. "Not for long."

She watched him. "I thought you might."

"Will you wait for me?"

It was Marsh who answered. "Yes. Of course we'll wait."

"You'll be all right?"

Emberley nodded. "We have enough food, and you brought me my Marsh. You do what you need to do. We'll be here, waiting."

Alasyr nodded. He looked at them both and then erupted into feathers.

"YOU CAME ALL THE WAY UP THIS MOUNTAIN? ON FOOT?"

Marsh still stared at the spot where Alasyr had stood only moments ago. The sense of emptiness at his absence was puzzling.

He thought he'd be relieved for this time alone with Emberley, but he felt as if a piece of him was missing.

He nodded. "It was Alasyr's idea. I thought he was crazy, but he was right. There was a way all along. I could never have done it without him."

"All these years and there was a path for men to follow, and no one knew."

"Some knew. They buried the knowledge, struck it from the maps and their memories."

Emberley nodded. "I don't know if these two worlds could ever exist together. If they even should."

"You look..." Marsh hesitated. "Alasyr told me..."

"I'm all right."

"Do you feel different? After dying?"

Emberley shook her head, but stopped mid-movement.

"A little. It isn't my flesh, or my bones that feel different, though, but something else. I don't know."

"But?"

She smiled. "You always know when I've left something unsaid, don't you?"

"It's because I know you, Emberley. I might not be as exciting as a Ravenwood, or—"

Emberley ended his self-reflection with a kiss. "That's nonsense, Marsh. Not everything has to be exciting."

"What about my eyes?"

"Your what?"

Marsh laughed. "Only something Eavan said. That you..." His smile faded as his thoughts moved on.

"What is it? What's wrong?"

"I... I spent those long days and nights on the mountain knowing that it wouldn't matter to me how you felt when I found you. All I cared about was seeing you safe. But now that I see you..." Marsh was again overcome with tears, but he wasn't ashamed of them now. "I find that isn't as true as I'd want it to be. All my strength is undone, sitting here before you now."

"You think I don't love you? Because of what I said at Wulfsgate?"

"You don't have to explain yourself to me. I've always known you're your own person. It was a gift to be given even a part of that."

Emberley pulled herself closer. "You aren't the only one who's been given too much time with their thoughts, Marsh."

"Too much of anything can be a bad thing, my father always said." He felt himself growing hard beneath her as she angled herself into his lap. He swallowed the lump in the back of his throat.

"Your father is a wise man, but on this, he and I disagree. I couldn't give you what you asked for then, because I wasn't fully myself yet. And now that I am, I can give knowing that it's with all of myself, my whole and full self, that I make this choice."

"I don't understand what you're saying," he said, chuckling to break the tension.

Ember pushed him back against the rock. She reached between his legs to unbuckle his trousers. "I'm saying that I *love* you, Marsh Tyndall. I'm saying it first this time, so you know it isn't from obligation."

Marsh groaned when her hand encircled him. Black stars danced behind his eyes as he was overcome with the immediacy of this pleasure. He wanted to say it back. How he loved her so much he couldn't breathe to think of it, but something else had stolen his breath just then.

Ember had wiggled out of her leather pants. His first thought was how she needed them on, how cold it was, but then she was sliding over him, and Marsh forgot every objection still waiting.

"You don't need to say anything this time," she said as she rolled over him. "It's my turn."

It was as if they'd known he was coming.

It was as if they'd been waiting all along.

There weren't many seers at Midnight Crest. Yet now he suspected there may have been more than ever felt safe confessing it, for seers wielded a dangerous power in a world where truth was decided by one person alone.

Arms from everywhere encircled Alasyr, ushering him quickly down the long hall of damp stones. His feet slipped on the slick unevenness, but they caught him, never letting him fall. He was so surrounded that he couldn't get his bearings. He didn't know where he was, so he couldn't discern where they might be taking him.

"What's happening?" he tried to ask, but his voice disappeared in the sea of leather and cloaks.

At last, he was ushered inside a room. He knew it was a room by the change from the cold to a cloying warmth, a kind you felt in too close quarters with others. A thunder of doors closing sounded behind him.

"Oh, mercy to the ancestors, he's here! You found him!"

Alasyr heard variations of all this around him in an echo of relieved cries, but it wasn't until his guardians broke away that he at last understood where he was. The Hall of Hours.

He almost didn't recognize the room. He'd stumbled in here as a boy, played upon the ornate floors. He'd always only seen it empty.

He knew some faces, but not all. He wondered how this could be possible in their small world, but the answer wasn't so elusive, not now, when his eyes were open.

His grandfather stepped forward. Rillyn. At his side was little Nevyn, Alasyr's only brother. What was he doing here? What were any of them doing here?

"What is this?" Alasyr demanded.

Rillyn pressed a hand to his heart. "The ancestors haven't abandoned us after all."

"What does that mean? Why am I here?"

"Your grandmother has gone the traitor's way. She is responsible for the deaths of my eldest children, of Varinya and Argentyn, and also an innocent half-blood. She manipulated hearts and minds of others to see it done. She would have killed Ravenna had Ravenna not been protected by something even our magic cannot penetrate."

Ravenna. Alasyr repeated this name, but it was all the other truths washing over him that silenced him from saying more. So his mother *was* dead. He hadn't imagined his father's lifeless body, either. It was true, all of it.

He'd hardly been gone, and in that time the whole of Midnight Crest had changed.

Heels clicked against the floor. All eyes turned toward the sound and Alasyr, too, followed where they looked.

It was Ravenna.

Alasyr opened his mouth, but nothing came out.

"You're here just in time, Alasyr," she said. But it wasn't her voice, for she, too, had changed.

"Time for what?" he managed, his voice more like a croak.

"For us to right the wrongs of Adynora Ravenwood."

35

SON OF DECIMA AND ISDEMUS

"Oh, you sweet girl." Gwyn practically smothered Lisbet into the folds of her gown. Khallum had to wonder if the girl could even breathe.

After several uncomfortable moments, she ended the embrace and dangled the girl at arm's length, drinking her in. "You poor thing. I was just so sorry to hear about your mother. In my heart, I know she and Holden will return. You cannot lose hope."

"I thank you for your kind words, Aunt Gwyn, though I wish I shared your confidence."

"Your mother has gone nowhere she cannot return from. There are no veils, Lisbet. So she must be out there, somewhere."

Lisbet stiffened. Her peel away from her aunt's attempt at consolation was gentle, but decisive.

Gwyn didn't seem to notice. "And Holden, well, he always finds his way back to duty, doesn't he? The war is long ended. They have no use for him, now. If he *was* dead, they would have taken credit for the deed. Helps no one to leave a lord in a ditch, does it?"

Khallum waited in impatience for his wife to see her fawning over their niece and poorly chosen words were misplaced. Lisbet placated Gwyn, allowing the affections while not requiring them in the least. She could teach her aunt a thing or two about toughness, he thought, especially when Khallum considered his wife's demeanor in recent days. She was always on the verge of some crying spell. He was afraid to say a single sideways word to her.

Khallum appraised the man with Lisbet. He was no Dereham, nor Quinlanden, and if he wasn't kin, then that made him wholly unfit to be alone with the young lass. Khallum bristled as he mulled over the possibilities of how his niece came to be with this stranger, as he waited for his turn to ask the questions.

Where did he know him from? Why could he not recollect this?

The nursemaid stepped out from beyond the eaves as she bounced Gemma. Gwyn had forbidden her from leaving their side with the bairn. On that, Khallum agreed.

Lisbet stepped forward and, smiling, peered behind the swaddling. "What a beautiful little one. Whose child is this?"

"'Tis a long tale, and it's fixin' to rain," Khallum grunted. "And aye, she is beautiful."

"Gemma is our greatest blessing, one I fear we don't deserve," Gwyn said, but her eyes had drifted off, and now she was lost to that hollow sadness he'd come to recognize so well.

At first, he'd ascribed it to all their losses. He still struggled to come to terms with them, so he supposed the women must be in a right state over matters in the Southerlands. But it was something else. Something he might spend more time sorting if he didn't have bigger problems.

"The Southerlands is no safe place for children right now," Khallum said. "Yet they keep sending them to me."

Lisbet nodded. "We're not looking for protections. Our arrival is intentional, not incidental. You might say we were called here."

He tried to pass a look to his wife, but she was again looking off into nothing.

"Called here?" Khallum repeated with a wry look. "Wasnae me who called ye."

Lisbet looked at her strange companion and sighed. "Not *here*, exactly. The Wastelands. We came here first, to see... well, I suppose we thought you might have some guidance for us. Failing that, then perhaps a way in that will not get us both killed?"

Khallum was utterly speechless. He choked out a rough sound. "You're *compelled* to the Wastelands, girl? Do ye have a death wish?"

"Not exactly," the man said.

"And who the feck are ye? I know you're no relation of Holden, nor Gretchen, so what are ye doing with the girl?"

The man passed his gaze evenly between all of them. "Lisbet wanted me here, and I'll be here until she decides she no longer wants me."

"We can tell him," Lisbet said in a near whisper. "I think he'll understand."

"Tell me what?" Khallum asked.

"Were famished. Can we talk about it over a meal?"

"Of course, dear!" Gwyn again came alive at a renewed promise of usefulness. "We'll have a proper feast prepared and some tankards of our finest ale sent down." To her husband, she asked, "Shall I have it all sent to the Hall of Warring?"

"What? Aye, that's fine." He was still staring at Gretchen's miniature. But this one had more fire. More... something that he couldn't define. The man at her side had it in him, too, and a sick feeling stabbed at his belly.

He knew who the man was.

"Gwyn, send someone for their horses and bags."

"Yes, dear."

"Come on, then. Let's get ye off your feet so I can hear this tale you've come all the way to the other end of the realm to tell."

It was all the same.

The great scholars and masters of the kingdom wrote in what Balfour liked to think of as High Kingdom. It wasn't a separate language, but a more affected way of writing that required the reader to go over the words more carefully. Most of their texts at the universities were written this way. The masters said it was to provoke the pupils to slow their learning, to take the needed time for truths and facts to be remembered.

There was little Balfour desired to remember from his days at Oldcastle. All except these last days with her.

He didn't mind how slow their progress was. It meant he could stay in this small room with her a little while longer. The only place in this world where the odd bond that had formed between them would ever be this intoxicating. He wasn't eager to give up the only thing that had ever lighted this sense of joy and purpose in him. If he could have found a thousand books for her to read, even that would not have been enough.

But they were both nearing the end of their books. They could return to the library, of course, but Assana's patience had been ground down into despair. Her mind was given over to finding the answer she'd come here for. She had room for nothing else. Balfour sensed that when these books failed her, she would move on and find her answers elsewhere.

He channeled his burning for her into the purpose she'd set him on. She offered the occasional reward,; a quick, but genuine smile, as she lay on the floor, looking up at him from over the top of her book. His heart swelled with each one. It would be broken soon, never again mended, for there was only one cure and she was also the cause. He slowed his reading to eke out this last bit, to prolong the terrible, inevitable end waiting when he'd spent his usefulness to her.

Then he saw it. "Assana," he practically croaked.

"Hmm?" she asked without looking up from her reading.

"Come here. Come up here."

"Why, what is it?"

"Read this."

When she pulled herself up on the small bed, he rambled on. "Read it. Read it aloud, I want to know how it sounds from you, so I know I'm not imagining this."

Assana flashed him an excited look before lowering her eyes to the book. With a shaky finger, he pointed to the passage. It wasn't hard to find. It was the final one in the book. The answer had come, at last, at the end.

"And thus it is the ultimate and foremost conclusion of this scholar, properly read into this elusive subject, that the conception of the veils must also be their undoing, and in their undoing thus also obliterates the cause. But it is also true when said that it is not the creators who will also deliver the needed ends, for evil cannot vanquish itself." She looked up. "I don't understand. It's all circular nonsense."

"The sorcerers, Assana. You read earlier that they were the ones who created the veils when they..." He shook his head. He hadn't been listening well enough.

"Tried to steal the Light?"

"Yes." He wagged his finger at the page. "The sorcerers created the veils. It must be the sorcerers who destroy the veils. It's in this part, *thus also destroys the cause in destroying the veils*. The sorcerers, too, will be destroyed. Destroyed, Assana. There it is. What you were looking for."

Asana sat up with a soft exhale. "Their fates are tied to the veils."

"I think so, yes."

She shook her head. "Does that help us? To destroy the veils would mean to destroy themselves. Why would they ever partake in such an act?"

"Assana." Balfour leaned in; his heart pulsed in his chest. "Not all sorcerers are responsible for the Sundering that created the veils."

"How can we ever know that?"

"You're the one who told me."

Assana started to retort, and then the light brightened behind her eyes. "You mean Dain?"

"Yes. I mean the one who was created here in this kingdom. Read this part again: *it is also true when said that it is not the creators who will also deliver the needed ends, for evil cannot vanquish itself*. If that doesn't mean Dain, what else could it mean?"

"But it's only rumor that his father was a sorcerer."

"Rumors often begin in truth."

"We don't even know if he's alive, or where to find him. Oldwin doesn't even know, and he has every reason to root him out and have him destroyed."

"What if he has children? There may yet be more of them. And do you really believe that none of the other sorcerers ever had children? There must be those who have been created here. Dain can't be the only one."

"Wouldn't we know?"

"Would we, though?"

"If there are..." Assana snapped the book closed. She crushed it tightly to her chest, like a reward. Tears pooled in her eyes. "What if this is it? If this is what I need to do?"

"We," he said with a lazy smile.

"You've already done more than I asked for."

He shrugged. "What else do I have going on?"

"Really?"

"Really."

Assana reached for his hand. "It's dangerous, you know. Not like when you go to the beach and a wave catches you, but dangerous like an assassin at the end of your bed."

"I know."

Assana pulled away with a grin. "Right, then. Now that I've pretended to care about your well-being."

Balfour cocked the outer corner of his mouth into a matching grin. "I might know where we can get some direction."

"Tell him," Lisbet said. "So Lord Warwick can stop looking at you as if you've kidnapped me."

Ash didn't share her confidence. He'd never met Khallum Warwick before, but he was aware of the man's reputation. He wasn't known for his imagination, but for his lack of it. His disdain for magic was legend. The Sepulchre supposedly received fewer Adherents each year from the Southerlands. It had been generations since the Warwicks employed Enchanters at their court.

What did Lisbet want him to say to this man, who would disbelieve any words spoken? That he was Lisbet's true father, and the two of them had come here on the back of some new magic that they didn't even understand?

"Go on," she urged. "He should hear it from you."

He didn't trust Khallum Warwick, but he trusted his daughter. He gave her a tight smile and then looked at the man whose energies were tied up in his anticipation of whatever Ash was about to say. "My name is Drystan Sylvaine, my lord. Most men call me Ash. Lisbet's mother was once my love, and because of that love, which persisted long after it should have, both Drystan and Lis—"

The death of Khallum's defiant, haughty look silenced Ash. The man paled. "I knew it! Say it again!"

Ash was even less confident when he replied. "I said my name is..." He trailed off again. Lord Warwick's jaw stretched and convulsed, as if he might dry heave at any moment. "Have I said something to offend you, my lord?" He flashed a worried look in Lisbet's direction, but her attention was fully on her uncle.

"Uncle Khallum?"

"Something to offend me?"

Ash tilted his head. "My lord, I don't understand."

"Do you know who you are?" Khallum demanded.

"I've just told you who I am, sir."

"Do you *know* who you are?" the man asked again.

Ash's response came with tiny head shakes. "I don't understand," he said again, more confused with every passing second. He again looked at Lisbet, but she stared straight ahead, and now it seemed she was intentionally avoiding him. "What is this?"

"I know who he is," Lisbet said shakily. The curiosity she'd worn in the beginning had faded, and now it was she who looked as if she might be ill. "But he doesn't, and I need to tell him before you say anything else. It should be me who does it."

Khallum scoffed. "How can that be? That you know, and he doesnae?"

"Someone told me, when I failed to see it for myself."

"Lisbet?" Ash's use of her name grew more demanding.

She lowered her eyes to her lap. "Forgive me, Ash. I wanted to tell you so many times. On our way to Wulfsgate. While we were there. On our travels here. I really, truly did. But every time I tried, my fear stopped me. I wasn't ready for everything to change between us. If I'd known that Lord Warwick knew... I would've said something sooner, so you didn't come to learn like this. You have to believe me."

Ash looked between Lord Warwick and his daughter. "The two of you have some shared secret, then? Is that it? Is that why you wanted to come here?"

"No," Lisbet insisted, her head shaking furiously. Still, she wouldn't look at him. "I didn't know Lord Warwick knew. I don't know how he does."

Khallum pointed at Ash. "He really doesnae know?" When Lisbet shook her head, he added, "Then why did you come? We sent our call into the Reaches for Drystan Sylvaine, and here you are. So if not answering this call, why are you here?"

"What is it the two of you aren't telling me?" Ash cried. He didn't like this. He no longer felt like her ally, but a cornered animal. "Lisbet!"

"You said you didn't know your birth family, Ash. You weren't supposed to know them. No one wanted you to know the truth, for it was enough to send this entire kingdom to its knees."

"Lisbet..."

"I'm sorry for not telling you. I'll say it again until you believe me, but I truly didn't have the words. This awakening we're both having, it's not an accident. It's because of who we are. Who we *really* are."

Ash looked at Lord Warwick for some sign of what was coming, but the man watched Lisbet intently.

With a drawn sigh, Lisbet went on. "You're the son of Decima Rhiagain and a sorcerer named Isdemus. King Khain never knew you weren't his son, and neither did anyone else in Duncarrow, other than Decima and Isdemus themselves. When he ordered your death, on the guidance of Oldwin, the man he tasked with it couldn't take the life of an innocent boy, so he instead placed you with the Sylvaines and returned to his king with a lie. They never knew where their son came from. No one could know your real name was Dain Rhiagain, or you'd never again be safe."

"No, that's not... I would know. I would've known," Ash retorted. His fingers tingled, threatening to go numb. His mouth felt stuffed with muslin cloth. "Those aren't the kind of secrets long kept in a kingdom like ours."

"Yet it was, and still is."

"It's nonsense, Lisbet! Listen to what you're saying! This sounds every bit the type of story we're told by our nans as babes!"

"You think it's nonsense?" Khallum asked with an eye roll. "Feckin' great. The one we've been waiting for would rather play skip the rocks."

"I don't know why it's happening now, Ash," Lisbet went on. "Only that we're meant to be here! I don't know what it means, but it does us no good, it does no one any good, to deny this truth."

Ash had a powerful urge to run his hands into the knife's blade edge of the table.

"Father, look at me."

Ash's entire resolve crumbled at the use of that word. When he turned toward her, he could hardly see her at all through the blur of his tears. All the little pieces of his life at last added up, began to make sense. *It cannot be true,* he kept repeating in his head, but Lisbet's tortured belief dulled the words from coming out, and the impatient lack of surprise from Lord Warwick's eyes killed them altogether. This man without imagination had no trouble at all believing he was sitting across the table from Dain Rhiagain, who was also, Lisbet claimed, a bloody sorcerer.

"If you love me, you'll trust that I wouldn't deceive you, especially not about something like this. You brought us to the Medvedev for a reason."

"Lisbet, you *wanted* to go there! You were aimed there all along. I was simply helping you make the voyage safely."

"No. You knew we belonged there, you never questioned it."

"Now that we've shared stories, can we talk about why you're here?" Khallum asked. "You didnae just land at my keep on coincidence alone, and ye know that now, so let's get on with it."

"Do you know, then, who his other child is?"

"Other child?" Khallum repeated. "What other child?"

"Ash has another child out there. We just don't know who they are. We'd hoped you might know."

"How the feck would I know?"

Ash pressed both hands over his mouth. Those long nights under the leaves of purple and pink were thrust to the front of his mind. "Yanna," he whispered. "Maybe we were wrong coming here, Lisbet. Maybe we were in the right place all along, as Yseult's prisoners."

"What was that name, again?" Khallum angled his head to the side. "Say it once more."

"Her name was Yanna. It was only a season, if even that long. And then I returned to the Easterlands, and Gretchen and I made our amends, and it was like that never happened at all. I'd almost forgotten about those nights. I *had* forgotten until we were again in those lands. I knew nothing about a child. She never said a word. But she was the only other woman I'd ever been with, aside from Gretchen."

Khallum pressed back from the table. He put his hands on either side of his beard, tugging. "Yanna, ye say? Not a name I've heard but twice, and the second time was you saying it just now."

"Who was the first?" Lisbet asked.

"Said she came from Bythesea, but we all knew t'was a lie. She didnae look like any woman from Bythesea that we'd known."

"It cannot be the same woman, though, can it?" Ash closed his eyes to slow his thoughts, spinning beyond his control. It was all too much. None of it connected in a way that comforted him, and yet it *was* connected, and both Lisbet and Khallum could see what he could not.

"She was with child when Hamish found her, barefoot and filth-ridden, at Bythesea. He never knew the name of the father. He would've killed him, and rightfully so, for leaving her like that."

"If Yanna was with child, Lord Warwick, that wasn't something I ever knew."

But Khallum was already lost in another thought. "But that means... Jesse. Oh, feck it all."

"Jesse?" Lisbet pressed.

"Oh, *feck it all*, I should've known there wasnae more than holes in that boy's story! Running around, saying he'd 'felt' things! And now he's gone, and Guardians know when he'll be back."

"Lord Warwick, who's Jesse?"

Khallum leaned in over the table. He dropped his palms inches from the serrated edge, a practiced move of a man who'd been perfecting this for years. "Aye, who's Jesse? Well, I ken Jesse Strong is now the husband of my Esmerelda. And if what ye say is true, then he's both Medvedev and sorcerer, and maybe it was *him* all along I've been waiting for. Right under my bloody nose!"

Lisbet whispered, "Did you say Esmerelda? She's alive?"

"Ah, and so it was never this Dain, this *Ash*, but the same man responsible for my only daughter. My own son, in the eyes of the law."

"What do you mean, waiting for him?"

"To destroy the veil! The one in the Westerlands I ken ye both came here for!"

"But we don't *know* why we're here."

"Ye donnae need to know, girl, for *I* know why you're here. To find it, and then destroy it."

"I have another son?" Ash asked. He could hardly keep up with the two of them in their rapid exchange, their shared understanding of something still eluding him. "His name is Jesse?"

"Yes!" Lisbet and Khallum said in tandem impatience.

"He's here?"

"He left. I donnae know when he'll return, and we donnae have the time to wait for him." Khallum shook his head. "No. It has to be you."

"Do you know where it is, Uncle?"

"Nay, girl, if I knew, I'd already be there!"

Lisbet slumped in her seat.

"It has to be you. You're here, now, and so it has to be you."

"We'll leave tonight, then," she said.

"Tomorrow. You'll need a fair rest for that place. Gives me time to collect the men who'll join us."

"You're going with us?"

"Aye, well, ye cannae very well just walk in all by yourself, can ye? The crown has men crawling all over the place. You willnae make it far like that."

"But..." Lisbet sighed. "If you don't know where this veil is, how do you know it exists at all?"

"My ancestors," Khallum said. "They've defended it for hundreds of years, waiting for someone to come along to destroy it."

"Why haven't you destroyed it?"

"If men could destroy it, donnae ye think we would've already? 'Tis a sorcerer who opened it, must be a sorcerer to close it for good."

Lisbet slowly nodded. "But why does it need to be destroyed?"

"I donnae know all, girl! But if you're here, it can only be the Guardians who've sent ye, at last, to finish what the Warwicks started. It finally makes sense! It's the only thing that does!"

"Sorcerers," she said again with a short, tight laugh. "You've been waiting for us hundreds of years, and now it all comes down to this moment, doesn't it?"

Khallum nodded. "Aye, I ken it does."

"We destroy it, and then what?"

"Oldwin loses, and his reign of terror ends."

Ash's eyes swam with dark stars. That was the last thing he saw before he slipped out of the chair and hit the floor.

IN THIS WORLD OR THE NEXT

36
THE VOW

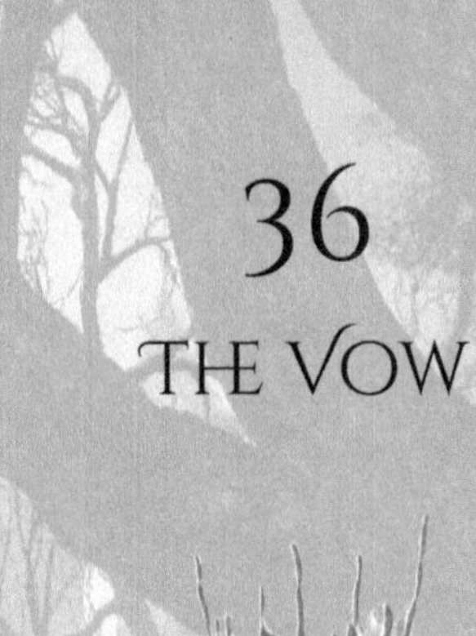

"We'll have to leave the horses here," Jesse said as his eyes scanned the forest.

"Why?" Esmerelda asked.

"It's only a feeling. I could be wrong."

"I trust your instincts, Jesse. So we leave them."

He nodded as he looked around. He avoided looking straight ahead. The answer was already there, but charging into the unknown left him hesitant.

"You seem like you can see something I can't."

"Aye. You're right. I can." The wonder of this strange realization washed over him like a warm bath. He *could* see it. This time was markedly different from his last attempt to bring her to the Hinterlands, approaching it with—he now knew—no chance of success. This time he'd known where to go at every turn. Each step their horses took felt like the right ones. There was never a moment where he stopped to question. He'd never needed to.

Jesse flattened his palm and let it hover inches from the bark. It seemed to throb and bow in response to the promise of his touch. And was it glowing? Could she see this, too?

"This time is different, isn't it?" she said, and it wasn't their first time on the trip she was in his head.

Jesse nodded. He wanted to explain it to her, but she understood as well as she could, and it wasn't his words she was after anymore, if it had ever been.

They'd ridden hard on their way north. Esmerelda kept a grueling pace without complaint. When he'd ask her if she needed a reprieve, she bristled, wanting to push another hour, another town. Without the need to travel under the cover of disguise, they enjoyed easier passage.

They'd hit the Compass Road near Termonglen. As they approached, he realized this was the place where the irrevocable shift started in his relationship with Esmerelda. In his dreams, he still saw her singing and dancing as she played that damned lute, heard her careful, eager words as she lay next to him in the moth-eaten bed. He saw himself softening to her, despite himself. Only later would this become something more, but it was here they'd begun to understand one another.

As they'd rounded the turn to take the Compass Road north, Esmerelda's posture had changed, too, slowing, drawing closer to him. Her hand dropped out between their horses and he'd taken it, without words, and then memory was once again a memory.

They'd said little on the trip north, beyond practical needs. They ate their meals in silence, and when they turned in each night, she'd press her cheek to his chest, and he'd draw her close, arm looped around her back. Her little sigh would soon turn to soft snores, and that was his own signal for peace; an end to the long days.

"That's it, isn't it?" She moved her horse forward, coming up alongside him.

He nodded.

"I can't see it like you can. What if that means I can't enter?"

Jesse dropped off his mare. He reached up to give her mane a loving stroke and then whispered in her ear. With a light snuff, she moved off at a slow gait.

Esmerelda understood he needed her to do the same. She

dismounted and clucked gently before sending her own horse off, and together, the two beasts wandered off into the woods.

"What did you say to her?"

Jesse nodded toward the woods. "I told her to find food and water, and we'd come back for them when we could."

Esmerelda cocked her head to the side. "Aye, you can speak to horses, can ye?"

He grinned. "Who knows? I ken you should hope so, or we'll be making the return trip on foot."

Esmerelda dusted herself off, stretching off the long ride. She wore the leather of a man, and the pants she'd chosen were cuffed at the ankle; too long. There'd been no time to commission something new, so she'd borrowed from her younger brother, Claybourne. "Then let's just hope you're as charming with the bears as you are the horses."

Jesse's smile faded. He reached for her hand. "I'm glad you're here, Esme. That ye came."

"You better be," she teased. "Or at least have the good sense to lie about it."

"You asked if you can enter here? Well, I willnae go without you. So close your eyes, and hold fast to me, and we'll give it our best go."

She did as he asked. "I'm not afraid," she lied, breathless.

"No? Well, I am." He laced each of his fingers through hers, one by one, tightening his grip as he took a single but bold step forward. She moved with him, and as their feet landed, he knew something had changed. He opened his eyes, and the first thing that stole his attention was the change in colors. Emerald became cyan. Sepia was now violet. A shimmering song rippled through the leaves of the trees that looked similar to the ones he knew, but were not the same. He knew this in the same way he'd known how to find this door, to this world that was his, as much as the one he'd left behind.

Esmerelda lengthened her posture with a sharp inhalation. She released his hand as she stumbled to the side, her head fallen back in wonder. "Jesse... oh. Would you look?"

"Aye, I see."

"I can hardly believe it."

"Nor I."

"Jamesan," a voice as foreign as this world said. They both turned to see a young man with violet hair. His hawk soared above, dipping low but not landing. Medvedev. Jesse had a sense of knowing him, though he was certain they'd never actually met.

"My name is Kian," the young man said, stepping forward. He nodded at Esmerelda. "And you, Esmerelda, are also welcome here, among us."

"Thank you," she managed.

"Kian," Jesse said. "I've heard that name. Somewhere."

"Your mother and mine were sisters. I waited a long time to see the son of Yanna with my own eyes, but not as long as my mother. I wear her regret that she didn't live to get this chance."

"I'm sorry to hear about your mother. Did you know mine?"

Kian shook his head. "She was gone before I was born. I only know her through my mother's eyes."

"You'd do me a great honor, sharing any of her stories with me."

"If time allows for it, it will be my gift to you."

Jesse gestured around. "These are Saleen lands?" He asked the question he knew the answer to, one last vestige of control, before surrendering himself.

"Yes."

"Is it true, what they say? That all of them are gone now?"

"Most of them," Kian said. "A few remain."

"Why are you here, and not in the Drumain lands? And why I am here, if my mother was Drumain?" Jesse cleared his throat. "I ken ye *have* been waiting for me?"

Kian nodded and settled his hands into a V-formation before him. "Will you allow me to show you to your tent and offer a warm meal? I cannot say how many of these we have left to share, but it is not many."

Jesse felt the question in Esmerelda's eyes as she watched him from the side. "Of course. Thank you."

Jesse re-linked hands with Esmerelda and followed Kian de Medvedev into the land of the Saleen.

RYAN RODE WELL AHEAD OF THE OTHERS. EVEN WITH THE DISTANCE between them, he could hear Lord Warwick's cutting remarks, as he speculated on Ryan's motivations for riding alone. He didn't rightly care what they thought. He didn't care, because they hadn't cared what asking him to return to the Wastelands might do to him.

Lord Warwick hadn't sounded at all remorseful when he commanded him to come along.

What good can I bring? I've no memory. It was a half-lie, but the full truth only lived within Ryan now.

Aye, and what if this triggers it?

And what if it doesnae?

I'm willing to take that risk.

What about me? What about what it might do to me, to remember it like that?

What about you? Ye got my daughter with child and then refused to marry her.

'Tis not true. I didnae refuse.

Aye, and what's the feckin' difference in the end? Fixin' to split hairs over that, are we? Ye left her with a broken heart, and that's all that matters to her father.

Seems my brother is doing a fine enough job mending it.

Aye, and we thank the Guardians for it, we do.

These days, all conversations ended like this, Ryan lingering just on the cliff's edge; a hair's breadth from the truth. To say more risked revealing things he still didn't understand, and wasn't sure he wanted to. Everyone looked at him like they knew him better than he knew himself. Maybe they did. Maybe these memories returning were only accumulations of all the things people had said to him about who he was.

But then, maybe they weren't.

Theirs was the most unusual group of brigands he'd ever seen.

Lord Warwick and Ryan's father were the only two who had even swung a sword in combat, he was certain of it. The nameless man—the one they called Ash, but that was no real name—fancied himself a Rush Rider, apparently, with a bow long enough to nearly drag the ground mounted. And the Dereham girl, who Khallum should have sent back to Wulfsgate the moment she arrived. This was no place for a girl, just like it was no place for the Blackwood boy who hardly had hair on his scrote. And, sure, they'd told him why, why they were going to the Wastelands, what they were going to do there. They'd told him all about the Warwick Defenders, and some supposed "veil" that would save or end the world. They could say it a hundred times, it still wouldn't make any sense.

What Ryan wanted to know was why not send in the entire Warwick Guard to storm to place? What would the six of them have against the Knights of Duncarrow? If it wasn't the Knights, it would be guards. The whole place was crawling with the crown's men. They didn't stand a chance. Khallum leaving his heir behind as a precaution confirmed he knew it, too.

He envied Rutland, who'd been chosen to stay behind and see after the defense of Warwicktown.

"You were the one that was in there?" Ryan's thoughts were interrupted by the girl, Lisbet. He hadn't even heard the hooves as she rode up beside him. He spent so much time in his head he'd forget the world outside still moved forward, with or without him. "The Wastelands?"

"So they say."

"I also heard you lost your memory."

"They say that, too."

"You didn't, then? It seems like the kind of place that would be hard to forget."

"I didn't say they were wrong."

"Ahh." She said nothing else, but she didn't fall back to the others, either.

"You're Lord Dereham's girl."

"Well... that's the thing." The girl laughed. "I always thought so.

Had no reason to believe otherwise. But that man back there, Ash? Seems he's my father."

Ryan's jaw went slack. "Ye don't feckin' say so? Does Lord Dereham know?"

"No, and he never will now."

"You think he's dead, then?"

"No other explanation makes more sense than that."

"Apologies for your loss, then."

"Apologies for yours."

"How do ye ken?"

"Esmerelda?"

Ryan shook his head. "You think I lost her?"

"Sorry if I misunderstood. I thought she'd married your brother."

"Nothing simple about that situation. What would ye know about it?"

"I haven't been here long, but seems to be more fishwives than warriors in the Southerlands."

"Aye? Don't be letting Lord Warwick hear you speaking like that."

Lisbet shrugged. "Well, I suppose it's not much of a loss, losing your love like that, if you don't even remember."

"Aye."

"Still, for not remembering the Wastelands, you're apprehensive enough about going."

"Oh? And are ye not 'apprehensive' about slipping into a prison camp crawling with our enemies?"

Lisbet shook her head. "No. Not really."

"Really."

"Really," she insisted.

"All right, Lady Lisbet, what does make ye apprehensive then?"

She looked straight ahead as she rode. "When this is all over, and I'm just Lisbet Dereham again, a prize to be bartered to the highest bidder."

"I take it ye dinnae want to be wed, then?"

"Why would I?"

Ryan laughed. "Donnae all young lasses want that?"

"You're not the first man who believed he had eyes into the mind of all lasses."

"I meant no disrespect."

"I know. It doesn't matter. But no, I don't fear the Wastelands, Ryan. I fear what comes after."

He cocked his head. "Well, I hear you're quite good at doing a runner when it suits ye."

"And I suppose I'll do it again, when the time comes."

"Kingdom is only so big. Aren't worried you'll run out of adventures?"

"Who said my next adventure will be in *this* kingdom?" She grinned from the side.

"Ryan!" Lord Warwick called. "Slow your pace. We're turning off here!"

Ryan stopped and called back. "Why?"

"Need to refill our provisions. Might know the place. Rutland brought ye there on the way to the infirmary, after they pulled you out of the Wastelands."

"You don't remember that, either, do you?" Lisbet asked.

"I remember enough to regret coming."

"Maybe I can help," she said as they angled down the path Khallum had directed them down.

"Aye? And how could *you* help me?"

"I know a few jests."

"Eh?"

"Jests. You know, to make you laugh. When you're feeling awful."

"Jests."

"That word mean something else down here?"

He held up one hand in a partial shrug. "Aye, all right, then. Tell me one now."

Lisbet seemed surprised that he'd taken her up on it. She settled back and lifted her head in thought. "Okay. A Knight of Duncarrow finds himself in a pub for the evening."

"What would one of the king's rats be doing in a pub with the lot of us?"

"It's a jest, not real. Let's say... it's a pub for knights, if that pleases you."

"No, it doesnae please me."

Lisbet sighed. "The knight, he brings with him his favorite weapon. It's a big one. Biggest one the pubkeep ever saw."

"I've seen the steel they carry. T'isnae that big."

"Well, this pubkeep hasn't seen anything bigger. He pours the knight a glass, and what does he say next?"

Ryan shrugged. "How should I know?"

Lisbet's mouth stretched into a mischievous grin. "Why the long mace?"

"Why the..." Ryan sighed, shaking his head. "All right, then. Ye got me."

"I have more."

"I know ye dinnae learn this stuff from other lasses."

"Seems to me," Lisbet teased, "that you don't know nearly as much about lasses as you'd like to think you do."

With one last grin, she returned to riding in silence.

THE WARM PRICKLE BEHIND HIS EYES WAS ONE HE KNEW, BUT NEARLY failed to recognize. It had been so long since such an intrusion. Hundreds... no, thousands. *Thousands* of years since a Medvedev had infiltrated his thoughts to send him a sighted vision.

The Meduwyn didn't communicate this way. If they had a message to send on far, they would ignite the water, the air, the fires in hearths and appear thus. They didn't steal into one another's minds like thieves, taking over where they were not wanted.

There was an unspoken rule about this. Only with permission. Never without. And yet... here it was, happening to him now.

He soon had his answer as the Medvedev appeared behind his eyes. It was as if he was seeing him from the inside out.

Who are you? Oldwin demanded.

A friend.

I have no friends. Least of all of your ilk.

I have been your friend for many years, though you have not known it.

You don't speak like other Medvedev. You must be one of the young ones, who knows no better than to break the sacred rules.

I speak the way you understand. It was said with derision.

You assault me. Then you insult me. You would do well to tread carefully here. Child.

I do not fear a dying Meduwyn.

Oldwin didn't answer this. He scowled and pressed himself further against the crop of rocks.

But it does not have to be this way, sorcerer.

It is your people who have made it this way, Medvedev.

We were cast out, same as you.

No. Not you. You're a young one, a babe. What could you know about it that was not told to you by others also too young to ever know about it? Ones who did not think to warn you of the danger of sending a sighted vision. The danger to you, in case you're unclear.

The Hidden Kingdom is my birthright, same as it is yours.

Yet you have never been there! If you had, you'd know it was never called that when we lived there. You know not of what you speak!

Not yet. But I will.

What do you want? I have no time nor desire to spar with one who is not half my equal.

You aim for the Hinterlands, but I see now, inside you, and you have not the energy for it, do you? You are already spent, Oldwin of Ilynglass.

What do you *want, Medvedev?*

Kael. Kael is my name. We wouldn't want you wasting what's left of your vigor on harder words.

Kael. Your mother is the Chieftainess of the Drumain. What trick is this?

The only trick is the one she's played on all of us, forcing us into an existence of half-truths.

Where is she?

I killed her. He said this without remorse or hesitation.

Well. You must be so beloved by your people.

You will not make it to the Hinterlands, Oldwin. Even you must know this.

Others who have underestimated me have not fared well. Kael.

Take it as you will. But there's another way. A better way.

What way? What is this nonsense of a child?

You already know. You spent the past hundreds of years searching for it.

Is that your answer? The Wastelands? Then you know I have not found it.

Your search was always a fool's one. The magic was never open to you. It is still not. You only thought it was, because you did not know any better. Even the Medvedev did not know it was created not by the Meduwyn betrayal, but by an overly curious Medvedev, who, like me, did not accept our way.

You think you're clever. You know what others have allowed you to know. Nothing more.

The child and grandchild of Isdemus are on their way now, right as we share these words together. They will find the veil, for they are not among the forsaken, as you are. All you must do is find them.

Jamesan Strong will be in the Hinterlands by now.

Oh, did you not know there are others? You nearly had one of them in your grasp, Oldwin, if she had not run off before marrying your boy king.

You're a liar. And he was never my king.

As you say.

You must desire something in exchange for this betrayal of your people.

They are not my people, so it is no betrayal. But I will tell you what I want. It's not enough for a Medvedev to travel back to Ilynglass. We must go together, Meduwyn and Medvedev, as one.

We were never one.

My people, as you call them, and what's left of yours, they want the Light closed from us forever. Well, so do I. But I want to be on the other side when it closes. You want this, too.

We cannot close it. Not you or me. You know this already, or you would not have sought me out.

What if we could?

You have already given me what I need to get there.

To get here, yes. But only a Medvedev can ensure your protection. Once you have passed through the veil into our realm, you are subject to our magic.

Why do you need me?

There are others coming. On both sides. Those who would stop us. We are stronger together. Jamesan has already arrived in the Hinterlands. Soon the others will come and will show him how to destroy the veil and close the Light from us, the chosen ones, forever. It cannot be undone.

Oldwin pushed his own thoughts on the matter of Jamesan from his mind. Kael wanted to stop the boy, but Oldwin saw him for what he was: a tool, either for or against him. Against, he was a formidable foe. For, he was the greatest weapon Oldwin had ever wielded.

But he would wield nothing if he couldn't get there. His trust for this Kael was shorter than his temper, but where Kael was young, impetuous, foolish, Oldwin was wise, calculating. There would be no union of Medvedev and Meduwyn, for it was unnatural. It had been so then, and was still.

Kael, in his youth, could be controlled, without ever knowing.

I go to the Wastelands. And then what?

It seemed as if they'd been walking forever. Kian led them through a dense forest, making the path as they went. The farther they walked, the greater Esmerelda's helpless panic stole over her, tickling at all her worst fears.

She'd come because she didn't trust the sorcerers' intentions with Jesse. But she hadn't allowed herself to think about what that might actually mean. She'd been too afraid to let her thoughts wander and get the best of her. But as they were pulled farther away from the world they knew, the more her own dread deepened. Her deepest fears were just around the corner now.

Kian didn't stoke these fears. He meant them no harm, though

Esmerelda now understood all too well that one's intentions didn't always determine outcomes.

Jesse seemed pulled forward by an invisible force, while she struggled to keep pace, unable to help drinking in the strangeness and wild beauty of the Hinterlands. He was single-minded in his task, aimed straight ahead. He wanted to be done with it all, for her, and for Gemma, but it wouldn't be so simple, even she knew that.

At last they came to a clearing. A huddle of tents were scattered about the edges, surrounding a large but unlit bonfire.

"You asked about the Saleen. This is what remains. What few survived," Kian said, solemn.

"What will they do?" Esmerelda couldn't help asking. "Is there hope for them? Will they rebuild?"

"There is always hope, Esmerelda."

Kian approached one of the tents and stepped through. He held out his hand to guide them in. Esmerelda ducked to make herself fit through the small gap, but then immediately felt foolish as she stepped inside. From outside, it hardly seemed big enough for them to even rest in. But she saw now it was as spacious as any room. There was a bed in the corner, made from less sturdy things than the ones she was used to, but still large enough for the both of them. Three chairs and a small table marked the center of the room, and at the other end, a chest, for their things.

"How?" she asked.

Kian smiled. "Anyone versed in magic knows there is no satisfying answer to 'how.' Will you sit?"

Esmerelda broke away from Jesse to take her chair. The hand that had been joined to his was swollen and red from how tightly she'd held to him; it throbbed at the absence of his touch. She flexed it and buried it in her lap with the other one.

She felt Jesse's eyes on her, and she flashed a tight, unconvincing smile.

"Where are Isdemus and Lysanor?" he asked.

Kian drummed his fingers on the small table. "They will not be coming."

Jesse pressed his palms to the table. "How's that? They're meeting me here."

"I'm afraid they will not be able to do so."

"Not be able to do so?" Jesse was incredulous.

"I'm sorry, but no."

"I donnae even know what I'm doing here! They were supposed to tell me."

"Their strength fades, Jamesan. It has faded almost beyond their control. Perhaps they will find another way to come to you, to explain themselves. I cannot say. But you will not be seeing them here. Nor ever again, in the flesh."

"Why would that be?"

"Once you have done as they ask of you, the Meduwyn—that is, the sorcerers—will be no more. Their fates are bound to the existence of the veils created by their treachery. You might say that when the veils are destroyed, they will be set free. Your sorcerers perhaps believe that, which is why they have gone against the others."

"But they haven't asked me to do anything!" Jesse declared.

"What will happen to them?" Esmerelda asked.

"I do not precisely know," Kian said. "But they will cease to exist in the way they once did."

"But Jesse is... he's..."

Kian nodded. "Jamesan is also Meduwyn. But he was not among those who participated in the betrayal. He is a pure blood, as some would say, as his father is, as his sister is."

Jesse perked up at the mention of this. "Do you know my father and sister?"

"I know them both."

"Will you tell me about them, or is this to be another secret I'm not allowed to have?"

"Everything happens when it should, Jamesan. You ask this of me now because you were meant to, and I was meant to answer in kind. I understand the sorcerers showed you your father's story. Your brother and sister—Drystan and Lisbet—came later, from an affair Dain had with Gretchen Dereham."

Jesse recoiled. "Lord Dereham's children, ye mean?"

"No," Esmerelda said, shaking her head. "Drystan and Lisbet are my kin. My mother is sister to Lord Dereham. I'd *know* if Lord Dereham wasn't their father, and as he isn't here to defend himself, it seems quite unfair to say such things."

"There is truth, and there is what we wish to be truth. Jamesan asked about his kin, and I have spoken the truth as I know it."

Esmerelda wanted to argue further, but this now felt like many things did as she'd come of age, all the little tethers to her childhood; the strung together lies. Each thread cut was a longer step forward, away from who she'd once been.

"I find myself absent words," Jesse said, exhaling between pursed lips. "I met Drystan once, years ago, on a stop in Wulfsgate. I might've seen Lisbet too, and just not remembered. And where are they now, my father and sister?"

"They have their own path to follow, just as you do."

"Speak plainly!" Esmerelda exclaimed. "Jesse is asking you something he has every right to know! That's his *kin*. His blood." She waited for Jesse to reach for her hand, to still her heat, but it didn't come.

"There is a veil," Kian said. "In the Wastelands. It must be destroyed before Oldwin finds it. He has been searching for hundreds of years now, and as he grows weaker, his desperation rises. Ash goes there to do what he must, and Lisbet, to give him the strength to go through with it. Just as you have come here. Just as Drystan found his way to Whitechurch, to bring about the end of Mortain."

"Aye, and will they? Destroy it?" Jesse pressed.

"I cannot see everything."

"Seems like you conveniently see plenty to me."

"I see what I'm given. Have you not known seers in your life? Scrying is not so different for us. Medvedev are more skilled at interpretation, but we have no more control than men do."

"Sounds more like a curse than magic," Esmerelda pointed out.

Kian smiled lightly. "It can feel like that. We are given enough to know the path we must take. But if we see the end of the path and not simply the way lighted for us, we would lose courage to do what we must. Our visions reassure us of what we already know we must do. That is all."

Jesse leaned across the table. "I see. Well, if Isdemus and Lysanor willnae come, then we can consider my promise fulfilled."

"That is not how this works."

"Aye? Then *you tell me. You* tell me why they went to such trouble to hunt me down and send me here, and why I had no choice. Why I sit here now, instead of at home, with my wife and daughter."

"There is always choice."

"Oh, that is such shite! You know he had no choice!" Esmerelda snapped. "What ye said about the visions? Aye, that proves it! He was always going to be here, so tell him. Tell him what he wants to know, what those foul magicians wouldnae!"

Jesse looked down at his lap and grinned.

"Not all Meduwyn would do evil," Kian said after a careful pause. "Some have sought redemption, like Jamesan's grandfather. Like Lysanor. In their redemption, they have turned their energies toward righting what they were part of making wrong."

"And does that redemption involve my husband coming to harm?"

Kian lowered his eyes. "The Sundering created the veils that left the Light vulnerable. It has been the charge of the Medvedev to protect it ever since. We traded immortality for honor, and we waited for one to come along who was of both worlds. I cannot close the veil just as Lysanor cannot, as Isdemus cannot. I cannot, for it was not my people who caused it, and they cannot, for it was. But you, Jamesan, are one of only four who have the blood of the Meduwyn, but not the dishonor and shame. Now you are three. But as Ash and Lisbet have their path set, so yours has brought you here."

Jesse held up his hands. "So that's all ye want? For me to close a veil? Why could they not just say so?"

The dread burning inside Esmerelda rolled to a boil. No, that wasn't all. That wasn't why the sorcerers had kept their secrets, leaving him in the dark. Her breath faltered as she waited for Kian to say what she had already guessed.

"It is not about when I want, but what you must do, what you were born to do."

"I wasn't born to do anything, but I made a vow and I'll fulfill it. But then we'll agree, there'll be nothing more asked of me. My wife and I will leave this place, and they'll let us be." He reached for Esmerelda's hand under the table, his eyes never leaving Kian. "Do ye ken? We understand one another?"

"No, Jamesan," Kian said. "That will not be the way of things."

"I'm telling you the way of things."

Kian shook his head. "There is only one way to close the veil. Only one way to protect the Light, and to end these years of madness."

"I donnae even know what the Light is! When I tell ye no one has taught me anything, I donnae think ye understand that I truly do mean nothing."

"It is your past as much as mine, though neither of us was there for it."

Esmerelda didn't care about the Light, or the past, or secrets. Her heart raced as she asked, "One way, you said. What does that mean?"

"It cannot be closed from this side. Only from the other. Once Jamesan steps through..."

Her understanding at last rose in crashing tandem with the stabbing, crushing feeling pushing her chest inward, choking her. "Then why... why cannae someone on the other side do this? Why, why would you take my husband?" Jesse's hand went limp in her own. She felt the shudder pass through him as his fingers twitched against her palm. "Nay. Nay, you find someone else," Esmerelda cried. "Jesse, this isnae what you agreed to, is it?"

He couldn't look at her.

"They didnae even have the decency to tell him! And since he didnae know what he was even agreeing to, I ken that means he's free to go!"

"I just wanted to find you," he said softly, his voice dropping lower. He was going somewhere else; somewhere she couldn't go. "I just wanted to protect you."

"Well, I donnae need your protection, do I?" Esmerelda leapt to her feet. "I refuse it! I tell ye now, I'll nay accept it again, and so then ye must stay here, with me, in our world, and they'll find someone else."

"There is no one else," Kian said. "Except Oldwin. And though he is weakened, he is not so weak that he cannot finish what Enivera began. There is only one way that puts an end to all of this now."

Jesse looked up with reddened eyes. "Now I know why they told me nothing."

"You say he must go?" Esmerelda said. "Aye, well fine, then I go with him."

"You cannot pass through the veil, Esmerelda."

"Oh, aye? Try and stop me!"

"It will not be me who stops you," Kian said sadly.

"Jesse!" she cried. She wagged her hand at Kian. "Tell him! Tell him you willnae do it!"

"How can I be a man of honor when it suits me, and only then? How could I be anything without my word?"

"I donnae give a plum about your honor, Jesse Strong. You're my husband. You promised me. You promised when ye asked for my hand that it was for always. That ye'd never leave me."

He turned his head away from her.

"Oh, now ye willnae even look at me?"

Kian rose from his chair. He reached for Esmerelda, but she swatted him away. "I used to think you were gods. But gods wouldnae destroy a man, for something he has naught to do with."

"Sit, Esmerelda."

She pulled her head back, aghast. "I donnae answer to ye!"

"Sit, and I shall tell you both. Why this has everything to do with you. Yes, even you, Esmerelda, and your little one, Gemmasyn, who will not have a life ahead of her at all if Jesse cannot do what he must."

She pointed a finger in his eye. Her hand shook. "Donnae ye ever invoke my daughter's name."

"Sit. Please."

"Why, so I can watch ye force my husband to do yer bidding?"

"I do not have the power to force Jamesan to do anything. He is here because he has chosen to come, and whether he steps through that veil and closes it forever, or turns his back on his destiny, it will not be me who has the power to decide either path. But I can tell you why you should care, and why this choice is not as simple a matter of honor."

She clutched the back of her chair, but didn't sit. "Then what?" Esmerelda sobbed. "Then what is this a matter of?"

"Whether tomorrow this kingdom will soon exist at all."

MASTER FROST SAT, STOIC, ON THE OTHER SIDE OF THE DESK, PASSING a stern look between them. Balfour couldn't tell if the man was angry, frustrated, or something more hopeful: curious.

He did this long enough for Balfour and Assana to share anxious looks between them. Finally, he leaned forward. It was Assana his eyes fell upon. "Many people are looking for you, girl."

Balfour pressed his toes deeper into his boots. He held his breath.

"I don't know what you mean, sir," she said.

"We both know you shouldn't be calling me sir, my lady. If I've put that together, others will as well, you can count on it."

"How?" Balfour asked. "I only knew because she's kin."

"And when did you last see her, Pupil Dereham? You've been here since you were a boy."

"I don't remember exactly when, but I must have."

Master Frost leaned back. "The Quinlandens are our liege lords in the Easterlands. Their portraits line the walls of our universities. They hang in the guild halls, even some taverns and inns. The whole of the Easterlands knows she's missing, and the kingdom besides."

"I've stayed scarce since returning."

"Your own brothers are here, in Ambercastle."

"And they're no closer to knowing I'm here."

"It's a dangerous game you play, if you want to pass through this world with that face."

"We'll travel with care," she insisted. "After all, I made it all the way here without anyone recognizing me."

"Travel," Frost said slowly. "You have plans, then?"

"Yes," Assana said.

"And what's that to do with me?"

Balfour grunted. He wasn't ready to tell his master, but here they were. "You're the only one with a mind for this. Who didn't piss it away over nonsense."

"You'll remember yourself, Pupil Dereham."

Balfour lowered his eyes. "Sorry. Sir."

"All right, then. You have my attention. A mind for what?"

Balfour dropped both hands onto the desk. "I've come to the end of what I can find here, sir. What I've found tells me my answers don't live in a book."

"You're speaking, of course, of what you've come to me about before."

"Yes."

He thumbed at Assana. "What does this have to do with her?"

"I'm here in search of the same answers," she jumped in, and Balfour thought, well, that's not even a lie, really, is it? How strange it was that their paths had seemed so distant in the beginning and now were so intertwined that it seemed to him they'd done nothing but waste time before finding each other.

"And what answers would those be, Lady Quinlanden? Or is it Queen Assana?"

Her voice dropped lower. "Please don't call me either of those things. I was never a queen, and I'm not a Quinlanden. Not anymore."

Frost's nod was contrite. "Very well. What answers, Nameless One?"

She licked her lips. Balfour felt the sudden nervousness coming over her. "I came here... I came to learn about the veils, and fate brought me to Balfour. Together, we want to find one for ourselves. To try and step through, so we can at least understand what is beyond them, on the other side..." She trailed off. They'd agreed to leave it there. Introducing the sorcerers to this discussion would complicate it, and might compel Frost to stop them altogether.

Frost raised his brows at Balfour. "And all these years, you thought you were alone."

"All those years, I was."

"Well, this is an intriguing notion the two of you have come up with. But why have you come to me? What more can I give you that I haven't already? I've shown you, at great personal risk, what few books might provide the answers you've craved. Beyond that, I have little to add and everything to risk in saying more. So, I hope the two of you haven't hung all your hopes on me."

"You gave Balfour that key for a reason. You said you wanted him to learn, right? But the real answers are out there. A man with enough interest to hide these books in a secret room of our school library must have even more brewing in his well of curiosity that he has not yet shared."

Frost bristled. "You assume much, girl."

"Am I wrong?"

He linked his hands at the fingers and spread them. "I'll ask you again. Why have you come to me? I've taught you to be clear in your requests, Pupil Dereham, and I expect nothing less just because we are beyond the walls of the classroom."

"We want to know where to find a veil."

Frost laughed. "You already know! Your father stepped through one, did he not?"

"You know he's never found it again, or people wouldn't say what they say about him. And if the man who found himself on the other side cannot find it again, how could we?"

"The question you should ask is why can *he* not find it again."

"And would you have an answer?" Assana pressed.

"Not an answer, only supposition."

She held her hands out, waiting.

"If veils are so simple to pass through, there'd be more stories of men passing through them, no?"

"Yeah. Perhaps."

"So then we must assume the veils only open under specific conditions."

"Are you assuming that, or do you know and you just won't say?" Assana demanded.

Balfour wanted to tell her to ease off, but she was right. Frost had daintily led Balfour down this path. Never committing to anything, never speaking in absolutes or full truths. He had more answers than he wanted Balfour to know he had, and these were answers they needed.

"I've never been through a veil myself, if that's what you're asking," Frost replied coolly. "Nor have I seen one with my own eyes. But there are others, others who have, who spend their days and nights and all hours in between in pubs, drowning their experiences in bad ale, unable to work, to live. They've lost trades, wives, children. You hear enough of them telling their sad tales and you start to think well, perhaps they're not so mad after all. Perchance there's something to this." Frost sighed and fell back in his chair. "Of course, the simplest answer is often the correct one. Perhaps they are just mad, in the end."

"You don't believe that."

"*Belief* is strengthened by experience, as I've always taught my pupils, which you'd know if you ever took one of my classes. There is nothing to be found in a classroom, or book, or library, that will ever be more valuable to you than what your own eyes see."

"What did they say, then, the men in the pubs?"

"Oh, they had their theories. Many were driven to madness and ruin by their inability to return, and all they had left was to gather in their little clubs, you might say, and tell their tales. And I, a few tables over, would listen. They all believed, each in their own ways, that the veils only opened in certain circumstances, and oh, how they debated this. One man claimed a veil opened twice for him, each time as he was in mortal danger, chased by the man he was in debt to. He paid off the debt and tried to return, but he was no longer in danger and the veil had no use for him. It was as if it didn't exist. So he said. And there was another, another who said he could enter only when he bled for it. Each time he had to cut himself open. One day, he stopped returning to the pub. The other men think he either bled to death or decided to make a life of it, in wherever was on the other side."

Assana screwed her mouth into a frown.

"So we just need to cut ourselves, then, is that what you're suggesting?" Balfour asked.

"Those aren't the only stories, Pupil Dereham. There are many, many different interpretations of what the veils have required from each man who dared enter, and for those ever more daring, attempted in desperation to recreate the conditions in order to return."

"How do we know what a veil demands?"

"By trying, until you at last get it right, or surrender. You're really determined to leave, then?"

"Yes, Master."

"They'll send a raven to your mother and father when you don't turn up for your courses, Balfour."

Frost nodded.

Assana turned to Balfour. "There's still Torrin's Pass. That one we know is real. We should leave soon. The voyage is long enough without our need to stick to the less traveled paths."

"Torrin's Pass?" Frost asked. "Why would you travel all the way to the Northerlands?"

"We were clear, we're in search of a veil. We asked you, and you—"

"Did you even read the book?"

"Yes, sir, but it's all speculation. There was nothing *real* in there, only the guessing of a man who'd never seen a veil with his own eyes. The only one I am certain of is the one my father went through."

"That makes it no different from the veils the men in the pub speak of, boy. If you yourself haven't seen it, then is it not still just speculation?"

"I believe my father!"

"Still, there's said to be one in Blackpool. Just south of here. There's an abandoned farm with a cellar large enough to house a proper crown dungeon, so I hear. More than one man has told tales of this one."

"Tales," Assana repeated.

"I'm wrong? It sets you back a day. I'm right? You've saved yourself a mighty long trip to the Northern Reach, and a pass that will kill a good man on a fair day. As a Frost man, I can speak with experience you'll be glad you don't have. My brother doesn't even leave his keep these days, living on the wrong side of the Northerland Range. Sees no aim in it."

"He's right," Assana said. "How do we find this farm?"

"Oh, you won't have much trouble there. I expect most folks in Blackpool think the place is haunted by more ghosts than they have people. Ask for the hallowed place, someone will point you true."

Assana half-bowed and shifted around, eager to be done with the conversation. "Thank you, Master Frost."

Balfour lingered. "You could come with us."

The older man laughed. He ran his hand over the stubble of a beard not yet formed. "Tempting as the offer is, I'm nearing my golden years, aren't I? The universities will care for me until the Guardians deem my promise spent. My interest in this matter is coming upon an end, where yours is only beginning."

"Aren't you even curious?"

"More than I feel I should say."

"I appreciate what you've done for me, Master Frost. You could have treated me as all the others did, but you chose to be kind, and to point me to the answers I needed."

Balfour looked at Assana and then back at his master. "When we find it, sir, we'll go to the nearest rookery and send a raven. If a second one doesn't arrive right behind it, you'll know we've stepped through."

"I would very much like that." The old man's eyes glassed over. "Does that mean you intend to stay on the other side?"

"Yes," he said, just as Assana said, "No."

Master Frost smiled. "Seems the two of you still have much to discuss before you move on. I take my leave and look forward to news of your grand adventures."

When he was gone, Assana spun on Balfour. "Stay! Why ever would we stay there? We have two purposes. To confirm your father's claim and to destroy the sorcerers."

"I have more confidence in our first purpose than the second. But there's only one sorcerer we know of in this kingdom, and we can't reach him, can we? Yet, they aren't from our world, so what's to say there aren't more of them in other worlds? Maybe ones less hidden away than Oldwin, and if we can find them, Assana, we can follow through on your desire to bring them to a veil and destroy it."

"When you say it aloud, it sounds so foolish," she said quietly. "I sound foolish."

"No," he insisted. He took her by the shoulders. "You aren't foolish. This is just hard, that's all. We have no chance of getting to Oldwin, but what if we could get to one in another world?"

Assana choked back tears. "What if we can't?"

"Then we are well rid of the lot of them. And everyone else who has made our lives not worth living in *this* world."

"No, Jesse, you heard him, same as I did."

"If Isdemus and Lysanor could only *get* here—"

"They aren't coming!" Esmerelda dropped the satchel on the floor of their tent. He'd watched her channel her angst into transferring their meager belongings into the chest provided. She sank down next to the jumbled contents. "It's over."

"It's not over, Esme. It's not over until it is." He imagined him dropping behind her, wrapping her in his arms and finding all the right words to ease her. But had it ever been so simple between them? It seemed to him their closeness had instead formed between the gaps of all they couldn't say.

"Tomorrow it will be," she said. He could hardly hear her with her head bowed so low. She reached in jerky movements for their belongings. "Tomorrow you'll fulfill that vow you swore without knowing what it meant."

"You know why I did it."

She pulled her hair aside and looked back at him over her shoulder. "You think this makes it easier for me? Knowing that it was your care of me that will send you to this fate? That it's..." Her face twisted as she fought back tears. "My fault."

"No. It's not your fault." Why couldn't he go to her? Why couldn't he say the things burning at the back his throat? Why, when if he kept them down much longer, he would choke? "I made this choice."

"What kind of man swears a vow without knowing his end?" Soundless tears trickled down her face, angry at herself for showing such emotion, at him for bringing it down on her.

Jesse moved closer. He pulled a chair out and sat by her. "I willnae ask ye to forgive me. But I need to know that ye donnae hate me. I cannae do what I promised I'd do if I think you'll go the rest of your days wishing we'd never met."

"How could you..." Esmerelda swallowed her bottom lip. "How dare ye suggest..."

"When I asked ye to be my wife, it was with the conviction that I'd give up anything, do anything, to keep ye safe. And though it may not feel like it now, that's exactly what I have to do tomorrow." He buried his face in his hands. "Just not the way I saw it happening."

Esmerelda chucked things into the chest, one by one, each creating a sound that deepened the now-growing silence.

"You incredible fool," she hissed. She spun on her knees, abandoning her frenzied tidying. "Do you even know where my anger comes from?"

"I donnae know anything anymore, Esme."

"Aye, well, ye can be mad at anyone, can't ye? The blacksmith, for getting the seams wrong on your armor. The cook, for not using enough spices. But anger? Rage? You get that when you care too much, when the object of that care has brought you to such a place that all you can see and feel is the powerful, suffocating darkness that comes from caring so feckin' much you donnae even know yourself anymore."

Jesse tried to speak, but all that escaped was a sigh. The sight of her made him want to fall to his knees. All those things that had driven him mad in the early days were now the same things that tied his heart into knots. The freckles dotting her nose and cheeks. The pout of her parted mouth; how her dark hair was so unruly that even in the height of what she was feeling, she had to stop to push it away.

How had he gone his whole life not knowing this feeling, only to find it on the eve of having to surrender it forever?

"I donnae regret marrying ye, Jesse Strong." She dropped her hands to her lap in defeat. "I regret it wasnae enough for ye, for the time ye were here."

"Not enough?"

"You and me, we weren't friends as bairns, were we? Even then, ye thought I was only the spoiled daughter of the lord, and it must have *killed* ye, when Ryan started looking at me different. But you're a man of honor. Ye were then, ye are now. That honor brought ye to me, protected me, and loved me, in your own way."

"My own way?" *Stop repeating her words*, he thought, *and just say them. Say your own. Say the ones you mean.*

"I know you would've gone all the way to the end of our lives, protecting me and Gemma. I know that. But..." Esmerelda turned her head to the side. She bit her lip again. "But there's more to life, aye? More than being safe from harm. And if I have one regret, 'tis that I didnae see your offer for what it was, for then I could've protected my heart from the way it breaks now."

Jesse shook his head. "No," he said. He reached down and cupped her face in both his palms. "No. You couldnae have it any more wrong than that."

"I thought I might've been wrong," she said. Tears ran down into his palm. "On our wedding night, I tried... and... what a fool I am, I thought, and now he'll only remember this and feel sorry for me, and try to make it up to me. Sad little me, who thought this was more than what it was."

Jesse's breath choked. "Ye think I donnae want ye?"

"Isnae what I *think*. It's what I know. It's what you've shown me."

"Esmerelda." He sighed. "I have never wanted anyone, or anything, more than I want you."

She fell back on her heels. His hands slipped away. "What?"

His heart beat so hard he feared he might not finish his words before it exploded. "I spent so long trying to understand how Ryan could give up everything to spend the rest of his life with you. And now, all that's running through my mind is that I'd give up everything for even one *night* with you."

Esmerelda pulled her hands to her face. She trapped her sob there.

"Esme?" He pushed the chair away and sank down to the floor, to his knees. "What have I said?"

"You tell me this now, in the end."

"I didnae know how to say it before now. I feared offending ye. Hurting ye."

She peeled her hands away. The sight of her sad face broke his heart, but it wasn't only sadness he saw there, but the very thing, the one thing, capable of sending his resolve to tatters. It lived in her eyes, the shape of her mouth, the tilt of her chin.

Esmerelda sprang up and kissed him. Her arms draped around his neck, and he fell back from the force of her desire, landing against the soft fabric of the tent floor pressed against earth. Her hair dangled down, tickling his face, as she watched him, someone else, but still the same Esmerelda he'd protected, befriended, and then loved.

"Tell me you want me, Jesse. Say the words. Again, so I can remember them in just this way."

"I want you. Ahh, Esmerelda. How I want you."

He slid his hands up the side of her leather trousers. He didn't know how to get her out of them quick enough, but she pushed herself up off the floor and slid them down before he could think of a tactic. Then her hands were between his legs. The snap of his belt pulled him forth, into reality; that he was here, with her, and this was happening, and it would be nothing like he'd imagined, but that was fine. Because his imagination had never been enough.

His head fell back in a groan when her hand found his cock. She wasn't coy in her desire; her grip tightened, sliding down the length, learning it.

Hands on her hips, he lifted her and slid her over him. Their cries sounded in tandem, in longing and anticipation and everything else that had lived between them, unsaid, for so long.

Esmerelda pressed her palms to his chest and guided herself slowly into the motion. Her eyes never left his. She was still crying, but now he understood her tears came from another place, and though he'd been the cause, this time that was all right.

He ran his hands up under her shirt, across the soft warm flesh of her back. She shivered under his touch and quickened her pace. He braced himself, digging his heels into the floor to keep from finishing too soon.

Jesse held tight to her as he flipped them. Now she looked up at him, her hair splayed about her like a dark halo. The sight of filled him with even more desperate longing. Her eyes rolled back as her jaw fell open in in a gasp.

He slowed. "Have I hurt ye?"

"Oh, no, no, you have not," she purred, lifting her hips higher to receive him. "Don't stop."

Jesse peppered her with kisses, finding a new place for his lips to land with every hungered stroke. She cried out again, and again, and he understood she was having her own pleasure, something he'd only heard about.

Esmerelda took his hand and pressed it between her thighs. She moaned louder, and he knew what she wanted, vowing, before the night was over, to learn her, all of her, and to deliver her everything she desired until she was entirely spent of it.

She wrapped her legs around his waist. Looking up at him, cheeks flushed, eyes glassy, she whispered, "Go on, then. I want to feel my husband. I want to know him before he's no longer mine."

A sea of stars filled Jesse's vision as he spilled, the both of them shuddering into it, all tangled limbs and harried sighs as they fell to the side.

"How I love ye," he whispered through his ragged breaths. "How I love ye, Esmerelda."

She slipped against him and raised her hand to his face. "Donnae tell me, Jamesan. Ye have all night, and I expect ye to show me."

37
WHAT WAS

Alasyr gaped at his sister. He tried to understand her, set to the backdrop of a sea of raven hair and pale, eager faces. Why she'd come here, come back to this. How well she fit into this picture, and yet didn't belong, not at all.

He'd been subjected to hours of her addressing their kin, of fielding questions and volleying many back, the kind that had only one answer. Things like, *is this how you want to live forever, subjugated by others who are just like you, no better? Is this what you want for your children?*

It was here he learned how his mother and father were murdered. That Adynora was imprisoned for her crimes that led to it. That Lady Blackwood had flown away. That they were more concerned for the fate of a half-blood—Emberley—than they were sad for the loss of their esteemed leaders.

Ravenna was aflame with her rage, with some newfound power emanating from her as she stood before all of them, assuming the role she was born for, but in a way none of the women before her could have foreseen or approved of. Tear it all down, she might have said, for that was the message she'd sent rippling through their kin.

When Rillyn had the floor, Alasyr took his chance. He yanked her by the hand, not relenting when she resisted, pulling her through a break in the crowd, realizing too late he should've been pointed toward the entrance and not the back. The madness rolling through the hundreds gathered was deafening. It dulled his senses, whittling the finer points to soft edges until sight and sound were nothing but a blur.

He could hear her saying his name in defiance, but he was so focused on finding a way out of the melee, and at last he saw it: a door. It would lead them deeper in, not out, but he only needed away from the others.

Alasyr flung open the door and nudged her inside. She nearly tripped on the way in. Once he was clear of the threshold, he slammed the door and threw his weight against it. His heavy breaths made his chest heave.

"What are you doing?" she demanded.

Alasyr suddenly knew what this room was. The velvets and silks. Heels too high and pointed for anyone daring to walk on the uneven stone of The Rookery. The forgotten dresses that had no place here, but for one night alone.

This was where they took the future High Priestesses to prepare for their Langenacht.

"Yes," she snapped, seemingly reading his thoughts, "I know very well what this room is for."

"You've been here?"

"Of course I have. Every year on my birthday, a reminder of what I had to look forward to. More like, what all the men had to look forward to. Their sick fantasy of watching a girl, a child, be taken by all of them."

Alasyr swallowed hard. "I know. I see it now for what it is."

"Do you?"

"It's wrong, all of it. Not only the Langenacht, Ravenna. But everything the Ravenwoods stand for, all we've built. The lies, the fear they've sown. A feigned war with men—"

"You may have become enamored of one of them, but that doesn't mean you know them."

"And you do?" Alasyr took a step closer, but didn't move far from the door. "You've been gone months, not years. You're no wiser than me, even if you came around to things before I did."

"What did it take, then, for you? It wasn't anything I said."

"It's not what anyone said," Alasyr replied. "But what I saw, with my own eyes. Father. Mother. Do you know, there's a very fine line between self-preservation and evildoing? I do, for I saw it in both of them."

"What they did to your Emberley, you mean."

"She's not mine," Alasyr said with a soft laugh. "She's not anyone's. Much like you, Ravenna. You remind me of her."

Ravenna crossed her arms. "You're right about one thing. She's not yours. And if you try to make her so, you will drive her to a fate that will haunt you for your remaining days."

"Drystan, you mean? Marsh told me. I'm sorry. I was so angry that you'd left for him, but I know you loved him."

"I didn't leave for my love of him," Ravenna said. The fire had died away. "But he died for his love of me."

"I hear he died with honor."

"Is death not all the same?"

"Why did you come back?"

"That's between me and the women who upheld the lie."

Alasyr shook his head. "I don't know what that means."

"And you? Why are you here? Adynora said you'd forsaken this life."

"Grandmother lied to you, as she has lied to all of us."

"On that we can agree."

"Do we really disagree on so much, Ravenna?"

"Why *did* you return, Alasyr?"

And there it was. The question without an answer. Why had he returned? He was done with Midnight Crest and the legacy of lies, but still, he was called here. Called home, and no matter how he tried to erase that word, that feeling, it was still that to him. Home.

"Ahh," she said. "You don't know, do you?"

He shook his head. "I can't think of anywhere I'd rather be less, and yet there's nowhere I need to be more."

"You want vengeance for her?"

"No," Alasyr said. "I don't need vengeance. Emberley lives."

Ravenna scoffed. "No one would survive the fall from our skies."

Alasyr's heart jumped. He started to tell her what he'd done, but for the first time in his life, he was afraid of Ravenna. Afraid of her, in the way he'd only come to understand he always should have been afraid of his mother and grandmother, of every High Priestess. "I'll need to return to her. Soon."

"We cannot have both worlds, Alasyr," Ravenna said. "You standing here before me tells me, in your heart, you've already made the choice."

"No," he said. He backed straight into the door. "I don't know why I came, all right? I was pulled here, as if something was left unfinished, and now that I've seen you, I know what that thing was. I needed to tell you how sorry I was. I should have never cast my lot for you. I should have taken you away then, and helped free you myself."

Ravenna bowed her head, nodding. "I require no apology from you, Alasyr. I *needed* to leave in anger, or I would've never left. I would've never seen the things I've seen, learned what I know now. Your eyes wouldn't have ever been opened." She looked up. Her eyes were splotched with red, but she was smiling. "Don't you see? We are precisely where we both need to be now."

Alasyr swallowed. He spread his palms against the door behind him. His fear of her deepened. "You want to lead Midnight Crest? You want to be their High Priestess?"

"And why not? It doesn't have to be as it was before. Ravenwoods divided by a caste system without sense or reason. One priestess holding all the power." She shook her head. "The High Priestess never should have been more than a figurehead, Alasyr. A symbol of hope, never oppression, or fear, as you say. It's the fear, the lies, that have tainted our blood, not the Blackwoods, nor the men of this kingdom who have long since lost interest in us."

Alasyr was speechless.

"You don't think your own return foretells the same fate? That we were meant to come together, once more, this time by choice, and lead our people into a new way?"

He didn't have the right words for what she was asking. A new way was needed—he could see that—but it wasn't Ravenna who was meant to bring it along. He saw this in her wild, tortured eyes. What had *she* seen? What wouldn't she tell him?

"Alasyr?"

"You aren't meant to be here," he said finally, voice barely above a whisper. "You weren't meant to come back. You don't belong here."

"What are you talking about?"

"You never have." He again stepped away from the door. "It's not about the Langenacht, or any of it. You're meant for something else."

"Why are you saying this? You spent months pining after me. Grandmother told me. She told me how you replaced that feeling with the love of a girl, and I wonder, did you do that to know me better? To know what I was thinking, when I so cruelly left you?"

"No!" Alasyr screamed. The sound slashed through a brief lull in the rumble of voices beyond the door. "Not everything is about you! I never wanted to even know Emberley Blackwood, and yet, I kept finding myself watching her, standing before her. Talking to her, knowing her. So, yes, I suppose I do know you better, because at last now I can see how you would leave everything behind for an outsider."

"But I was *wrong*, Alasyr, don't you see? I cared for Drystan, but it wasn't the love he deserved. Had he never left Wulfsgate, he'd be safe in his bed, right now. Instead, he's gone to the Guardians he believed so strongly in. Is that what you want for Emberley? For your passing fancy to be the end of her?"

Alasyr's head shook. "You're not me. I'm not you. I wouldn't have left for someone I didn't care that much for. I wouldn't have done that to Drystan, as you did."

Ravenna recoiled as if struck. "You think so little of me?"

Alasyr folded his hands in front of his mouth. "What I think, Ravenna, is that you've come back for the same reason as me. To make your peace with what was. Not to once again become a part of what you were never meant for. Your place isn't here. Nor is mine. Let the Ravenwoods rebuild the world *they* want."

"You'll go back to her, then?"

Alasyr nodded.

"Why?"

Tears burned at the back of his eyes. "Because I love her."

"You love her?"

"Yes." His voice cracked. "I loved her enough to restore her to life, and I love her enough that I'll protect her for the rest of it."

"Restored her... what does that mean?"

He shook his head. He couldn't tell her.

Ravenna's mouth parted in shock. "You won't stay?"

Alasyr bit back his fear and approached his sister. He tentatively reached for her arms, unwinding them. He took her hands in his. "Nor should you. I came here for answers to questions I didn't even know how to form. And now I see. You're called somewhere else, Ravenna. I don't know where. Perhaps you do. Perhaps that answer lives in your secrets that you'll never tell. But it isn't here."

"You'll find only a curse at the end of a path with man," she said.

"That was your path," he said gently. "Not mine. My path is wherever Emberley Blackwood leads me. And..." He smiled as he said it. "Marsh Tyndall."

"Who's Marsh?" She shook her head. "You really have changed, haven't you?"

"We both have."

She dropped her eyes. Tears spilled onto their joined hands.

"Go, Ravenna. Before they convince you to stay. Go and be free."

"Free?" She laughed. "When have we ever been free?"

Alasyr pressed one hand to her chest. "You'll know it here, when you find it."

. . .

MARSH STOOD AT THE EDGE OF THE CAVE, ONE HAND PROPPED against what Emberley had called the door. It wasn't a door. It was cold and jagged, and, with the wrong move, an invitation to death. "Do you think he's coming back?"

"He said he would, so he will."

"I believe *him*," Marsh said. "But he's afraid of them. Of his people. After what they did to you. It's why he made us trek up the mountain, why he wouldn't let me bring an entire search party to recover you. He didn't want to draw their eyes."

"I know he won't come back any sooner just because you're standing there," Emberley said. "It's so much warmer by the fire, Marsh."

"It's only... you said earlier that maybe you were ready to fly again. What if you left? You could go back to Wulfsgate, and I could wait for him."

"Marsh."

"We have plenty of food. I could last another fortnight without more supplies. I think."

"*Marsh.*"

He turned toward her.

"You've hardly said a word to me. If I didn't know better, I'd say you were afraid to look at me."

Marsh flushed. "I did more than look at you when we arrived, you know."

"I remember," she said. "Because it was the last time you wanted anything to do with me."

His shoulders sagged. "That's not true."

"Isn't it?"

Marsh reluctantly left the safety of the entrance. That he even thought of it as this was proof she was right. He didn't want to be near her, though even he didn't understand why.

"What is it? Tell me." She pushed. She held her hands out to him, but he didn't take them. Instead, he settled across the fire from her, keeping some distance between them.

Emberley sighed. "Is it Alasyr? Are you upset with me because

I've been here, with him?"

Marsh shook his head. He kept his eyes focused on his hands, upturned in his lap.

"Then what?"

"I don't know," he confessed. "I don't know what it is. All this time, all I wanted was to be near you, to see you and hold you, and now I feel... I feel as if..." It came to him as he spoke. "As if I'm not who you really wish was sitting across from you." He immediately regretted the words. He wasn't jealous of Alasyr. It was more complicated than that.

"You don't believe that, do you?"

"Nothing I've ever believed has served me on this journey to you."

Emberley held out her hands. "What can I do, to ease your heart? Because I do love you, Marsh. Not because you came for me, or because you followed me on my mad whim to leave the Westerlands and come here. I love you because you're not like me at all, and yet you make me more of who I am."

"And Alasyr?"

She nodded.

He nodded with her. "Yeah."

"For you, too?" She didn't seem surprised.

Marsh shrugged. "I don't see him as I see you, and I also can't say he's a brother to me, either. It's not like that with Jonah."

"Maybe it isn't something you need to understand."

He laughed. "When have you ever known me not to need something to make sense?"

She smiled.

"That's why... in Wulfsgate. I wanted to support you, Emberley. I did. I wanted to understand what you were going through, but every time I tried, it seemed like it pushed us further apart. That it pulled you into a world where I couldn't go."

Emberley shook her head. "I'm sorry. I was afraid and overwhelmed, and I knew you didn't have the answers I needed, so I turned to the one who would. And I know now, I see now, it was never about one or the other. You're both part of me, and I know that's not fair to either of you—"

"When has fair had anything to do with it?" He sighed and scooted closer to her. She leaned into his open arms. "Look. It won't be me who asks you to choose. All right?"

She nodded against him.

"But please, I beg you, don't push me into the darkness again. I want to see. I want to know. Even if I'll never understand, I'm asking you to trust that I at least want to try."

Emberley tilted her head up to kiss him. "If I ever go anywhere that you can't come, I'll make a way for you, Marsh. I promise."

"ARE YOU SURE YOU WANT TO SEE HER?" RAVENNA GUIDED ALASYR down the long hall leading to the room where the others had imprisoned Adynora.

"I am." Alasyr kept up, but lingered a step or two behind. If there was a sign of how things were different now between them, it was in the intentional, but not unkind, distance he needed from her.

"She'll only have lies for you. That's all she knows."

"She conspired to murder our parents, Ravenna. They had their faults, but she raised them to be great, only to later create their fall. I want to know why."

Ravenna stopped and turned. "She'll spew some nonsense about duty and tradition, but it won't come close to satisfying the gash in your heart. I know this, because I had the same questions for her, and all that's come of my asking is a raw anger that I find myself powerless against."

Alasyr lifted the corner of his mouth. "You? You've never been powerless. Why else would she have tried so hard to destroy you?"

"Let the other Ravenwoods deal with her, Alasyr. It's with their magic that she's bound now. None have suffered under our ways more than the ones who had no reward for being called Ravenwood."

"You're implying that to be a High Priestess is a reward?"

"That's the way our world was set up."

Alasyr laughed. "Coming from the one who fled that life."

Ravenna tilted her head. "It's all perception, isn't it? If you're a Ravenwood guard, you dream of spending your days in the grand suites occupied by the High Priestess and her family, eating your meals at long tables, resting your head against silk. But when you're doing those things, all you want is the freedom others enjoy."

"I still want to see her."

Ravenna's light smile disappeared.

"You don't have to come."

"I will, just the same."

They came to the end of the long hall. There was no lock on the door. None was needed. Adynora was bound to her velvet chair with the magic of a hundred furious Ravenwoods.

Adynora was unsurprised to see Ravenna, but at the sight of Alasyr behind her, the older woman's grin turned to a sneer. "You had to do it, didn't you? Bring him back? Selfish girl."

"I didn't come back for Ravenna," Alasyr said, stepping to Ravenna's side. "Or anyone."

"I wouldn't have sent anyone after him." Adynora was still speaking to her directly. Ravenna bristled at what she knew was an attempt to break her; even now, when her grandmother had no power beyond her words. "He was innocent in this all, just like Ryandyr, and the twins."

"Your distorted ideas about right and wrong are why Midnight Crest is on the verge of collapse," Alasyr said. He pushed past Ravenna, moving ahead of her. "Why my mother and father are dead."

"Let us not forget the girl." Adynora smiled with her entire face.

Alasyr lifted his hands. He wiggled his fingers. "The one who lives, because of me? That one?"

Adynora's smile melted into a sneer. "You want me to believe you raised the dead? You?"

"It's no matter to me what you believe," Alasyr said. "Emberley Blackwood lives. She lives, and her magic is no trifle, as you wanted us to believe. I thought you should know, before you meet the ancestors."

Ravenna's blood cooled. He'd hinted at this earlier, and she'd been too afraid to push him. Adynora might need time to come around to his confession, but Ravenna knew her brother. He wasn't lying. If he wasn't lying, then not only was Emberley returned to life, but she would have inherited some of Alasyr's power. Like healing, but more potent. As healers, those receiving their magic often found themselves with a temporary surge of power. But to resurrect someone was to make this permanent.

Did he know?

Had that been his intention?

Adynora tore at the invisible bonds. "There hasn't been a Ravenwood capable of necromancy in generations."

"Is it that," Alasyr asked, approaching her with his head cocked, "or that the others are too fearful to share who they really are, so they bury it? Like the seers?"

Adynora fell back in the chair. "Why did you come to me? To taunt an old woman?"

"You won't even see fifty years before the Ravenwoods deal with you," he countered. "Which is more than fair, seeing as my mother hardly saw thirty before your manipulations stole what should have been remaining to her."

"Ah, then yes. To taunt me."

"Alasyr," Ravenna whispered. "Why *are* we here?"

Alasyr held up a hand to her. "No, Grandmother. Not to taunt you. I watched you drive my father to do terrible things. I know it was you who helped bring Lady Blackwood to The Rookery. You who killed that Rhiagain princess. Who pushed my mother to discover father's deception. And as I've thought about it, these long days alone in the skies, left to my thoughts, I remember now you encouraging Ravenna to follow her heart. I couldn't know what that meant then, but once she left... now, I see. Did you also trick Ravenna into loving that boy?"

Adynora inhaled through her nose, closing her eyes through the long exhale. "Would it matter if I had?"

Ravenna gasped. Both hands flew to her mouth. She dropped them away just as fast, shaken but unwilling to give Adynora any further satisfaction.

Alasyr half-turned. "You see? Save your guilt. It doesn't belong to you."

Adynora turned her wrists up. "Ahh. Now I see why you've come. Go on, then, Alasyr. Ask what you came for, really."

"Let's go," Ravenna hissed. "She's full of lies. I told you."

"Are they lies, Ravenna, or are they truths that are too difficult for you?" Adynora asked sweetly. "Go on, Alasyr."

He turned toward Ravenna. "You were right. There's nothing here." He pushed past her and out the door before Adynora could say any parting words.

"You want to know about the Blackwood girl!" she called back. "Whether I did to you what I did to your sister?"

"Whatever you did or did not do to Alasyr," Ravenna said, drawing near, until she was so close her breath mingled with her grandmother's in the musty air of the small room-turned-cell. "Will die with you. You've taken enough. You will take no more."

"I had no hand in your brother's foolish dalliance with that girl, and if you don't believe that, then ask yourself why I would concern myself with someone so unimportant as Alasyr."

"Nothing is beneath you, Adynora."

"You think so little of me. That's only because you were not made for this, like I was. Like most who came before me. You were not made for this, because your mother was weak, and she made you. But one day you might face a trial of your own, Ravenna. One where your choice is between your heart and your world. A weak woman battles her will to prove to herself that when she chooses her heart, it was no simple choice. But a strong woman? Well, she knows all along that there was only ever one choice. And when she makes it, she leaves the weak ones to question and judge her charge, but she makes it just the same." Adynora nodded. "She makes it just the same, Ravenna."

38
MONSTERS

Gretchen found her son squatting at the bank of the river. The Azylria sat at the base of the winding city of Malfenza, on the desert side, where the unknown lived. Its water was the clearest blue, in stunning contrast to the barren landscape that seemed to stretch forever and go nowhere.

Most of their water came from the Azylria, and to bring it up the hill was an arduous chore that took most of the day, and sometimes part of the evening. They tried to cart up enough to not need to repeat the task for some time, but it seemed she'd already helped them with the water bringing enough times for it to feel like tradition to her.

She'd asked Maura where the river went, for in Gretchen's world, rivers eventually found pardon at the opening of a sea, but Maura didn't like the question. She saw it for what it was; told Gretchen she could spend her life following a stream of water, or watering the land she was given. There really was no one Gretchen could talk to about the way she was feeling. They all took her curiosity as an affront, instead of entertaining the inquisitiveness that anyone would have, coming into a new world.

"Yesterday was water day," she said, as her shadow fell over

Pieter. He dumped smaller buckets of water into the larger basin, which would require the muscle of the four of them to pull up the hills and back to the pinnacle of Malfenza. The wheels were old and falling off. Curran had been trying to replace them, searching through the abandoned homes and stalls for something comparable, but so far had found nothing suitable.

Despite that this wasn't a one-man job, Pieter was alone. "We didn't get enough."

"Why are you here without the others?"

"The others will come."

"Can I help? I know you'd hate to miss temple this evening."

Pieter wiped his arm across his brow and gazed up at her, straining against the noonday sun. "Why have you come all the way down here, Mother?"

"Brahim said he saw you headed toward the river. He thought maybe you'd left something here, from yesterday. He mentioned nothing about needing more."

"Hmph."

"I've tried coming by your home and speaking with you there. But it seems I always arrive at the wrong times."

Pieter dunked another bucket full of water in the basin. "It may not seem like it to you, but I do have plenty to keep my attention here, to keep me busy. My hands are needed and appreciated."

"I didn't think otherwise."

"Malfenza may not be full of people anymore, like Wulfsgate, but the work to keep it from falling entirely into a grown-over relic is never-ending. It's on us, the ones who stayed, to keep that from happening." He was in full defense. She'd incited it, or her presence had, but it was the very last thing she wanted.

"Pieter, I didn't come to argue with you."

Pieter laughed. The muscles in his shoulders flexed as he pulled another bucket of water from the river, hoisting it up over the bank. "You tried the veil, didn't you? Tried, failed, and now you've come to confess it, when I tried to tell you all along, but you didn't trust me enough to believe."

She shook her head, though he was turned away from her. "I didn't go."

Peter fell back on his heels, shaking his head. "Come to try to convince me again, then? Save your words. I won't change my mind."

"No," she said, "I didn't come about the veil." Pieter should have been the one she could talk to about the ones left behind. Of Nyssa and Torrin, and all their sweetness and fire. Of Holden. Of Drystan, who might yet come home, and Lisbet, who she'd swear to go easier on, if only she could see her again, even just once. And Christian, who would make such a fine leader if he wouldn't keep his heart so guarded, and though she'd given up hoping for it, she would, to see him again. She'd pushed every one of them, children and husband, to be what *she* believed they should be, when all this had done was lead them into dark places where happiness would forever elude them.

But there was still Pieter. And could this new world not also offer her a chance to begin again and do things right, as Curran had said, with a tenderness she did not yet trust. It didn't have to be this way. So hard.

"I came to apologize, cub."

Pieter set the bucket aside. He looked away from her, out into the expanse of desert that had not a tree, not a rock, to focus upon. It promised nothing. "To apologize."

"You've been here years, but I... this is all so new to me, Son. I've been, all my life, prepared for the next thing that would threaten my survival. I've always done what was needed to protect my family and myself and now... now I'm faced with knowing I'll never see any of them again; that my protections cannot reach them." Gretchen trapped the sob in her throat. "Except you."

"Except me. And is that not enough? Is that what you mean to say, but cannot?" He turned then. His eyes were heavy with an accusation that masked his grief.

Gretchen dropped by his side. She tried to smile as she pressed her palm to his cheek. Even as a man, his flesh was so soft, so unmarred that it took little to conjure him as she remembered him best. "Pieter, you and I have always been close, haven't we? You didn't have the pressures Christian and Drystan had. It was easier to love you, for I never had to be hard on you, as I had no choice but to be with your older brothers, knowing what future awaited them. I liked that you preferred me to your father. I liked that he noticed it, and that it angered him. For you are *my* boy, in a way Christian and Drystan never were and never could be. When the king took you…" Gretchen faltered here, as she neared her confession. "When the king took you," she started again, "I begged and bartered with the Guardians. I told them I would give up all the others, all my children, my husband, my food and warmth and joy. If I could only have you back." Her shoulders rolled forward as she sighed. "And now you know my darkest secret, the one I keep far from my heart for fear it will burn it to ash."

Peter twitched his mouth into a sad smile. "Mother."

She bowed her head as the tears spilled. "The Guardians have upheld their end. And so must I."

Pieter pushed forward off his heels and wrapped his arms around her. "Is that what you think, that you're being punished?"

She nodded against him.

"And I always thought you were the wisest person I knew. It doesn't work that way, Mama. The Guardians are a creation of our world, not this one. Not all the worlds. Tenestela has their own gods, but they're a comfort, that's all. It gives the people something to hope for. To blame when the hope fails."

"No, Pieter. The Guardians, fate, it doesn't matter the name. The reason my heart is so heavy is that I'm filled with such joy to be reunited with you, once more. And I would still…" Gretchen sniffed. "I would still, even now, trade them all for you. I have to live with knowing that this is the only truth about myself that will ever matter when my life is weighed and measured in my final hours."

"All right, come on, then," Pieter whispered as he held her.

. . .

"Not now!" Christian barked at the unwelcome sound beating against his father's chamber door. He still thought of this way, his father's, as if Holden would appear to take it all back.

But Holden wasn't coming back. He was dead. As dead as Christian's once hopeful way of looking at the world ahead, as dead as his marriage; as dead as the plants outside begging for rebirth as they fought off the onslaught of an unwelcome springtide snow.

For the better, Christian thought. He wouldn't even recognize his family as they were now. His wife, defected. One child missing, one dead, and two of them belonging to another man entirely.

And then there was Christian. The prodigal failure.

"It's me." A small voice. It took him longer than it should have to place it. Torrin. Christian's guilt spread across his tight chest. Now, with this new understanding, he pushed himself back and saw the moment again, differently. Booming knocks became the rap of tiny, tentative fists.

"Come in, Torrin," he said, sighing through the words.

The door cracked open. Torrin was a small boy, even for his age, but against the giant slab of wood he seemed only a baby. He hovered in the space between, waiting.

Christian waved him in. "Come on, then." The hearth fire lit the otherwise darkened room, but it wasn't enough to see his brother's face. "I know you didn't come down here to stand in my doorway and say nothing."

Torrin turned his whole body to the back of the door to close it, hesitating there. His fear spread across the room, casting a shadow.

Christian stood and pushed his chair across the wooden floor. Torrin swelled with a deep breath and turned, but didn't come any closer. His eyes fell on the chair, but Christian may as well have been offering the pointy end of his sword.

"All right, then. What is it?"

"Uncle Alric is gone. And Aunt Earwyn."

"Gone?"

Torrin dug his hands into his trouser pockets. "They aren't coming back. That's what they said to Lady Aylen."

Christian crossed his arms. "They talked to Lady Aylen?"

Torrin nodded.

"When was this? When did they talk to her?" He shook his head quickly. "When did they leave?"

Torrin glanced back toward the door.

"Torrin."

"I... I don't know. Aunt Earwyn was going to teach me to keep better track of time, but..."

"Who told you?"

Torrin just stared at him.

"Who told you they left?"

"I—"

"Did they say where they were going?"

"I... I don't know."

"What do you know, then? Who told you?"

"Lady Aylen!" Torrin dropped his head even lower. "She told Nyssa and me when we asked her where Aunt and Uncle were."

"When did Lady Aylen tell you this? How long has she known?"

Torrin lifted his shoulders.

"And why did she send *you* to tell me this?" Christian hadn't seen his wife in days. She'd taken to sleeping in Lisbet's chambers. She no longer came to see him during the day, either. Her hollow appeals weren't welcome, but it didn't mean her absence wasn't felt.

"She didn't... send me," Torrin said. "Nyssa and I, we thought you should know, since everyone else does, and you don't come to meals with us anymore."

"Lady Aylen didn't think I should know that my aunt and uncle had left?"

Torrin shifted in visible discomfort. "Lady Aylen has been unwell."

A hard chill passed through Christian. "What do you mean, unwell?"

"She hasn't left her bed in two days."

"Well, has anyone called for a physician?" Christian demanded.

Torrin's shrug this time seemed to cause him physical pain. His lips parted, but fear held his tongue. Was he really so afraid of him? Had Christian given him cause for this? *There are no monsters,* his father would say, when Christian insisted some were attempting to sneak into his room by moonlight. *Not unless you give them life.*

Torrin looked at him the way Christian had once stared in horror at his bedroom door, blanket pulled to his chin, awaiting the horror he knew, he just knew, was on the other side.

"Say it, Torrin. It's all right." He tried to sound more like his father.

"Nyssa!" Torrin blurted. He took his time before he spoke again. "Nyssa has... seen things." He pointed to his head. "Seen like you see."

Christian stepped closer. "Visions?"

Torrin nodded.

Was his little sister a seer, then? Was it possible? Some families had magic that rippled through them, but it had always only been Christian. "What has she seen, Torrin?"

"Lady Aylen..."

"What about Lady Aylen, Torrin?"

But Torrin had spent the sum of his bravery. He turned and fled, disappearing through the crack he'd left in the door, his harried footfalls disappearing down the hall.

RHYDIAN SAT PERCHED AT THE VERY END OF HER BED, AT THE READY. Arturo paced, his sword belt clanging with the heavier steps, pausing by the windows every few steps to reflect, as if the answers to this sudden and terrible conundrum lived just beyond.

It had all happened so swiftly. The woman who had once been filled from temples to toes with the very stuff of life, was now slowly losing this same magic.

Lady Asherley floated in and out of consciousness. He stayed close; in his hand he clutched the delicately folded cloth, now stained entirely with her blood. He'd folded it as many times as he could, and there was no longer a clean square for her to cough upon. He needed to find another one soon, though that would mean leaving her side.

"Is she dying then?" Arturo asked. He stood at the window, arms crossed, still looking out.

"You know I can't answer that."

"Because you know the answer will enrage me."

"Arturo."

"Rhydian."

"Well," Rhydian said, sighing. "The physicians have no answers. The healers have come and gone. You already know this."

"Maybe it's time to let him in." Arturo nodded toward the door with a nervous, jittery energy. As if someone was on the other side, just awaiting invite.

"Rosewood again? Really?"

"It's what she would do. He's her man. Why should he not still be, when she cannot speak for herself?"

"He's long past spent his usefulness. He'll only upset her now." Rhydian shook his head. The more he entertained the notion, the worse it sounded. "You know how he is, Turo. He doesn't *think* before he opens his mouth. For all we know, she can hear every word still."

"He's an old fool, but she trusts him. And you heard what he said to her, Rhydian. He told her I was coming, and how could he have known that? He also said she'd die if she stayed in Wulfsgate. And now..." Arturo pointed to the bed. "He might know something."

Rhydian laughed, humorless. "As I said."

"I dismissed them all! All the children. Yes, I *know* some of them are grown, ready to lead their own families, but they're still babes in the ways that matter."

Both men turned toward the sound of Asherley's delirium. They were used to these sudden outbursts now. She'd been sleeping since her collapse, but not restfully. Periodically, she'd wake long enough to speak something strange, often nonsensical. It seemed to Rhydian that the person she was speaking to was Lord Byrne.

Arturo approached the bed in silence, listening. Rhydian went still.

"Oh, he's so like you. Brandyn's every bit his father's son. You would've chosen your friends, too, wouldn't you, you silly man?" She laughed wistfully. "No matter now. They've gone back to their mothers and fathers, where they belong. Yes, Storm, too, and Brandyn won't forgive me for that one so soon."

Rhydian tried to speak, but Arturo hushed him with a finger at his mouth. He nodded at her as if to say, *listen*.

Rhydian held his sigh. Arturo believed Asherley's feverish mumblings were confessions, and that it was their duty to hear them.

Her thoughts seemed to travel elsewhere. "You think so? Well, I say, I deserve this. I've earned it. Why should I not die here, meet the same death as our Hollyn? Why not, when it was I who didn't protect her from it to begin with? I shouldn't have left her with that traveler so easily. I told her it was to prepare her, but really, I was just too busy to be bothered."

Rhydian tried again to get Arturo's attention, and this time it worked. He whispered the words. "Do you hear that?"

Arturo nodded.

"Could that be what this is? The same affliction that took Lady Hollyn?"

"How can I know?" Arturo barked.

"I'm only thinking aloud—"

"Only thinking, when we should be *doing*."

Rhydian rose to his feet. "And what more can we do, that we haven't done? We aren't smiths of miracles. We are only men."

"The Guardians have never thought well of me, my love. But it seems they do have a sense of humor, yes?" Asherley said with a light laugh. She moaned and rolled to her side, returning to her silence.

"Joran," Arturo said more firmly.

Rhydian shook his head. "That old fool will have her swilling rabbit's foot stew before he'd come with anything of use."

Arturo stepped closer. His sweet, hot breath calmed Rhydian's racing heart. "Your disdain of anything magic is yours to bear, but don't let it come between our lady—our *friend*—and a chance for life."

Rhydian turned away. "I don't... it's not *magic* I have a disdain for. I sent for the healers myself, did I not?"

"And were practically giddy when they failed to heal her."

"That's not true, Turo."

"No? Then you won't begrudge me when I leave this room and find the old Enchanter. He served her well for years. He may yet have some service left to provide her."

Rhydian scoffed. "I won't stop you."

Arturo reached for his hands. Rhydian looked down at their bond, which had kept him safe, kept him warm, all these years. "Rhydian, please. I need more from you now than your indifference."

Rhydian sighed. "We'll speak with him together."

GRETCHEN HUDDLED UNDER THE MEAGER EAVES OF THE SMALL entryway. Beyond, the rain pelted the sandy hills, rolling waves of mud into ditches and down into the valley. There'd be flooding, perhaps landslides. Maura had said so. Gretchen thought, how lovely it would be to ride the whole mess down the sloping, winding hills of Malfenza, let it take her where it would, to whatever end.

The door opened, startling her out of her strange melancholy. Curran stood, one hand propped against the doorframe. At first annoyed, and then, as he regarded her more closely, alarmed.

"Gretchen?"

It wasn't the first time he'd called her by her name, instead of that terrible slur, Intrusa, but the kindness in his tone caused the swell of emotion rising within to overflow. She buried her face in her hands in place of a response. It wasn't right to be here, any more than it had been for her to share her innermost thoughts with

Pieter. Her burdens were her own to live with, and one day, perhaps sooner than she'd ever imagined, to die with.

She shook her head; which wasn't a lie, because it wasn't *some-thing*, was it? It was everything. Her whole life, tragedy upon tragedy, pain stacked upon pain, often self-inflicted.

And where had there been joy, but in the glimpses of light peeking between the stones? Her brief but charged moments with Ash; the all too short years where her children still liked her. The occasional exchanged laugh with Holden, who was a good man, better than she deserved with her constant attempts to cut through to the center of him, to burrow in with her strong intentions and cutting judgments. Maybe from the inside, she could make him the man she wanted, and it wouldn't matter that he hadn't chosen her, either.

Curran stepped aside. She glanced at the open door before her eyes fell back on him. And yes, she saw now, it was an invitation. One that wouldn't again be extended if she refused it now, and, if taken, would lead her down a path there would be no return from, like stepping through another veil.

Gretchen Quinlanden Dereham pulled her shoulders back, held her head high, and once more stepped through a door to a new life.

39
THE HALF-BLOODS

The Wastelands were appropriately named, Lisbet thought. Even when the narrow peninsula had been in Warwick hands, it had never been fit for life beyond the stinging critters that would take a grown man down, she remembered her father saying.

They'd expected a melee at the border. Ryan conspired an elaborate misdirection, but they never got to see it play out. The border was empty. The guard stand stood abandoned, discarded bowls and knives and unwashed clothing gathered off in somewhat neat piles at the side of the narrow road, as if the wind had attempted to tidy up in their absence.

Lord Warwick wasn't nearly thrilled enough about the lack of resistance. She was already nervous, without wondering where his head was. She'd put on a brave face and confidently declared that her instincts had called her here, but in private she wrestled with what it all might mean, and the responsibility that was hers alone to figure out. A year ago she was no less the daughter of Dain Rhiagain than she was now, but back then, she'd had no sign of the magic in her blood. No sense that she was special, or that this specialness could be of use beyond the walls of Wulfsgate Keep. Leaving with

Drystan had been a whim—a meticulous one, but a whim nonetheless—that had nothing to do with any of this. But that very decision had been the one to bring her here, and nothing that had happened to her since was inconsequential.

It nearly made her believe in the idea of fate.

Mostly it made her head hurt.

"So it was all true, then. Lake's claims," Ryan remarked as they drifted through the remnants of what had once been the great pride of the Rhiagains.

They moved farther in, approaching the camps. It was even more of the same. Lisbet was relieved to see the place abandoned, and so was Ryan, who'd gone uncomfortably quiet. The older men huddled together, as if they knew something the younger ones did not.

"Camp Atonement," said Hamish unnecessarily, as they'd passed below an unkempt sign declaring the same. He cast a rueful look at his son, who had dismounted and wandered off toward the rows and rows of tents. Half of them were hardly upright anymore. "A right awful place."

Lisbet dismounted and headed toward Ryan. When Ash tried to follow, she held up a hand behind her.

She ducked into the tent. Ryan stood stiffly at the center of a long line of small cots, arms straight at his sides, hardly moving save for the soft lift of his shoulders as he breathed.

"Was this where you stayed?" she asked.

Ryan nodded.

"You and the prince?"

"Aye."

Lisbet bit back the rest of her questions. She searched for words of comfort, but there weren't any for the horrors men experienced in a place like this. The kind few ever lived to tell about.

"Ye aren't going to ask me what it was like, then?" His voice was small, like a child's.

"Would you like me to?"

"Nay." He made like he was going to drop down and sit at the edge of one of the filthy bed rolls, but recoiled in disgust. "So, where is this veil, then?"

Lisbet shook her head. "I don't know."

"Aye? Well, how do they expect us to find it then?"

"Well. It was our instincts, and our dreams, that brought us this far. I can only hope they'll take us the rest of the way. If not, then... then I don't know."

He watched her over his shoulder without turning. "What are they like?"

"The dreams?"

"Aye."

"Unclear," Lisbet answered. She sighed. "But undeniable. I can't say I understand them, most of the time, but each one leaves me with this sense of immediacy, that I must follow them... that if I don't..."

"If you donnae, what?"

Lisbet lifted her shoulders in a shrug. "Nothing good."

"Aye, but how can ye *know* that?"

"I can't explain it."

"Aye." Ryan spun around, taking in the dusty, ragged remains of the tent. "Just like I cannae explain where my memory went."

"You seem like you remember this place."

"Aye, but it's like..." Ryan pointed at his head. "Flashes, ye ken? Pieces. I feel *ill* being here, like the most terrible things I've endured happened right in this spot, but I cannae decide if what's happening is me remembering, or me putting together all the things Darrick told me about our time here. Lake? The man who told us about the bodies in the pit?" He shook his head and made a face. "I cannae picture him. So am I remembering, or am I putting a story together that was told to me?"

Brandyn peeked his head inside. "Hey, you guys about done? Lord Warwick wants to get a move on."

"Aye." Ryan passed a look to Lisbet as he moved around her. Ash was waiting at the doorway for her. She watched Ryan mount his horse.

"What was that about?"

"Lord Warwick never should've made him come here. It wasn't right."

Ash rested a hand on her shoulder. "Perhaps, but there's no gain in getting too deeply involved in it, Lisbet. We have our own concerns."

"Who said I was getting involved?" She shook her hand off and then, with a wince, turned in apology. "Are we okay? We haven't really spoken after that day in the Hall of Warring."

"Of course." He was lying.

"Ash."

"We should go. The others are waiting."

"I should've told you sooner. I know that."

"And I understand why you didn't. There will be time enough to ruminate on all of it, but I don't want to be in this forsaken place any longer than we have to. Do you?"

She nodded. "No."

They both jumped at the sound of steel drawn in imperfect unison. Instinct prompted Ash to reach for his longbow as he rushed back toward the other men. Lisbet strafed across the hard desert sand, shielding her eyes from the blinding sun. She didn't see them at first, but once she did, her hand traveled to her sword belt.

"Knights of Duncarrow," Hamish muttered.

"Easy," Khallum warned. "There's nay more than a dozen."

"Only a dozen? Only a dozen *knights?*"

Ryan smirked. "We'll make quick work of this."

"The knights are the best the crown has in this kingdom," Hamish argued. "Ye ken ye can do better?"

Khallum held his free hand to the side. He kept his sword down, but drawn, as he rode forward a few paces.

"Lisbet, you stay back," Ash said.

"No chance." Lisbet reached for the reins of her horse and swung up, falling in next to Ryan and Brandyn.

"Would ye look at them," Ryan said. "Skin and bones. Best warriors the crown can find, and they donnae even feed them."

"Captain General Gilgowan!" their leader announced. His uniform confirmed his words, but his gaunt, hung face, and the sallowness living in the expressions of all the men behind him, made it easier to believe they'd stolen these threads and titles.

Something very wrong had happened here.

"Have you come on behalf of the crown at Duncarrow?"

"Nay. The Warwicks are done serving Rhiagains." Khallum spat at his feet. "Any still slinging their shingle for this crown is no friend of ours." He spat again. "Sir."

"Here we go," Ryan said under his breath.

Gilgowan looked at his men at the left, and then the right. "Then it seems we have a common interest, for the crown has forsaken us, and we... well, men, what are we now?"

"Rebels!"

"Outcasts!"

"Treasonous ratsbanes!"

"That so?" Khallum asked.

Hamish tightened his grip on his hilt. He looked ready and eager for battle. "What's your business here?" he barked.

Gilgowan laughed. "I would've slit you from ear to ear for asking me that, not so long ago. Now, what care have I? We haven't eaten a proper meal in weeks. Or has it been months? We stay for fear of the blade promised to traitors, but I think we'd all rather face a swift death than let the starvation take us, now that we've seen it with our own bellies, isn't that right, men?"

The others murmured in weary agreement.

"But why have you not eaten?" Brandyn asked. "You're knights of the crown. After the king, there is none higher."

"Were you not listening when I said the crown had forsaken us, boy?"

"We have no quarrel with you," Khallum said. "We have business here, and we'll be on our way now."

"Hold on," Ryan said. He reached into a satchel and pulled out several bundles rolled in cloth, tied by the women who'd prepared them. He held them out. Gilgowan rode forward slowly to accept them. The hunger in his eyes bordered on feral as he bowed to Ryan in gratitude. His men shuffled behind him, restless, ravenous.

"Slake the curiosity of a dying knight," Gilgowan said, before returning to the others. "Why would the Lord of the Southerlands come to a place like this?"

Lisbet noted Khallum had told the general he was a Warwick, but not which one. Gilgowan might be starving, but he was still sharp.

"These are Warwick lands, lest ye forgot."

"They haven't been Warwick lands in generations."

"Our business is our own," Khallum gruffed.

Gilgowan swiped his tongue over his lips. "Warwicks. Yes. I think I know why you're here, and if there was a drop of humor left in me, I reckon your arrival might even be funny."

"What would ye know about any of it?" Khallum challenged.

Gilgowan wagged a finger over his shoulders. "We found it, you see. It's what we were sent here to do. Why these camps were cleared of men who were criminals, yes, but had committed no crime deserving of death." He laughed. "And we would've done our duty to the very end, right, men? As we always have. And if it were only me... but I watched my men die by the dozens. Ate some of them, too. You'll understand, if you ever look death in the eye. I didn't understand until I stared him straight down."

Lisbet and Brandyn exchanged a nervous look.

"Son of a crow," Khallum whispered. He eased up on his sword. "Aye, well, we've more food. Can send for more still."

Gilgowan shook his head. "We'll be clear of this place by night-fall, and will greet whatever fate awaits us. As knights." He spun his horse around, aimed the way they'd come. "Men, you have served well. And given all. None could say they've served harder, or given more. But your service is now ended. I free you of this burden that has killed many of our brothers."

"But, sir." The men were confused. "What about you? Are you not coming?"

"Not today."

"Where you go, we go."

"No. No, not this time." Gilgowan shook his head. "There is no more 'we,' men. Find your freedom, if you dare. Take the food these men have offered. My duty nears conclusion, but yours has already ended."

When the men had at last pushed on, reluctant but driven by the promise of food and a proper rest, Gilgowan said to Khallum, "The veil. That's what you've come for."

Khallum's head twitched. Then, with a sigh, he nodded.

"My lord," Hamish hissed.

"The king. His magician. Whoever. Wanted it pretty badly, didn't they?" Gilgowan laughed. It was a gravelly sound; the cry of the dead. "Well, all the more reason you should have it then. As you said. These are Warwick lands."

Khallum shifted on his horse. "You know where it is?"

Gilgowan passed a hand across his cracked and scabbing lips. "Yeah. I know where it is. And if you've a little more of that food to spare, I'll show you."

"Why's he helping us?" Lisbet wondered aloud.

"You can only push a man so far," Ash muttered.

"'Tis a trap," Hamish said. "Cannae trust this one not to turn on us."

Gilgowan tossed his head back and laughed. "If you look upon me, as I am now, and see a threat, then that, my friend, is more a reflection of your abilities than mine."

"Now what?" Lisbet whispered. "We follow him?"

Ryan whistled through his teeth. "Aye. We follow him."

"What is it?" Ash asked her when she didn't immediately fall in with the others.

"A sense. It may be nothing."

"No, we trust our senses now. Remember?"

Lisbet nodded. She gathered the reins and spurred her horse forward. "There's danger ahead. And I don't mean dying knights, either."

"Is there anything else you can see?"

She shook her head. "We should be ready for anything."

BRANDYN FELL INTO STEP NEXT TO LISBET AND RYAN AS THEY followed the disgraced general deeper into the Wastelands. They'd passed through three camps, each more derelict than the last. He'd never learned how many camps the Wastelands had, but he could do the math well enough to know what their emptiness represented. He thought of the pits of bodies Ryan mentioned with a chill.

"How much farther, do you think?" he asked Lisbet as she took a swig from her waterskin.

"I wish I could say."

"You haven't had another vision?"

"I thought for sure... if I could just *get* here, it would all make sense. But it's as if it's all gone dark."

Brandyn pointed to his own head. "You're not the only one. Failed seer here."

She smiled into her laugh. "Maybe it's this place?"

"You think?"

"Since we came through the camps, I feel... different." She glanced back at Ash, who had fallen behind enough to be out of earshot. "I don't like the feeling."

"I feel that way, too."

"You do?"

Brandyn nodded. "Heavier. You remember those cloaks your father made mourners wear for the dead-given rites? The ones heavier than the beasts that provided them?"

"One does not so quickly forget the Dereham mourning cloaks."

"It's like that," Brandyn said. "Except I can't take it off."

"It's like that for me, too." Lisbet looked off to the side, into the dark red mountain range, and beyond, to the black smoke that hovered just above the crater of the volcano. Brandyn had heard stories, passed down tales, of what it had been when it last erupted. Supposedly, the peninsula once dipped further inland, but the end had broken off into the sea, never to be seen again.

"Ryan, you've been here before," Brandyn prodded.

"Never this far," Ryan said. "Prisoners aren't given holidays, ye know. Not that I would've come here, anyway." His shoulders shook in a shiver.

"You feel it, too?"

"Donnae need to feel anything. It's all around us."

"But it's more than that," Lisbet said. She tapped her fingers against the leather of her pants. "There's something ahead, waiting. We shouldn't be here."

"Wasn't it your visions that brought us here?" Ryan quipped.

"I sense that too, Lisbet," Brandyn said. "You think it's the general?"

Lisbet hesitated, then shook her head. "He's not a danger to anyone. Not anymore."

"What if my father is right, and he's leading us into a trap?" Ryan said.

"Then I hope you know how to do more than wave that sword around."

Gilgowan slowed, then turned down a path that led them into a narrow canyon. Brandyn squeezed his shoulders closer together as they entered the gap in the mountains wide enough for their horses, and not much more. They fell into single file as they entered, one by one.

To Brandyn, it seemed the walls closed in tighter the deeper they moved in, and the air was thinner, like it was when they passed over the Seven Sisters. The horses ahead reared back. They didn't like it either.

The men ahead had put some distance on Brandyn and the others. He held his breath, as if he might need it later.

Ahead of him, Lisbet shot up straight in her saddle. "I can feel it!" She was panicked, her breaths too close together. "Oh, no, no, it's so strong now. Can you feel it?"

"Cannae feel a thing but these walls trying to swallow us alive," Ryan said. He was behind Brandyn, close, but his voice was so distant he might have been a mile away.

"I do," Brandyn said, breathless. He recoiled with a jolt. Here it was. Happening now. The feeling lodged in his throat as the seer's vision took hold. It was *strong*. Too strong. He'd waited so long for it to happen again, but now that it was again here, all he wanted to do was shake it off, to be free of its potent hold. But it wouldn't relent. "We shouldn't be here. We need to stop. We can't go any farther."

He tried to call ahead, but his voice bounced between the rock walls, trapped between them. "Lisbet, you have to stop! Stop, stop!"

Lisbet drew back on the reins. Her horse fought her, but after a moment she had him calm enough to stay still. She turned in the saddle.

Brandyn cupped his mouth and screamed ahead, but the three men heard nothing. They pushed on, oblivious.

"We cannae stay in here!" Ryan cried.

"This place is evil," Lisbet said. "It's all around us."

"I saw him! I saw him!" Brandyn blurted.

"Who?" Ryan asked.

"Lisbet? Brandyn? What's going on up there?" Ash's voice cut through a moment of silence. Brandyn had forgotten the man was even there.

Brandyn looked at Lisbet and heaved the name through clipped breaths. "Oldwin."

"Do you feel that?" Khallum whispered.

"Aye," Hamish answered, just as quiet.

"I can almost see it." He pointed ahead. "It's the air. 'Tis not the same here. You do feel it, Hamish?"

"Aye, Khallum, aye, I do." He was green in the face, like he was fighting off an illness. Khallum wanted to reassure him that there was no longer anything to fear, but he couldn't deceive them both. His own fears were reflected in the eyes of his old friend. A great malevolence, lying in wait.

"There." Gilgowan pointed, though he needn't have bothered. Though there was no door or sign, the light shimmer in the air was unmistakable. The air *moved* differently. It hovered above the red floor of the desert, wedged between two boulders. "None of my men would try it, but that has to be it, doesn't it? That's the only explanation for... *that.*"

"Where'd the others go?" Hamish asked, pulling back to turn and look.

Khallum rode on, drawing closer. All these years he'd believed in nothing, and here it was. It was a strange thing. When he'd said he could see it, he almost could, but it wasn't with his *eyes*. It was a sense, as if his hand would unflinchingly land true if he reached out to touch it; as if the very air would bend and bow to his touch.

Behind him, Hamish grunted, followed by a cry of pain. The sound of a man hitting dirt was unmistakable. Khallum turned, and it wasn't Hamish his eyes fell upon, but him. *Him.* It could only be him, because... ahh, Khallum ceased to breathe as he beheld him. How could anyone have ever mistaken a sorcerer for man? These were his only thoughts as he stared down his most formidable opponent.

Oldwin.

Hamish hovered in the air, held aloft by nothing tangible. Oldwin's hand was turned to the right, as if a twitch the other way would sever his hold on Hamish. Khallum gaped in horror. This wasn't a threat. Hamish was still alive, so Khallum could watch him die.

Even in his fear, he didn't miss the strain in the sorcerer's face. The light tremble of his bottom lip. The downward twitch his jaw made.

Gilgowan slowly drew his sword, but made no move to strike.

"You," Khallum boomed. "No longer see fit to hide in your fortress of sea and stone?"

"You've cursed my name from behind the safety of your doors and guards. Can you not say it now, when you at last have me before you? Is this not what you wanted, Khallum Warwick?"

Khallum pressed the name through his teeth with a sneer. "Oldwin. I have a long overdue debt to settle with ye. One ye cannae ever repay, but aye, we're gonna try anyway, I ken."

"Let me down," Hamish grunted.

Oldwin laughed. He flicked his wrist and sent Hamish hurling into a boulder. He dropped and rolled, coming to a startling stillness. Oldwin shook his hand.

"You will never have satisfaction from me, Khallum," he said. "But you can leave here with your life."

"If it costs me my life exacting my reprisal, that will be a cost well paid."

"Where are they, Khallum?"

"I donnae know who *they* are. I donnae care. Ye could be asking about the snakes we passed on the way in, and I still wouldnae tell ye. You've taken enough. I'll give ye no more."

"Don't toy with me. The half-bloods. I know they're here."

Khallum glanced to check on Hamish, but the man hadn't moved. "I know no half-bloods."

"I know they're here, because you didn't come to defend it this time, did you? No, those days are well behind you. And they were never *your* days at all, were they? You've come to close it, but you wouldn't have come all this way without the means to see it done."

"Why?"

Oldwin cocked his head to the side.

"Why my people? My Reach? Why Anabella, who'd already suffered enough?"

Oldwin held a hand aloft at his side, all fingers rippling in the shimmer's direction. "I think you know."

"Tell me anyway, so I can repeat the words as I remove the head from your shoulders."

"I needed to know where it was."

"Never thought to just ask?"

"Would you have told me?"

Khallum laughed. "Nay."

"I was wrong about you, though. I thought you cared more for your blood, your people."

"Aye? Well, I ken you'll see how just wrong ye are about me soon enough."

Oldwin was unconcerned. "You'd be killing the wrong monster. Aren't you even curious how I knew where to find the munitions? The others, whose names escape me. Your man, Law. Darrick's whore."

"Donnae listen to him!" Hamish groaned, finally awakened. Khallum sagged in relief to hear his voice. "He only knows lies!"

"I couldnae care less who you've bought from me, not anymore," Khallum said, though this, too, was a lie. But Hamish was right. There could be no truths from a creature such as this one. "You'll get nothing else."

"It wasn't ever you I needed anyway, as it turns out. Only my patience, which has served me well, in the end." Oldwin dropped his hand with a light sigh. "So tell me, Khallum, where I can find these half-bloods, and we can end this madness between us."

"Never."

"If I have to pull it from you, it won't be you who suffers for the refusal. It will be that sweet little bairn, cooing in her cradle, deceived by the very lord who was sworn to protect her life. And what of her mother? Her mother, whose life I traded for the names and locations of all the others I took from the Southerlands."

"Khallum, what does he mean by that?" Hamish asked.

Khallum licked his lips as he reached for his sword. The sound echoed off the boulders as he drew his steel with intention. "Ye wanna pull it from me, do ye? Aye, well, come and take it then."

The sound of Hamish drawing his sword from behind was a sweet relief. Gilgowan closed in from Khallum's left flank.

Oldwin held his hands to the sides. "It's a bold choice to die, when to live is within your grasp. Give me the half-bloods, Khallum. I have no quarrel with you."

"Oh, but I have a quarrel with ye, sorcerer."

Lisbet came rushing out from the pass. When they all turned, she came to an abrupt halt, dust kicking up around her boots. "You wanted a half-blood? Well, here I am!"

"You foolish girl!" Khallum yelled, but it was too late. He spun his horse around to ride toward her, but the look she sent him stopped him cold.

Lisbet dropped to the ground and spread her palms into the desert dust, fingers splayed. Khallum's horse was the first to notice the change, as she reared up, but then Khallum, too, felt it. He gripped her reins as a deep roar ripped through the canyon. Smaller rocks crumbled off the foothills, spreading in an uneven dance across the undulating ground. The boulder that had nearly taken Hamish out cracked down the center.

"Is she doing that? The girl?" Gilgowan panted.

"Aye. I think so," Khallum said.

"Lisbet! No!" Ash cried as he pushed out of the pass and into the open. He was thrust back against the wall by the force of the invisible storm swirling from the hands of Lisbet Dereham.

Oldwin, hands up to shield himself from the desert debris, strained through the magic to get to her. "This was your grandfather's favorite trick! Did he teach you this?"

"DO IT!" she screamed. "NOW!"

"'Tis a distraction," Hamish hissed. "She's helping us!"

Khallum's horse wouldn't go. She was too afraid. He leapt from her back and charged against the unseen wind, holding tight to the sword that felt as if it was being torn from his hands. Hamish strained at his side. Then Gilgowan was there too, at his back.

Ash pushed off the wall with one hand, the other wielding his swaying longbow as he neared in on Oldwin.

Lisbet screamed, "I can feel him! He can't fight me!"

"Are you so certain of that, little one?" Oldwin's face peeled back as he pushed harder.

"As certain as I was that I could stop you."

"Certain enough to stake all their lives upon it?" He stretched his arm out, groaning against the resistance. He was inches away now.

Lisbet roared as her head fell back. Every strand of her crimson and gold hair splayed in the hard wind. "NOW! RIGHT BLOODY NOW!" she yelled before collapsing forward, exhausted.

The storm abruptly ended.

Khallum, Hamish, Gilgowan, and Ash leapt to life, swarming in on the sorcerer from all sides. Oldwin brought up one hand to cast his defense, but Hamish's sword was quicker. It caught Oldwin just above the wrist, slicing clean through. The severed limb flopped to the desert floor.

Oldwin didn't waste time mourning the loss of his hand, instead raising the other, and this time, his magic was unanswered. Ash loaded his longbow, but was driven back against the rocks with a sickening thud. He slid down and slumped over. Lisbet screamed.

Oldwin's second of hesitation as he turned toward the sound of Lisbet's cry was enough for Khallum and Hamish to drive their swords into his chest. Their steel penetrated side by side. The sorcerer sounded a rattle and fell to his knees as they withdrew their swords. They didn't wait for his counterattack, plunging the steel again into him, through his back, exiting through his belly. Gilgowan spun to the front and jammed his sword tip into the center of the sorcerer's throat. Khallum and Hamish ducked away just as it protruded grotesquely out of the back of Oldwin's neck.

Oldwin fell to the ground. Khallum dropped to a crouch at his side, ready to cut the creature's head clean off, but Oldwin was spent. His handless arm bled the last of his life force into the sand.

"We did it. We killed him," Khallum said, looking up at the other men in wonder. "And they said it couldnae be done by mere man."

Lisbet crawled toward them. Khallum pulled her to her feet and held her aloft as she struggled against the fatigue. "Something's happened to him," she said.

"Aye, he's dead."

Ryan and Brandyn came riding out of the pass, the two rider-less horses behind them.

"He was weakened. He wouldn't have fallen to us otherwise."

"I donnae care what he was. He's done now. We can get on with it."

"I don't trust it," Lisbet said. Khallum dusted her off and released her. "Something isn't right, Uncle."

"Ye can see it with your own eyes. Dead."

"But it shouldn't have been so easy!"

"I ken your brother killed the other one easily enough," Khallum countered.

"Lisbet! What did you do? What was that?" Ash hobbled to her side. He was wounded, but seemed unaware of it as he reached for his daughter.

Lisbet gently shook him off. "I don't know. I don't know what it was. I only knew that I could do it." She cleared her head. "That I *needed* to do it."

Ryan handed her the ribbons that had flown from her hair. "I donnae know what to do with these."

Lisbet tried to laugh. "Nor would I expect you to."

"Lisbet. What you said before," Brandyn said. "Do you still feel it?"

Lisbet raised her hand to her bloodied lip. She nodded.

"Then we better be quick."

As the others started toward the veil, Khallum groaned, sucking in a gulp of air as he turned away from them. He looked down to see dark crimson cut through his mail, which hadn't been enough to protect him, not from the force of sharp stone carried on a fierce wind. He hid the growing wound in his belly with his hand, wincing through the sharp pain. It was bad, though if he didn't look, he wouldn't know, and if he didn't know, he could still do what he needed to, until the end.

"You got us this far," Ash said. "Now what, little one? How does one destroy a veil to another world?"

"*We* got us this far, Ash. Together. We both saw Duncarrow. The Wastelands. And I know you've seen other things too, things you're keeping from me."

"Not everything we see makes sense," Ash said, and she knew this, too, was a half-truth. "Does no good speaking of things prematurely."

"*None* of this made sense, or was clear," she countered.

"Right now, all that matters, Lisbet, is destroying that veil, right? It's why we came."

"I'm thinking," she said. She shook off his questions. She had enough of her own. What good were visions that pushed her all the way to the end and then abandoned her?

"A veil on one side, naught on the other," Ryan mused. "A man must enter what he intends to smother."

"What?" They all turned toward him.

He shrugged. "Something the old man used to say. He'd sing it. I ken he was always a little mad, though. He used to buy pints for the gulls when the pub was closing."

"What old man?" Lisbet asked.

Ryan nodded toward Khallum. "Odrahn."

"I never heard him say such a thing," Khallum volleyed.

"You never spent much time in the pubs, did ye?"

"Sir," Khallum reminded him.

Ryan was unfazed. "Man was always in his cups."

"Say it again," Lisbet urged. She was looking away, tangled in her thoughts. "Please."

"A veil on one side, naught on the other. A man must enter what he intends to smother." Ryan laughed. "Now that I hear it again, it's really quite nonsense, aye?"

"A man must enter what he intends to smother," Ash said. "If nothing else, we need to go through."

"You're going through? That?" Hamish pointed. "Do ye even know what a thing like tha' will do to a man?"

"No," Lisbet replied. "But we're not only men, are we?"

"Aye, should we do something about this one?" Ryan kicked at Oldwin's corpse.

"Don't do that," Brandyn warned.

"He gonna spring back to life, is he?"

"You don't have much experience with sorcerers, do you?" Brandyn challenged.

"He'll be returning with us. I have just the place for him, flying above the ramparts, for all to see," Khallum called back. To Lisbet he said, "I hope you know what you're doing, girl."

"I don't know anything!"

"Your mother will kill me, something happens to ye."

"Do *you* really know nothing about this?" she asked him. "How could one be a Defender without knowing anything about what they're defending?"

"I ken those who should've told me and didnae had their reasons. And you? You're here for a reason, too."

"That thing you did, Lisbet, to stop Oldwin. With your hands," Ash said. "Can you do it to the veil?"

"I can try," she said, turning back toward the shimmer.

"From the other side," Brandyn reminded her. "Like Odrahn's rhyme said."

Lisbet nodded. She looked again at her uncle. "Are you coming with us?"

Khallum shook his head. "I dinnae ken so, girl. My great-uncle said the Warwick Burden was to defend it, and one day find the one who could destroy it. That's all."

"Where does it lead?"

He shrugged. "Odrahn didn't say. But Oldwin was interested enough. Wherever it leads, is somewhere he very much wanted to go."

Lisbet looked again at the crumpled body of the sorcerer. She hadn't been there when Drystan had struck the fatal blow to Mortain, but maybe he'd looked this feeble and mortal in death, too. There was nothing special about Oldwin now. Nothing more than a broken form that had once housed a misspent life.

Lisbet looked at her father. "What if we can't come back from this?"

Ash nodded at the question, thinking through his answer. "You said to me when we left Wulfsgate that you didn't expect to see it again. Do you remember?"

"I remember."

"There's much you don't know, Lisbet. That *we* don't know. It worries us, keeps our minds spinning. But what is the one thing we do know now?"

"I don't know," she said.

He laughed. "You don't know what we know?"

"I don't know what you mean by it."

"We know the magic is fickle, but we know it's true." He pointed his hand behind him, toward the veil. "It brought us here, to a place the Warwicks have defended for many generations, while they waited for *us*. The very ones they needed to fulfill their duty are the ones who landed at Khallum's doorstep. You think I'm angry with you, for not telling me who I was?" He lowered his head with a light laugh. "Oh, sweet Lisbet. I'm *relieved* to finally understand it! To know that my lifetime of wandering hasn't been for nothing. Everything I've done, every place I've been, it's been for *this*. For *you*. For *us*. If you truly fear what will happen when you step through, then I'll take this burden for both of us. But if your fearlessness is not yet spent, daughter, then let us do this, together. Let us trust that the magic didn't bring us this far only to destroy us."

Lisbet thought to herself that the magic had led Drystan to his destruction, but he'd still faced it. He'd faced down his fears of what would be, and did what he was born to do.

"Thank you, Uncle Khallum. For taking us this far." She nodded at Hamish and Ryan. "You're good men." To Brandyn, she said, "If you see my mother, my father, or any of the others, you tell them I'm all right. When you say it, sound like you believe it."

He nodded. "I will."

"Remember when you said you didn't believe in veils?" Lisbet teased her father.

"Who said that's changed?"

Lisbet stretched a hand out. "If we don't do it now, I'll lose my courage."

"The both of us will," he said, with a squeamish look.

"Right. Since none here know any more than we do, and there are no more questions to be asked..."

"We go."

"We go."

Ash took her hand, and they approached, at first slowly. She felt the warmth of the veil as they came face-to-face with it. The air thrummed this close. She almost turned back, but they'd already gone beyond any place they could return to.

Ash nodded without looking, and together they stepped through.

"They're gone. Feck it all, they did it," Ryan whispered.

"It's still there," Brandyn said. "The veil."

"They have to destroy it, remember?" Ryan said. "They only just left."

"We should go," Hamish said with a light shiver. "I donnae wish to be here any longer than we must."

"We need to wait until it's gone," Brandyn said. "We need to know it was done."

"Aye, and why? The sorcerer is dead. Who else cares?"

"Do you know the answer to that question with certainty?" Brandyn countered. "If not, then I suggest we wait."

Hamish grunted, but made no further argument.

Khallum cried out and fell to his knees.

"My lord?" Hamish was the first at his side. Ryan dropped in front of Khallum and gasped.

"What? What is it?" Brandyn called as he rushed over.

"Where's Gilgowan?" Ryan asked.

"He... I don't know. He must have left after you felled Oldwin," Brandyn said. He passed his eyes around the canyon. "What's going on?"

"Lord Warwick is in a bad way, kid," Ryan said, loudly enough for the two of them. "We need to get him to someone who knows their way around a belly wound."

"But that'll take too long," Brandyn whispered.

"Aye, which is why, if we want to save him, we'll have to choose. His life, or stay and wait for your certainty."

Brandyn again looked back. The shimmer was still just as strong as it had been before Ash and Lisbet had entered. "Right. Okay. Let's patch what we can before we move him."

Ryan nodded and returned to Khallum's side. Brandyn stood, thinking, as father and son tore through their satchels.

Brandyn had been powerless to save his father, but he wouldn't let his uncle die.

"I'll ride ahead," he said, swinging up on his horse. "I'll send back aid to meet us here. He'll have a better chance than waiting until Whitecliffe."

"Aye," Ryan said with a nod. "Go. Quick."

Brandyn guided his horse back toward the path, but the scene before him left him frozen in place.

Oldwin, unfurling from the ground. Oldwin, winding up his arms as he took off in a horrifying sprint, his severed hand regrown. Oldwin, as he hurled himself, flipping forward into a grotesque roll across the air, passing through the same veil the Warwicks had fought all these years to keep him from.

Brandyn found his voice and screamed.

The veil disappeared.

40

AT LONG, LONG LAST

Alasyr should have left by now. He'd never intended to stay this long. It was Ravenna. Now, as before. She'd always been able to do this, to point him in the direction of her choosing. He'd tried telling her he was leaving, but she'd pushed, as she always had. *Come,* she'd said. *Just for a bit. Then you can go. Do it for me.*

He didn't want to follow Ravenna to the Hall of Hours again. It would be easy to blame his choice entirely on her, but she was only a part of it. His curiosity at this new society flourishing from within the Ravenwoods was stronger than he'd like it to be.

A nauseating dread lived in his belly as he approached the double doors. Both terror and excitement. These were once his people, if it was even fair to call them that. But he was no longer the eldest son of their High Priestess, but a man separated from it all by choice. He had no veil of tradition to protect him, and until now, he hadn't been aware of how much he'd relied upon this for the sense of safety he'd always enjoyed at The Rookery.

The gathered Ravenwoods went silent as Ravenna and Alasyr entered the room. A flurry of leather and feathers sounded and then settled as everyone took their seats.

Rillyn Ravenwood moved into the circle that marked the center of the hall. "We're all so happy you haven't yet left us." His mannerisms were welcoming, but this put Alasyr on edge more than ever before.

Rillyn's soft smile to Ravenna gave Alasyr a fresh chill.

"I'm not staying," Alasyr said to his grandfather, though his eyes were busy traveling around the faces of those perched in the tiered seating that wrapped around the room, and up, up into the dome. "Ravenna asked me to come see you once more. So here I am."

Rillyn passed a look to Ravenna. "We want to know, Alasyr, about Emberley Blackwood."

Alasyr's blood chilled in an instant. "Emberley?" And then, just as quickly, "She's dead. My mother killed her. If that's all you wanted to know, then it seems we're done here."

"It's all right," Ravenna urged, but it wasn't all right. Why were they asking about Emberley? Why her, and why now?

"We know," Rillyn said. "We know what you did. We know your strength saved her."

Alasyr whipped his gaze to Ravenna in a panic. But she was smiling, like their grandfather. "It's okay. Really, Alasyr, I promise you."

"You *told* them."

"I told our grandfather, who doesn't see Emberley the way Adynora does. Who doesn't feel that loathing for men that we were bred to feel. It's going to be all right. Please, you can tell them what you did."

"It wasn't yours to share!"

"You're not the only powerful one," she said, with a flush in her cheeks. "Don't you understand? I've listened to them all, all of them, tell the stories, the ones our mother and grandmother and all before them would say didn't matter, but they do! They're spectacular, all of them. More, even, than the women they were told were greater than all of them combined. Some have magic we've never seen before."

"Of course they have magic, they're Ravenwoods. But it's not the same as yours, is it? The rest of us don't have visions. We don't know our histories as you do, so we're at a great disadvantage, and you know it."

"There are no visions," she whispered. "Yes, another lie. Like so many other things. There are no *chosen* ones among us. There are only Ravenwoods."

"What?" Alasyr remembered the words of a dying man. He'd said something like this, too. But how could the women have held so tightly to their power if the visions weren't real?

"We only want to know her," Rillyn said. "We mean her no harm, Alasyr. Quite the opposite."

"Ravenna, what have you done?" Alasyr glared at her through bloodshot eyes.

"Just listen to them. Please. Do you trust me?"

He lifted both his shoulder. "I don't know anymore."

The crestfallen look that replaced her smile wounded him, but he had bigger problems than Ravenna's feelings. He had to get back to Emberley *now*. Was that what this was? A means of distracting him, while they sent others off to find her?

"What's she like?" Alasyr parroted. His face was feverish. It felt like his eyes were burning from the inside. He ran his hands over his dry mouth. "She's good and kind. She's strong and brave. Yes, brave, for who else would fly to a world where they were hated and face their death, to save someone they love?"

"She sounds like someone we would love to know better," Rillyn urged gently.

"Yeah? Well, you never will. Because I choose her. I will forever choose her over the horrors we've allowed to become our means and ways here at Midnight Crest."

"What your mother did was horrible," Ryessa said, stepping forward. His once beloved aunt. The second born, whose job it had been to raise her elder sister's children over having children of her own. "It's unforgivable. No one here would come to her defense."

"Maybe you wouldn't defend her, but you would've done the same, wouldn't you? To protect Midnight Crest?"

She shook her head. "This world that has sequestered us, kept us from a life worth living? You have it all wrong about us, our asking about Emberley. We want to know her, we do. We want to know what it's like to have our blood but her freedom."

"What's it like?" Alasyr asked, incredulous.

"What if you didn't have to choose?" Rillyn asked.

"There's only one choice! Her. And she doesn't belong here, any more than I do."

Rillyn and Ryessa passed a look between them. Rillyn nodded at his daughter to speak.

"Small numbers of Ravenwoods have always met in secret, or what felt like secret. The High Priestesses have always known. They understood they had to allow us this, or risk us rising up. But when Ravenna left, others, like me, who knew something was changing, that something *should* change... we found our way to the Hall of Hours, and six became twelve, became twenty, became..." She gestured around. "What you see. We didn't always speak so openly. You know the price for treason. Adynora knows it, too, and will soon pay it. But our fear of her and what she might do to us was replaced by something else, something beautiful. An emboldening, you might say. Fears were the mortar that bound us to the foundation of this world. But all mortar eventually cracks, and so our fears have, and there are more of us, Alasyr, more of us than ones like her."

"You mean more of you than there are those like Ravenna and me."

"Why did you leave?" Ryessa asked.

"Why did I leave? You know why!"

"And yet you still don't see how you belong in *here*, and not the Courtyard of Regents, or the richly decorated but sterile and lonely apartments of your mother and grandmother. You still don't see how you're more like us than them. How many of us have left, Alasyr? And until you and Ravenna, when have any of them come back?"

"You're one of us," Rillyn said. "One of us as we would like to be, not as we were."

Alasyr again looked at Ravenna, but she was fixed on something else. "I will ask one more time. Why am I here?"

"What if you didn't have to choose?"

"You keep saying that, but there is no other way for me."

"We'd like to meet her. Your Emberley."

Alasyr laughed. "Absolutely not."

"We see a future where Ravenwoods don't have to hide from men, but are their allies. Are not the Blackwoods proof we can live amongst them, that we don't have to be banished to the cold stones of The Rookery?"

Alasyr backed away. "Rhosyn wed herself to a man of power. The heir of his Reach. She was protected by that, and nothing more. What happened to her isn't a tale we should think would apply to the rest of us, should we attempt to fly down to their world and become one with them." He turned to his sister. "Ravenna, I'm leaving."

"Alasyr!"

"Let him go," he heard Rillyn say as Alasyr stormed out of the Hall of Hours. Ravenna's heels clicked their urgency a pace behind him as she followed him out.

"Alasyr, wait!"

He spun on her halfway down the hall. "You betrayed me."

"You're not understanding."

"If something happens to her..." Alasyr swallowed a surge of emotion. "If something happens to Emberley..."

Ravenna threw her arms up. "I know why you're afraid, but nothing is going to happen to her!" Her words turned to a yell as he resumed moving down the hall. "They want to know her. Emberley represents what could be."

"She represents everything we have been taught to hate, and you know this."

"You and me. Not them."

Alasyr scoffed. "You've always thought you knew more than

everyone around you. I used to think that was because of the visions, but now I know that wasn't it. Turns out, you know very little."

"I'm leaving." She dropped her eyes to the side. "Just as you said I should. You're right. This isn't where I belong. And you were right when you said my path isn't yours, but for different reasons than you realize. But maybe meeting Emberley wasn't an accident at all, but the needed twist of fate that will bring forth a new and better future for our people."

"You sound insane."

"Is not all powerful change led by the very mad? The fearless? The brave?"

Alasyr shook his head. "What would either of us know about that?"

"They want change," she said, pointing back toward the still open doors. "They *think* they want change, and they do, they're ready for something different, but no one wants their entire world turned around. Not once it happens to them. There must still be some comforts they can look to. Not the same traditions, no, but something like them."

"Do you even hear yourself?"

"What if you really didn't have to choose?"

He snickered. "Thank you, Rillyn."

"You still don't understand his question at all, do you?"

"I have no time for their questions, or the way they speak of Emberley as if she were a rare beast to be pulled apart for their curiosity."

"They see her, and they see hope."

"They'll only ever see her in their imagination. This isn't my home anymore."

"You think home is where she is," Ravenna said. She stepped closer. "But if you love her as much as you claim to, then what will you say when Emberley herself tells you that, she, too, was called here, just as you were called back?"

"You know nothing about her."

"No, but I know you. And I'd wager it was you who encouraged her to find her wings, wasn't it? And if it was, then you know she will never again be satisfied without them."

"WHAT DO WE DO?" HAMISH ASKED, PANTING. HE PASSED HIS attention between his lord and the air... the air that was now like all the other air around it. No shimmer. No promise of a magic that, until coming here, he hadn't believed in. Not a sign that it had ever existed.

The sound of hooves caught his attention as he saw Brandyn spin his horse around and press hard in flight. The boy aimed north, disappearing in a cloud of red dust. Seeing the Blackwood kid leave for aid reminded Hamish that his best mate was dying.

He turned back toward where Khallum lay in a growing pool of dark blood mingling with the foul dirt and volcanic sand. Ryan pulled one cloth, replacing it with another, and then another, in a frantic but futile cycle to stem the flow. Hamish hadn't even seen him get hit. What had it been? Was it magic? Something flying through the wind created by the girl?

"What do we do?" Ryan repeated, wiping his brow against his forearm. "Only thing we can."

"I meant..." Hamish glanced back toward where the veil had been. "He's gone after them! He'll kill 'em both."

"Aye? And what are we to do about it? We donnae even know where they went." The cloth Ryan held was already soaked. He shook his head as he searched for another.

Hamish glanced between his two responsibilities. Khallum would want him to care about the girl and the man. They'd been his charge, and Khallum was a man of service, a man who would give his life for his charges, his men, his Reach. He would want Hamish to act on his behalf.

"There has to be some way."

"There isnae. It's done. And Lord Warwick will be, too, if we cannae help him. So come help me." Ryan set the cloth aside and seemed to consider his options. *"Help me*, Father. We have to carry him out of here."

"No, Son. We move him, he'll die."

"If he stays, he'll die!"

"Aye, and tha's how it is, in battle. We keep 'em still, until help can come, and if it doesnae, we do what we can for 'em, in their last moments."

"What?"

"I ken you wanna act, ye get that from me. But we have to keep him from thrashing about, best we can. Ye move him, what's left of his blood will belong to the Wastelands."

"He's *dying*, Father."

"Aye, I know, Son."

"Donnae just stand there!"

Hamish closed his eyes. He imagined the Guardians before him, as he often did when faced with great troubles. He supposed his vision of them was probably not a very apt one, for in his estimation they all had horns and spikes and scales, and the most forked tongues you ever saw. But he liked seeing them this way, as villains, and not as heroes, as most others in the kingdom seemed to. For a man could reason with a villain, offer him some enticement to bend his will. A hero would die upon his will before he bent even a little.

"We're out of time, Ryan."

Ryan's tears cut through the red dirt crusted on his cheeks. Hamish didn't suppose his son was especially sad to be losing the same lord that had crushed his life inside his fist, but was feeling something more convoluted, an emotion that ran deeper than men ever spoke of; that he himself had known when facing down the Medvedev in the Easterlands.

"I cannae let him die."

"Ye have so much of yer mother in ye."

"Now isnae the time for this nonsense!"

"So much. And ye donnae even see it. But it's nay seeing I need from ye right now, Son. I need ye to feel it."

"You what?" Ryan shoved the clothes aside. He tore off his own shirt and pressed it against Khallum's belly. "You *what?*"

"He willnae make it out of here alive, Ryan. Doesnae matter how hard the boy rides."

"Why are you just standing there? He's your best mate! The man ye sold me out to, for all your love of him!"

"Your mother, she could heal. Ye remember?"

Ryan sank back on his heels. "I donnae... no, I donnae remember."

"I ken she told me once that there was naught to it. Her magic. She only needed think of wha' she needed, n'er wha' she wanted. Ye ken? What she needed. Her hands did the rest."

"I'm not a healer, if that's what you're saying. Do ye have more cloth in your bag?"

"You're half her, son. Half Yanna."

"I donnae have a drop of magic in me, and ye know that!"

"What if I say ye do? Ye do, and t'was me who kept ye from it."

"How does that help us now?" Ryan nodded at Khallum. "Help him?"

"It will either help him, or it willnae. But if ye donnae try, you'll always wonder if ye couldhae saved him."

Tears dropped onto the sand. "That's not fair. You cannae put that on me."

"Aye? And yet I am. Ye have to try. Ye have to try, for there is naught else we can do for him now."

Ryan sobbed as he regarded their dying lord. "What if I cannae?"

"Then we'll know the Guardians wanted him more."

OLDWIN'S VISION DOUBLED, THEN BLURRED, WHEN HE PASSED through the wavering veil. He felt the resistance in his bones as the magic fought him, attempting to expel him like a foreign object. If he'd waited even a second longer to follow them through, the way would have been closed to him. All veils stayed open, briefly, once entered. During that time, the veil was open to all, for good or ill.

Including the very sorcerer the magic was designed to keep out.

He spotted them several paces ahead. The girl and the man. They didn't know he was there, or they'd already be upon him. They were oblivious, caught in their confusion about where they'd landed.

This was why he so loathed the young ones, who had never seen the Light, never been close enough to breathe it in, to soak up the power that was both shared and withheld, leaving all creatures longing and confused. These new ones, they fought for ideas, but understood nothing.

Instinct brought the needed magic forth to be rid of them. He quelled it as quickly as he'd summoned it. They were half-bloods. If he failed with Jamesan, he could perhaps still use one of them.

Oldwin instead reached for another magic. When it rolled forth upon his palms, it was fainter than it should have been. His regrown hand shook. He was even more tempered in here, where their magic worked against his.

But it was enough. He shot his hands forward, and both Lisbet and Ash crumpled to the ground. Oldwin staggered as the magic left him. He reached for something to right himself, but caught only air.

Never let them see you this way. As long as they fear you, you're as powerful as you ever were.

He sank to his knees. The wind passing across the field burned his lungs in its assault. The overpowering scent of the strange flora rendered him dizzy with intoxication.

"You won't be able to stay here long, Meduwyn."

Kael.

Oldwin squinted up at him. The radiating rings of sunlight blinded him. He heard the high screech of a hawk.

He was not himself, no.

But he was here.

He was *here*.

At long last. At long, long last.

. . .

ALASYR ANGLED HIMSELF UNDER THE CLOUDS AND LANDED SEVERAL steps from the bench. Time had done nothing to change any of it; not the sweep of bare land around it, nor the trees that seemed to trap sound itself. It was just as he remembered from his youth.

"How did you do that? Change your color?" Alasyr demanded. "And why are you so much *faster* now?"

"Oh, are you angry that I beat you? For once?"

"Ravenna. You've been up to something. Something foul."

"Can we just agree that there are some things best not spoken of?"

Alasyr shot his hands out to the sides. Scoffed. "You're really not going to tell me?"

"No."

"Why not?"

"Because I'm leaving, and I'd rather spend these last moments with you, saying our goodbyes. Doing it right this time." She patted the seat beside her.

Alasyr sat with reluctance. He'd been wrong when he thought this place hadn't changed. It had. Because they had, both of them. They were foreign here, specters belonging to another place, another time.

"You never used to keep things from me."

Ravenna laughed. "Oh, come now. We both know *that's* not true. You never knew about Drystan."

"Maybe I did and said nothing."

"I never told you about the worst of the training, with Mother and Grandmother. Never told you I didn't have my vision."

Alasyr hunkered forward over his knees. He linked his fingers together. "I can't keep up with you. You changed your mind so fast. Seems only hours ago you were going to be the new and much improved High Priestess."

"Alasyr, I'm going to tell you something. It may not be the answer you were after, but perhaps it'll help you understand me better. I haven't ever said these words aloud. I'm only just now coming around to them."

"All right."

"I didn't leave for a boy. I didn't leave for love, nor for fear. I left because I wanted to know what it was to be needed. Not as a man needs a woman, nothing that simple. I wanted to know my presence, in the right place, was enough to change the course of things."

"And did you? Change things?"

She smiled sadly. "I don't know. Maybe? Probably not. And then I came back. Called, like you were. And I saw a glimpse of what it would be like to be needed, and by my own people. I saw in the Hall of Hours how desperate they are for something new! But I'm not something new, am I? I can call myself whatever I please, I can pretend, but it doesn't make it true, does it?"

Alasyr shook his head. "Yet you've been trying to convince *me* to stay. Even more of the same."

"With Emberley," Ravenna said. "You heard them. I know you have your doubts, but I believe them. They see hope in her. They see that perhaps there are lives for them beyond these icy walls that have become a prison, now that their eyes are opened. And now opened, they cannot be closed again, can they?"

"I will not stake her life on that, Ravenna."

"You love her that much?"

Alasyr pulled his hands apart and shrugged as he straightened, leaning back against the bench. "I don't know what love is. Does any Ravenwood? I only know I would stop breathing if she did."

"That sounds like love to me."

"Hmm."

"Think about it, Alasyr. That's all. Our grandmother's evil is not theirs. I sense no danger in them, no deception, and I would. I would feel it." She patted her chest. "Here."

"Your heart has gotten you into enough trouble, wouldn't you say?"

"Is that not what hearts are for?"

"Where will you go?"

Ravenna cast her gaze out into the mess of fog and snow. A quick wind sent snow from the canopy of trees showering down upon them. "I spent these months searching for where I belong. But I never stopped to consider that maybe I was coming about this wrong. Why do I *need* to belong *anywhere*?" She shook her head. "I have some friends I promised to come find. I'll start by keeping that promise."

"Will you ever come back?"

Ravenna moved closer. She dropped her head on his shoulder. "What is it the men of the Northerlands like to say? Find me at the first snow?"

Alasyr laughed. He kissed the top of her head and held her, enjoying the goodbye that was stolen from him the first time.

41

I WILL SEE TO IT

Lisbet's eyes fluttered open to the shocking sight of Kian de Medvedev, followed by a splitting pain in her head that nearly knocked her out again. "What is this? Was it the veil?" Eyes again closed from the pain, she reached her hands around on the grass. "Where's Ash? Ash? Why are *you* here, Kian?"

"The veil is closed," Kian answered.

"How? How did it close? I meant to destroy it!" Lisbet groaned as a hawk squawked in her ear. Aian. "Am I imagining you?"

"And you closed it. Are you hurt?"

"I'm here, Lisbet." She felt Ash's arms encircle her from behind.

"I did? How?" she asked Kian. She leaned back into her father and pressed her eyes to the cloth of his sleeve.

"By stepping through," he said, but looked almost as confused as she did.

"Others step through veils and don't destroy them!"

"You entered it with the intention of ending it." Kian knelt before her. She saw the outline of him through her eyelids. Felt his uncommon warmth. "Here. Let me ease you."

She recoiled, but then softened as his palms encircled her face. A slow but ever-increasing peace came over her. And then the pain was gone, as if it had never existed at all. She rolled forward just as Kian did the same for Ash.

"Explain it to me," Lisbet pressed. "If it were that simple, then someone else would've done it."

"There are few with blood capable," Kian answered. He helped Ash to his feet and returned to her. Examining her. "I don't know if I got it all. How are you feeling?"

"Confused."

"Aside from that."

"Frustrated."

"Aside from *that*."

"Aside from not knowing why I'm here, how I destroyed the veil simply by stepping through it, and why Oldwin tried to kill us all in the Wastelands, I'm perfectly fine!" Lisbet quipped. She brushed the grass off her leather pants.

"I cannot understand why he didn't kill you," Kian mused. "Unless he intends to use you."

"Intended," Ash corrected. "He's dead. We killed him."

"Are you certain?" He pointed to his head. "Was that before or after he followed you through the veil and rendered you unconscious?"

"*What?*" Lisbet coughed out. "No." But Kian was incapable of this lie. And she remembered, now, coming through; her eyes taking in the sight of something familiar. Taking it in. And then, nothing except the searing pain that came before the darkness. "Ash, what did I say? Before we came through? That it was all too simple! Too easy!"

"How?" Ash moved between them. "How could he come through? Lord Warwick said it had to be one of us."

"When a veil opens, the barrier between the worlds thins, until it can close again. In that time, anyone can enter. He knew this and waited for you."

"But..." Lisbet reached for her head to silence her competing questions. "How did it close, then? You said it was because I stepped through, but then he came after me."

"You're thinking too much into it," Kian said softly. "You entered it with the intention of closing it and had the blood to match your intention. Once it closed, it closed forever." He smiled at her. "Your heart should be full just now, not confused, or frustrated. I know it's hard for you to imagine this, but this kingdom has waited hundreds of years for you. The Warwicks swore their lives to this duty, for generations. And now it is done." His smile faded. "But Oldwin is now within our world. As we feared he might."

"Kian, how did he know we would be there? He asked Lord Warwick about the half-bloods. He knew we were coming. As you said, he waited for us."

"The answer is simple. Someone told him."

"Only a few people knew we were going there."

"You were not deceived by your friends, if that's weighing on your heart."

"Who, then?"

Kian didn't answer.

"Well, where is he now?"

"In hiding. He will not stay hidden forever. The Light is closed to him, but he will search for a vulnerability. We have little time to waste."

Ash reached for his sword, but Kian shook his head. "Did that serve you the first time? You cannot kill a sorcerer with steel, not when they can heal themselves."

"Mortain was killed that way," Lisbet countered. "By Drystan's hand."

"He was distracted. Oldwin will not be so careless."

"Then how?" Ash asked.

Kian pointed toward the forest. "There's someone you should both meet."

"We have bigger problems," Lisbet said.

"Just the same." Kian turned away. Lisbet raised her brows at Ash, but he wore the same look.

Lisbet fell into pace next to Kian while Ash dropped behind.

"I thought I'd never see you again," she said.

"As did I." He took an unintentional step to the right, creating more distance between them.

"How can that be? You knew what my destiny was."

Kian kept his eyes on the path. "I was only half-right. I thought your destiny was to convince Ash to step through the veil. I did not see you coming with him."

"Are you happy I did?"

Kian's cheek twitched.

"Did you miss me?"

"Did I miss you?"

"You heard me."

"I've had..." Kian cleared his throat. A light flush rose in his cheeks. "I've had my own duties to tend to here. They afford me little time for reflection."

Lisbet grinned. "You did. You missed me."

Kian's lip curled at the corner. He shot her a sideways look that she might have overlooked if she wasn't waiting for it.

"It looks different this time," she said.

"You're in Saleen lands now, Lisbet."

"Saleen?" Lisbet paled. "But..."

"Not all of them," he answered. "Some are still here."

"Why aren't you in the Drumain lands?"

"You ask questions of me because you trust my answers. Trust in your own instincts."

"If I didn't trust in my own instincts, Kian, I wouldn't be here at all."

"It was a Warwick who guided you to the end. You still have much to learn."

"Of course I do! And why won't you teach me?"

"That is not the way."

"Kian."

But he was done speaking.

Kian led them farther down the winding path until at last they came to a small clearing, scattered with tents. "In here," he said. He held open a flap. Once Ash and Lisbet were through, he turned to go.

"Where's he going?" Ash asked.

Lisbet spun around, taking in the tent. It was very like the one she'd lived in as a prisoner of the Drumain. Far larger on the inside than the outside betrayed. Only a single bed, but Kian had said he'd only expected Ash to come through.

"Do you think the others are okay?"

"Lord Warwick and his men?"

Lisbet nodded.

"They'll be fine. Thanks to you. Do you want to talk about that?"

"Not especially." Lisbet reached for a round, purple fruit from the small woven bowl. She mimicked throwing it to Ash, but he shook his head. She shrugged and took a bite.

The tent door parted once more. Lisbet and Ash turned toward it, but Kian wasn't alone. With him was a man Lisbet didn't recognize and—

"Esmerelda?" Lisbet dropped her fruit.

Esmerelda pressed past the man she'd come in with. She rushed over to Lisbet. "Lisbet? How..." Esmerelda didn't wait for an answer. She yanked Lisbet against her in a desperate hug. "What the Guardians are you doing here?"

Esmerelda turned back toward the man she'd come in with. He wore a dark, blank stare. The color had faded from his cheeks. "Jesse? What is it?"

"Did you say Jesse?" Lisbet asked. Her uncle's words came back. *Aye, who's Jesse? Well, I ken Jesse Strong is now the husband of my Esmerelda. And if what ye say is true, then he's both Medvedev and sorcerer, and maybe it was him all along I've been waiting for.*

Jesse was Lisbet's brother.

Ash stopped breathing.

"Where are we going?" Oldwin demanded.

"Your gratitude for rescuing you. Where is that?"

"We're farther from the Light, not closer."

"You'll know when we get there."

"That isn't how this works, Medvedev. You need me more than I need you."

"Says you." Kael snorted.

"No Medvedev would solicit the aid from a Meduwyn if there was another way. As I said, we are *going the wrong way.*"

"We go there now, they kill you."

"They cannot kill me!"

Kael's laugh sealed his fate. Oldwin *would* kill him when this was done. "A hundred years ago, perhaps. But now? A bad fall would end you now."

"You would do well to watch your words around me."

"But you were not here a hundred years ago. Do you want to know why?"

"Our opportunity narrows with every moment wasted."

"They find you, our opportunity is ended."

Oldwin had entertained the whims of this fledgling far too long. He fell back and held his hand aloft. But his magic failed him before he could even release it. In response, Kael raised his own hand and rendered Oldwin frozen in place. "You're in my land now, Meduwyn. Here on my invitation. One I can rescind as quickly as it was extended. I say where we go. How we get there." Kael dropped his hand. Oldwin bowed in response to being reanimated.

He simmered from within. Any words in response would further underscore his weakened state, which he could hardly bear as it was. He wouldn't have to bear it much longer. But he hadn't come this far to take commands from a fledgling.

There was nothing else Kael could offer him now. But Oldwin had something for Kael.

Kael stopped before a tree. This one looked no different from all the others they'd passed, the many dozens, but Kael bowed his head and laid his hands against the bark. A door appeared.

"No," Oldwin said. "I will not."

"As long as you're here, they will find you. Stop you. We must wait for others to come."

Oldwin slowly backed away, one step crunching in the under-growth, then another. He didn't know if he could fight the Medvedev if it came to it, but he could defeat him in other ways.

"I did not come for your games, Medvedev."

"My desires are yours."

"Your desires cannot possibly be mine!" Another step. "My desires span thousands of years, stuck by the barbs of a struggle you have not yourself endured and therefore could never grasp beyond your futile attempts to put words to the memories and experiences of others. You're a babe, lost, playing a game belonging to your betters." Another step. "Have you even seen the Light? You're no Keeper. Your brother is the Keeper. Ahh, and you think I do not know that? That I cannot know things about you? You look so surprised that I would know anything at all about the Medvedev, but we were once brethren. Child. I know you better than you know yourself, for I knew the ones who came before, the ones who *mattered*. So, you go, then, but I will not follow."

"Others will come," Kael pressed on, but his words sounded desperate now. The cracks in his confidence were now visible, spidering as his tenuous hold on the situation frayed. "They'll come."

"More infants sounding their curdling cries of 'no fair' to the skies, you mean?"

"You'll be found if you stay. They will destroy you."

"But I have already destroyed the Saleen." Another step, then another.

"There are more than Medvedev in there, Oldwin. You know this."

He had just enough strength in him to render himself invisible once more. But he couldn't be certain it would work. Not unless he tried. If he failed, Kael would strike at this weakness. "I know of the man. Jamesan. I followed his sister and father through the veil. But they are fledglings in their knowledge of self, as you are. They know nothing, as you know nothing. If you really understood any of this in the way you claim, you would see how you can use them. Instead, you look for war. But what is war, to a magician?" Oldwin laughed. "You watched from safety as I conspired to clear these lands, to clear the way for you to even come here, with your confused intentions. So that you and your little army could demand the Light, as if it were a toy stolen by another child."

Kael's jaw trembled as he glowered. He knew he'd lost the battle of words. He prepared now to wage one of magic. "If you really knew everything, it wouldn't have taken you thousands of years to accomplish what I will do in a mere twenty."

"And yet," Oldwin said. "In the end, you still needed me."

Kael's eyes glowed.

Now.

It had to be now.

With what strength remained to him, Oldwin lifted his palms to the side and willed himself unseen.

Jesse gathered with his father and sister around the small bonfire Kian and the others had lit. They each cradled the clay bowls in their palms, but none had enjoyed more than a few spoonfuls. He kept looking for Esmeralda, but Kian had taken her away to give the three of them some time alone. *How generous,* Jesse thought, *coming from the same man who will take it all away tomorrow.*

Jesse didn't want to be alone with them. There were expectations now, of the right words, of the weaving together of lives, and stories, and fates. These were all the things he'd never been good at. And this man, Ash, well, he was a bit like looking into a mirror, wasn't he? Though his eyes were light gray, and Jesse's a mossy green, they were the same in all other ways. The cut of their cheekbones, carved from the same artist. Even Ash's smile was familiar.

Jesse's stomach was in knots. This was his father, and also not his father. And Lisbet... how she reminded him of his sister, Gemma. There was no blood shared between his late sister and Lisbet Dereham, but could it really be coincidence that they were so alike? When she talked, when she laughed. It was almost painful to behold, but instead of pain, he felt he was being returned something that had been cruelly stolen.

And she'd been with Ryan before she arrived here. Had he taken to her, too, or was Jesse only imagining these things, his mind working around a way to accept this family that was now his.

"I was sorry to hear about your father. That is, Lord Dereham," Jesse said. He had to say something. Anything was better than the silence of the unsaid.

Lisbet relaxed. She nodded, tipping her mug of wine his way. "You'll come around to the idea of having two fathers one day, Jesse. But know that it is no betrayal of Steward Strong if you and Ash one day form a bond."

"Lisbet, go easy. He must be overwhelmed," Ash said, but he may as well have been speaking of himself. His eyes were wild as he tried and failed to stop watching and evaluating Jesse in the same way Jesse had been watching and evaluating him.

"Ken we all are," Jesse said. "Not easy spending your life knowing you're one thing, finding out you're another."

Ash sounded relieved as he laughed. Some of the tension had dissipated. "You could say it again and again, and there'd be no less truth to it."

Jesse dropped his eyes to his bowl. "And I, well... I was sorry to hear about Drystan, too. I remember him. He was a good lad."

Lisbet reached for her braid. He'd noticed her toying with it during their introductions. "I'm sorry you never got to know him."

"We'll try to make up for that, the three of us, yeah?" Ash added.

Jesse tried to smile. He couldn't say that there'd never be a chance for that; that tomorrow he'd step through the veil and never return.

Thinking of what awaited him caused him to look for Esmerelda again. This time when he looked her way, he spotted her, looking back at him. As their eyes locked, she rolled her shoulders back, pretending to appear detached from the emotions she'd showed during the night. He flushed to think of it. How had he waited this long to love her so? But there was no good answer to this, for his love for his brother had come first. There was no other time or place in this world where Jesse could have loved her as wholly as he did now.

There was a saying that Strong men were named aptly. But Jesse was no Strong man. He'd been reared by one, but he was a Rhiagain in blood, a Meduwyn, a Medvedev, and knowing all these things didn't mean he knew himself any better, but rather, less. What he knew now was confined to how he felt about her; about what it would mean to leave her behind.

"Your mother," Ash started. "Kian told me that her promise was ended."

Jesse nodded. "Some years back."

"I know this seems to be all we can say to one another tonight, but I am sorry to hear it. I mean that."

"She never told me about you. My father, Hamish, he never knew about you, either."

"I didn't know she was with child when I left her, or I wouldn't have left. No matter how much I missed Gretchen, I would not have left Yanna to carry that alone. I only wish she would've sent for me. I would've come back. I would."

"I dinnae think it was for your sake she said nothing." Now Jesse did smile. "Hamish would've killed ye."

"And then you would've never abandoned your duties in Rushwood to pine after my mother, which means I would've never been born," Lisbet pointed out. "Nor Drystan. And do you have other children we should know about? They seem to pop up like springtide flowers."

"Amusing," Ash said drily.

"It was a fair question."

"Yseult always said that we're where we need to be. I always thought it was horseshit." Ash laughed. "But maybe sometimes it's not."

"Hmm," Jesse agreed. "How was my mother when you knew her?"

Ash blew through pursed lips. "Well, I knew her for such a short time. A couple of months. But she was easy to love, Yanna. She made it so simple to forget my worries, even if I knew it could never last. She did all right, then, with your father?"

"Aye, well, there are only so many dyes for hair, and she was the only one in the Reach with a pet fox. I ken it was the worst kept secret in the Southerlands, though Ryan and I didnae know a thing until just before she died."

Ash laughed. "And no one cared your father had wed a Medvedev?"

"If they knew, they said nothing. The men in the Southerlands, we look after each other. My father's loyalty is his currency, and he offers it freely to others. This earns him theirs."

"I saw your brother in the Wastelands. He's a fine young man."

"Lord Warwick was wrong for making him return there," Lisbet said. "I think he's remembering things. He shouldn't have had to go there a second time."

"What do you mean, remembering?" Jesse asked.

Kian appeared at the far end of the bonfire. "I want to show you all something before the night is ended. Will you come with me?"

Jesse hung on the promise of Lisbet's answer. Perhaps she was mistaken. Ryan would never have treated Esmerelda as he had, if his memory had returned.

Ash was the first to stand. "It doesn't seem any of us will be eating much tonight, so why not?"

Kian had already turned and departed. Ash jogged to keep up, but Jesse hung back with Lisbet, gathering their bowls and mugs into the neat piles. "Do you really think he's remembering?"

"Not about Esmeralda, if that's what got you worried."

"I only want what's best for her."

Lisbet patted his arm. "Seems to me that's what you did, what was best for her. Her child has a father, and she seems happy enough. Too late for regrets now, Jesse. What's done is done."

But it wasn't regret Jesse felt. It was a renewed sense of hope that he'd thought was lost to him since Kian's startling reveal. He could put aside his own grief of being separated from Esmeralda if he knew someone else, someone who had loved her as much as he did, might be waiting.

"What's going through your mind?"

He smirked. "Eh. I'm always looking ahead, thinking of what's coming."

"Nah, it's more than that. I can sense it. You're afraid." They started in the direction Kian and Ash had gone.

"Did Kian tell ye why I'm here?"

"I didn't know you would be. I'd *hoped* our paths might cross, but I didn't know how to make it happen. And then, here you are! So, I don't know if I believe in fate, but if I did, I'd say that's why you're here to meet us."

He stopped in the path. "Lisbet. They say I'm the one who has to do it. Who has to close the way to the Light."

"Oh!" She shook her head, smiling. "There's nothing to be afraid of with that. Ash and I closed the one that brought us here from the Wastelands. It was nothing at all. I don't even remember doing anything, only arriving, and then... Oldwin." Her smile died.

"Esmerelda has crossed that creature's path. If he's here, we're not safe."

"Kian says we're protected as long as we stay within this barrier he created for us. He seems confident it will hold. Just don't wander off into the forest alone, yeah?"

"It willnae need to hold much longer. Oldwin will be destroyed when I pass through."

"But that's a good thing."

"And so will the veils. All of them. And that means there willnae be one left for my return."

Lisbet went still. Her thoughts came to a halt. "No. That can't be. Kian wouldn't ask that of you."

"But he has. And so have Isdemus and Lysanor."

"There has to be another way." She choked out a nervous laugh. "No, that can't be right. That can't be what he really means."

"Kian was more than clear in his meaning. And our grandfather, Isdemus, he was the one who pointed me here. He did it, knowing what I'd have to do. To protect this kingdom, and Esmerelda, and Gemma, and Ryan, and my father, and you and Ash and *everyone*, I have no other choice." The words came out in a single, desperate breath.

"No," she said. "No. We'll find another way."

"There's no time."

"I don't care. We'll find one. I've lost two brothers now. I'll not lose another, not when I've only just met him."

Jesse bowed his head. "I wish it were different, Lisbet. I would like to know you."

"And you will." The fire in her eyes cooled his blood. "You will. If no one else will find a way, I'll see to it."

"Lisbet! Jesse! You coming?"

"You mark my words, Jesse. You're not going through that veil unless we can find a way for you to come back."

KIAN CALLED IT A TEMPLE, BUT ASH HAD SEEN TEMPLES BEFORE. Mainly in the Easterlands, where the men of the Reach saw fit to enshrine everything.

This temple was constructed only from that which they had in their own forests. There was no marble or hard stone but woven wooden steps, climbing unevenly up toward the small enclosure. The pillars were twined with colorful leaves that snaked up and then back down again, spiraling into the earth.

Ash stumbled through the handful of steps. There'd been no smoothing down, no finer carpentry here. They paid their honor through modesty. Jesse and Lisbet managed the last step together and then settled in on either side of him. Once acknowledged, he hardly noticed them anymore, for his attentions weren't pulled but yanked forth, consumed by the call of what Kian kept calling the Light. Jesse and Lisbet felt it too. He sensed their awe radiating.

"The veil grows thin. Little separates our world, or any world, from The Hidden Kingdom anymore. We have never in our history been more on the edge of such peril."

"I'm not doing it now," Jesse said. He backed up a step, as if the Light might reach through the veil and pull him through. "I'll have one more night with my wife. I'm not asking."

"Tomorrow is later than tonight. Tomorrow brings us closer to the end, to more uncertainty. Yet it is *your* choice. I have said that from the beginning."

"His choice to do what, exactly?" Ash asked. He looked between Kian and Jesse. "To do what?"

Jesse's chest rose as he inhaled through his nose.

"What does he have to do, Kian?"

"He doesn't *have* to do anything. He's always had a choice."

"Tell me what's going on here," he demanded, still looking at Jesse, whose eyes were closed. "Jesse? What has he asked of you?"

"Kian says he has to go through," Lisbet shot back. Her nose was scrunched, her eyes narrowed. "Except he has no return for him if he does, right, Kian?"

"Though it is unfortunate, yes."

"No return?" Ash repeated. "What does that mean, no return?"

"Aye, I ken it means exactly as it sounds," Jesse spat.

"I don't believe it," Lisbet said. Her braid swung as she shook her head. "I don't believe our entire future, the future of this kingdom, rests only upon Jesse."

"I wish it were not so, but we are out of time," Kian said. "He is here for only one reason."

"*You* are out of time. *I* still have until sunrise to find another way." She watched Jesse as he spoke, but he only had eyes for the veil.

Ash laid his palm at the center of Jesse's back. His fingers trembled. "Set it down, for now. It does no good, thinking about it."

"We'll find a way," Lisbet insisted. "There is another way. There must be."

"We'll find it. We'll find it," Ash said. *For I will not lose another son when I have only just found him.*

Jesse backed away and then spun around, crashing into Ash before he found his path. He fled down the steps and ran.

Ash started after him, but Lisbet grabbed his arm. "There's only one thing we can do for him." She turned her dark eyes on Kian. "And it will be more than you tried to do, won't it?"

Ash heaved out a hard breath.

The visions.

The ones he'd kept from Lisbet, claiming not to understand them.

He thought maybe he understood them now.

Jesse and Esmerelda met Ravenna in the Forest of All, just beyond where the veil released them back into the Hinterlands. And they now knew, when they had passed into Saleen lands, they were no longer in the Hinterlands at all. There was relief in stepping back through that same veil, to a world more familiar.

Jesse had a sense Ravenna was near. When he told Esmerelda, she was eager to come greet Ravenna with him. In the time he'd been separated from them, they'd evolved from enemies to sisters.

"You just appeared from nowhere!" Ravenna exclaimed. "That's some trick."

"That's the way, over here," Jesse said as he regarded the changes that had come over her in the short time since he'd seen her last. Every time he saw Ravenna Ravenwood, she was someone new. Like looking upon the same face, worn by different people.

"You came," Esmerelda whispered.

Ravenna held her hands out. Esmeralda took them. They stayed this way, watching each other in silent adoration, until Ravenna finally said, "I promised you I would, didn't I?"

"I knew you would. Only I didn't expect to see you so soon." Esmerelda shook her head. "Did you find what you were looking for?"

Ravenna nodded. She brought Esmerelda's hands to her mouth and kissed them both. "I did. And you?"

Esmerelda's face fell.

"What is it, Esme?"

"Not out here," Jesse said. A fresh wave of relief came over him. It was as if the Guardians conspired to ease his heart on the matter of his wife and kindle his courage for tomorrow. Ravenna was here now. She'd help Esmerelda through what she must endure on the morrow, and take her to the man who would see after her, when it was done.

There was guilt, too, at thinking of Esmerelda in this way, when he knew better than to assume she needed any of it. But it wasn't for Esmerelda that he felt this relief. Selfishly, it was for him.

Ravenna pointed behind him with a sideways grin. "You want me to go in there?" She wagged her finger. "Wherever *there* is. I can't even see it."

"Aye, unless ye intend to make camp out here, all by yourself."

"Come," Esmerelda said, practically giddy. How nice it was to see her happy again. She'd again taken Ravenna's hands in hers. "Oh, I'm so glad you're here."

"As am I." Ravenna kissed her. She glanced at Jesse as her lips connected with the soft flesh of Esmerelda's flushed cheek. Then he understood. She already knew. She knew and would make him say it anyway, as she had before when he'd needed her guidance.

"Why did you come?" he asked.

"Well, I promised Esmerelda at her wedding, and I couldn't break such a promise."

"But why here? Why did you come here?"

Ravenna shook her head. "Jesse. You know why. And since it seems we are short on time, let us not squander it."

42

A FIGHTING CHANCE

Brandyn navigated without sight. The mingled sweat and filth kicking up from his hard ride burned his eyes, rendering him effectively blind. Beside him, Gilgowan pushed just as hard. He hoped the captain general knew where to go, because if it was up to Brandyn, the cause was lost. He couldn't make heads or feet of his senses. It seemed he'd been riding his whole life.

Behind them rode the remaining stragglers of the Seventeenth Artifact of the Knights of Duncarrow. They'd been steps from freedom when Brandyn—accompanied by Gilgowan, who he'd found lingering just beyond the canyon, preparing to fall on his sword—found them near the south entrance to Camp Atonement. Brandyn had first given over the remaining food in his satchel and then rolled right into his pitch, listing out the riches and titles he could offer them, but they stopped him before he could finish. They required no payment for their honor. They would rise to the aid of Lord Warwick, because they were soldiers, and soldiers left no man behind.

"How much longer?" he called out to Gilgowan. "I can't see anything in this wind."

"Not much." He barely heard the response over the crash of hooves.

"What's not much?"

"You'll recognize it soon enough."

Brandyn couldn't stop thinking about the knights. Would he be willing to give up his life for someone he didn't know? Was that not one of the core tenants of being a soldier, to serve something greater than yourself? And in that way, was being a lord really so different? His mind ran circles around these thoughts, where he would alternately reassure himself that all he'd done on behalf of the Reach had been for the goal of service, but also how true it was that vengeance had fueled his war with the Easterlands. A hatred for those who had taken his father from him, who had dared spread their filthy hands over the land belonging to his mother. Even playing the benevolent lord for the long-suffering tradesmen in Newcarrow had been less about coming to their aid and more about showing others he wasn't a boy any longer and could lead without hanging on his mother's dresses.

He was ashamed of this pride he'd worn like a banner. His mother had sent him here to become a lord, but that had never been his passion, only his birthright. He could no more see himself holding court upon his mother's golden throne than returning to the Sepulchre to finish his training. And *that* revelation was the most terrifying of all. Was this something all men endured on the verge of becoming one? Or was this truly a call elsewhere, to the unknown of something entirely new?

Brandyn closed his mouth tight and held his breath as they entered the narrow canyon. Gilgowan was right. He was now well acquainted with their bearings. He hardly remembered riding through here to go find the captain general, but his memory of passing through it hours before would never leave him. Nor would the terrible vision he'd had here.

Gilgowan launched into a gallop when he cleared the pass. Brandyn had no desire to be alone in there for even the final few moments it took to catch up. He tapped his palm against his thigh in anticipation of the freedom beckoning ahead.

When at last he broke into the open, he bolted after the captain general. He didn't have to ride far from here. He came to a shuddering halt just before his uncle, kicking up a fair amount of dust.

Khallum stood upright, braced against a boulder on one side and Hamish on the other. He was *standing*. Brandyn could hardly believe it. He jumped from his horse.

"How are you doing?" he asked. "When I left..."

Khallum nodded to his left, where Ryan was crouched against the other boulder, face buried in the underside of his forearms.

"I don't understand," Brandyn said.

Khallum cried out and winced, almost bowling over before Gilgowan slipped under his other arm, his full weight now borne by both men. His uncle might be standing, but he wasn't well.

"Was Ryan, got him this far," Hamish said. His eyes were ringed with red. "Now, it's for us to get him the rest of the way." He offered Brandyn a slow, reverent nod. "Ye did right bringing these men here. I ken we'll need every last one, even if they are just skin and bones."

Brandyn glanced down at Ryan. "You healed him?"

"I donnae know what I did." He waved without looking up. "He isnae leaving here on his feet, though, I know that."

"It'll be enough," Hamish insisted. "'Cos it has to be."

Khallum dropped to his knees before the men could stop the fall.

"Men of the Seventeenth Artifact!" Gilgowan cried out. "We returned to deliver Lord Warwick of this wretched place, and so we will. Take the bedroll we lifted from Camp Atonement and fashion it into a proper gurney. He can't sit atop a horse. We've no time to squander."

The men, once on the verge of death and now animated into new life, flew into action at their general's command.

Brandyn approached his uncle as Hamish worked to right him again. "We'll get you out of here, Uncle. Get you back to Aunt Gwyn, and the boys, and Esme. I swear it."

Khallum spat a wad of blood into the dirt. His teeth were covered in it when he grinned. "If I had more time to train ye proper, first thing I would've taught ye was to never make a promise beyond the ones ye can keep."

"The kingdom *needs* you."

"Aye, once, perhaps. But it was the young ones who had the courage to stand against what they knew to be wrong. Even the great Khallum Warwick wouldnae have stopped the king from taking his own daughter. Every one of those lasses took their fate into their own hands, and most are better for it. The kingdom is better for it."

Brandyn shot a glance at Hamish. "You give him the last of your flask or something?"

Hamish shrugged, as confused as Brandyn was.

"Well, if you died, *I'd* not be better for it. So let's get you home and get a proper healer to lay hands on you."

"Is it really done, then?" Khallum's eyes were trained on something behind him.

Brandyn turned around. "The veil, you mean?"

"It's truly closed?"

Brandyn nodded. "It seems to be. But Oldwin made it through, in the end. Went in after them. We have to hope the Guardians are on their side. It's out of our hands now."

Khallum grimaced as a fresh pain seized him. The wind howled as it bounced off the canyon walls. It sounded like a scream.

"We can't wait anymore. We have to get him out of here now," Brandyn said to Hamish. "Gurney or no."

"Why wouldn't he tell me where the veil went? How can I defend them if I donnae know where they are?" Khallum murmured.

Hamish eased him back down to the canyon floor. "Easy does it, my lord. Save your piss and fire for when ye have the coal to fuel it, aye?"

Brandyn knelt by Ryan. "What did you do, exactly?"

Ryan shrugged.

"Will he live?"

"His wound is closed, but I ken there's more going on." He pointed at his belly. "On the inside."

"Come on." Brandyn held his hand out. "Let's help the knights, so we can give him a fighting chance."

Gabi should look at her mother. It was the right thing to do, the proper thing. She had to do it. Asherley would chide her for it later when this had passed, for not possessing the mettle to face the hard stuff. One of her favorite things to say was that toughness was wrongly ascribed to men, for it was the women who had to not only endure but persist. The true business of a lady was to do what the men couldn't.

Each time she'd angle her eyes a little too far to the left, taking in the edges of her mother's sallow flesh and sunken eyes, she knew she wasn't made of the same stuff as her mother. Or Emberley, who her mother undoubtedly wished was the one sitting before her now.

"Gabrianna," her mother croaked. "My sweet one."

"Mother." Gabi's voice shook. She couldn't make herself look down when Asherley wrapped her bony fingers over the top of her hand, which she'd tried to bury into the soft velvet of the bedding. She lacked the courage to face seeing with her eyes what her flesh felt and her heart knew. That this was Hollyn all over again.

That her mother was dying.

"You're afraid," Asherley said. "I did not raise you to be afraid."

"If I'm afraid it's because I don't understand."

"What don't you understand?"

"You were *fine* when you arrived here. You were fine! I saw you, you looked as you always have, and now—"

"I wasn't fine, Gabi, though I understand how troubling it has been for you to see me decline so quickly. It hasn't been easy for me to know I have so little time to conclude what remains of my business as Lady of the Rush."

Gabi looked up with a start. Her mother's gaunt face was a greater shock than she was ready for. She struggled with her words. "You're giving up?"

"It's not giving up, Gabi, when you were already defeated."

"You aren't defeated! Not as long as you still draw breath."

"I'm defeated by something that has no cure."

Gabi reared back. "But there is a cure! I heard Blackfen talking to the Grand Minister."

Asherley tried to laugh. Her body trembled at the effort. "Then you heard them say only a sorcerer can cure me, and where, my dearest, might we find one of those? One that would not kill me for my efforts."

"What about Joran's Life Vision?"

"What about it?" Asherley coughed into a bloodied wad of silk. "My darling, Joran has served us well. But there is none who will help. There is no grand voyage for me to take, where relief awaits me at the end. The end is merely the end." Asherley squeezed her hand. "I watched my own mother die a terrible death. I wouldn't have wished this upon you, but I didn't raise children incapable of facing that which would break others, did I?"

Gabi shook her head. She licked away the tears that had caught at the edges of her lips on their way down.

"Right, so we agree. There will be no more talk of it." Asherley's cracked lips curved into a grin. "I called you here for a reason, you know."

"Oh?"

"Blackfen and Tyndall will prepare you for what comes next."

"For what comes next?"

"Yes. When I'm gone."

"What?"

"When you become our Lady of the Rush. The Lady of the Westerlands. I won't be here to show you how it's done. But you can trust them, my dear. And the rest of my counsel. It will be your choice, but I hope you choose to keep them, for they will steer you true, always."

"Mother." Gabi wiped away her tears. "I'm not Ember. It's me, Gabrianna."

"Don't condescend to me, Gabi. I know who you are. I'm not delirious. Just as I know my Emberley isn't coming home to me. Her fate is set, and it doesn't intersect with ours. Nor does Brandyn's, though I was slower to see that. Slower to understand."

"Why? Why would he not return? He's supposed to be our lord! Isn't that why you sent him away?" Gabi's desperation rose in her chest. She could hardly breathe. "Why are you saying these things?"

"I need to know you'll be ready."

"Mother!"

"I need to *know*. And if you are not, that you will take the counsel from those who would help you get there."

"No," Gabi said. "No! Mother! You cannot mean me! I'm not the strong one. I'm not the pretty one, nor the wise one. I'm not—"

"Gabrianna Blackwood, you are only not these things if you say you are not. I'm not your father. I'll not indulge your cataloguing of weaknesses. Nor your need for comparison to siblings who are all very different from you, in their own ways, as you are different from them. You are no less the daughter of a lady, and a lord. You have no less Blackwood or Warwick blood. You are the vines that tie the Westerlands together, and the salt and sand poised to protect them. You are more than I could have ever asked for, and you will lead this Reach, not if, but when. That when is upon us now. This very day, even."

"Don't say that." Gabi recoiled at her mother's attempt to soothe her. "How can you say this? How can you just surrender? You say you taught us not to be afraid, but you also taught us to fight! To never lie down, for anyone or anything."

Asherley reached beside the bed for the small bell. She rang it. Two guards opened the door from the outside.

"And now you're dismissing me, after you've just destroyed my heart?"

"I haven't the strength to spar with you, my sweet one. Go now. Think on my words, for I will rest easier if I know your heart has come around to what you must do before I've spent the last of my promise."

Arturo spun just in time to catch Gabi before she ran herself straight off the balcony.

"Whoa there, Lady Gabrianna. Did you forget the stonesmiths were doing repairs? You almost went over."

"Maybe I'd like to go over!" she cried, thrashing in his arms. He turned her and saw her face splotched with dark red. "Gabi, what's wrong? Is it your mother?"

"Is it not always my mother? The mother who sent us all away. Who let Hollyn die, when she was *in* Duncarrow, in reach of a cure, but was more inclined toward her machinations. Who let Brandyn almost destroy our Reach because she has always loved Emberley the best of all!"

Arturo didn't relent. He held her tight against him until she relaxed. It was the same trick he used with his mare, and people were not so different. When her breathing had slowed, he released her. "Then she told you."

"That she's dying? And that it will be me who has to pick up all the shattered pieces she's left behind? Because *everyone* has left me. Everyone I've ever loved is *gone*."

"Do you not think she would change the course of this, if she had the power?"

"She knows what she needs to do, she just won't do it!"

Arturo sighed. "Oldwin is no longer even in Duncarrow, they say. And even if he was, she made a proper fool of him in front of the entire kingdom when she slipped away in the night."

Gabi crossed her arms. She seemed to draw inward. "Joran saw a way for her to live. He wouldn't have said anything of the sort if it wasn't true. He's an old fool, but he has no deceit in him."

Arturo was aware of Gabrianna's belief that she was less essential than the other children of Lady Asherley, but he saw so much of her mother in her now that it sent a chill down his spine.

"Nothing is so simple, though, is it?"

"But it is!" she insisted. "You know what I think? I think she doesn't *want* to be healed. I think she misses Father that much that she wants to return to him. Well, we all do! But we have responsibilities here, don't we?"

"Gabrianna," he said. "You're the empath. Did you not feel her agony when she gave you your charge?"

Gabi turned away. Arturo threw a look over his shoulder to the door of the room from which he'd emerged just before Gabi had come flying down the hall. Joran and Tyndall were still in there. He should be, too, but he'd left to check on Lady Blackwood.

"Come, Gabi. You'll be our lady soon. You should be a part of this. You have a right."

Her eyes narrowed. "A part of what?"

"You aren't the only one who still believes your mother can be saved."

THEY WEREN'T LISTENING.

They never listened. Any of them. They heard what they wanted, weaving his words into the narrative best suited to pairing with theirs. Lady Asherley was different. She wasn't like these others, these men who were fascinated by magic but had no respect for it. She pushed, but always knew when she had gone too far. She recognized when her desire for clarity in vision had become wish fulfillment instead.

These men, though, these men were desperate. They were good men. Asherley couldn't have better ones to serve her. But they weren't listening.

"She was meant to leave when she arrived. Once Brandyn was on his way," Joran managed to say, in a rare break of the heated verbal exchange passing across the table.

"Well, she didn't. Did she?" Tyndall challenged. "Or we wouldn't be conspiring over candles and stale wine without her."

Joran felt the Grand Minister's loathing like quills from a spined possum. He expected it; was used to it. It no longer bothered him. Few things did these days. Even so...

His walking stick tapped against the table. The tremor in his hands was worse now. He set it aside before Arturo murdered him with that glare.

"Even then what, Enchanter?"

"What I did not tell Lady Asherley, then..." Joran coughed into his sleeve. Was he really going to tell these men what he wouldn't tell his own mistress? If he did, then he could no longer claim to have served her with immutable loyalty.

"Tell us, Joran," Gabi pleaded in her soft, pliant voice. It was for *her* that he would say what he was about to say. He would serve her as he had served her mother, though his time was coming, was near ending, and he didn't think he'd be serving her for very long.

"I saw many outcomes to your mother's illness, my lady. She did not recover in most of them."

Gabi's lower lip trembled. "Why would you have given her hope, then?"

"Your mother surrendered her freedom, and will soon surrender her life, for her children. Lady Emberley now has a life ahead of her, but she would not have if your mother had stayed in Wulfsgate, for her obsession would have pulled your sister under. Lord Brandyn, too, has a path ahead of him, one that might never bring him home to you. And you, Lady Gabi, your future here is what I saw, in almost every outcome. But none of this could have been so had she not returned. And so I said what I needed to bring her home." He coughed again. "I did not lie to her. I only showed her a less likely ending to stir her to act."

"Less likely doesn't mean impossible," Gabi said.

Arturo leaned over the table. "Yes, but you also said she could travel somewhere, for aid. Let us come back to that."

"She cannot travel anywhere now, can she?"

"Why does it have to be her? Why not one of us?"

"Who else could convince a sorcerer to proffer his aid?"

Arturo pointed to his longbow against the wall. "I can be quite persuasive when required, Enchanter."

"You said Oldwin would kill her, though," Gabi charged. "You speak from both sides of your mouth, Enchanter."

"Who said I was talking about Oldwin?"

"You keep too much to yourself," Arturo warned. "Too much."

Joran sagged in his chair. He would need to lie down soon. His back could hardly support his weight anymore. Everything ached, from the crown of his head to the tips of his toes.

When he responded, it was to Gabi he directed his words. "There are others like old Oldwin. He is not the only one who can help your mother."

A new hope rose into the flush of Gabi's cheeks, her expectant eyes. He almost hated himself for it. He had no right to give it to her. He should have crushed it underfoot before it took shape.

"Where?"

"The Hinterlands."

"Of course," Tyndall said with a roll of his eyes. "Of course they would be in the one place we cannot get to in this kingdom. How convenient."

Arturo pushed off from the table. "Oh, no? Watch me."

"I'm coming with you," Gabi said. She jumped to her feet, smoothing her dress down, affecting her best attempt at feigned bravery. "I'm coming."

"No, my lady. That is not what your mother would have wanted. Your place is here."

"Wait, Turo, you're not seriously thinking of going there? You cannot enter those lands," Tyndall countered.

"I can try."

"No, I mean..." Tyndall seemed to wrestle with himself. "You could walk those lands the rest of your life and still never cross paths with a single Medvedev."

Gabi let out a small, excited gasp. "I remember now. It was as if we had crossed some threshold. Some..."

"Veil," Tyndall finished for her. "You step through a veil to enter Drumain lands. Saleen lands. Mayke lands. Asgill lands. Not one are in the Hinterlands at all. They don't exist in our world."

"And how would you know about the veils, Minister?" Joran challenged. He still had some fire in him yet. Could still spar with the young ones.

"Enough to know we can't enter them without invitation."

"Then I will demand one," Arturo said.

"Yes? Then I wish you fair tidings." Shaking, Joran moved to his feet. Gabi rushed to his side to help him, but he gently chided her. When the day at last arrived that he could no longer help himself to his feet, that he must be aided by one he once helped deliver to this world, he would know with certainty his service was ended.

"That's all. That's all you have to say?" Arturo challenged.

"What more is there? Your mind is made. Gabrianna and I will stay with Lady Blackwood until the end."

"There won't be an end," Arturo contested, "not for many years."

"Turo, please. What will our lady think if you're not there when she asks for you?" Tyndall pleaded.

He turned his palms up. "Stay with me, or pray over her. Do what you feel is right, Rhy. I'll think no less of you. But I'll never rest another night in my life if I knew there was a way, and I was too much of a coward to take it."

When Tyndall hesitated, Arturo grabbed his longbow and left.

"He's a hotheaded fool. Will get himself killed, acting like that," Joran said. "If he truly meant to serve his lady, he would serve her daughter, as were her wishes. Not abandon Gabi when she most needs his counsel."

"He's a man of great *honor*," Tyndall hissed. "And if he gets himself killed, his blood will be a stain upon your legacy, for it was you, Enchanter, who sent him on this fool's errand. You, the wise one who didn't even have the good sense to lie when it mattered."

Tyndall spun, his minister's robe whirling behind him as he departed behind his lover.

"Is it really so dangerous?" Gabi asked Joran. "The Medvedev were kind to us once they knew we meant them no harm."

"It isn't the Medvedev he need fear."

"Then who?"

"The worst kind of danger, Lady Gabi, is the one we cannot foresee."

43

AWAKEN THE LION

Alasyr didn't know how much time had passed. He'd been sitting on the same bench since Ravenna had flown off.

He liked it here. He could stay here forever. Ember and Marsh waited for him, though. That was, if they hadn't already tried to make their way down the mountain. They'd likely given up on him when he didn't return promptly. They were right about him all along, they'd say, glad to be well rid of him.

This is your grandmother speaking. Her influence. She's always been in your mind, twisting your thoughts to cause you to believe your worth was limited to one thing alone.

She would die soon. Her execution was set. For all his resentment of her, all the hurt she'd caused, he didn't want to be here to see it carried out. It seemed arcane to ascribe a death sentence, now, when the other Ravenwoods looked to a future that was supposed to be different, not more of the same.

He didn't see the raven descend through the trees. It wasn't until his grandfather, Rillyn, unfolded before him that Alasyr realized he wasn't alone anymore.

"How did you know to find me here?"

"You knew about this place because Varinya and Argentyn told you, yes?"

Alasyr nodded.

"And I told them, years past, just as my mother and father told me when I was around your age. I saw it as the one place I could go to be someone else for even a little while. Adynora rarely joined me, even when we were very young. She'd become anxious if she was away from The Rookery too long, as if her very health and happiness were determined by her proximity to the power at the center of Midnight Crest."

"Isn't it that way for most High Priestesses?"

"Not as much as it was for her. She didn't learn her unshakable zealousness from our mother. Maybe she was born with it."

"You're really going to let them put her to death? Your own wife and sister?"

Rillyn joined him on the bench. "You think we're no better than she is, don't you?"

"I think if it's change you're after, then change."

Rillyn relaxed some. "I don't think, in the end, that she'll die at their hands. They'll see it isn't the way forward, after all. As you said, to change, we must change."

"It isn't up to you?"

"The others look to me as an elder, whose wisdom can act as a guide through this. But I'm not their High Priest anymore. I'm not their leader. I'm not the one who can take us forth into the new era."

Alasyr laughed. He dropped his hands to his knees as he bent forward. "You're implying me again. Me and Ember."

"I know your hesitations. I would have them, too, if I were you."

"They're more than hesitations. What happens when she's no longer so novel to them? When they tire of her? When they, again, want change, and she doesn't fit into what that looks like?"

"You think they want it all to change?" Rillyn shook his head. He spread his arms over the back of the bench. "No matter what they might say, Alasyr, we both know why the idea of the High Priestess, the all-powerful, has been tolerated for as long as it has. There is comfort in knowing what will be. What is. They don't want to tear The Rookery down stone by stone. It's their home, the only one they've known. They only want access to the parts that have been closed to them."

Alasyr shrugged. "Ravenna gave me the same speech. You don't need me for that."

"They see in your Ember a sign of hope. A glimmer of what might be."

"You keep saying that, but not why I should believe it."

"What if I told you there were a hundred of us, at least, who would swear the blood vow to never lay hands upon her? More than that, to protect her should others try?"

Alasyr scoffed. "We don't swear blood oaths in Midnight Crest. Not anymore. Too many died for it."

"Yes, because they're life binding. It isn't only their own lives bound to the vow, but all others who joined in making it. If any of us were to break the vow, any of us who took it, we would all suffer the same death. We would fall to ash."

"You expect me to believe they would all risk their lives like that?" Alasyr laughed, shaking his head. "For a half-blood."

"What do you call her when you hold her against your chest? Not that, I assume."

Alasyr turned his head away. "Ember. Just Ember."

"Your mother was beloved, Alasyr, not for who fate decided she should be, but because she was the first in a very long line of priest-esses to confront the sacred ways. She paid with her life. They would see her son continue this work."

"My mother is not a martyr. Let's not rewrite history, Rillyn. She shouldn't have been murdered, but she wasn't innocent."

"When have the boundaries of good and evil ever been clearly drawn?"

"Why, why does it have to be me?"

"It doesn't. But do you really want to leave this world behind, or is it the lies you want to push into the past?" Before Alasyr could answer, Rillyn pressed on. "You care for Emberley. You know what she can do now, but so does she, and she'll never be content to be so far from the source of our magic again. Has she said this to you? For if she hasn't, it doesn't mean that she hasn't thought about it. It will never be far from her thoughts."

"It's more than her now," Alasyr said. He couldn't believe he was entertaining this, but Rillyn's words sank into the holes of his heart that he hadn't yet learned to fill in any other way. They played at his fears, but also his hopes. Ones he didn't even know he had. "A man, a boy."

"Marsh, yes?"

Alasyr didn't bother asking how he knew. He nodded.

"Would he come?"

"Would he come? You did hear me when I said he's a man?"

"Do you love him, too?" There was no cleverness in the question. Rillyn watched him closely for his answer.

Alistair snorted. "Love. You and Ravenna throw that word around as if any of us have ever understood the meaning."

"All right, but do you?"

"He won't leave Ember. So how I feel has no bearing here."

"But would *you* leave *him*?"

Alasyr had no answer for this.

"What if they would swear the blood vow for Marsh as well?"

"That's absurd! For a man?"

"I didn't ask whether you thought it was possible, I asked if it would change your mind."

"He's from the Westerlands. He's not used to the cold."

"Alasyr."

"I don't know how I feel about it, or him! I don't know how I *should* feel about it, and isn't that strange, when my whole life has been people telling me how I should feel about everything?"

"Go back to them. Think on it."

"I can think on it until I'm spent, but he's still a man lacking wings."

"Let us consider ways of overcoming that."

Alasyr looked at the skies. The clouds had parted, and at last the way was clear for a swift, easy return to the cave. It was time. He'd lingered far too long.

He stood and moved toward the cliff's edge.

"Think on it, Alasyr, that's all we ask. Talk it over with your Ember, your Marsh. We'll be waiting."

Alasyr exploded into feathers.

"Where?" Earwyn asked. She wrapped her furs tighter as the mountain wind's assault drove her repeatedly back off the path.

"There." Alric pointed. Where she felt as if there was an unseen force looking to expel her from this place, he'd come alive, more and more, as they approached the neck of the pass, and the pear-apple tree that had forever changed his life. Even his limp was less pronounced, and she wondered, if they could pass through, and her idea to recreate this experience for Alric hadn't been merely a dream, would his physical limitations disappear entirely?

"I see nothing but the tree," she called back. The bitter cold made talking hard. Her mare bucked as they drew closer. Soon, she'd have to let her go, but now that the time was upon her, she found the idea harder to accept. The finality of such a move was the first time she was shocked by her plan.

"You can't see it, but it can see us."

"What does that mean, it can see us?"

"I don't know. I don't know half as much as I wish I did about this cursed thing." Alric left his pony on the path, giving her one final, tender kiss and a quick rubdown. Whispering all sorts of sweet words men rarely wasted for beasts, but Alric was a rare man.

Alric ambled down the thigh-deep snow. The drifts he passed by were taller than he was. A terrible feeling rumbled up from the depths of Earwyn's belly. "Be careful, Al!" she called down, but her voice disappeared in a fresh, unrelenting wind whipping down the pass. Had she done right in bringing him here? She hadn't known what else to do, how else to make him whole. What if instead she was sending him to his doom?

He planted his feet. His hand came up against his brow, shielding himself as he strained to see her. "This is it, Earwyn, this is the place."

"But it's not there, is it?" She carefully stepped down the uneven path he cut through the snow.

"Of course it's there. It's always there. Watching us." He held his hand out to her and helped her down the final few paces. "Can you feel it?"

She shook her head.

Alric cast a mournful look at the air beneath the tree. "No, nor can I. It only came alive for me when I needed it."

"I'd say you need it now more than ever. You've been lost, ever since it spat you back out and left you in a world that gave up on you years ago."

Alric switched his gaze from the tree to her. "The world, Earwyn, not you. If you decided not to go, I'd never go without you. You do know that? We go together, or we don't go at all."

Earwyn shook her head. "Do you know what a burden that is to me, to know that your choosing me could come at the expense of your own happiness?"

"You've mistaken the source of my happiness if you believe that. Do you want to go home? Say the word, and it will be as if we never talked about this at all."

Earwyn wiped her tears on the snowy cloak, afraid they would freeze if she didn't tend to them quick enough. "No, you old fool. This was my idea, wasn't it? I'm committed to this, Alric, I'm committed to you. But unless we can make the veil appear for us, then we'll find nothing but misery here when the storm from the north makes its way."

His mouth curled. "Would you like me to entice another bear?"

"Is that a serious question?"

Alric chuckled. "If I could command the world around me, I'd contrive another avalanche, like the one we believe sent Gretchen through."

Earwyn didn't say it, but it seemed far more likely that Gretchen

Dereham had met a grizzly ending on the pass. Any outcome she could conjure in her mind was far more likely than a fickle veil granting her passage.

She hoped she was wrong.

"I could try to kill you," she offered, only half joking. "Would that open it?"

"It's possible, but what if it closed on you, and we were separated? The bear was forbidden from following me last time."

"Well, it's all speculation, isn't it? Everything we know about this veil, or any veil, is a series of guesses based on an experience from years past. It might, it might not."

Alric looked around them, thinking. She knew he'd been thinking about this their entire way up the pass; a thought that first began over two decades ago. But there were no easy answers here, away from the world of men, subject to the whims of the elements. A storm might come in that threatened their lives, but it might not. Another avalanche might come rumbling down the tree line, but it might not.

"Do you hear that?" Alric half-hobbled up the elevation leading from the tree. "On the pass? Can you see if someone is coming? We could solicit their aid!"

"Help us how?" she murmured to herself, reaching inside her cloak, to the vest where her daggers were stitched. Alric anticipated an opportunity, so she must be the one to anticipate danger.

"Alric!" she whispered, as loud as she dared, watching him move more swiftly toward the path. "Where are you going?"

He held up his hand as if to say, it's all right, but it wasn't all right. The first fingers of dread spread around her heart, tightening it in a vise.

The hooves had slowed as they crested the hill. Then they stopped.

"Is that..."

"It's Eavan," Alric said. He looked back at her. Now, at last, he had the good sense to be concerned. "Oh, Guardians. Earwyn. It's Eavan."

· · ·

THEY ARRIVED IN BLACKPOOL AT THE FIRST WHISPER OF DUSK, BUT even at this early hour, the town was bereft of life. Assana thought to herself, well, they must be in the taverns, that's where people go in sad little towns like these, but she had a deeper sense that was stronger, one that told her that even the establishments serving decent ale would be empty. Everything would be. The only thing Blackpool and Oldcastle had in common was their proximity on a map.

"I really don't like this place," she said with a shiver.

"I thought the Quinlandens contested these lands. That you were trying to take them off the Southerlands."

"Guardians, no!"

"At least don't act like you've never been here."

"Well, I haven't."

"I don't believe that," Balfour challenged. He watched her from the corner of his gaze. "Uncle Holden dragged his little ones all over the Northerlands a dozen times before they were even out of their swaddling."

"My father isn't Lord Dereham, is he?"

The dark pall that hung over the main road spread across everything, shrouding the businesses lining the right and left. Most looked abandoned, if not for the beady eyes regarding them with suspicion from the shadows, peering through the slats in doors and the boarded-up windows.

"Every Reach has a town like this," Balfour offered. "A place where the rest of the kingdom moved on, but they stood still."

"You're so well-traveled, are you?"

"Well read, and that's the next best thing."

"Well, look, there's an inn." She squinted at the broken tile swaying from one end. "At least, that's what the sign says."

"That's a generous name for it," Balfour mumbled. "We should've stopped off at the Reliquary. We'll need a blessing in a place like this."

Assana waited outside while Balfour ran in. He returned only moments later.

Her face fell. "No rooms, then? Is the innkeeper's corpse rotting in his chair?"

"Every room was available. He gave me my pick of them." Balfour dangled a key.

"You stole it, didn't you?"

"I could have, but no, I didn't."

"You weren't in there long enough for any of that!"

"I dropped the gold on the desk. He pointed at the keys. I took one. I wish all dealings were so simple."

Assana groaned. "This is where we die, isn't it?"

"Probably. Shall we?"

Assana huddled close to him as they entered through a narrow door. She kept her eyes down when they passed by the small desk lit by a dim lantern, but still, she felt the old man's eyes on her. Wondering, probably, what the two of them were doing in a place like this.

She practically pushed Balfour up the small staircase. She finally chanced a look down into the tavern of the inn, but the old man had moved on. He was picking scabs from his feet.

"Disgusting," she said, as Balfour closed the door behind them.

He counted his words off on his fingers. "The town? The old man? The tavern? This room? Me?"

She rolled her eyes. "Must I choose just one?"

Balfour frowned at the closed door. "I was hoping for a hot meal here tonight. I didn't see a barkeep. Did you?"

"With business this booming?"

"That's a no, I take it."

"The old hen probably handles matters himself, and I'd not eat a thing he touched, nor even looked at."

"Dried fruits it is!" Balfour dropped his satchel on the bed and dug out the small wrapping of food they'd packed. It wasn't much. It wasn't nearly enough if they couldn't restock here. The thought of taking these meager rations into another world, through the veil, left her unsettled.

If there even was a veil.

"Should we talk about this?" Balfour asked, mouth full of food.

"What more can be said about Blackpool other than I'd rather spend the night in the Wastelands? At least their meals are served hot."

"You knew what I meant. About tomorrow."

Assana pretended to rifle through her own bag. What was it with him, always wanting to talk? Always wanting to understand things? What good was there in that? "What about it? We find the veil. If it's there, we go through."

"Assana."

"Balfour."

"All right. I'll be more direct with my questions. What if we can't get through?"

She threw her hands up. "I don't know what you want me to say! We keep trying?" She reached for the sack of fruit, but none of it sounded good. "We keep trying until we find the way. What else is there?"

"You don't have to be so cross with me."

"It's your foolish questions I'm cross with. Don't ask them, and I'll be less cross."

Balfour cocked his head. "None of this is playing out in your thoughts at all?"

"No," she lied. "Not really."

"I don't believe you."

"How disappointing."

"Assana, all right, what if we *do* cross over, and then we can't return?"

"Doesn't do us any good to waste our minds on what might be! We go, we find our way forward. We see where it leads. Hopefully, as you've suggested, to a sorcerer."

Balfour dropped onto the bed next to her. "What do you want from life, Assana? When this is over?"

Assana threw her head back with a groan. "I'm weary of talking. I'm weary of this place. The Southerlands don't agree with me. Can we instead just be silent?"

"Once you've exhausted your vengeance," he went on. "What then?"

"I don't know! No one ever knows where their life will lead them. Who could ever answer a question like that with anything resembling truth?"

"Do you want to return home?"

"I have no home. I thought you understood that."

"Make a new life for yourself somewhere else?"

"I told you, I don't know!"

He grinned. "May I suggest Blackpool? One season, all year, and you'll never wait in the queue for anything."

Assana dropped her head and gave him the laugh he'd earned. "I said I don't know. And I mean it. I can't think of *anything* else right now. I'm of a single mind." And she couldn't, because she'd faced her vengeance with a fearlessness that would make even the boldest man envious, but there was nothing more terrifying to Assana than trying to discern what she might do once her vengeance was spent.

Balfour set his food aside. He leaned back on his hands. "I've never known, either, so you know. What comes after. I'd stay at Oldcastle forever, if they'd allow it. I have land awaiting me in the Northerlands for nothing more than being a Dereham. I suppose I'll take it. Live like Steward Frost, confined to my four walls for the rest of my days."

"If you're trying to make me feel sorry for you, you've failed. That doesn't sound so bad to me."

"There is peace in anonymity," he agreed. "And I guess that's where I'm going with this. If we do manage to cross over, but then can't return..." Balfour slowed his speech. "Or, should we choose *not* to return..."

"Choose not to return?" Her mouth parted.

"I wouldn't be opposed to the idea of finding a new way, in a place where no one knows the names Dereham or Quinlanden. That's all I wanted to say."

"That's all?" She shook her head to clear it. "I'd say that's more than enough."

"I didn't mean to upset you."

"Don't forget our purpose, Balfour."

He sat back up. Recovered his food. "Right. Of course not."

EAVAN WAITED UNTIL SHE'D COME A FEW MORE PACES DOWN THE HILL before dismounting her horse. She'd never liked riding, and now liked it even less being with child. But it was *for* her child that she'd done this, come all this way, with this insane idea.

"Eavan, what's gotten into you?" Earwyn comically flapped through the snow, working against nature to get to her faster than her body could take her.

Alric was already there. He only had eyes for what she'd dragged in behind her, though.

"Well. Caught yourself a snow lion." He kept muttering about it, mostly intelligible exclamations to himself as he rubbed his gloved hands over the stubble dotting his face. He didn't ask why she'd come all the way up the pass by herself.

Earwyn would, though. She'd have a thousand questions. And she'd see through any lie given in response. She might not be a reader of whispers, like Asherley, but she was just as sharp.

Eavan had all the answers prepared, but she didn't need them. She was a woman grown. She didn't come seeking permission. She could make this decision herself.

"Careful. It's not dead," she said when Alric knelt to examine the black and white spotted beast, poking it with his finger.

"Not dead? Why go to the trouble of trussing it like this just to parade it around where no one can see it?"

"Alric Dereham, the way your mind works sometimes!" Earwyn exclaimed. She pointed to Eavan. "You're so concerned with a snow lion, are you? But not with your niece at the top of Torrin's Pass, swollen with child? Are you going to ask her, or shall I?"

"It needs to be alive when we wake it up," Eavan said. She walked back and joined her uncle at the side of the animal. Its breaths were shallow, but regular. She sighed in relief. She hadn't used too much, then. Maeryn would be proud of her, but then, Eavan had no care what Maeryn thought of her anymore. Her mother's turn as a traitor was one of the many reasons Eavan now found herself here.

"Oh, I know you did not say wake it!" Earwyn laughed, incredulous. "Have you come this way by accident? No, that's not... that doesn't happen. Someone is after you, then?"

"No. No, one is after me."

"Oh, girl. You must know I have a thousand questions."

Eavan chuckled. "I know you do. So let me come to it."

Earwyn flashed her husband a conspiratorial glance, looking for an ally. But he had his hand on the chin of the lion, regarding it with much more interest than he seemed willing to spare for his wife's confusion.

"I know what you plan to do. I heard you both, on the ramparts."

"My dear. It's so kind of you to want to come and try to speak sense into us," Earwyn said. "But our minds are made. We do this because we must." She nodded at the snow lion. "Have you brought us food? Is that what this is?"

"I didn't bring him for us to kill him, or for him to feed us. We're going to be *his* food. Or, we'll let him think so, that is."

Earwyn brought both hands to her mouth.

Alric finally joined the conversation. "Ahh, a proper idea, Eavan. Easing him. Offering us up as bait. Well, he isn't killing anyone like this, is he?"

Eavan looked at Earwyn. "Mother taught me her botany. To heal, to ease, to hasten. It may be the only useful thing she taught me. I didn't know... if it would be enough, or too much. She only showed me how to use her concoctions on men. I made more, in case it was needed. Ah, and I have the nettles to mix with the bruiseweed, for when we're ready to bring him back."

Earwyn cast her eyes to the snow lion with a heavy sigh. "Oh, Eavan, I can see the wisdom in it. Your heart is good, to want to help us like this. But what if he kills us? More worrisome to me is, what if he kills you?" She laid a hand on the swelling under Eavan's furs. "Or your little baby?"

"This little baby," Eavan began, heart racing. Here it was, the moment she'd rehearsed the whole grueling ride here. She had made her choice and would do this no matter what they said, but she wanted their blessing. Right now, it was the closest thing she had to love. "This baby is why I do this. Aunt Asherley can speak her pretty words to me about arranging a marriage, or finding me a place in the Rush, but we both know that's all they are. Pretty words. There's no place for me here, now, nor my little one. Each day, I'd awaken and think of ways to die, until Marsh came around, and showed me how it felt to hope for something again. He's gone on to risk his life for the one he loves." Eavan clutched her belly. "I never wanted to love this baby, but I do, and to love it, I have to give it a chance. A *real* chance. So I'm coming with you. That's what I'm saying. Don't try to talk me out of it, or think you can just send me home. There's no home for me now, the way I came."

"Oh, Eavan," Earwyn said. "Poor, sweet Eavan."

Alric exhaled. He put his hands on his hips. Here it was. He'd finally lay his authority down, try to dissuade her. "What happens when you wake it up?"

Eavan stumbled through her response. "I... uh... I can't say for sure."

"Alric, snow lions kill men much bigger than you," Earwyn said.

"Yes, and you're a better shot with a bow than most men."

"You want to let loose this beast, let it come for your neck, and you expect me to aim well enough to kill it?"

"Only if we can't escape before it kills us," he said reasonably. "Earwyn, this is precisely what we were discussing before Eavan arrived. Like a gift from the Guardians! With a ready-made answer, that will deliver us the one thing we still needed to see this through."

He shook his head, his eyes growing wilder with joy the more he spoke. "I don't believe the Guardians would abandon us now."

"What if you're wrong?" Earwyn's face flushed dark with her fear. "I'm not going to sacrifice this girl on a guess!"

"What would Aunt Asherley do?" Eavan asked.

The question took Earwyn back. "What?"

"Ask yourself, what would Aunt Asherley do?"

"But we're not Asherley, dear, are we?"

Eavan gathered her breath. "She'd awaken the lion."

Earwyn shook her head. "Eavan, this could go so wrong, in so many ways."

But Alric was already staging their approach. He hobbled sideways, downward. "All right. Earwyn, you stand back by the tree, where I showed you before. Have your bow drawn and ready. Eavan will be with you."

"I have to do it," Eavan said.

"Nonsense. You think I'd let you die up here?" Alric smiled. "Give me the herbs, Eavan. I'll awaken the lion."

"Oh, Guardians." Earwyn turned into her exhale. She looked ready to collapse.

"If it seems the situation is beyond our control, you shoot. And we find another way."

"I've never shot a lion, Alric! Only elk kind, or deer, creatures who are perfectly still when I aim and fire. Not a ferocious, not to mention *furious*, beast hurling itself at your throat!"

"Then you'll have to be extra cautious, won't you? Eavan, how much do I need to give him?"

"You'll only get one chance. So all of it."

"You're certain?"

"Even half awake, he could take your face."

"Alric," Earwyn pressed. "Are you certain? Is there no other way? Shouldn't we think this through? We don't *have* to do this now."

"There's nothing to think through, darling." To Eavan he said, "How do I give it to him?"

"Put it..." Eavan mimicked opening the lion's mouth. "Under his tongue."

"How long will it take?"

"On a man, moments. For a lion? I don't know. But I'd be running before his mouth closes."

"I haven't run since I was a boy, but I won't be lingering, don't you worry."

"Alric," Earwyn pleaded, but resignation had crept into her rebuttals now.

"Go now. Both of you. Remember, if the veil opens, it'll be near the center of the tree. Or, it was, for me."

"And if that thing eats you, silly man, what then?"

"Then you better hope I'm enough of a meal to keep him satisfied long enough for you to go through."

Earwyn wrapped her arm around Eavan and led her through the dense snow. "If this does work, I don't know what'll happen. Once we pass through. I don't even know if we can return at all, so Eavan, you must be certain. Before he awakens that beast, be sure you want to do this. It's not too late to go."

"It is too late," Eavan said. "And I am certain. For once, I'm resolved. And we are kin, are we not? It will not be so terrible, all of us together."

Earwyn squeezed her tighter. "No, darling, of course not. Now we just have to hope that whatever might await us on the other side is as welcoming of us as we are of each other."

When they reached the spot, Alric waved, then pressed his hand firm against the air as if to say, *stop*. She thought she saw him smile at Earwyn before kneeling down at the lion's side.

Eavan held her breath as the beast's jaw rose in Alric's fist. With his other hand, he reached inside.

Eavan pressed her face into her aunt's chest.

44
THE VESPERTINE TWILIGHT

Kian insisted they stay away from the forest. The remaining Saleen kept watch at the perimeter of the clearing, an area extending from the lake on one side to the cluster of tents on the other.

The Medvedevs' choice to remain on the edges of this night to give the men their final hours seemed to infer a respect for what Jesse would do for all of them, tomorrow; how they'd all be forever changed by his choice.

And while they measured out his final hours, Oldwin was out there. Kian claimed Oldwin wouldn't come this close without protection. This didn't put Jesse's mind at ease, because Kian's voice wavered as he said it.

"Try to enjoy this evening you insisted on, Jamesan. He will not come tonight. He won't come until you are ready to approach the Light. Because when you do, the Light will be more vulnerable than it has been since Enivera reached her hands in and demanded what was not hers. That is when he will come."

"Then why the guards?"

"Because you think we need them. This is the least we can do for you, when you will do everything for us."

One of the Saleen had used her magic to light the trees when darkness descended. Thousands of tiny, glowing dots lit up the branches, casting a shower of shimmering brilliance all around them. It was the most incredible thing Jesse had ever beheld. He'd always seen magic as a tool employed of practicality. Never this, a show purely for their own enjoyment.

They gathered at the banks of the moonlit lake behind the temple. The water was unusually still; the edges lined by sparkles of tiny silver plants resembling bells. Kian had asked them not to enter the sacred waters, but Jesse required no such warning. He feared what even a dip of his toe might do to dishonor it.

Esmerelda laughed with Lisbet as the two caught up. Both had been promised to the king as brides, and both had taken their futures into their own hands. One of their own choosing. They were cousins, and now also bonded by this. He'd be robbed of this same familiarity with Lisbet, but at least she'd be around for Esmerelda.

All of his thoughts were like this now. Centered on the life his wife would have when he was gone, and how he could still influence this, still protect her, help keep her from wandering too far down the darker paths.

"You're so beautiful," Jesse whispered as he slipped his arms around her from behind.

"Aye? Those aren't *your* words, for Jesse Strong wouldnae ever say such a thing about naught but the sea."

"Well, I just did, didn't I? No sea anywhere in sight."

"Only because you feel guilty about leaving me." She spun in his arms. Her eyes twinkled, playful. "I have my whole life to think on what I've lost, but that's not how I want to remember you."

Jesse kissed her, lingering so long Lisbet made a gagging sound. "Let's dance, then."

Esmerelda burst into surprised, delighted laughter. "Dance! To what music? This isn't exactly a fete, now, is it?"

"Well, *I* have a very clear memory of you cutting your toes to feck all at Termonglen. *That* Esmerelda didnae *need* music to dance."

"That isnae quite how I remember it, Steward Strong. I recall singing a song that you couldnae wait for me to stop singing."

"So what's stopping you now? Is it because it's not only you and me now? Not only you and me, and the moldy curtains, and that broken lute?"

"Oh, aye, you're issuing a *challenge*, I see." She backed out of his arms and curtsied. "I accept."

"I'm, eh, gonna go find Kian," Lisbet murmured.

Esmerelda fell into perfect form before he could even find his feet. She had them moving, swaying, across the silvery shores, her hair flying behind her in a wind created by their movement. She was right, he'd been so embarrassed when she'd last asked him to dance that he'd made fun of her. But even then, he'd been snared by her easy way with herself. She was a child born of duty, but grown of fire and salt and sand, and also softness, and light. She was the safest place he'd ever known.

Esmerelda may not want to speak about what would happen in the morning, but it was all he could think about. *I love you. I loved you even before I knew what the word meant. I loved you for all the wrong reasons, and all the right ones. You're my last thought in the evening, and my first in the morning. The sun in my oft dark sky; the moon lighting my favorite time of night. You're my reason, in a world without. And it has been an honor to be yours, if only for a little while.*

But these were only reminders of what his absence would bring, not what he now, in the flesh, on fire for her, could still give her.

Her hand snaked across his cheeks, winding through his hair. No one in all his life had ever looked upon him with the intensity Esmerelda Warwick Strong now offered him. She was reading him, drinking him in, saving him for later.

Jesse couldn't say any of this without breaking the spell she'd created from her sorrow, but he wanted her to love again. Selfishly, it soothed him to think there could be only one Jesse, but it was Esmerelda who was the rare gem. The one whose heart was hard won and well treasured.

Perhaps it would be Ryan in the end, as it had been in the beginning.

Instead, Jesse said nothing.

He closed his eyes and followed her lead as she moved them through the effortless steps of a dance created from her heart; as the rest of the world fell away entirely into the vespertine twilight.

RAVENNA STOOD SENTRY UPON THE EVENING AT THE FAR EDGE OF THE lake, arms crossed, mug pressed against her arm, untouched. The raven beheld the others with the trained eyes of a hawk. She'd come here either from loyalty or a life debt, either of which had to have been formed and settled in the months since he'd last seen her, taking off into the night sky and leaving them all behind.

"I don't like the feel of this. Standing around, waiting for Oldwin to come attack us."

"If anyone understands him well enough to possess such a fear, it's me," Ravenna said. "But he won't come here. Not like this. Sorcerer or no, this world limits him."

Ash was shocked. "You're acquainted with him, then?"

"In a manner of speaking."

"We are talking about the same creature here?"

"Yes."

He could tell she would say no more. He changed topics. "Is it just me, or do you feel like an outsider here, too?"

"Because I'm a Ravenwood?" she returned without looking his way. She had her eyes on Jesse and Esmerelda. Her gaze traveled with them as they moved. So it was for them she was here.

"Are we not friends, after all we've been through?"

"After all we've been through, and all that's happened, I should think I'm the last person you'd want to see."

Ash didn't want to talk about Drystan tonight. Not when he was hours from losing another son. "You know, I've known plenty of other Ravenwoods. You aren't the only one."

She snickered. "Have you?"

"Well, by plenty, of course, I mean two, or maybe three. From when I was in Wulfsgate."

"Ah, yes, bedding Lord Dereham's wife. Or was that another apprentice blacksmith?"

Ash laughed. He liked her direct way of speaking. It was refreshing, when so many around him, including himself, preferred to save their meaning, spreading it thin. He didn't remember her being this way. She'd changed, and he liked her better now.

"He'll come to you," Ravenna said. She hadn't moved her arms. She motioned to Jesse with her head, nodding. "He's just afraid to leave her when he's only just found her."

"Oh, don't trouble yourself over how I'm feeling. I'd understand if he never came to me. I wouldn't come to a father who arrived in my life so far into it."

"You didn't know."

"Would that make me feel better, if I were him? I don't think so."

"Where did Lisbet go?"

"She's off with Kian. I think he's soft on her, and she him."

"It won't last."

"No, no, of course not."

Ravenna half-turned. "Is it true that you didn't know?"

"Who I was?"

She nodded.

"I knew... I knew, I suppose, that there was something more to my birth than a forgotten child left in a basket for a childless family. But a Rhiagain? A sorcerer? That's the stuff of fables, Ravenna. Of the stories children tell when they're playing deep in their imaginations. And even knowing everything I know now, I'm still only Ash, son of Drystan. I'm no different than I was."

"Oh, now that's a lie."

"Sorry?"

"There's how you feel, Ash. And then there's how you *are*."

"Mostly what I feel right now is a powerful, consuming emptiness."

"You're not going to wax poetic on me, are you?"

"No, I'm quite serious, Ravenna. I feel as if I've arrived here too late, and that this terrible timing of my arrival was no accident at all. That it's my fate to meet my son, and then watch him leave everything he loves behind, powerless to stop it. I've seen it, in my dreams, and at last I understand it, what it means, what it *will* mean when it's over and done. My punishment began with my birth, continued when the king's man failed to do his duty and end my life, and it continues even now."

Ravenna shoved her drink at him. "You clearly need this more than I do."

Ash eyed the drink strangely before accepting. "You're suggesting I should be even more in my cups?"

"Is that where you place this blame? You're drunk?"

"I would like to be. Anything is better than this utter helplessness."

Ravenna dropped her arms to the sides. She pointed at Lisbet. "You've got it all wrong about Lis. She's not flirting with Kian. She's pressing him for information. She's doing exactly what she said she would do, Ash, and using what hours remain to her to find another way for Jesse. Perhaps if you joined her, you might discover a means of exhausting some of this helplessness plaguing you."

Ash was taken aback by her suggestion he was moping. "You don't think I'm doing the same? That my thoughts haven't been consumed with just this?"

"Standing here with me, whinging over your ale?"

"And why are you here, Ravenna? Where have you been all these months, only to reappear here, now? Who are Jesse and Esmerelda to you?"

Ravenna returned her gaze forward. "It's mostly for Esmerelda."

"What of Jesse?"

"What of him?" She watched him from the side. "Oh, you think *I've* come to find another way to orchestrate some last hour means of saving him? You think I have that power? I don't. Nor do you. Jesse's fate was sealed when he answered the call of the sorcerers.

All we can do now is be there as he fulfills his vow, to give him strength."

"There is no emotion in you at all, is there? Did you ever love Drystan?" He regretted saying it as the words left his lips.

Ravenna sighed. She squeezed his arm with a placating smile. "I'm not having this conversation tonight. But it *is* nice to see you and Lisbet again, even if these were the conditions required to make it so."

Esmerelda felt the searching eyes of Jesse's father and Lisbet upon her. They each wanted their turn with him and she, selfishly, had stolen what time he had left, fearful of being parted from him for even a single moment ahead of the final one.

Ahh, how her life had changed so much, so fast.

She understood now that she hadn't left her life behind all those months ago so that she might chase the excitement of a past envisioned with Ryan, but to discover the perfect beauty of a love she was made for with Jesse.

However fleeting.

"Go to them," she whispered against his cheek, where he'd let his beard grow again. She couldn't say these words looking into his eyes. She'd lose her courage there.

"No. I willnae leave you."

"But I'm asking you to, because I've had so much more of you than either of them. It's their turn."

He crushed her tighter. "I'd rather be here, with you."

"You'd rather have a whole life to get to know them. But you don't have that. You have tonight."

Jesse stopped dancing. "Are you certain?"

"Of course I am. I think I might lie down for a few and catch my breath. My energy isn't fully recovered after Gemma." She grinned. "Or last night."

Jesse kissed her. "I willnae be long. I'll find you there?"

"If you don't, I'll come hunting for you. 'Tis no empty threat, either, Steward. A woman capable of regicide is capable of anything."

Jesse laughed. "No one knows better than me what you're capable of."

"Go." Esmerelda gave him a gentle push. She bit her lip to stave the tears. "Go on."

LISBET FOLLOWED HIM WHEN HE SLIPPED AWAY FROM THE OTHERS. IT was something in his eyes that told her this was the right thing to do. What he *wanted* her to do.

She'd gotten nowhere questioning Kian. For every idea that came to her, he had a rebuttal ready. It had always been Jesse, he insisted. He'd always been the one in their visions. First, his mother's, then, as he'd matured into his role as Keeper, his. The visions didn't lie. Even if she found a way, the course would still correct to the way it was meant to be, the circle closing at last.

Well, Kian didn't know everything, did he? She hadn't lost hope, even if everyone else had.

But there was another part of their conversation playing in her head now.

I know why you told me who I am, instead of waiting for me to see it.
Why is that?
Because you like me. In spite of yourself, you like me.
I like many.
But you like me in a way that's more than that.
My like for you has limitations. You're Meduwyn.
Don't forget, it's a Meduwyn you now look to, to save all of you.
Us. And Jamesan is equally Medvedev.
So you can't like me because of the blood running through me, that I have no control over? That I did not ask for?
I am a Keeper. My call for duty surpasses any unnatural wants I might possess.
So I'm unnatural to you.
You are a surprise to me, Lisbet. We will leave it at this.

She hadn't known what she'd actually wanted from this. Pushing him like that. Certainly it wasn't from any desire to pursue some unexplored feelings between them. She was already eager to be rid of this place.

Lisbet wasn't used to seeing him so wound. This only incited her own fears. The man who feared nothing was afraid now.

They made so many turns in the path that she didn't know if she could return without his guidance. She tried to commit their route to memory, but they were deep in the forest, now, beyond the rutted ways created by paths well-traveled. She kept her hands before her face to shield it from the branches whipping at her with every long step.

"It was you," Kian declared.

Lisbet went still at the shock of his voice. She looked around for a place to duck into.

"You have forgotten the faces of those who came before you. I will speak as a man for you."

She knew this voice, too. Kael, who had unsettled her so much before. The one who had betrayed his people. Lisbet could've sworn she heard Eithne say that Kael had even killed his own mother. She didn't want to believe this could be true. Yseult couldn't have been so easily slain. Could she?

"It was you," Kian repeated.

"You will have to be more specific than that, brother."

"How could you bring Oldwin here? He has spent hundreds of years trying to bring death upon us, and all it took was an invitation from you."

"How could you keep the Light from us? We can both ask questions the other has no desire to answer, can't we?"

"He is Meduwyn, Kael. He is the reason for the great sorrow. The cause of the rupture in all things."

"You bring a Meduwyn here for your own aims. How are you better than me?"

"It was not me who brought him. If you were a Keeper, you

would know this. It was his own kind who created him, and then aimed him to us."

"He will die soon. Your Meduwyn. The young one."

"No. The Light will protect him."

"That is not how he will die."

Lisbet's heart was ready to jump from her chest. She crouched lower.

"He is protected and is powerful in his own right. You cannot harm him."

"I will not need to harm him," Kael spat. "What you would have him do is against our ways."

"It is the very reason for our ways!"

"You think I do not know, because I was not trained as you were?" Kael laughed. "I took that which was not freely given. Just as you have taken from all of us."

"You are wrong, brother. You cannot know how far you have strayed from the path."

"Her path."

"Is it true?" Kian's voice dropped, softer. "How could you have done it? No matter what darkness lives in you. She was our mother."

Kael snorted. "It was not as easy as you would like to think. But she wanted me to do it. She challenged me! All but begged me."

"I don't believe you."

Kael shrugged.

"Why, why would she beg you? Why would she want this?"

"Why do you think? So that I could do what she would not. What she was not strong enough to do."

"You know that isn't true, even as you say it."

The two said nothing for so long, Lisbet wondered if she'd missed them moving deeper into the forest.

"Oldwin intends to use your Meduwyn for himself," Kael finally offered.

"He is your ally. Why tell me this?"

"He is no one's ally. I should not have brought him here. I'll admit, that was a poor choice. You and I, this is how it should be. I see that now."

"There is no you and I, Kael. Not anymore."

"Oldwin will come for him. He is weakened, yes, but lacks none for cunning. Where he will fail in strength, he will win in wit. You must be prepared for him."

"He is yours to deal with. You brought him here."

Kael's voice rose in pitch. "We can still end this, brother! Dispose of all who carry the tainted Meduwyn blood, return our people to the Light, where they belong. We have no need to defend that which is ours, if they're gone. The Light *chose* us! Why would we continue to suffer?"

"You would take from the Light, as Enivera once did."

"I would not!"

"You have already tasted darkness, Kael."

"He will come for you, Kian. It does not have to be this way."

"You made it this way, when you killed Mother. When you invited a traitor to our lands."

Kian's steps crunched once more. He was coming her way.

Kael sounded his cackle into the night air. "Oldwin will take from you before this night is ended. Unless we stop him, together. I can help you."

"I see now, it was you all along I needed to stop," Kian said to himself. He pressed through the brush to where she hunkered. He looked down. "You see now? It is not only one battle we fight. We cannot afford your hopeful whims. If Jamesan cannot do what he must, then all is lost."

"That's not what I took from this at all!" Lisbet countered as she leapt to join him. She struggled to keep pace with him as he stormed back toward their camp. "I see an enemy divided, and we can strike upon that!"

"You see nothing," Kian said. His voice was cutting. "And was that not the problem all along, Lisbet?"

. . .

ASH HUDDLED WITH HIS SON UPON THE SMALL LOG. *HIS SON.* THIS WAS less natural than it had been with Drystan. He'd had seventeen years to come around to Drystan being his boy; he'd known the moment he looked upon him in the cradle. It was only when he was older that he'd been allowed to enjoy the time with him, but in his mind he'd always been his father.

Jesse was different. It wasn't only his blood. He'd been raised in another world entirely. The men of salt and sand had always seemed as if they belonged to another kingdom. They were hardy of constitution, full of passions, quick to draw sword, far slower to cool. Jesse was both like and not like these men, and Ash couldn't help wondering if it was his own contribution to the boy causing this confusion in him.

"I really thought Isdemus and Lysanor would come."

"Maybe it's as Kian said. They're too weak now."

Jesse pointed at the forest. "Yet Oldwin is here."

Ash bowed his head. This was all the time they would get, and he should know what to say. But he was as lost to the task as Jesse seemed to be.

"What are they like?"

"The sorcerers?"

Ash nodded. "I've never met one myself. I saw one, moments before..."

Jesse put a hand on his knee, ever briefly. "You donnae have to speak of it."

"It's how I know they can be killed."

Jesse touched his sword. "Anything can be killed." He looked back out over the still lake. "Lysanor, she's... full of fire. She wants to save the world, but has no care for who she takes down to do it. Isdemus, though, he's made of a different mold. He's kinder. I donnae know if this is because he's my blood kin, or if it's what lives in him, but he helped me get back to Esmeralda. He's always seemed more conflicted about what they would ask me to do."

"He never told you what it was, though?"

Jesse shook his head. "Probably for the best."

"You wouldn't have agreed to it, you mean."

"For Esmerelda, I would've walked through fire." He grinned. "Aye, I would've agreed to it, but with decidedly less courage."

"She won't be alone. Lisbet and I. Ravenna. Your brother, too?"

"Aye. I'm counting on it."

"There's a little one. I saw her in Warwicktown." He tried not to sound as hopeful as he felt at the idea of a grandchild.

"There is, aye. She's Ryan's, Gemma. It was Ryan Esmerelda loved first. It was for him, she gave up everything. For him she sent this entire kingdom to its knees."

"Seems she's done the same for you now."

Jesse turned on the log. "Would you take a message to my father for me? Tell him what I did here. Tell him he's to give everything I have to Esme, and the bairn. She doesnae need it, being a Warwick, but I want her to have something of me."

Ash swallowed. "Of course. Of course I will."

"Did you tell them who you were, when you went to Warwicktown?"

"I did."

"And you're still breathing air?"

"Fortunately for me, Lord Warwick saw the sense in keeping that truth from him, for the time being."

They laughed together. Ash watched him. Jesse had his eyes. The color was different, but he knew them well; they were Drystan's eyes, too, and Lisbet's.

"I know Hamish is your father. I would never ask for the same name. But I want you to know, there's nothing I wouldn't do for you, Jesse. We only just met, and I would move this entire world to save you."

Jesse nodded slowly. "Aye, I know. It comforts me, knowing Esmeralda willnae lack for the care of others."

"Do you believe in the Guardians?"

Jesse gave a light shrug. "I suppose."

"Do you believe they are inherently good?"

"It's what the Reliquary would have us believe. Even the Guardian of the Unpromised Future has his role to play. Why?"

"They've never been especially good to me. Eh, don't mind me. Just the musings of a man at the middle of his life, with no aim for the end."

"Aye, the ale *is* good, innit?"

Jesse was smiling when Ash turned to look at him. It was Yanna's smile. It spread to Ash's own face.

Then it froze. Melting away, as Jesse's eyes widened, wild, fearful.

"What? What is it?"

"Esme," Jesse whispered. "It's Esme. She's gone."

45
MORTAR AND PESTLE

Christian regarded the letter with the same suspicion he'd afford a man accused of murder. His mother's perfect scrawl taunted him. He lacked the courage to read the words, or to burn the paper, so there it had sat. First upon his father's desk, and then, deep in the drawer. He didn't recall pulling it out this time, but there it was, fraying at one end; the words, *With Love, Mother* exposed, a challenge.

It will haunt you for the rest of your life if you don't do something. Read it. Then burn it. Be done with it. Be done with her.

Christian wiped the moisture from his eyes with a sleeve. The smoke of his always working hearth burned his vision, his lungs, all of him. How much longer could he stay in here before it became too much?

"All right then. Let's be done with each other, as you've already been done with me." Christian didn't bother with the letter opener. He tore at the spot already half-opened, treating the letter with the same respect his mother had given him.

My Dearest Son, he read. Already the words were a lie. *At last, we understand each other.*

I have judged you since the day you chose life with the enchanters over your own blood. I have called down my greatest anger, and it was for you alone. I told myself how I loved you, how that love should beget understanding of your choice, but it never did. You might say that was because I never loved you enough. But I would say it was because I have loved you far too much. More than a mother should.

It is only now, when I must leave our world for another, called by something bigger than myself, that I finally see your choice was not about me.

It is a strange thing to feel as if your home is no longer one. You might think I am choosing Pieter over the rest of you, but it is less tidy than that, just as your own leaving was never so simple or straightforward. I am choosing to follow my conscience, which has worn havoc on me ever since I failed to fight hard enough for Lisbet. For not seeing through to the truth of you, and Drystan. These are crimes I cannot undo, but I can still make it right for Pieter. And, if the Guardians are kind, I will do precisely that.

I do not know what my return looks like, or if there even is a return. I will not come back without him. But if I have arrived too late, then I may lie down beside him and face my own unpromised future, for I have no further failure left in me to give.

As for you. Stay. Go. I now know how wrong it was for me to expect you to step to the places I had laid for you. There are other Derehams, if it isn't to be you. But this life is the one we get. We must not leave it with regret, Son.

Please apologize to Aylen on my behalf. If I have upset her with my words about your choice to remain childless, it was not my intent. She is good for you. I know we had someone else in mind for you, and that we crossed more than words on the matter. But I could not have chosen better for you than Aylen Wynter. I see this now. Wherever you go, you would be wise to ensure she is at your side.

If we do meet again, I hope it will be under a fairer understanding of one another.

And if we do not, know that I love you.
I am proud of the man you have become.

And we will see each other once more, if not in this world, then the next.

With Love, Mother.

Christian crumpled the letter in his fist. He heaved it at the fire with an exhausted grunt that quickly turned to a sob. He watched the edges curl inward, blacken. All evidence of this gift she'd given him, surrendered to ash.

Mother.

He dropped to the floor and crawled to the fire, reaching his hand into the flame to retrieve the letter before it was too late. He flattened the vellum in desperation, but he'd only saved half of it. Christian pressed his face against the scorched letter and cried silently into his mother's final words to him.

Stefan had little to say on their journey across the kingdom. In the beginning, he couldn't stop asking about Anabella, as if she'd simply gone to market. He hadn't grasped that when Darrick said she was gone, her absence was permanent. It seemed cruel that a child should only understand death when experiencing it with the one closest to them.

He'd perked up when they passed through Wulfsgate, for it was the first time Darrick allowed him to interact with anyone. Darrick had intended to speak with the young Lord Dereham, but was instead greeted by his wife, a striking silver-haired Enchanter with a face that reminded him so much of his Anabella that it nearly clipped him at the knees. She was a true Northerland woman, of as fine of breeding as Anabella herself had been. She hadn't recognized him, but she immediately knew Stefan.

I know it was you who kept my wife and son fed and safe when I could not. How I wish she could be here now to share her gratitude.

Your Grace, she'd whispered.

Darrick, please. I have not been Your Grace for too long, and I hope never to be again.

I was so fond of Anabella. We were friends as girls, and then to see her again, after all those years gone, it was as if she was returned from the dead. I was so aggrieved to hear of your loss. Truly, is there anything I can do? Anything at all.

I'm only passing through, but Lord Warwick sent me with an inquiry for you. About a certain Drystan Sylvaine. You might know him as Ash.

Her face had gone dark at the name. *You've not long missed him. He came to cause havoc here, and then left again, with Lisbet.*

Where were they headed?

They didn't say.

Your husband, madam, would do well to support the Southerlands in their cause. I understand he is not eager to the task, but Oldwin plays a dangerous game. One he cannot win, but nor can the kingdom as long as he plays it.

My husband, as you seem to know, has taken a reprieve from duty. I will do what I can in his stead.

I thank you. Lord Warwick does as well.

You've come all this way, to tell us this?

As I said, only passing through. To take him home, to Whitecap.

Is Steward Weatherford expecting you, then?

No, and I'd rather he not know.

Very well, at least allow me to restock your provisions and change out your horses for beasts better suited to the north. The pass is treacherous, even in springtide, and you'll need more than what you came with.

I would owe you another great debt.

You owe me nothing. Any kindness given in expectation is not kindness at all.

She'd been right about the pass, but what he hadn't anticipated was how Stefan had come alive as they crested the summit, easing down toward the eastern side. Now he had more than enough to say. He animatedly spoke of how Wyat had been teaching him to use the bow; how both Ransom and Pieter played with him, protected him. He'd liked Lady Blackwood, he said, but the other, the princess, was scary. Darrick confessed Assyria had always scared him a little, too.

Still, he said a silent entreaty to her, at the place where she had met her end in her plight to help him.

Once on the other side, the trip became markedly easier. They'd passed a couple of quiet nights in Wulfshead Haven before making the final push on to Whitecap.

"What has your mother told you about your grandfather, Stefan?" Darrick asked as they traveled the Long Road. It was called this, Anabella once told him, because the way from Wulfshead Haven to Whitecap seemed endless, with no landmarks to break it up, no inns to ease the monotony. In a storm, a man traveled on blind faith alone. It was said to have driven some mad.

"That he made furs?"

"That's right. The best in the Northerlands. Nay, the kingdom."

Stefan tugged at the heavy cape Lady Aylen had given him. "Did he make this one?"

"Well, that I'm not sure about. We can ask him."

"You said to Lady Aylen that Grandfather doesn't know we're coming. Will he be mad?"

"Mad? No, I don't believe so." But this was precisely what Darrick feared as they rode slowly beneath the snow-covered iron gates reading Weatherford Hall. His own wife's ancestral home, and this would be his first visit. Perhaps his last.

Four guards stepped into the path. They wore the sleepy, disordered looks of men who didn't expect to see a visitor today.

"State your name and your business."

Darrick started to respond, but these were Stefan's people. He nodded to his son. "Go on, then. Tell them. Like we practiced."

Stefan twisted in the saddle. He looked back at Darrick once more for approval. Darrick nodded once more.

He straightened and said in a small but commanding voice. "My name is Stefan Weatherford. I've come to meet my grandfather."

Christian was drawn by the high trilling sound. It came from within. It sounded like the dead calling the living.

He followed where the deafening sound led him. It didn't feel like a choice at all, but a command. He hadn't left his father's apartments for anyone or anything, but he was doing it now, for something he couldn't even define, let alone explain.

The sound led him down the hall, to the end, where it split two ways, revealing the children's apartments. Where he'd once lived. One door was cracked. Lisbet's bedroom. But it wasn't Lisbet sleeping here these days, but Aylen.

There was a fire in the hearth, indicating she was still awake. He didn't want to go in. He saw this now for what it was: a true seer's dream, like the one that had come to him when Brandyn needed his aid. He wouldn't wake from this and put it out of mind. Whatever he saw in this room, would be. A truth undisputed. A future that would come to pass.

Christian nudged the door just wide enough to see inside. Aylen's back was to him. She wore the sleeping robe Earwyn had made for her, a mix of the silver of her chosen life and the furs of her born life. Her long hair cascaded over the hood and down her back. She was so beautiful. How had he ever forgotten this? Forgotten how it felt to want her, to want desperately to take her into his arms and disappear into whatever she was offering.

Christian walked up to the side of her. She couldn't see him. But now he could see her, and he could see that she was crying. She worked diligently through her tears, twisting the pestle into the mortar, breaking down the herbs to ready them. He leaned in closer to read some of the names. Graviolas. Pennyroyal. Rudaflower. What he didn't know about herbs could fill a larger book than what he did, but he knew these. These were the herbs sequestered into the chambers of women after dark, to deliver them of things unwanted.

Christian again studied his wife's purposeful face. She did what she must, alone. Alone because of him. With child, because of him.

Aylen, no. No, look at me. Please look at me.

But she couldn't hear him.

Aylen! He danced around her, waving his hands, desperate to break through and find a way to her, even though he knew how futile it was.

At last finished with the grinding of herbs, she wiped her brow and then went to the fire at her room's hearth where the small kettle brewed. She dusted the herbs from her palm, stirring with the large ladle.

No, Aylen. I'm here. I'm here now. I know I wasn't before, but I am now, and you don't have to do this!

That task done, she sank into the rocking chair just beside the hearth. She buried her face in her hands and sobbed.

WREGAN WEATHERFORD HELD COURT IN HIS TALL, RED CHAIR, staring straight at the space between them with an uncomfortable detachment. Anabella had told Darrick about this chair. He'd purchased it from a traveling merchant on a whim, at first leaving it outside from his buyer's regret at such an ornamented piece, but over time he grew attached to it. It became his one indulgence in his otherwise practical, albeit privileged, life.

He waited for the servant to pour and pass the tea. The only glances were casual. The way his eyes landed on his grandson, briefly, giving him the same regard he gave everything else in the otherwise bland sitting room.

When the young woman at last left them, the steward crossed his legs. He folded his arms over them. "I remember you. I sold you fur. You kept sending back for more."

Darrick felt like laughing, if not for the knot in his belly. There was no *Your Grace* or *Prince*, or even *sir*. It shouldn't bother him, for he'd given these things up. They'd never meant much to him to begin with. It was for his son, only, that the steward's indifference rankled him.

"You did. The very finest."

"Paid well, too. I might have taken less, had I known you'd steal my daughter."

So he meant to get right down to it. "My intentions with Anabella were always honest. I wanted her to be my queen. My brother had other ideas, as he often did."

"Were you correcting me, or agreeing with me?"

Darrick held his growing frustration. "I didn't come to argue with you, sir."

"So I'm sir to you?" Wregan challenged. "Go on, drink your tea. It's not poisoned, though you'll find it less agreeable than those fancy Everhart blends you Rhiagains import from the Easterlands."

"Go on," Darrick urged his son. Stefan looked scared, but obliged.

"Why, then, did you come? To offer me the news that has already reached me?" The steward tossed a log into the fire from the tall stack next to his chair. The fire rushed up at the fresh addition, crackling in happy response. "You needn't have. I got the same raven everyone else in the kingdom received, about the return of my daughter and her prince. Perhaps the one intended just for me, her father, was lost in flight."

"Steward Weatherford—"

"And now you've come to tell me that my joy at hearing of my Bella's resurrection was only fresh torture. Now she's truly dead, isn't she?"

Darrick looked down at his hands. "I wish more than anything that wasn't why I was here."

Wregan held out his hands. "Well, I already knew. A man knows when his child is lost to him. I never mourned the first time, for I knew she was still out there, long after everyone else had given up on her. And that scholar. Edevane. He'd never tell me the truth, but why else would the man visit me, year after year?"

"She wanted to come to you. We planned to, when it was safe. When the kingdom was safe."

"When has the kingdom ever been safe, Darrick? It hasn't been safe since the Rhiagains washed up on our shores, claiming to be gods. Yes, I see what Anabella saw in you. There's intrigue in your eyes, and she always did love to cultivate her imagination, let it run. But you? You never stopped to think, did you? Of what it would do to her, loving her? Never considered that she could have a fine marriage, a happy one, instead of whatever it was she had with you."

Wregan waved his hands with these last words, as if to say he thought little of whatever *it* had been.

"Regret is a powerful thing, Steward. It has legs, arms, a mind of its own. Whenever I begin to regret loving her, instead I look upon him." He pointed to Stefan. "Her son. My son. Your grandson."

Wregan scoffed. "The ends do not justify the means just because you've worked to convince yourself otherwise."

"Look at him, sir. His name is Stefan. He's the very image of his mother, and I'll wager he looks like your wife, too."

"My wife is turning in her crypt, seeing you here, searching for forgiveness."

Darrick shook his head. "There is no forgiveness for me, not in this lifetime. You're mistaken if you've taken that as my intent." He stood and urged Stefan to do the same. "Go on. Go see your grandfather."

"Don't take another step, boy."

"Listen to me, Stefan. Do as I say." If the older man pushed him away, Stefan would be wounded, and he'd already borne so much. But it had to be here. Here, he could be safe, loved by his own people. Anabella's sisters all had families of their own, children for Stefan to play with. A life yet awaited him. A life better than what Darrick could provide for him.

But it would all come down to this.

Stefan slowly shuffled across the rug to his grandfather. He held his head low, looping his hands behind his back. He wore his reluctance like a shroud.

"Look at him, Steward. I cannot bring Anabella back, but Stefan *is* Anabella, through and through. He is more Weatherford than Rhiagain, and I would see that chasm grow wider still."

The steward tapped his foot against his knee, and then, with a defiant glare, finally looked upon his grandson. "What do you want from me, then, boy?"

Stefan burst into tears. "Right. Right, easy now." Wregan reached forward tentatively and grasped the boy's shoulders. "Easy does it.

There's no crying here. None of my girls ever cried, and I'll not take it from you, either."

Stefan hopped into the old man's lap as if the words were an invitation and buried his face in his chest. The steward gaped at him, confused at the strange assault. Awkwardly, he attempted to comfort him.

"You want me to take him in, is that it?"

Darrick waited, then nodded. He did want this. Everything inside of him screamed against being parted from his son, but it wasn't about his own wants. His wants had gotten Anabella killed. He wouldn't chance the same happening to Stefan.

"You'd abandon your own son, when he's only just lost his mother?"

"I would see Stefan with his people."

"Are you not his people?"

"He'll never be safe with me. The kingdom knows my face. They will know his."

Wregan snorted. "We have little use for the kingdom up here." He bounced Stefan in his arms the way a child might bounce a cat. His displeasure now was playacted. Darrick saw the warmth Anabella had told him about coming through. "No Rhiagains have ever come this far north. Not until you, anyhow."

"Stefan may be a Rhiagain, but that isn't the life I want for him."

"I'm an old man now. What can I give this boy, other than his mother's name?"

"Kin. And safety."

"And you? Where will you go, once you're free of this burden?"

"Stefan could never be a burden." Darrick's voice choked. "And I will never be free."

"That's not an answer."

"I don't yet know."

"Only a fool or a letch would leave his son." The steward eased Stefan back down. "All right, now, that's done, isn't it? Enough of that." He dusted his trousers off. "He's *your* son, and I have neither the time nor the strength to look after him. So if you want your boy to stay, then you'll stay with him."

"Sir—"

"The groundskeeper's cottage has long been empty. The guards tend things now, for some extra coin. Needs a woman's touch, and I don't suppose *you'd* have that skill, but you'll sort it out, same as you sorted this matter, I expect."

Darrick fought the surge of emotion pressing on all sides of his chest. "Steward, your kindness. I don't deserve it."

"You'd do well to remember that it's Anabella's kindness that brings us together now. As I must remember it, if I'm to warm up to this little one. If I'm to learn to forgive, and in that forgiveness, allow you to live."

Darrick bowed. "Then let us honor Anabella, together, through her son."

The steward nodded. He seemed as if he would say more, but he kept his counsel.

AYLEN AWOKE WITH THE WORLD IN MOTION. ROUGH HANDS SHOOK her. The assault was such a shock that all she could do was lift her arms to block it. She pulled her legs back to disarm her assailant, and then she saw who it was.

Christian.

"What are you *doing*?" She swatted him away, tugging against the blanket to cover herself again, in modesty. As if she was a maid and he was here improperly.

But he was here improperly. She hadn't invited him, and he wasn't welcome.

"Have you done it? Is it done?" He said the words over and over until she shook her head.

"Is what done? What's gotten into you?"

Christian moved back to the edge of the bed. Rocking. Panting. She sensed fear from him, and loathing, though not for her.

"Please tell me there's still time to make this right. That you can forgive me."

"Are you drunk?" She curled her lips in disgust. "Do that in your own chambers."

Christian whipped his head up. "Drunk on my sorrow. My terrible regret. Oh, Aylen, I've been so wrong. I've wronged you, wronged us, and now..." His eyes traveled down.

Now she understood. He'd had a seer's dream. He'd seen her with the herbs. Aylen turned away. She'd wanted to hear these words from him for weeks now, but her heart was too wounded for them to sink any deeper than the air around them.

"Please, Aylen. Tell me it's not too late. Tell me it's not done."

She shook her head, still looking away.

"Oh, Guardians. Aylen. Aylen. Please look at me."

"Would you stop saying my name like that? I don't like it. I don't like the way it sounds, when you're like this."

"I'm so sorry. I am so, so sorry."

"I haven't done it, but that isn't because I've had second thoughts. I only wanted to wait until morning, to give the herbs time to steep. I didn't want to have to do it twice."

Christian reached for her hands, but she clutched the blanket tighter, peeling away from him. "Don't do it."

"You have one bad dream and now you want children with me? Now you love me again?"

"I've always loved you." He crawled closer. "It was the love I didn't bear myself that has brought me to this."

"Just because you've had a revelation? It doesn't erase the hurt." She dropped the blanket and spun on him. "No one has *ever* hurt me as you have, Christian. No one. And it isn't for you that I would be rid of this child, but for me, so that I do not have to look upon him or her and see their father and fear that would prevent me from loving them as a mother should."

Christian's breathing slowed. "Is that true?"

She buried her face in her hands and shook her head. "No."

"I have no excuse for how I've behaved. None. Only this terrible sadness at the thought of losing you."

"And when the dream wears off and you return to your self-loathing tomorrow?"

"No." He reached for her. "No. I promise you, that won't happen. I swear to you. I'll be better. I'll try to fill the heavy boots left by my father. I'll be the husband you deserve, and... and the father."

"You don't want children!"

"I didn't, until I thought..." Christian glanced at the hearth, where the kettle had cooled. "Until..."

"That is not a reason."

"People can change, Aylen. They do it all the time."

"There's nothing that will drive me farther from you than an empty promise, Christian. Our marriage won't survive such deep hurt a second time."

Christian reached for her hair, tangling the silver strands in his fingers. "I love you. I have loved you since I was a boy. I followed you to the Sepulchre, not because I wanted to leave home, but because I couldn't bear to be parted from you. I couldn't sleep at night, thinking of you falling in love with some Enchanter in their palace in the sky."

"That's not the man who's ignored me these weeks. Yelled at me. Belittled me."

"I know. I hate the man I've become. I wish him dead."

"What am I supposed to say to that?"

"I want to tell you why returning home was so abhorrent to me."

She laughed. "*Now* you'll tell me, when you've already ground my heart into dust. When I've asked you hundreds of times to help it make sense."

"I was betrothed to Raissa Aldenwood."

"So? I was betrothed to one of the Arranden boys when I was a girl. All that went away when we became Adherents."

"For you. But I was the son of a lord, and it was always expected I'd come home when my training was done. In their letters, my parents told me Raissa waited patiently for my studies to complete.

Her father took our betrothal with the seriousness he believed it deserved and would entertain no other offers for her. When I told my mother that I was in love with you, and that she should call off the betrothal, she called me a fool. She said that any bonds forged here would be meaningless upon my return."

"But..." Aylen shook her head. "You're a grown man! You don't answer to your mother."

"Do you know what happened to Raissa?"

"No."

"When my mother was no help, I wrote to Steward Aldenwood myself and told him of my intentions toward you, that he was free to find another match for Raissa. But that isn't what he did. He blamed his daughter. Said that I'd been so put off at the thought of being her husband, that I'd contrived some gentleman's excuse to get out of it. So instead he sent her to live with the dowager widows of the Reliquary. Ruined, for me."

"That was a terrible thing her father did," Aylen whispered, "but that isn't your fault."

"Of course it's my fault! I ruined her, and the whole Reach knows it! They know their lord is responsible for this, because he loved someone he shouldn't."

"I won't respond to the last thing you said, for both our sakes, but if the whole Reach knew it, why then am I only learning of this now?"

"I don't know. But I was afraid to tell you, because I was ashamed. Ashamed that I'd been weak as a boy, putting aside my duty for love, and then again, when duty called once more, and I chose my heart. How could that man ever lead a Reach? If he couldn't even be trusted to do as his father and mother had commanded him?"

"If you'd only told me, I could have spared you this agony so much sooner. Instead..." Aylen dropped her eyes. She had more to say to him, but he was already at his lowest, and she feared striking the fatal wound.

"I didn't know how much rage lived within me until my father surrendered himself to our enemy. And then, my mother... she had *two* children by another man, and then *abandoned* the rest, for what do we matter, in her eyes?"

"Your mother is imperfect, like all of us are. But neither of these things should be your burdens. They do not have to be *your* legacy."

"No? Is what I did with Raissa not proof of the son carrying the sins of the father and mother?"

"You... do you know, *you* have the power to undo what happened to Raissa. Don't you?"

"What?"

"The word of a lord is the greatest in the land. But instead, you hide yourself away, when you alone have the power to help her. You can still make this right for her, Christian. You could find her a respectable match and send for her to return, ending her exile. Instead, you hunker in your father's rooms and pretend like there's nothing here for you."

He laughed under his breath. "Can it really be so easy?"

"Nothing is ever easy when you're alone. Don't you see that?"

"I never wanted to be alone."

"Yet you chose it." Aylen's heart was still so broken. It would take time to heal and forgive. But wasn't this what she wanted, for him to see how he'd been wrong, to find his way back to her? If it wasn't, then she must accept that she had no life here at all.

"Can I really be this man? Is it possible?"

Aylen pulled him close. His face fell into her neck, where he sounded a soft cry against her flesh. "Anything is possible if you want it badly enough, and will do what's needed to see it done."

"I'll have your kettle discarded."

"Don't say that if you don't mean it. It was my fault. I wasn't careful enough. I knew how to prevent it, but I was careless, with everything we had to deal with here."

"I mean it. Don't drink it, Aylen."

"I cannot bear your regrets later."

He angled his head up and pressed his lips to the underside of her chin. "My only regrets are the ones that pushed you away from me. I can do anything with you by my side. Will you let me prove to you I can be the man you thought me to be? The one my mother and father raised me to be?"

Aylen tilted her head sideways and kissed him properly. How she'd missed this. Missed him.

But her heart was still too tender to commit.

"I promise to think on it."

46

THE LIGHT WIELDER

"**S**he's not in her tent!" Jesse called back to the others in a panic. "Check the others! Check all of them!"

Ash flew into action, tearing back flap after flap back in concert with the others, who looked as afraid as Jesse did. But Ash knew she wouldn't be there, same as Jesse did.

"Ravenna, Lisbet, check the lake, and the temple!" Ash directed. "Where's Kian?"

Jesse vaulted away from the camp and into the forest. Ash went after him. "Jesse, wait!"

Jesse had one of his daggers out of his boot without slowing. He slashed at the brush, piercing through places they both know she wouldn't be.

"Jesse."

"If she's not out there, she has to be in here!"

"You know she isn't."

"Why would you say that? She has to be!"

Ash reached for his arm. He didn't know if it would work, and even if it did, if it would work on his own son, who had even more magic flowing through him than he did. But Jesse's irises receded.

His breath returned to normal. His heartbeat no longer a frenzied hammer beating upon drums.

"What did you do to me?"

"Look at me. I saw it in your eyes. You know she's not there. So think, Jesse. Listen, to yourself."

"All I can think about is that I let her go, so I could be with you."

Ash had no time to nurse the bruise left by that. "I saw you. I saw you when you felt it. You knew she wouldn't be in her tent. You saw her. If you saw her, you can find her."

"I didn't see her, I..." Jesse stopped his thrashing of the bushes and touched his fist to his to his heart. "I felt it like, like a dagger made with ice."

"What do you feel now?"

"Fear." Jesse bit so hard into his lower lip it sent a trail of blood down his chin. "Fury."

"At Oldwin?"

"Isdemus. For leading me here and then leaving me. He found her last time. He could find her again, if he *was here*."

"You have his blood, Jesse," Ash urged. "Use it."

"What do ye mean, use it? I donnae even know what magic is! No one's trained me, no one..." He shook his head. "We're standing here sparring, when she's out there, he has her!"

"Who?"

"Aye, ye know who." Jesse's words faltered. He turned left, then right, then whipped his head to the sky. He drew his sword.

"What's happening?"

"Shh."

Jesse went still. His head tilted, listening. His dagger hand dropped lower until the steel fell to the ground.

His mouth parted. First in wonder. Then, anger.

Ash wanted to push him harder, but he was afraid of interrupting his thrall.

"Ash!" Lisbet cried. He shot a glance back in the direction her voice had called from, then looked back at Jesse. "Ash, I need you!"

But he couldn't leave Jesse. Not like this.

"Ash, where are you?"

"Go to her," Jesse said. Dazed. "I'll be fine. I ken I understand now."

"Understand what?"

"Ash!" Lisbet's cry now had a frenzied pitch.

"Go to her. I'll find you."

"I'll be right back," Ash promised.

LISBET KNELT AT THE FOREST'S EDGE, CLUTCHING THE TORN BLANKET soaked in blood. Blood that could only be Esmerelda's. If not hers, they were meant to believe it was.

"Let it go," Ash said, gently tugging to pull it away from her. "Jesse's gone into the forest to find her. He knew something was wrong. He would know if it was too late."

"This is a lot of blood, Ash! It's a lot of blood!"

"And it does us no good here, wondering about it, does it? We need to get back to Jesse. He's in the forest. We can help him."

Ravenna moved several paces away from them. In the distance, she spotted Kian gathering with the Saleen. Would they search for Esmerelda, or was there nothing more important to them than their temple? Their Light?

Even if they helped, they wouldn't find her. Not where they were looking.

It wasn't Ravenna's magic that told her this, but Oldwin himself.

And in the end, raven, phoenix, whatever you are... I upheld my end of the deal and I let her live. But you can only buy someone's life once. This time, she belongs to me, and I will decide her fate, just as I decided yours.

Oldwin had at last found his vengeance. He couldn't attack her body, so instead, he went for her heart. He wanted her to know it was her own failures that would cost Esmerelda her life.

Ravenna knelt down and pressed her hands to the earth. She closed her eyes, and at last, listened to the voices that had been calling for her all along.

. . .

Yes, there you are. Aimed true now.

Where are you, sorcerer?

Your father wasn't going to leave you without some intervention, was he? He'll be coming upon a bit of Esmerelda's blood at the forest's edge. Now, I should think.

If you've harmed her—

You're in no position for ultimatums, Jamesan. But your fortune looks up, for I already spared her life once. I can do it again.

Where are you?

Keep walking. You'll find me. Us.

What do ye want, that you'd have to pull me away from the others to get it from me?

Don't you want to lay eyes upon her first, to see that I've not killed her?

I know Esme isn't dead. I have no patience for games.

Something tells me that this is the most talkative you'll ever be in our short but valuable acquaintance.

I've no unnecessary words for you. Only the end of my sword.

How unimaginative for the one who has within him the most unique magic in all the worlds.

Aye? Isdemus said you didnae know anything about me, all these years. That's the power of magic.

I don't fear your magic, Jamesan. I want your help.

And how could I help you?

Well, you could quicken your pace before I lose patience and do something terrible.

Jesse stumbled over roots protruding from the ground. He fell forward, but instead of hitting earth, the air caught him. It was just as it had been in Greystone Abbey, when the magic had intervened to keep him from launching over the stairwell.

When he recovered his footing, he pushed through the next patch of brush, and there he was.

Oldwin.

Holding Esmeralda, with a longblade to her throat.

"Esme!" Jesse cried out. He held his hands forward. "Donnae move, not even a little! That blade is lethal."

Esmerelda almost nodded from instinct, but stopped. She widened her terrified eyes instead to show she understood.

"Here we are, then," Oldwin said, as if they were gathering for supper. "Just you and me, at last."

"Release her, and we can talk."

"I don't think that will be happening."

"There'll be no business between us if I cannae even think straight."

"It isn't your thoughts that will serve you, or her, but your action."

Jesse was afraid to look at her. Fresh rage boiled from deep within. If he dared feed it any more, it would erupt beyond his control.

He swallowed and met the sorcerer's eyes. "Tell me, then."

"I want you to go through the veil, to the Light."

"You know that's why I'm here, aye? Are ye always so clever?"

Oldwin tilted the knife up. "I'll show you clever."

"All right!"

Oldwin dodged the question. "Tonight."

"Look, at least just lower the blade. She cannae even breathe."

"Tonight. But you will not be alone."

Jesse swallowed his laugh. "They brought me here to stop you, not aid you. That is what ye want, aye? To go through, with me?"

"I *will* go through, and I'll do it with your aid, for if you refuse this, I bleed her dry before you can even make it the ten paces to try and take her from me."

Esmerelda's cheeks flexed in fear. She strained to be still. Her eyes closed.

"And if I do, what happens then?"

"She lives."

"And to the veils? The Light?"

"Do you care?"

Jesse realized he did care. He might not have wanted this, but it was his just the same.

"Do you care about this kingdom more than you care about her? For that is really what we're talking about here, Jamesan. Nothing more complicated than her life."

Esmeralda's whimper pierced his heart. "Are they not the same? For if you take the Light, as Enivera once tried, is her life not forfeit, anyway, along with all the others?"

"You sound so much like Isdemus, weighing the moral quandaries of his tender heart. Make your choice, Jamesan. It can only be made once. And know that if you let her die here, that does not mean you have won. I will truss myself to your legs and push you through myself before this night is ended."

"Esmerelda," Jesse said. He gripped his sword tighter. His eyes filled with stars. Oldwin meant to kill her. Either way, no matter the choice he made. "Everything's gonna be all right."

"If you will not choose, then I will do it for you!" Oldwin drew his blade across her throat. Esmeralda's eyes fluttered. She gurgled as he released her and collapsed to the ground.

"NO!" Jesse's scream pierced the night, splitting into the simultaneous cries of a thousand versions of himself. He leapt forward, but it was his own magic stopping him, his own magic keeping him from her. And then he saw that Oldwin, too, was aware of this shift, and it wasn't wonder he saw in the sorcerer's eyes, but raw, unrealized fear.

Jesse's arms flew out. His head fell back, and as he rose up off the ground, rising higher and higher, everything, everything exploded into light.

LISBET SHIELDED HER EYES AS NIGHT ERUPTED INTO DAY. SHE BIT INTO her jerkin to keep from screaming. It wasn't only her eyes under assault, but her ears, everything; her very flesh burned with whatever Jesse had done and was still doing.

Eyes still covered, she crawled across the forest floor, belly pressed tight to the tangled undergrowth. Blind in all the ways that mattered, she called upon the magic that was still so new to her, still untested, to take her to Esmerelda. To find her without eyes.

She chanced a peek and saw Jesse still levitating above the earth. She'd never seen anyone do anything like it, but there wasn't time to think about it. Farther ahead, Oldwin had dropped into a protective crouch, waiting for the horrors to end.

Was it killing him? She hoped it was. She prayed it was. But that hope was naively optimistic, for she lived, and were they not made from the same things?

Where was everyone? She'd lost track of Ravenna, and Ash, and Kian, and all the rest when the light pierced the world.

At last, her hand connected with Esmeralda's upturned boot. She traced a path up her leg, one hand at a time, stopping at her waist only long enough to bring herself closer, inching across the ground. Farther still, to her chest and...

Lisbet cried out as her hand connected with the gash at Esmeralda's throat.

"You won't die this way, Esmerelda. You've cheated death once. You can do it again." Lisbet cupped her hands around her cousin's throat, where the blood still pulsed as it flowed away from her. But where there was blood, there was life, still. She squeezed her eyes shut and called deep within herself, to where she knew this power must live. It had to be there. This magic that eluded her all her life couldn't fail her now, when she actually *needed* it, just as it had come to her aid in the Wastelands when Oldwin bore down on them.

"Heal. *Please* heal."

Someone fell in beside her. She didn't have to look up to see it was Ravenna. She seemed unaffected by the magic coming off Jesse, and, looking straight at Lisbet, said, "Together. Focus now. We do it together."

Esmeralda's chest heaved upward as she lifted, her arms dropping to the sides, her fingers brushing the earth as the two women reached deep within themselves for the magic needed to save her. Lisbet screamed from the inside, pushing it out of her. *Take it. Take my own life force, give some to her. But don't let it end like this!*

Esmeralda sent Lisbet stumbling backward when she sounded a deep gasp into the blinding night. She rolled to her side, clutching at her throat. Then, clawing at the ground for purchase, she screamed.

"Guardians," Lisbet whispered. She squeezed her eyes shut.

"The Magic of Need," Kian said as he watched Jesse. She sensed the others had also come. The other Saleen. Ash. "You cannot summon this magic by command. It reveals itself only for those worthy of wielding it." He sounded not merely surprised, but in awe.

"What's he doing? What is this?" Lisbet asked. She buried her face in her cloak. Her dinner rose to the back of her throat, and she retched into the dirt.

She'd thought this was like what she'd done in the Wastelands, but it wasn't. It was so much more devastating.

"Even he does not know that he's just called the Light."

Lisbet screamed against the inside of her wrist. Jesse's magic was in her head now, pressing at the sides of her skull, inward, outward. It was unbearable. She couldn't stay here. None of them could. She had to grab Esmerelda, to get them both away.

But then it was over. The light drew back, retreating into Jesse. He descended, lowering back to the ground.

He doesn't know. He doesn't know that he's just saved her. That in slowing Oldwin, he's given us the time to bring her back.

The Magic of Need. Could there be a better name for it?

"Only a Light Wielder can call upon that magic!" Oldwin cried. He pushed back to his feet, unsteady. Swaying, he reached for the branch of a nearby tree, and when he missed, he fell back to his knees, where he remained. "You are no Light Wielder, Jamesan! No sorcerer can wield the Light if they have not first taken it for themselves!"

Jesse held his sword at his side, sweat pouring from every inch of him. "You've taken everything from me, and now, I will take everything from you."

Ash withdrew his own sword. Lisbet went for hers, but then Jesse stopped. His fighting stance eased.

The sound of Esmeralda's feral scream called the eyes of all gathered. Lisbet turned to see her standing over Oldwin, his thin hair gathered in her fist as she drew her own dagger across his throat. Her howling escalated as she sawed through his flesh in haphazard strokes; as he flailed beneath her, weakened by whatever Jesse had called down.

She sounded another cry and then ripped backward, tripping over the ground as his head came loose. She regarded it in delighted surprise, then held it aloft, her whole body undulating with her uneven, harried breaths.

"And once again, it is I who have done what other men could not!" she cried. Her voice was hoarse. A thin pink line stretched across her throat. "It's done, and now *you will leave my husband alone!*"

"Esme," Lisbet whispered. She recovered her wits and scrambled to her feet and ran to her. She felt Jesse right behind her, but the magic had taken something from him. He dragged himself forward by will alone.

Lisbet gaped at the horrors in both Esmerelda's hands. She tried to take something from her, anything. The dagger. The head. But Esmeralda would relinquish neither.

"You can put it down now, Esme. It's done. You've done it."

Jesse limped toward them faster now. Esmerelda's crazed vibrations eased as he neared, as if his presence were the only power capable to calm this tempest she'd stirred to life.

She dropped both arms to her sides. The dagger was the first to fall. The head was next, bouncing upon the ground twice before rolling off to lie in the dirt.

And then she, too, fell, but not before Jesse caught her.

"Let it go. I'm here."

Esmerelda collapsed into his arms.

"We cannot stay here," Kian called to them. "We cannot waste even a single moment."

"Did you not see what happened? It's done!" Ash exclaimed. "It's over. Can you not let them have even this?"

"It's not over. It will not be over until The Hidden Kingdom is closed to everyone, forever."

47
FOR THE ONE WHO CANNOT FLY

"You're back!"

"We thought they'd wooed you into staying!"

Marsh and Emberley gathered on each arm as they guided him inside, peppering him with questions too fast for him to answer. He couldn't quite be sure, but it seemed they *were* happy to see him. He'd still half-expected them to be gone. That he'd arrive and find only the remnants of their time there, as they'd moved on without him.

"Tell us everything," Emberley said. "How was it? Did you find what you were after?" She moved back to their fire and rifled through the food bag, withdrawing some root vegetable that Marsh had chosen. It turned his stomach. "Here, you should have something to eat before we get going. Did you eat anything at all while you were there?"

Alasyr shook his head at the offering. "I'm not hungry."

"Is everything okay?" Marsh handed him a mug of wine. This Alasyr accepted.

"My mother and father are dead," he said, after a long sip. "I thought they might be. Now I have confirmation."

"Alasyr!"

"My grandmother will be tried as a traitor. I don't know what the outcome will be." He looked at them both with a wry smile. "And… I saw Ravenna. For a little while."

Ember set the bag aside and moved to him. "She came back? Why?"

"Same reason as me. She had her questions. I had mine."

"She's gone again?" Marsh asked. "Already?"

"She got her answers."

Ember laid a hand against his face. Her troubled eyes wore more concern than he'd ever gotten from either of his parents. "What happened to you there? You've changed."

"No, I'm not changed, I…" He grabbed her hand and brought it to his mouth. "I have to ask you both something that I don't know how to ask."

"When you wanted something from me, you didn't hesitate," Marsh said. He'd come closer, but leaned against the cave wall. He was more confident than when Alasyr had seen him last. More sure of himself. Alasyr tried not to think of why that might be. "You didn't care how mad it might sound. How much danger it put me in."

"No, I didn't care, because I knew you'd do it, for her. But are there limits to that, Marsh, to what you would for Emberley?"

"I haven't met one yet."

"Just say it," Emberley pressed.

"I need to know, Ember. What life waits for you when we leave this mountain?"

She seemed surprised by the question. "Well, I suppose I don't know. I've tried not to dwell on it, because there's no place for me now, is there? I'm having a hard time seeing myself anywhere."

"But you've known you weren't going home," Marsh said, gentle. "You knew that before you flew here."

She nodded. "But what else is there, if not the Rush, if not this other world I belong to, that has already turned me out? Then what am I meant for?"

A welcome warmth was taking over inside Alasyr, one that

threatened to crush the ever spreading darkness. He would say it and let come what may. He would say it, because even if they turned him down, they wouldn't turn their backs on him.

"A revolution is happening in Midnight Crest." He laughed to himself. "Started by my grandmother, of all people. In trying to protect her way of things, she upended it all. Change is coming. Maybe the Ravenwoods are at last ready for it."

"Are we in danger here?" Emberley asked.

He shook his head. He felt Marsh's eyes on him from across the cave. "They want..." Alasyr bowed his head in his folded hands, drawing strength. When he again looked up, he met her gaze. "You, Emberley. They want you to come to Midnight Crest."

She stumbled back a step. "Me? Last time, your mother *murdered* me, in case you'd forgotten."

"She's gone now, and the others condemn what my mother did to you. They see you, and they see things could be different for them, too." Alasyr channeled his grandfather now, hoping desperately that he was doing the right thing. "They see hope. They don't turn their noses at the story of Rhosyn at all. They're inspired by her. They revere her. She's a symbol of what could be, if they weren't held like prisoners in a small northern kingdom, but instead allowed to live among men."

"They'd become curiosities of men, taken as slaves. Killed." Marsh was green in his face as he said the words. "The kingdom regulates the use of magic so carefully. We all know the penalty for not following their laws."

"Rarely enforced," Ember said. "My mother and all her children have practiced magic for years. My grandmother. We all have magic in us. Your own mother, Clarissant, is a witch, is she not?"

"You know it would be different if thousands of Ravenwoods were walking our Reaches, eating in our taverns, living in our towns, marrying our men and women. We, *us*, we'd welcome it, but we aren't everyone else."

Ember nodded. "He's right. Even Rhosyn had to temper her powers when she came to live in Longwood Rush."

Alasyr shook his head. "What you describe is generations away. It'll never happen in our lifetimes. But that isn't what they're hoping for, or what they've offered me."

"What, exactly, have they offered you?" Marsh's patience had turned to suspicion. Alasyr would have to speak quickly before it returned to distrust.

"They want Ember to come to Midnight Crest, not as an adversary, or a curiosity, but as a beginning of what could be for all of them."

"I see." Marsh ran his hands over his new beard.

Emberley moved across the cave, stopping before Alasyr. "You did tell them I go nowhere without Marsh?"

"I did, and that he was a man, without wings. They said they'd find a way, if Marsh was willing. He represents something to them, too. The kingdom of men that has been closed to them their entire history here."

"They want *me* to come?" Marsh asked.

"They've extended the invite to you as well, yes."

"Are we really considering this?" Marsh asked her, but the sharp concern of his earlier words was absent now. Alasyr felt his rush of heartbeat, his whirl of thoughts. Marsh was a practical man, a planner, and this passed across his face as he imagined tomorrow, a year from now, ten. "You really believe we could be safe there? All of us? Because, I'd be trapped there, you know. At your mercy."

Alasyr nodded. "I would never let anything happen to you. Either of you."

"And when we get there?"

"I don't know. They want us to help them find a way forward, with the best of who we are, not the worst of it."

"And what do you want?" Marsh asked, and Alasyr realized that, until now, no one had ever asked him this.

"I want to be wherever the two of you are," he said. He felt no shame in saying these words now, and that freedom of thought made his heart swell even more. It made him brave. "I want to go wherever you go."

Marsh peeled off the wall and joined them in the center of the cave. "I guess I'd be all right with that. Ember?"

She nodded. She dropped her hands to her sides, offering one to each of them. "I don't know what I did to deserve this. You. Both of you."

Marsh's eyes widened, mouth parting in growing wonder as he beheld the new spectacle just beyond the cave entrance. Alasyr already knew what he was seeing; he'd felt them, all of them, the hundreds of Ravenwoods as they left The Rookery and traveled together south, swarming in perfect formation.

Ember turned and gasped. "Look at them all. What are they doing? Alasyr?"

"They're here for Marsh. For the one who cannot fly."

"And me," Ember whispered. "The one who forgot how."

Marsh pushed her matted hair back off her face, kissing her right beside her ear. "If you tried now, I believe you could do it."

"Do you?"

Alasyr pressed his lips to her other temple. "You're ready, Emberley."

Ember laughed to keep them from seeing her tears. "Have we decided, then? You both think there's nothing more to discuss? And you, Marsh, you'd just give up your birthright, for a life with strangers?"

"I could never take that title, unless it meant you were with me, and I see now, Ember, that you aren't made for that life. You weren't meant to preside over banquets, or the blessing of babies. That was never your path. I used to wish it was, to fit you neatly into the same life I was made for, but it was fear behind that wish. I took my love for you up this mountain, and I'll take it higher still, if that's where you're called, for I'll always be called to wherever you are."

Tears streamed down her face as she turned to Alasyr. "And you? Would you really return to the same place that you fled?"

"It's not that place anymore. The place I fled is a relic, on its last breath. I think... I think I'd like to be a part of building what comes next. The Ravenwoods aren't defined by one person. We all matter."

The symphony of wings in the skies beyond the cave grew louder. "I think you're both right," Ember said. "I think I can fly now."

When Master Frost had given them the counsel to ask around about the old farm, he'd failed to mention that first they'd have to find someone to ask.

Balfour and Assana wandered from the taverns to inns to shops, weaving in and out of the derelict structures that weren't quite abandoned, but neither were they fit for patrons. Balfour couldn't help wondering what had happened here. Whether it was beyond repair. If someone with enough coin would ever come and breathe new life into a place that had once been one of the Great Cities.

They had to leave the town proper to find anyone willing to talk to them. This was where they came across the dairy maid, tending her cattle at the edge of town. Maid, though, was perhaps not the right word for her. She was old enough to have remembered when the Wastelands was still Southerlands territory. Her white, rheumy eyes had been blind long enough for her to learn her comfort with it. She navigated her task with surprising ease.

"Haunted? Aye, that's what they told ye? That doesnae even crack it." She cackled under her breath. "Right fools, then, both of ye. Highborns too, from the smell of it. You'd both benefit from the paddle."

"But do you know of it?" Assana replied in annoyance. "We were told the locals would know."

"There isnae such thing as ghosts, pubes. But if ye've an urge to disappear from this world, nay to return, then aye, travel up the road another half kip, and you'll see it, where the path splits. Top of the hill. There's no road. No one tends it now, for why would they? We're all waiting for the one with the courage to burn it down." She laughed again. "But then, aye, it might rebuild itself, aye?"

Balfour thanked her and nudged Assana along. He could see the old woman's words had shaken her.

"Don't let her under your skin. There no such thing as ghosts, she said so herself."

"Then what do you think all that was, about people disappearing?"

"If a veil is there, that would explain it."

"But never to return?"

"You know what I know." Balfour kicked at a large rock in the road, sending it into the remnants of a nearby fence. "If you want to stop now, then go."

"Of course I don't want to stop. Can't I voice concerns without you thinking I'm having doubts?"

"No need in getting us both scared, that's all."

"I'll be sure to keep my words to myself, then."

It was as the old woman said. When they came upon it, they knew. Though the day had boasted some sunshine, not a drop of it fell over this place, forsaken by light, forgotten by time.

"What do you think could have happened here? For it to look like it does?" Assana asked.

"Children going missing comes to mind."

"But if so many have been lost here, then it can't be so hard to enter, can it? If some can fall through, without intending to?"

"I don't know," he said, but he was shaking his head. "That would be too easy."

"It could be," she went on, "that these men, the ones coming back to tell their tales, have complicated it needlessly. Whatever payment the veils demand, it could be as simple as asking. Couldn't it? Why does it have to be the letting of blood, or the call of danger?"

"Do you want an answer, or are you thinking aloud?"

"Your mood has soured, but you should be happy. We made it." She took his hand as he lifted her up a small embankment where the road had fallen away.

"I'll save my joy for when we have confirmation we haven't been sent on a fool's task."

Balfour hesitated when they reached the door. It loomed high above him, higher than it should. It seemed to him that the entrance to the house could be the veil, for when he stepped through, he was quite certain he'd belong to another world than the one outside. The musk of wet soil and old boards repulsed him. He held his breath.

Assana pushed through the doorway ahead of him.

"Watch your footing. There's a cellar beneath. I wouldn't trust the floor at all."

She bent her knees and gently bounced. "Let's find that cellar, quickly."

She pushed on ahead, past rotting furniture, and windows snaked with dying vines. Even the plants wouldn't grow here, he thought with a chill, and then he saw she'd found the stairs.

"It's so dark down here," she called back, already descending. "I told you we should've brought the lantern."

"Do you know how heavy a lantern is? It would have slowed us."

"Not seeing a thing will slow us well enough."

"We'll have to make do with the bit of light coming through from outside, though, won't we? It's the best we've got. It's—"

Assana stopped when she reached the floor. The daylight from behind him lit her well enough for him to see the horror spreading across her face.

"What is it? What's down there?"

"We may have just answered one question," she said, struggling for breath. "Balfour. It's here."

"What is?"

"You know what."

Balfour shuffled down the first few stairs and then hesitated. "Maybe we should go."

"Go? Why would we go? That's your fear talking. We're here. We've done it. And it wasn't even so hard, was it?"

"You can see it? With your eyes?"

"Get down here already!"

"Are you certain that's what it is, and not some other… malevolence? It should be invisible, Assana. My father said as much. That he only felt it. He could never see it."

"Not this one," Assana said, and then she disappeared from his view as she moved farther into the cellar. "And yes, I'm quite certain."

"Assana!"

Balfour angled himself sideways down the remaining steps, one foot, then the other. He didn't know where this fear had come from. He'd never been afraid of anything, certainly not this, which he'd been chasing for so long.

"It's all right, Balfour."

"Are you sure? I can't stop thinking about those missing children. I think you should come back up. We can talk about it first."

"I don't think there's evil here. But it's..."

"It's what?" Balfour called back. Sweat dripped into his eyes. "It's what?"

"I think it wants us to enter. I don't think we'll have to do anything at all to appease it, other than accept."

Balfour leaned back against the stairwell, gasping for breath. Why was this happening to him? Why now, when he'd done it, at last? Where was his courage?

"I'm gonna step through," she called back. He didn't like the way her voice changed. It chilled him straight to the bone.

"No, wait!"

"It wants me to. It's... calling to me. It's been waiting for me."

"Assana!"

No response came.

"Assana? Wait! I'm coming. I'm coming down. Just wait for me!" He gripped the railing, eyes closed. His feet searched for purchase, and at last connected with the cool dirt.

Next foot. Next foot, he commanded. When his balance was secure, he pushed back off from the stairwell and opened his eyes.

"Ahh," he exhaled. There it was. It was... it was...

Balfour took a step. Then another. He wasn't in command of himself anymore. He responded to something bigger than himself. Assana wasn't there anymore, but he didn't need to look for her, for she'd already gone through, just as she'd said she would.

Balfour came to a stop just before the strange shimmer in the air of the cold cellar. It was warmer here, and the thought entered his head that he was feeling the warmth from the other side.

"Father," Balfour whispered. He took the last step, angling his foot forward, and then—

EAVAN WOULD NEVER FORGET WHAT HAPPENED WHEN ALRIC WOKE THE lion.

Earwyn wouldn't let go of her. Eavan strained in her arms, desperate to see, but her aunt held her back with the strength of a man.

"It should've been me. He's not quick enough, the poor bastard," she kept muttering, over and over, but she didn't go to take his place, either. Neither woman could move. Neither could take their eyes off Alric's gentle dance around the lion's mouth.

"Get your bow ready," Eavan said. "He's not wasting time."

Earwyn stumbled off to one side, searching for stable ground. She gathered her skirts and found solid footing. She never dropped her eyes off her husband as she reached into the quiver.

Eavan could just barely make out Alric's leap to his feet. The look of surprise he wore, and then panic.

"His eyes are open! They're open! It's already working! Earwyn, be ready!"

"I've got sight," Earwyn said. "But he needs to move before I'll get any clean shot off."

Alric was already running when the lion ambled to his feet. The beast shook off his sleep like the remains of a good nap.

"He's on his feet, Alric, move!"

Eavan backed up, instinct bidding her to be as far away from this beast as her feet could carry her. But then her foot connected with something warm. It was snow; it was...

"Aunt Earwyn. It's open. It's open!"

"Go on, then, girl! I'll take care of the lion."

Eavan shifted, now more afraid for them than for herself. She left her foot anchored within, in case the veil tried to close again.

But she was frozen, horrified by the sight unfolding. Alric, bounding through snow. The lion, faster.

"Shoot!" he cried. "For Guardian's sake, shoot!"

Earwyn pulled back on the bow. Her hand shook. Eavan reached her own hand over and laid it over her aunt's. Earwyn's smile was tense.

"Now," Eavan whispered. The arrow sailed through the falling snow and embedded in the lion's upper front thigh. He yelped, but it hardly slowed him at all.

"Another, another," Eavan urged. She pulled the next arrow out for her aunt, helping her nock it. "He's almost on him."

"I'm going as fast as I can! Alric, run!"

Earwyn loosed an arrow once more, this time hitting the lion at the side of his neck. This one stopped him, long enough to swat it with his paw. The arrow snapped, the end falling away as the lion leapt back into action. But it was enough to give Alric a small lead.

He almost fell on them both as he tripped on something buried in snow. "Go, go," he cried, and then Eavan watched the rest happen as if looking through a window. She was pushed, falling, falling, through air, through warmth. Earwyn was pulled into the veil with her. Then she saw Alric turning to face down the beast, sword drawn.

Eavan looked up from the sand of a desert to see her uncle turning and leaping through the veil as the lion's jaws yawned open to claim its prize.

And then the lion was gone. The snow was gone.

"Is it still there?"

"It didn't come through." Earwyn exhaled. "It didn't come." She stretched her hand forward. "I can't see it. The veil. Is it still there?"

"I don't know. I don't know," Alric panted. "But we didn't step through just to return again, did we?" Alric threw his head back and laughed. "We came through! We did it! We're here!"

But Earwyn had already gone on ahead. Eavan could almost read her thoughts as her aunt toiled over more practical matters, all of which could be summed up with the question, *what now?* She wandered in the direction of a forest that seemed so oddly placed in the middle of all the sand and sun. Eavan lifted her own skirts and followed her. Alric lingered only a short while longer before coming after them.

It didn't seem so different from the forests she was used to in the Easterlands. There were fruit-like things growing in the trees. She wanted to eat from them, but this wasn't her world, where she knew what was safe and what wasn't. It wasn't only her own life she needed to consider now.

Tacked against trees every few paces were scraps of red cloth, held in place by honey. Eavan knew this trick. She could guess why she was seeing it here, now.

Alric was the one who spotted the stream. He fell to his knees and drank of the water without stopping to wonder if he should. Eavan and her aunt watched him in wary anticipation, but the sickness never came. "It's water, just like ours."

Eavan dropped down and lapped hungrily from the slow-moving water. At her side, Earwyn moaned at the fresh assault. Nothing had ever tasted so good, and she thought, yes, let's stay here, where we can drink of this water for the rest of our lives.

Alric leaned back as a shadow passed over them.

Not one shadow, but two.

An old man and an old woman.

Eavan drew back, but the old woman held her hands aloft to show there was no threat to them. The man did the same.

"It seems we were too late this time," he said. "They're here to stay, I suppose."

"We were too late," she agreed. "But… could this be the man Gretchen talked about? She said he would try to come again. The timing is right."

"Gretchen!" Earwyn exclaimed. "You've seen her? Is Pieter here, too?"

"Are you Alric?" the woman asked.

He nodded. "Is this real?"

She turned to Earwyn. "And you must be Earwyn."

"Where's Gretchen?"

"And you..." the old woman knelt before Eavan. "There's two of you."

Eavan nodded.

"There are no little ones here. But perhaps it will be different for you. Your child is of your world, not ours."

"Where's Gretchen?" Earwyn demanded.

The man and woman exchanged a look. "Fill your skins. There's still enough light left to make it to the top, but only just."

"Where are you taking us?"

"You said you were looking for Gretchen? Well, you won't find her in here."

The old woman planted her walking stick into the dirt and turned. Her husband joined her.

"We aren't really going with them, are we?" Earwyn asked.

"We came in search of something else. This is something else," Alric said, radiating with nervous, charged energy.

"How do we know it's safe? How do we know they won't slit our throats and steal our things?"

Eavan pushed to her feet. "We don't. But we didn't come all this way to cower in fear, with our doubts, did we?"

She fell in behind their new guides and prepared to face whatever *something else* might await them.

ALASYR LED MARSH TO THE MOUTH OF THE CAVE. MARSH'S FEAR WAS palpable, but his step was true. He didn't falter. A surge of pride coursed through Alasyr. In some small way, he'd been a part of helping him find this courage.

And what was Marsh to him? He watched him from the corner of his eye. It was hard to conjure the derision he'd once felt. He supposed Marsh was his friend, but that missed the mark, too. He wanted him near. He was better in his presence. It was like this with Emberley, too, but with her it had become so much more. Maybe it could be like that with Marsh, too. And if it could, he wouldn't shy away from it.

Emberley, at Marsh's other side, took his hand as they neared the edge. They didn't ask if Marsh was ready. This was a true leap of faith, where thought and hesitation had no place.

Alasyr grabbed his other hand, and together, they hoisted him up and out, into the frigid mountain air. Marsh sucked in a fearful breath as he soared forth, but the expected fall never came, as the ravens knitted their form into a protective cushion.

"I can't believe this is happening. Do you see this? I'm flying!"

"Don't get ahead of yourself, Wildwood. You're still a man," Alasyr countered.

Ember was next. She closed her eyes as her head tilted back. And then her arms arced out at her sides, forming the perfect half-circle, her palms connecting just as she snapped into the form she was meant for. She took to the skies and soared, wings stretched, making several indulgent loops before settling in with the other ravens who were there to take Marsh to Midnight Crest.

"She's stunning. She's absolutely perfect," Marsh whispered.

"Yes," Alasyr agreed. "She is."

It was his turn to take the step to the edge. He looked out upon the sea of black feathers, a unification born of love, and of a newfound faith. Marsh had rolled forward on his hands and knees to brace himself better, but he no longer looked so terrified.

"I'll see you at the top," Alasyr said and erupted into feathers.

48

THE ROT FROM WITHIN

Gwyn wrung out the bloodied cloth once more. The faceless nurses had been in and out, replacing the filthy for the clean, but the slow bleed in Khallum's abdomen was relentless. He would live, they said. *They* being the physicians and the healers who traveled south to Warwicktown in a rush. The lone seer in the keep had a positive outlook to share as well. The Nye girl had brought the woman with her. She'd refused to come without her. Khallum allowed it for the sake of keeping peace at the wedding, but everyone knew he would be rid of the soothsayer before long. As he dealt with all things unpleasant to him.

He would have to wake first.

But though they all said he would live, none could explain why Khallum's wound wouldn't close.

"How is he?" Little Brandyn stood in the doorway. But he wasn't so little anymore, was he? Though his body hadn't caught up with his deeds, his face belied the many traumas he'd endured to get here. This same boy had led a war. Had saved her husband.

She shook her head.

"Will he ever wake?"

"They say he will. Where's Ransom?"

646

"With Rutland and Hamish." Brandyn shifted uncomfortably. "Training."

"Ahh." Gwyn returned to her ministrations. Training was a kind and over simplistic way to say what Brandyn really meant. Ransom was being prepared to replace his father, for even his own men had such a void of hope that they saw no choice but to enact the succession protocols.

It was a strange thing to regard her husband in his stillness. Khallum was never calm. He was even a restless sleeper. The last time she'd seen him so perfectly inanimate was the day of the Blessed Union, when he'd awaited Khain's decree to decide which young highborn he would marry. Gwyn remembered very little about that day, other than the tears, the heartbreak caused to others with so few words. But she remembered the light twitch at the corner of Khallum's mouth, the smallest hint of approval, when her name was read with his.

He'd assessed his options as they were all paraded upon the dais and had picked her. And then he'd won her.

Gwyn wondered at many points throughout their two decades together whether she'd failed or succeeded at fulfilling her husband's expectations formed on that day.

But if she *had* succeeded, then it was predicated on a great betrayal. The greatest ever told.

Brandyn lingered a moment longer and then slipped back down the hall.

Gwyn rose from her husband's side and moved across the room to the door. She closed it, pressing her body against the old wood as she latched the bolt. She half expected him to leap out of bed, railing at her for locking him in. But he didn't move.

"Khallum," she began. She twisted her hands together. Was she really going to say this? Now? And would it even count when he wasn't present to hear the words? Or would they find him somewhere, like ash riding a wind?

"Khallum, I... there's something I have to tell you." She lowered herself back into her chair at his bedside. "I don't know how. I didn't then, when I should have, and it's not gotten any easier since. But I can't hold it inside me anymore. It's eroding away at what's left of me. I would have told you, eventually. I would have! I meant to, so many times, but there was always something else. But no matter what the physicians or healers have said, you are not as you once were, darling, and I won't chance your promise spending itself without me telling you true, for once."

Gwyn reached for his hand, then drew it back to her lap. She didn't deserve the comfort his touch would bring. He wouldn't consent to give it if he knew what she was about to say.

"I know what a great shock to you it was to know our Esmerelda was alive, after all those months of mourning her. Imagine how it was for me, her mother! The one child of four I was allowed to love as my own. To nurse, and play with, and decide the manner of her upbringing. It still amazes me how she ended up more like you, but that only made me love her more."

Gwyn squeezed her eyes to push back the tears. She wouldn't cry. She wasn't searching for pity, nor redemption. Only an end to the secrets.

"So, when a stranger reached out to me, claiming to have Esmerelda in his grasp, I..." Gwyn shook her head. "No, I'll not make more lies upon the ones already grown. It was Oldwin who came to me. He wore another face, but was free with his name, and his intentions. He said he had Esmerelda, she was carrying her first child, and I could have her! He was going to give her back to me. All I had to do was tell him one thing. That was all, he said. And it was only by chance that I knew where the munitions were stored at all. I heard Rutland speaking of it, to Law, in the hall one day when I passed. The men never think to whisper around the women; they think we're too daft to ever know a thing. But I did know it, and it seemed such a small thing to have my heart back. To know I could give you that gift, too, and the boys. Garrick especially took her loss so hard. Munitions could be replaced. Esmerelda could not.

"But then... ah, I should have known. A sorcerer with his powers, he could've found the munitions on his own. He read my hesitation well and played upon it. He knew that I knew Esmerelda would never be safe again, nor her child, unless I continued to pay for that safety. But if I'd known that our arrangement would cost the lives of Nye's family... of Law... of poor Anabella... well, I..." Gwyn hung her head. "No, I would've done the same. I would've done just about anything, to have Esmerelda home again."

Now she cried. The weight hadn't been lifted. It never could. But the shroud of her betrayal had been turned back, and now Khallum knew her for who she was.

Gwyn screamed when she was lifted in the air by her hair. The pain was immediate, absolute, blinding. Her feet dangled as she was hoisted higher, off her chair. She clawed at the source, but she knew these arms, these hands.

"You... treacherous... bitch."

"Khallum, let me down. You're hurting me! Let me down and we can talk!"

"My own wife. *My own wife!*" Khallum yanked, and she went flying. Her feet landed upon the floor and slid as he moved faster, pausing only to draw the bolt on the door. "Talk? Ye wanna talk, do ye? Aye, well, get the words out now, while ye can."

"Khallum, please!" she pleaded. Oh, she deserved this, but the pain was beyond anything she'd known. She thrashed in his arms until some of her scalp tore away, sending a searing agony through her. He flipped her against a wall as he turned the corner, and she felt something break.

"Please? Donnae ye think any of the dead might have asked the same, before your treachery bought their promises?"

"I know the wrong I've done, but..." Gwyn screamed again as she connected with another corner. "Please, just put me down! You can take your sword to me, but let me walk on my own feet!"

"The nerve in asking me for anything. Ye donnae even know what this is, do ye? For you were never salt and sand. You never bled for this Reach, like we have. Ahh, but ye will. My own wife!"

"Where are we going?"

"You've seen me deal with traitors aplenty. Only this time, you'll be on the sharp end of it."

KHALLUM DRAGGED GWYN FROM THE KEEP, AWARE OF THE EYES ON him, gathering quickly into a crowd that followed him. But though they were curious, none said a word in her defense. None stopped to ask why the lord was dragging his lady like a common housemaid across the courtyard and down to the coast, toward the Warwick Throne. This enraged him more. Had they seen in her what he would not? Could not?

She sounded a shrill cry when he pulled her into the sand. Her legs kicked behind her, but she found even less purchase here than she had on the dirt. His hands slipped from the blood he'd drawn at her scalp, so he switched hands, gathering more hair this time.

"Please," she whimpered. Didn't even have the mettle to scream anymore. She was weak, and her weakness had cost good men and women their lives, and it couldn't be borne! It could not be borne from anyone, least of all the wife of the one man responsible for all of them.

"Father! Father, what the Guardians are you doing?" Ransom. At last someone was here to speak for her. Well, he could speak all he wanted. There was nothing for Khallum to hear that he hadn't already. Nothing that could right that wrong.

More cries of *father, father*. The other boys, then. He regretted they'd see this, but perhaps it was time for them to know the business of men applied to all.

Brandyn was the next to call out for him, and then Rutland, and then more voices he recognized, men and boys and even women who couldn't fathom what had gotten into their lord. Probably thought he was addle-brained from his injuries. Khallum grunted, tugging harder. So, they'd all bear witness to this, then. There'd be no whispering in halls later, about what might have happened between Lord Warwick and his wife, because they'd all have seen it themselves, with their own eyes. He would make her speak her words again, for all to hear, so none could say Khallum Warwick had not ruled evenly.

He yanked harder as he scaled the hill of the Warwick Throne. He'd underestimated how badly his injuries had slowed him. He'd led with anger, but now the wound in his belly screamed at him. The blood on his nightshirt meant it was reopening, again.

"On your feet, you bitch!" he screamed, and she tried, but his grip was too tight. He released her and shoved her to the ground. She landed on her knees, sobbing.

"Khallum, what's gotten into you? That's your wife!" Rutland. So he was to be the replacement for Law. His new voice of reason.

"Aye, wife is she? Well, what would ye do, Erran, if it was *your* wife who was the rat on the inside, feeding information to our enemy?"

"Gwyn? No. There must be a mistake." Rutland reached for him, but Khallum shook him off. "You're not well. You should be resting."

"Tell him yourself." Khallum kicked at her. "Tell him!"

"It was me," Gwyn cried. "It *was* me, but I did it for Esmerelda! What was I supposed to do? She's my daughter! She's my daughter!"

"Son of a crow," Rutland whispered. "All right, then. Aye, let's, uh, let's take this back inside, aye? We can discuss it. Decide what should be done about it, like men."

"She killed Samuel!"

"Aye, I heard ye, but we can talk about it, then we'll deal with it."

"There's only one way we deal with traitors in this land!" Khallum boomed. "And ye know that. Ye know it."

"We also afford them a proper trial, Khallum. Aye? A trial, where other men will decide her guilt."

"You heard her!" Khallum drew his sword and turned to Rutland. "You heard her, with your own ears! There isnae a matter of inno-cence, not anymore. She isnae denying her guilt."

"Mother!" Ransom cried and tried to go to this mother's side.

Khallum pointed his sword at him. "She isnae your mother anymore, Ransom. She's the witch who sold our Reach. The blood is on her hands."

"It cannae be true." Ransom sobbed. "Mother, tell him you're lying. Tell him anything."

"Aye, but it is," Khallum said. "And it's just as well ye see how we deal with traitors, no matter what their name may be."

"But she's our mother! Your wife! You cannae just take her head, without even a trial!"

Garrick howled. Khallum saw Claybourne comforting his brother, crying with him. They didn't understand, but they would. One day, they would. They'd remember that their father was made of tougher stuff. He wasn't a weak man, unwilling to hold his own wife to the same account he'd hold others.

His belly was on fire. He reached down to touch it, and his hand was soaked in his own blood. What good were healers, if the feckin' wound wouldn't even stay closed?

Khallum turned back to his wife. She cowered like a deserter, arms drawn over her head, as if he couldn't peel them away to reach her neck. Gwyn. How he'd loved her. Trusted her. He'd trusted her almost as much as any man, and he'd paid for that lapse. Others had paid for his lapse. He wanted to kick her off the cliff, straight into the sea, but that wasn't how the Southerlands dealt with treason.

"You cannae do it!" Hamish called, huffing up the hill. "She's your wife, my lord. There are some things you cannae return from!"

"Listen to reason, Khallum. I know you're angry. We all are." Rutland, trying and failing to sound like the one man who was ever good at it, Law.

"If ye donnae have the stomach for this, *then leave me.*"

"Uncle." Brandyn pressed his hands to his waist as he caught his breath. "Don't do it. I'm begging you. You don't want to do this, no matter what she's done."

"Ye missed the part where she confessed, boy. It's done." He called out to the gathered crowd. "Stay and bear witness, or go! It's naught to me!"

"Uncle, will you listen to me? Only for a moment. Please."

"Cowards, the lot of ye. You'd let your own wives trod dirty, wouldnae ye?"

"I still have nightmares, about what I did to Mads Waters. Almost every night. I know he was guilty. I know he stood and watched Lord Quinlanden murder my father, a crime that required answer. But in killing him like I did, I was the one who suffered. I'm still suffering. Taking a man's head like that, you don't know how it feels until you do. His suffering is ended, but mine has only begun."

"I donnae have nightmares, boy."

"Father, please," Ransom pleaded. "She's sorry. She'd do it all differently, if she could. I know she would. Look at her! She's helpless. This is wrong, and you know it!"

Gwyn lowered her arms. Her eyes were red, but dry now. "No, Ransom. I wouldn't do it differently." She moved warily to her feet, swaying closer to the edge to create distance from Khallum and his sword. "No mother would. And I reckon your father, he would've done the same, too. Can you tell me, Khallum, that if Oldwin had come to you, dangling your emerald at an unthinkable cost, that you would've refused him?"

Khallum pointed at her with his sword. "Are ye asking me if I'd turn traitor against my own Reach?"

Gwyn's hair was a bloody, matted mess. But it was her belly she clutched as she backed closer to the edge. "No. I'm asking you if you could have set your love aside for your own daughter so easily."

"How dare ye." He edged forward. "How dare ye suggest such a thing?"

Gwyn held out her arms. They stretched from side to side. Her gnarled hair caught the wind. "My crimes weigh on my heart. They're never gone. No joy erases them. But my Esmerelda is alive, and her Gemma is alive, and though I wish I were a better woman, who could put the needs of others over her own, I know now I am utterly incapable of this when it involves the matter of my own children." She shook her head. "I'm sorry. But I am not remorseful. I would *not* choose differently, but I would've told you sooner, Khallum. That is my one regret. That I didn't tell you once we had her safe in our arms again, so that we could fight him together, come what may."

Khallum tightened the grip on his sword hilt. It felt suddenly heavier. He struggled to hoist it. "Aye, but ye didnae, did ye? Didnae even trust your own husband enough to help you find a better way."

"I was afraid. Of this." Gwyn lowered her arms. She nodded at his sword. "That all the good I brought to your life could be erased by a mother's fear. All your love for me, poised at the end of a sword meant for my neck."

"Do ye think I want to kill ye, Gwyn?" Khallum's voice choked. "Do ye think this is easy for me, that my own wife…" He stuck his fist in his mouth to stave the emotion. "My own heart?"

"No." She shook her head. "I don't think this is easy for you at all. But I think you'll do it, just the same."

"Khallum." Rutland's warning was harder now. "Khallum, set it down. She's your wife. We'll find another punishment for her. There's no coming back from this. Not for you. Not for the Southerlands. You think your people want this, but they donnae. They donnae want this, not this."

"He knows his own mind, Erran. He always has." Gwyn took another step back. "But I'll not have the last thing I see be my husband swinging a sword down on me. Ransom, Garrick, Claybourne. Take care of your father. Take care of Esmerelda, and Gemma. And take care with your memories of me, for this last one will haunt you if you let it."

Gwyn took one more step back, and she swayed backward as she fell back over the edge.

"No!" Khallum dropped his sword and flew forward. He caught her by the foot just as she disappeared over the edge. He wrapped his fist tight around it; and then Rutland, too, was there, and Hamish, and the boys, and they'd pulled her up and laid her against the grassy cliff.

Khallum crawled closer so he could see her face. "Gwyn." He lay down beside her. "You'd take that from me, too, would ye, you crazy wench?"

Gwyn turned her head toward him. She tried to smile. "You still think everything is about you."

The boys gathered around, winding themselves around her arms, her legs, as if to show Khallum he would have more to contend with if he still meant to see this through.

But his heart had stilled. And then rose, for the one who'd stolen it, against all odds.

Even now.

The words he could never, would never, say to her, lived within him, in the hard knot formed at the center of his chest.

For Esmerelda, I would've done it, too. All the rest be damned. My soul be damned.

Her crimes required an answer, but he wouldn't be the one to mete it.

"Your wound," she whispered. "Khallum."

Rutland and Hamish leaned down to hoist him, one under each arm. "Come now, Khallum. Let's get ye back to bed."

49
ALL THAT REMAINS

Kael was already there. He was alone, despite his claims to have stirred others to his cause. He stood at the base of the steps to the temple, waiting.

Waiting, for him.

Jesse held tight to Esmerelda's hand. He'd hold her until he couldn't anymore. Last time he'd let her go, he'd watched, helpless, as another tried to murder her. The thin pink line ringing her throat confirmed none of it had been a nightmare.

Lisbet kept pace with Kian on the trek back and was still locked to his side as he approached Kael.

"Come stand with me, Lisbet," Ash called. She ignored him, watching Kian with nervous anticipation. "Lisbet."

"We have dealt with your mess," Kian said. He'd cast aside his pleasantries. "You are not welcome here, Kael of the Drumain."

"Was the girl who dealt with it. But it is very like you to take what is not yours," Kael returned.

"Why is it so hard for you to be one of us? You were not always this way."

Kael snorted. "I was always this way. You were the blind one. Then and now."

"You cannot succeed," Kian said. "Nor can you return to what was. You decided your fate when you brought one of the Light Enders into our sacred lands."

"You aren't going to tempt me with a lie, then? Lure me into submission with empty promises?"

"I've never lied to you, Kael."

Kael laughed, gesturing wildly behind him. "What is this, if not the greatest lie ever told to all Medvedev?"

"You'll never see it as it is. I no longer desire to convince you. You'll step aside, willingly, or you will be moved aside, with force."

Kael laughed. "You really are the son of Yseult. You think speaking your desires makes them so. Well, I will not step aside, Kian. I will not let you use your half-blood to destroy what belongs to all of us."

"For myself," Kian said. "I would stay my hand against you. But for everyone else, I will do whatever is necessary to stop you."

"What's going to happen?" Esmerelda whispered. Her voice was hoarse; another reminder of her fate at the end of the longblade. A reminder he'd not been quick enough, or clever enough, to protect her from it.

Jesse tightened his grip on her hand. The remaining hope still within him showed him a different future; one where the Medvedev brothers' battle would be another way to end this. But he knew better. If Kael fell, there would be others. There were always others.

From the corner of his eye, Jesse saw Ravenna make slow, purposeful steps in the direction of the temple.

Then Ash, too, made his way forward.

Don't do it. He'll feel you both coming. He wanted to scream these words before Kael saw them sneaking in to attack from behind, but his tongue was weighted by this fear. He reached for his sword instead, but Esmerelda shook her head.

"Whatever is necessary," Kael repeated slowly. "Do you remember when I told you that you were weakened by your attachment to man?" He flipped his hand and Lisbet went soaring into the air. He turned his wrist, moving her in slow circles above him. "This one, in particular."

"Lisbet!" Ash cried. "Kael, look at me. Whatever you want from her, I can give you. I'm older than she is. More powerful."

Kael's side-eyed scowl to Ash was his only answer.

"Harming her to harm me?" Kian asked. "You have strayed so far even from your own fractured purpose."

Jesse withdrew his sword. He released Esmerelda's hand. She slowly knelt, reaching inside her boot for her remaining dagger.

"Stay close to me. No naps in the tent, aye?"

"That you could make jests, now."

"If not now, then when, Princess?"

"Jesse." She sighed.

"You were so fixated on this one." Kael pointed at Jesse. "Your chosen one. The *only* one. When all that made him that was his Medvedev mother."

"It's more than that," Kian insisted. "You would know that, if you were a Keeper. If you could be trusted to be one."

"No, Kian. You saw him as your savior because the others could not enter our world. *Never considering* that you might have invited them here yourself."

Lisbet spun above him, face frozen in the same expression she'd worn before his magic trapped her.

"If that were so, I would have known," Kian said. "Mother would have known. We would have seen others, and not him."

"No, Kian. You have done precisely what Mother trained you not to do. You are blinded by your importance. You have seen what you wanted, no more. The girl is just as capable of entering this veil." Kael shook his head, smiling. "Let me prove it to you."

"Stop!" Ash cried, just as Jesse cried, "No!"

Kael switched his gaze between the two men. "I have no care which of you goes with me. But I will go through." He cocked his head at Jesse. "Perhaps *this* was the meaning of their visions, after all. Would you let another take your place? Your own sister?"

"Let her down, Kael," Jesse said, sword down, but at his side. "Let her down, and we can decide what to do. She isnae involved in this. This is between us."

"I have already decided what to do. And it seems, so have you." Kael pivoted and began ascending the steps, Lisbet floating above him.

"Let her down!" Jesse cried. "This is my burden, Kael!"

Jesse yelped as Kael's magic pulled him to the steps in a violent rush. He sent Lisbet hurling into the dirt, where she rolled, stopping when she hit a tree. "So it is."

"Jesse!" Esmerelda screamed. She pitched forward, but something unseen stopped her.

"This isnae how I saw this happening," he called to her, as Kael's magic dragged him up the stairs and toward the veil. "If I tell you all the ways I love you, my courage will fail. But I donnae need to say any of it, Esmerelda, do I?"

"Saleen!" Kian cried. "Rise, rise now, or fall!" He held his hands out, and the others appeared from the forests, doing the same. Their familiars, on land and in air, gathered around. "Call down all you are, or he will take it from you!"

"Jesse, I'm not strong enough for this! I thought I was, *oh, Guardians*, I thought I was, but I'm not!"

The heat from the veil's shimmer scorched his flesh. He squeezed his eyes, wincing through the onslaught. "I *will* find you, Esmerelda! In this world, or the next! In another lifetime, under different skies, *I will always find you!*"

Esmerelda howled as she struggled against the invisible magic. "JESSE!"

"NOW! IT MUST BE NOW!" Kian cried. Jesse held his breath as Kian and the remaining Saleen launch their magic. He braced himself for impact.

Esmerelda fell to her knees, sobbing. She reached for him.

The world rushed up as Jesse thudded against the edge of the stone steps. He moaned in pain and rolled over, expecting to see Kian and the Saleen heading their way, but what he saw instead stopped his heart.

Lisbet, mouth wide, locked in a silent scream.

"NO!" Esmerelda screamed. No longer a prisoner of Kael's magic, she found her legs and sprinted forward and up the stairs.

She ran past Jesse and straight at the veil.

Esmerelda beat against the air with her fists. "No! You give her back! She wasnae supposed to go! She wasnae even supposed to be here!"

Jesse tried to pull himself to his feet, but he fell back over.

"Kian, you have to get her back!" she demanded.

Lisbet's scream pierced the air. "FATHER!"

"What have you done?" Esmerelda asked. "What have you—"

He is my son. My flesh and bone. There is only one thing I can do for him now, and only I can do it. At last, I understand what my dreams were telling me to do.

Ravenna thought of Ash's cryptic words as she found her way alongside the back edges of the temple. She'd guessed what he intended to do, and the revelation wasn't surprising to her. There was only one way his words could be taken now, with the end so near.

Ash's distraction when Lisbet was taken by Kael gave her the chance to hurry up the back steps without being seen. As she drew closer to where the shimmer in the air belied the veil's presence, it felt as if she was approaching the sun itself. She forced herself to face the magic, against the very real resistance of it, to feel the burn and welcome it. In return, the magic became visible. It revealed itself to her, in its repeating pattern of red and gold, like the mane of the great lions of lore.

She reached her hand forward in wonder. Her fingers blackened at the nearness to it, and she withdrew. Even burnt, the lure to step even closer was strong, almost overriding her senses, but even a phoenix wasn't impervious to flame.

Your purpose isn't here. It's never been here. Had Alasyr realized his meaning was bigger than Midnight Crest? Ravenna had traveled this kingdom, north to south, and had come no closer to belonging; to herself, or to something bigger. She could keep searching, of course she could, but in her heart she knew the answers weren't waiting for her here.

They might be waiting nowhere. But for the first time in her short but remarkable life, Ravenna Ravenwood knew it wouldn't be until she was willing to sacrifice everything that the enlightenment she'd sought her whole life would follow.

For Esmerelda, so that she doesn't lose what she has only just gained.

For Drystan, who wouldn't have wanted his father to be alone.

But most of all, for me.

The gleam of the veil distorted her view of events on the other side. She thought she saw Jesse pulled forth by Kael's magic, and then pulled inward; the end near. Ash would see this for what it was, and she searched for him in a panic, afraid she might have missed him in the melee.

She jumped when he came up behind her. He didn't stop to ask why she was there, to impart any final words. He rushed forward, single-minded, determined to make it before Kael could drag his son to another world.

Just before he vanished, Ravenna thrust her hand forth and clutched tight to one of his. He had just enough time to turn back and register the surprise, and then he disappeared inside the magic. She, too, was pulled forth, and then she was inside as well, and it was all light and *she* was light, and there was nothing, nothing but the light, the glorious indestructible light, and the rough flesh of Ash Sylvaine's hand, still clutched tightly to hers, as they stepped from one world into the next.

ARTURO CLOSED THE DOOR TO LADY BLACKWOOD'S CHAMBERS, careful not to let the noise wake her. He swayed on his feet, cursing himself, blaming the drink, blaming his own inadequacy with it. But as he braced himself with a sconce upon the wall, everything around him still moved; the stones undulated from beneath them, forming an unnatural wave. Some crumbled away into piles of rubble in the hallway.

Arturo opened his mouth to scream, but he had no idea who to call for.

CHRISTIAN PRESSED THE HILT OF ICEBORNE INTO TORRIN'S HAND, teaching him precisely where to place his thumb and forefinger, just as Holden had once taught him. Torrin had just wrapped his hand into place when he pitched forward and tossed himself into the hay. The sword nearly broke his fall, deciding things in another way.

"You have to be more sure-footed than that, or you'll take your own eye out!" Christian chastised just before he, too, went crashing to the armory floor. Torrin cried out in terror as he rolled away from him. Christian tried to reassure him that everything was fine, but it wasn't fine, it wasn't only them, but everything. It was—

YESENIA WARWICK FELT HER HUSBAND CLOSE IN ON HIS CLIMAX AS HE bucked his hips beneath her. She thought she might draw it out, as she liked to do when he threatened to spill this fast, but tonight it felt so incredible that instead of slowing him, she urged him on, begging him to go faster. She screamed as the orgasm rocked through her, Corin's own cries joining hers. She started to tell him it should always be this good, but then he was thrusting inside her once more, something he hadn't been able to do for over a decade, back when he was a much younger man. But it was the look in his eyes that killed her passion.

"Yesenia, it's not me. It's—"

"GRETCHEN," CURRAN WHISPERED AS HE AWOKE TO THE SOUND OF things crashing. The destruction came from all over. "Wake up." He dropped his legs over the side of the bed and then recoiled in horror when the floor moved. It *moved*. It *was* moving. "Gretchen, Gretchen, wake up. Wake up! The world is ending, it's—"

"Something's wrong. Go back," Balfour pleaded. "Assana, this is wrong. It's all around us. It's all wrong, and we don't belong here."

"It's already gone," she said as she fell into the bush she'd been standing beside. The roar of stampeding animals drew closer. "Look."

"We have to go back!"

"There's no going back now. But don't you see? Don't you see, Balfour?" Assana crawled out of the bush with a frenzied, excited look. "This has to mean someone *did it*. Someone did what we couldn't, and the sorcerers are no more."

He shook his head. Only the thin branches of the strange bowing tree kept him from rolling down the hill. "Then we missed the part that said it was the end for us, too!"

Assana screamed as a handful of the bush broke away and she went tumbling away from him.

It was the high swell of tide that Gwyn noticed first. She could hear the sea from inside her cell, of course, but she couldn't see it, not unless standing at the window. She'd been reading from the book Khallum had left her, trying, but mostly failing, to keep her mind from thinking too much.

It was only a glance, but it was enough to know the sea shouldn't appear for her this high in the window. She rushed to the bars, clutching them tight in her fear as the sea rose up and coiled back, like the head of a snake.

Wyat Edevane checked and double-checked his trunk. It was all there, everything he'd owned or collected in his tenure as Scholar of the Reliquary. This wasn't his first return home, but it was his final one. The news of his father's death meant another kind of death for Wyat, as he traded his scholar's life for one as the heir of Oldcastle.

The stained glass in the window of his small chambers rattled. This was common in a storm. He went to double check the latch was secure, but the moment his feet hit the floor, the rest of him no longer cooperated. He tripped, crashing into the desk where he'd written thousands of missives over the years.

Wyat looked up just in time to see the colored glass shatter into pieces.

"WHAT IS THAT? WHAT'S HAPPENING?" ESMERELDA WAVERED ON HER feet and then lost her balance altogether. Jesse caught her as she tumbled, but she was still shaking. Except it wasn't Esmerelda at all, it was everything. The whole earth trembled.

Jesse covered her as heavy branches came loose from the temple, crashing around them. "We have to get out of here," he said. "This whole thing is coming down."

Jesse wrapped his arms around his wife and ushered them down the steps that were already falling away, returning to the earth. He spotted Lisbet shrieking in Kian's arms as she clawed at him, calling for her father.

"It's like the world is screaming!" Esmerelda's voice was loud, high as she strained to be heard over the sharp pitch that had fallen over everything around them.

They tripped over the erupting earth, dodging new erosions as they popped up, one after the other, as everything around them ripped itself apart.

He made his way to Lisbet and grabbed her from Kian.

"The trees," Kian said. "The trees will protect you. Go."

Jesse huddled between Esmerelda and Lisbet and aimed them for the forest. Kian was right. It wasn't as bad here. Once their feet connected with the forest floor, the earth stopped moving. He set them both against the thick bark of the nearest tree and turned to see what they had left behind.

Everything that had been there moments before was gone.

The ground.

The temple.

The tents, the bonfire, everything, gone, swallowed by the chasm formed by the closing of the veil.

"It's gone. It's closed," Jesse whispered. He searched around for Ash. Maybe he'd fallen in, maybe...

"He did it. The fool went in," Lisbet sobbed. "He went in without saying goodbye. He left me! He left me. I didn't even get... I didn't even get to say..."

Esmerelda held her, whispering something soft, comforting. Still, Jesse searched. If he could only find Ash, he could make this right. And Ravenna, where was she?

You give her back! She wasn't supposed to go.

"No," he said. "Oh, Ravenna."

Jesse peered into the still trembling world beyond the forest's edge. The vibrations knocked him back when he came too close, and he stumbled farther still, coming to a halt when the tree broke his steps.

He looked down to see his wife and sister still locked in embrace, comforting each other through the shock of the impossible choice Ash and Ravenna made when none of them were looking.

He watched the two of them in stunned silence. The rumble beyond the forest was almost deafening. He imagined a very different ending, where Lisbet comforted Esmerelda, where they whispered of the love that had been taken from her.

But that wasn't what had happened.

The man Jesse had never called Father had taken his place.

A sacrifice that had given Jesse his life back, but had taken something else.

Jesse slid down the rough bark, mouth parted in awe as he watched the world fall away. He reached for the two women and they wrapped themselves in his arms, and they held each other like this as they waited for the tremors to stop.

LYSANOR'S EYES FLASHED OPEN. SHE'D BEEN SLEEPING FAR TOO LONG. She'd never needed this rest before. It seemed so cruel to her that her final days must be spent in such exhaustion.

"Isdemus. Isdemus!"

"I know," he said, as calm as always. "Can you feel it?"

"Is this really happening?"

Isdemus held out his arms, and she climbed into them. "Yes."

"He did well. You were right, as you always are."

"He did well," Isdemus agreed, "because he's one of us."

"I don't know if I'm ready. I thought I was, but what if we cannot find each other? What if this is the last time we're ever together?" She looked up at his serene face, committing it to the records of her mind. With this assessment came all the memories. Even as far back as children, when they were pulled away from their mother and father to become Meduwyn in their own right. Fortune had kept them together all the years since, beyond the odds.

"This is not the end, Lysanor." His arm went lax as he regarded the night sky for the last time. "Or if it is, it's a fair one, is it not?"

"You're my heart and my strength," she whispered as the tears fell. "Can I call upon these things one final time, when my courage is failing me?"

"Call upon me anywhere. I will always find you, sister."

Lysanor tried to speak, but there were no words, and then there was nothing at all.

GILFORD RHIAGAIN WAS IN THE COURTYARD WHEN IT HAPPENED. HE felt it first, of course, but he only gained a surer understanding of the situation at hand when he looked up to see the keep at Duncarrow crumbling, stone by stone. He wanted to laugh, because it seemed like something the very brave did when staring down the end, but he was not very brave, and decided he didn't have the heart to pretend, either.

He looked up to see the crossed swords of the Rhiagains flapping against the wind. He found a nice, flat rock from which to observe the end of the world, as he repeated the words of the prophecy that had started all of this, and would now be the end of it all.

From Khain's son will spring a line that will undo his legacy and restore each of the Reaches to their own kingdoms. He will bring Duncarrow down to the rocks, and all that would remain would be salt and ash.

50

THE DAY

Erran and Hamish had been trading off their vigil in Khallum's chambers. Lem Garrick, and Allarick Nye had both been by a few times over the preceding weeks since The Day. Nathenial Law had replaced his father as a permanent fixture on the shadow council, which was the only name Erran could find for what they were doing, meeting without their lord to guide them. Ransom had stepped in, but he didn't command the respect his father always had, and his grandfather before him. Erran couldn't help feeling like Khallum's mental decline foretold the end of something, but he didn't yet know what.

They'd moved Khallum and the capital to Whitecliffe for the time being. The keep in Warwicktown had been washed away on The Day, when the tide came in and took most of the town with it. Hamish promised Khallum they would rebuild, but Erran thought now might be as good a time as any to reassess the location of the Southern capital. Warwicktown had always been at the mercy of the weather. It wasn't even the first time the keep had been rebuilt.

Warwicktown wasn't the only casualty from The Day. Messages came pouring in from all over the kingdom, of entire cities lost, people missing and still not recovered. Everyone had their thoughts on what The Day even was, and what it meant, but most agreed on one thing, at least. It had to do with the Rhiagains, and a reckoning long coming. Duncarrow had been reduced to the stones it had been built with. No one knew how many Rhiagains were buried under the wreckage. None had bothered attempting any recovery missions.

"We did it. Erran, we did it," Khallum mumbled. Drool spilled from the corner of his dry mouth as his head rolled to the side on the pillow. "We closed it."

"Aye, my lord. 'Tis done." *Been done*, he wanted to add, but he'd stopped correcting Khallum after the first few days. Time was fluid now for the Lord of the Southerlands.

"The Warwick Burden is ended."

"That it is."

"Can ye ask Gwyn to make me her special tea? She'll ken what ye mean, say it just like that. Special tea."

"Of course," Erran said, wincing inwardly, as he did anytime Gwyn's name came up. Khallum's decline began after he'd almost taken her head in front of all of Warwicktown. But it had become something tangible when they had to tell him she'd been trapped in her cell when the sea water came. They'd all been so consumed with the shock of the unprecedented storm surge that they'd been unable to get to her on time.

At least, that's what they told themselves. Rutland knew they'd only thought of the prisoners until everyone else was already safe.

Ransom sputtered something unintelligible as he awoke from his spot on the chair across the room. "Sorry. Sorry. I'm awake now."

"Take your rest where ye can get it," Erran said. "Naught ye can do here, anyway. The wife might appreciate seeing ye, once in a while."

"My wife understands why I need to be here."

"Stewardess Rutland mentioned she's with child now. That you're going to be a father."

"The business of women," Ransom said. "I already made my contribution to the effort."

Erran chuckled. "Just the same."

"Did I hear him speak?" Ransom nodded to the bed, where Khallum was again snoring away.

"More of the same." Erran rubbed his beard. "Ye ken Esmerelda knows how to make your mother's tea?"

"Aye, she might. If not, we can ask Lisbet. Mother learned it in the Northerlands."

"Have them show the kitchen maids. He'll want it sent daily. He mentions something once, it'll keep coming up."

Ransom nodded and pushed himself from the chair with some effort. Erran had proper chambers prepared for him, but he preferred to stay here, with his father. He'd even refused a better chair. Erran suspected there was something inside the boy that made him crave suffering. If so, he'd inherited that from Khallum, who'd always equated the salt and sand life with the degree of a man's travails.

"He'll get there," Erran said when Ransom had hobbled to the door. "'Tis none stronger than your father. He's all salt and sand."

Ransom grinned from the corner of his mouth. "Aye, there might be others who'll appreciate the lies, Rutland, but I know better. And so do you. He's a broken man. There are some wounds men donnae wish to return from. He told me so himself once."

Erran nodded at the boy who would likely soon become their lord. "Aye, perhaps you're right. But I ken I'll carry enough hope for the both of us, just the same."

"You've stayed longer than I thought you would."

Lisbet looked up to see Brandyn coming in from the back entrance, the one she used. He shut out the daylight momentarily when he stepped into the grotto. He was only one of a few who knew she liked to come here. She'd been happy to find it when they arrived with the caravan from Warwicktown. It was a place she could be truly alone with her thoughts. These days, more and more, she craved that solitude.

"Maybe I'm enjoying the beautiful views in Whitecliffe."

Brandyn laughed and joined her on her favorite boulder. From here, she could see the whole enclave. She could watch the tides, and know when she was cutting it close, playing too hard against the odds. She wasn't afraid of the sea, but after what happened to Aunt Gwyn, she wouldn't cause unneeded worry in the others, either. Steward Rutland in particular always had a wary look for her when he saw her heading this way.

"It is really nice here. I see why they call it the jewel of the Southerlands," Brandyn said.

"Are you sure they didn't mean that giant statue?"

"Aren't you even a little tempted to climb it?"

"Who says I haven't?"

Brandyn nudged her with his shoulder, smiling. "I should be home, too. Nothing for me here, as long as my uncle is still in a bad way."

"So what's keeping you here, then?"

Brandyn pivoted on the rock so he was facing her. "Do you remember some of the things we said to each other, in the Wastelands? About our senses, and that sometimes, we just *know* things, even if we don't really understand them?"

Lisbet nodded.

"Well," Brandyn said. "It's something to do with that."

"What do you feel?"

"That I don't belong here," he said, nodding to himself. "But I also have this powerful feeling that I'm not meant to return to Longwood Rush, either. It's so strong that when I even think of my mother, or Gabi, or Ember, my mind pushes my thoughts elsewhere, pointing me away from them, never toward them."

"That's tough," she said. "But I understand. I know I'll probably never see Wulfsgate again, either."

"Where will you go, then?"

"Somewhere I've never been," Lisbet mused. She'd all but decided what she would do. It was the how still eluding her.

"That could be many places," Brandyn pointed out in a teasing tone. "Even for a highborn lady of the realm, who's done her share of traveling. You must have somewhere in mind, as much as you come here to think."

"You know," she said, "when we, Ash and I, were about to step through that veil, I secretly hoped we'd end up in another place entirely, somewhere beyond the kingdom. I was even a little *disappointed* when we weren't."

"And now the veils are all closed," Brandyn said. "I'm sorry you won't ever get that chance."

"Something, though, has been weighing on me, ever since we returned," Lisbet went on. She sorted through her convoluted thoughts as she tried to respond in a way he would understand. "We call them other worlds, but Kian, he said they're all part of the same world. That it was broken, torn apart, when the sorcerers betrayed the Light." She turned to him. "And the Rhiagains. They washed ashore from somewhere out there. They didn't come through a veil to get here."

"You don't know that," Brandyn said. "The shipwreck could've been part of their story, too. Everything else they said was a lie."

"It could've been," she agreed. "But I don't think so. Brandyn, I think this kingdom is only a small part of a larger world."

"Even if that were true..." Brandyn trailed off. He seemed to be coming to his own conclusions.

"I know," she said. "I know. No one has ever successfully taken a ship more than a few miles from our shores. I know that, and I still can't help but wonder..."

"Lisbet Dereham. You want to go find out for yourself, don't you?"

"What if I did? Let's play pretend here, for a moment. What would you tell me if you thought I was seriously considering it?"

Brandyn rolled his tongue around in his mouth. "Well, first, I'd ask why you think the outcome would be any different for a fourteen-year-old girl than it was for all the experienced seamen who've failed."

"Fifteen now. I think. And I'd respond to that, how many of those seamen had sorcerer's blood in them?"

"And to that I'd say, what does your blood have anything to do with captaining a sea vessel??"

"And I'd respond that I do not know, exactly, but if four sorcerers can cross the White Sea with a ship full of Rhiagains, what might I be able to do?"

Brandyn shook his head. "Are we done pretending now?"

"If you like."

"Lisbet, do you really think what you're suggesting is possible?"

"Possible, yes."

"But?"

"But it would take a great deal of courage to try, not knowing for sure. Wouldn't it?"

"You're going to try. Aren't you?"

She nodded. "I just need to find a ship."

His mouth dropped open as he laughed. "Do you even know how to sail one?"

"Not in the slightest."

"Of course. Of course that wouldn't stop you. Why would it?" He shook his head, incredulous.

"I'm sure I can pay some downtrodden trader to join us."

"Us?" Brandyn raised his brows. "You think I'm coming?"

"Sure sounds like you were angling for an invitation."

He pulled his legs up under him, watching the water beyond the cave as the tide changed. "I guess I am."

"I won't be so terribly lonely, then." Lisbet jumped to her feet, dusting the sand off her bottom. "We won't be leaving from the Southerlands, though."

"Where would we leave from, if not here?"

"Longwood Rush," she said. "I have something your mother needs. And, well, I think you'll feel better, too, if you make your amends before you take to the high seas, for Guardians knows what future awaits us."

. . .

"You really intend to do this, then? I cannae talk ye out of it, with some proper sense about the dangers of the White Sea?"

Lisbet shook her head. She leaned against the open window in the Hall of Warring, arms crossed. "I didn't come here for you to tell me all the ways this could go wrong. I came to say goodbye, for now."

Jesse's mouth twisted. "Right."

Lisbet pushed back from the window. "For now, Jesse. I *will* come back."

"Any proper seaman knows better than to make a promise like that," Jesse said. "I suppose it would be selfish of me, to ask ye to reconsider. So I willnae do that. But I'll see that ye have the right men, the right resources, a proper vessel, because I'll not mourn another sister, Lisbet. Ye understand?"

Lisbet nodded. Her eyes stung. "Yes." She swallowed. "Thank you."

Jesse pointed beyond the window, to the sea. "And if ye come across any trouble, any at all—"

"We'll turn back. I know."

"I know you know. I have less confidence in you following it." He shook his head. "I ken this was always my lot in my life. My wife and my sister, both as hardheaded as bulls."

"I'm leaving Starcaller with you."

"Your horse?"

"She's more than a horse. And she's still got enough years in her that she'll be a good companion for Gemma, when she's ready."

Jesse nodded. "Aye. We'll take good care of her for you."

"Jesse, look..." Lisbet stepped closer. "I know you might be tempted to be taking the blame on yourself, for what Ash did."

"Ahh, I—"

"No, listen to me. Because when I'm gone, you'll have one less person here to remind you, and I'm the one who knew him best. Next to my mother, I knew Ash best, and I know he didn't take your place so that you could wallow in your guilt, brooding, sounding your 'what-ifs' to the skies. So if you find you cannot let it go for yourself, let it go for him. Because *that* is how you honor him. By going forth into the life he left here for you."

"You're right. I'm trying."

"You're going to brood, aren't you?"

"Aye, I might." He held up his fingers, pinching his thumb and forefinger together. "Just a little."

Lisbet flew into his arms without thinking. "I know you don't think I'm coming back, but I still have to get to know my brother, don't I?"

Jesse wrapped his arms around her. He pressed his face to the top of her head. "I'm gonna hold ye to it. Make you swear the seaman's oath."

She pulled back. "What's that?"

"Oh, it's very serious."

She grinned. "Is it now?"

"Aye, it is." He sighed. "All right, then. I'll send some ravens to some of our men in the Westerlands. Have ye sent off proper."

"Thank you, Jesse."

Jesse nodded. He blinked away the budding tears. "Aye. Course."

RYAN SAT ACROSS FROM ESMERELDA IN THE ROSE GARDEN. HE'D ASKED her to come here, to walk with him, and she waited for him to say something. He wrung his hands in his lap, telling himself he should meet her eyes; it was the right thing to do.

He spotted Jesse coming down the path. Jesse turned to come back the way he'd come when he saw them, but Ryan called his name, waving him down.

"I didnae mean to intrude," Jesse said. "Rutland was asking after Esmerelda. About some tea. It can wait."

"No, it's good you're here," Ryan said. "I wanted to talk with both of ye, if that's all right."

Jesse nodded. He leaned against a walled area of the garden, wearing a guarded look. *Probably expecting me to tell him I've remembered I'm in love with his wife.* The spray of a nearby waterfall—the one, Ryan had heard, Steward Rutland had installed for his wife, and if that wasn't true love—rained a fine mist down upon all three of them, and he could no longer differentiate it from the nervous sweat that had been accumulating since swaying Esmerelda's attention away from her handmaids.

"If ye wish," Jesse said.

"I owe ye both a proper apology," Ryan began. "For how I've behaved. Particularly you, Esmerelda."

Esmerelda reached forward and untangled his hands, clasping them both in hers. The kindness in her touch made his chest ache. "Save your apologies, Ryan. These past months have been troubling for us all. There's not a one of us who has been relieved from tragedy. I should have been more understanding, when you came back to us, so lost. What you needed was my friendship, and instead I gave you the weapon of my wounded heart, my poison tongue."

Guardians, how her touch stung. How familiar it was, like an old but still perfect comfort. He saw her lying beside him in the barn as they watched the moon through the break in the rafters. The flush in her cheeks when she stole a kiss from him at a banquet thrown by her father. How she laughed when he passed her some filthy words on a torn scrap of vellum, at the wedding for one of the Law girls. How later he'd fulfilled every one of them.

"Not at all," he managed, swallowing the thickness spread throughout his mouth and throat. He released her hands before he was lost to the memory of how they felt running down his abdomen, tracing her fingers over all his scars. "It's as ye said. We all had our troubles." He wiped his sweaty hands on his trousers. "Jesse. I want ye to know. I *am* happy for ye. You're my brother, and I couldnae ask for anything more than your contentment. I should have..." Ryan cleared his throat. "Said it at yer wedding, I know, but I'm saying it now."

Jesse nodded. "No use in dwelling. We all need to turn our eyes to rebuilding this Reach."

"Aye," Ryan said, nodding. He closed his eyes. "Aye, but I'll nay be here for that, will I?"

"What?" Jesse peeled back off the wall. "Why would ye not be?"

Ryan felt Esmerelda's intense gaze, waiting with Jesse for his answer. "I'm leaving the Southerlands. For the time being. Nay, that's a lie. I donnae when I'll come back, if I even do."

"Why?" Esmerelda whispered. "This is your home. Your kin, they're all here. And Jesse. And.... Gemma."

"So they are," Ryan said. He couldn't look at either of them. "But, eh, Gemma, she's got a father already. A better one than I could be. Maybe ye donnae even tell her about me."

"Why wouldn't we tell her?" Jesse's steps drawing closer on the stone made Ryan feel even sicker. Why couldn't they just accept it? Why did there have to be questions? He had answers for them, all right, but they'd all be better if he took them with him to the pyre after his promise was spent.

"It's all wrong," Ryan said. He finally looked up. "For me, I mean. It's all wrong here."

Esmerelda leaned in. "Ryan, your memory may still come back."

He shook his head. "Nay, 'tis more than that. I cannae explain it to ye. There's no sense to be had."

"Whatever you think is broken, brother, it can be repaired." Jesse laid a hand on his shoulder. "Between us, it already is."

Just let me go. Let me leave, now, before I say what I really mean, or do what I really wish to, which is to throw the explosive burning a hole in my pocket straight into the center of the marriage that never should have been.

"Where will you go?" Esmerelda asked. "Everyone you know is here."

"I have some friends who need use of my skills."

"Friends," Jesse repeated. He didn't believe him. He knew there was more than what he was saying. This was the bond they'd always enjoyed, and it was for that, even more than for his wounded heart, that he needed to be free of them, of the Southerlands, of all of it. He wanted to remember Jesse as it was between them then, not as it was now.

"If it's that Kaslan James, up to no good again, I'll have the skin on his neck," Esmerelda warned.

Ryan dropped his head and smiled. "Nay. 'Tis not Kaslan." He decided to tell them. If they knew where he was going, they'd know better than to search for him. "I kenned Lisbet and Brandyn had it in their fool heads to take a vessel to sea, when we all know both of them would drown swimming in the shallows."

"You're going to be their captain," Jesse said slowly. "You want to go with them, into the unknown."

"Aye, Jesse, I do. I want to find myself again, and I cannae do it here, with all the people who know me as someone else."

Esmerelda looked at Jesse. "There's no one I'd trust on such a voyage other than a Strong man, and Ryan here might be the only one foolish enough to actually do it."

They all laughed together. Ryan ran his nose over his fist, sniffling. "Anyway, I said what I needed to say. I ken we're still kin, whether I'm here or there."

"In this world, or the next," Jesse said. He held out his hand.

Ryan took it. "Aye, Jesse. But most probably the next."

ESMERELDA LAID HER DAUGHTER BACK IN THE CRADLE HER FATHER HAD crafted with his own hands, working long into the night when she'd gone into labor. She couldn't have appreciated it then, as she did now, when he was incapable of even taking care of himself. Now, it was her most prized possession; it would keep all her children safe through the years, and, one day, Gemma would use it for her own bairns.

She was such a wonder. A small bundle of joy and curiosity. It was too soon to say with any certainty, but her little nose and mouth were the same as Gwyn's, which would be a bittersweet gift. Gemma would never know her grandmother. Esmerelda would need to decide later whether to tell her about the choice Gwyn Warwick had made that had torn their whole Reach down the center.

Whether to tell Gemma about the things Esmerelda had done,

she thought, as she reached for the scar on her neck that would never fade.

She didn't allow her thoughts to dwell on any of it overlong. She redirected herself to tending her father, and settling into a marriage and family life that they'd earned with their own blood; the blood of others.

Jesse's breath warmed her neck. She angled forward to better receive his kisses. His hands brought her to life again, running down and over her belly, which would never be as smooth as it once had been. He knew this bothered her, and at night, when there were no duties to distract them from one another, he saved most of her kisses just for this spot.

She would never tire of this.

She would take none of it for granted.

She knew now the worth of it all.

The cost.

Every day mattered.

Every hour.

Every second.

"What are you thinking?" he asked against her ear. He parted her hair to kiss her there, too.

"Wishing I was a seer."

"Why would you ever want that curse?"

She turned in his arms. "Not for me. For our people. Will it ever be the same, do you think? Can we come back from this?"

"Maybe," he said, running his hands through her hair, "another question to ask is, should we?"

"You don't think we should rebuild?"

"What I think doesnae matter, aye? We will rebuild. We already are. It's what we do. But I sense something new in this rebirth. Maybe something better, aye, maybe worse."

"You've always been so inspiring with your words."

Jesse laughed. "'Tis why I offer them so sparingly."

"Will you be all right if we stay here a while longer?"

"Your father," he said, understanding immediately. "There's no rush for us. Home is wherever we need it to be. Sandycove. White-cliffe. Duncarrow."

Esmerelda pretended to hit him. "Your jests are terrible. You should work on that, with all that idle time you have now that the Reach is in rubble."

"Tired of me already, Princess?"

"You must be aching to return to the sea. No?"

"Aye, I miss it." He wrapped her tighter. "But my hands are needed more here."

"And here," she purred, taking one of his hands and dropping it between her legs.

"Calm down, woman. I meant this rebuild yer so passionate about."

"Aye, I know what you meant. And I ken ye know who ye answer to, in the end."

"Watch it with the commands. I just might follow them." Jesse lifted her and set her atop the desk. Her heart quickened at what would come next. A sadness fell over his eyes instead.

She sighed, curling her bottom lip. "I think about them all the time, too."

He sagged into his words. "Lisbet says we honor them by moving on. But I'll always wonder what happened when they landed on the other side. Whether they've done all right, made a new life of it. I'd like to think they're happy together."

"As will I. But the wondering will drive us mad if we let it." Esmerelda craned her neck up to kiss him. "I almost lost you once, and I'll never let it happen again. Nothing will do that like the darkness."

"I've not done enough to strike that from your fears," Jesse said. "But I will. I may lack for words, but I can show you. And I'll keep showing you until you put it out of your mind for good."

"I welcome that," she said. "But let's do it in a way that keeps them alive for us, still."

He nodded. "Aye. Let's do that."

"I do still owe you a son," she said. She leaned in, taking his bottom lip between her teeth, running her tongue over it before releasing it again. "He'll already have a name, won't he? We'll name him for his grandfather. And if he's a girl, well, we have that covered, too, don't we?"

"You donnae owe me anything, Esmerelda, now or ever. But I'll always take whatever ye have to give me."

EPILOGUE

"We've been waiting for you," one of them said as they fell in around Lisbet, flanking her on all sides, practically carrying her down the corridor of the Halls of Longwood. Among them, the Grand Minister, though she'd already forgotten his real name, and her aunt's seer, Joran.

She knew Blackfen, the Rush Rider, mostly from the legends told in his name. He came from a long line of strong, brave men, all gallant and storied Riders.

But she'd first met him weeks before, when they'd been expelled from the Saleen lands, after all the veils closed. She'd never considered that it would leave the Medvedev separated from the kingdom forever as well. She'd never see Kian again, and hadn't decided yet how she felt about that.

They'd been spat out, as if from a lion's gullet. Dazed, devastated, Jesse had stumbled around the Forest of All, calling for their horses. And then they'd come, but they weren't alone. Blackfen had ridden out on his own awe-inducing mare, leading Jesse and Esmerelda's without rope or rein.

"Where are the sorcerers?" he'd demanded.

Lisbet had been too exhausted to consider whether it would be wiser to lie. She'd pointed between herself and Jesse, and said, "And what of it?"

His skepticism sat plainly upon his face, but he didn't challenge her assertion, either. He wore an exhaustion almost as heavy as her own. "My name is Arturo Blackfen, First Rider of the Rush Riders of the Western Reach. Your presence is requested in the Westerlands." He tilted his head when he saw Jesse kneeling by a tree with Esmerelda. "Is that Jesse Strong? The trader's son with nothing more to offer the world?"

"Don't worry about him. Unless you can present a more compelling offer, I can't afford a detour right now." She almost added, *after what we've been through*, but she didn't have the heart to explain it.

"What's your name?"

"Lisbet."

"Lisbet." He let the name sit with him. "You wouldn't by chance be the same Lisbet missing from the Northern Reach?"

"Let's agree that I'm not."

"Who your parents are isn't what matters to me, Lisbet. Lady Blackwood is dying, and as I understand it, from those with more experience and knowledge than me, her illness came from another world and can only be healed by those who come from the same."

"But how could she have come across such an illness?"

"It doesn't matter how," Blackfen said, but something behind the question made him flush. "All that matters, is what is. And what will be, if we cannot find a cure for what ails her."

Lisbet looked back at Jesse and Esmerelda. Esmerelda had injured her ankle in the exodus, and Jesse was more concerned with this than the enigmatic Rush Rider beseeching Lisbet.

"I've only ever healed someone once. And I had help, so I can't even be sure it was me."

"Even your lack of confidence in yourself is greater than what we can offer her."

"I want to help," Lisbet said. "But right now, they need me, too."

And I won't be separated from my brother, when I have only just lost my father.

Blackfen reared up on his horse. "The Enchanter says he and his brethren can sustain her as she is for another thirty days, give or take. Beyond that, her fate is up to the Guardians."

"Why would their heals have such an expiration?"

"It isn't their heals keeping her alive. They've placed her under a protection, where she is neither living, nor dead. It can only sustain her for so long. At least, that's how it was explained to me. Magic has never made much sense."

"A month, you say?"

"I have no authority to command you, but I will ask you, and if need be, I'll beg you. Be there before this time expires, or both of us will wear her fate on our armor for the rest of our days."

"I'll come," Lisbet said. "I will."

"I'm still within the thirty days, am I not?" Lisbet shot back to her growing escort. She'd left Ryan in the courtyard with some very attentive ladies of the Blackwood court, but Brandyn was right at her side.

"You played this one close," Blackfen shot back. "But you're here, and I'll say nothing more about it."

"Here," the Grand Minister said. He held his arm toward an open door at the end of the hall.

Lisbet was confronted with the horror as soon as she'd stepped into the chambers. The flesh barely holding on to her aunt's bones. She'd lost some of her beautiful chestnut hair, and parts of her scalp were visible, red and angry.

"Take Lord Blackwood out of here," Lisbet called back as the others shuffled in. "Brandyn shouldn't see his mother like this. If her daughters are here, keep them away until I tell you otherwise."

She vaguely heard Brandyn arguing with the men as they guided him away, but Lisbet's attention was now fully on the woman she'd called aunt her whole life, despite that there were no blood ties between them. The Epoch of the Accordant had joined all the houses, in multiple ways, but the Blackwoods had joined her family through Alric.

None of this made what she was seeing easier to bear.

"Lisbet Dereham." The old Enchanter was speaking to her. "So the old prophecies are true, and Dain's line lives on, with the blood of the ones who would have destroyed it all. And one of them was right under our noses, a daughter of a great lord."

"I'm not here to talk about it," she shot back. "I'm here to save her."

"Are you confident in your magic? Once we release her from the protection, there will nothing left keeping her from leaving this life for the next."

"Yes," Lisbet said, hoping he couldn't hear the lie.

But she needn't have concerned herself with her own abilities. As the Enchanters released their magic, Lisbet took immediate charge of her own. She threw herself over the emaciated form of Asherley Blackwood, fearful her hands alone wouldn't be enough. It wasn't like it had been with Esmerelda. Nor did she have Ravenna there to pick up where she'd faltered.

The collective gasps were her first sign she'd done something. The bed trembled as she pulled the sickness away and sent it sailing into nothing.

When her aunt bucked beneath her, Lisbet leapt off of her. She scrambled to the edge of the bed. Joran's sobs were the only sound in the otherwise quiet room. Lisbet held her breath, waiting.

Asherley rolled her head to the side and smiled. "That cannot be little Lisbet, can it?"

THEIR WAGON ROLLED ALONG THE UNEVEN ROAD, PASSING BENEATH the tall wooden gates. The sign reading Dunwoode had already greeted them several paces back. Christian hadn't been to Dunwoode since he was a boy, but the stories of the weeks' long lines to enter the town in recent months had filtered up to Wulfsgate, and beyond. Their easy passage could be no better signal that the realm had entered a period of peace. However long it lasted, they would embrace it and make the most of what they were given.

Dunwoode's proximity to the border had always put them in the forefront for security, but in return for keeping the borders safe, Steward Haddenfoot rarely enjoyed the same attentions of his lord, or even his peers farther north.

The whole of the town had come to greet them. The snow here had melted away, revealing the promise of a true springtide. A proper one. Fresh blooms of white and pink rained down upon their path, and as Christian looked out into the densely packed crowd, he saw the women and girls were wearing crowns of it. The men had pinned the blooms to their right breast. Cries of "springtide has come to the Northerlands," were as loud as their calls for Aylen, their Silver Lady.

She looked so beautiful at his side. Her silver hair had been braided and wrapped around their own blossoms, the only ones they had right now, from the cherry trees in the Wintergarden. Her sapphire-colored dress was new, spun from cloth of gold and the finest velvet he could send for, and he liked her in it. He told her so. He'd made a habit of telling her things like this, instead of keeping them within, where they helped no one.

Aylen waved to them all. She was theirs, and they loved her. In the back, Nyssa and Torrin were the perfect little mirrors of their brother, and sister-in-law, shoulders pulled erect, their hands cupped in waves just as they were shown when Aylen worked to dress them for the occasion.

The wagon came to a halt. The guards traveling with their litter made a path in the crowd for them. Christian climbed down, then reached back to offer his wife a hand. When Aylen exited the wagon, the cheers of joy grew so loud he couldn't hear what she was trying to say to him.

He read it upon her lips, just the same. *You've done well, husband.*

They were led along the road toward the town square. A stone fountain towered in the center, and in front of this, a dais had been erected.

Christian mounted the steps, still waving. He swelled with their approval; their surprise that he'd chosen *them* this time, when his predecessors had only excuses for their exclusion.

Aylen guided the twins into place. Nyssa, at her right. Torrin, at his left. When she had taken her own spot next to him, the town council lowered their hands to the crowd to indicate their lord was ready to speak.

"Greetings, Dunwoode!" Christian called when the din had died away. These words got them going again, though, and he was happy to hear it. It buoyed him, giving him what he needed to keep his promise to his wife and his Reach.

"'Tis an historic day for our Reach, is it not?" More cheers, escalating now. They knew where he was taking them and were eager to go there with him. "For hundreds of years, the Northerlands has celebrated Torrin's Day, a reminder of the man who bravely broke ground in the north when no one else would. Leave the forests and the gardens for the lesser men, he said. We're made of tougher stuff."

Aylen smiled from his side, clapping along with them.

"But where better to celebrate this man, than in the town who has fought the hardest to defend us from those who would take what is not ours. This may be our first time breaking bread and pouring wine on Torrin's Day in Dunwoode, but it will not be our last!"

It took much longer for the crowd to settle this time, but when they did, Christian offered them one last thing to celebrate on this day. "The past was laid by great men like Torrin Dereham, but it is our own children who set the way for the future. And I am proud and humbled to tell you all now, before we have even told our own people in Wulfsgate, that Aylen and I will welcome our heir by midwinter."

The people of Dunwoode cried out their joy and felicitations to the couple, many of them in tears. It was easy to forget that they, too, had endured. The disappearance of Lord Holden and Lady Gretchen, the loss of the beloved Dereham children, had left them in the dark; as much as the Derehams themselves.

Christian nodded to the men, and they again created a way forward. He took Aylen's hand, and each of them took one of the twin's, and together they made their traditional walk down the main street of Dunwoode, as the original Torrin Dereham had once done, they said, when he chose Wulfsgate as his capital.

"Will you forgive me for saying something to you that you might wish I hadn't?" Aylen asked. She smiled and waved as she spoke. Still theirs, but also his.

"What's that?"

"You were made for this, Christian. You couldn't see this day in your mind's eye, but I could. It doesn't take a seer to know you are home, where you belong. And I thank the Guardians every night that you saw it when you did, so that we could be here, now, together."

"You can say it whenever you like," Christian told her. "You need no permission from me for anything, ever. You are more than my wife. You're the savior of this Reach, even if none of them will ever know it."

"I don't need them to think of me this way," she said, and now her smile was for him alone. "For you already do."

Assana kept watch in the tower, if it could even be fairly called this. She and Balfour had built it together, from wood, not stone, by day, and never night. At night, the herds emerged, and if they weren't on higher, safer ground, they wouldn't survive to see morning. In this flatland, that often meant climbing as high as they could.

They'd built quickly, eager to put their days of sleeping in the strange, flat-topped trees behind them. Because they'd rushed the construction, they then spent their subsequent days fortifying, and, eventually, addressing their own comfort. Balfour cobbled together a roughshod table and chair, where they took their meals, when it was safe to make a fire. Assana patched together a mattress from moss she found in the forest, and the hides of the thin, tall beasts that Balfour killed for their meals—the only beasts they could defeat in this world of strange and inexplicable creatures.

They shared this bed, as they shared this new life. They never spoke of this choice, to unite beyond practical needs, but not everything needed to be said, Assana realized. Often the loudest words were the ones kept to yourself.

She tapped her foot, anxious. The orange sun, bigger in this world than theirs, spread its arms over the horizon, lighting the blades of the dry grass that spread for miles.

And then she saw him. The black-and-white striped animal was draped over his shoulders, something he hadn't been able to do when they first came through. But, then, she wouldn't have guessed herself capable of half the things she'd learned here out of necessity.

Balfour stopped when he reached the strange bush shaped like a cat. He knelt behind it, awaiting her signal. She'd already made four circles around the upper deck, and there was nothing. Of course, she'd made that mistake before and almost gotten him killed. But tonight was a quiet one. The sky was full of stars, which in her old life was where the Guardians lived, but now they were just there. Guiding Balfour across the plain and back to her.

Assana waved both of her hands over her head. He popped up again, waving back before making his final sprint to safety.

Her heart slowed to a more comfortable set of beats as he made it to the ladder and began his climb to her. This never got easier, but she was getting better at being his scout, and that meant he could count more days ahead of him.

She traded a kiss for his knife, which she'd clean well in the river, when the night was at its highest.

"He's bigger than the last."

"Yes." She folded his dagger into the waist of her dress. "You're improving all the time."

"Maybe tomorrow we can try again, in the forest."

"Maybe."

Balfour stripped out of his bloodied shirt. It was only one of two he had here. They'd packed so little. "I'll come with you, when you go to the river tonight."

Assana smiled. "I'd like that."

Balfour returned the smile.

This wasn't the life Assana had imagined they'd find here, but it was fair enough. It was more than fair enough.

She only wished they'd remembered to send that raven to Master Frost, like they'd promised.

"Have you gathered all you'll need?" Kian asked. "The pile is thin."

Eithne nodded. "We require little. As you know."

"You can still choose to stay," Kian said. He looked around at what remained of their camp after the world had caved in. It wasn't only their tents lost to the permanent chasm. Some of their own had fallen in, never to return. And Kael. Kian had watched his brother as he fell, helpless to do anything except find his forgiveness in the seconds that ticked down the rest of his life. "The threat to you is ended. Whether you are one or many, you are just as safe."

"Yes, I know, however..." Eithne dropped her eyes. "I still feel as if you have more to teach me, Kian."

"The way of the Keepers is no more. Now, we are simply who we are, no less or more."

"The doctrine of a Keeper is only the beginning of what I did not know. If you would prefer I stay here, I will. If you will have me, I would still come."

"You know you are welcome with the Drumain."

"And with you?"

Kian flushed. "And with me."

Eithne reached for his hand and squeezed it. "You may have been only a Keeper of the Light, but to me, you are the light. I can see the hope you will offer, following in the steps of your mother."

"It is not my role to take."

"Unless you had a daughter."

Kian hadn't expected her to be so forward. "That was my mother's hope, that I would continue the line for her."

"You will." She released his hand, grinning as she turned away. "I know you had hoped to find Kael. To hold him to proper account."

"He gave his life for his crimes, which is more than I would've taken," Kian said, sighing.

"What is the punishment for a traitor? I have never known one."

Kian nodded at the other Saleen, who'd finished securing what little they would take with them to the ponies. "A punishment is only a crime turned against the offender. Any who would conspire against the safety of their own become the safety itself."

"I don't know what that means."

He reached for the reigns of his own pony and swung up. "The veils that used to keep us protected from the rest of the kingdom were made of those who once wielded them as a weapon."

"Kael would have been sentenced to live inside the veil?"

He reached down for her. "He would have become the veil itself. His magic, keeping us from others like him."

"A fitting punishment," she said. She settled herself in front of him on the pony. "But now that there are no veils, we no longer need protection."

"We are no longer connected to the kingdom," Kian said as they fell in line behind the remaining Saleen. "Now it is for us to keep things safe from within."

CURRAN FINISHED NAILING THE WOODEN PLAQUE TO THE POSTS THAT Gretchen had passed through many years past. Maura and Curran had gone around a bit on where to place the memorial, but it was Curran who found the words to say why this should be the place.

Brahim was a father to all. Not only Malfenza, for whom he gave all, but for those travelers lost. All who come to Malfenza should know his name.

She remembered when he would've said this with disdain dripping from every word, but now he smiled at her. At Pieter. At Pieter's wife, Eavan, and their daughter, Lisbet.

There may be no more travelers to our world anymore, but the ones who come after us should know what he did.

Maura hobbled forth, shifting most of her weight to the cane Pieter had fashioned for her. Gretchen's son was now the age she had been when she'd come to Tenestela. He'd been only a little younger when Eavan, Alric, and Earwyn had made their way through the veil, putting an end to a story Alric had started when he was hardly more than a boy. When Pieter had seen Eavan's condition, a look had come over him, one his mother knew well. They'd made a marriage of practicality, but it had become a union of love.

"Easy, Maura. The daylight is still ours," Alric chided. He hovered with his hands just under her elbows. "We have time to do this properly."

Curran passed Gretchen a look across their gathered family. She couldn't say when she'd began to think of them all like this, but nor could she remember what it was like to share a bed with Holden, when she'd lain next to Curran for so long. Eavan called her mother, and that, too, had happened naturally.

Even Ash had become her distant past.

Gretchen would miss her other children until her final breath, but she had no lingering regrets about coming here in search of Pieter. What she'd found wasn't a replacement for that life, but a fork in the path she'd been on, offering her another way.

The heat was oppressive, and the foul desert wind carrying stinging sand was too much for little Lisbet, who erupted in tears. Pieter swung her up into his arms and held her there, Eavan leaning against him as she wore a smile bigger and brighter than any Gretchen had seen on her in the kingdom.

"Brahim was a man unlike any other," Maura began. "I first met him as a girl, here in Malfenza, when the children's plague was still only a cautious whisper in the markets. I bore him two children, and both, we sent away. We had no choice. But then, we discovered that there might be another way for us to care for others."

"He was like a father," Earwyn added. She wrapped her shawl tighter about her face to block the sand, but her tears were visible. "I hadn't known how much I still needed one until he took us in and made us one of you."

"When we kissed our children and sent them away, it was the last we ever saw of them." Maura moved slowly to Earwyn. She patted her on the arm. "But our hearts were full, just the same."

"We all owe you both our lives, as they are now," Gretchen said.

Maura made a tsk sound. "It was Brahim whose heart melted first. He was the one who said, we cannot abandon them, Maura. They're here for a reason, and we're part of that reason. They've lost something, and we cannot find it for them, but we can show them another way."

"I have Brahim to thank for my wife," Curran said.

"And mine," Pieter added.

"And I," Gretchen said, "have received more than any debt would repay."

Curran wrapped his arm around her and pulled her close. He kissed the hollow of her cheek.

"But you can repay it," Maura said. The deep wrinkles in her old face contorted into a soft smile. "For when I am gone to join Brahim, it will be all of you who will bring the children back to Malfenza, at last."

"I hate you," Gabrianna teased. "I just absolutely loathe you, and I'll be sure you know it before you leave me here."

"We both know it was never going to be me," Brandyn said as he hugged her. "I'm not cut out to be a lord."

"Of course it wasn't going to be you, you daft boy! Everyone knew Mother preferred Ember!"

"Thanks, Gabi."

"But do you see her here, now? No. And now, you've left it all to me. You're selfish, Brandyn Blackwood, and I hope you know that when you do return, and yes, I said *when*, you'll remain unforgiven until you've made proper amends."

Brandyn kissed her cheek. "You'll forgive me. *If* I come back."

"Your sister's right. *When* you come back. It's an order from your mother," Asherley said. The sound her boots made was uneven as she made her way down the ramp. Her limp hadn't eased since her illness, not even after repeated attempts from Lisbet to see her right again, but she was otherwise restored to the woman he remembered, bursting with life and mischief.

Lisbet waved from the starboard bow. Behind her, the mainsail snapped into place. He caught glimpses of Ryan rushing around behind it, doing all the things Brandyn would never have known to do on his own. Then he saw Storm, too, just behind Ryan, caught between her desire to learn and her inability to hold her tongue.

"Where will you go?" Gabi asked, as if the prior hundred times hadn't counted.

"Wherever Lisbet leads us."

"Lisbet is still a girl. Hardly older than me, you know. Storm, too, even if she isn't afraid to stab a man. You'd do well to listen to the other one. Ryan."

"He's reckless and impulsive, and I half expect him to sink us to the bottom of the White Sea, just for the fun of it." Brandyn laughed. "But he's also one of the best seamen in the realm. We couldn't be in better hands unless Hamish Strong himself was at the helm."

"Should have finished your studies at the Sepulchre. You might then know how to see something like that coming," his mother said. He'd missed this side of her; how playful and witty she'd been before the dark times had come to them all.

"Well, when you come back, you can take your not-so-rightful place as mother's heir again," Gabi said. "While she finds me a fine match. Perhaps Jonah Tyndall, who'll become a steward, now that Marsh isn't returning."

"You still have some years before I'll seriously consider any offers for you," Asherley reminded her. "Brandyn, don't get up to anything your mother wouldn't."

"So nothing is off-limits."

She laughed and kissed the top of his head. "You're a good boy. I couldn't have asked for better. But if you don't find your way back to me, I'll channel the dead and send your father after you, and yes, you're wondering now if I can even do that, aren't you? Well, disobey me and find out."

Brandyn backed away and down the ramp with his hands up. "I know better than to challenge the temper of a Blackwood woman. I've been surrounded by them my whole life! Will be refreshing to have a reprieve, I think!"

"You cheeky little bastard. Be safe." She blew him a kiss. After she aimed a look at Gabi, his sister did the same.

Brandyn took them both in one last time. He'd be happy to remember them just like this, side by side, their hair blowing in the wind, cheeks flushed with good health and an eye to a better future than they'd all known in recent days. It was because of this he could leave.

It was because of this, he could live.

Ryan had the anchor up no sooner than Brandyn's feet hit the deck planks. The wind was with them that day and the ship launched into its journey without lingering for more emotional goodbyes, or second thoughts.

Brandyn himself had none.

He had three mates with whom he'd trust with his life—and might yet get a chance to put that to test—and an open sea awaiting.

As Ryan eased them around the bend, Brandyn caught one final glimpse of The Hidden Cave. It was the last place he and his sisters had all been together. With Hollyn gone, and Emberley chasing another fate, it would remain so, forever. A treasured memory.

Brandyn placed his hand to his heart as they passed and looked boldly to the future.

EMBERLEY LIFTED HER CHIN TO EXTEND HER NECK, AS THE OTHER women fastened the pins all around her dark dress. The high feathers, sewn into the edges beneath the lining of furs, tickled her ears as the women brushed against them in their work. She wanted to swat them away each time, but resisted this urge, reminding herself that she was here because of her skill at adaptation.

"You were made for this," one of the women, Velusine, said as she examined her work. Emberley committed that name to memory, the moment of their introduction. Alasyr told her that his mother and grandmother rarely bothered to learn the names of the others. If she wanted to bring them something different, she must show them something different.

Another, Rysah, watched her with a shaking head. "That red hair. What I wouldn't give for it."

"It came from my father," Emberley answered, proud of this. Proud of who she was, where she came from. She wanted them to see it, to never forget that she was only here, now, because of their own curiosity of what life could be like beyond these walls.

"Where can we find more of these redheaded men?" Velusine quipped. She spun her around. "Yes. Just so. Rysah?"

"Beautiful," Rysah said, sweeping her eyes over the gown of velvet and furs with an appraising look. Alasyr would certainly have something clever to say about it later, after all the teasing she'd given him about his own wardrobe.

"You don't think it's too much?" Ember asked.

"This is what we know. Not everything about our life was so bad, was it?" Ryessa lifted herself from the chair in the corner, where she'd been observing the final fitting. "Are you ready, Emberley?"

She nodded, determined that none would see the storm raging within her, swirling around her anxiousness and fear as she carried the weight of the entire future of the Ravenwoods under the mountain of black feathers. "I'm ready."

The guards opened the door to the dressing room and Emberley was ushered down the hall, flanked by Velusine and Rysah. She sucked in a gulp of arctic air, trapping it her in lungs. *Give me strength. Harden me, but never so much that I forget who I am.*

They rounded the corner at the end of the hall. And then, she saw it. The entrance to the Courtyard of Regents. Her heart sped as they neared, and then she saw *them*. Alasyr and Marsh, dressed in all black to match her, hands folded in front, the anticipation in their eyes clear enough for anyone to read.

Beside Alasyr stood a beautiful silver goat.

Ryessa waited at the arch. She placed a gentle hand at her back, and eased her forward. Alasyr tapped his foot to suppress his grin. Marsh closed his eyes, exhaling.

She slipped into place between them as she took an arm from each. Her two loves. The keepers of both halves of her heart.

Together, they exited the icy courtyard and returned to the stone, following Ryessa and the other women to the Hall of Hours.

The double doors stretched open before the women could reach for them. The low roar of hundreds of voices inside rooted Emberley in place. All of them strong enough to kill her and her men. Her trust in Alasyr's promise was all she had to go on, but if she couldn't trust that, then all was lost.

Emberley tightened her grip on both men.

"Go on." Alasyr leaned in and whispered, "We're here."

Emberley found her steps once more. Together, with her men, each representing the two worlds, and she, the marriage of the two, entered the Hall of Hours to a thunder of welcome applause.

"How is he?"

"When he's awake, he's just as much spit and fire as always," Esmerelda said. She mopped her brow against her sleeve. Her cheeks were flushed with the remains of the day. "I almost prefer him sleeping these days."

"You're a good daughter," Jesse said. He untied her apron from behind while she propped herself against the wall. He looked past her and caught a glimpse of the rope from their wedding laying atop the hearth, the promise they'd made, and were still making. "He knows this, too, even if he'll never say it."

She flounced down in the chair with a sigh. "He's improving. But I rather think he enjoys tormenting us all. You should hear the way he speaks to Ransom. You've never heard a list of faults so long."

Jesse raised his brows. "I've been on the wrong end of his anger. I donnae require a demonstration."

Esmerelda reached a hand forward. He took it. "Is it time?"

"The sun is near spent. I've placed everything just as ye asked."

"You're a keeper, Jesse Strong. I dinnae care what my father says about ye." She grinned as he pulled her back to her feet.

They moved into the adjoining room. True to her instruction, Jesse had arranged the candle in the center of the table that stood against the tall window. Beside it was the single orange feather Esmerelda had found the night of their wedding, the one Ravenna had left behind when she took to the skies.

Esmerelda didn't believe her finding it was an accident, but an intentional gift from a dear friend and sister, left behind for this very purpose.

He'd never say to her the words that would smolder the hope still living inside her. Ravenna would never find them again; not in this world. Nor could he force his wife to talk about the deeds weighing heaviest on her heart; the two lives she'd taken, to protect the ones she loved most. The scar at her throat she touched, now, without realizing.

But he could love her, in the ways she needed. He could set up the candle, and the feather, and say the words with her, and even mean them, because for Esmerelda, he could and would do anything.

"Come back to us," she whispered as she lit the candle. She slid the feather through the thumb hold. "If anyone can find a way, Ravenna, I know it's you. I know what you are. I know who you are. You can always be who you are, with us."

Jesse folded her into his arms from behind and repeated her words, adding in his father's name.

They said them again, and then once more, to be certain the Guardians were paying mind.

They knew the words were for themselves, and the wounds that would never close.

They said them anyway.

They said them in gratitude.

In love.

Esmerelda leaned back into him and closed her eyes. She swayed a little in her exhaustion, and then was asleep.

Jesse lifted his wife into his arms and carried her back to their bedchamber, where he would lie down beside her, night after night, and remember what others had given for him so that he could be here, with her, where his life began, and where one day, it would end.

But not before he had lived.

THE HIDDEN KINGDOM DIDN'T INITIALLY WELCOME THEM.

Most of those early days were lost to the upheaval, and Ravenna had little memory of coming through at all. Her last clear recollection was the look on Ash's face when she grabbed his hand, when he realized what she was doing.

Time seemed different here, though it was only a feeling. Feelings could either be trusted or not, and they were of no use to her here.

In the beginning, they'd been stuck upon an island of land, seemingly created by the chaos she could only guess had been wrought when Ash passed through and destroyed all the veils. Her first thought had been, we'll die here like this, of starvation, of thirst, only shortly thereafter replaced by wonder as Ash pointed out a small bush that hadn't been there when they landed. Beside it, a pool of water that ran deep, like a well.

The island had provided, though it hadn't yet decided what to do with them.

Ravenna tried to use her wings, but could go no farther than the small patch of land they'd been given.

Then the bush bore fruit, and when they finished what it gave them, more grew. The well never ran dry.

Time, she decided, wasn't only different here, but meaningless.

She understood more about herself now, though. For one, it wasn't Ash who had pulled her through the veil, but the pure blood of new life, Meduwyn and Ravenwood, growing within her. No longer the curse Oldwin had intended for her, but something new to hope for.

Over time, the island added to itself, multiplying in circumference. The chasm between them and the rest of this new world was now a crack.

The scent of rich pines carried all the way to them, their first taste of what was out there. There was no longer anything dividing them from the rest of the world. The ground was mended. Her vision no longer blurred as she strained to discern what, if anything, was out there. The forest before her was clear as the one she'd left behind, but greener, taller. It beckoned to her in a silent but commanding voice, calling her forward; to surrender all she didn't know for all that she could.

If she took to the air now, she knew she would be free to soar. That their purgatory had ended.

Ash stretched his arms, as if awakening from a very long nap. "Now what?"

Ravenna turned her eyes to the sky with a mischievous grin. He nodded.

She didn't check to see who might be looking. That wasn't needed here. She could be who she was.

Ravenna transformed into a phoenix, twirling as she rose higher and higher, the show as much for Ash as for herself; as for The Hidden Kingdom, her new master and servant alike.

Ash shook his head at her display as he chuckled. He took his first step beyond their small known world and into the promise of the unknown.

"All right, then. You lead the way."

THE KINGDOM OF THE WHITE SEA trilogy has ended, but there is so much more coming from this world. The histories of the kingdom are rich, full of tales of forbidden love and incredible treachery. In The Book of All Things, we explore these stories, one by one. Start with *The Raven and the Rush*.

JOIN THE KINGDOM OF THE WHITE SEA OFFICIAL READER GROUP ON Facebook, for latest news and exclusive content.

IF YOU ENJOYED THIS NOVEL, AN HONEST REVIEW IS ALWAYS appreciated.

In Memoriam

In remembrance of the deceased of the kingdom, in imperfect order.

Prisoner Hill

Susannah the Horse

Hollyn Blackwood

Byrne Warwick

Maye, Byrne's Handmaiden

Assyria Rhiagain

Mason Wakesell

Mortain of Ilynglass

Drystan Sylvaine

Chieftainess Ohsmha

Clahnn Saleen

Mads Waters

Eoghan Rhiagain

Aiden Quinlanden

Argentyn Ravenwood

Varinya Ravenwood
Correen Rhiagain
Rehana and Drystan Dereham of Malfenza
Chieftainess Yseult of the Drumain
Stewardess Nye & Daughter
Samuel Law
Men of the Seventeenth Artifact
Men of Camps Atonement and Restitution
Maeryn Blackwood Quinlanden
Anabella Weatherford Rhiagain
Oldwin of Ilynglass
Kael of the Drumain
The Many Rhiagains of Duncarrow
Gwyn Dereham Warwick
Brahim of Malfenza

Northerlands
THE NORTHERN REACH

Lord and Lady:
Lord Christian Dereham and Lady Aylen Wynter Dereham

Lord Holden Dereham is believed dead
Lady Gretchen Dereham is missing

Capital:
Wulfsgate

Standard:
The jagged mountaintop

Siblings:
Drystan, 17 (deceased)
Lisbet, 15
Pieter, 14
Nyssa and Torrin, 10 (twins)

Greater Families/Stewards:

Aldenwood, Turick, Hardeham, Frost, Horne, Arranden, Wynter, Haddenfoot, Claybourne, Weatherford

Key Towns:
Whitecap, Midwinter Rest, Westport, Eastport, Salthill, Darkwood Run, Witchwood Cross, Wulfshead Haven, Torrin's Pass, Dunwoode

Landmarks:
Northerland Range, Icebolt Mountain, Torrin's Pass, Forest of Lycana, Frozen Vale

Notable Northerlanders:
Alric Dereham & Earwyn Blackwood Dereham of Wulfsgate
Anabella Weatherford Rhiagain of Whitecap (wife of Darrick)
Wregan Weatherford, Steward of Whitecap
Steward Frost and daughter Elena of Midwinter Rest

SOUTHERLANDS
THE SOUTHERN REACH

Lord and Lady:
Lord Khallum Warwick & Lady Gwyn Dereham Warwick

Capital:
Warwicktown

Standard:
The crested wave

Children:
Ransom, 19
Esmerelda, 18
Niall, 15
Garrick, 13

Greater Families/Stewards:
Strong, Rutland, Bradford, Clayton, Garrick, Holton, Leecaster,
Law, Nye, Thorpe

Key Towns:

SOUTHERLANDS

Sandycove, Iron Hill, Sandymount, Whitecliffe, Stone Mawr,
Blackpool, Leecaster Bay, Hornsea, Goldthorpe, Port Worthing

Landmarks:
The Golden Coast, The Warwick Throne, Drummond's Cock

Notable Southerlanders:
Jesse Strong of Sandycove
Ryan Strong of Sandycove
Hamish and Andrija Strong, Steward and Stewardess of Sandycove
Khoulter Warwick, prior Lord of the Southerlands (deceased)
Lem Garrick, Steward of Iron Hill
Barne Holton, Steward of Sandymount
Samuel Law, Steward of Port Worthing, & son Nathenial
Erran and Mariel Rutland, Steward and Stewardess of Whitecliffe,
& daughters Agnes and Esther
Odrahn Warwick, Great-Uncle to Lord Warwick

EASTERLANDS
THE EASTERN REACH

Lord and Lady:
Lord Cian Quinlanden

Lord Aiden Quinlanden is deceased, and died a traitor
Lady Maeryn Blackwood Quinlanden is being held as a traitor,
awaiting trial

Capital:
Whitechurch

The Resplendent Reliquary of the Guardians is located in
Riverchapel
The Consortium of the Sepulchre in the Skies is located in
Briarhaven
The Council of Universities are in Oldcastle

Standard:
The oaken tree

Siblings:

EASTERLANDS

Eavan, 19
Assana, 17
Cian, 16
Breandan, 14
Dorrin, 13

Greater Families/Stewards:
Oakenwell, Sylvaine, Forrest, Skylark, Rowan, Rosewood, Waters, Edevane

Key Towns:
Streamstowne, Rushwood, Riverchapel, Oldcastle, Everleigh Pike, Everhart Thicket, Greenfen, Briarhaven, Bythesea, Oak Hill

Landmarks:
Fionn's Pass, Gap of Ever, The Sparkling Beck

Notable Easterlanders:
Lord Corin Quinlanden and Lady Yesenia Warwick of Whitechurch
Chasten Quinlanden and Mariana Skylark Quinlanden, prior Lord and Lady (deceased)
Drystan "Ash" Sylvaine of Rushwood
Enchanter Joran Rosewood of Greenfen
Mads Waters, Steward of Bythesea (deceased)
Stirling Oakenwell, Steward of Oak Hill
Wyat Edevane of Oldcastle
Rolph Edevane of Oldcastle
Drystan and Raychelle Sylvaine, Steward and Stewardess of Rushwood
Barrie Sylvaine of Rushwood
Mortain the Sorcerer

WESTERLANDS
THE WESTERN REACH

Lord and Lady:
Lord Brandyn Blackwood (interim)

Lady Asherley Blackwood is away tending to a personal matter

Capital:
Longwood Rush

Standard:
The providing mother

Siblings:
Hollyn (deceased)
Emberley, 16
Gabrianna, 15
Brandyn, 12

Greater Families/Stewards:
Tyndall, Glenlannan, Ashenhurst, Bristol, Blakewell, James,
Stanhope, Richland, Derry, Wakesell

Key Towns:
Wildwood Falls, Pine Bluff, Windwatch Grove, Whispering Wood,
Valleybrooke, Greencastle, East Derry, Greystone Abbey,
Newcarrow, Whitewood

Landmarks:
The Seven Sisters of the West, The River Rush, Whispering Wood,
The Whitewood, The Hidden Cave, Halls of Longwood, Sky Dome

Notable Westerlanders:
Easlan James, Steward of Greystone Abbey & son Kaslan
Griffath and Clarissant Tyndall, Steward and Stewardess of
Wildwood Falls, & children Marsh, Jonah, and Lyria
Glen and Fleur Ashenhurst, Steward and Stewardess of Windwatch
Grove, & children Meadow and Brook
Mason (deceased) and Jasmine Wakesell, Steward and Stewardess of
Whitewood, & daughter Storm
Arturo Blackfen, Rush Rider
Grand Minister Rhydian Tyndall

HINTERLANDS
THE LAND OF THE MEDVEDEV

Chieftainesses:
Yseult de Medvedev, Drumain Clahnn
Ohsmha de Medvedev, Saleen Clahnn (deceased)

Clahnns:
Drumain
Asgill
Mayke
Saleen

Yseult's Children:
Kian, 17
Kael, 15

Landmarks:
Forest of All

Other Notable Medvedev:
Yanna de Medvedev of Clahnn Drumain (sister of Yseult, deceased)
Eithne of Clahnn Saleen

DUNCARROW
SEAT OF THE RHIAGAINS

King:
The crown is presently kingless
Oldwin of Ilynglass has claimed power

Standard:
The crossed swords

Rhiagains:
Eoghan- Last King (deceased)
Khain- Father (deceased)
Florian- Mother (deceased)
Dain- Brother (deceased)
Assyria- Sister (deceased)
Correen- Sister (deceased)
Darrick- Brother
Anabella- Wife of Darrick
Stefan- Son of Darrick

Notable Rhiagains of Past:
King Carrow the Original

DUNCARROW

King Carrick the Dreamer
King Karsein
King Fynne the Good

Known Rhiagain Sorcerers:
Oldwin
Mortain
Lysanor
Isdemus

Landmarks:
The sky dungeon, Isle of Belcarrow

MIDNIGHT CREST
HAVEN OF THE RAVENWOODS

High Priestess & Priest:
Adynora Ravenwood is interim High Priestess

Castle:
The Rookery

Sigil:
The raven

Grandchildren:
Alasyr, 18
Ravenna, 16
Ryandyr, 13
Ashara, 11
Nyana & Nevyn, 8 (twins)

Landmarks:
Courtyard of Regents, Hall of Hours

Notable Ravenwoods:

Varinya and Argentyn (both deceased)
Rillyn
Ryessa
Corridyn (deceased)
Aryc
Sandyr
Ailyn
Rhosyn (defected)

THE CONSORTIUM OF THE SEPULCHRE IN THE SKIES
THE ACADEMY OF MAGIC AND RULING COUNCIL OF ELDERS

Head Magus:
Head Magus Tymagen

Location:
Briarhaven, in the Easterlands

Adherents- students
Enchanters/Enchantresses- magic practitioners who have finished their studies and been assigned into the world. May also be called by their discipline (i.e. Healers, Seers, etc.)
Magi- Instructors of magic at the Sepulchre
Elder Magi- A position of tenure that allows access to the Sacred Halls
Head Magus- The head of the Sepulchre

Notable Magi:
Magi Christian Dereham (on banishment)
Magi Aylen Wynter (on banishment)
Elder Magi Rorric Dereham
Elder Thorsen

Notable Adherents:
Brandyn Blackwood (on leave)
Esther Rutland

THE COUNCIL OF UNIVERSITIES

Location:
Oldcastle

Universities:
Onyxcastle
Emeraldcastle
Crimsoncastle
Ambercastle
Azurecastle

Pupils- students
Masters- teachers
Wardens- keepers of certain posts

Notable Masters & Wardens:
Master Frost
Master Dilliswhane
Warden Liddle

Notable Pupils:

Balfour Dereham
Breandan Quinlanden
Dorin Quinlanden
Fairchild Bristol
Firth Garrick
Rolph Edevane

Oldcastle Landmarks:
Wayfarer's Inn, Ever the Gap, The Golden Castle

TENESTELA

Leaders:
Brahim and Maura

Province:
Malfenza

Others:
Curran
Jassmyn

Landmarks:
Azylria River, Cadsella, the Malcazara

WASTELANDS
CROWN LABOR CAMPS

Land seized by the crown and turned into prison labor camps, including Camp Atonement and Camp Restitution.

Notable Past Prisoners & Their Number:
Cap- WCNM999
Hill- SHNT1 (deceased)
Andy- SCST8769

Prisoner Numbers Decoded:
City- Reach-Crime-Number Correlating to Crime
I.E. Cap, from Whitecap in the Northerlands, was the 999th person
imprisoned for the crime of murder.

Seventeenth Artifact of the Knights of Duncarrow:
Captain General Gilgowan
Lieutenant Worley
And many others

ALSO BY SARAH M. CRADIT

KINGDOM OF THE WHITE SEA

<u>Kingdom of the White Sea Trilogy</u>

The Kingless Crown

The Broken Realm

The Hidden Kingdom

<u>The Book of All Things</u>

The Raven and the Rush

The Sylvan and the Sand

The Altruist and the Assassin

The Melody and the Master

The Claw and the Crowned

The Priestess and the Paladin

THE SAGA OF CRIMSON & CLOVER

<u>The House of Crimson and Clover Series</u>

The Storm and the Darkness

Shattered

The Illusions of Eventide

Bound

Midnight Dynasty

Asunder

Empire of Shadows

Myths of Midwinter

The Hinterland Veil

The Secrets Amongst the Cypress

Within the Garden of Twilight

House of Dusk, House of Dawn

<u>Midnight Dynasty Series</u>

A Tempest of Discovery

A Storm of Revelations

A Torrent of Deceit

<u>The Seven Series</u>

1970

1972

1973

1974

1975

1976

1980

<u>Vampires of the Merovingi Series</u>

The Island

and more

<u>The Dusk Trilogy</u>

St. Charles at Dusk: The Story of Oz and Adrienne

Flourish: The Story of Anne Fontaine

Banshee: The Story of Giselle Deschanel

<u>Crimson & Clover Stories</u>

Surrender: The Story of Oz and Ana

Shame: The Story of Jonathan St. Andrews

Fire & Ice: The Story of Remy & Fleur

Dark Blessing: The Landry Triplets

Pandora's Box: The Story of Jasper & Pandora

The Menagerie: Oriana's Den of Iniquities

A Band of Heather: The Story of Colleen and Noah

The Ephemeral: The Story of Autumn & Gabriel

Bayou's Edge: The Landry Triplets

For more information, and exciting bonus material, visit www. sarahmcradit.com

ABOUT THE AUTHOR

Sarah is the USA Today and International Bestselling Author of over forty contemporary and epic fantasy stories, and the creator of the Kingdom of the White Sea and Saga of Crimson & Clover universes.

Born a geek, Sarah spends her time crafting rich and multilayered worlds, obsessing over history, playing her retribution paladin (and sometimes destruction warlock), and settling provocative Tolkien debates, such as why the Great Eagles are not Gandalf's personal taxi service. Passionate about travel, she's been to over twenty countries collecting sparks of inspiration, and is always planning her next adventure.

Sarah and her husband live in a beautiful corner of SE Pennsylvania with their three tiny benevolent pug dictators.

www.sarahmcradit.com